A CAREER IN BOOKS

ALSO BY KATE GAVINO

Sanpaku
Last Night's Reading

A CAREER IN BOOKS

A Novel about Friends, Money, and the Occasional Duck Bun

Written and Illustrated by

KATE GAVINO

PLUME

PLUME

An imprint of Penguin Random House LLC
penguinrandomhouse.com

PLUME and P colophon are registered trademarks of
Penguin Random House LLC

LIBRARY OF CONGRESS CATALOGING-IN-PUBLICATION DATA
has been applied for.

ISBN 9780593185483 (hardcover)
ISBN 9780593185490 (ebook)

Printed in the United States of America
1st Printing

For 3R

A CAREER IN BOOKS

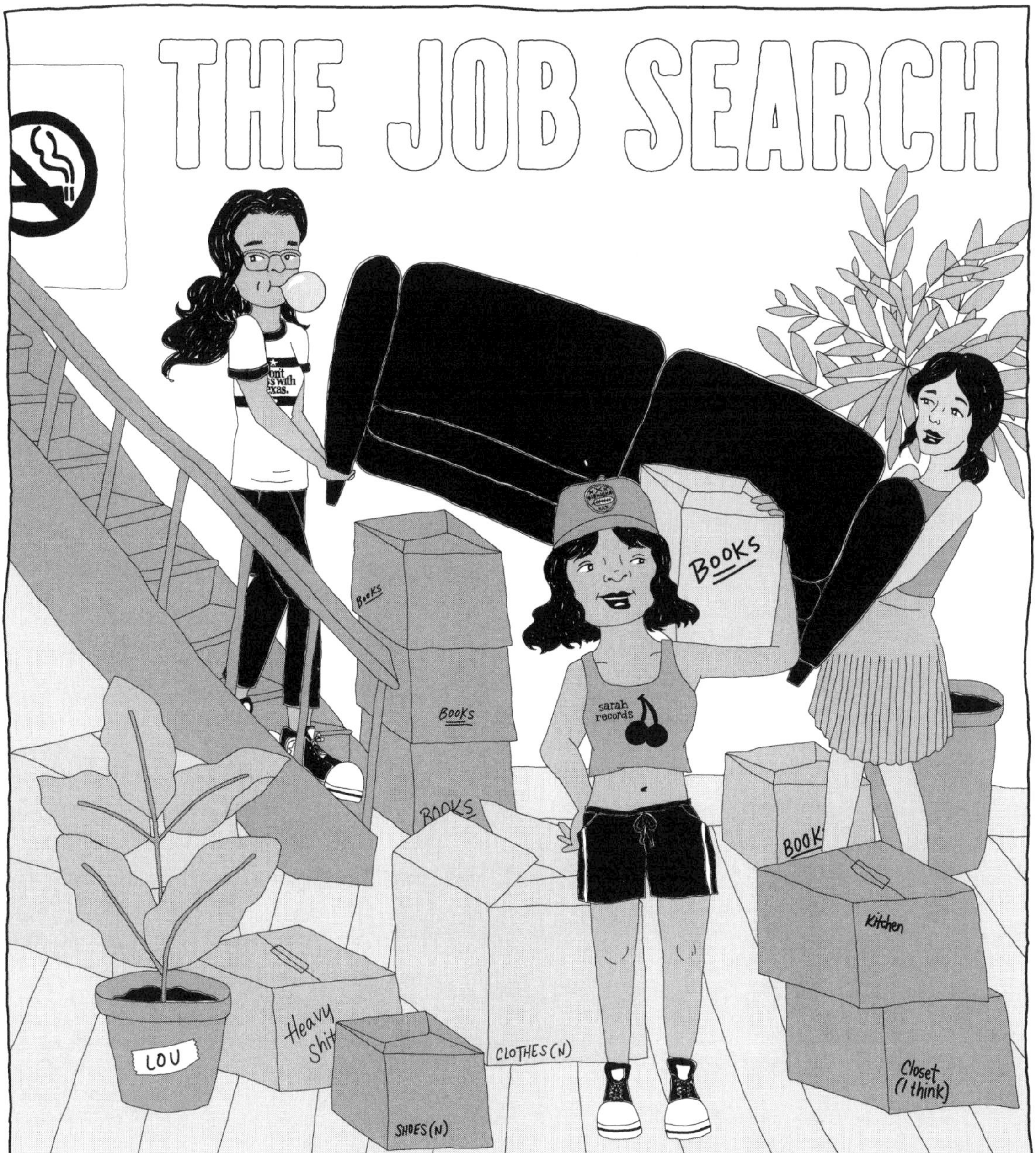
THE JOB SEARCH
BOOKS
Books
Books
BOOKS
sarah records
Kitchen
Heavy
LOU
CLOTHES (N)
SHOES (N)
Closet (I think)

NINA WAS THE FIRST ONE HIRED.

DUBSTEP-OBSESSED BROS

NINA, SILVIA, AND SHIRIN LIVE HERE

THEY THINK AN OLD LADY LIVES HERE? NOT SURE.

SHIRIN CLAIMS TO HAVE SEEN STEVE BUSCEMI PEEING HERE ONCE.

219

SHE BREEZED THROUGH THREE ROUNDS OF INTERVIEWS WITH POISE AND CONFIDENCE, CONJURING UP DAZZLING REFERENCES AND GRACIOUS THANK-YOU EMAILS.

"Love is or it ain't." ♥♥♥ - Toni Morrison

JUNE 2011

THE POSITION PAID A MERE $30,000 A YEAR, BUT NINA LIVED IN THE SMALLEST, WINDOWLESS ROOM IN THE APARTMENT, SO HER RENT WAS ONLY $500/MONTH.

DICTEE

TOKYO

おはよう

2046

THE SECRET HISTORY DONNA TARTT

THIS WAS A STEAL FOR GREENPOINT, A NEIGHBORHOOD WHOSE POLISH MOM-AND-POP SHOPS WERE BEING DISPLACED BY WINE BARS AND 16 HANDLES FRANCHISES.

NINA COULD GET BY MOSTLY WITH THE HELP OF HER BOYFRIEND, TAISHI, WHO PAID HER MONTHLY STUDENT LOAN BILL ($251.23).

FAVORITE MOVIE: IRON MAN 2
FAVORITE BOOK: OF MICE AND MEN (?!?)
FAVORITE BAND: OKKERVIL RIVER
FAVORITE FOOD: CHICKEN KATSU CURRY

HE CALLS HIS PARENTS EVERY SUNDAY MORNING AND INFORMS THEM EVERY TIME HE GOES TO THE DOCTOR, EVEN WHEN HE TOOK NINA TO GET HER IUD.

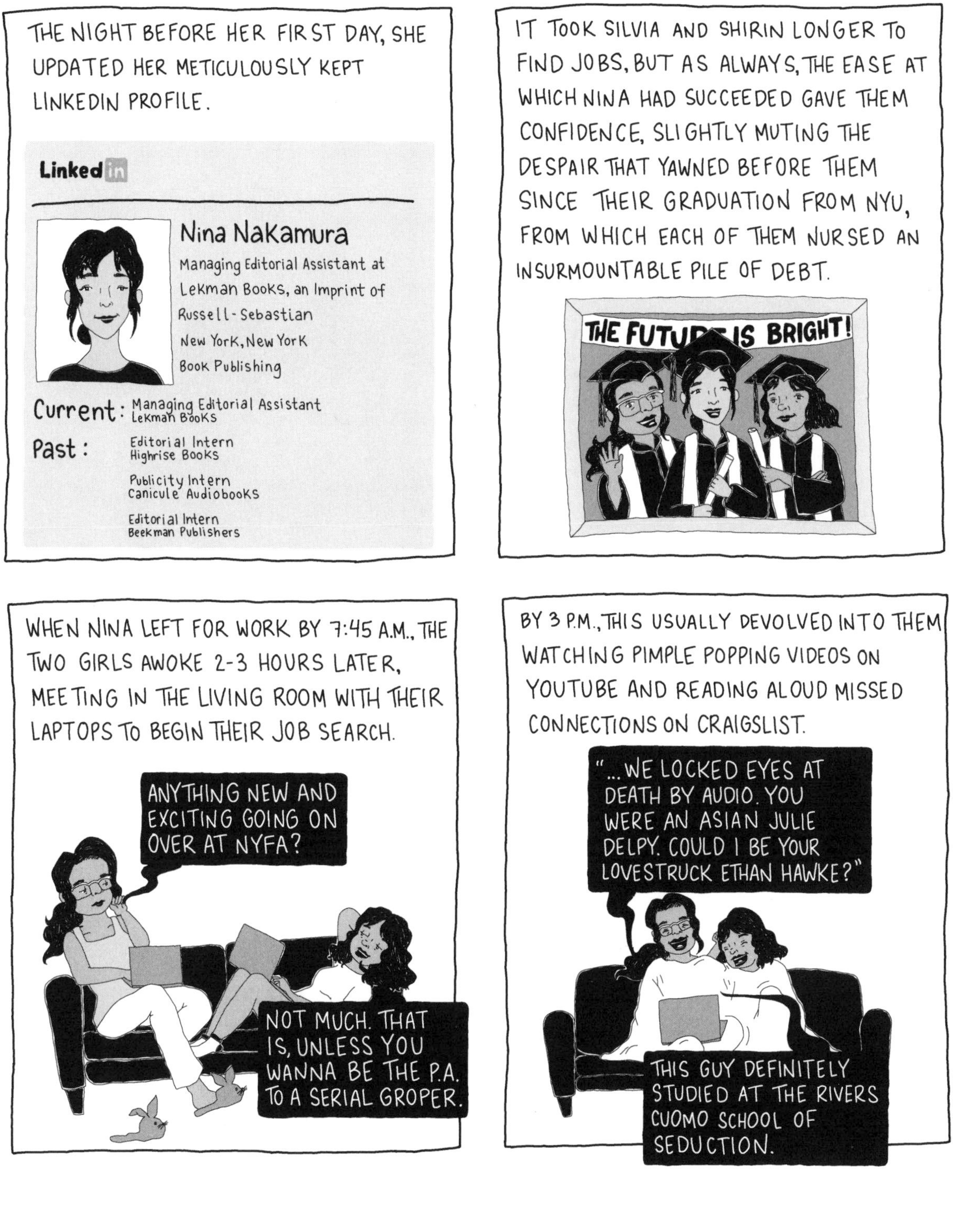
THE NIGHT BEFORE HER FIRST DAY, SHE UPDATED HER METICULOUSLY KEPT LINKEDIN PROFILE.
LinkedIn
Nina NaKamura
Managing Editorial Assistant at Lekman Books, an Imprint of Russell-Sebastian
New York, New York
Book Publishing
Current: Managing Editorial Assistant Lekman Books
Past: Editorial Intern Highrise Books
Publicity Intern Canicule Audiobooks
Editorial Intern Beekman Publishers
IT TOOK SILVIA AND SHIRIN LONGER TO FIND JOBS, BUT AS ALWAYS, THE EASE AT WHICH NINA HAD SUCCEEDED GAVE THEM CONFIDENCE, SLIGHTLY MUTING THE DESPAIR THAT YAWNED BEFORE THEM SINCE THEIR GRADUATION FROM NYU, FROM WHICH EACH OF THEM NURSED AN INSURMOUNTABLE PILE OF DEBT.
WHEN NINA LEFT FOR WORK BY 7:45 A.M., THE TWO GIRLS AWOKE 2-3 HOURS LATER, MEETING IN THE LIVING ROOM WITH THEIR LAPTOPS TO BEGIN THEIR JOB SEARCH.
ANYTHING NEW AND EXCITING GOING ON OVER AT NYFA?
NOT MUCH. THAT IS, UNLESS YOU WANNA BE THE P.A. TO A SERIAL GROPER.
BY 3 P.M., THIS USUALLY DEVOLVED INTO THEM WATCHING PIMPLE POPPING VIDEOS ON YOUTUBE AND READING ALOUD MISSED CONNECTIONS ON CRAIGSLIST.
"...WE LOCKED EYES AT DEATH BY AUDIO. YOU WERE AN ASIAN JULIE DELPY. COULD I BE YOUR LOVESTRUCK ETHAN HAWKE?"
THIS GUY DEFINITELY STUDIED AT THE RIVERS CUOMO SCHOOL OF SEDUCTION.

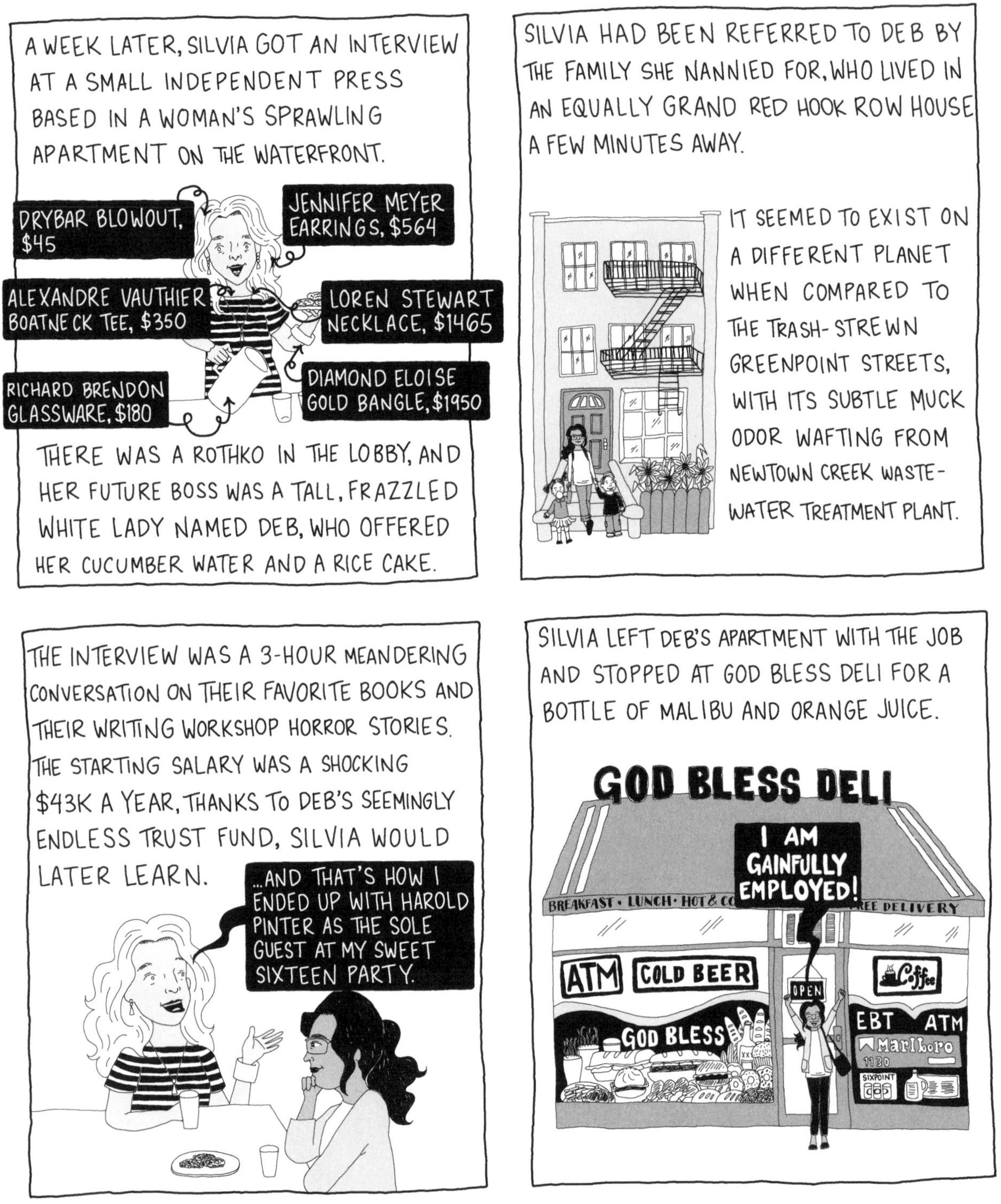
A WEEK LATER, SILVIA GOT AN INTERVIEW AT A SMALL INDEPENDENT PRESS BASED IN A WOMAN'S SPRAWLING APARTMENT ON THE WATERFRONT.
DRYBAR BLOWOUT, $45
JENNIFER MEYER EARRINGS, $564
ALEXANDRE VAUTHIER BOATNECK TEE, $350
LOREN STEWART NECKLACE, $1465
RICHARD BRENDON GLASSWARE, $180
DIAMOND ELOISE GOLD BANGLE, $1950
THERE WAS A ROTHKO IN THE LOBBY, AND HER FUTURE BOSS WAS A TALL, FRAZZLED WHITE LADY NAMED DEB, WHO OFFERED HER CUCUMBER WATER AND A RICE CAKE.
SILVIA HAD BEEN REFERRED TO DEB BY THE FAMILY SHE NANNIED FOR, WHO LIVED IN AN EQUALLY GRAND RED HOOK ROW HOUSE A FEW MINUTES AWAY.
IT SEEMED TO EXIST ON A DIFFERENT PLANET WHEN COMPARED TO THE TRASH-STREWN GREENPOINT STREETS, WITH ITS SUBTLE MUCK ODOR WAFTING FROM NEWTOWN CREEK WASTE-WATER TREATMENT PLANT.
THE INTERVIEW WAS A 3-HOUR MEANDERING CONVERSATION ON THEIR FAVORITE BOOKS AND THEIR WRITING WORKSHOP HORROR STORIES. THE STARTING SALARY WAS A SHOCKING $43K A YEAR, THANKS TO DEB'S SEEMINGLY ENDLESS TRUST FUND, SILVIA WOULD LATER LEARN.
...AND THAT'S HOW I ENDED UP WITH HAROLD PINTER AS THE SOLE GUEST AT MY SWEET SIXTEEN PARTY.
SILVIA LEFT DEB'S APARTMENT WITH THE JOB AND STOPPED AT GOD BLESS DELI FOR A BOTTLE OF MALIBU AND ORANGE JUICE.
GOD BLESS DELI
I AM GAINFULLY EMPLOYED!
ATM
COLD BEER
Coffee
OPEN
GOD BLESS
EBT
ATM
Marlboro

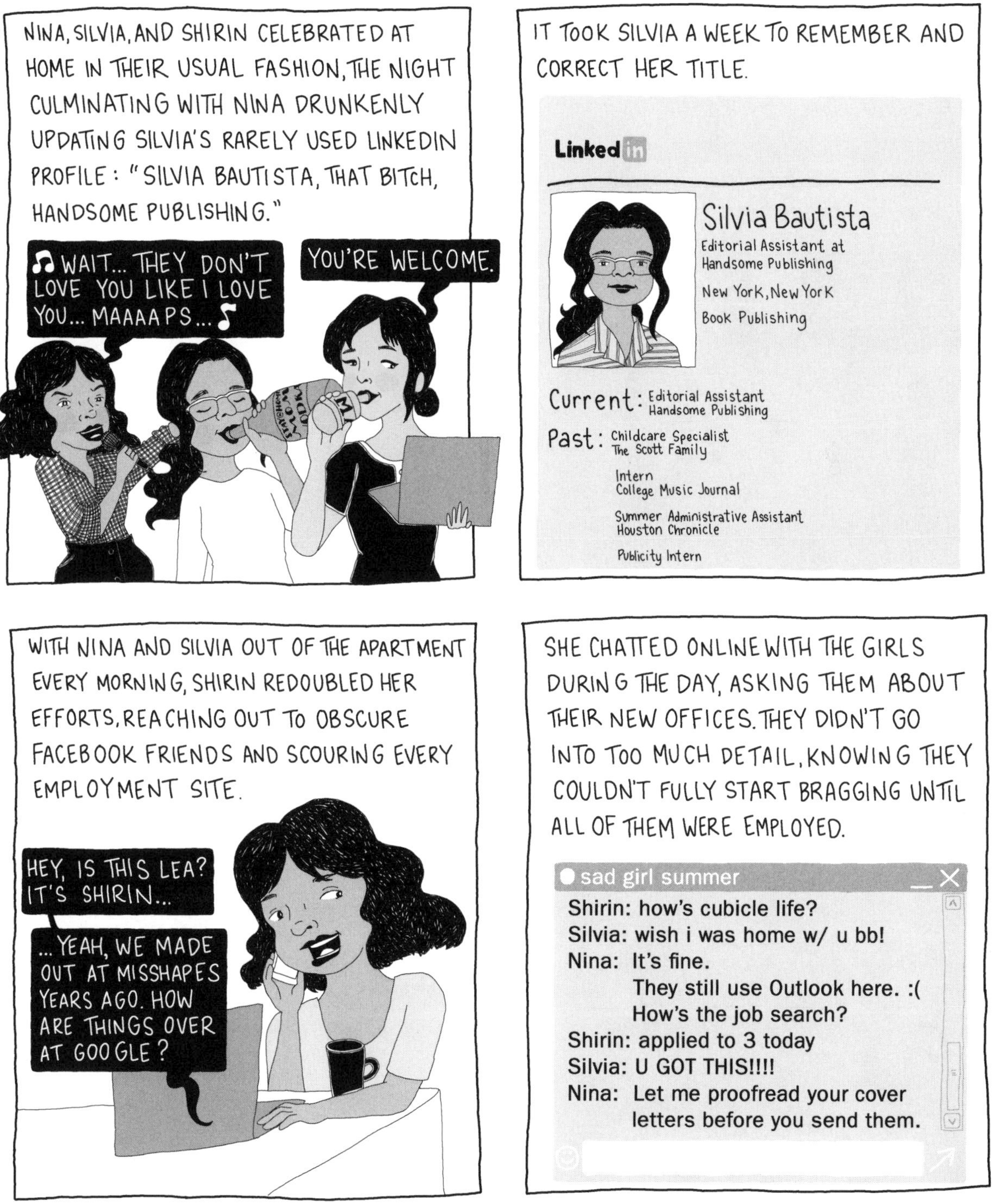
NINA, SILVIA, AND SHIRIN CELEBRATED AT HOME IN THEIR USUAL FASHION, THE NIGHT CULMINATING WITH NINA DRUNKENLY UPDATING SILVIA'S RARELY USED LINKEDIN PROFILE: "SILVIA BAUTISTA, THAT BITCH, HANDSOME PUBLISHING."
♫ WAIT... THEY DON'T LOVE YOU LIKE I LOVE YOU... MAAAAPS... ♪
YOU'RE WELCOME.
IT TOOK SILVIA A WEEK TO REMEMBER AND CORRECT HER TITLE.
Linked in
Silvia Bautista
Editorial Assistant at Handsome Publishing
New York, New York
Book Publishing
Current: Editorial Assistant
Handsome Publishing
Past: Childcare Specialist
The Scott Family
Intern
College Music Journal
Summer Administrative Assistant
Houston Chronicle
Publicity Intern
WITH NINA AND SILVIA OUT OF THE APARTMENT EVERY MORNING, SHIRIN REDOUBLED HER EFFORTS, REACHING OUT TO OBSCURE FACEBOOK FRIENDS AND SCOURING EVERY EMPLOYMENT SITE.
HEY, IS THIS LEA? IT'S SHIRIN...
...YEAH, WE MADE OUT AT MISSHAPES YEARS AGO. HOW ARE THINGS OVER AT GOOGLE?
SHE CHATTED ONLINE WITH THE GIRLS DURING THE DAY, ASKING THEM ABOUT THEIR NEW OFFICES. THEY DIDN'T GO INTO TOO MUCH DETAIL, KNOWING THEY COULDN'T FULLY START BRAGGING UNTIL ALL OF THEM WERE EMPLOYED.
sad girl summer
Shirin: how's cubicle life?
Silvia: wish i was home w/ u bb!
Nina: It's fine.
They still use Outlook here. :(
How's the job search?
Shirin: applied to 3 today
Silvia: U GOT THIS!!!!
Nina: Let me proofread your cover letters before you send them.

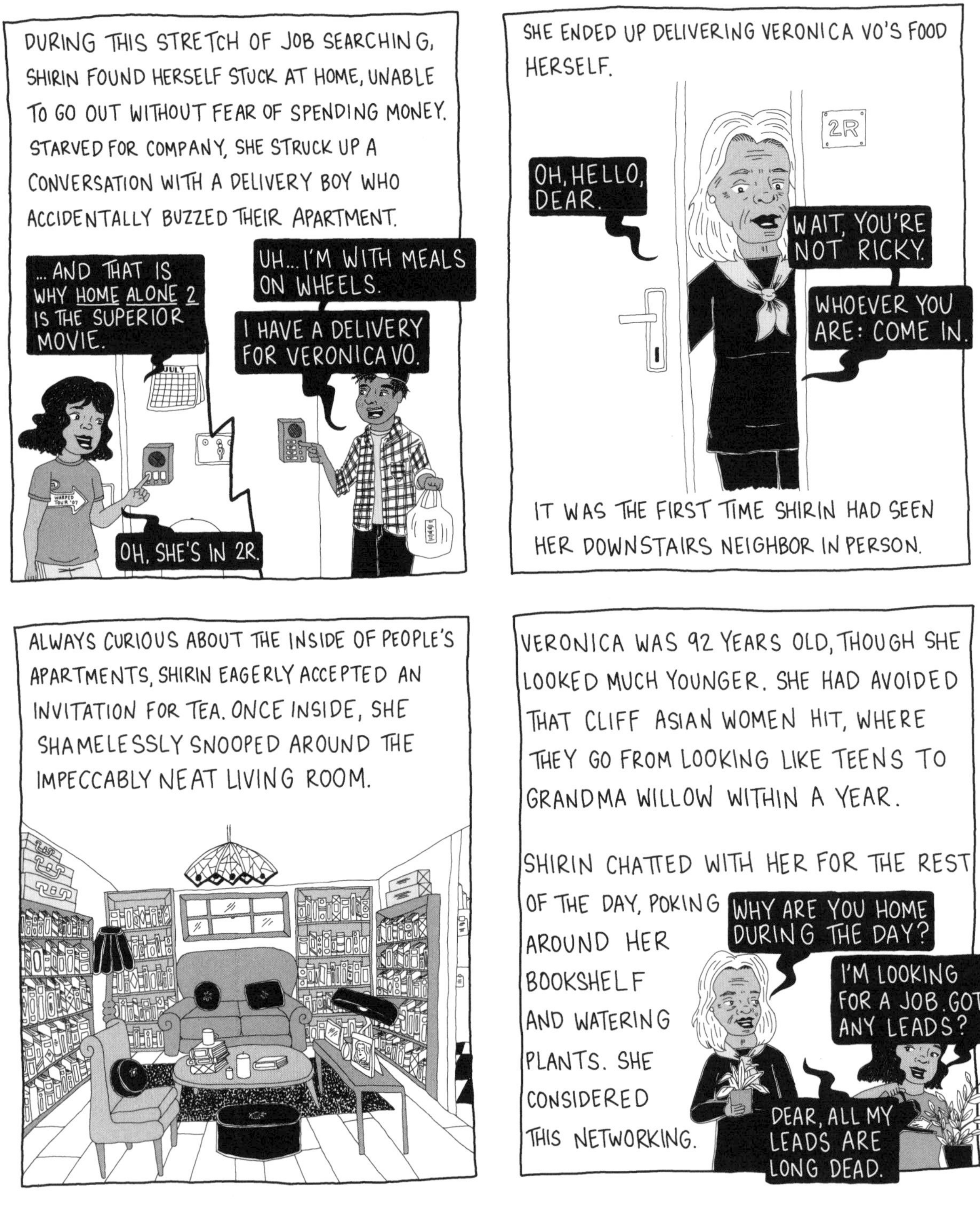
DURING THIS STRETCH OF JOB SEARCHING, SHIRIN FOUND HERSELF STUCK AT HOME, UNABLE TO GO OUT WITHOUT FEAR OF SPENDING MONEY. STARVED FOR COMPANY, SHE STRUCK UP A CONVERSATION WITH A DELIVERY BOY WHO ACCIDENTALLY BUZZED THEIR APARTMENT.
... AND THAT IS WHY HOME ALONE 2 IS THE SUPERIOR MOVIE.
UH... I'M WITH MEALS ON WHEELS.
I HAVE A DELIVERY FOR VERONICA VO.
OH, SHE'S IN 2R.
SHE ENDED UP DELIVERING VERONICA VO'S FOOD HERSELF.
2R
OH, HELLO, DEAR.
WAIT, YOU'RE NOT RICKY.
WHOEVER YOU ARE: COME IN.
IT WAS THE FIRST TIME SHIRIN HAD SEEN HER DOWNSTAIRS NEIGHBOR IN PERSON.
ALWAYS CURIOUS ABOUT THE INSIDE OF PEOPLE'S APARTMENTS, SHIRIN EAGERLY ACCEPTED AN INVITATION FOR TEA. ONCE INSIDE, SHE SHAMELESSLY SNOOPED AROUND THE IMPECCABLY NEAT LIVING ROOM.
VERONICA WAS 92 YEARS OLD, THOUGH SHE LOOKED MUCH YOUNGER. SHE HAD AVOIDED THAT CLIFF ASIAN WOMEN HIT, WHERE THEY GO FROM LOOKING LIKE TEENS TO GRANDMA WILLOW WITHIN A YEAR.
SHIRIN CHATTED WITH HER FOR THE REST OF THE DAY, POKING AROUND HER BOOKSHELF AND WATERING PLANTS. SHE CONSIDERED THIS NETWORKING.
WHY ARE YOU HOME DURING THE DAY?
I'M LOOKING FOR A JOB. GOT ANY LEADS?
DEAR, ALL MY LEADS ARE LONG DEAD.

DAYS LATER, SHIRIN CAME ACROSS A 2-MONTH-OLD JOB POST ON MEDIABISTRO, SEEKING AN EDITORIAL ASSISTANT AT MASSELIN UNIVERSITY PRESS, AN ACADEMIC PUBLISHER BASED IN PARIS WITH A MIDSIZE SATELITE OFFICE IN SOHO.

JOB POSTING   SAVE   APPLY

Company: Masselin University Press

Salary and Benefits: Competitive

Job Duration: Full Time

Job Location: New York, NY

Requirements: Primary responsibilities include working on the Eastern History list, providing administrative support to editors, and reviewing and processing manuscripts. This is a great opportunity for those looking to begin a career in publishing.

Masselin University Press is an Equal Opportunity/Affirmative Action Employer

SHE WAS SO NERVOUS BEFORE THE FIRST INTERVIEW THAT SHE VOMITED UP HER BREAKFAST IN THE BATHROOM OF A NEARBY CRATE & BARREL.

(IT'S SO YOU.)

Crate & Barrel

NOTICE
EMPLOYEES MUST WASH HANDS BEFORE RETURNING TO WORK

DUDE, DON'T BE A LITTLE BITCH TODAY.

YOUR LOLO WAS IN WW2. YOU CAN HANDLE ONE JOB INTERVIEW.

BUT SHE PULLED HERSELF TOGETHER AND GOT THE JOB AFTER THREE MORE ROUNDS OF INTERVIEWS AND A BACKGROUND CHECK.

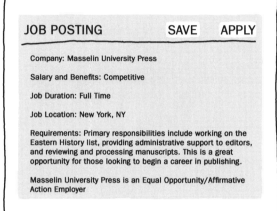

MASSELIN UNIVERSITY PRESS
SHIRIN YAP
EDITORIAL

SHE WOULD BE THE ASSISTANT TO THE EASTERN HISTORY EDITOR, WHO LIVED IN PARIS BUT CAME TO NEW YORK EVERY FEW WEEKS.

THE JOB PAID 28K A YEAR, SO SHIRIN WOULD HAVE TO KEEP HER WEEKEND HOSTESS JOB AT BIBINGKA, A TRENDY EAST VILLAGE FUSION RESTAURANT.

"THE MOST EXCITING GASTRONOMIC EXPERIENCE EVER!" -4-STAR YELP REVIEW

BIBINGKA
EST. 2007

"MY LOLA WOULD DISOWN ME FOR EATING HERE." -1-STAR YELP REVIEW

FILIPINO FUSION

592

MABUHAY!

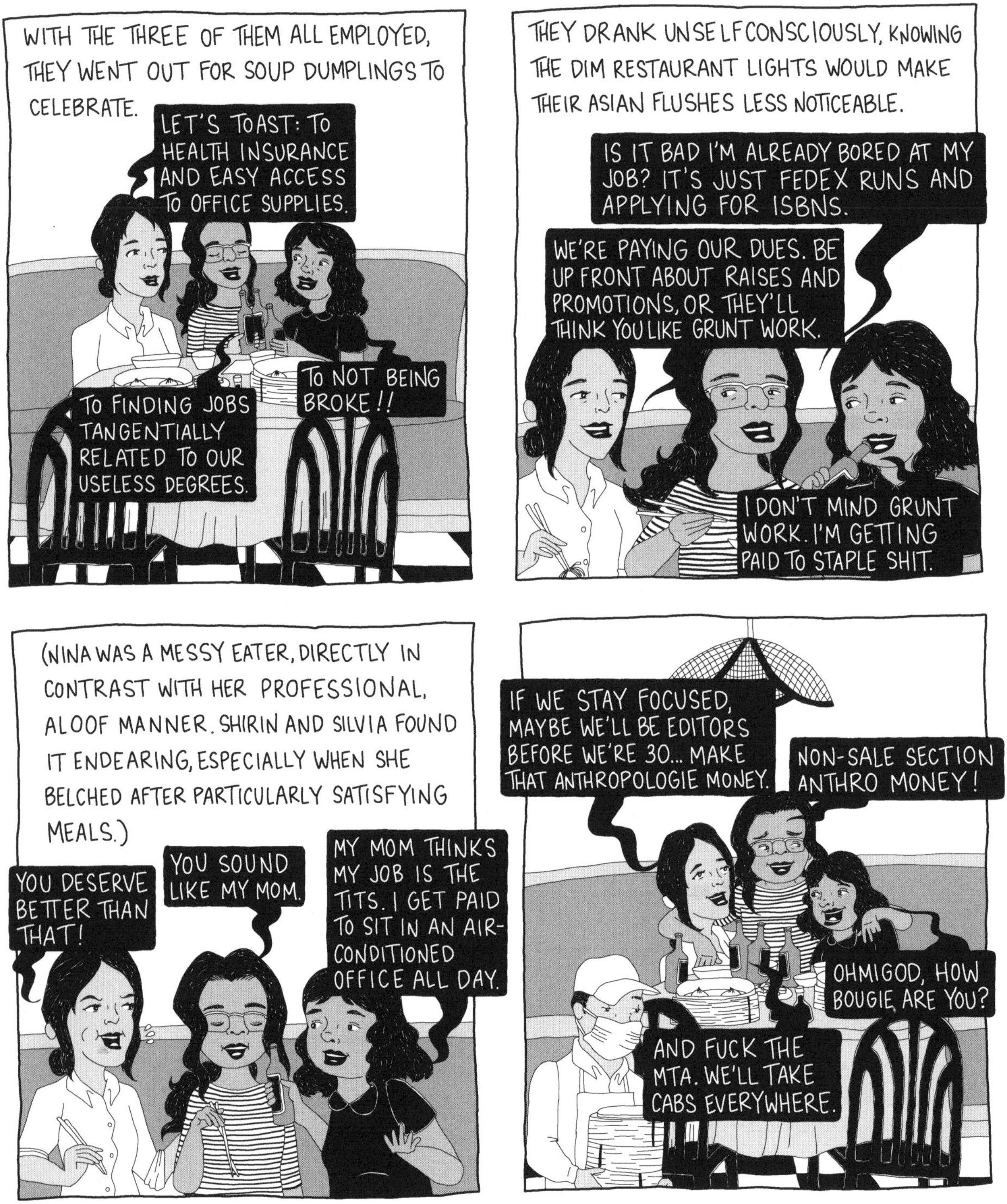
WITH THE THREE OF THEM ALL EMPLOYED, THEY WENT OUT FOR SOUP DUMPLINGS TO CELEBRATE.
LET'S TOAST: TO HEALTH INSURANCE AND EASY ACCESS TO OFFICE SUPPLIES.
TO FINDING JOBS TANGENTIALLY RELATED TO OUR USELESS DEGREES.
TO NOT BEING BROKE!!
THEY DRANK UNSELFCONSCIOUSLY, KNOWING THE DIM RESTAURANT LIGHTS WOULD MAKE THEIR ASIAN FLUSHES LESS NOTICEABLE.
IS IT BAD I'M ALREADY BORED AT MY JOB? IT'S JUST FEDEX RUNS AND APPLYING FOR ISBNS.
WE'RE PAYING OUR DUES. BE UP FRONT ABOUT RAISES AND PROMOTIONS, OR THEY'LL THINK YOU LIKE GRUNT WORK.
I DON'T MIND GRUNT WORK. I'M GETTING PAID TO STAPLE SHIT.
(NINA WAS A MESSY EATER, DIRECTLY IN CONTRAST WITH HER PROFESSIONAL, ALOOF MANNER. SHIRIN AND SILVIA FOUND IT ENDEARING, ESPECIALLY WHEN SHE BELCHED AFTER PARTICULARLY SATISFYING MEALS.)
YOU DESERVE BETTER THAN THAT!
YOU SOUND LIKE MY MOM.
MY MOM THINKS MY JOB IS THE TITS. I GET PAID TO SIT IN AN AIR-CONDITIONED OFFICE ALL DAY.
IF WE STAY FOCUSED, MAYBE WE'LL BE EDITORS BEFORE WE'RE 30... MAKE THAT ANTHROPOLOGIE MONEY.
NON-SALE SECTION ANTHRO MONEY!
OHMIGOD, HOW BOUGIE ARE YOU?
AND FUCK THE MTA. WE'LL TAKE CABS EVERYWHERE.

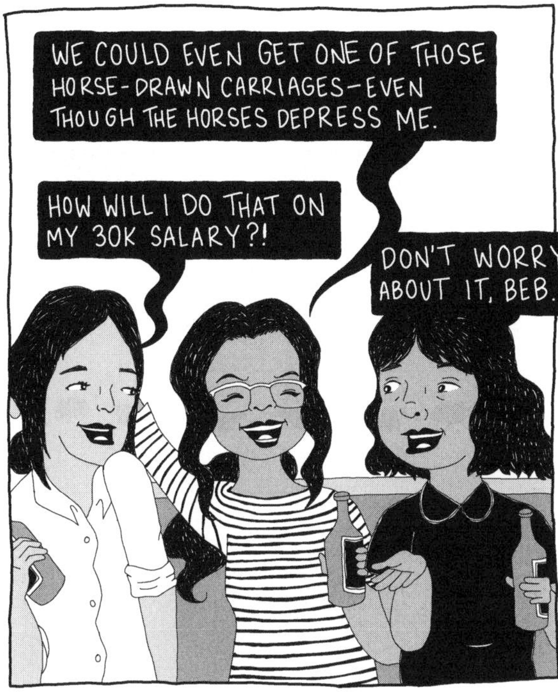
WE COULD EVEN GET ONE OF THOSE HORSE-DRAWN CARRIAGES—EVEN THOUGH THE HORSES DEPRESS ME.
HOW WILL I DO THAT ON MY 30K SALARY?!
DON'T WORRY ABOUT IT, BEB.

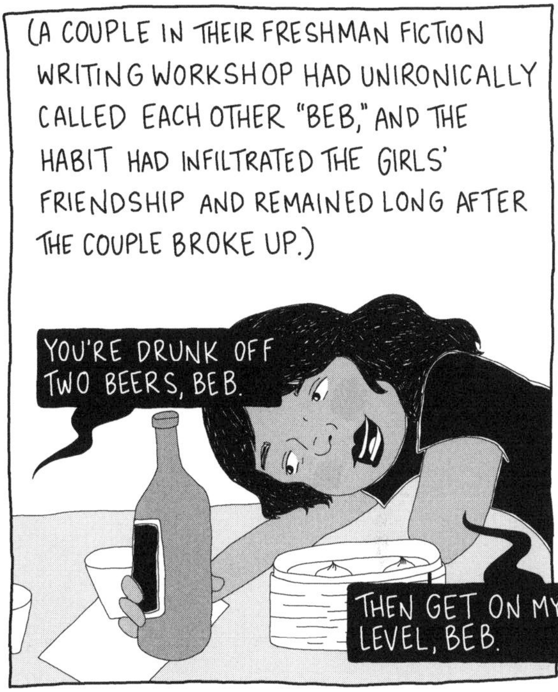
(A COUPLE IN THEIR FRESHMAN FICTION WRITING WORKSHOP HAD UNIRONICALLY CALLED EACH OTHER "BEB," AND THE HABIT HAD INFILTRATED THE GIRLS' FRIENDSHIP AND REMAINED LONG AFTER THE COUPLE BROKE UP.)
YOU'RE DRUNK OFF TWO BEERS, BEB.
THEN GET ON MY LEVEL, BEB.

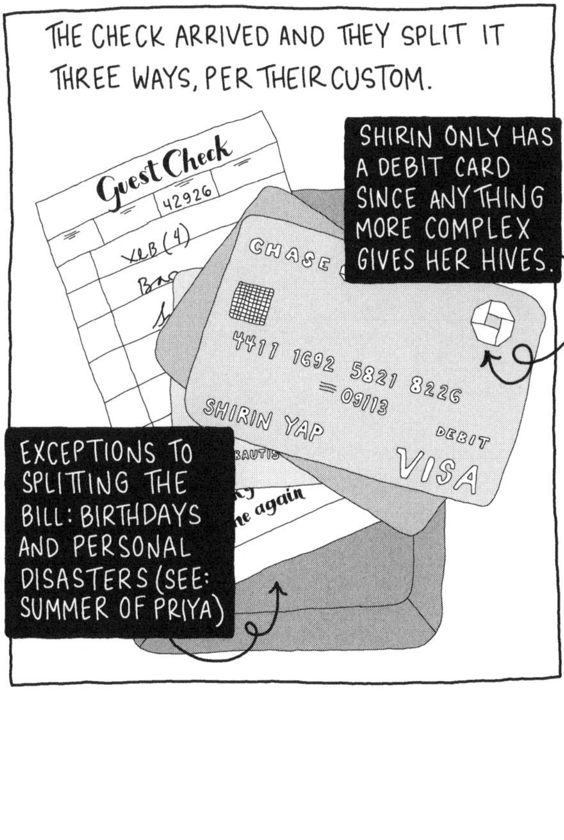
THE CHECK ARRIVED AND THEY SPLIT IT THREE WAYS, PER THEIR CUSTOM.
Guest Check
42926
SHIRIN ONLY HAS A DEBIT CARD SINCE ANYTHING MORE COMPLEX GIVES HER HIVES.
CHASE
4411 1692 5821 8226
09113
SHIRIN YAP
DEBIT
VISA
EXCEPTIONS TO SPLITTING THE BILL: BIRTHDAYS AND PERSONAL DISASTERS (SEE: SUMMER OF PRIYA)

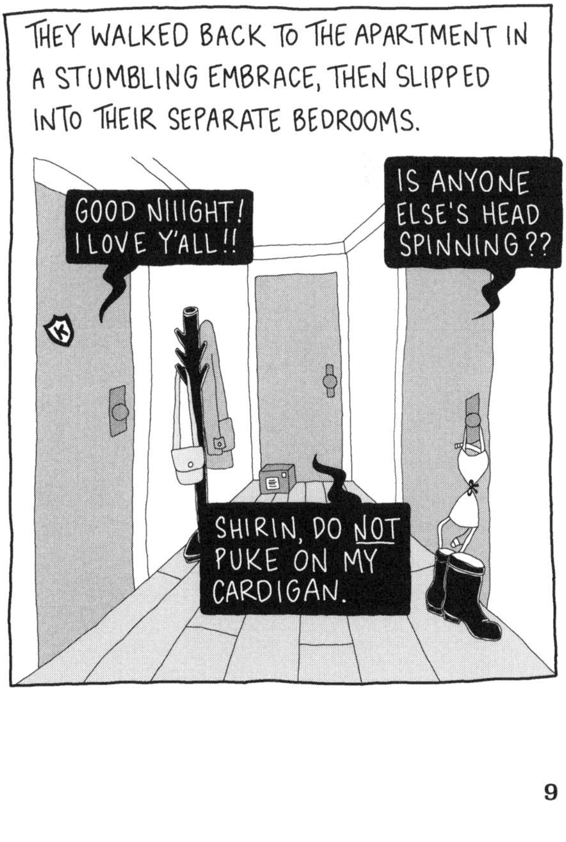
THEY WALKED BACK TO THE APARTMENT IN A STUMBLING EMBRACE, THEN SLIPPED INTO THEIR SEPARATE BEDROOMS.
GOOD NIIIGHT! I LOVE Y'ALL!!
IS ANYONE ELSE'S HEAD SPINNING??
SHIRIN, DO NOT PUKE ON MY CARDIGAN.

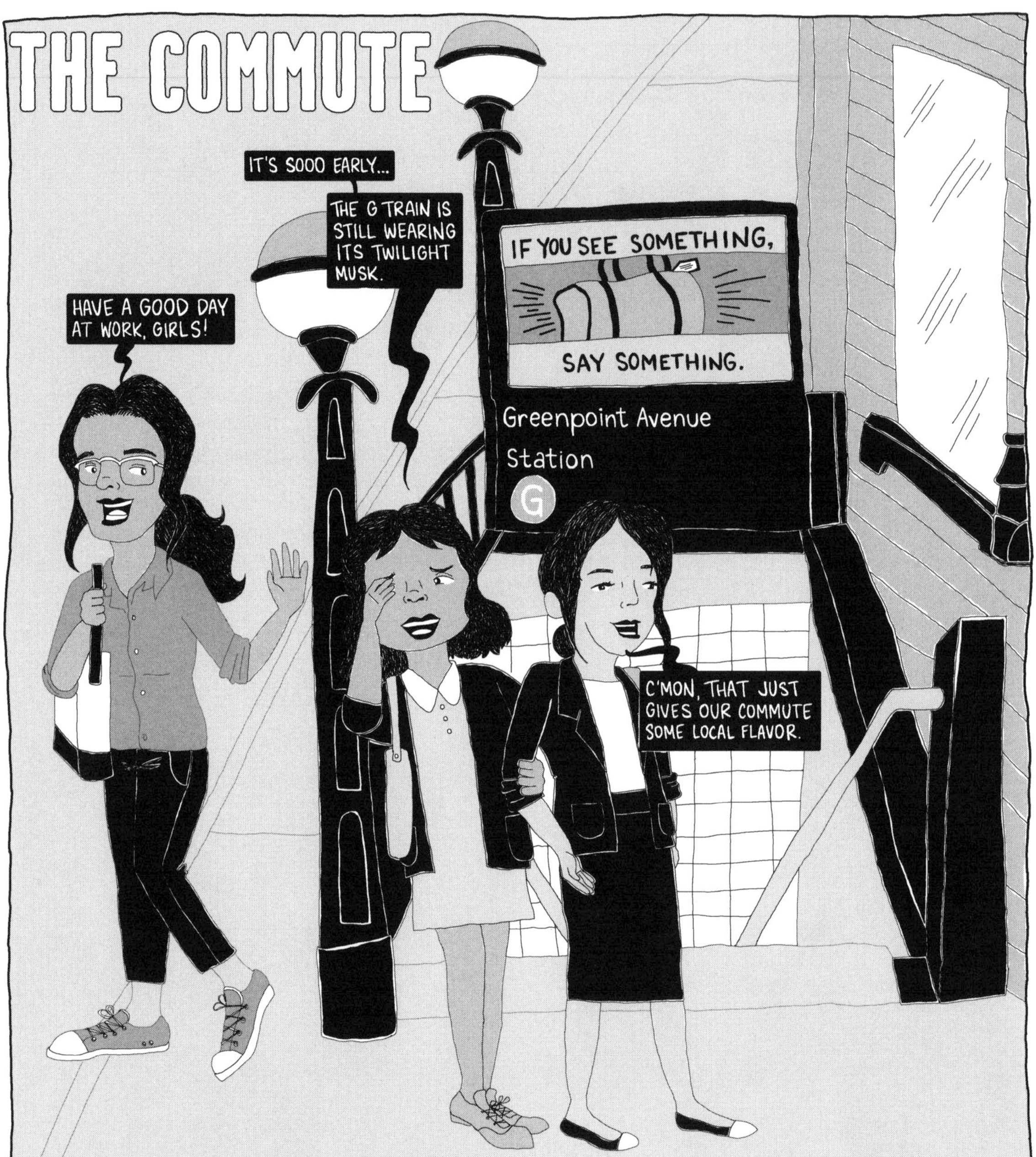
THE COMMUTE
IT'S SOOO EARLY...
THE G TRAIN IS STILL WEARING ITS TWILIGHT MUSK.
HAVE A GOOD DAY AT WORK, GIRLS!
IF YOU SEE SOMETHING,
SAY SOMETHING.
Greenpoint Avenue Station
G
C'MON, THAT JUST GIVES OUR COMMUTE SOME LOCAL FLAVOR.

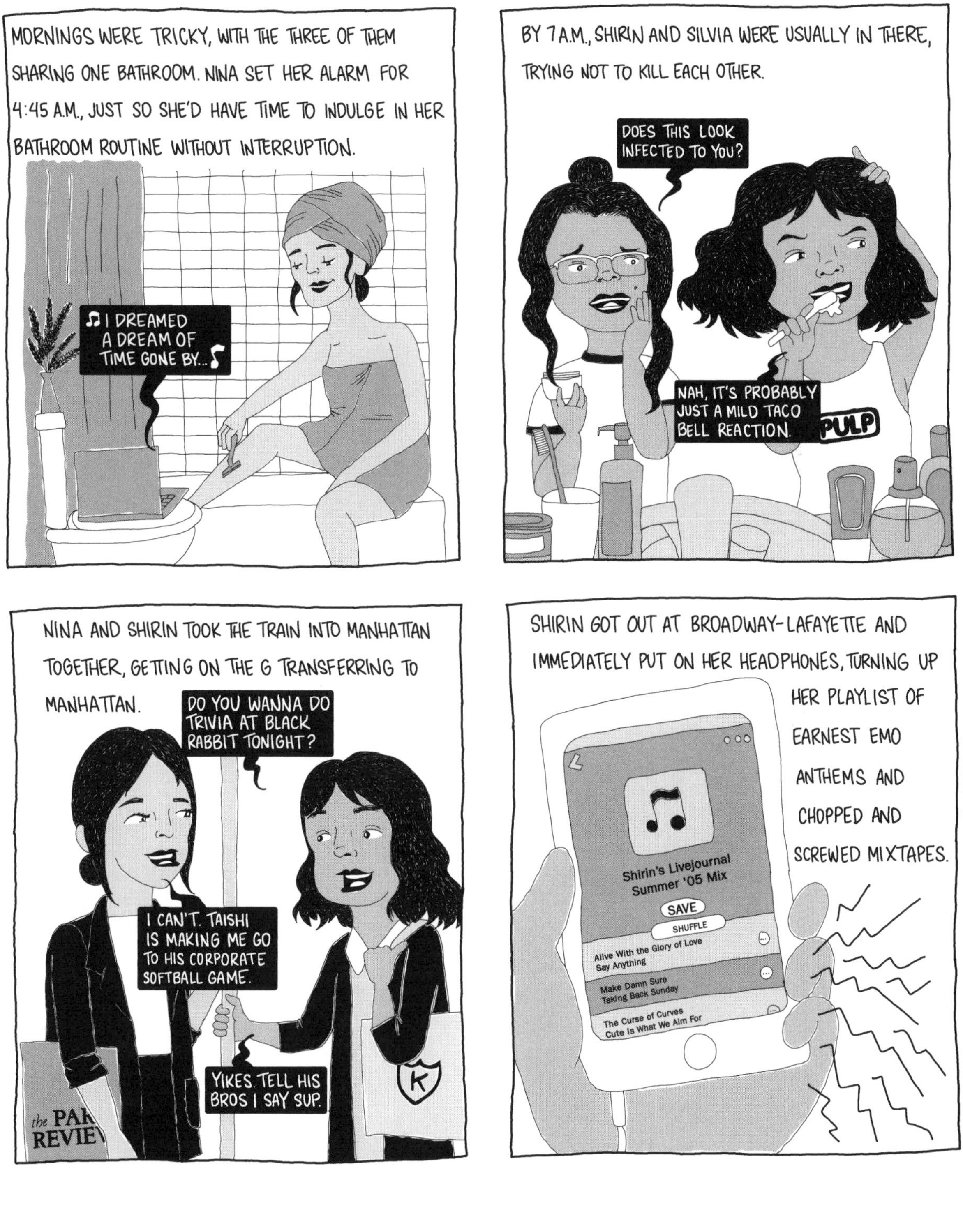
MORNINGS WERE TRICKY, WITH THE THREE OF THEM SHARING ONE BATHROOM. NINA SET HER ALARM FOR 4:45 A.M., JUST SO SHE'D HAVE TIME TO INDULGE IN HER BATHROOM ROUTINE WITHOUT INTERRUPTION.
♫ I DREAMED A DREAM OF TIME GONE BY... ♪
BY 7 A.M., SHIRIN AND SILVIA WERE USUALLY IN THERE, TRYING NOT TO KILL EACH OTHER.
DOES THIS LOOK INFECTED TO YOU?
NAH, IT'S PROBABLY JUST A MILD TACO BELL REACTION.
PULP
NINA AND SHIRIN TOOK THE TRAIN INTO MANHATTAN TOGETHER, GETTING ON THE G TRANSFERRING TO MANHATTAN.
DO YOU WANNA DO TRIVIA AT BLACK RABBIT TONIGHT?
I CAN'T. TAISHI IS MAKING ME GO TO HIS CORPORATE SOFTBALL GAME.
YIKES. TELL HIS BROS I SAY SUP.
SHIRIN GOT OUT AT BROADWAY-LAFAYETTE AND IMMEDIATELY PUT ON HER HEADPHONES, TURNING UP HER PLAYLIST OF EARNEST EMO ANTHEMS AND CHOPPED AND SCREWED MIXTAPES.
Shirin's Livejournal Summer '05 Mix
SAVE
SHUFFLE
Alive With the Glory of Love
Say Anything
Make Damn Sure
Taking Back Sunday
The Curse of Curves
Cute Is What We Aim For

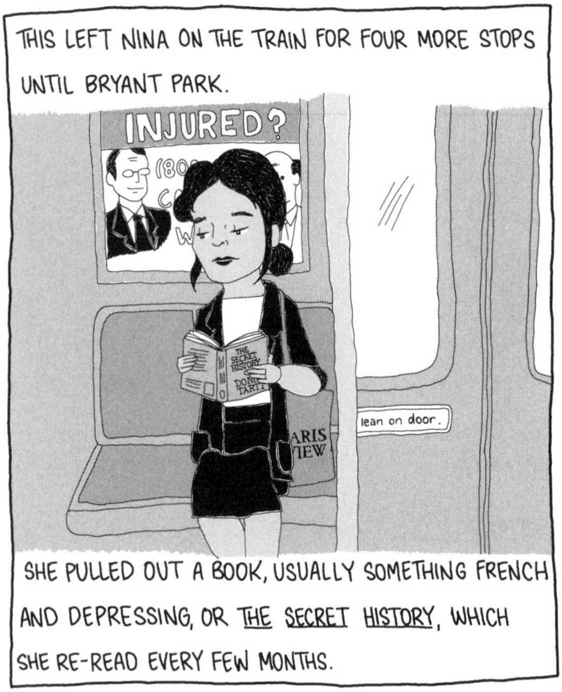
THIS LEFT NINA ON THE TRAIN FOR FOUR MORE STOPS UNTIL BRYANT PARK.
INJURED?
lean on door.
SHE PULLED OUT A BOOK, USUALLY SOMETHING FRENCH AND DEPRESSING, OR THE SECRET HISTORY, WHICH SHE RE-READ EVERY FEW MONTHS.

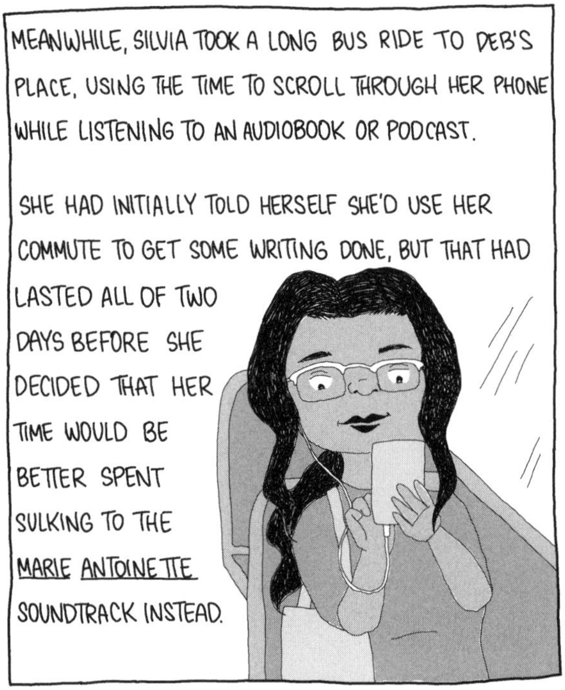
MEANWHILE, SILVIA TOOK A LONG BUS RIDE TO DEB'S PLACE, USING THE TIME TO SCROLL THROUGH HER PHONE WHILE LISTENING TO AN AUDIOBOOK OR PODCAST.
SHE HAD INITIALLY TOLD HERSELF SHE'D USE HER COMMUTE TO GET SOME WRITING DONE, BUT THAT HAD LASTED ALL OF TWO DAYS BEFORE SHE DECIDED THAT HER TIME WOULD BE BETTER SPENT SULKING TO THE MARIE ANTOINETTE SOUNDTRACK INSTEAD.

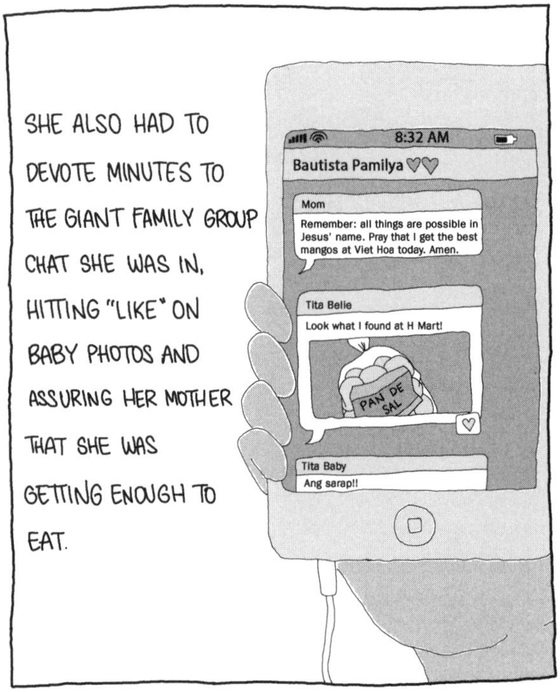
SHE ALSO HAD TO DEVOTE MINUTES TO THE GIANT FAMILY GROUP CHAT SHE WAS IN, HITTING "LIKE" ON BABY PHOTOS AND ASSURING HER MOTHER THAT SHE WAS GETTING ENOUGH TO EAT.
8:32 AM
Bautista Pamilya ♡♡
Mom
Remember: all things are possible in Jesus' name. Pray that I get the best mangos at Viet Hoa today. Amen.
Tita Belle
Look what I found at H Mart!
PAN DE SAL
Tita Baby
Ang sarap!!

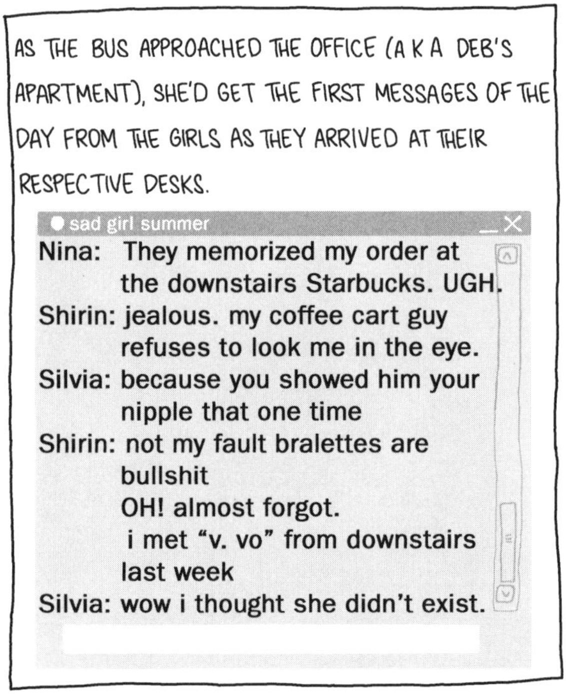
AS THE BUS APPROACHED THE OFFICE (A K A DEB'S APARTMENT), SHE'D GET THE FIRST MESSAGES OF THE DAY FROM THE GIRLS AS THEY ARRIVED AT THEIR RESPECTIVE DESKS.
sad girl summer
Nina: They memorized my order at the downstairs Starbucks. UGH.
Shirin: jealous. my coffee cart guy refuses to look me in the eye.
Silvia: because you showed him your nipple that one time
Shirin: not my fault bralettes are bullshit
OH! almost forgot.
i met "v. vo" from downstairs last week
Silvia: wow i thought she didn't exist.

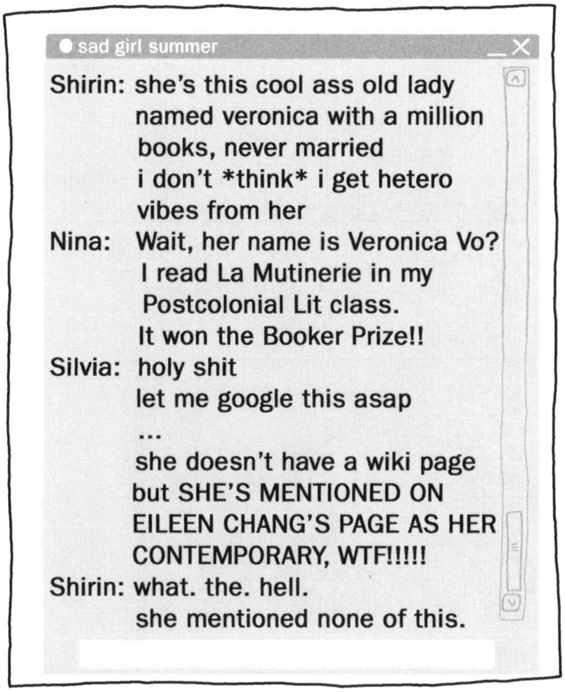
sad girl summer
Shirin: she's this cool ass old lady
named veronica with a million
books, never married
i don't *think* i get hetero
vibes from her
Nina: Wait, her name is Veronica Vo?
I read La Mutinerie in my
Postcolonial Lit class.
It won the Booker Prize!!
Silvia: holy shit
let me google this asap
...
she doesn't have a wiki page
but SHE'S MENTIONED ON
EILEEN CHANG'S PAGE AS HER
CONTEMPORARY, WTF!!!!!
Shirin: what. the. hell.
she mentioned none of this.

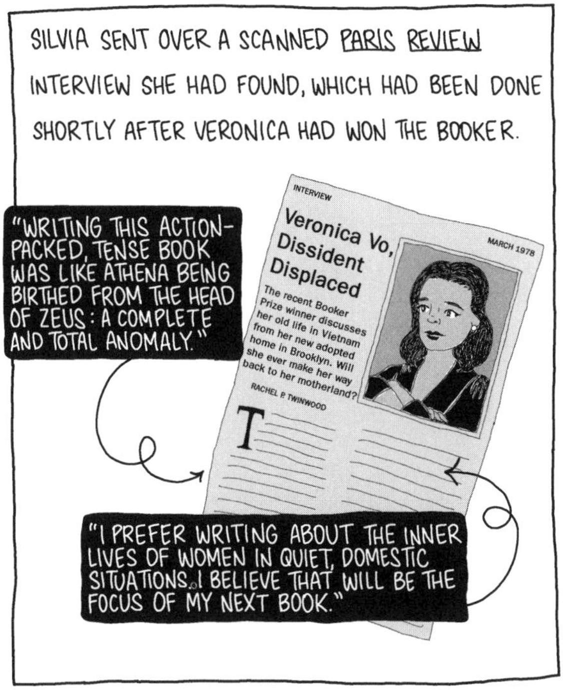
SILVIA SENT OVER A SCANNED PARIS REVIEW INTERVIEW SHE HAD FOUND, WHICH HAD BEEN DONE SHORTLY AFTER VERONICA HAD WON THE BOOKER.
"WRITING THIS ACTION-PACKED, TENSE BOOK WAS LIKE ATHENA BEING BIRTHED FROM THE HEAD OF ZEUS: A COMPLETE AND TOTAL ANOMALY."
INTERVIEW
Veronica Vo, Dissident Displaced
MARCH 1978
The recent Booker Prize winner discusses her old life in Vietnam from her new adopted home in Brooklyn. Will she ever make her way back to her motherland?
RACHEL P. TWINWOOD
"I PREFER WRITING ABOUT THE INNER LIVES OF WOMEN IN QUIET, DOMESTIC SITUATIONS. I BELIEVE THAT WILL BE THE FOCUS OF MY NEXT BOOK."

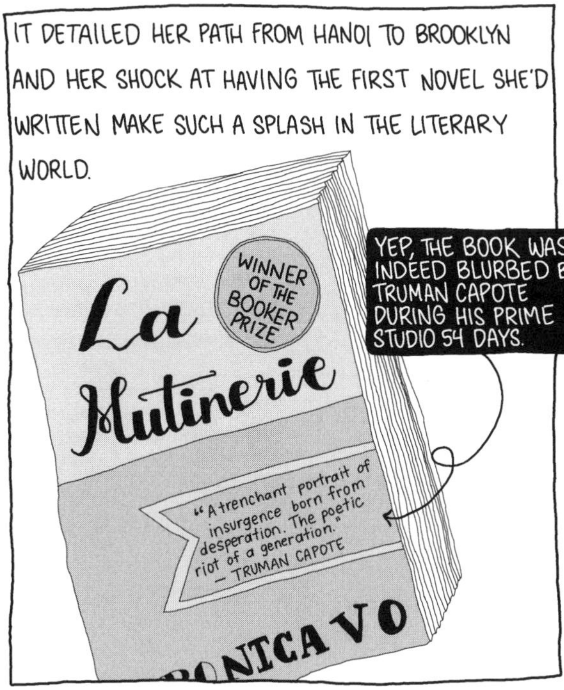
IT DETAILED HER PATH FROM HANOI TO BROOKLYN AND HER SHOCK AT HAVING THE FIRST NOVEL SHE'D WRITTEN MAKE SUCH A SPLASH IN THE LITERARY WORLD.
YEP, THE BOOK WAS INDEED BLURBED BY TRUMAN CAPOTE DURING HIS PRIME STUDIO 54 DAYS.
WINNER OF THE BOOKER PRIZE
La Mutinerie
"A trenchant portrait of insurgence born from desperation. The poetic riot of a generation."
— TRUMAN CAPOTE

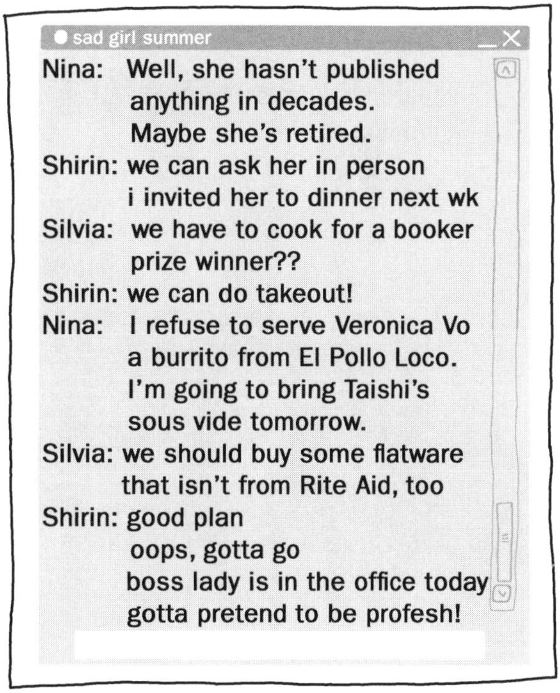
sad girl summer
Nina: Well, she hasn't published
anything in decades.
Maybe she's retired.
Shirin: we can ask her in person
i invited her to dinner next wk
Silvia: we have to cook for a booker
prize winner??
Shirin: we can do takeout!
Nina: I refuse to serve Veronica Vo
a burrito from El Pollo Loco.
I'm going to bring Taishi's
sous vide tomorrow.
Silvia: we should buy some flatware
that isn't from Rite Aid, too
Shirin: good plan
oops, gotta go
boss lady is in the office today
gotta pretend to be profesh!

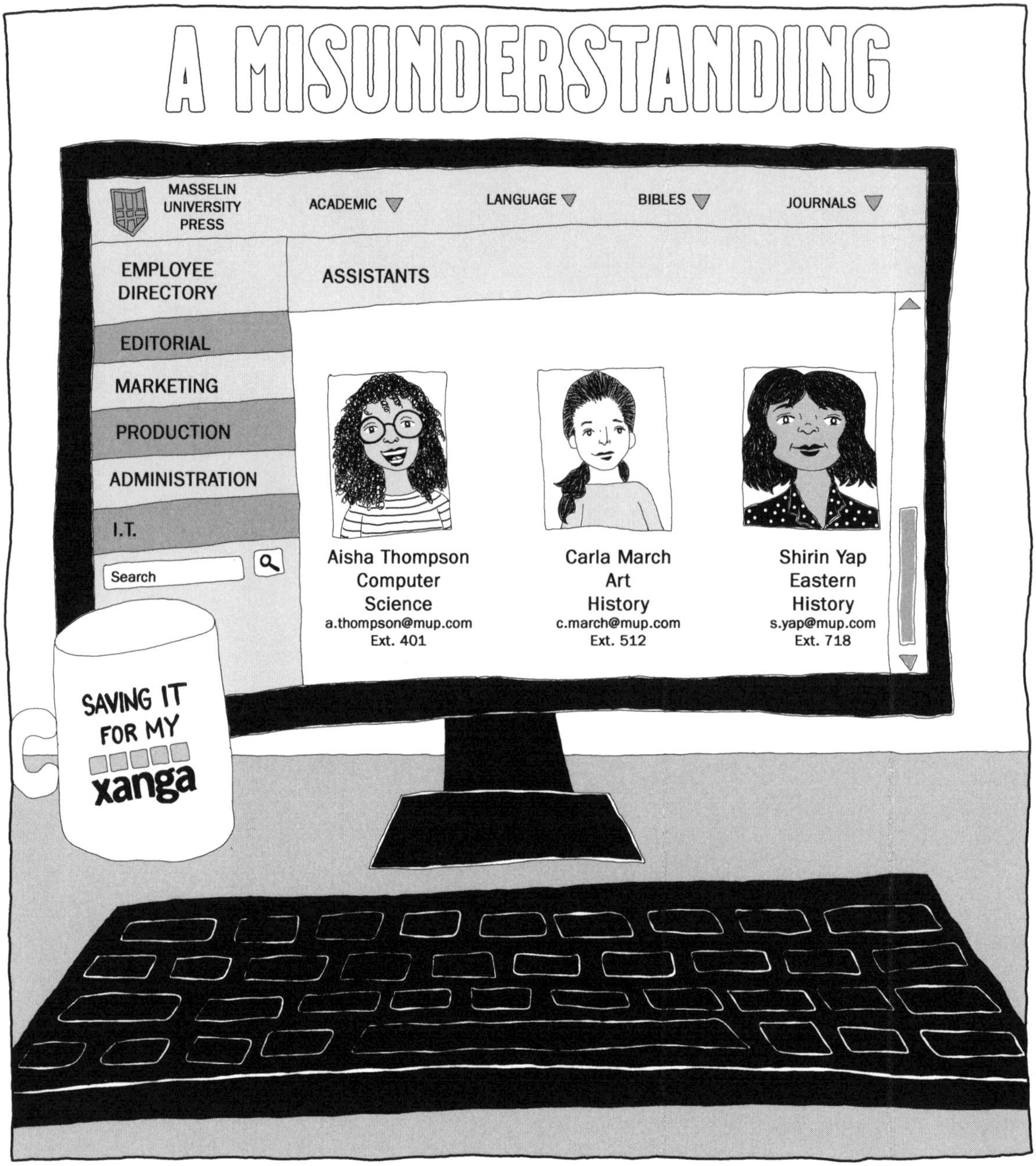
A MISUNDERSTANDING
MASSELIN UNIVERSITY PRESS
ACADEMIC
LANGUAGE
BIBLES
JOURNALS
EMPLOYEE DIRECTORY
EDITORIAL
MARKETING
PRODUCTION
ADMINISTRATION
I.T.
Search
ASSISTANTS
Aisha Thompson
Computer Science
a.thompson@mup.com
Ext. 401
Carla March
Art History
c.march@mup.com
Ext. 512
Shirin Yap
Eastern History
s.yap@mup.com
Ext. 718
SAVING IT FOR MY
xanga

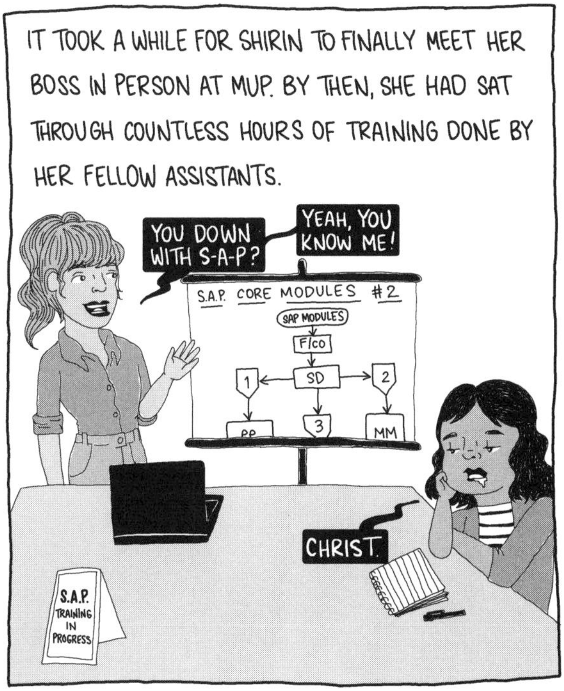
IT TOOK A WHILE FOR SHIRIN TO FINALLY MEET HER BOSS IN PERSON AT MUP. BY THEN, SHE HAD SAT THROUGH COUNTLESS HOURS OF TRAINING DONE BY HER FELLOW ASSISTANTS.
YOU DOWN WITH S-A-P?
YEAH, YOU KNOW ME!
S.A.P. CORE MODULES #2
SAP MODULES
F/CO
SD
1
2
3
MM
CHRIST.
S.A.P. TRAINING IN PROGRESS

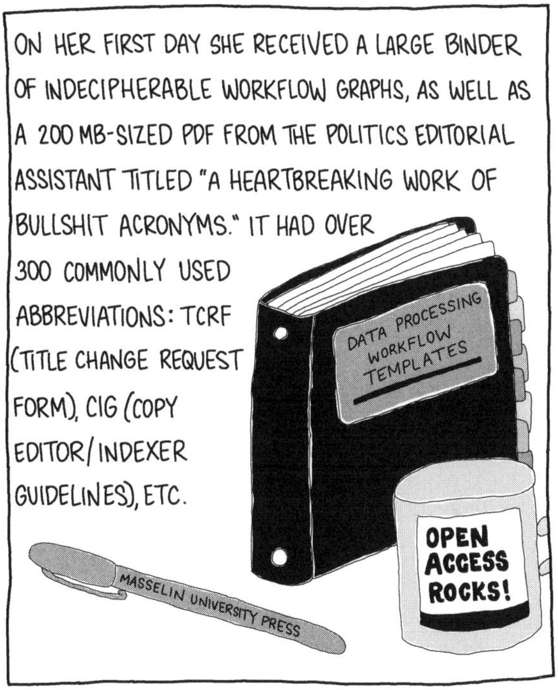
ON HER FIRST DAY SHE RECEIVED A LARGE BINDER OF INDECIPHERABLE WORKFLOW GRAPHS, AS WELL AS A 200 MB-SIZED PDF FROM THE POLITICS EDITORIAL ASSISTANT TITLED "A HEARTBREAKING WORK OF BULLSHIT ACRONYMS." IT HAD OVER 300 COMMONLY USED ABBREVIATIONS: TCRF (TITLE CHANGE REQUEST FORM), CIG (COPY EDITOR/INDEXER GUIDELINES), ETC.
DATA PROCESSING WORKFLOW TEMPLATES
OPEN ACCESS ROCKS!
MASSELIN UNIVERSITY PRESS

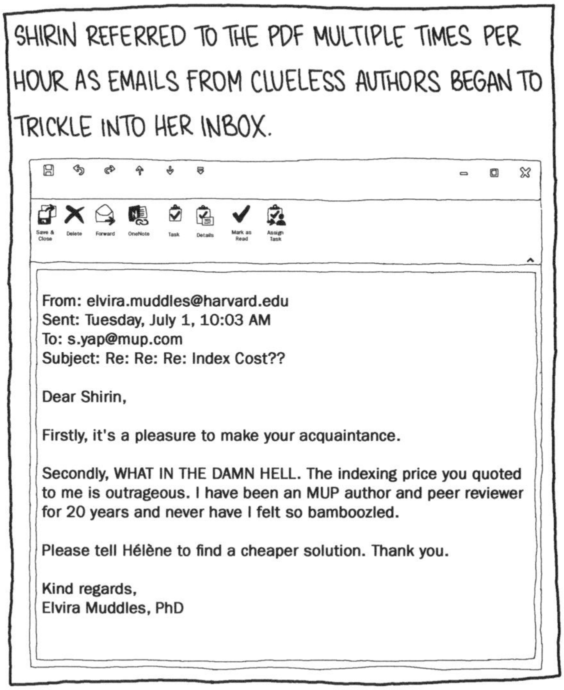
SHIRIN REFERRED TO THE PDF MULTIPLE TIMES PER HOUR AS EMAILS FROM CLUELESS AUTHORS BEGAN TO TRICKLE INTO HER INBOX.
Save & Close
Delete
Forward
OneNote
Task
Details
Mark as Read
Assign Task
From: elvira.muddles@harvard.edu
Sent: Tuesday, July 1, 10:03 AM
To: s.yap@mup.com
Subject: Re: Re: Re: Index Cost??
Dear Shirin,
Firstly, it's a pleasure to make your acquaintance.
Secondly, WHAT IN THE DAMN HELL. The indexing price you quoted to me is outrageous. I have been an MUP author and peer reviewer for 20 years and never have I felt so bamboozled.
Please tell Hélène to find a cheaper solution. Thank you.
Kind regards,
Elvira Muddles, PhD

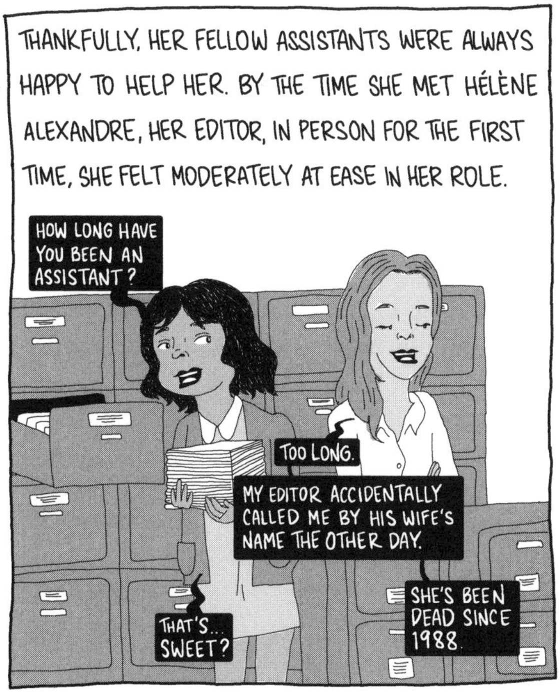
THANKFULLY, HER FELLOW ASSISTANTS WERE ALWAYS HAPPY TO HELP HER. BY THE TIME SHE MET HÉLÈNE ALEXANDRE, HER EDITOR, IN PERSON FOR THE FIRST TIME, SHE FELT MODERATELY AT EASE IN HER ROLE.
HOW LONG HAVE YOU BEEN AN ASSISTANT?
TOO LONG.
MY EDITOR ACCIDENTALLY CALLED ME BY HIS WIFE'S NAME THE OTHER DAY.
THAT'S... SWEET?
SHE'S BEEN DEAD SINCE 1988.

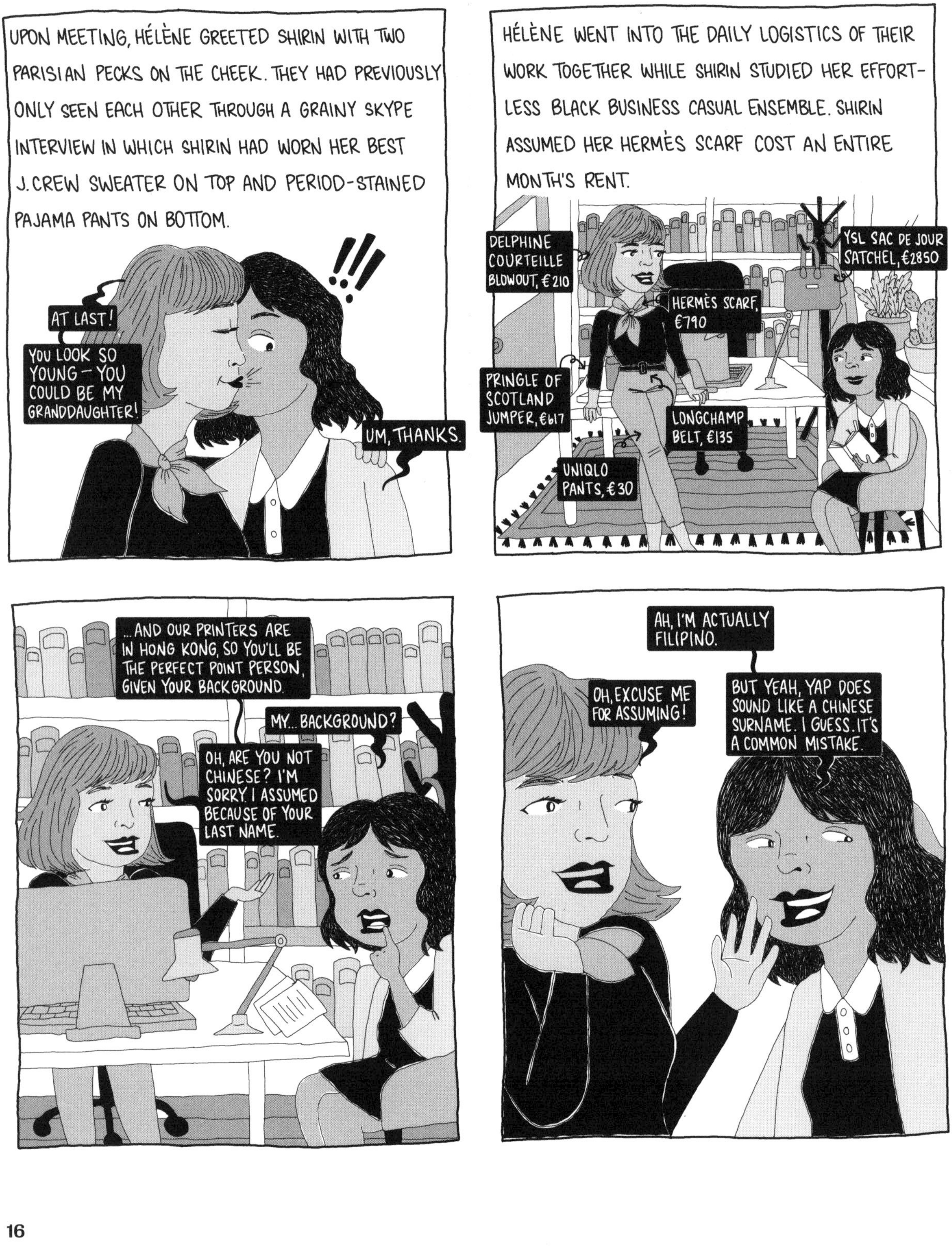
UPON MEETING, HÉLÈNE GREETED SHIRIN WITH TWO PARISIAN PECKS ON THE CHEEK. THEY HAD PREVIOUSLY ONLY SEEN EACH OTHER THROUGH A GRAINY SKYPE INTERVIEW IN WHICH SHIRIN HAD WORN HER BEST J.CREW SWEATER ON TOP AND PERIOD-STAINED PAJAMA PANTS ON BOTTOM.
!!!
AT LAST!
YOU LOOK SO YOUNG – YOU COULD BE MY GRANDDAUGHTER!
UM, THANKS.
HÉLÈNE WENT INTO THE DAILY LOGISTICS OF THEIR WORK TOGETHER WHILE SHIRIN STUDIED HER EFFORTLESS BLACK BUSINESS CASUAL ENSEMBLE. SHIRIN ASSUMED HER HERMÈS SCARF COST AN ENTIRE MONTH'S RENT.
DELPHINE COURTEILLE BLOWOUT, €210
YSL SAC DE JOUR SATCHEL, €2850
HERMÈS SCARF, €790
PRINGLE OF SCOTLAND JUMPER, €617
LONGCHAMP BELT, €135
UNIQLO PANTS, €30
...AND OUR PRINTERS ARE IN HONG KONG, SO YOU'LL BE THE PERFECT POINT PERSON, GIVEN YOUR BACKGROUND.
MY... BACKGROUND?
OH, ARE YOU NOT CHINESE? I'M SORRY. I ASSUMED BECAUSE OF YOUR LAST NAME.
AH, I'M ACTUALLY FILIPINO.
OH, EXCUSE ME FOR ASSUMING!
BUT YEAH, YAP DOES SOUND LIKE A CHINESE SURNAME. I GUESS. IT'S A COMMON MISTAKE.

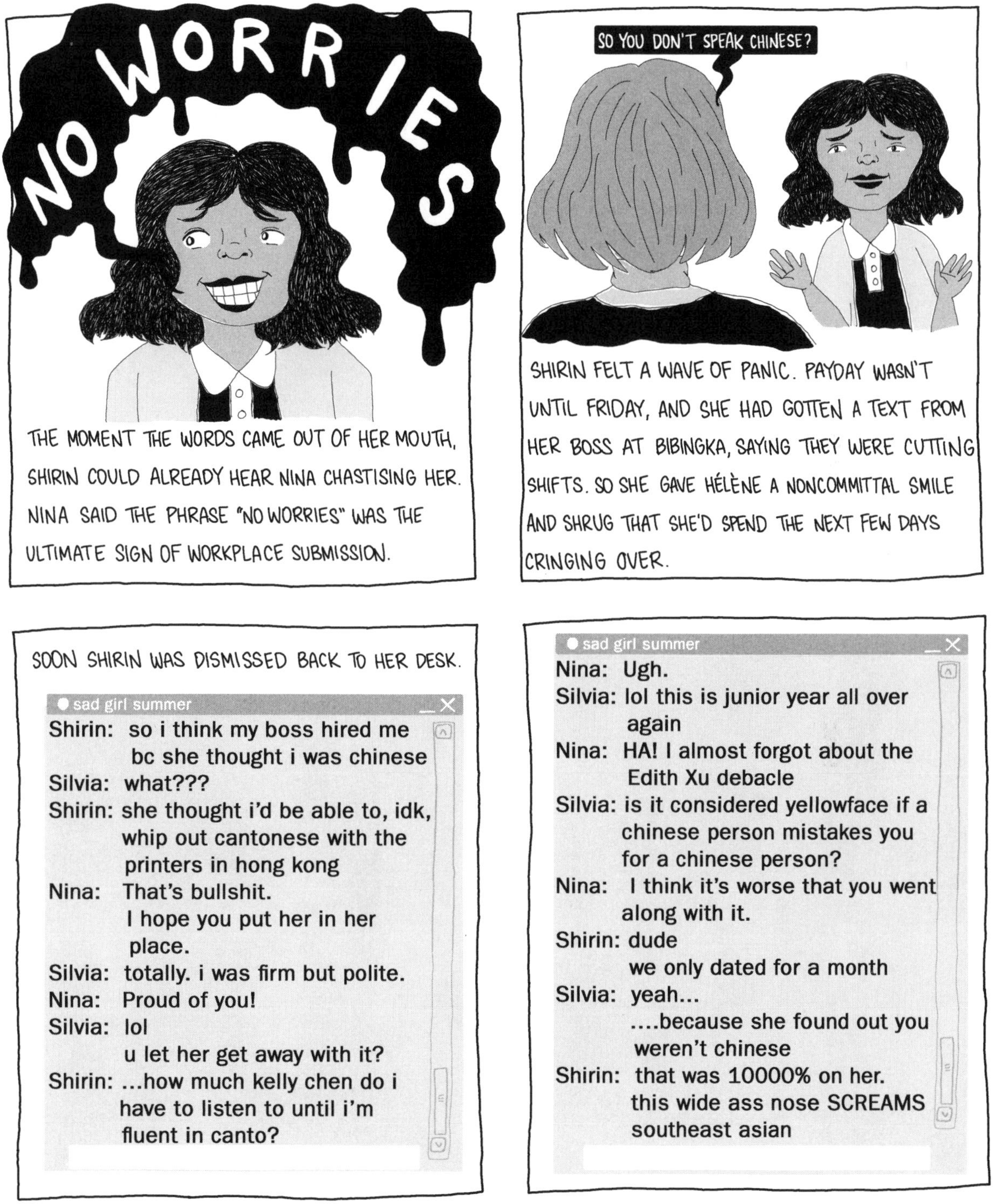
NO WORRIES
THE MOMENT THE WORDS CAME OUT OF HER MOUTH, SHIRIN COULD ALREADY HEAR NINA CHASTISING HER. NINA SAID THE PHRASE "NO WORRIES" WAS THE ULTIMATE SIGN OF WORKPLACE SUBMISSION.
SO YOU DON'T SPEAK CHINESE?
SHIRIN FELT A WAVE OF PANIC. PAYDAY WASN'T UNTIL FRIDAY, AND SHE HAD GOTTEN A TEXT FROM HER BOSS AT BIBINGKA, SAYING THEY WERE CUTTING SHIFTS. SO SHE GAVE HÉLÈNE A NONCOMMITTAL SMILE AND SHRUG THAT SHE'D SPEND THE NEXT FEW DAYS CRINGING OVER.
SOON SHIRIN WAS DISMISSED BACK TO HER DESK.
sad girl summer
Shirin: so i think my boss hired me bc she thought i was chinese
Silvia: what???
Shirin: she thought i'd be able to, idk, whip out cantonese with the printers in hong kong
Nina: That's bullshit.
I hope you put her in her place.
Silvia: totally. i was firm but polite.
Nina: Proud of you!
Silvia: lol
u let her get away with it?
Shirin: ...how much kelly chen do i have to listen to until i'm fluent in canto?
sad girl summer
Nina: Ugh.
Silvia: lol this is junior year all over again
Nina: HA! I almost forgot about the Edith Xu debacle
Silvia: is it considered yellowface if a chinese person mistakes you for a chinese person?
Nina: I think it's worse that you went along with it.
Shirin: dude
we only dated for a month
Silvia: yeah...
....because she found out you weren't chinese
Shirin: that was 10000% on her.
this wide ass nose SCREAMS southeast asian

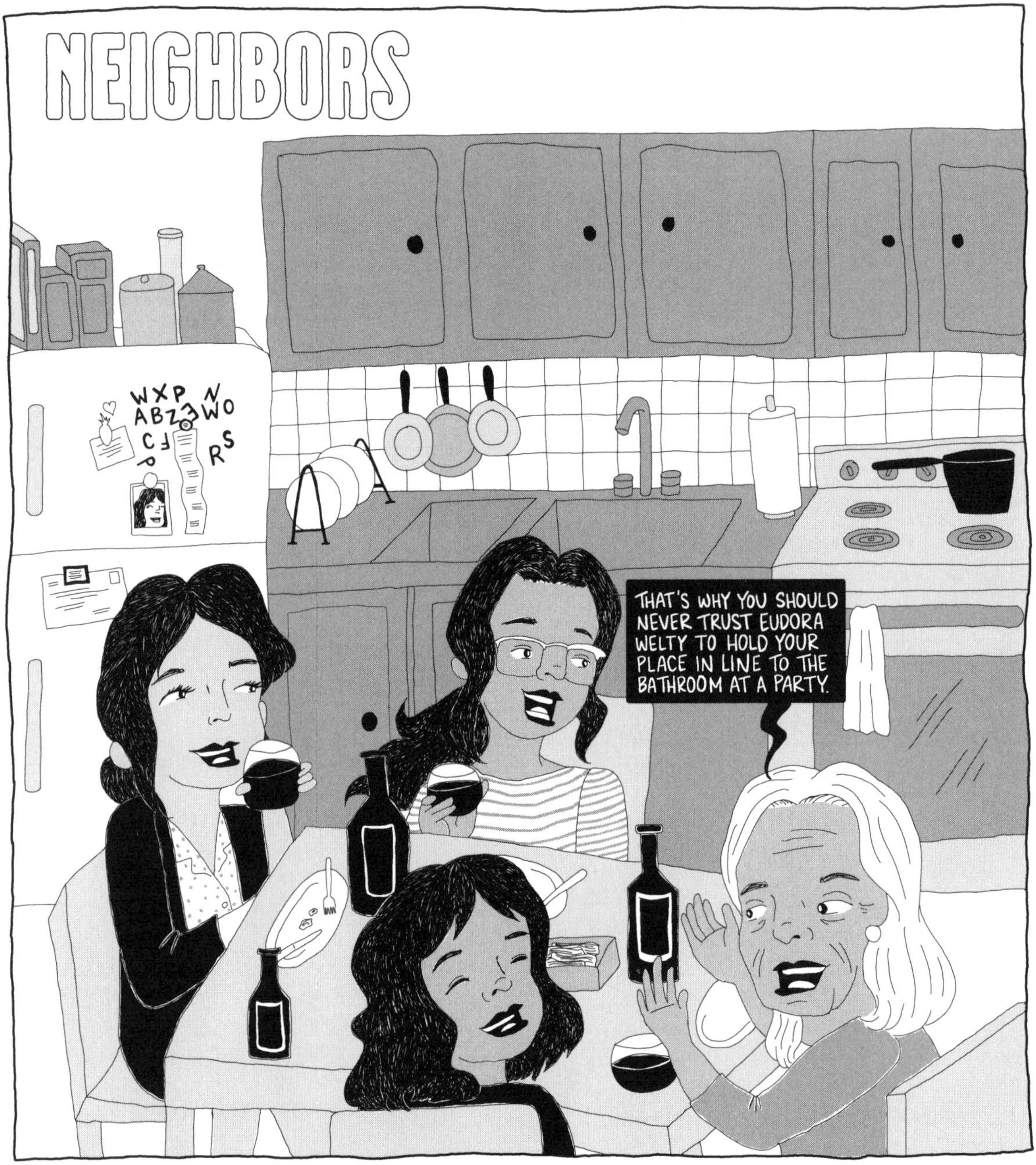
NEIGHBORS
THAT'S WHY YOU SHOULD NEVER TRUST EUDORA WELTY TO HOLD YOUR PLACE IN LINE TO THE BATHROOM AT A PARTY.

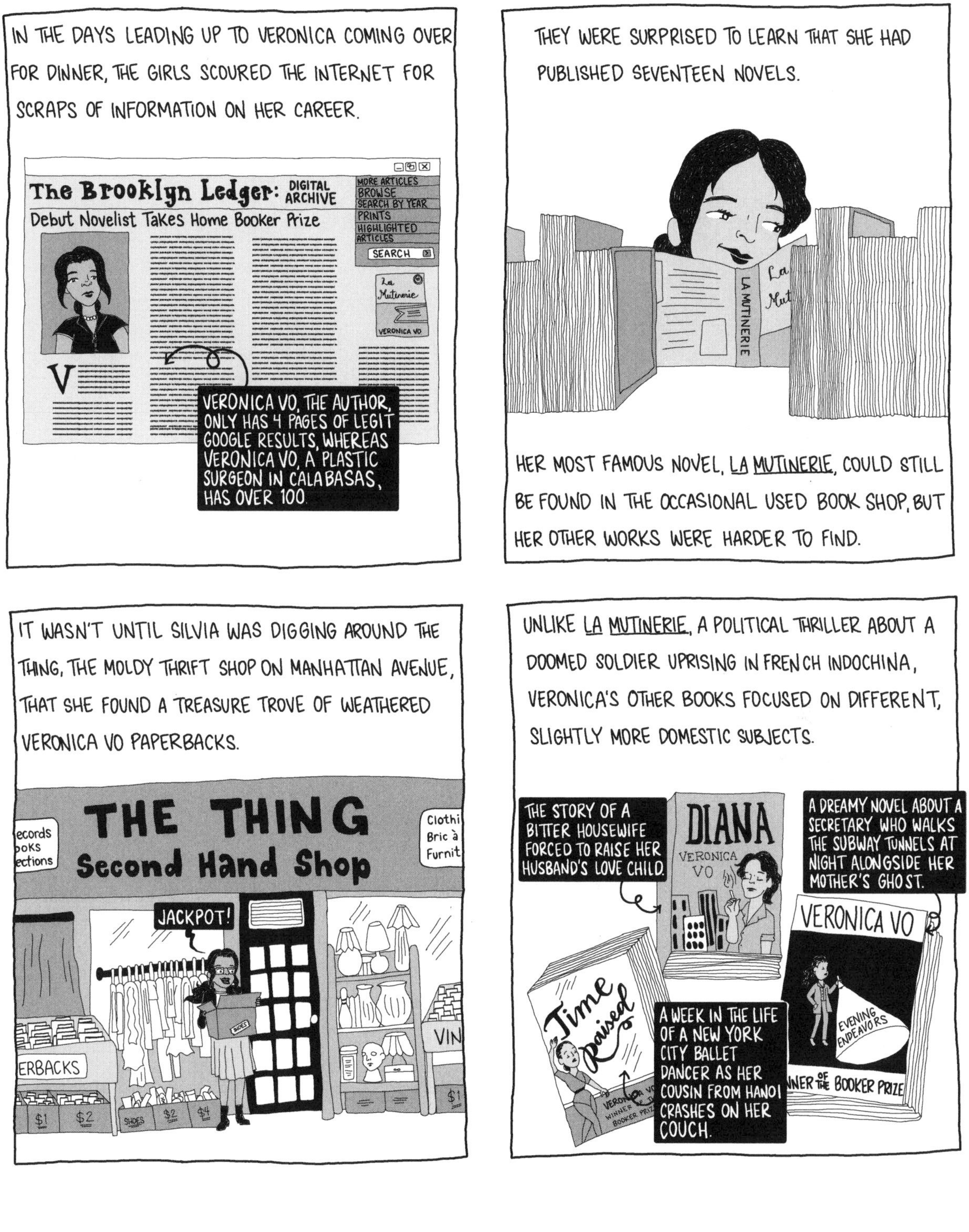
IN THE DAYS LEADING UP TO VERONICA COMING OVER FOR DINNER, THE GIRLS SCOURED THE INTERNET FOR SCRAPS OF INFORMATION ON HER CAREER.
The Brooklyn Ledger: DIGITAL ARCHIVE
MORE ARTICLES
BROWSE
SEARCH BY YEAR
PRINTS
HIGHLIGHTED ARTICLES
SEARCH
Debut Novelist Takes Home Booker Prize
La Mutinerie
VERONICA VO
VERONICA VO, THE AUTHOR, ONLY HAS 4 PAGES OF LEGIT GOOGLE RESULTS, WHEREAS VERONICA VO, A PLASTIC SURGEON IN CALABASAS, HAS OVER 100.
THEY WERE SURPRISED TO LEARN THAT SHE HAD PUBLISHED SEVENTEEN NOVELS.
LA MUTINERIE
HER MOST FAMOUS NOVEL, LA MUTINERIE, COULD STILL BE FOUND IN THE OCCASIONAL USED BOOK SHOP, BUT HER OTHER WORKS WERE HARDER TO FIND.
IT WASN'T UNTIL SILVIA WAS DIGGING AROUND THE THING, THE MOLDY THRIFT SHOP ON MANHATTAN AVENUE, THAT SHE FOUND A TREASURE TROVE OF WEATHERED VERONICA VO PAPERBACKS.
THE THING
Second Hand Shop
JACKPOT!
UNLIKE LA MUTINERIE, A POLITICAL THRILLER ABOUT A DOOMED SOLDIER UPRISING IN FRENCH INDOCHINA, VERONICA'S OTHER BOOKS FOCUSED ON DIFFERENT, SLIGHTLY MORE DOMESTIC SUBJECTS.
THE STORY OF A BITTER HOUSEWIFE FORCED TO RAISE HER HUSBAND'S LOVE CHILD.
DIANA
VERONICA VO
A DREAMY NOVEL ABOUT A SECRETARY WHO WALKS THE SUBWAY TUNNELS AT NIGHT ALONGSIDE HER MOTHER'S GHOST.
VERONICA VO
EVENING ENDEAVORS
Time Raised
A WEEK IN THE LIFE OF A NEW YORK CITY BALLET DANCER AS HER COUSIN FROM HANOI CRASHES ON HER COUCH.

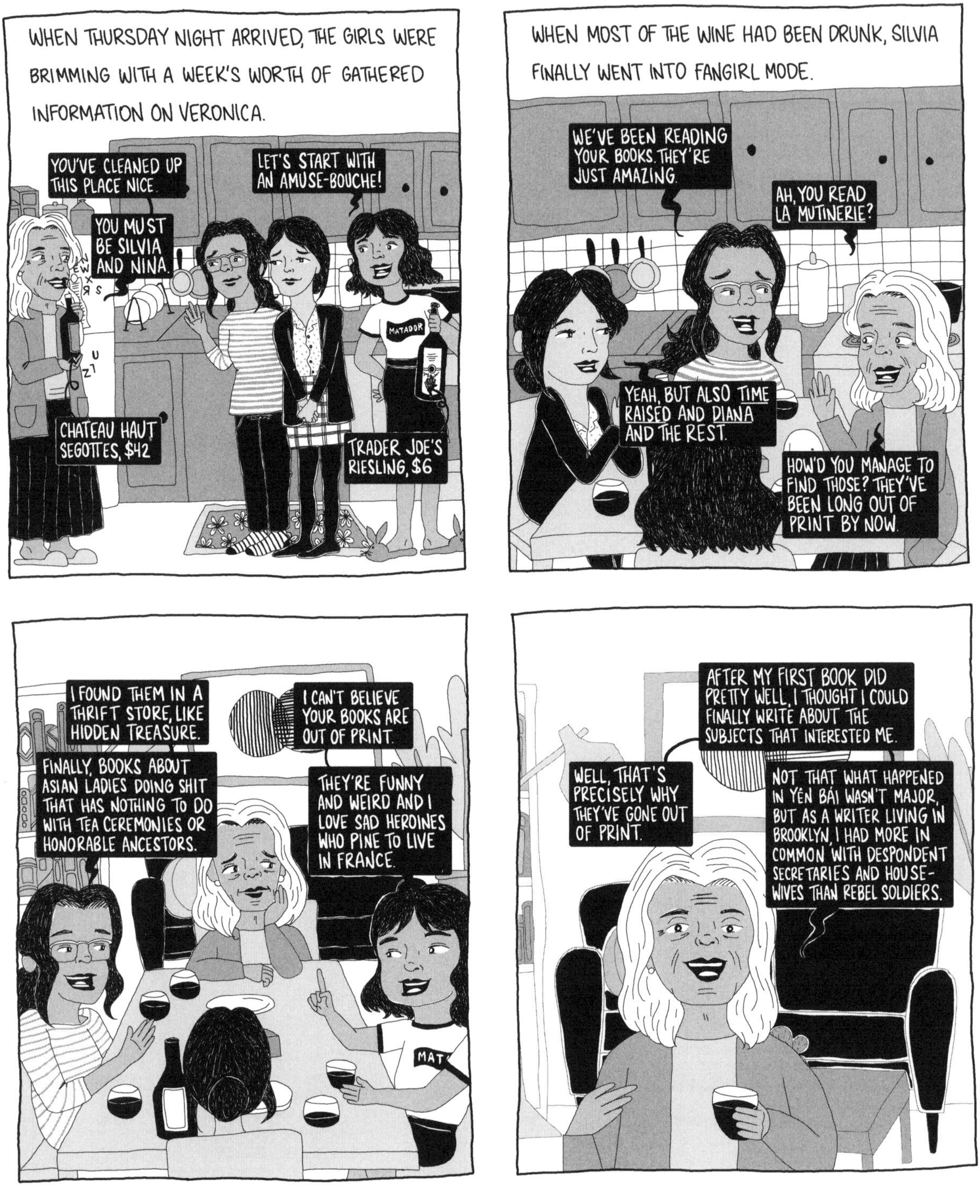
WHEN THURSDAY NIGHT ARRIVED, THE GIRLS WERE BRIMMING WITH A WEEK'S WORTH OF GATHERED INFORMATION ON VERONICA.
YOU'VE CLEANED UP THIS PLACE NICE.
LET'S START WITH AN AMUSE-BOUCHE!
YOU MUST BE SILVIA AND NINA.
MATADOR
CHATEAU HAUT SEGOTTES, $42
TRADER JOE'S RIESLING, $6
WHEN MOST OF THE WINE HAD BEEN DRUNK, SILVIA FINALLY WENT INTO FANGIRL MODE.
WE'VE BEEN READING YOUR BOOKS. THEY'RE JUST AMAZING.
AH, YOU READ LA MUTINERIE?
YEAH, BUT ALSO TIME RAISED AND DIANA AND THE REST.
HOW'D YOU MANAGE TO FIND THOSE? THEY'VE BEEN LONG OUT OF PRINT BY NOW.
I FOUND THEM IN A THRIFT STORE, LIKE HIDDEN TREASURE.
I CAN'T BELIEVE YOUR BOOKS ARE OUT OF PRINT.
FINALLY, BOOKS ABOUT ASIAN LADIES DOING SHIT THAT HAS NOTHING TO DO WITH TEA CEREMONIES OR HONORABLE ANCESTORS.
THEY'RE FUNNY AND WEIRD AND I LOVE SAD HEROINES WHO PINE TO LIVE IN FRANCE.
MAT
AFTER MY FIRST BOOK DID PRETTY WELL, I THOUGHT I COULD FINALLY WRITE ABOUT THE SUBJECTS THAT INTERESTED ME.
WELL, THAT'S PRECISELY WHY THEY'VE GONE OUT OF PRINT.
NOT THAT WHAT HAPPENED IN YÊN BÁI WASN'T MAJOR, BUT AS A WRITER LIVING IN BROOKLYN, I HAD MORE IN COMMON WITH DESPONDENT SECRETARIES AND HOUSE-WIVES THAN REBEL SOLDIERS.

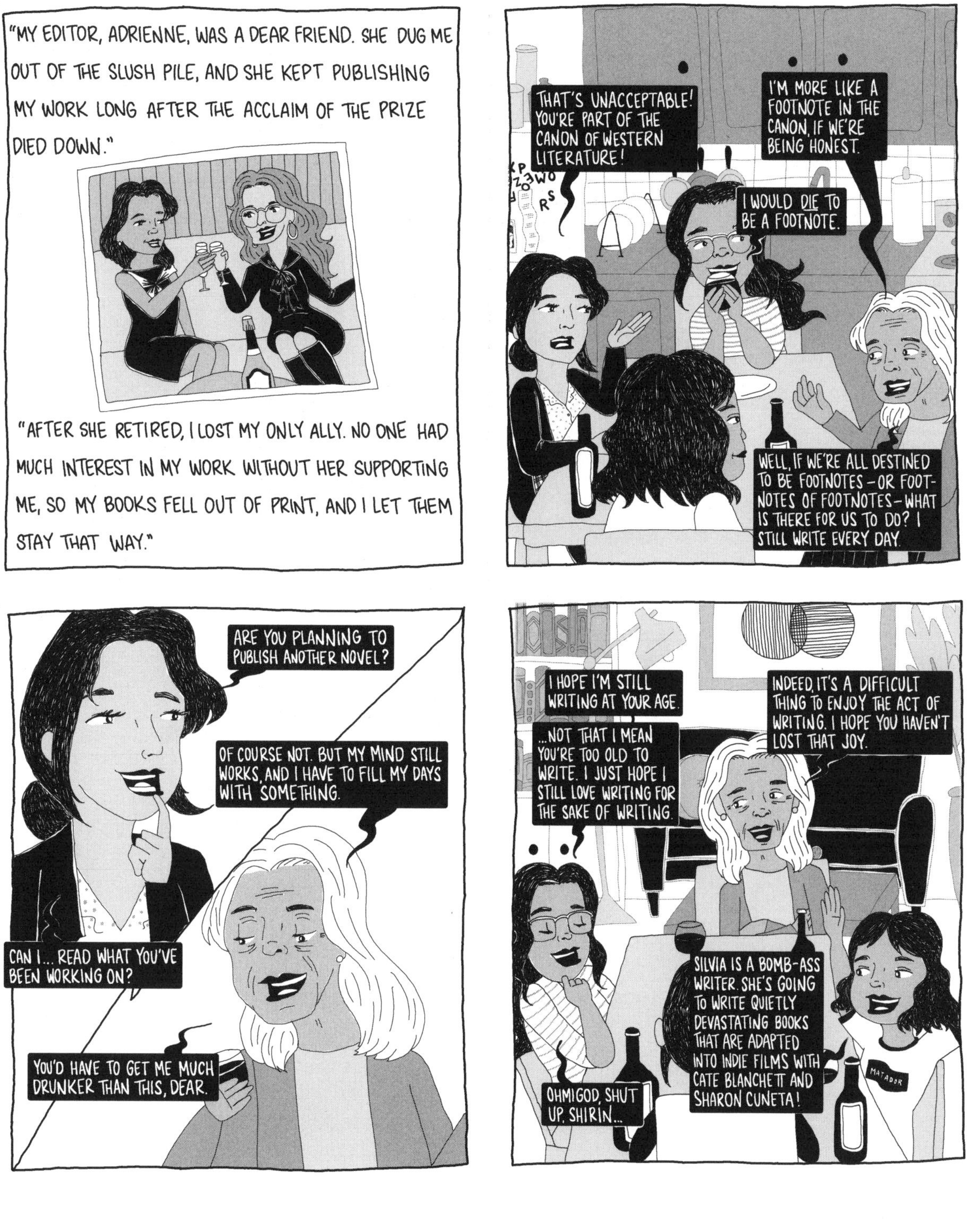
"MY EDITOR, ADRIENNE, WAS A DEAR FRIEND. SHE DUG ME OUT OF THE SLUSH PILE, AND SHE KEPT PUBLISHING MY WORK LONG AFTER THE ACCLAIM OF THE PRIZE DIED DOWN."
"AFTER SHE RETIRED, I LOST MY ONLY ALLY. NO ONE HAD MUCH INTEREST IN MY WORK WITHOUT HER SUPPORTING ME, SO MY BOOKS FELL OUT OF PRINT, AND I LET THEM STAY THAT WAY."
THAT'S UNACCEPTABLE! YOU'RE PART OF THE CANON OF WESTERN LITERATURE!
I'M MORE LIKE A FOOTNOTE IN THE CANON, IF WE'RE BEING HONEST.
I WOULD DIE TO BE A FOOTNOTE.
WELL, IF WE'RE ALL DESTINED TO BE FOOTNOTES—OR FOOTNOTES OF FOOTNOTES—WHAT IS THERE FOR US TO DO? I STILL WRITE EVERY DAY.
ARE YOU PLANNING TO PUBLISH ANOTHER NOVEL?
OF COURSE NOT. BUT MY MIND STILL WORKS, AND I HAVE TO FILL MY DAYS WITH SOMETHING.
CAN I... READ WHAT YOU'VE BEEN WORKING ON?
YOU'D HAVE TO GET ME MUCH DRUNKER THAN THIS, DEAR.
I HOPE I'M STILL WRITING AT YOUR AGE.
...NOT THAT I MEAN YOU'RE TOO OLD TO WRITE. I JUST HOPE I STILL LOVE WRITING FOR THE SAKE OF WRITING.
INDEED, IT'S A DIFFICULT THING TO ENJOY THE ACT OF WRITING. I HOPE YOU HAVEN'T LOST THAT JOY.
SILVIA IS A BOMB-ASS WRITER. SHE'S GOING TO WRITE QUIETLY DEVASTATING BOOKS THAT ARE ADAPTED INTO INDIE FILMS WITH CATE BLANCHETT AND SHARON CUNETA!
OHMIGOD, SHUT UP, SHIRIN...
MATADOR

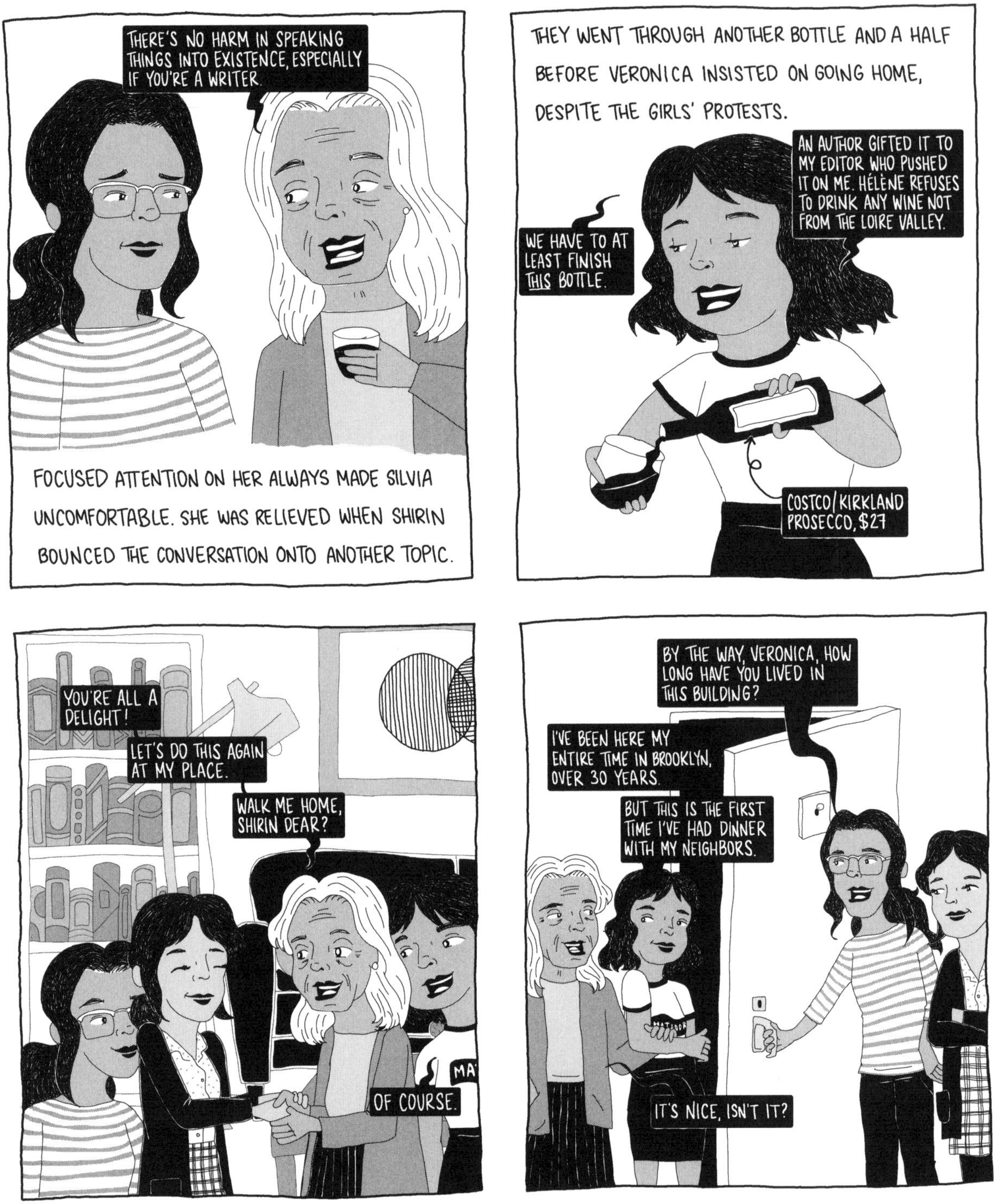
THERE'S NO HARM IN SPEAKING THINGS INTO EXISTENCE, ESPECIALLY IF YOU'RE A WRITER.
FOCUSED ATTENTION ON HER ALWAYS MADE SILVIA UNCOMFORTABLE. SHE WAS RELIEVED WHEN SHIRIN BOUNCED THE CONVERSATION ONTO ANOTHER TOPIC.
THEY WENT THROUGH ANOTHER BOTTLE AND A HALF BEFORE VERONICA INSISTED ON GOING HOME, DESPITE THE GIRLS' PROTESTS.
WE HAVE TO AT LEAST FINISH THIS BOTTLE.
AN AUTHOR GIFTED IT TO MY EDITOR WHO PUSHED IT ON ME. HÉLÈNE REFUSES TO DRINK ANY WINE NOT FROM THE LOIRE VALLEY.
COSTCO/KIRKLAND PROSECCO, $27
YOU'RE ALL A DELIGHT!
LET'S DO THIS AGAIN AT MY PLACE.
WALK ME HOME, SHIRIN DEAR?
OF COURSE.
BY THE WAY, VERONICA, HOW LONG HAVE YOU LIVED IN THIS BUILDING?
I'VE BEEN HERE MY ENTIRE TIME IN BROOKLYN, OVER 30 YEARS.
BUT THIS IS THE FIRST TIME I'VE HAD DINNER WITH MY NEIGHBORS.
IT'S NICE, ISN'T IT?

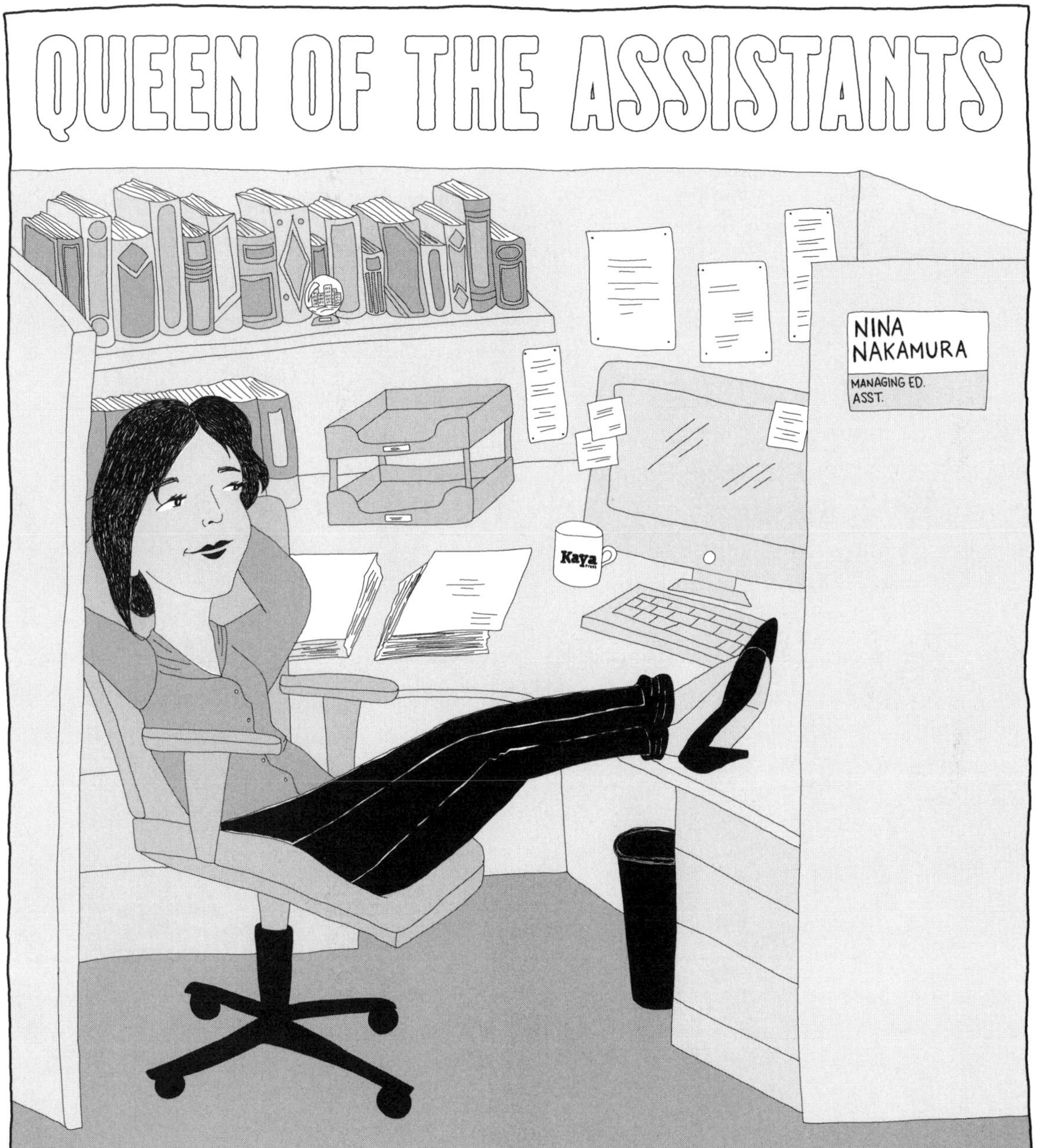
QUEEN OF THE ASSISTANTS
NINA
NAKAMURA
MANAGING ED.
ASST.
Kaya

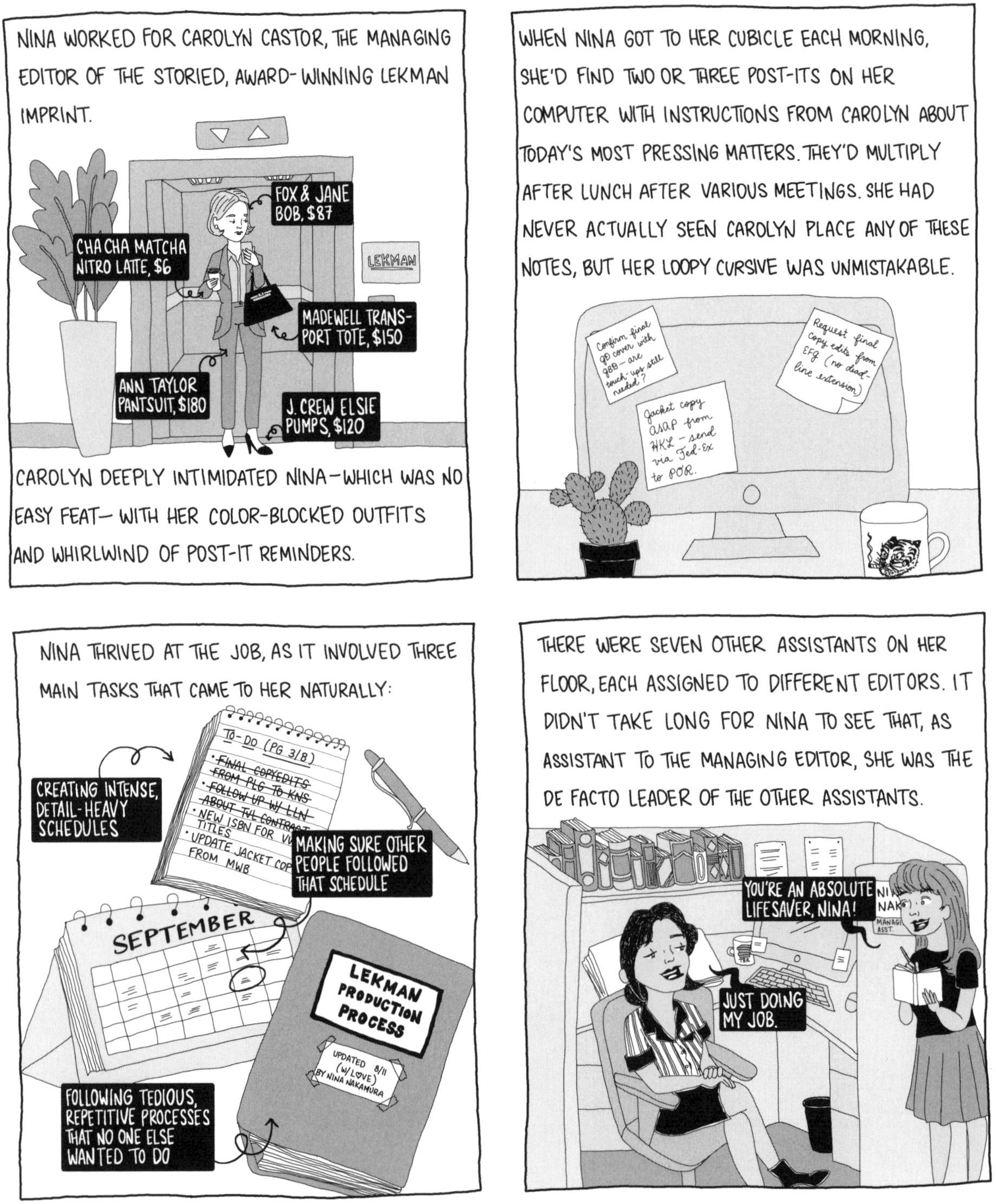
NINA WORKED FOR CAROLYN CASTOR, THE MANAGING EDITOR OF THE STORIED, AWARD-WINNING LEKMAN IMPRINT.
FOX & JANE BOB, $87
CHA CHA MATCHA NITRO LATTE, $6
LEKMAN
MADEWELL TRANSPORT TOTE, $150
ANN TAYLOR PANTSUIT, $180
J.CREW ELSIE PUMPS, $120
CAROLYN DEEPLY INTIMIDATED NINA—WHICH WAS NO EASY FEAT—WITH HER COLOR-BLOCKED OUTFITS AND WHIRLWIND OF POST-IT REMINDERS.
WHEN NINA GOT TO HER CUBICLE EACH MORNING, SHE'D FIND TWO OR THREE POST-ITS ON HER COMPUTER WITH INSTRUCTIONS FROM CAROLYN ABOUT TODAY'S MOST PRESSING MATTERS. THEY'D MULTIPLY AFTER LUNCH AFTER VARIOUS MEETINGS. SHE HAD NEVER ACTUALLY SEEN CAROLYN PLACE ANY OF THESE NOTES, BUT HER LOOPY CURSIVE WAS UNMISTAKABLE.
Confirm final QD cover with QBB—are touch-ups still needed?
Request final copy edits from EFG (no deadline extension)
Jacket copy asap from HKL—send via Fed-Ex to POR.
NINA THRIVED AT THE JOB, AS IT INVOLVED THREE MAIN TASKS THAT CAME TO HER NATURALLY:
TO-DO (PG 3/8)
• FINAL COPYEDITS FROM PLG TO KNS
• FOLLOW UP W/ LLN ABOUT TVL CONTRACT
• NEW ISBN FOR VU TITLES
• UPDATE JACKET COPY FROM MWB
CREATING INTENSE, DETAIL-HEAVY SCHEDULES
MAKING SURE OTHER PEOPLE FOLLOWED THAT SCHEDULE
SEPTEMBER
LEKMAN PRODUCTION PROCESS
UPDATED 8/11 (W/ LOVE) BY NINA NAKAMURA
FOLLOWING TEDIOUS, REPETITIVE PROCESSES THAT NO ONE ELSE WANTED TO DO
THERE WERE SEVEN OTHER ASSISTANTS ON HER FLOOR, EACH ASSIGNED TO DIFFERENT EDITORS. IT DIDN'T TAKE LONG FOR NINA TO SEE THAT, AS ASSISTANT TO THE MANAGING EDITOR, SHE WAS THE DE FACTO LEADER OF THE OTHER ASSISTANTS.
YOU'RE AN ABSOLUTE LIFESAVER, NINA!
JUST DOING MY JOB.

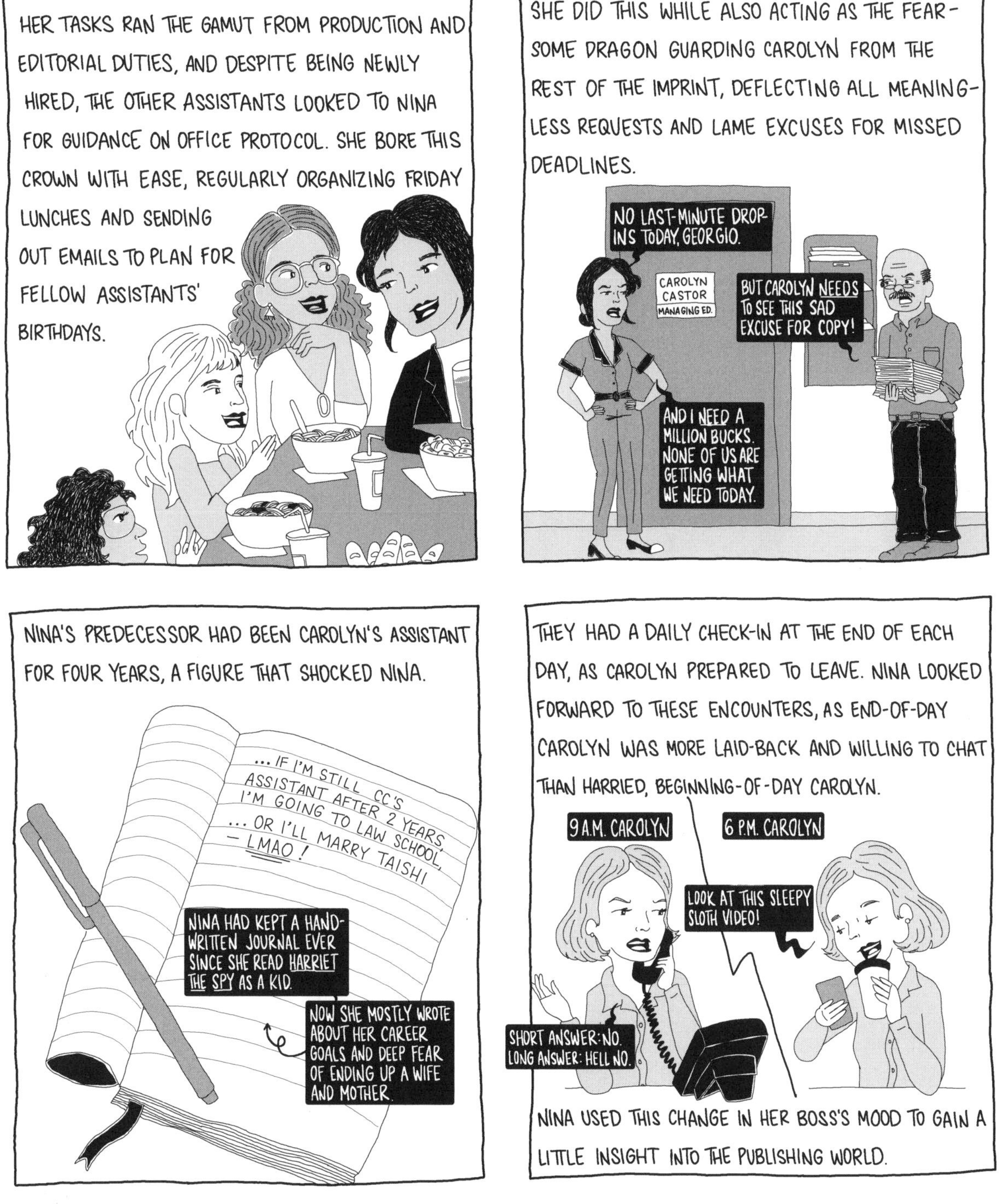
HER TASKS RAN THE GAMUT FROM PRODUCTION AND EDITORIAL DUTIES, AND DESPITE BEING NEWLY HIRED, THE OTHER ASSISTANTS LOOKED TO NINA FOR GUIDANCE ON OFFICE PROTOCOL. SHE BORE THIS CROWN WITH EASE, REGULARLY ORGANIZING FRIDAY LUNCHES AND SENDING OUT EMAILS TO PLAN FOR FELLOW ASSISTANTS' BIRTHDAYS.
SHE DID THIS WHILE ALSO ACTING AS THE FEARSOME DRAGON GUARDING CAROLYN FROM THE REST OF THE IMPRINT, DEFLECTING ALL MEANINGLESS REQUESTS AND LAME EXCUSES FOR MISSED DEADLINES.
NO LAST-MINUTE DROP-INS TODAY, GEORGIO.
CAROLYN CASTOR
MANAGING ED.
BUT CAROLYN NEEDS TO SEE THIS SAD EXCUSE FOR COPY!
AND I NEED A MILLION BUCKS. NONE OF US ARE GETTING WHAT WE NEED TODAY.
NINA'S PREDECESSOR HAD BEEN CAROLYN'S ASSISTANT FOR FOUR YEARS, A FIGURE THAT SHOCKED NINA.
... IF I'M STILL CC'S ASSISTANT AFTER 2 YEARS, I'M GOING TO LAW SCHOOL, ... OR I'LL MARRY TAISHI – LMAO!
NINA HAD KEPT A HANDWRITTEN JOURNAL EVER SINCE SHE READ HARRIET THE SPY AS A KID.
NOW SHE MOSTLY WROTE ABOUT HER CAREER GOALS AND DEEP FEAR OF ENDING UP A WIFE AND MOTHER.
THEY HAD A DAILY CHECK-IN AT THE END OF EACH DAY, AS CAROLYN PREPARED TO LEAVE. NINA LOOKED FORWARD TO THESE ENCOUNTERS, AS END-OF-DAY CAROLYN WAS MORE LAID-BACK AND WILLING TO CHAT THAN HARRIED, BEGINNING-OF-DAY CAROLYN.
9 A.M. CAROLYN
6 P.M. CAROLYN
LOOK AT THIS SLEEPY SLOTH VIDEO!
SHORT ANSWER: NO. LONG ANSWER: HELL NO.
NINA USED THIS CHANGE IN HER BOSS'S MOOD TO GAIN A LITTLE INSIGHT INTO THE PUBLISHING WORLD.

CAROLYN, HAVE YOU READ ANY VERONICA VO?

VERONICA VO? SHE SOUNDS FAMILIAR.

HER FIRST NOVEL WON THE BOOKER PRIZE IN THE 70s. LA MUTINERIE.

NEVER READ IT, BUT HER NAME RINGS A BELL. I THINK SHE WAS A PART OF PERRY'S CROWD.

PERRY COPELAND WAS ONE OF THE FOUNDING EDITORS AT RUSSEL-SEBASTIAN. HE HAD DIED A FEW YEARS AGO, LEAVING BEHIND HIS MEMOIRS, NEARLY 400 PAGES THAT DESCRIBED KEY PARTIES, ILLICIT DRUGS, AND A FASCINATION WITH CHINESE CRESTED DOGS.

HIS DOG, BASHŌ, LIVED AN UNPRECEDENTED 22 YEARS, AND HIS ASHES REMAIN SOMEWHERE IN A FORGOTTEN OFFICE FILING CABINET.

HER BOOKS ARE GREAT, EVEN THOUGH SHE ONLY GETS CREDIT FOR THE FIRST ONE.

THEY'RE ALL OUT OF PRINT NOW, BUT I THINK THEY'D BE WORTH REISSUING.

HMMM...

YOU KNOW, WITH NEW COVER ART AND A FOREWORD BY SOMEONE YOUNG.

NINA COULD TELL CAROLYN'S MIND WAS ALREADY OUTSIDE THE OFFICE. SHE DECIDED NOT TO PUSH ON ANY FURTHER.

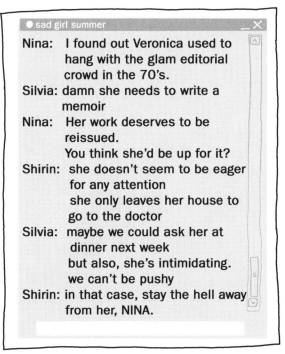

● sad girl summer

Nina: I found out Veronica used to hang with the glam editorial crowd in the 70's.

Silvia: damn she needs to write a memoir

Nina: Her work deserves to be reissued.
You think she'd be up for it?

Shirin: she doesn't seem to be eager for any attention
she only leaves her house to go to the doctor

Silvia: maybe we could ask her at dinner next week
but also, she's intimidating. we can't be pushy

Shirin: in that case, stay the hell away from her, NINA.

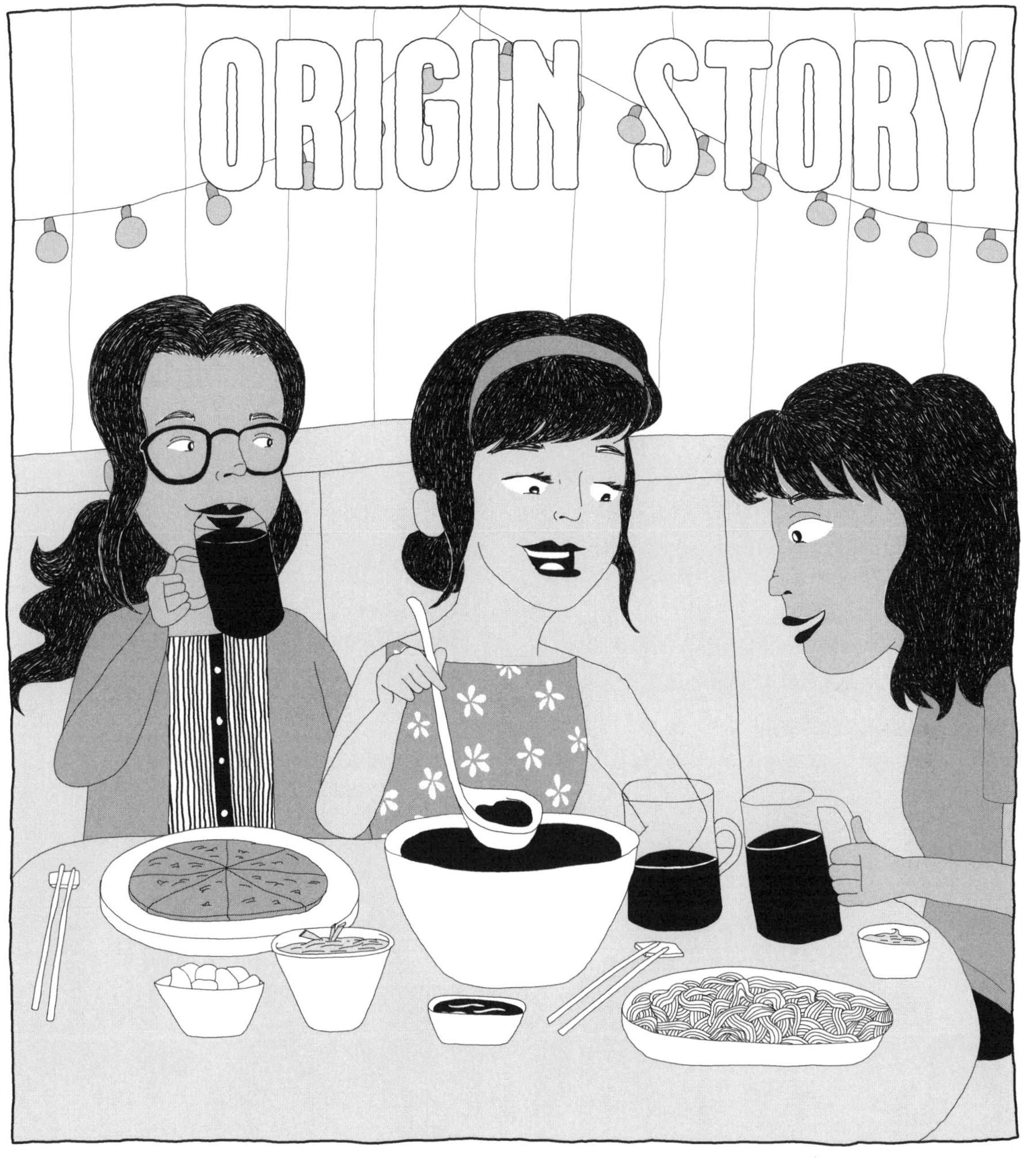
ORIGIN STORY

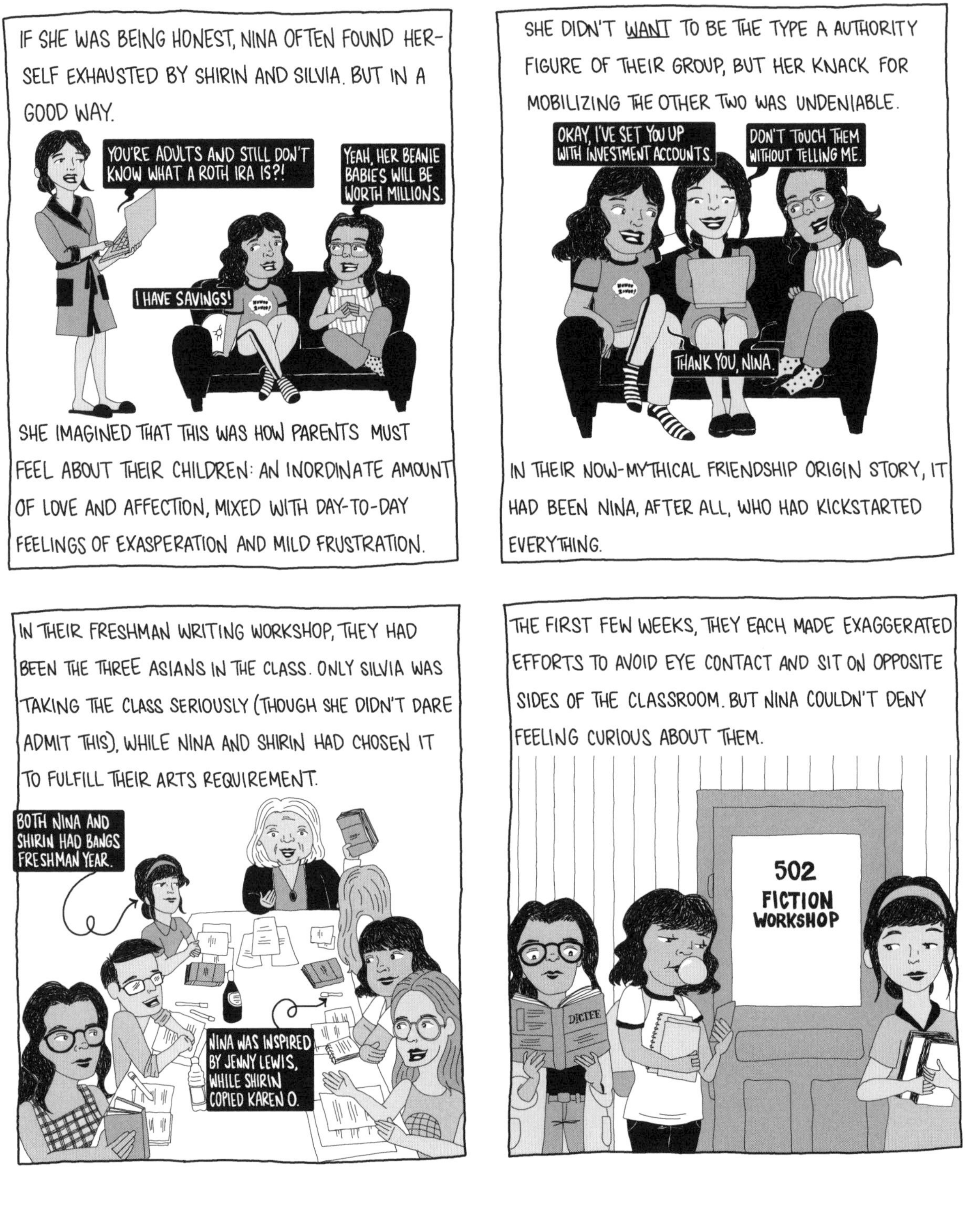

IF SHE WAS BEING HONEST, NINA OFTEN FOUND HER-SELF EXHAUSTED BY SHIRIN AND SILVIA. BUT IN A GOOD WAY.
YOU'RE ADULTS AND STILL DON'T KNOW WHAT A ROTH IRA IS?!
YEAH, HER BEANIE BABIES WILL BE WORTH MILLIONS.
I HAVE SAVINGS!
SHE IMAGINED THAT THIS WAS HOW PARENTS MUST FEEL ABOUT THEIR CHILDREN: AN INORDINATE AMOUNT OF LOVE AND AFFECTION, MIXED WITH DAY-TO-DAY FEELINGS OF EXASPERATION AND MILD FRUSTRATION.
SHE DIDN'T WANT TO BE THE TYPE A AUTHORITY FIGURE OF THEIR GROUP, BUT HER KNACK FOR MOBILIZING THE OTHER TWO WAS UNDENIABLE.
OKAY, I'VE SET YOU UP WITH INVESTMENT ACCOUNTS.
DON'T TOUCH THEM WITHOUT TELLING ME.
THANK YOU, NINA.
IN THEIR NOW-MYTHICAL FRIENDSHIP ORIGIN STORY, IT HAD BEEN NINA, AFTER ALL, WHO HAD KICKSTARTED EVERYTHING.
IN THEIR FRESHMAN WRITING WORKSHOP, THEY HAD BEEN THE THREE ASIANS IN THE CLASS. ONLY SILVIA WAS TAKING THE CLASS SERIOUSLY (THOUGH SHE DIDN'T DARE ADMIT THIS), WHILE NINA AND SHIRIN HAD CHOSEN IT TO FULFILL THEIR ARTS REQUIREMENT.
BOTH NINA AND SHIRIN HAD BANGS FRESHMAN YEAR.
NINA WAS INSPIRED BY JENNY LEWIS, WHILE SHIRIN COPIED KAREN O.
THE FIRST FEW WEEKS, THEY EACH MADE EXAGGERATED EFFORTS TO AVOID EYE CONTACT AND SIT ON OPPOSITE SIDES OF THE CLASSROOM. BUT NINA COULDN'T DENY FEELING CURIOUS ABOUT THEM.
502
FICTION WORKSHOP
DICTEE

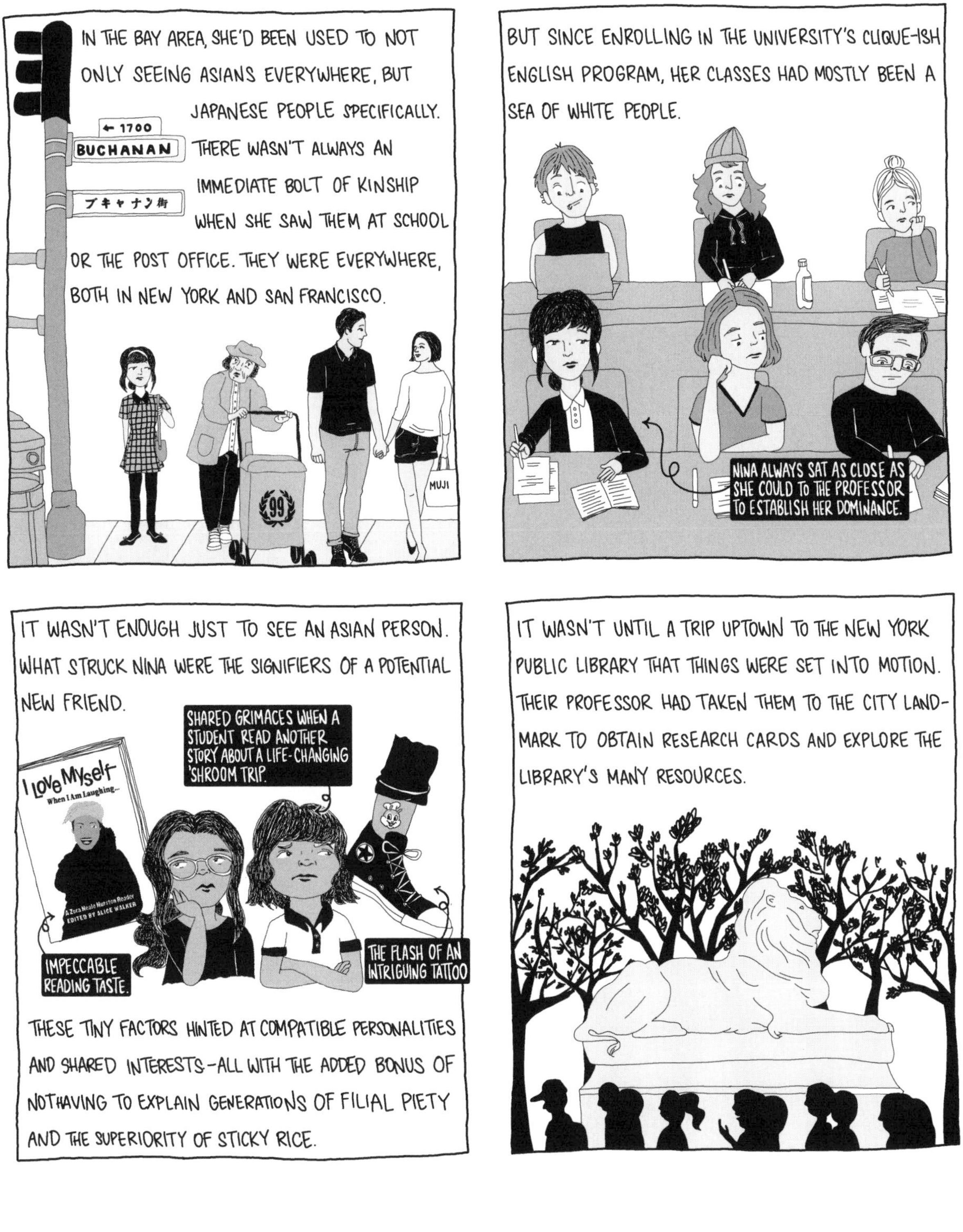
IN THE BAY AREA, SHE'D BEEN USED TO NOT ONLY SEEING ASIANS EVERYWHERE, BUT JAPANESE PEOPLE SPECIFICALLY. THERE WASN'T ALWAYS AN IMMEDIATE BOLT OF KINSHIP WHEN SHE SAW THEM AT SCHOOL OR THE POST OFFICE. THEY WERE EVERYWHERE, BOTH IN NEW YORK AND SAN FRANCISCO.
← 1700
BUCHANAN
ブキャナン街
99
MUJI
BUT SINCE ENROLLING IN THE UNIVERSITY'S CLIQUE-ISH ENGLISH PROGRAM, HER CLASSES HAD MOSTLY BEEN A SEA OF WHITE PEOPLE.
NINA ALWAYS SAT AS CLOSE AS SHE COULD TO THE PROFESSOR TO ESTABLISH HER DOMINANCE.
IT WASN'T ENOUGH JUST TO SEE AN ASIAN PERSON. WHAT STRUCK NINA WERE THE SIGNIFIERS OF A POTENTIAL NEW FRIEND.
I Love Myself When I Am Laughing...
A Zora Neale Hurston Reader
EDITED BY ALICE WALKER
IMPECCABLE READING TASTE.
SHARED GRIMACES WHEN A STUDENT READ ANOTHER STORY ABOUT A LIFE-CHANGING 'SHROOM TRIP.
THE FLASH OF AN INTRIGUING TATTOO
THESE TINY FACTORS HINTED AT COMPATIBLE PERSONALITIES AND SHARED INTERESTS—ALL WITH THE ADDED BONUS OF NOT HAVING TO EXPLAIN GENERATIONS OF FILIAL PIETY AND THE SUPERIORITY OF STICKY RICE.
IT WASN'T UNTIL A TRIP UPTOWN TO THE NEW YORK PUBLIC LIBRARY THAT THINGS WERE SET INTO MOTION. THEIR PROFESSOR HAD TAKEN THEM TO THE CITY LANDMARK TO OBTAIN RESEARCH CARDS AND EXPLORE THE LIBRARY'S MANY RESOURCES.

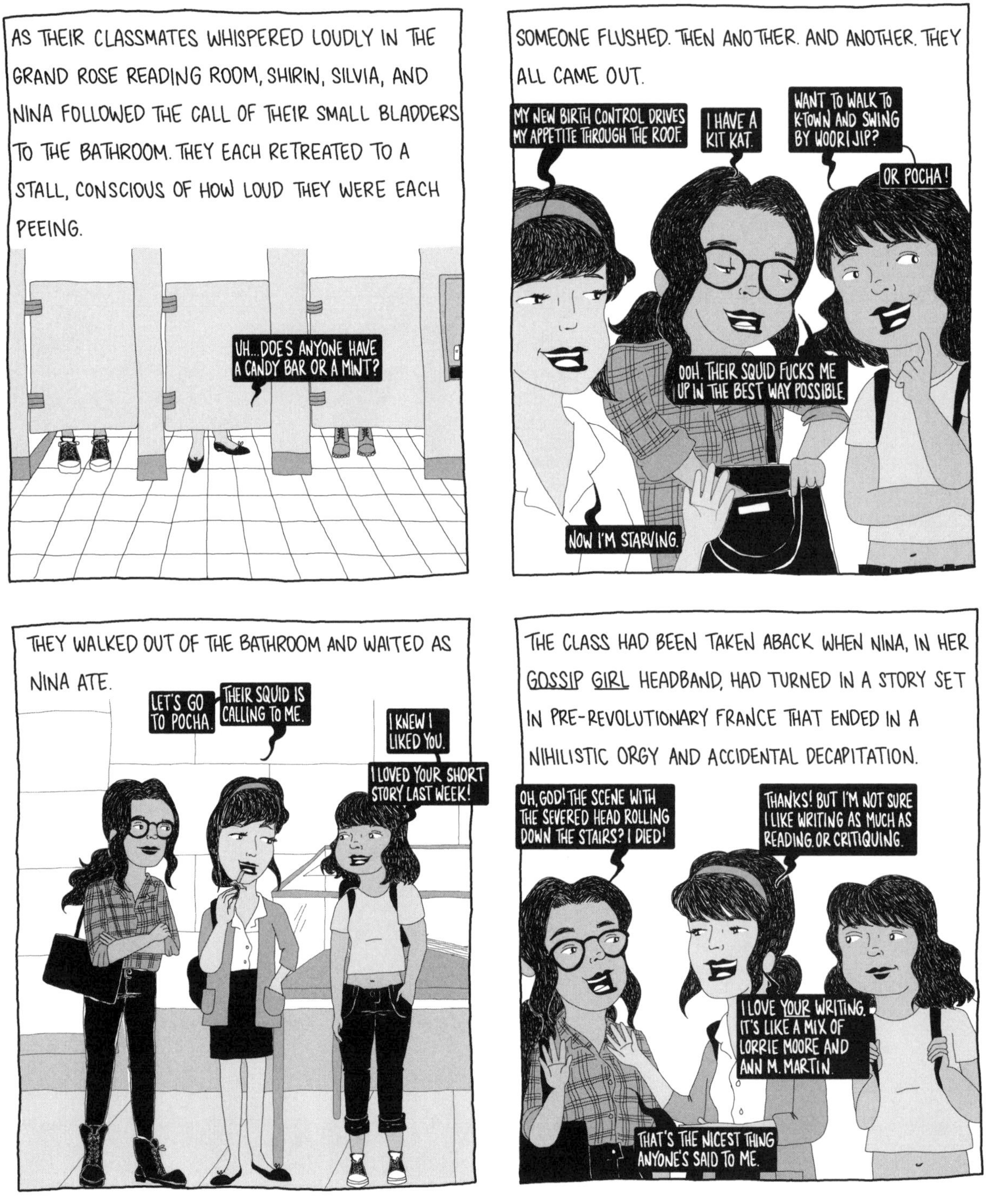
AS THEIR CLASSMATES WHISPERED LOUDLY IN THE GRAND ROSE READING ROOM, SHIRIN, SILVIA, AND NINA FOLLOWED THE CALL OF THEIR SMALL BLADDERS TO THE BATHROOM. THEY EACH RETREATED TO A STALL, CONSCIOUS OF HOW LOUD THEY WERE EACH PEEING.
UH...DOES ANYONE HAVE A CANDY BAR OR A MINT?
SOMEONE FLUSHED. THEN ANOTHER. AND ANOTHER. THEY ALL CAME OUT.
MY NEW BIRTH CONTROL DRIVES MY APPETITE THROUGH THE ROOF.
I HAVE A KIT KAT.
WANT TO WALK TO K-TOWN AND SWING BY WOORI JIP?
OR POCHA!
OOH. THEIR SQUID FUCKS ME UP IN THE BEST WAY POSSIBLE.
NOW I'M STARVING.
THEY WALKED OUT OF THE BATHROOM AND WAITED AS NINA ATE.
LET'S GO TO POCHA.
THEIR SQUID IS CALLING TO ME.
I KNEW I LIKED YOU.
I LOVED YOUR SHORT STORY LAST WEEK!
THE CLASS HAD BEEN TAKEN ABACK WHEN NINA, IN HER GOSSIP GIRL HEADBAND, HAD TURNED IN A STORY SET IN PRE-REVOLUTIONARY FRANCE THAT ENDED IN A NIHILISTIC ORGY AND ACCIDENTAL DECAPITATION.
OH, GOD! THE SCENE WITH THE SEVERED HEAD ROLLING DOWN THE STAIRS? I DIED!
THANKS! BUT I'M NOT SURE I LIKE WRITING AS MUCH AS READING. OR CRITIQUING.
I LOVE YOUR WRITING. IT'S LIKE A MIX OF LORRIE MOORE AND ANN M. MARTIN.
THAT'S THE NICEST THING ANYONE'S SAID TO ME.

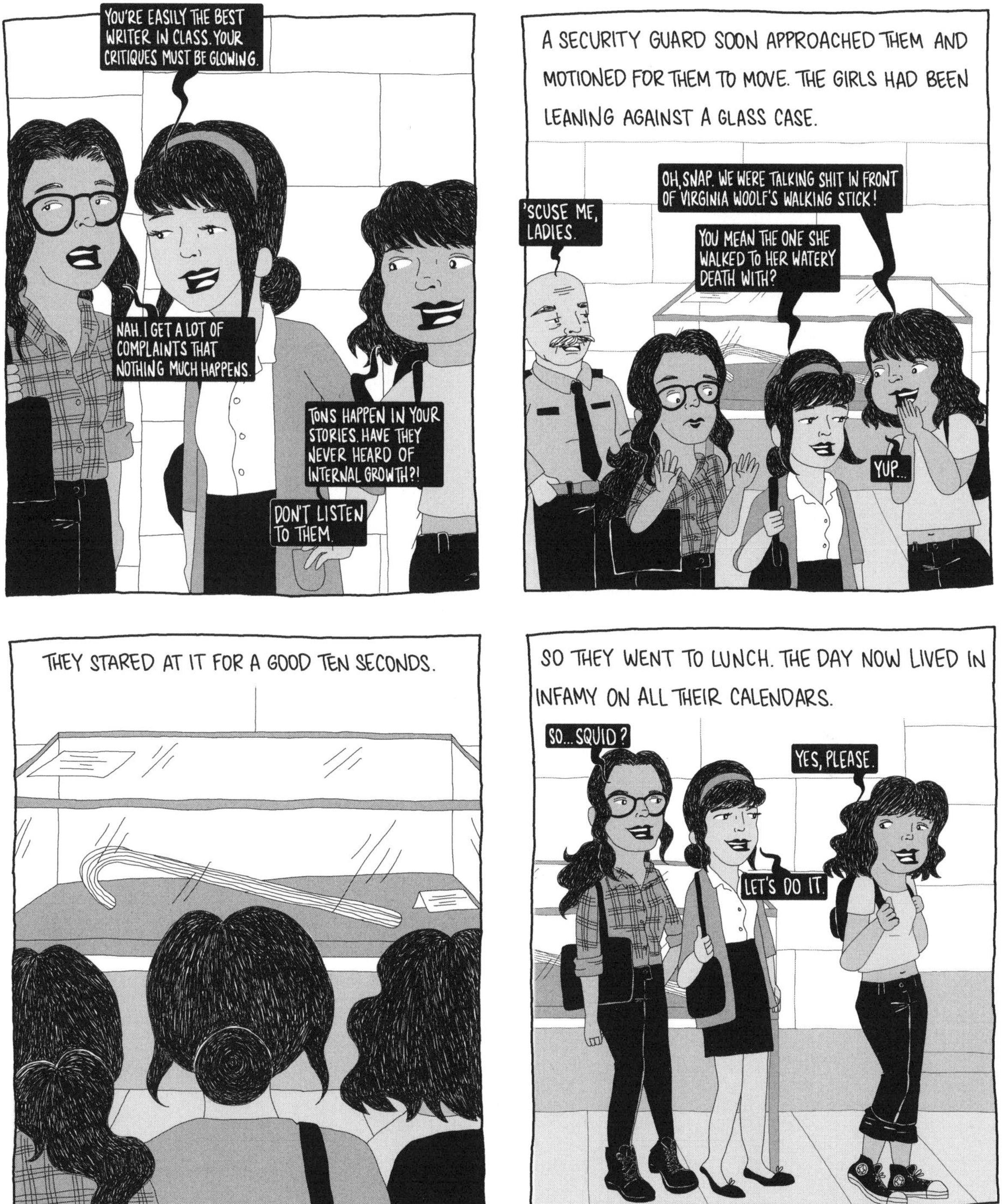
YOU'RE EASILY THE BEST WRITER IN CLASS. YOUR CRITIQUES MUST BE GLOWING.
NAH. I GET A LOT OF COMPLAINTS THAT NOTHING MUCH HAPPENS.
TONS HAPPEN IN YOUR STORIES. HAVE THEY NEVER HEARD OF INTERNAL GROWTH?!
DON'T LISTEN TO THEM.
A SECURITY GUARD SOON APPROACHED THEM AND MOTIONED FOR THEM TO MOVE. THE GIRLS HAD BEEN LEANING AGAINST A GLASS CASE.
'SCUSE ME, LADIES.
OH, SNAP. WE WERE TALKING SHIT IN FRONT OF VIRGINIA WOOLF'S WALKING STICK!
YOU MEAN THE ONE SHE WALKED TO HER WATERY DEATH WITH?
YUP...
THEY STARED AT IT FOR A GOOD TEN SECONDS.
SO THEY WENT TO LUNCH. THE DAY NOW LIVED IN INFAMY ON ALL THEIR CALENDARS.
SO... SQUID?
YES, PLEASE.
LET'S DO IT.

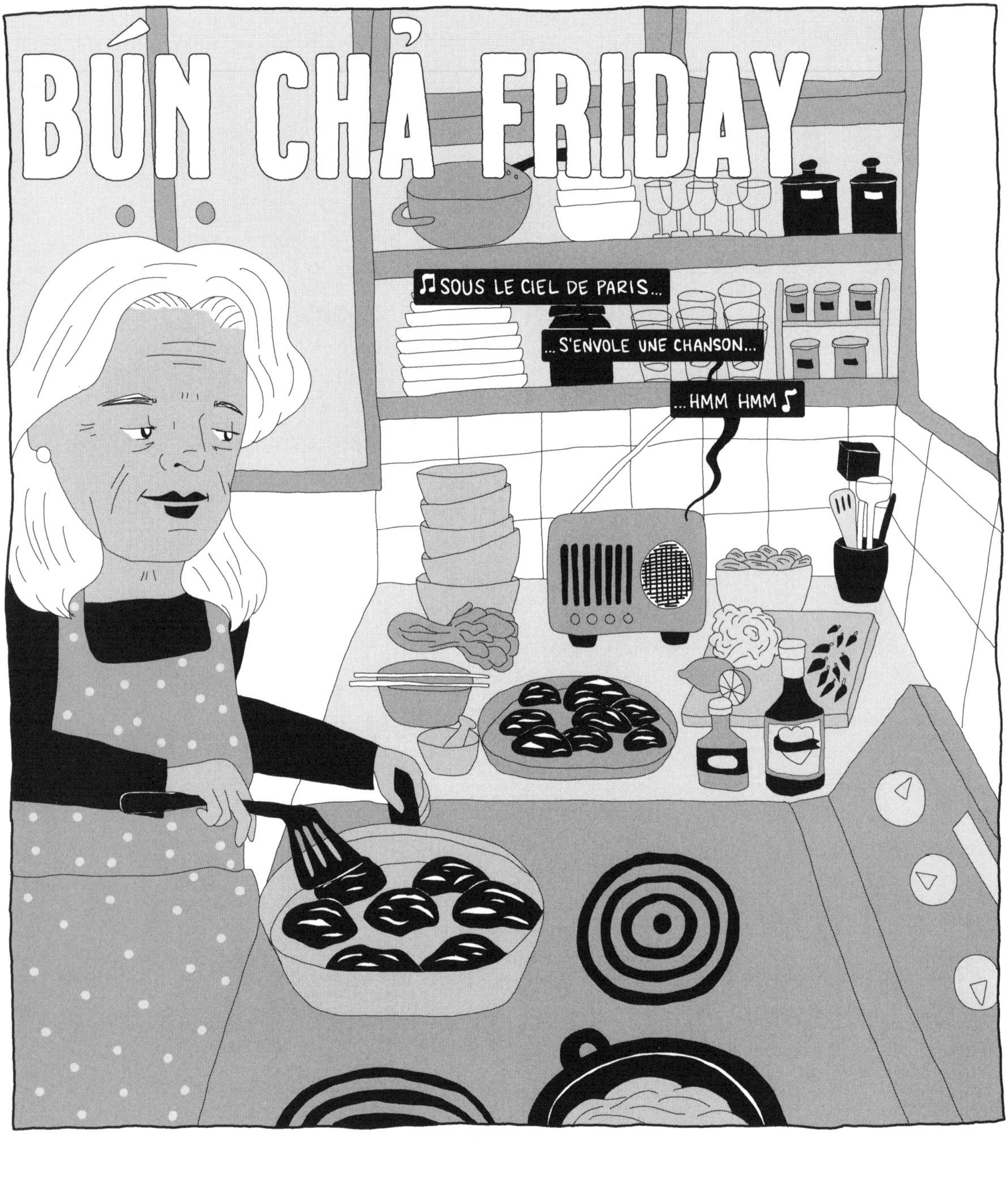
BÚN CHẢ FRIDAY
♫ SOUS LE CIEL DE PARIS...
... S'ENVOLE UNE CHANSON...
... HMM HMM ♪

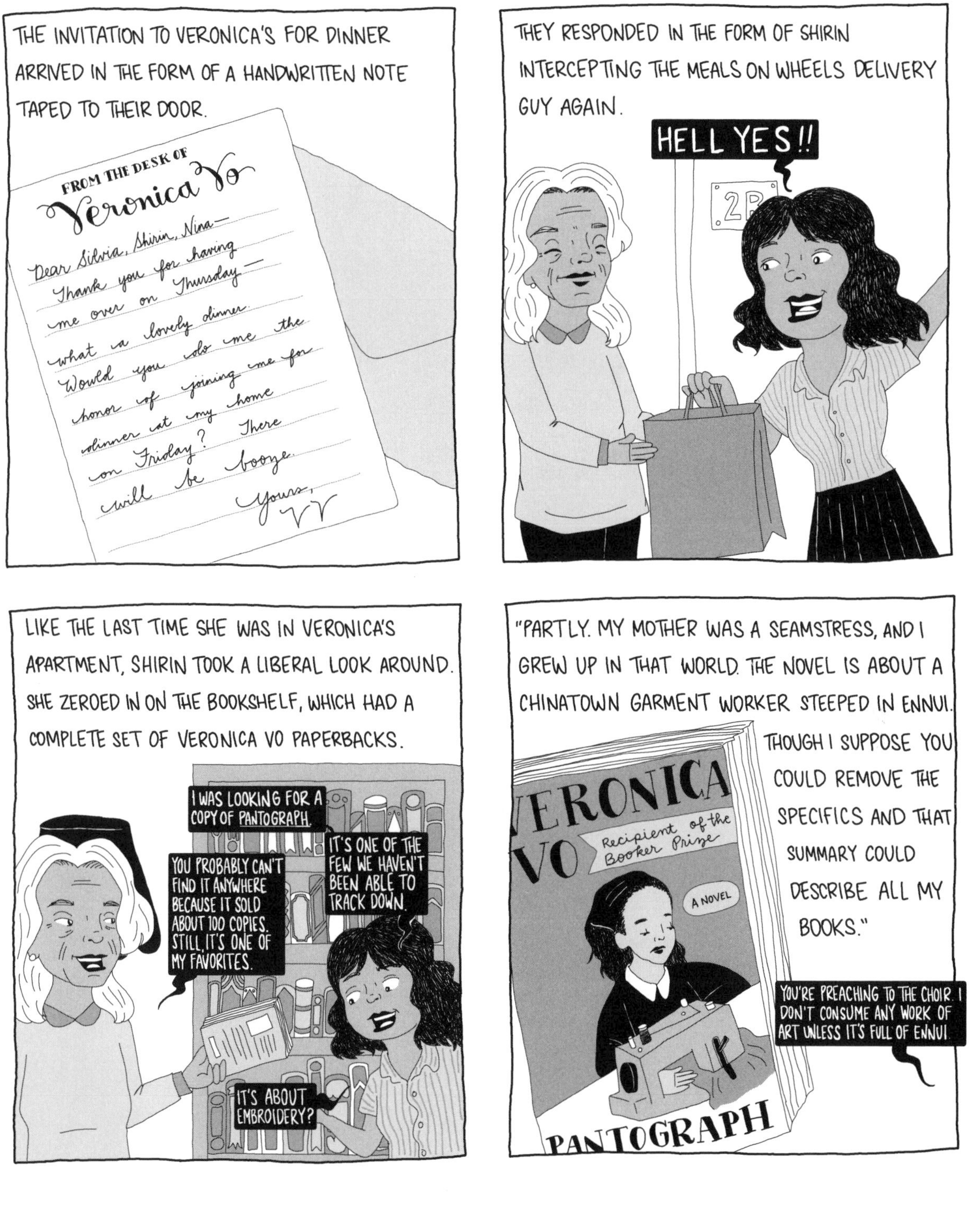
THE INVITATION TO VERONICA'S FOR DINNER ARRIVED IN THE FORM OF A HANDWRITTEN NOTE TAPED TO THEIR DOOR.
FROM THE DESK OF
Veronica Vo
Dear Silvia, Shirin, Nina—
Thank you for having me over on Thursday—
what a lovely dinner.
Would you do me the honor of joining me for dinner at my home on Friday? There will be booze.
Yours,
VV
THEY RESPONDED IN THE FORM OF SHIRIN INTERCEPTING THE MEALS ON WHEELS DELIVERY GUY AGAIN.
HELL YES!!
2B
LIKE THE LAST TIME SHE WAS IN VERONICA'S APARTMENT, SHIRIN TOOK A LIBERAL LOOK AROUND. SHE ZEROED IN ON THE BOOKSHELF, WHICH HAD A COMPLETE SET OF VERONICA VO PAPERBACKS.
I WAS LOOKING FOR A COPY OF PANTOGRAPH.
IT'S ONE OF THE FEW WE HAVEN'T BEEN ABLE TO TRACK DOWN.
YOU PROBABLY CAN'T FIND IT ANYWHERE BECAUSE IT SOLD ABOUT 100 COPIES. STILL, IT'S ONE OF MY FAVORITES.
IT'S ABOUT EMBROIDERY?
"PARTLY. MY MOTHER WAS A SEAMSTRESS, AND I GREW UP IN THAT WORLD. THE NOVEL IS ABOUT A CHINATOWN GARMENT WORKER STEEPED IN ENNUI.
VERONICA VO
Recipient of the Booker Prize
A NOVEL
PANTOGRAPH
THOUGH I SUPPOSE YOU COULD REMOVE THE SPECIFICS AND THAT SUMMARY COULD DESCRIBE ALL MY BOOKS."
YOU'RE PREACHING TO THE CHOIR. I DON'T CONSUME ANY WORK OF ART UNLESS IT'S FULL OF ENNUI.

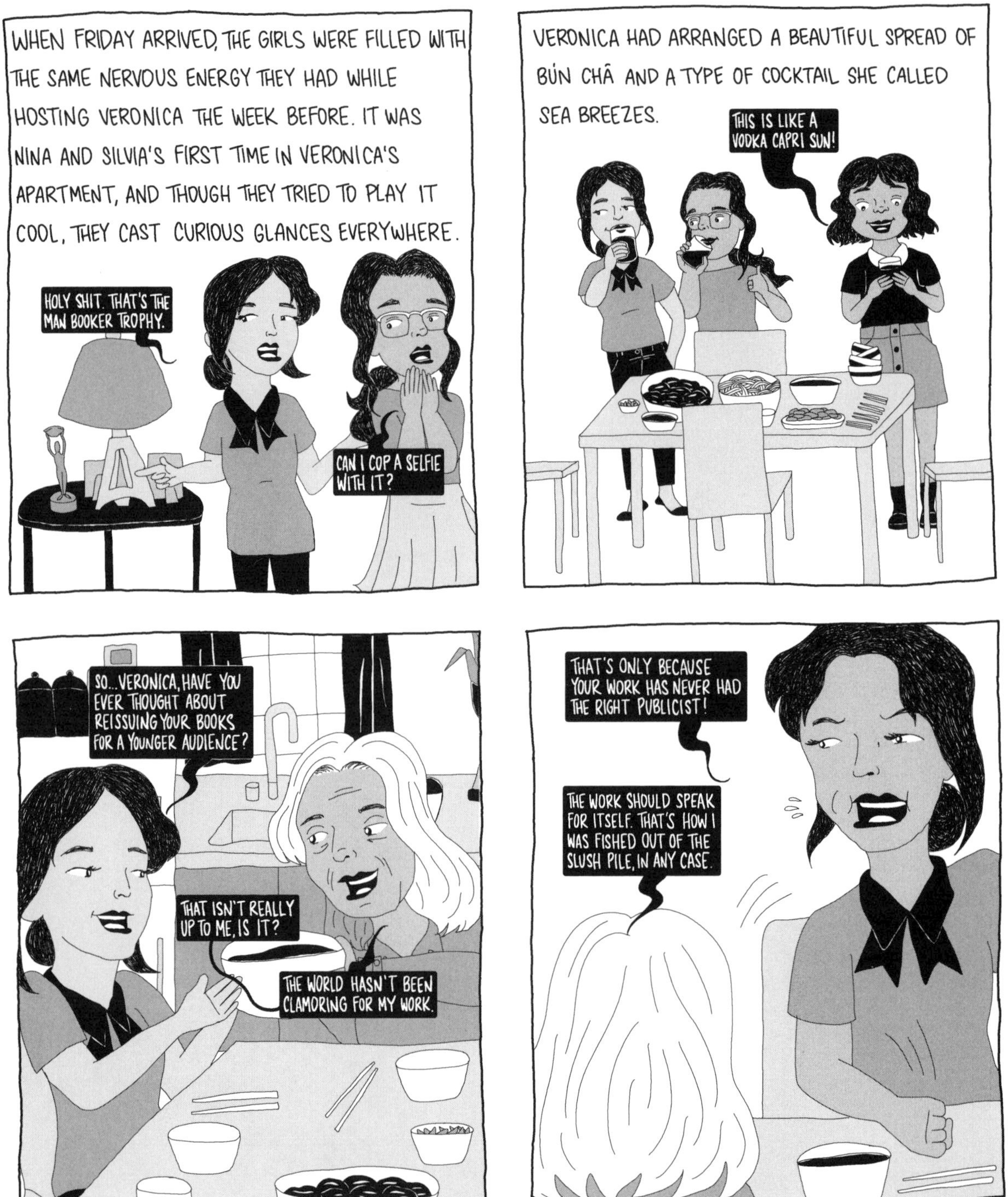
WHEN FRIDAY ARRIVED, THE GIRLS WERE FILLED WITH THE SAME NERVOUS ENERGY THEY HAD WHILE HOSTING VERONICA THE WEEK BEFORE. IT WAS NINA AND SILVIA'S FIRST TIME IN VERONICA'S APARTMENT, AND THOUGH THEY TRIED TO PLAY IT COOL, THEY CAST CURIOUS GLANCES EVERYWHERE.
HOLY SHIT. THAT'S THE MAN BOOKER TROPHY.
CAN I COP A SELFIE WITH IT?
VERONICA HAD ARRANGED A BEAUTIFUL SPREAD OF BÚN CHÂ AND A TYPE OF COCKTAIL SHE CALLED SEA BREEZES.
THIS IS LIKE A VODKA CAPRI SUN!
SO... VERONICA, HAVE YOU EVER THOUGHT ABOUT REISSUING YOUR BOOKS FOR A YOUNGER AUDIENCE?
THAT ISN'T REALLY UP TO ME, IS IT?
THE WORLD HASN'T BEEN CLAMORING FOR MY WORK.
THAT'S ONLY BECAUSE YOUR WORK HAS NEVER HAD THE RIGHT PUBLICIST!
THE WORK SHOULD SPEAK FOR ITSELF. THAT'S HOW I WAS FISHED OUT OF THE SLUSH PILE, IN ANY CASE.

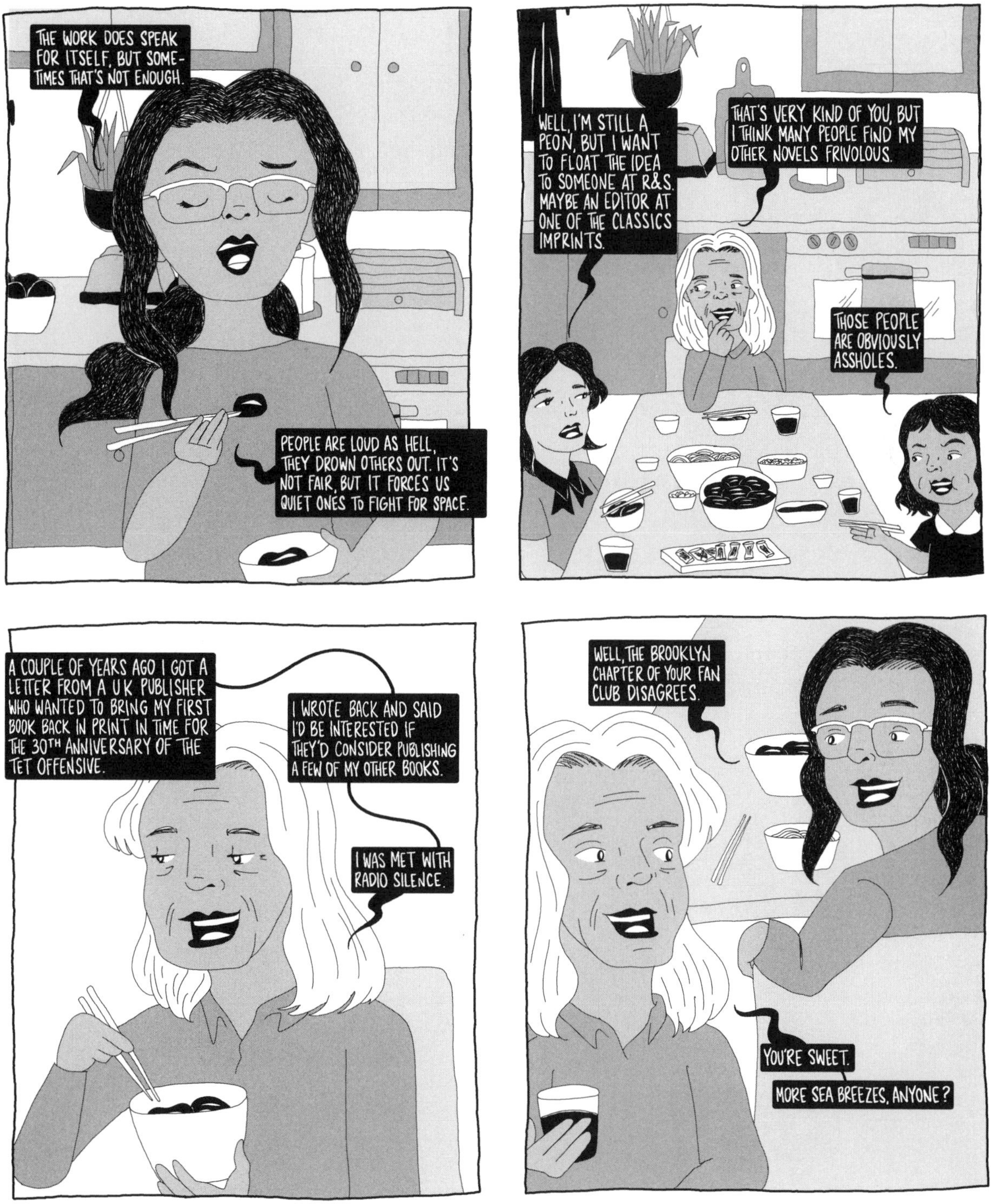
THE WORK DOES SPEAK FOR ITSELF, BUT SOMETIMES THAT'S NOT ENOUGH.
PEOPLE ARE LOUD AS HELL, THEY DROWN OTHERS OUT. IT'S NOT FAIR, BUT IT FORCES US QUIET ONES TO FIGHT FOR SPACE.
WELL, I'M STILL A PEON, BUT I WANT TO FLOAT THE IDEA TO SOMEONE AT R&S. MAYBE AN EDITOR AT ONE OF THE CLASSICS IMPRINTS.
THAT'S VERY KIND OF YOU, BUT I THINK MANY PEOPLE FIND MY OTHER NOVELS FRIVOLOUS.
THOSE PEOPLE ARE OBVIOUSLY ASSHOLES.
A COUPLE OF YEARS AGO I GOT A LETTER FROM A UK PUBLISHER WHO WANTED TO BRING MY FIRST BOOK BACK IN PRINT IN TIME FOR THE 30TH ANNIVERSARY OF THE TET OFFENSIVE.
I WROTE BACK AND SAID I'D BE INTERESTED IF THEY'D CONSIDER PUBLISHING A FEW OF MY OTHER BOOKS.
I WAS MET WITH RADIO SILENCE.
WELL, THE BROOKLYN CHAPTER OF YOUR FAN CLUB DISAGREES.
YOU'RE SWEET.
MORE SEA BREEZES, ANYONE?

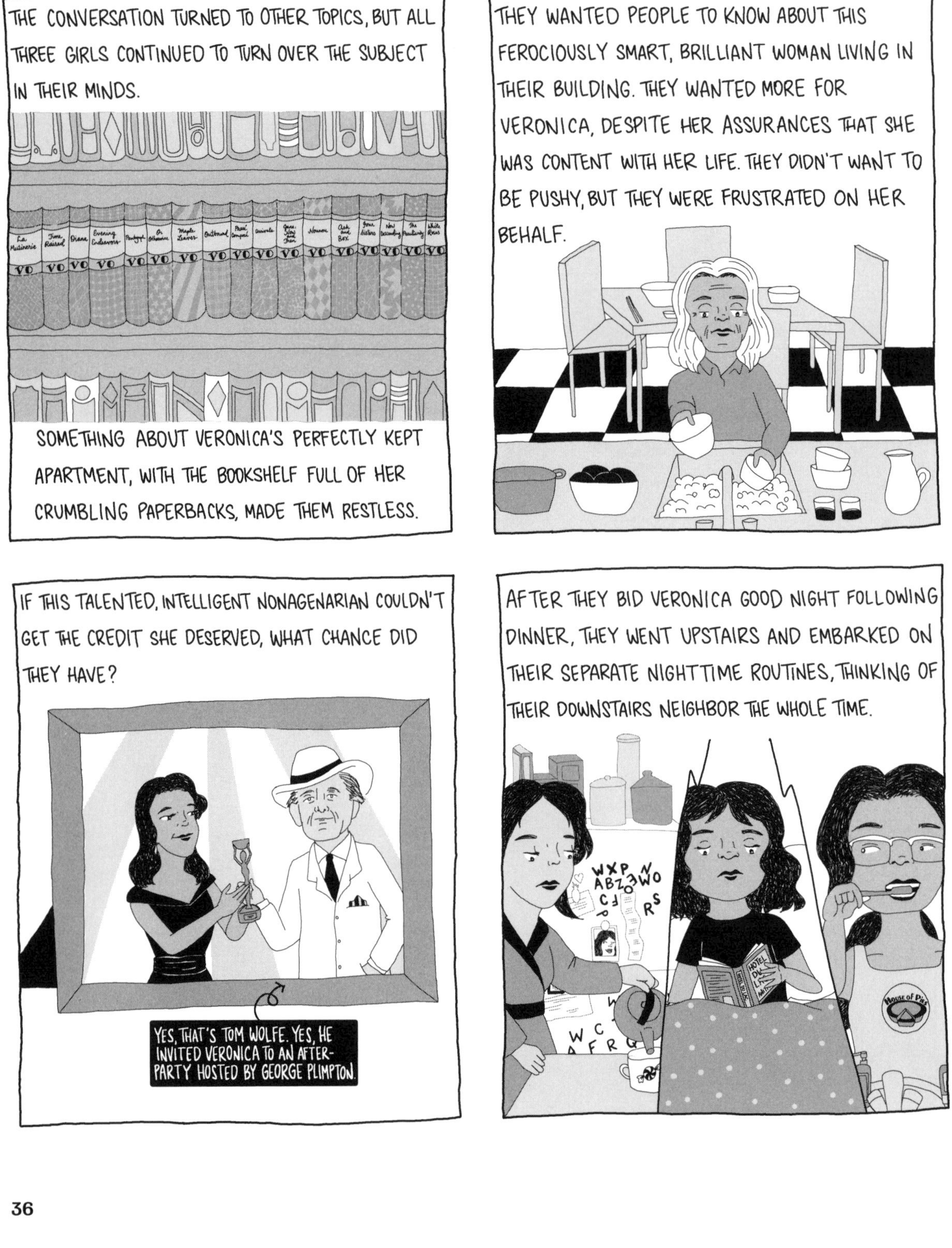
THE CONVERSATION TURNED TO OTHER TOPICS, BUT ALL THREE GIRLS CONTINUED TO TURN OVER THE SUBJECT IN THEIR MINDS.
SOMETHING ABOUT VERONICA'S PERFECTLY KEPT APARTMENT, WITH THE BOOKSHELF FULL OF HER CRUMBLING PAPERBACKS, MADE THEM RESTLESS.
THEY WANTED PEOPLE TO KNOW ABOUT THIS FEROCIOUSLY SMART, BRILLIANT WOMAN LIVING IN THEIR BUILDING. THEY WANTED MORE FOR VERONICA, DESPITE HER ASSURANCES THAT SHE WAS CONTENT WITH HER LIFE. THEY DIDN'T WANT TO BE PUSHY, BUT THEY WERE FRUSTRATED ON HER BEHALF.
IF THIS TALENTED, INTELLIGENT NONAGENARIAN COULDN'T GET THE CREDIT SHE DESERVED, WHAT CHANCE DID THEY HAVE?
YES, THAT'S TOM WOLFE. YES, HE INVITED VERONICA TO AN AFTER-PARTY HOSTED BY GEORGE PLIMPTON.
AFTER THEY BID VERONICA GOOD NIGHT FOLLOWING DINNER, THEY WENT UPSTAIRS AND EMBARKED ON THEIR SEPARATE NIGHTTIME ROUTINES, THINKING OF THEIR DOWNSTAIRS NEIGHBOR THE WHOLE TIME.

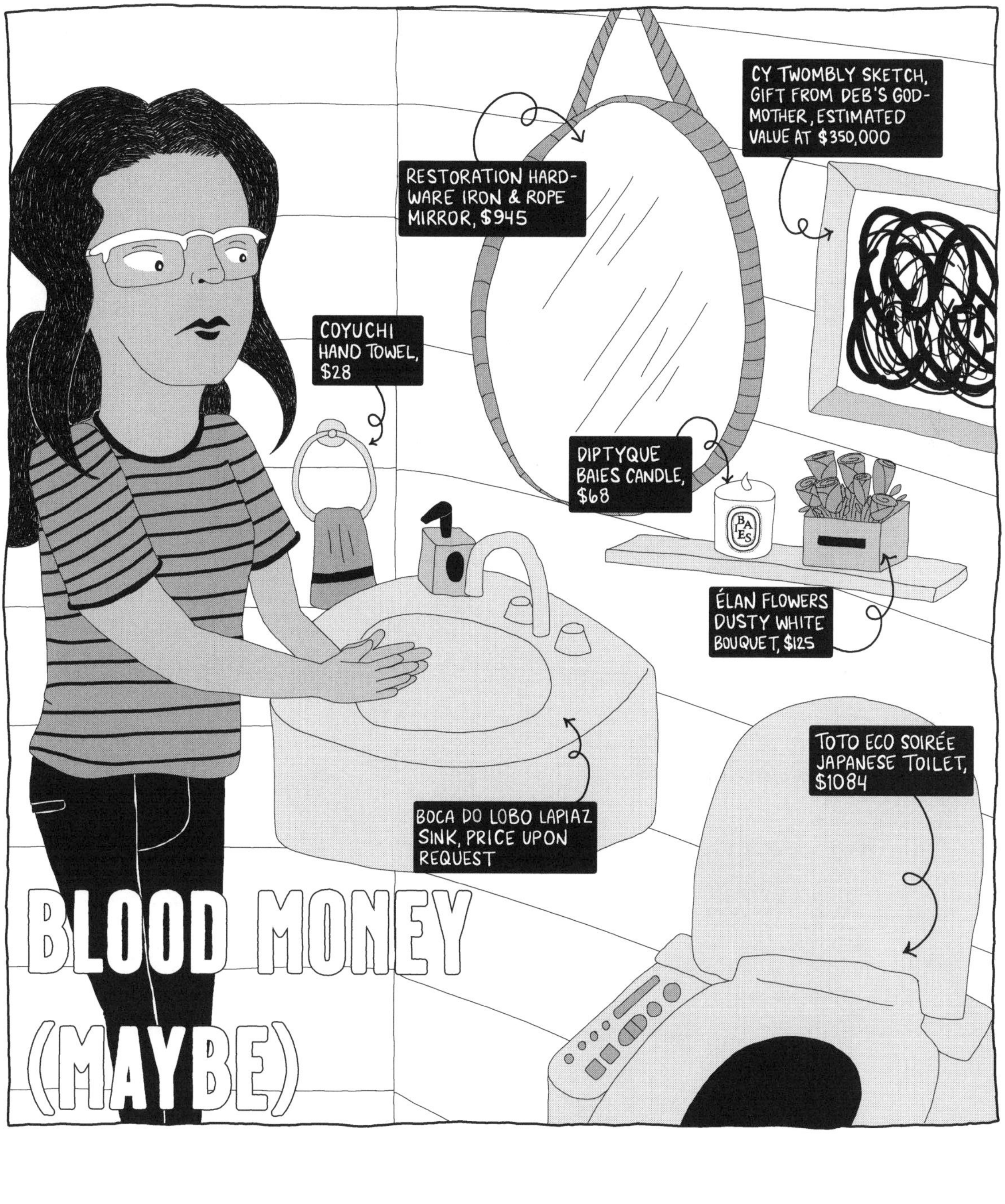
CY TWOMBLY SKETCH, GIFT FROM DEB'S GOD-MOTHER, ESTIMATED VALUE AT $350,000
RESTORATION HARDWARE IRON & ROPE MIRROR, $945
COYUCHI HAND TOWEL, $28
DIPTYQUE BAIES CANDLE, $68
BAIES
ÉLAN FLOWERS DUSTY WHITE BOUQUET, $125
TOTO ECO SOIRÉE JAPANESE TOILET, $1084
BOCA DO LOBO LAPIAZ SINK, PRICE UPON REQUEST
BLOOD MONEY
(MAYBE)

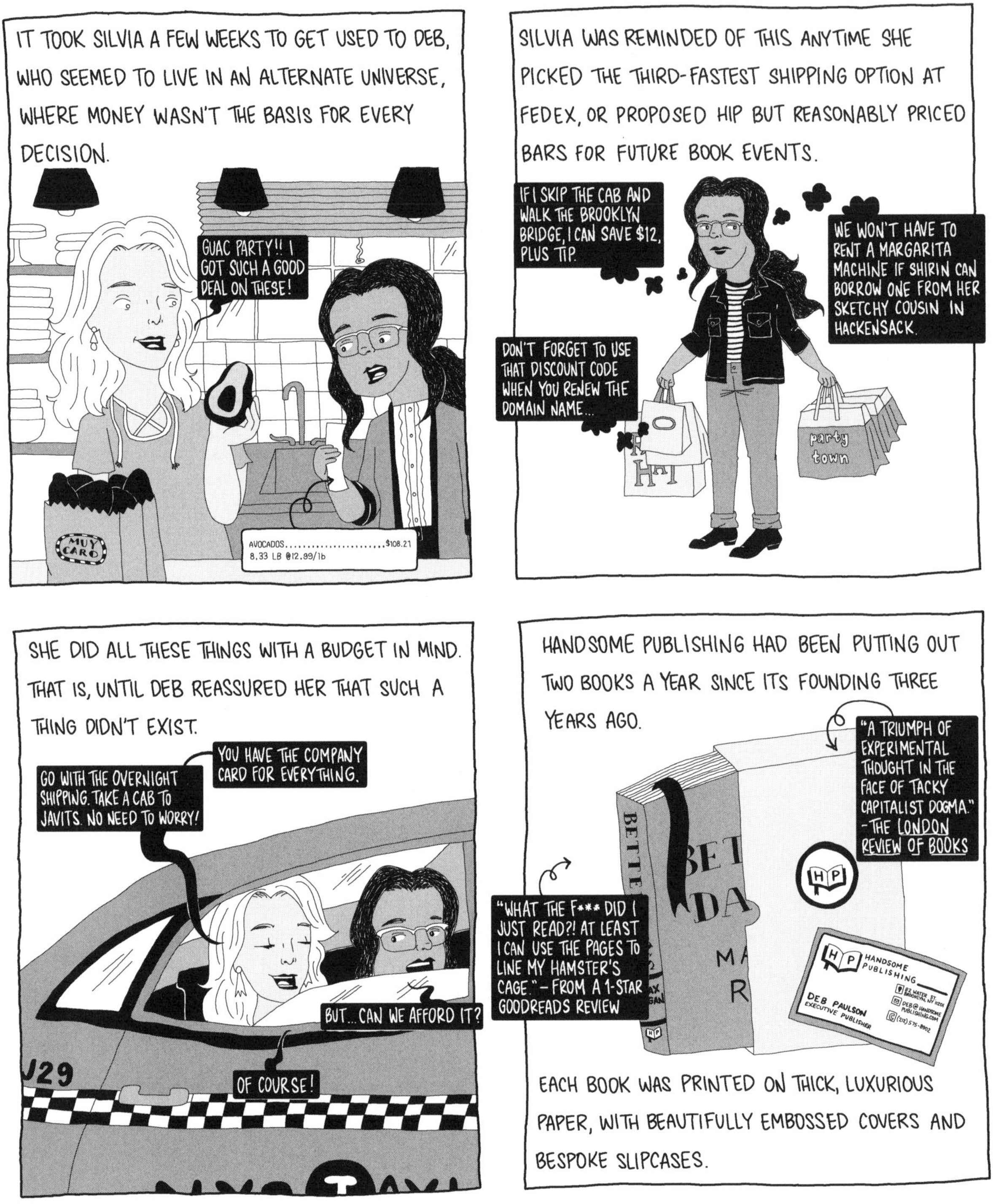
IT TOOK SILVIA A FEW WEEKS TO GET USED TO DEB, WHO SEEMED TO LIVE IN AN ALTERNATE UNIVERSE, WHERE MONEY WASN'T THE BASIS FOR EVERY DECISION.
GUAC PARTY!! I GOT SUCH A GOOD DEAL ON THESE!
MUY CARO
AVOCADOS......................$108.21
8.33 LB @12.99/lb
SILVIA WAS REMINDED OF THIS ANYTIME SHE PICKED THE THIRD-FASTEST SHIPPING OPTION AT FEDEX, OR PROPOSED HIP BUT REASONABLY PRICED BARS FOR FUTURE BOOK EVENTS.
IF I SKIP THE CAB AND WALK THE BROOKLYN BRIDGE, I CAN SAVE $12, PLUS TIP.
WE WON'T HAVE TO RENT A MARGARITA MACHINE IF SHIRIN CAN BORROW ONE FROM HER SKETCHY COUSIN IN HACKENSACK.
DON'T FORGET TO USE THAT DISCOUNT CODE WHEN YOU RENEW THE DOMAIN NAME...
party town
SHE DID ALL THESE THINGS WITH A BUDGET IN MIND. THAT IS, UNTIL DEB REASSURED HER THAT SUCH A THING DIDN'T EXIST.
YOU HAVE THE COMPANY CARD FOR EVERYTHING.
GO WITH THE OVERNIGHT SHIPPING. TAKE A CAB TO JAVITS. NO NEED TO WORRY!
BUT... CAN WE AFFORD IT?
OF COURSE!
HANDSOME PUBLISHING HAD BEEN PUTTING OUT TWO BOOKS A YEAR SINCE ITS FOUNDING THREE YEARS AGO.
"A TRIUMPH OF EXPERIMENTAL THOUGHT IN THE FACE OF TACKY CAPITALIST DOGMA." -THE LONDON REVIEW OF BOOKS
"WHAT THE F*** DID I JUST READ?! AT LEAST I CAN USE THE PAGES TO LINE MY HAMSTER'S CAGE." - FROM A 1-STAR GOODREADS REVIEW
HANDSOME PUBLISHING
DEB PAULSON
EXECUTIVE PUBLISHER
EACH BOOK WAS PRINTED ON THICK, LUXURIOUS PAPER, WITH BEAUTIFULLY EMBOSSED COVERS AND BESPOKE SLIPCASES.

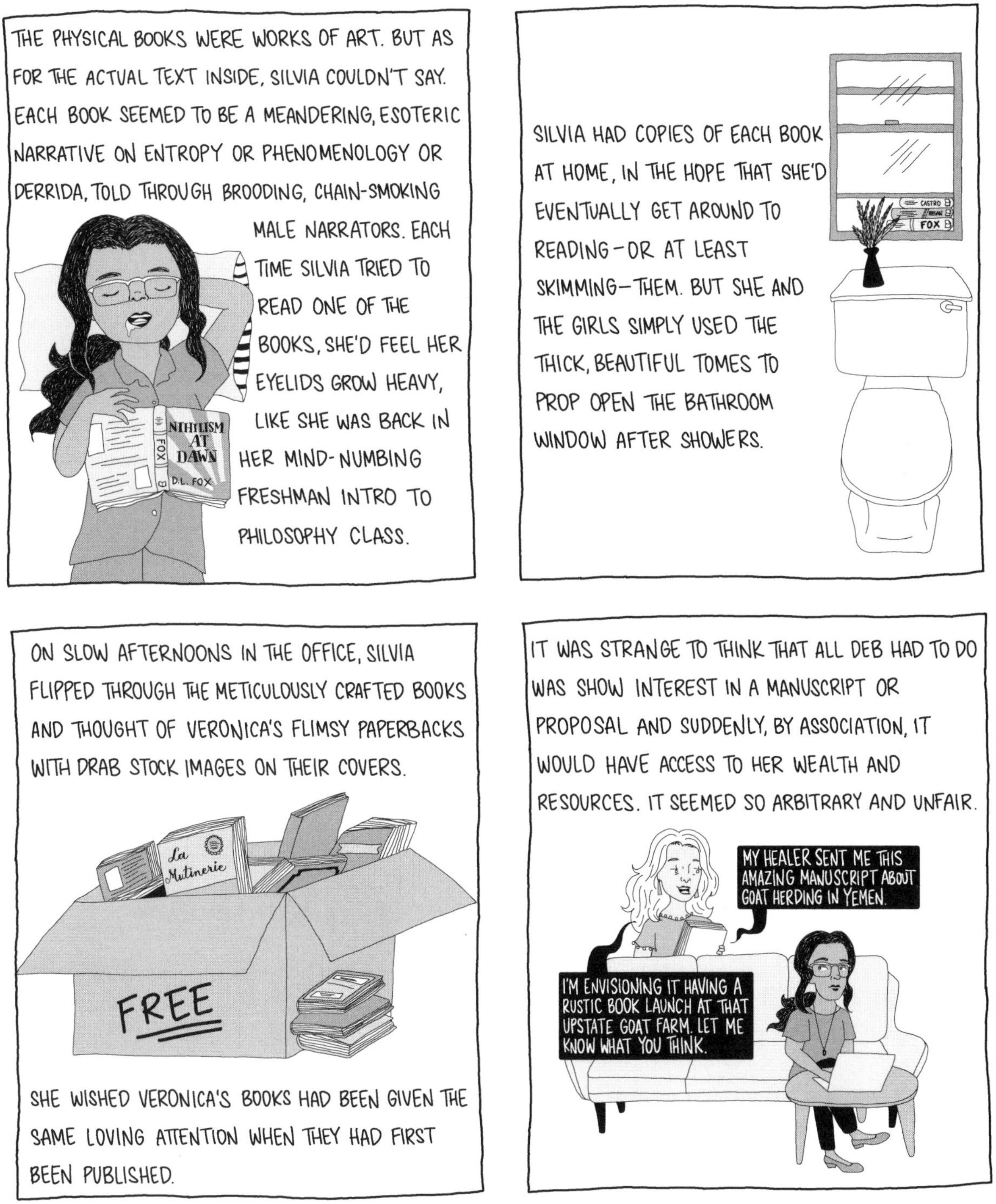
THE PHYSICAL BOOKS WERE WORKS OF ART. BUT AS FOR THE ACTUAL TEXT INSIDE, SILVIA COULDN'T SAY. EACH BOOK SEEMED TO BE A MEANDERING, ESOTERIC NARRATIVE ON ENTROPY OR PHENOMENOLOGY OR DERRIDA, TOLD THROUGH BROODING, CHAIN-SMOKING MALE NARRATORS. EACH TIME SILVIA TRIED TO READ ONE OF THE BOOKS, SHE'D FEEL HER EYELIDS GROW HEAVY, LIKE SHE WAS BACK IN HER MIND-NUMBING FRESHMAN INTRO TO PHILOSOPHY CLASS.
NIHILISM AT DAWN
FOX
D.L. FOX
SILVIA HAD COPIES OF EACH BOOK AT HOME, IN THE HOPE THAT SHE'D EVENTUALLY GET AROUND TO READING—OR AT LEAST SKIMMING—THEM. BUT SHE AND THE GIRLS SIMPLY USED THE THICK, BEAUTIFUL TOMES TO PROP OPEN THE BATHROOM WINDOW AFTER SHOWERS.
CASTRO
FOX
ON SLOW AFTERNOONS IN THE OFFICE, SILVIA FLIPPED THROUGH THE METICULOUSLY CRAFTED BOOKS AND THOUGHT OF VERONICA'S FLIMSY PAPERBACKS WITH DRAB STOCK IMAGES ON THEIR COVERS.
La Mutinerie
FREE
SHE WISHED VERONICA'S BOOKS HAD BEEN GIVEN THE SAME LOVING ATTENTION WHEN THEY HAD FIRST BEEN PUBLISHED.
IT WAS STRANGE TO THINK THAT ALL DEB HAD TO DO WAS SHOW INTEREST IN A MANUSCRIPT OR PROPOSAL AND SUDDENLY, BY ASSOCIATION, IT WOULD HAVE ACCESS TO HER WEALTH AND RESOURCES. IT SEEMED SO ARBITRARY AND UNFAIR.
MY HEALER SENT ME THIS AMAZING MANUSCRIPT ABOUT GOAT HERDING IN YEMEN.
I'M ENVISIONING IT HAVING A RUSTIC BOOK LAUNCH AT THAT UPSTATE GOAT FARM. LET ME KNOW WHAT YOU THINK.

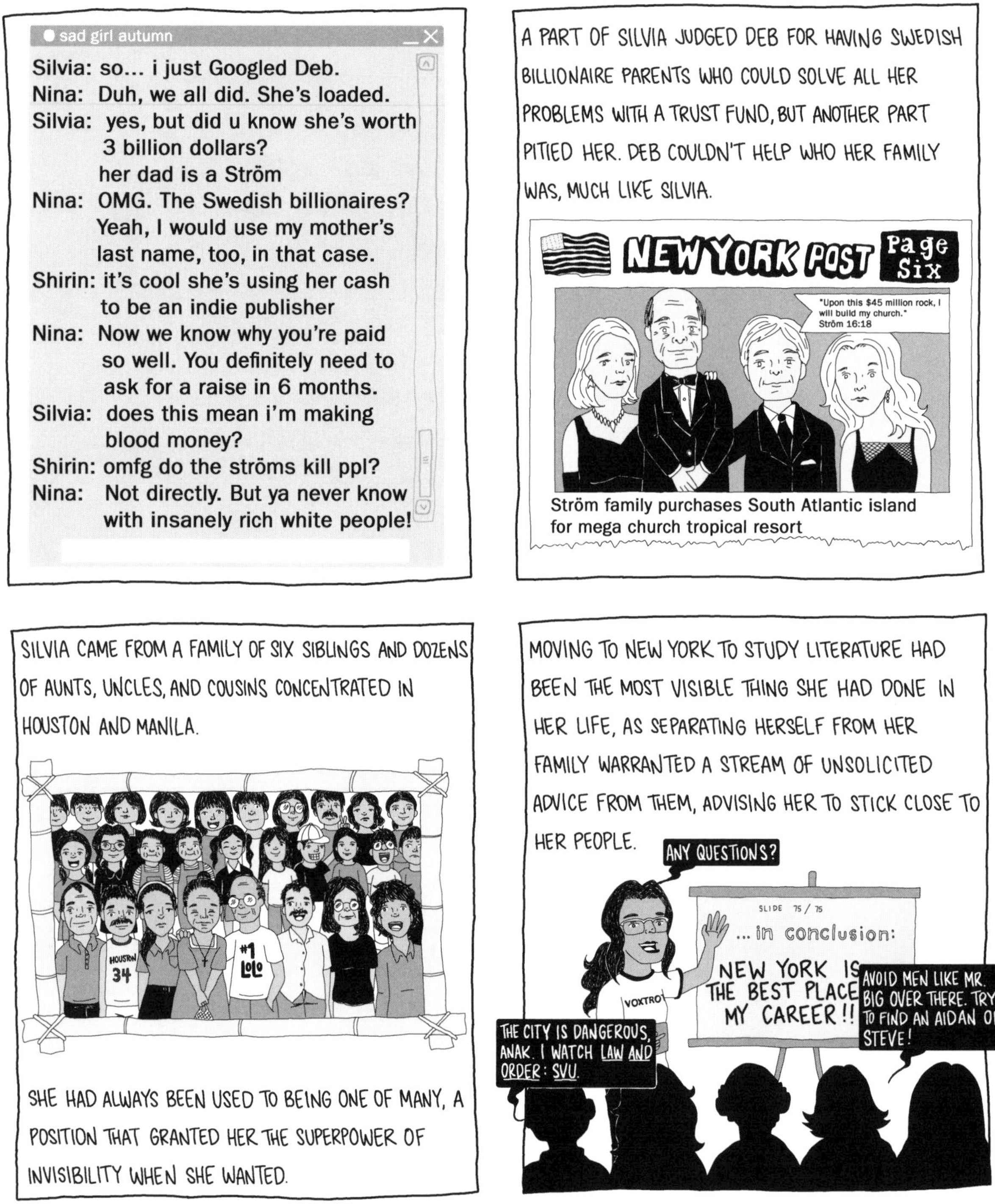
sad girl autumn
Silvia: so... i just Googled Deb.
Nina: Duh, we all did. She's loaded.
Silvia: yes, but did u know she's worth 3 billion dollars?
her dad is a Ström
Nina: OMG. The Swedish billionaires? Yeah, I would use my mother's last name, too, in that case.
Shirin: it's cool she's using her cash to be an indie publisher
Nina: Now we know why you're paid so well. You definitely need to ask for a raise in 6 months.
Silvia: does this mean i'm making blood money?
Shirin: omfg do the ströms kill ppl?
Nina: Not directly. But ya never know with insanely rich white people!
A PART OF SILVIA JUDGED DEB FOR HAVING SWEDISH BILLIONAIRE PARENTS WHO COULD SOLVE ALL HER PROBLEMS WITH A TRUST FUND, BUT ANOTHER PART PITIED HER. DEB COULDN'T HELP WHO HER FAMILY WAS, MUCH LIKE SILVIA.
NEW YORK POST
Page Six
"Upon this $45 million rock, I will build my church." Ström 16:18
Ström family purchases South Atlantic island for mega church tropical resort
SILVIA CAME FROM A FAMILY OF SIX SIBLINGS AND DOZENS OF AUNTS, UNCLES, AND COUSINS CONCENTRATED IN HOUSTON AND MANILA.
HOUSTON 34
#1 LOLO
SHE HAD ALWAYS BEEN USED TO BEING ONE OF MANY, A POSITION THAT GRANTED HER THE SUPERPOWER OF INVISIBILITY WHEN SHE WANTED.
MOVING TO NEW YORK TO STUDY LITERATURE HAD BEEN THE MOST VISIBLE THING SHE HAD DONE IN HER LIFE, AS SEPARATING HERSELF FROM HER FAMILY WARRANTED A STREAM OF UNSOLICITED ADVICE FROM THEM, ADVISING HER TO STICK CLOSE TO HER PEOPLE.
ANY QUESTIONS?
SLIDE 75 / 75
... in conclusion:
NEW YORK IS THE BEST PLACE MY CAREER!!
VOXTRO
THE CITY IS DANGEROUS, ANAK. I WATCH LAW AND ORDER: SVU.
AVOID MEN LIKE MR. BIG OVER THERE. TRY TO FIND AN AIDAN OR STEVE!

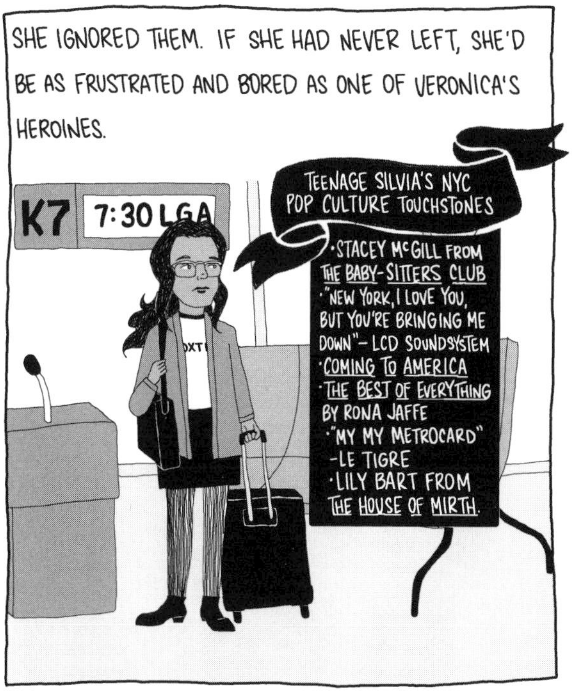
SHE IGNORED THEM. IF SHE HAD NEVER LEFT, SHE'D BE AS FRUSTRATED AND BORED AS ONE OF VERONICA'S HEROINES.
K7 7:30 LGA
TEENAGE SILVIA'S NYC POP CULTURE TOUCHSTONES
•STACEY McGILL FROM THE BABY-SITTERS CLUB
•"NEW YORK, I LOVE YOU, BUT YOU'RE BRINGING ME DOWN"– LCD SOUNDSYSTEM
•COMING TO AMERICA
•THE BEST OF EVERYTHING BY RONA JAFFE
•"MY MY METROCARD" –LE TIGRE
•LILY BART FROM THE HOUSE OF MIRTH.

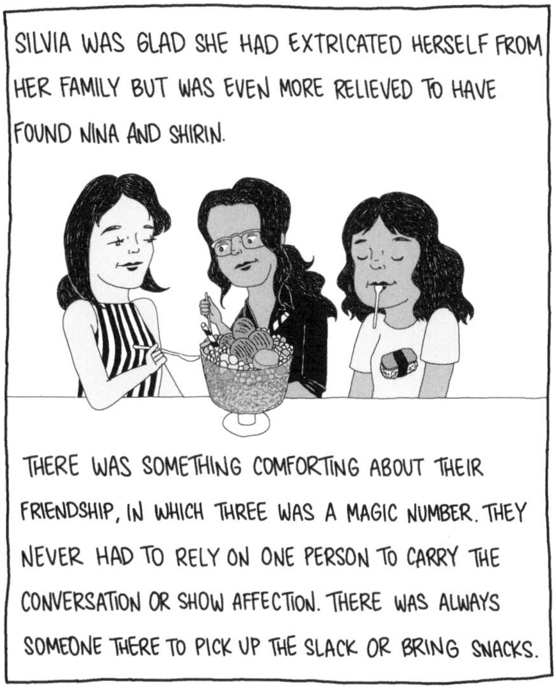
SILVIA WAS GLAD SHE HAD EXTRICATED HERSELF FROM HER FAMILY BUT WAS EVEN MORE RELIEVED TO HAVE FOUND NINA AND SHIRIN.
THERE WAS SOMETHING COMFORTING ABOUT THEIR FRIENDSHIP, IN WHICH THREE WAS A MAGIC NUMBER. THEY NEVER HAD TO RELY ON ONE PERSON TO CARRY THE CONVERSATION OR SHOW AFFECTION. THERE WAS ALWAYS SOMEONE THERE TO PICK UP THE SLACK OR BRING SNACKS.

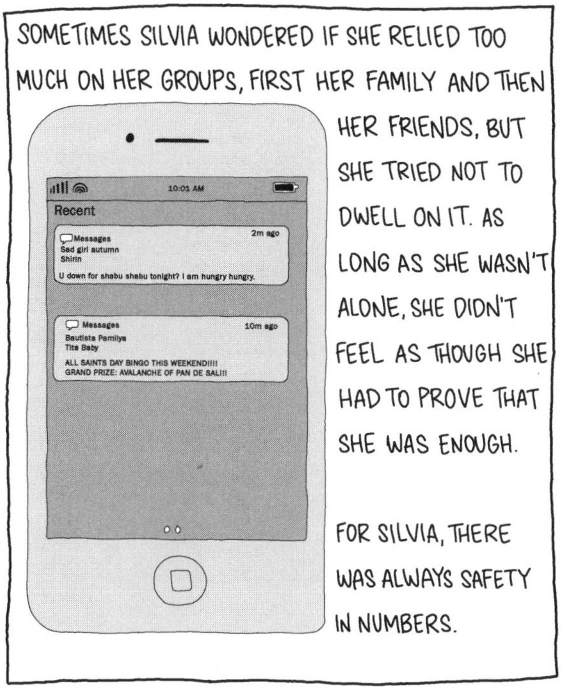
SOMETIMES SILVIA WONDERED IF SHE RELIED TOO MUCH ON HER GROUPS, FIRST HER FAMILY AND THEN HER FRIENDS, BUT SHE TRIED NOT TO DWELL ON IT. AS LONG AS SHE WASN'T ALONE, SHE DIDN'T FEEL AS THOUGH SHE HAD TO PROVE THAT SHE WAS ENOUGH.
10:01 AM
Recent
Messages
2m ago
Sad girl autumn
Shirin
U down for shabu shabu tonight? I am hungry hungry.
Messages
10m ago
Bautista Pamilya
Tita Baby
ALL SAINTS DAY BINGO THIS WEEKEND!!!!
GRAND PRIZE: AVALANCHE OF PAN DE SAL!!!
FOR SILVIA, THERE WAS ALWAYS SAFETY IN NUMBERS.

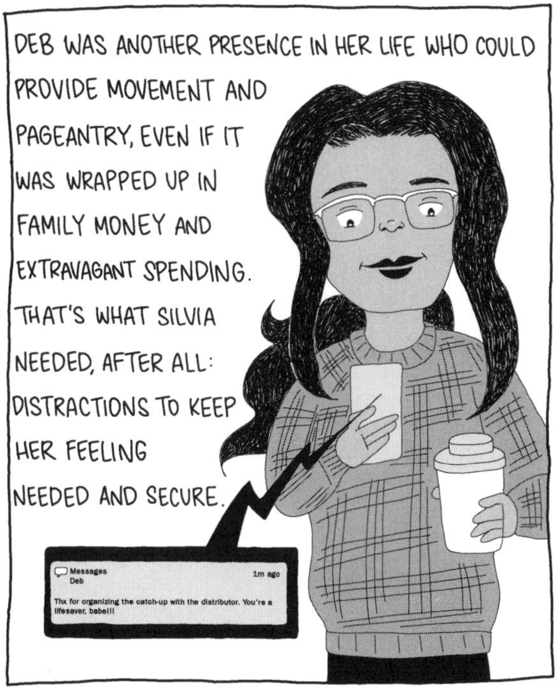
DEB WAS ANOTHER PRESENCE IN HER LIFE WHO COULD PROVIDE MOVEMENT AND PAGEANTRY, EVEN IF IT WAS WRAPPED UP IN FAMILY MONEY AND EXTRAVAGANT SPENDING. THAT'S WHAT SILVIA NEEDED, AFTER ALL: DISTRACTIONS TO KEEP HER FEELING NEEDED AND SECURE.
Messages
Deb
1m ago
Thx for organizing the catch-up with the distributor. You're a lifesaver, babe!!!

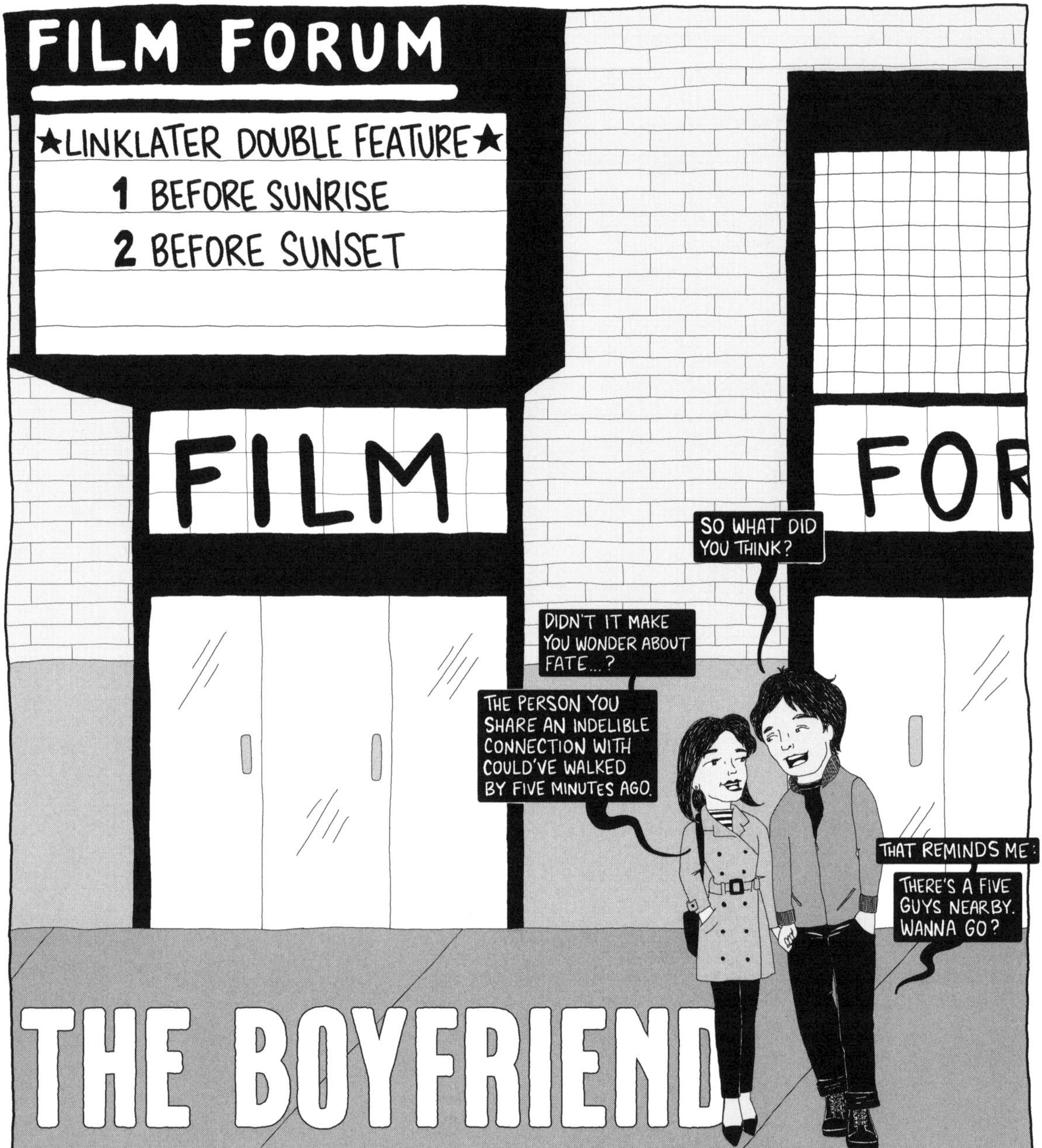
FILM FORUM
★LINKLATER DOUBLE FEATURE★
1 BEFORE SUNRISE
2 BEFORE SUNSET
FILM
FOR
SO WHAT DID YOU THINK?
DIDN'T IT MAKE YOU WONDER ABOUT FATE...?
THE PERSON YOU SHARE AN INDELIBLE CONNECTION WITH COULD'VE WALKED BY FIVE MINUTES AGO.
THAT REMINDS ME:
THERE'S A FIVE GUYS NEARBY. WANNA GO?
THE BOYFRIEND

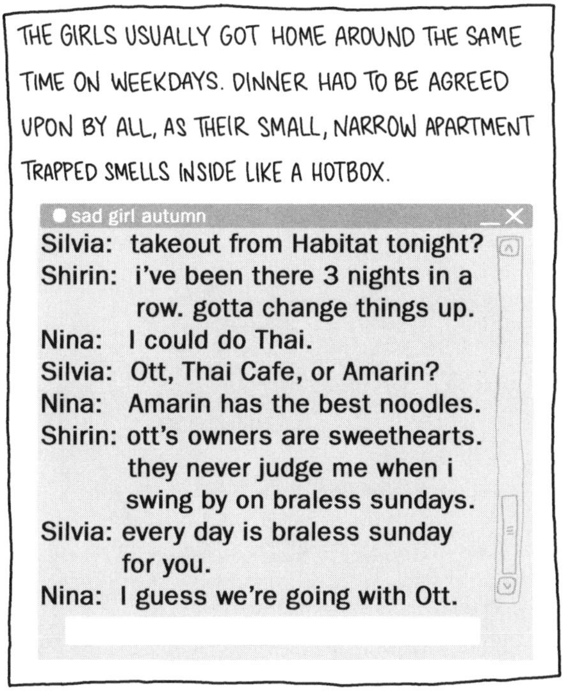
THE GIRLS USUALLY GOT HOME AROUND THE SAME TIME ON WEEKDAYS. DINNER HAD TO BE AGREED UPON BY ALL, AS THEIR SMALL, NARROW APARTMENT TRAPPED SMELLS INSIDE LIKE A HOTBOX.
sad girl autumn
Silvia: takeout from Habitat tonight?
Shirin: i've been there 3 nights in a row. gotta change things up.
Nina: I could do Thai.
Silvia: Ott, Thai Cafe, or Amarin?
Nina: Amarin has the best noodles.
Shirin: ott's owners are sweethearts. they never judge me when i swing by on braless sundays.
Silvia: every day is braless sunday for you.
Nina: I guess we're going with Ott.

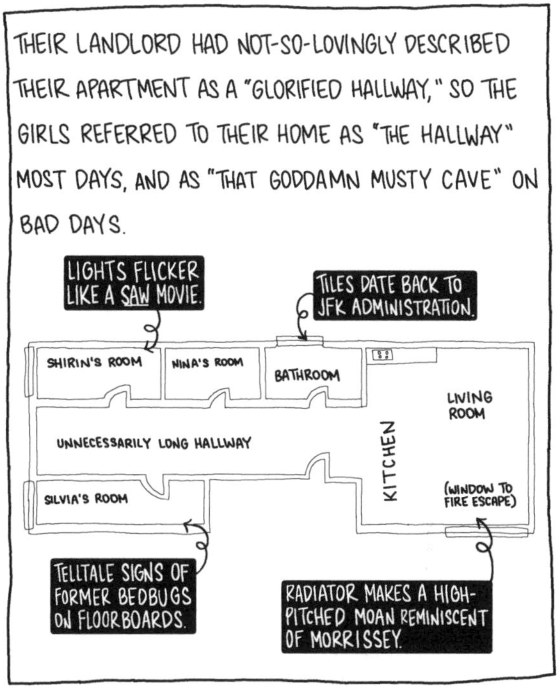
THEIR LANDLORD HAD NOT-SO-LOVINGLY DESCRIBED THEIR APARTMENT AS A "GLORIFIED HALLWAY," SO THE GIRLS REFERRED TO THEIR HOME AS "THE HALLWAY" MOST DAYS, AND AS "THAT GODDAMN MUSTY CAVE" ON BAD DAYS.
LIGHTS FLICKER LIKE A SAW MOVIE.
TILES DATE BACK TO JFK ADMINISTRATION.
SHIRIN'S ROOM
NINA'S ROOM
BATHROOM
LIVING ROOM
UNNECESSARILY LONG HALLWAY
KITCHEN
SILVIA'S ROOM
(WINDOW TO FIRE ESCAPE)
TELLTALE SIGNS OF FORMER BEDBUGS ON FLOORBOARDS.
RADIATOR MAKES A HIGH-PITCHED MOAN REMINISCENT OF MORRISSEY.

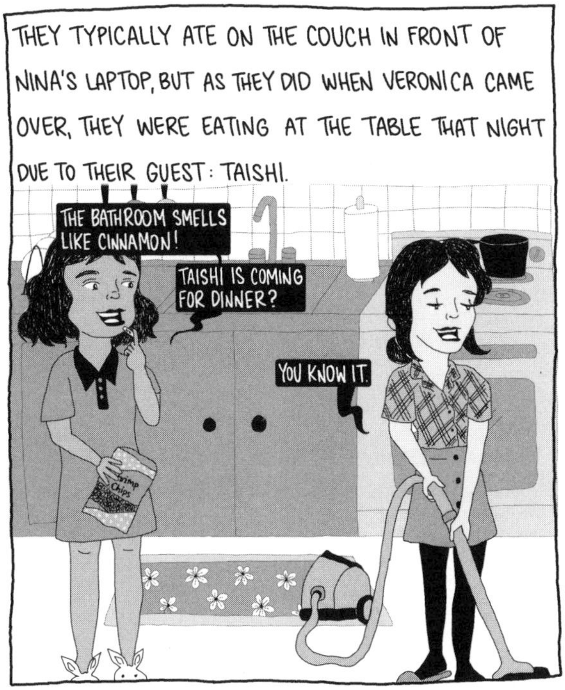
THEY TYPICALLY ATE ON THE COUCH IN FRONT OF NINA'S LAPTOP, BUT AS THEY DID WHEN VERONICA CAME OVER, THEY WERE EATING AT THE TABLE THAT NIGHT DUE TO THEIR GUEST: TAISHI.
THE BATHROOM SMELLS LIKE CINNAMON!
TAISHI IS COMING FOR DINNER?
YOU KNOW IT.

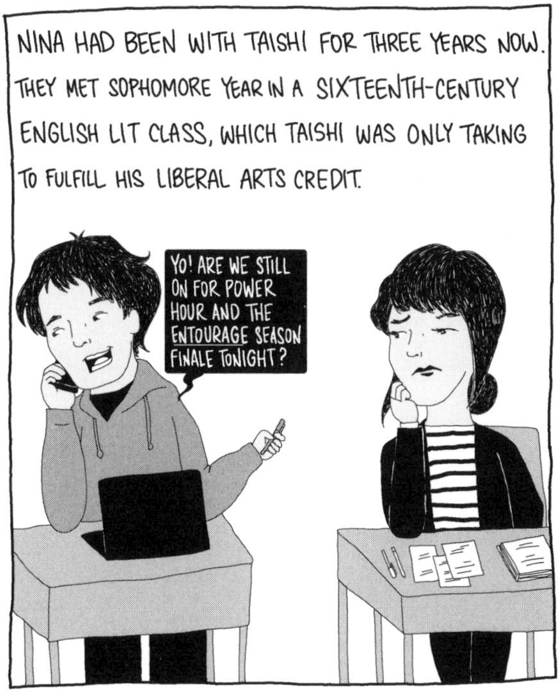
NINA HAD BEEN WITH TAISHI FOR THREE YEARS NOW. THEY MET SOPHOMORE YEAR IN A SIXTEENTH-CENTURY ENGLISH LIT CLASS, WHICH TAISHI WAS ONLY TAKING TO FULFILL HIS LIBERAL ARTS CREDIT.
YO! ARE WE STILL ON FOR POWER HOUR AND THE ENTOURAGE SEASON FINALE TONIGHT?

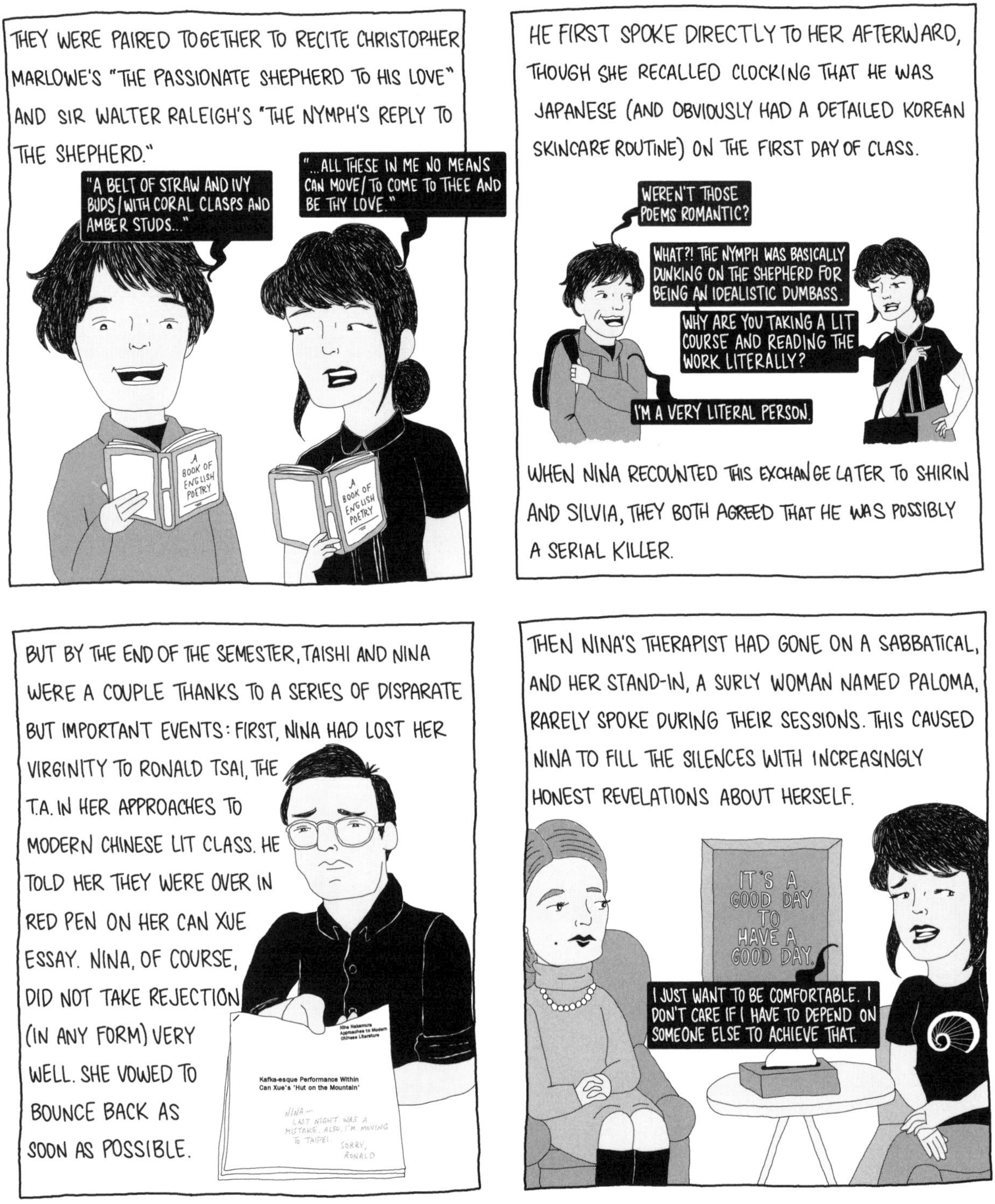
THEY WERE PAIRED TOGETHER TO RECITE CHRISTOPHER MARLOWE'S "THE PASSIONATE SHEPHERD TO HIS LOVE" AND SIR WALTER RALEIGH'S "THE NYMPH'S REPLY TO THE SHEPHERD."
"A BELT OF STRAW AND IVY BUDS/WITH CORAL CLASPS AND AMBER STUDS..."
"...ALL THESE IN ME NO MEANS CAN MOVE/TO COME TO THEE AND BE THY LOVE."
A BOOK OF ENGLISH POETRY
A BOOK OF ENGLISH POETRY
HE FIRST SPOKE DIRECTLY TO HER AFTERWARD, THOUGH SHE RECALLED CLOCKING THAT HE WAS JAPANESE (AND OBVIOUSLY HAD A DETAILED KOREAN SKINCARE ROUTINE) ON THE FIRST DAY OF CLASS.
WEREN'T THOSE POEMS ROMANTIC?
WHAT?! THE NYMPH WAS BASICALLY DUNKING ON THE SHEPHERD FOR BEING AN IDEALISTIC DUMBASS.
WHY ARE YOU TAKING A LIT COURSE AND READING THE WORK LITERALLY?
I'M A VERY LITERAL PERSON.
WHEN NINA RECOUNTED THIS EXCHANGE LATER TO SHIRIN AND SILVIA, THEY BOTH AGREED THAT HE WAS POSSIBLY A SERIAL KILLER.
BUT BY THE END OF THE SEMESTER, TAISHI AND NINA WERE A COUPLE THANKS TO A SERIES OF DISPARATE BUT IMPORTANT EVENTS: FIRST, NINA HAD LOST HER VIRGINITY TO RONALD TSAI, THE T.A. IN HER APPROACHES TO MODERN CHINESE LIT CLASS. HE TOLD HER THEY WERE OVER IN RED PEN ON HER CAN XUE ESSAY. NINA, OF COURSE, DID NOT TAKE REJECTION (IN ANY FORM) VERY WELL. SHE VOWED TO BOUNCE BACK AS SOON AS POSSIBLE.
Nina Nakamura Approaches to Modern Chinese Literature
Kafka-esque Performance Within Can Xue's 'Hut on the Mountain'
NINA— LAST NIGHT WAS A MISTAKE. ALSO, I'M MOVING TO TAIPEI. SORRY, RONALD
THEN NINA'S THERAPIST HAD GONE ON A SABBATICAL, AND HER STAND-IN, A SURLY WOMAN NAMED PALOMA, RARELY SPOKE DURING THEIR SESSIONS. THIS CAUSED NINA TO FILL THE SILENCES WITH INCREASINGLY HONEST REVELATIONS ABOUT HERSELF.
IT'S A GOOD DAY TO HAVE A GOOD DAY.
I JUST WANT TO BE COMFORTABLE. I DON'T CARE IF I HAVE TO DEPEND ON SOMEONE ELSE TO ACHIEVE THAT.

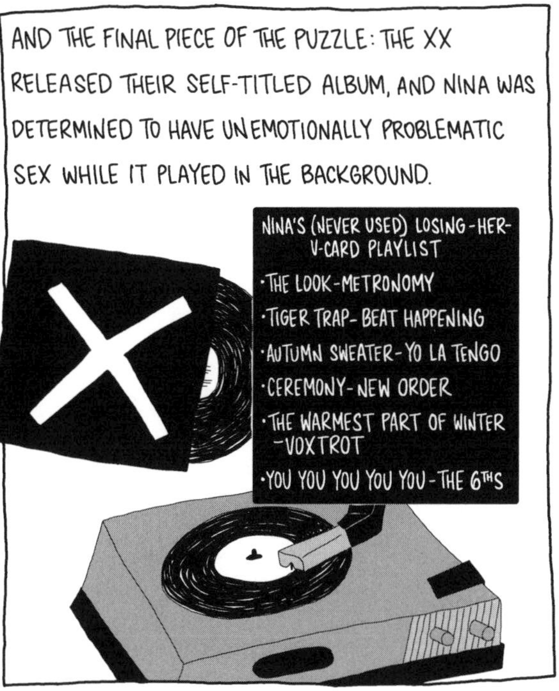
AND THE FINAL PIECE OF THE PUZZLE: THE XX RELEASED THEIR SELF-TITLED ALBUM, AND NINA WAS DETERMINED TO HAVE UNEMOTIONALLY PROBLEMATIC SEX WHILE IT PLAYED IN THE BACKGROUND.
NINA'S (NEVER USED) LOSING-HER-V-CARD PLAYLIST
·THE LOOK-METRONOMY
·TIGER TRAP-BEAT HAPPENING
·AUTUMN SWEATER-YO LA TENGO
·CEREMONY-NEW ORDER
·THE WARMEST PART OF WINTER -VOXTROT
·YOU YOU YOU YOU YOU-THE 6THS

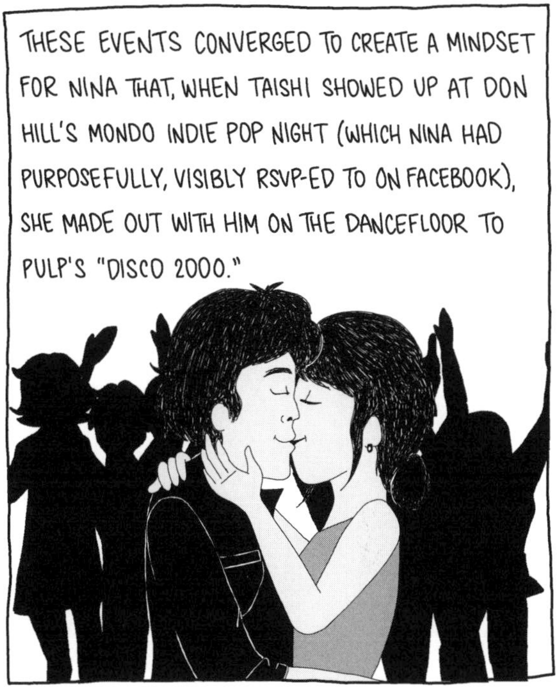
THESE EVENTS CONVERGED TO CREATE A MINDSET FOR NINA THAT, WHEN TAISHI SHOWED UP AT DON HILL'S MONDO INDIE POP NIGHT (WHICH NINA HAD PURPOSEFULLY, VISIBLY RSVP-ED TO ON FACEBOOK), SHE MADE OUT WITH HIM ON THE DANCEFLOOR TO PULP'S "DISCO 2000."

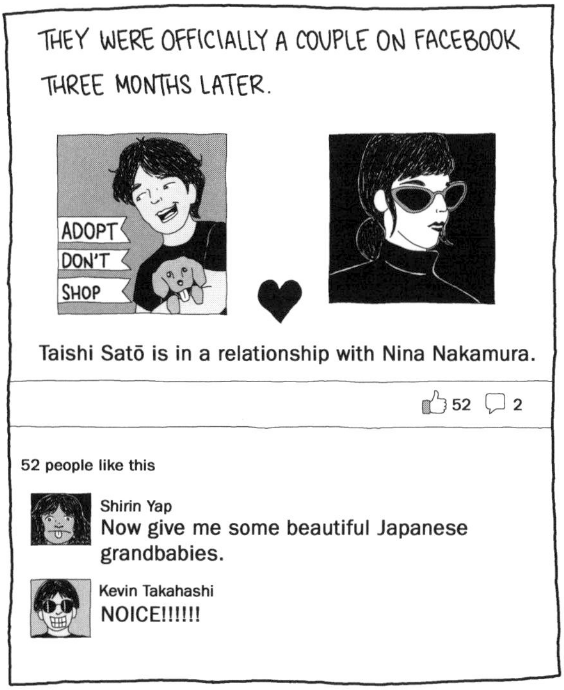
THEY WERE OFFICIALLY A COUPLE ON FACEBOOK THREE MONTHS LATER.
ADOPT
DON'T
SHOP
Taishi Satō is in a relationship with Nina Nakamura.
52
2
52 people like this
Shirin Yap
Now give me some beautiful Japanese grandbabies.
Kevin Takahashi
NOICE!!!!!!

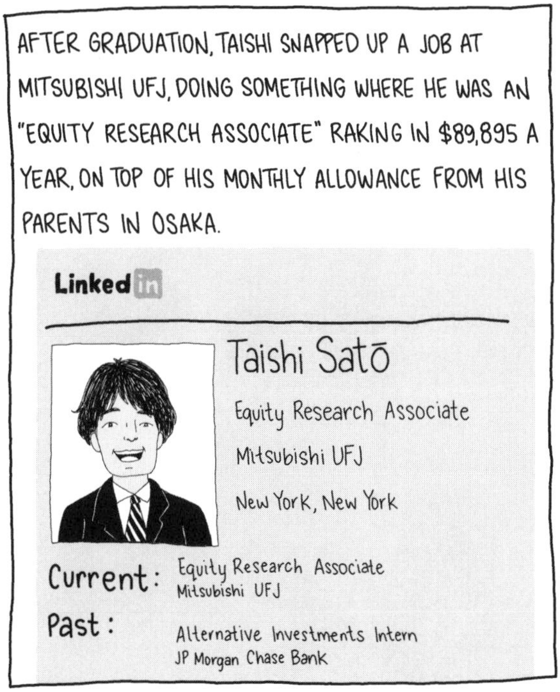
AFTER GRADUATION, TAISHI SNAPPED UP A JOB AT MITSUBISHI UFJ, DOING SOMETHING WHERE HE WAS AN "EQUITY RESEARCH ASSOCIATE" RAKING IN $89,895 A YEAR, ON TOP OF HIS MONTHLY ALLOWANCE FROM HIS PARENTS IN OSAKA.
Linkedin
Taishi Satō
Equity Research Associate
Mitsubishi UFJ
New York, New York
Current: Equity Research Associate
Mitsubishi UFJ
Past: Alternative Investments Intern
JP Morgan Chase Bank

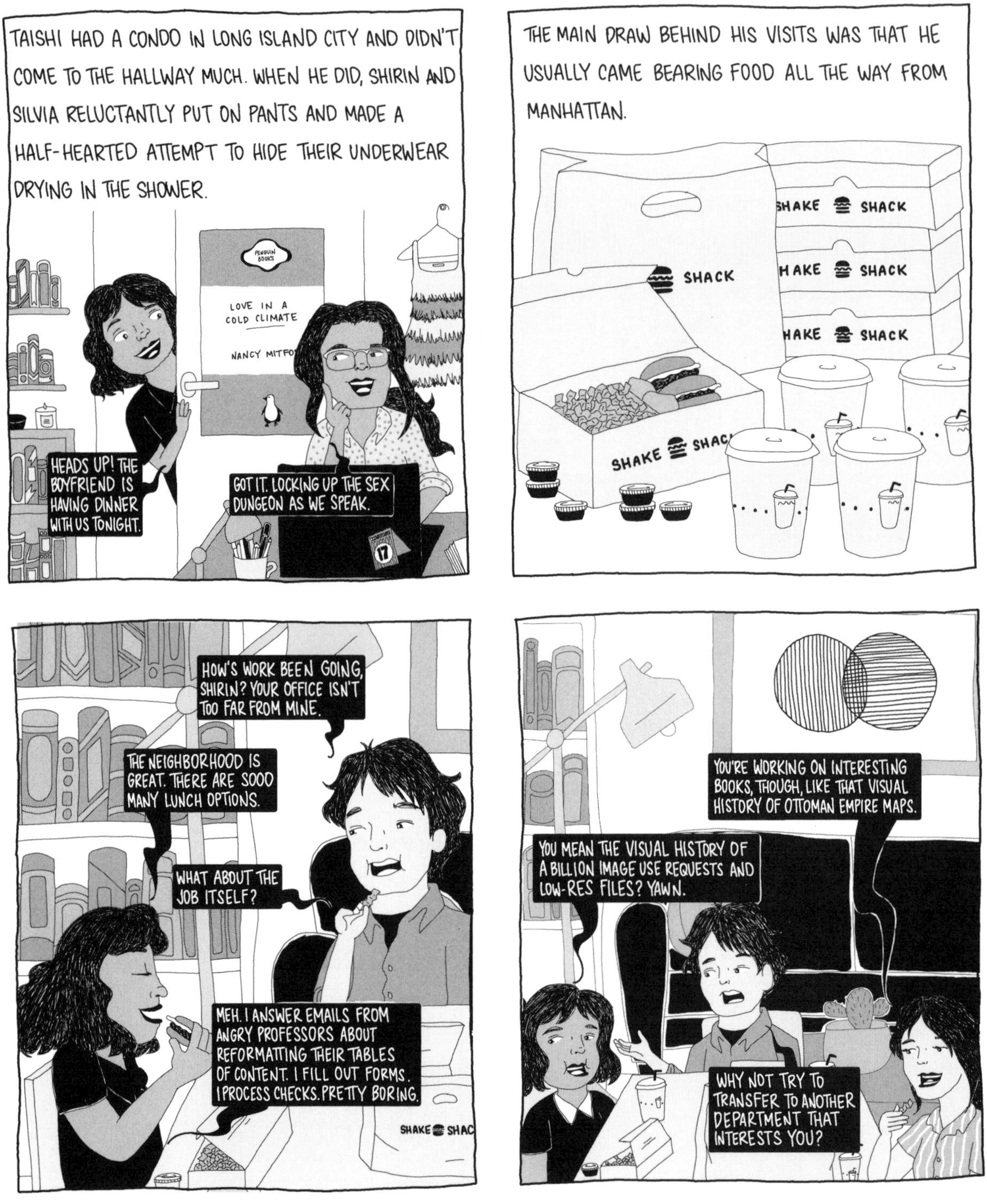
TAISHI HAD A CONDO IN LONG ISLAND CITY AND DIDN'T COME TO THE HALLWAY MUCH. WHEN HE DID, SHIRIN AND SILVIA RELUCTANTLY PUT ON PANTS AND MADE A HALF-HEARTED ATTEMPT TO HIDE THEIR UNDERWEAR DRYING IN THE SHOWER.
PENGUIN BOOKS
LOVE IN A COLD CLIMATE
HEADS UP! THE BOYFRIEND IS HAVING DINNER WITH US TONIGHT.
GOT IT. LOCKING UP THE SEX DUNGEON AS WE SPEAK.
THE MAIN DRAW BEHIND HIS VISITS WAS THAT HE USUALLY CAME BEARING FOOD ALL THE WAY FROM MANHATTAN.
HOW'S WORK BEEN GOING, SHIRIN? YOUR OFFICE ISN'T TOO FAR FROM MINE.
THE NEIGHBORHOOD IS GREAT. THERE ARE SOOO MANY LUNCH OPTIONS.
WHAT ABOUT THE JOB ITSELF?
MEH. I ANSWER EMAILS FROM ANGRY PROFESSORS ABOUT REFORMATTING THEIR TABLES OF CONTENT. I FILL OUT FORMS. I PROCESS CHECKS. PRETTY BORING.
YOU'RE WORKING ON INTERESTING BOOKS, THOUGH, LIKE THAT VISUAL HISTORY OF OTTOMAN EMPIRE MAPS.
YOU MEAN THE VISUAL HISTORY OF A BILLION IMAGE USE REQUESTS AND LOW-RES FILES? YAWN.
WHY NOT TRY TO TRANSFER TO ANOTHER DEPARTMENT THAT INTERESTS YOU?

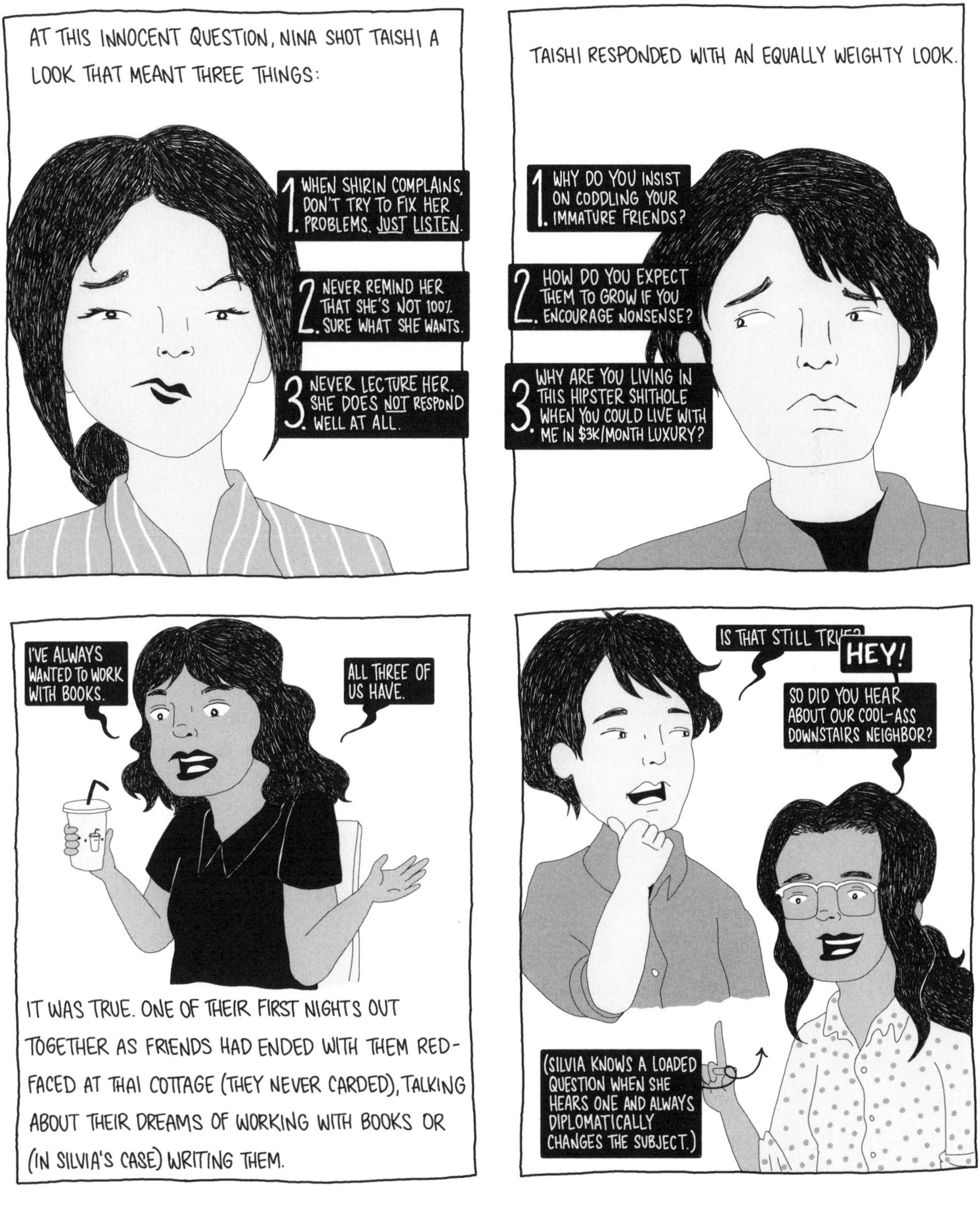

AT THIS INNOCENT QUESTION, NINA SHOT TAISHI A LOOK THAT MEANT THREE THINGS:
1. WHEN SHIRIN COMPLAINS, DON'T TRY TO FIX HER PROBLEMS. JUST LISTEN.
2. NEVER REMIND HER THAT SHE'S NOT 100% SURE WHAT SHE WANTS.
3. NEVER LECTURE HER. SHE DOES NOT RESPOND WELL AT ALL.
TAISHI RESPONDED WITH AN EQUALLY WEIGHTY LOOK.
1. WHY DO YOU INSIST ON CODDLING YOUR IMMATURE FRIENDS?
2. HOW DO YOU EXPECT THEM TO GROW IF YOU ENCOURAGE NONSENSE?
3. WHY ARE YOU LIVING IN THIS HIPSTER SHITHOLE WHEN YOU COULD LIVE WITH ME IN $3K/MONTH LUXURY?
I'VE ALWAYS WANTED TO WORK WITH BOOKS.
ALL THREE OF US HAVE.
IT WAS TRUE. ONE OF THEIR FIRST NIGHTS OUT TOGETHER AS FRIENDS HAD ENDED WITH THEM RED-FACED AT THAI COTTAGE (THEY NEVER CARDED), TALKING ABOUT THEIR DREAMS OF WORKING WITH BOOKS OR (IN SILVIA'S CASE) WRITING THEM.
IS THAT STILL TRU
HEY!
SO DID YOU HEAR ABOUT OUR COOL-ASS DOWNSTAIRS NEIGHBOR?
(SILVIA KNOWS A LOADED QUESTION WHEN SHE HEARS ONE AND ALWAYS DIPLOMATICALLY CHANGES THE SUBJECT.)

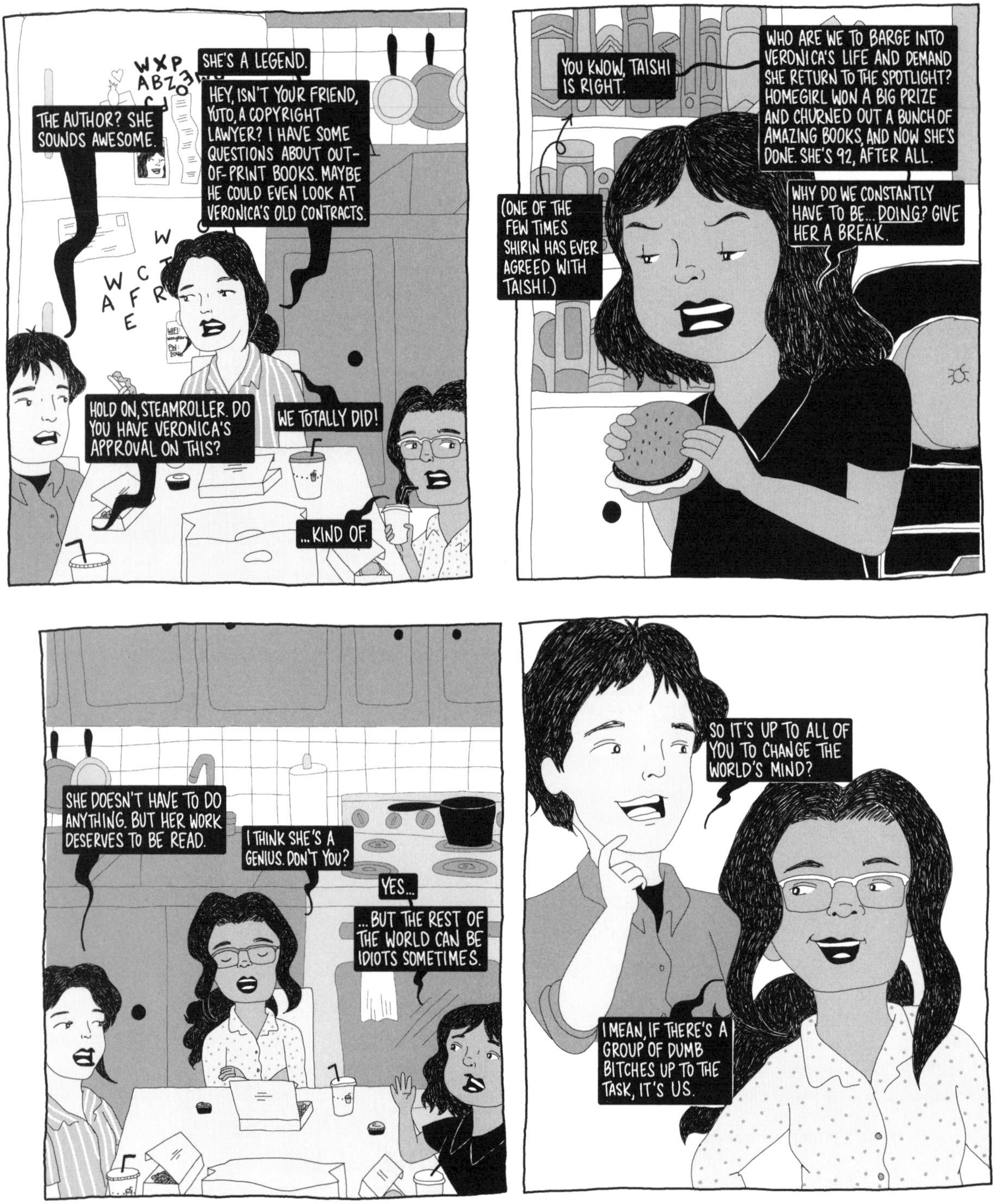
THE AUTHOR? SHE SOUNDS AWESOME.
SHE'S A LEGEND.
HEY, ISN'T YOUR FRIEND, YUTO, A COPYRIGHT LAWYER? I HAVE SOME QUESTIONS ABOUT OUT-OF-PRINT BOOKS. MAYBE HE COULD EVEN LOOK AT VERONICA'S OLD CONTRACTS.
HOLD ON, STEAMROLLER. DO YOU HAVE VERONICA'S APPROVAL ON THIS?
WE TOTALLY DID!
...KIND OF.
YOU KNOW, TAISHI IS RIGHT.
(ONE OF THE FEW TIMES SHIRIN HAS EVER AGREED WITH TAISHI.)
WHO ARE WE TO BARGE INTO VERONICA'S LIFE AND DEMAND SHE RETURN TO THE SPOTLIGHT? HOMEGIRL WON A BIG PRIZE AND CHURNED OUT A BUNCH OF AMAZING BOOKS, AND NOW SHE'S DONE. SHE'S 92, AFTER ALL.
WHY DO WE CONSTANTLY HAVE TO BE... DOING? GIVE HER A BREAK.
SHE DOESN'T HAVE TO DO ANYTHING. BUT HER WORK DESERVES TO BE READ.
I THINK SHE'S A GENIUS. DON'T YOU?
YES...
...BUT THE REST OF THE WORLD CAN BE IDIOTS SOMETIMES.
SO IT'S UP TO ALL OF YOU TO CHANGE THE WORLD'S MIND?
I MEAN, IF THERE'S A GROUP OF DUMB BITCHES UP TO THE TASK, IT'S US.

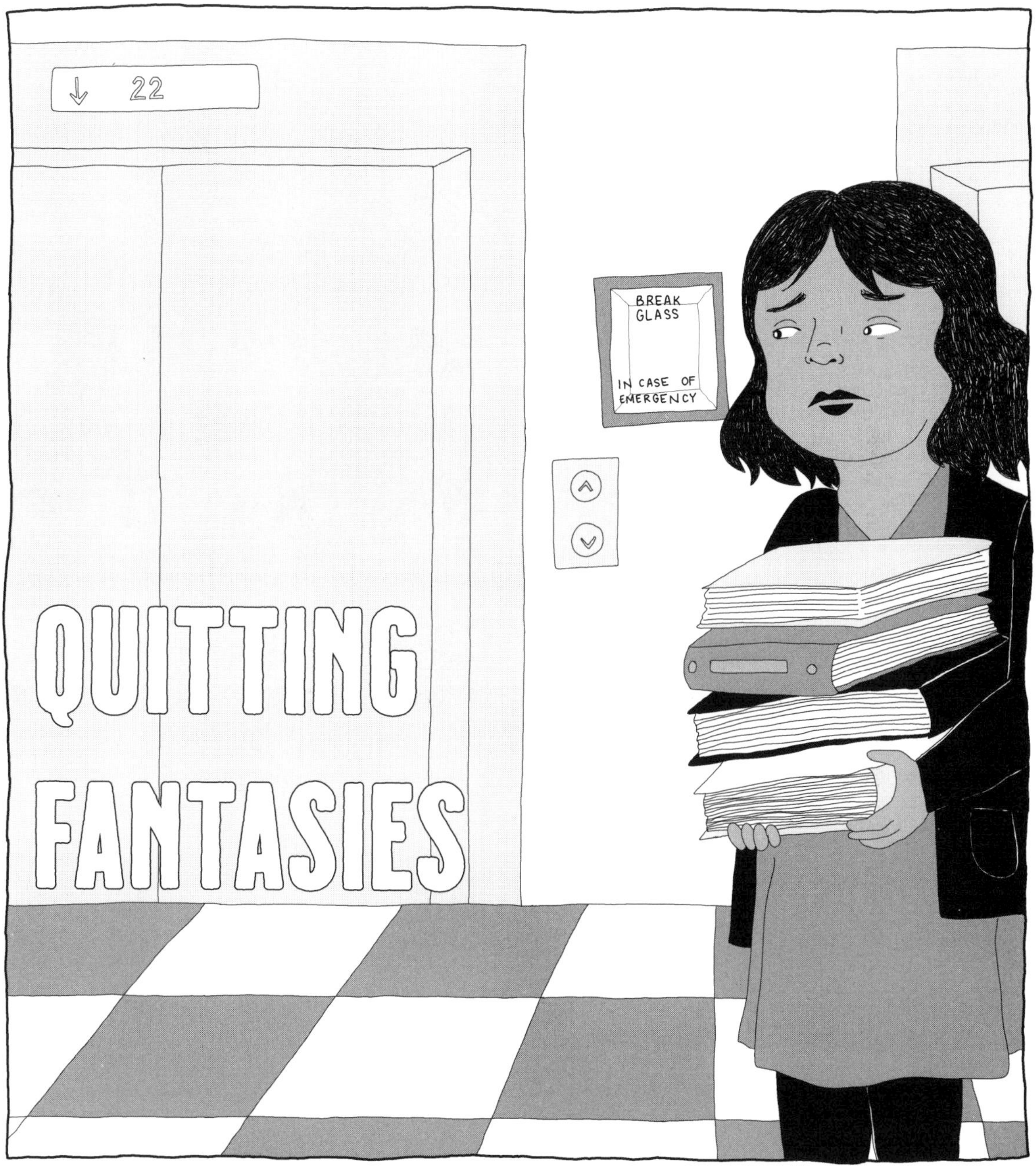
22
BREAK GLASS
IN CASE OF EMERGENCY
QUITTING FANTASIES

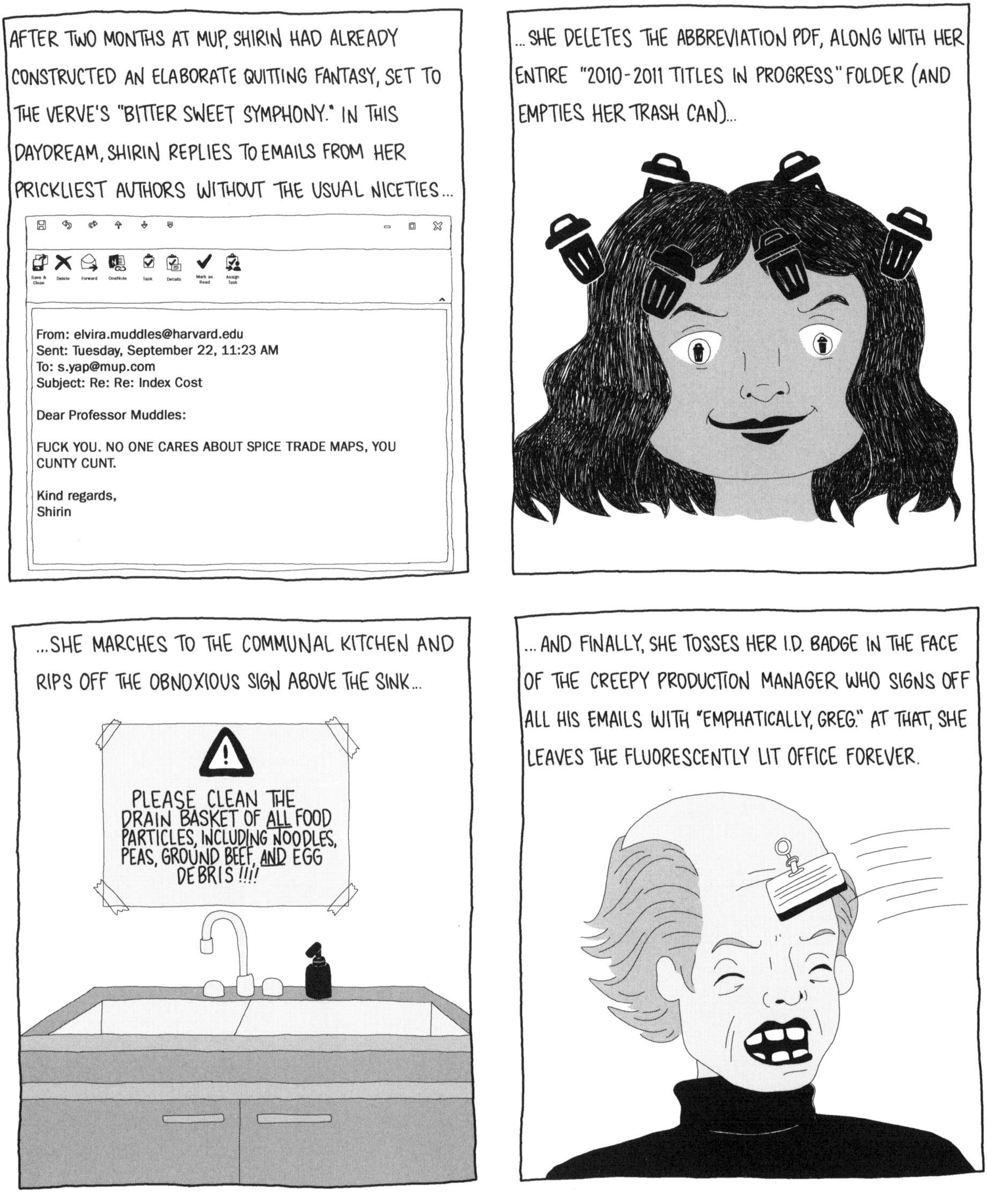
AFTER TWO MONTHS AT MUP, SHIRIN HAD ALREADY CONSTRUCTED AN ELABORATE QUITTING FANTASY, SET TO THE VERVE'S "BITTER SWEET SYMPHONY." IN THIS DAYDREAM, SHIRIN REPLIES TO EMAILS FROM HER PRICKLIEST AUTHORS WITHOUT THE USUAL NICETIES...
Save & Close
Delete
Forward
OneNote
Task
Details
Mark as Read
Assign Task
From: elvira.muddles@harvard.edu
Sent: Tuesday, September 22, 11:23 AM
To: s.yap@mup.com
Subject: Re: Re: Index Cost
Dear Professor Muddles:
FUCK YOU. NO ONE CARES ABOUT SPICE TRADE MAPS, YOU CUNTY CUNT.
Kind regards,
Shirin
...SHE DELETES THE ABBREVIATION PDF, ALONG WITH HER ENTIRE "2010-2011 TITLES IN PROGRESS" FOLDER (AND EMPTIES HER TRASH CAN)...
...SHE MARCHES TO THE COMMUNAL KITCHEN AND RIPS OFF THE OBNOXIOUS SIGN ABOVE THE SINK...
PLEASE CLEAN THE DRAIN BASKET OF ALL FOOD PARTICLES, INCLUDING NOODLES, PEAS, GROUND BEEF, AND EGG DEBRIS!!!!
...AND FINALLY, SHE TOSSES HER I.D. BADGE IN THE FACE OF THE CREEPY PRODUCTION MANAGER WHO SIGNS OFF ALL HIS EMAILS WITH "EMPHATICALLY, GREG." AT THAT, SHE LEAVES THE FLUORESCENTLY LIT OFFICE FOREVER.

THIS IS WHAT SHIRIN IMAGINED AS SHE RECEIVED HER FOURTH EMAIL OF THE DAY FROM ELVIRA MUDDLES, HÉLÈNE'S NEEDIEST AUTHOR. SHIRIN SKIMMED ALL HER EMAILS BEFORE FORWARDING THEM TO HER BOSS AND ADDING "PLS ADVISE."

IT WAS 3 P.M. IN NEW YORK AND 9 P.M. IN PARIS. AT THIS POINT, HÉLÈNE HAD SIGNED OFF FOR THE DAY.

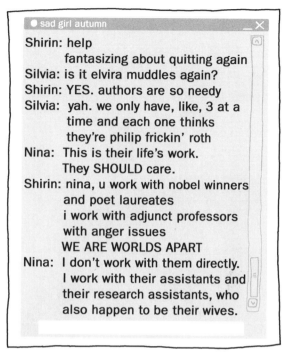

● sad girl autumn

Shirin: help
fantasizing about quitting again
Silvia: is it elvira muddles again?
Shirin: YES. authors are so needy
Silvia: yah. we only have, like, 3 at a time and each one thinks they're philip frickin' roth
Nina: This is their life's work. They SHOULD care.
Shirin: nina, u work with nobel winners and poet laureates i work with adjunct professors with anger issues WE ARE WORLDS APART
Nina: I don't work with them directly. I work with their assistants and their research assistants, who also happen to be their wives.

TO SHIRIN'S SURPRISE, HER DESK PHONE BEGAN RINGING. ONLY ONE PERSON CALLED HER ON IT.

HI, HÉLÈNE?

HELLO, SHIRIN.

ISN'T IT LATE OVER THERE?

YES, BUT MY DINNER DATE STOOD ME UP, SO HERE I AM, CHECKING MY EMAIL.

SHIRIN IMAGINED HÉLÈNE IN A DIMLY LIT BRASSERIE, SMOKING AND ADJUSTING HER SCARVES, LIGHT-YEARS AWAY FROM SHIRIN'S CUBICLE AND FILE CABINETS.

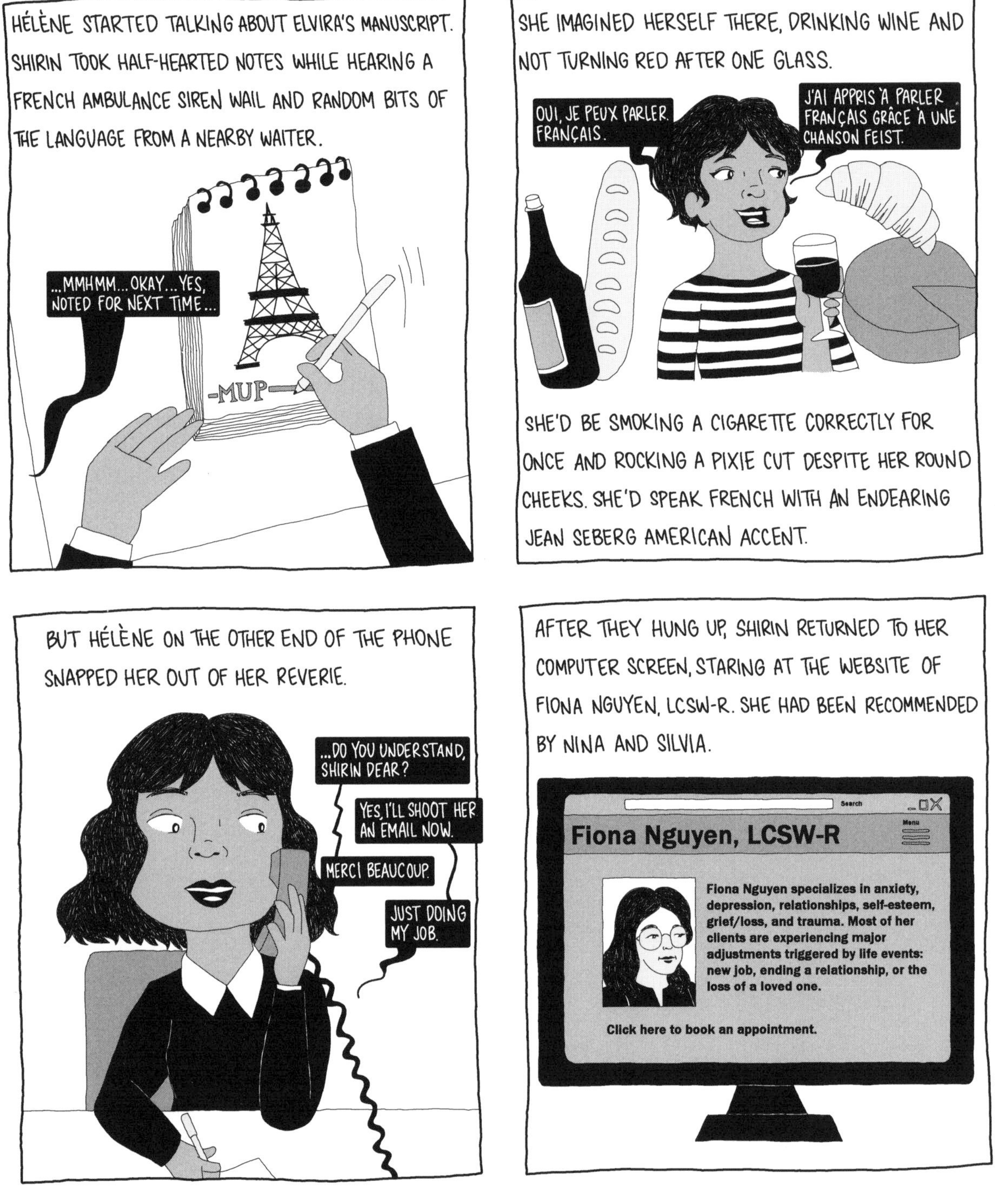
HÉLÈNE STARTED TALKING ABOUT ELVIRA'S MANUSCRIPT. SHIRIN TOOK HALF-HEARTED NOTES WHILE HEARING A FRENCH AMBULANCE SIREN WAIL AND RANDOM BITS OF THE LANGUAGE FROM A NEARBY WAITER.
...MMHMM... OKAY... YES, NOTED FOR NEXT TIME...
-MUP
SHE IMAGINED HERSELF THERE, DRINKING WINE AND NOT TURNING RED AFTER ONE GLASS.
OUI, JE PEUX PARLER FRANÇAIS.
J'AI APPRIS À PARLER FRANÇAIS GRÂCE À UNE CHANSON FEIST.
SHE'D BE SMOKING A CIGARETTE CORRECTLY FOR ONCE AND ROCKING A PIXIE CUT DESPITE HER ROUND CHEEKS. SHE'D SPEAK FRENCH WITH AN ENDEARING JEAN SEBERG AMERICAN ACCENT.
BUT HÉLÈNE ON THE OTHER END OF THE PHONE SNAPPED HER OUT OF HER REVERIE.
...DO YOU UNDERSTAND, SHIRIN DEAR?
YES, I'LL SHOOT HER AN EMAIL NOW.
MERCI BEAUCOUP.
JUST DOING MY JOB.
AFTER THEY HUNG UP, SHIRIN RETURNED TO HER COMPUTER SCREEN, STARING AT THE WEBSITE OF FIONA NGUYEN, LCSW-R. SHE HAD BEEN RECOMMENDED BY NINA AND SILVIA.
Search
Fiona Nguyen, LCSW-R
Menu
Fiona Nguyen specializes in anxiety, depression, relationships, self-esteem, grief/loss, and trauma. Most of her clients are experiencing major adjustments triggered by life events: new job, ending a relationship, or the loss of a loved one.
Click here to book an appointment.

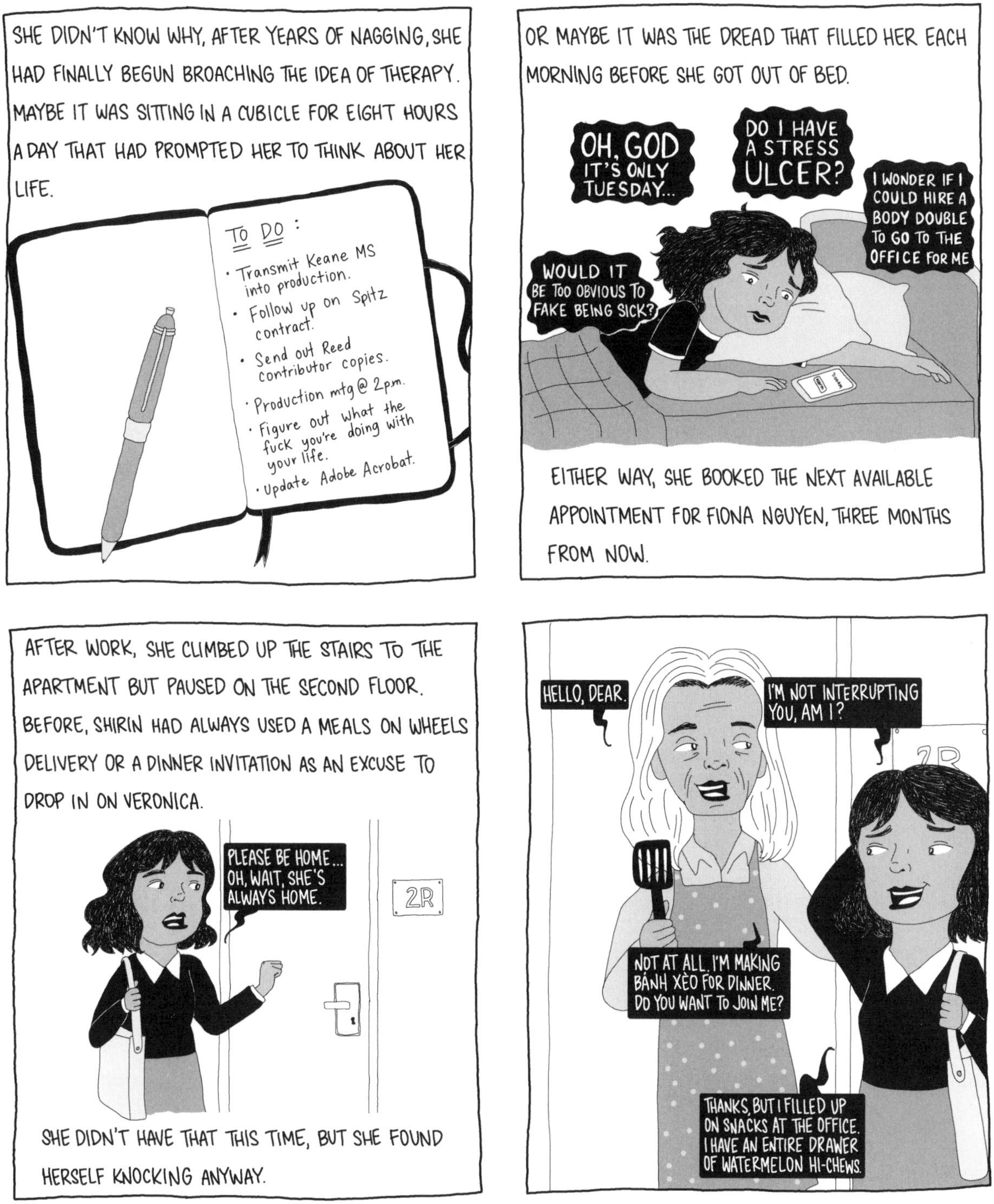
SHE DIDN'T KNOW WHY, AFTER YEARS OF NAGGING, SHE HAD FINALLY BEGUN BROACHING THE IDEA OF THERAPY. MAYBE IT WAS SITTING IN A CUBICLE FOR EIGHT HOURS A DAY THAT HAD PROMPTED HER TO THINK ABOUT HER LIFE.
TO DO:
• Transmit Keane MS into production.
• Follow up on Spitz contract.
• Send out Reed contributor copies.
• Production mtg @ 2p.m.
• Figure out what the fuck you're doing with your life.
• Update Adobe Acrobat.
OR MAYBE IT WAS THE DREAD THAT FILLED HER EACH MORNING BEFORE SHE GOT OUT OF BED.
OH, GOD IT'S ONLY TUESDAY...
DO I HAVE A STRESS ULCER?
I WONDER IF I COULD HIRE A BODY DOUBLE TO GO TO THE OFFICE FOR ME
WOULD IT BE TOO OBVIOUS TO FAKE BEING SICK?
EITHER WAY, SHE BOOKED THE NEXT AVAILABLE APPOINTMENT FOR FIONA NGUYEN, THREE MONTHS FROM NOW.
AFTER WORK, SHE CLIMBED UP THE STAIRS TO THE APARTMENT BUT PAUSED ON THE SECOND FLOOR. BEFORE, SHIRIN HAD ALWAYS USED A MEALS ON WHEELS DELIVERY OR A DINNER INVITATION AS AN EXCUSE TO DROP IN ON VERONICA.
PLEASE BE HOME... OH, WAIT, SHE'S ALWAYS HOME.
2R
SHE DIDN'T HAVE THAT THIS TIME, BUT SHE FOUND HERSELF KNOCKING ANYWAY.
HELLO, DEAR.
I'M NOT INTERRUPTING YOU, AM I?
2R
NOT AT ALL. I'M MAKING BÁNH XÈO FOR DINNER. DO YOU WANT TO JOIN ME?
THANKS, BUT I FILLED UP ON SNACKS AT THE OFFICE. I HAVE AN ENTIRE DRAWER OF WATERMELON HI-CHEWS.

WHAT CAN I HELP YOU WITH?
I WAS WONDERING: WHY DID YOU MOVE TO NEW YORK? AND WHY NEW YORK SPECIFICALLY?
EVERYONE WAS LEAVING VIETNAM ANYWAY, AND I WENT TO LOUISIANA FIRST BECAUSE THAT'S WHERE EVERYONE I KNEW HAD GONE.
BUT I HAD NO REASON TO STAY THERE, SO I TOOK A TRAIN TO NEW YORK BECAUSE OF THAT GODDAMN JOAN DIDION ESSAY.
"GOODBYE TO ALL THAT"?!
MY EX HAD A LINE FROM IT TATTOOED ON HER CLAVICLE.
GOOD THING SHE'S YOUR EX NOW.
"ANYWAY, JOAN-AND EVERY OTHER WRITER I READ-MADE THE CITY SOUND SO APPEALING. I SPOKE VIETNAMESE, FRENCH, AND ENGLISH, SO I HOPED TO GET A JOB IN AN OFFICE OR EMBASSY AND WRITE AT NIGHT. I WORKED AS A TYPIST FOR A JEWELRY WHOLESALER FOR A YEAR AND A HALF BEFORE LA MUTINERIE."
DID YOU HATE IT?
NATURALLY.
HOW'D YOU SURVIVE?
WELL, I HAD LIVED THROUGH A COUPLE OF WARS AND THE DESTRUCTION OF MY HOME COUNTRY, SO WORKING IN AN OFFICE WAS A BREEZE, DEAR.
COOL, COOL, COOL.

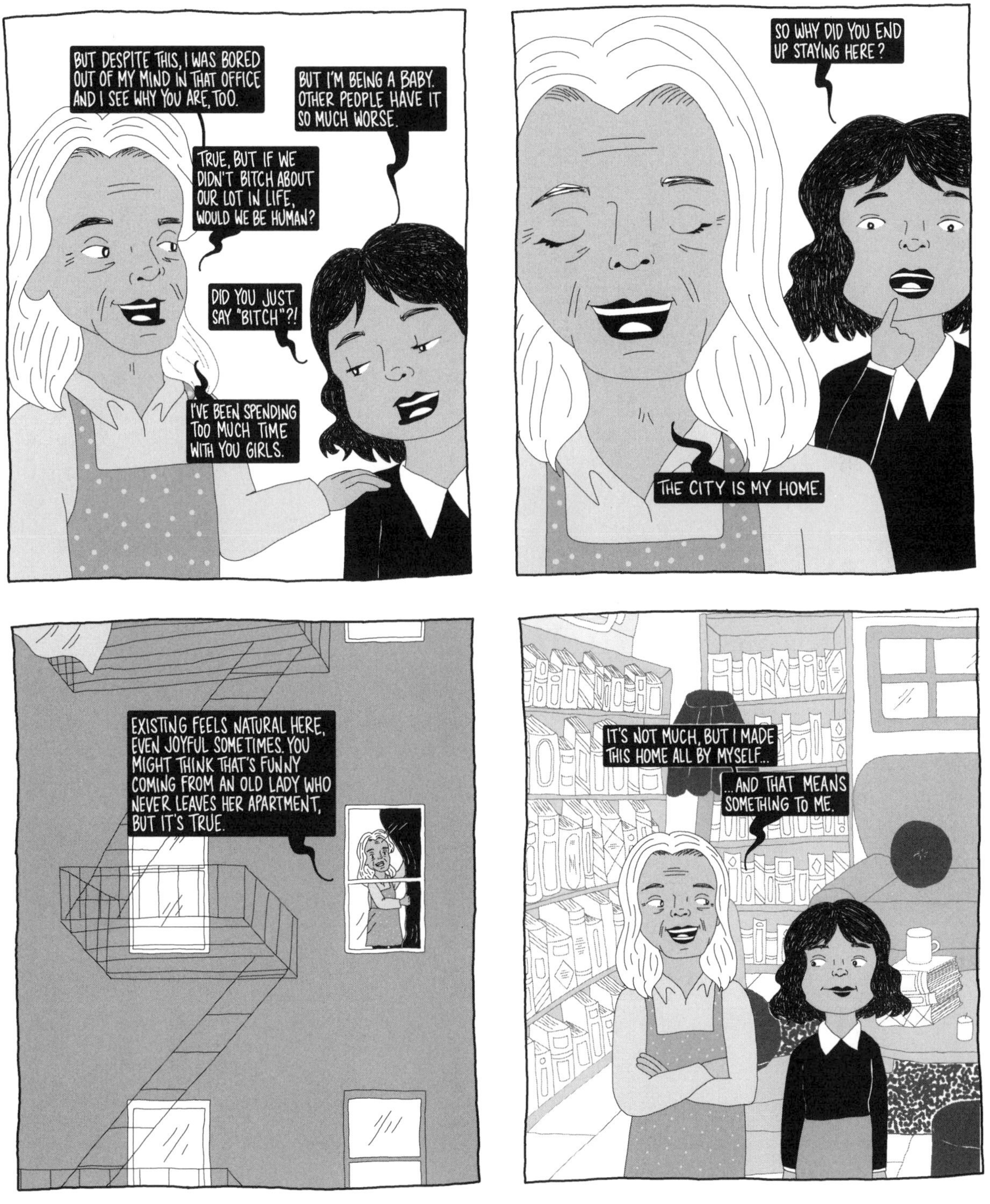
BUT DESPITE THIS, I WAS BORED OUT OF MY MIND IN THAT OFFICE AND I SEE WHY YOU ARE, TOO.
BUT I'M BEING A BABY. OTHER PEOPLE HAVE IT SO MUCH WORSE.
TRUE, BUT IF WE DIDN'T BITCH ABOUT OUR LOT IN LIFE, WOULD WE BE HUMAN?
DID YOU JUST SAY "BITCH"?!
I'VE BEEN SPENDING TOO MUCH TIME WITH YOU GIRLS.
SO WHY DID YOU END UP STAYING HERE?
THE CITY IS MY HOME.
EXISTING FEELS NATURAL HERE, EVEN JOYFUL SOMETIMES. YOU MIGHT THINK THAT'S FUNNY COMING FROM AN OLD LADY WHO NEVER LEAVES HER APARTMENT, BUT IT'S TRUE.
IT'S NOT MUCH, BUT I MADE THIS HOME ALL BY MYSELF...
...AND THAT MEANS SOMETHING TO ME.

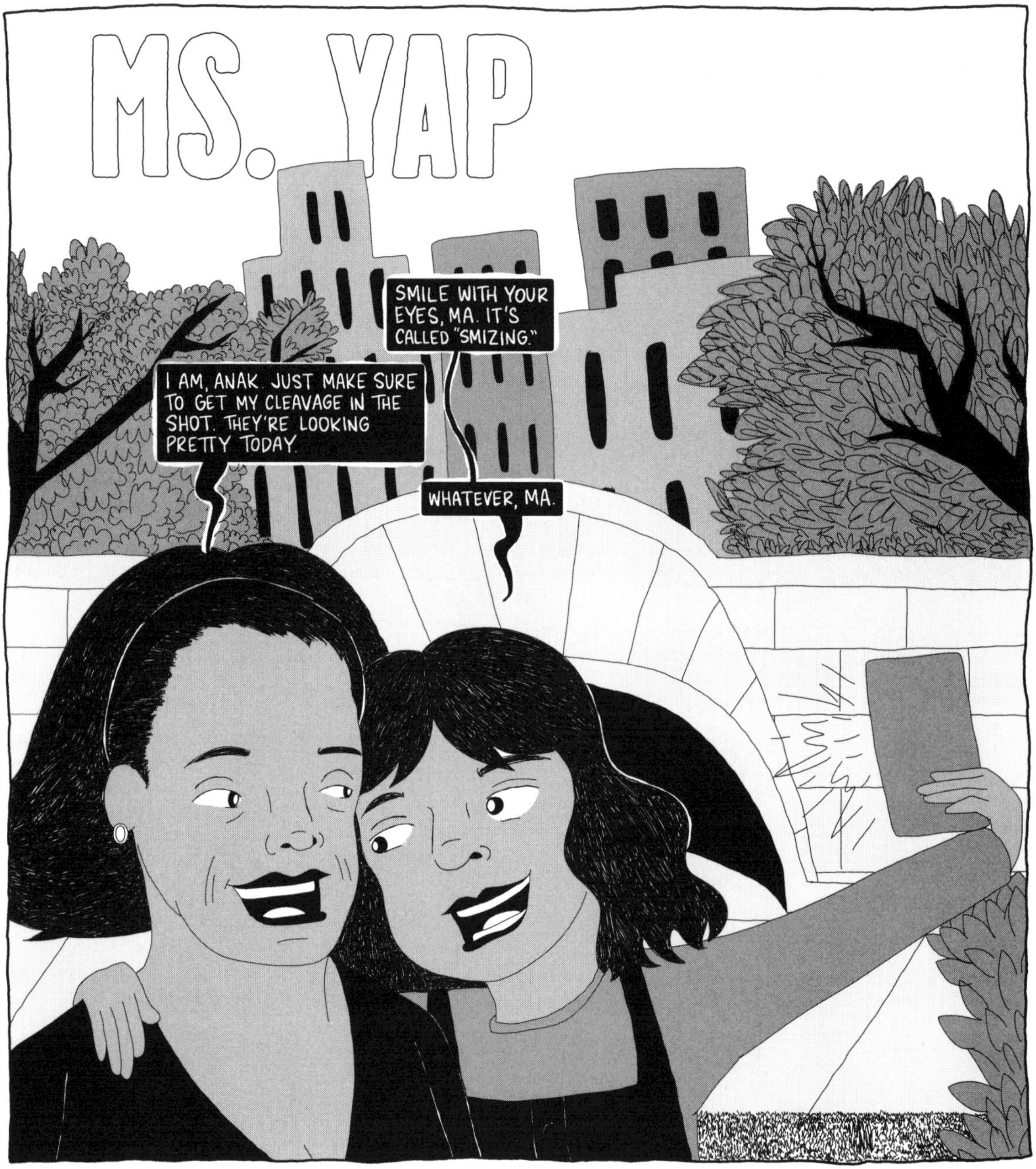
MS. YAP
I AM, ANAK. JUST MAKE SURE TO GET MY CLEAVAGE IN THE SHOT. THEY'RE LOOKING PRETTY TODAY.
SMILE WITH YOUR EYES, MA. IT'S CALLED "SMIZING."
WHATEVER, MA.

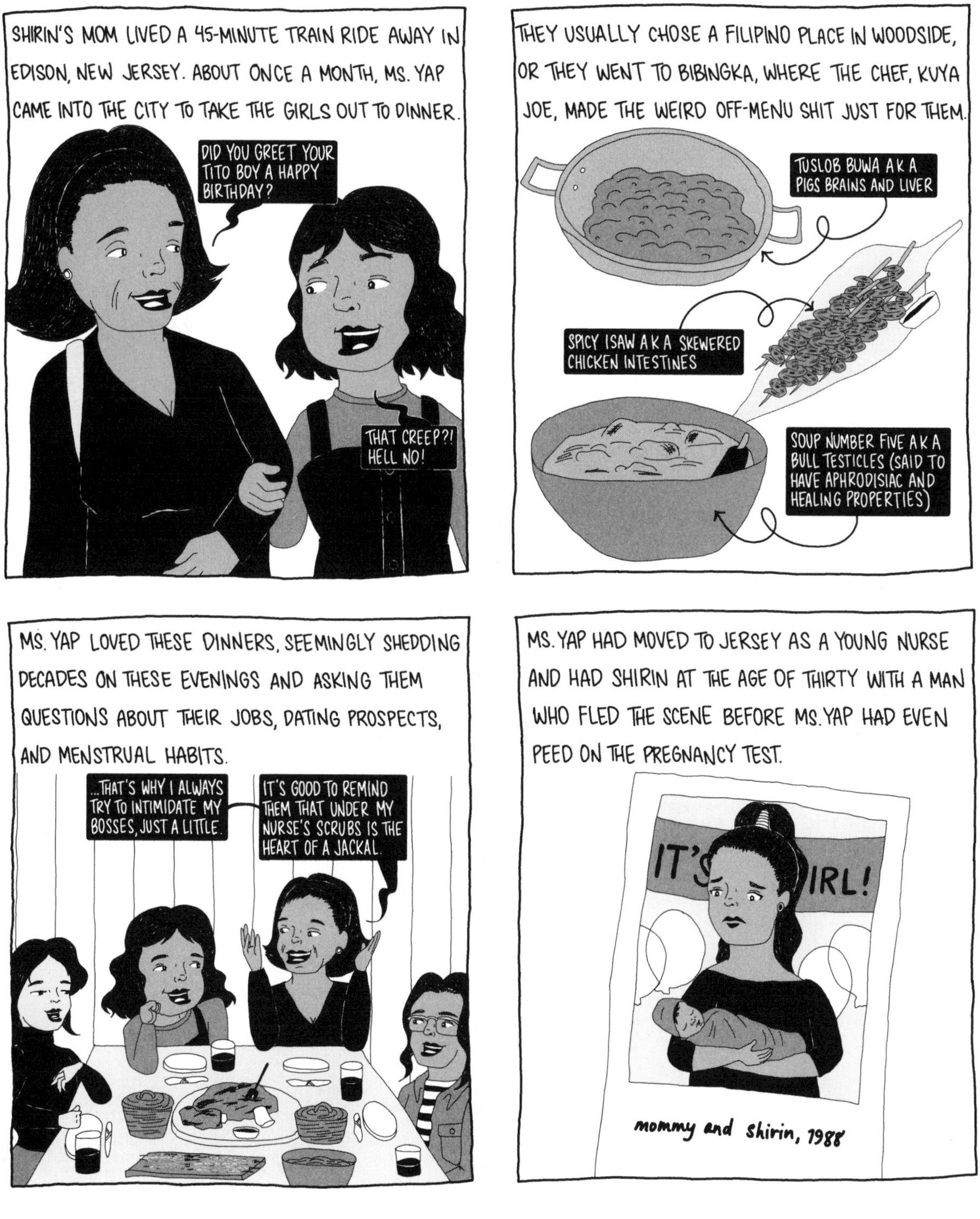
SHIRIN'S MOM LIVED A 45-MINUTE TRAIN RIDE AWAY IN EDISON, NEW JERSEY. ABOUT ONCE A MONTH, MS. YAP CAME INTO THE CITY TO TAKE THE GIRLS OUT TO DINNER.
DID YOU GREET YOUR TITO BOY A HAPPY BIRTHDAY?
THAT CREEP?! HELL NO!
THEY USUALLY CHOSE A FILIPINO PLACE IN WOODSIDE, OR THEY WENT TO BIBINGKA, WHERE THE CHEF, KUYA JOE, MADE THE WEIRD OFF-MENU SHIT JUST FOR THEM.
TUSLOB BUWA AKA PIGS BRAINS AND LIVER
SPICY ISAW AKA SKEWERED CHICKEN INTESTINES
SOUP NUMBER FIVE AKA BULL TESTICLES (SAID TO HAVE APHRODISIAC AND HEALING PROPERTIES)
MS. YAP LOVED THESE DINNERS, SEEMINGLY SHEDDING DECADES ON THESE EVENINGS AND ASKING THEM QUESTIONS ABOUT THEIR JOBS, DATING PROSPECTS, AND MENSTRUAL HABITS.
...THAT'S WHY I ALWAYS TRY TO INTIMIDATE MY BOSSES, JUST A LITTLE.
IT'S GOOD TO REMIND THEM THAT UNDER MY NURSE'S SCRUBS IS THE HEART OF A JACKAL.
MS. YAP HAD MOVED TO JERSEY AS A YOUNG NURSE AND HAD SHIRIN AT THE AGE OF THIRTY WITH A MAN WHO FLED THE SCENE BEFORE MS. YAP HAD EVEN PEED ON THE PREGNANCY TEST.
IT'S IRL!
mommy and shirin, 1988

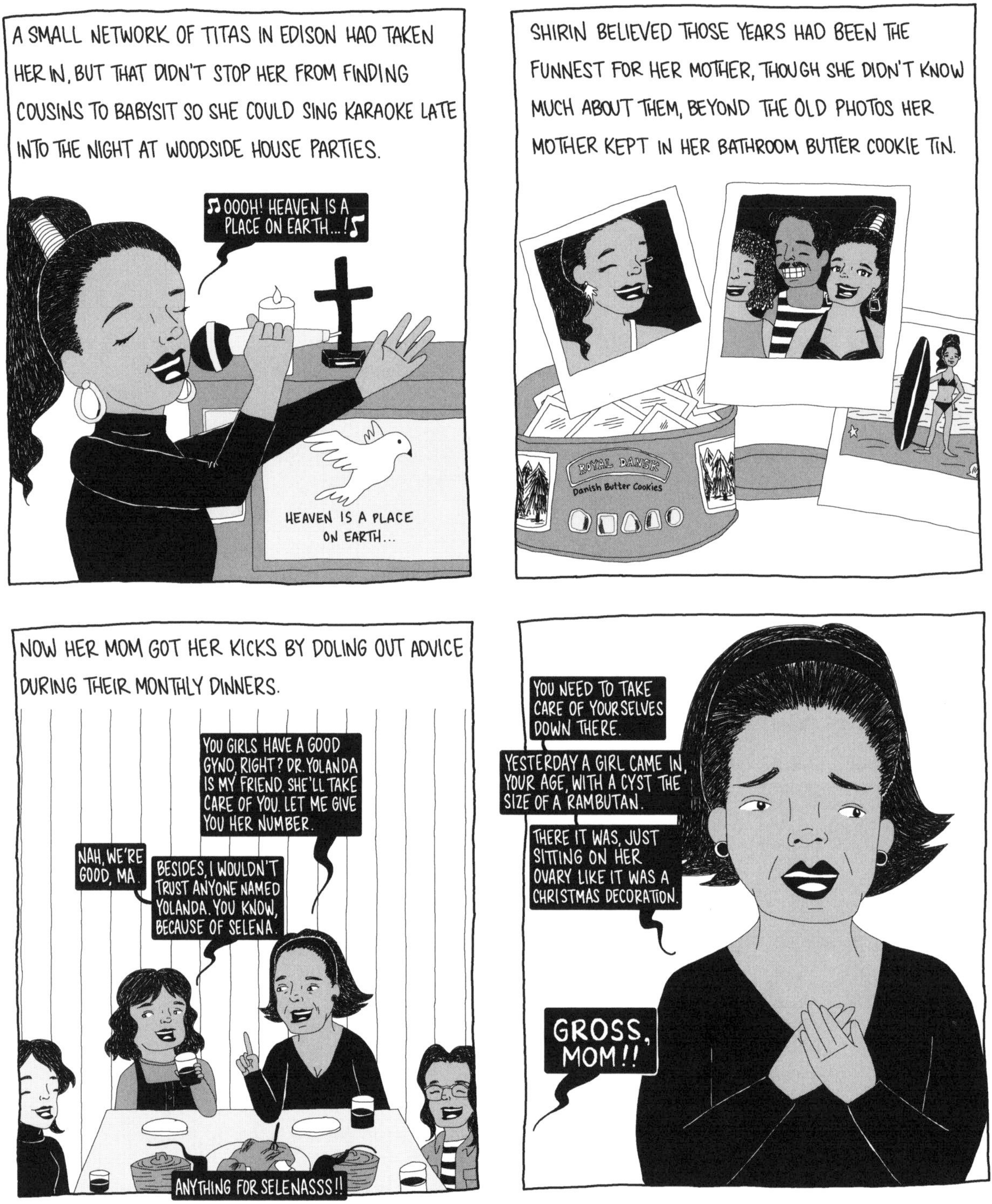
A SMALL NETWORK OF TITAS IN EDISON HAD TAKEN HER IN, BUT THAT DIDN'T STOP HER FROM FINDING COUSINS TO BABYSIT SO SHE COULD SING KARAOKE LATE INTO THE NIGHT AT WOODSIDE HOUSE PARTIES.
OOOH! HEAVEN IS A PLACE ON EARTH...!
HEAVEN IS A PLACE ON EARTH...
SHIRIN BELIEVED THOSE YEARS HAD BEEN THE FUNNEST FOR HER MOTHER, THOUGH SHE DIDN'T KNOW MUCH ABOUT THEM, BEYOND THE OLD PHOTOS HER MOTHER KEPT IN HER BATHROOM BUTTER COOKIE TIN.
ROYAL DANSK
Danish Butter Cookies
NOW HER MOM GOT HER KICKS BY DOLING OUT ADVICE DURING THEIR MONTHLY DINNERS.
YOU GIRLS HAVE A GOOD GYNO, RIGHT? DR. YOLANDA IS MY FRIEND. SHE'LL TAKE CARE OF YOU. LET ME GIVE YOU HER NUMBER.
NAH, WE'RE GOOD, MA.
BESIDES, I WOULDN'T TRUST ANYONE NAMED YOLANDA. YOU KNOW, BECAUSE OF SELENA.
ANYTHING FOR SELENASSS!!
YOU NEED TO TAKE CARE OF YOURSELVES DOWN THERE.
YESTERDAY A GIRL CAME IN, YOUR AGE, WITH A CYST THE SIZE OF A RAMBUTAN.
THERE IT WAS, JUST SITTING ON HER OVARY LIKE IT WAS A CHRISTMAS DECORATION.
GROSS, MOM!!

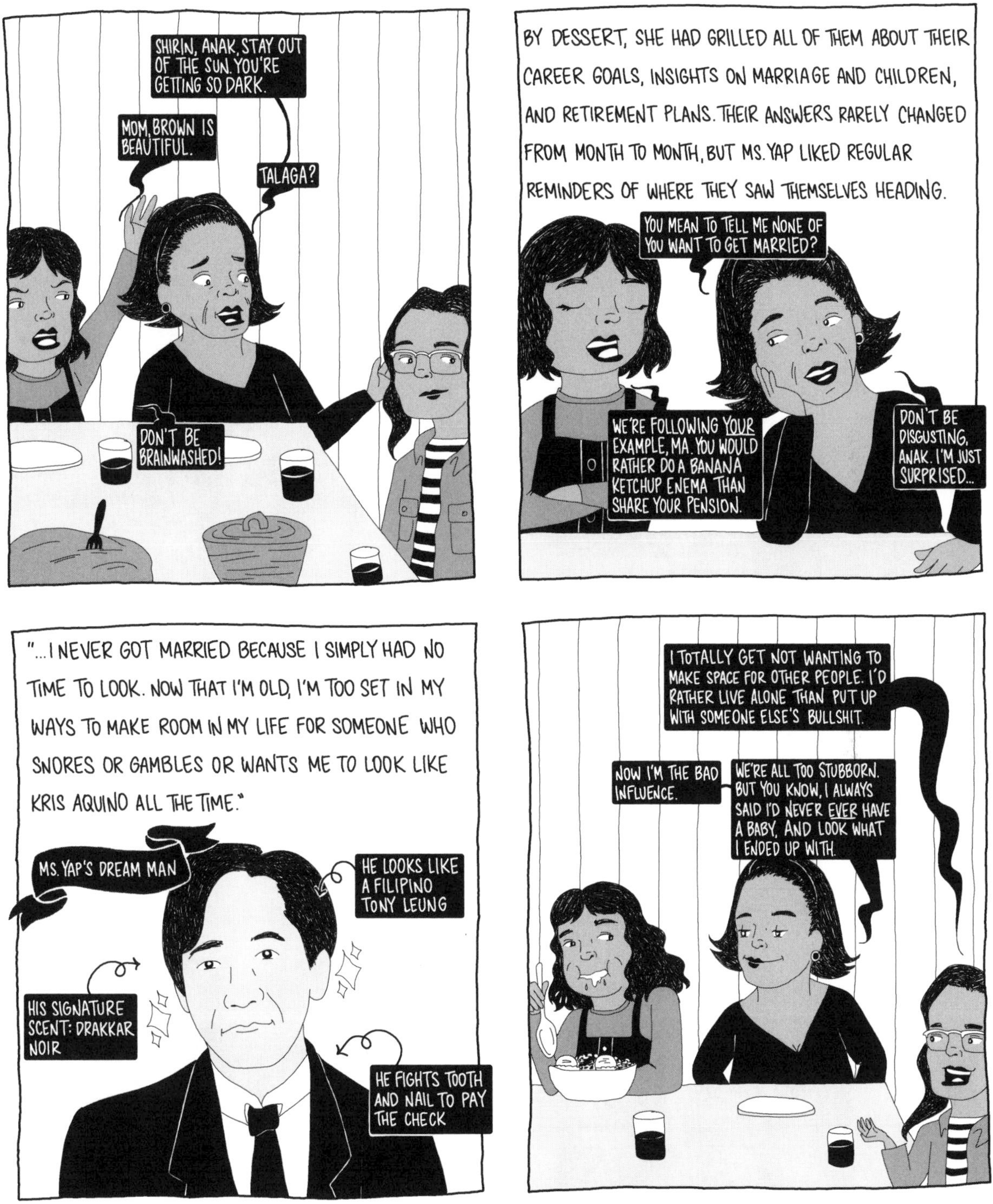
SHIRIN, ANAK, STAY OUT OF THE SUN. YOU'RE GETTING SO DARK.
MOM, BROWN IS BEAUTIFUL.
TALAGA?
DON'T BE BRAINWASHED!
BY DESSERT, SHE HAD GRILLED ALL OF THEM ABOUT THEIR CAREER GOALS, INSIGHTS ON MARRIAGE AND CHILDREN, AND RETIREMENT PLANS. THEIR ANSWERS RARELY CHANGED FROM MONTH TO MONTH, BUT MS. YAP LIKED REGULAR REMINDERS OF WHERE THEY SAW THEMSELVES HEADING.
YOU MEAN TO TELL ME NONE OF YOU WANT TO GET MARRIED?
WE'RE FOLLOWING YOUR EXAMPLE, MA. YOU WOULD RATHER DO A BANANA KETCHUP ENEMA THAN SHARE YOUR PENSION.
DON'T BE DISGUSTING, ANAK. I'M JUST SURPRISED...
"...I NEVER GOT MARRIED BECAUSE I SIMPLY HAD NO TIME TO LOOK. NOW THAT I'M OLD, I'M TOO SET IN MY WAYS TO MAKE ROOM IN MY LIFE FOR SOMEONE WHO SNORES OR GAMBLES OR WANTS ME TO LOOK LIKE KRIS AQUINO ALL THE TIME."
MS. YAP'S DREAM MAN
HE LOOKS LIKE A FILIPINO TONY LEUNG
HIS SIGNATURE SCENT: DRAKKAR NOIR
HE FIGHTS TOOTH AND NAIL TO PAY THE CHECK
I TOTALLY GET NOT WANTING TO MAKE SPACE FOR OTHER PEOPLE. I'D RATHER LIVE ALONE THAN PUT UP WITH SOMEONE ELSE'S BULLSHIT.
NOW I'M THE BAD INFLUENCE.
WE'RE ALL TOO STUBBORN. BUT YOU KNOW, I ALWAYS SAID I'D NEVER EVER HAVE A BABY, AND LOOK WHAT I ENDED UP WITH.

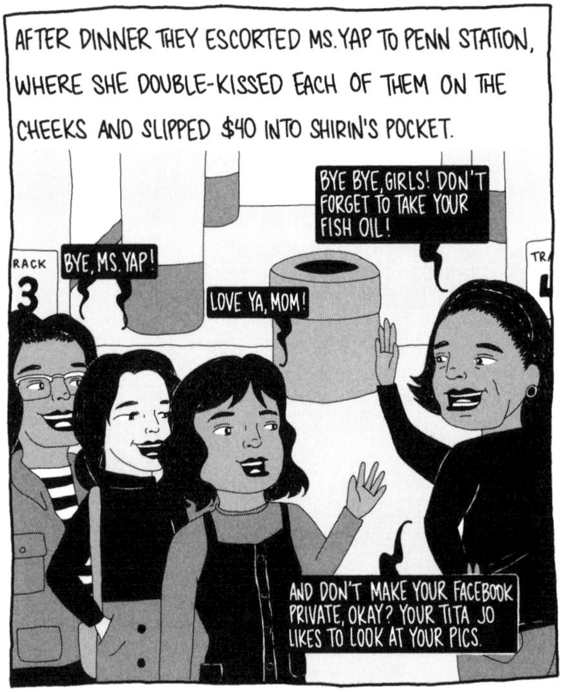
AFTER DINNER THEY ESCORTED MS. YAP TO PENN STATION, WHERE SHE DOUBLE-KISSED EACH OF THEM ON THE CHEEKS AND SLIPPED $40 INTO SHIRIN'S POCKET.
BYE BYE, GIRLS! DON'T FORGET TO TAKE YOUR FISH OIL!
BYE, MS. YAP!
LOVE YA, MOM!
AND DON'T MAKE YOUR FACEBOOK PRIVATE, OKAY? YOUR TITA JO LIKES TO LOOK AT YOUR PICS.

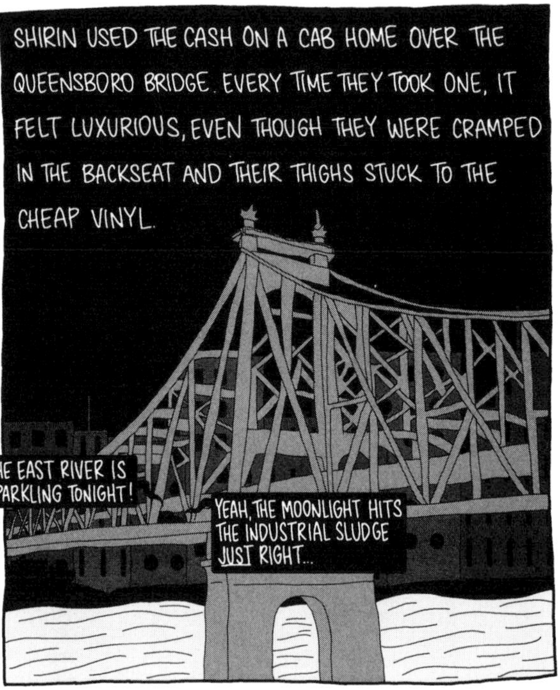
SHIRIN USED THE CASH ON A CAB HOME OVER THE QUEENSBORO BRIDGE. EVERY TIME THEY TOOK ONE, IT FELT LUXURIOUS, EVEN THOUGH THEY WERE CRAMPED IN THE BACKSEAT AND THEIR THIGHS STUCK TO THE CHEAP VINYL.
THE EAST RIVER IS SPARKLING TONIGHT!
YEAH, THE MOONLIGHT HITS THE INDUSTRIAL SLUDGE JUST RIGHT...

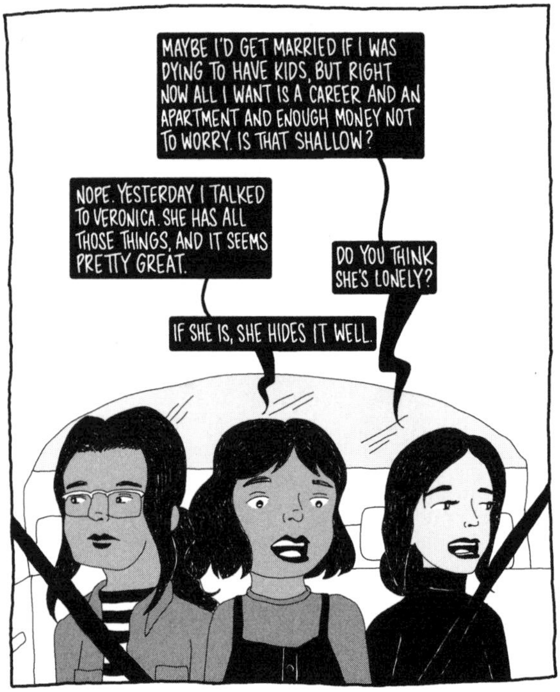
MAYBE I'D GET MARRIED IF I WAS DYING TO HAVE KIDS, BUT RIGHT NOW ALL I WANT IS A CAREER AND AN APARTMENT AND ENOUGH MONEY NOT TO WORRY. IS THAT SHALLOW?
NOPE. YESTERDAY I TALKED TO VERONICA. SHE HAS ALL THOSE THINGS, AND IT SEEMS PRETTY GREAT.
DO YOU THINK SHE'S LONELY?
IF SHE IS, SHE HIDES IT WELL.

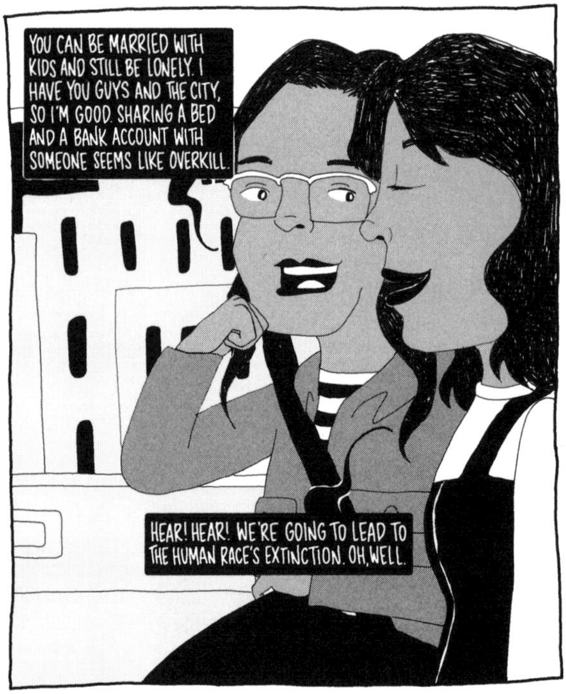
YOU CAN BE MARRIED WITH KIDS AND STILL BE LONELY. I HAVE YOU GUYS AND THE CITY, SO I'M GOOD. SHARING A BED AND A BANK ACCOUNT WITH SOMEONE SEEMS LIKE OVERKILL.
HEAR! HEAR! WE'RE GOING TO LEAD TO THE HUMAN RACE'S EXTINCTION. OH, WELL.

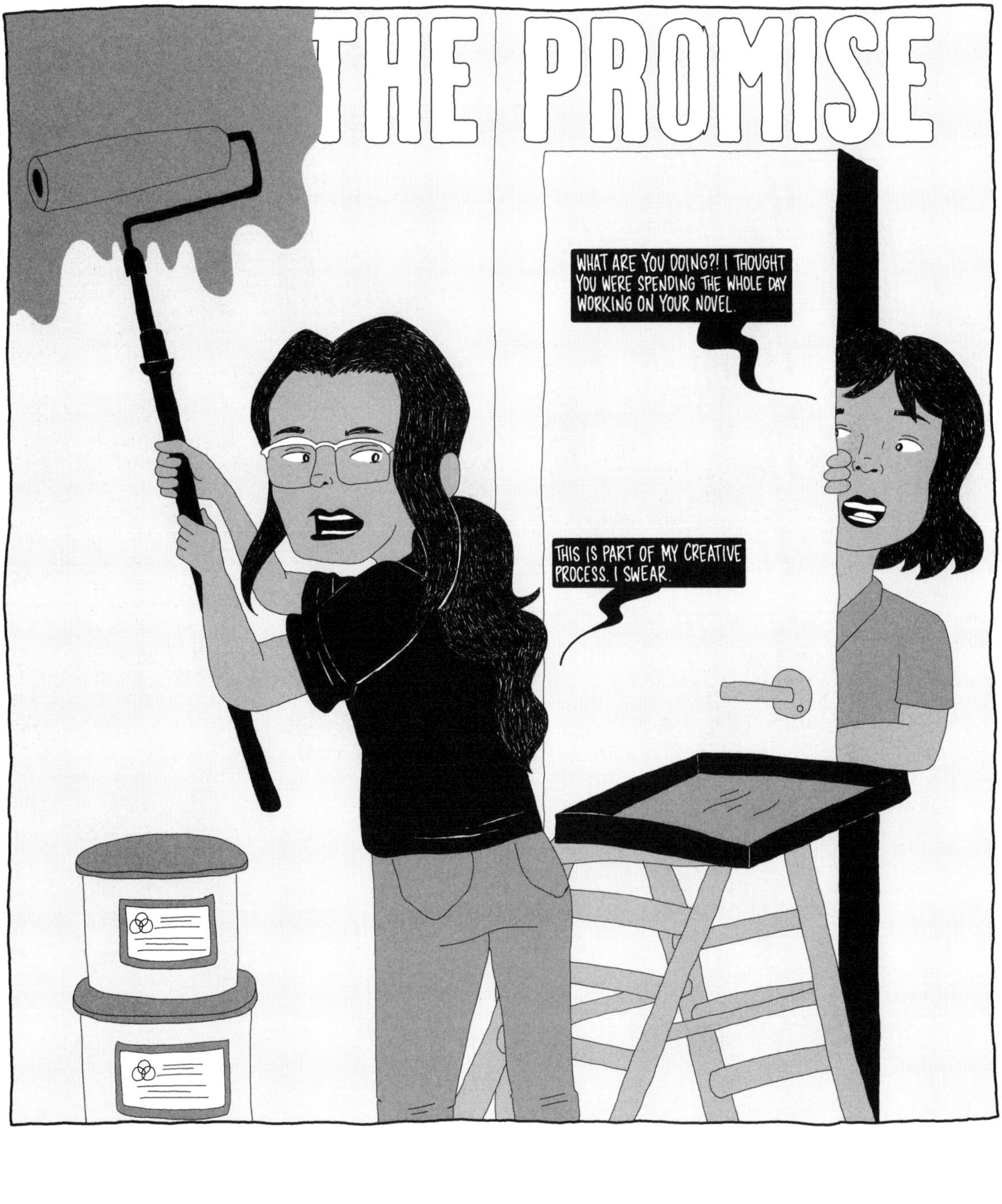
THE PROMISE
WHAT ARE YOU DOING?! I THOUGHT YOU WERE SPENDING THE WHOLE DAY WORKING ON YOUR NOVEL.
THIS IS PART OF MY CREATIVE PROCESS. I SWEAR.

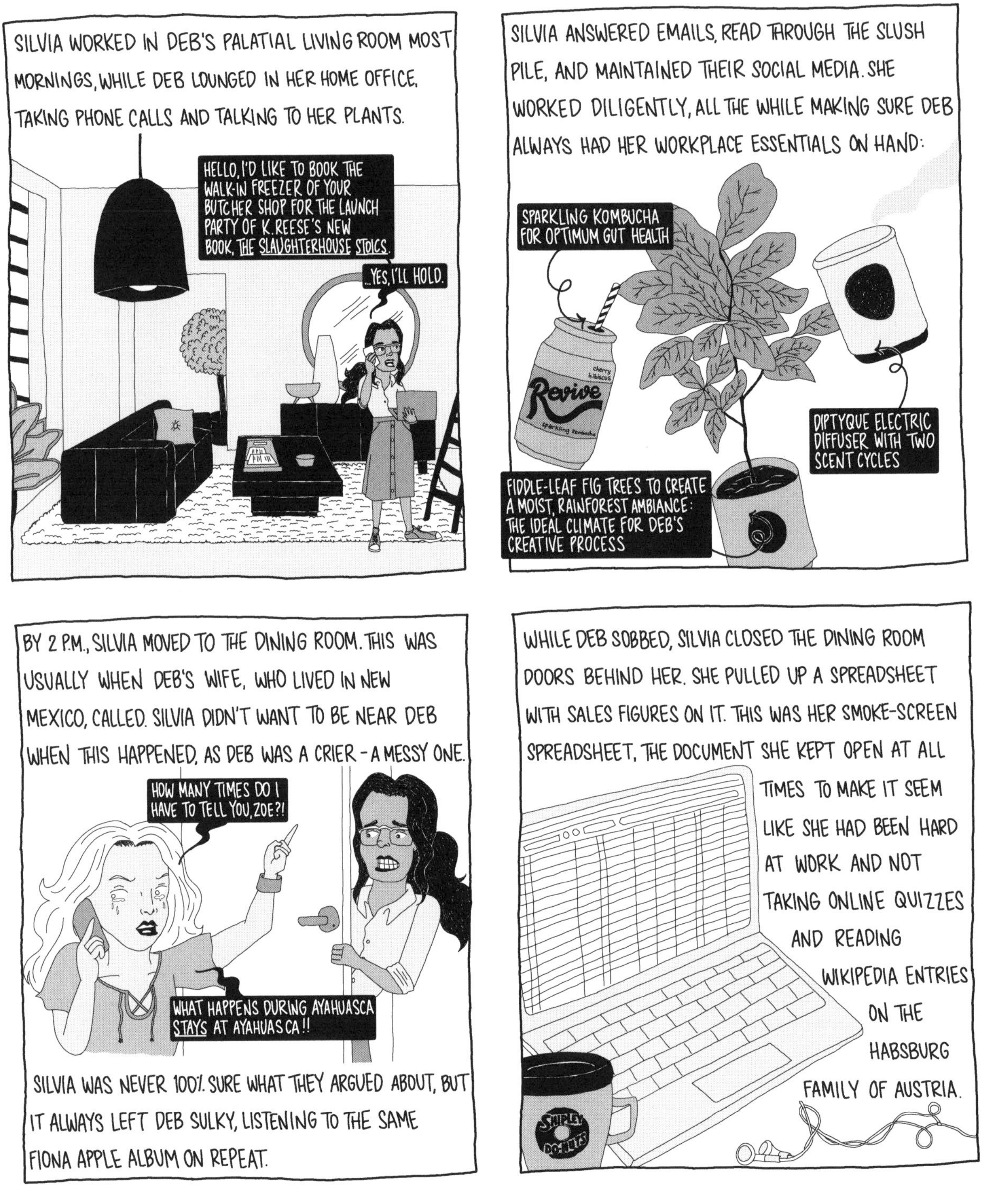
SILVIA WORKED IN DEB'S PALATIAL LIVING ROOM MOST MORNINGS, WHILE DEB LOUNGED IN HER HOME OFFICE. TAKING PHONE CALLS AND TALKING TO HER PLANTS.
HELLO, I'D LIKE TO BOOK THE WALK-IN FREEZER OF YOUR BUTCHER SHOP FOR THE LAUNCH PARTY OF K. REESE'S NEW BOOK, THE SLAUGHTERHOUSE STOICS.
...YES, I'LL HOLD.
SILVIA ANSWERED EMAILS, READ THROUGH THE SLUSH PILE, AND MAINTAINED THEIR SOCIAL MEDIA. SHE WORKED DILIGENTLY, ALL THE WHILE MAKING SURE DEB ALWAYS HAD HER WORKPLACE ESSENTIALS ON HAND:
SPARKLING KOMBUCHA FOR OPTIMUM GUT HEALTH
Revive
DIPTYQUE ELECTRIC DIFFUSER WITH TWO SCENT CYCLES
FIDDLE-LEAF FIG TREES TO CREATE A MOIST, RAINFOREST AMBIANCE: THE IDEAL CLIMATE FOR DEB'S CREATIVE PROCESS
BY 2 P.M., SILVIA MOVED TO THE DINING ROOM. THIS WAS USUALLY WHEN DEB'S WIFE, WHO LIVED IN NEW MEXICO, CALLED. SILVIA DIDN'T WANT TO BE NEAR DEB WHEN THIS HAPPENED, AS DEB WAS A CRIER - A MESSY ONE.
HOW MANY TIMES DO I HAVE TO TELL YOU, ZOE?!
WHAT HAPPENS DURING AYAHUASCA STAYS AT AYAHUASCA!!
SILVIA WAS NEVER 100% SURE WHAT THEY ARGUED ABOUT, BUT IT ALWAYS LEFT DEB SULKY, LISTENING TO THE SAME FIONA APPLE ALBUM ON REPEAT.
WHILE DEB SOBBED, SILVIA CLOSED THE DINING ROOM DOORS BEHIND HER. SHE PULLED UP A SPREADSHEET WITH SALES FIGURES ON IT. THIS WAS HER SMOKE-SCREEN SPREADSHEET, THE DOCUMENT SHE KEPT OPEN AT ALL TIMES TO MAKE IT SEEM LIKE SHE HAD BEEN HARD AT WORK AND NOT TAKING ONLINE QUIZZES AND READING WIKIPEDIA ENTRIES ON THE HABSBURG FAMILY OF AUSTRIA.
SHIPLEY DO-NUTS

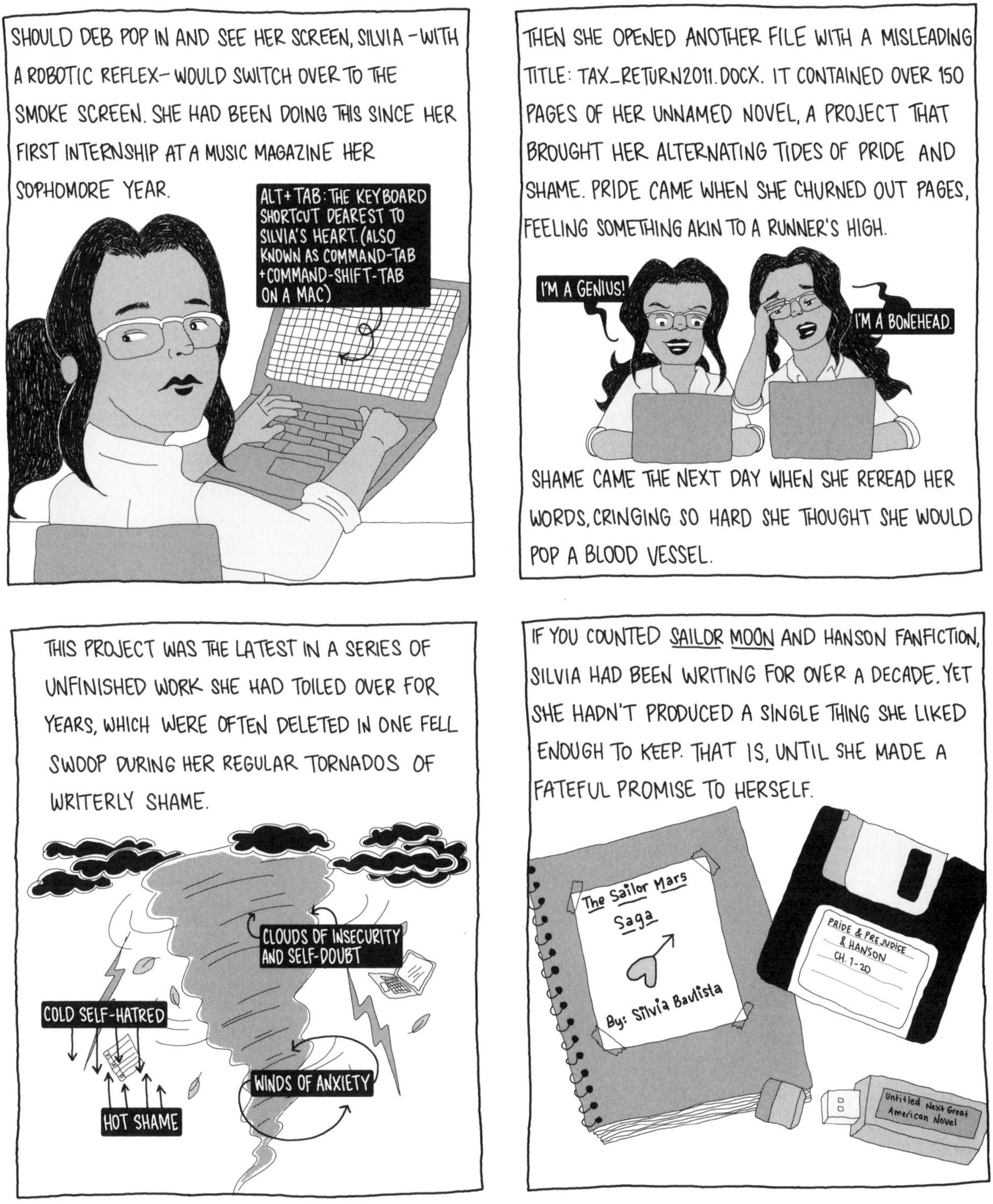
SHOULD DEB POP IN AND SEE HER SCREEN, SILVIA—WITH A ROBOTIC REFLEX—WOULD SWITCH OVER TO THE SMOKE SCREEN. SHE HAD BEEN DOING THIS SINCE HER FIRST INTERNSHIP AT A MUSIC MAGAZINE HER SOPHOMORE YEAR.
ALT+TAB: THE KEYBOARD SHORTCUT DEAREST TO SILVIA'S HEART. (ALSO KNOWN AS COMMAND-TAB +COMMAND-SHIFT-TAB ON A MAC)
THEN SHE OPENED ANOTHER FILE WITH A MISLEADING TITLE: TAX_RETURN2011.DOCX. IT CONTAINED OVER 150 PAGES OF HER UNNAMED NOVEL, A PROJECT THAT BROUGHT HER ALTERNATING TIDES OF PRIDE AND SHAME. PRIDE CAME WHEN SHE CHURNED OUT PAGES, FEELING SOMETHING AKIN TO A RUNNER'S HIGH.
I'M A GENIUS!
I'M A BONEHEAD.
SHAME CAME THE NEXT DAY WHEN SHE REREAD HER WORDS, CRINGING SO HARD SHE THOUGHT SHE WOULD POP A BLOOD VESSEL.
THIS PROJECT WAS THE LATEST IN A SERIES OF UNFINISHED WORK SHE HAD TOILED OVER FOR YEARS, WHICH WERE OFTEN DELETED IN ONE FELL SWOOP DURING HER REGULAR TORNADOS OF WRITERLY SHAME.
CLOUDS OF INSECURITY AND SELF-DOUBT
COLD SELF-HATRED
HOT SHAME
WINDS OF ANXIETY
IF YOU COUNTED SAILOR MOON AND HANSON FANFICTION, SILVIA HAD BEEN WRITING FOR OVER A DECADE. YET SHE HADN'T PRODUCED A SINGLE THING SHE LIKED ENOUGH TO KEEP. THAT IS, UNTIL SHE MADE A FATEFUL PROMISE TO HERSELF.
The Sailor Mars Saga
By: Silvia Bautista
PRIDE & PREJUDICE & HANSON
CH. 1-20
Untitled Next Great American Novel

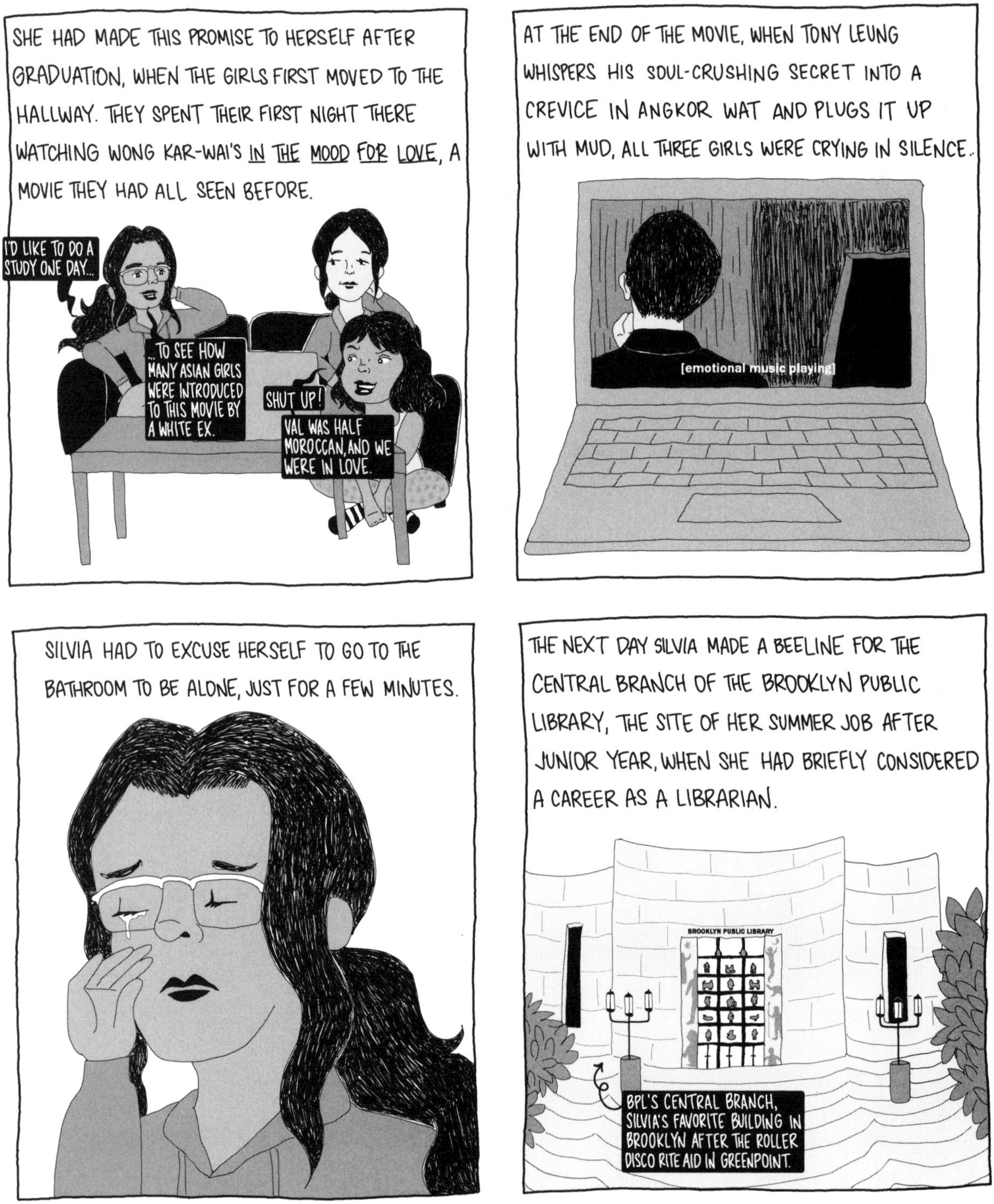
SHE HAD MADE THIS PROMISE TO HERSELF AFTER GRADUATION, WHEN THE GIRLS FIRST MOVED TO THE HALLWAY. THEY SPENT THEIR FIRST NIGHT THERE WATCHING WONG KAR-WAI'S IN THE MOOD FOR LOVE, A MOVIE THEY HAD ALL SEEN BEFORE.
I'D LIKE TO DO A STUDY ONE DAY...
...TO SEE HOW MANY ASIAN GIRLS WERE INTRODUCED TO THIS MOVIE BY A WHITE EX.
SHUT UP!
VAL WAS HALF MOROCCAN, AND WE WERE IN LOVE.
AT THE END OF THE MOVIE, WHEN TONY LEUNG WHISPERS HIS SOUL-CRUSHING SECRET INTO A CREVICE IN ANGKOR WAT AND PLUGS IT UP WITH MUD, ALL THREE GIRLS WERE CRYING IN SILENCE..
[emotional music playing]
SILVIA HAD TO EXCUSE HERSELF TO GO TO THE BATHROOM TO BE ALONE, JUST FOR A FEW MINUTES.
THE NEXT DAY SILVIA MADE A BEELINE FOR THE CENTRAL BRANCH OF THE BROOKLYN PUBLIC LIBRARY, THE SITE OF HER SUMMER JOB AFTER JUNIOR YEAR, WHEN SHE HAD BRIEFLY CONSIDERED A CAREER AS A LIBRARIAN.
BROOKLYN PUBLIC LIBRARY
BPL'S CENTRAL BRANCH, SILVIA'S FAVORITE BUILDING IN BROOKLYN AFTER THE ROLLER DISCO RITE AID IN GREENPOINT.

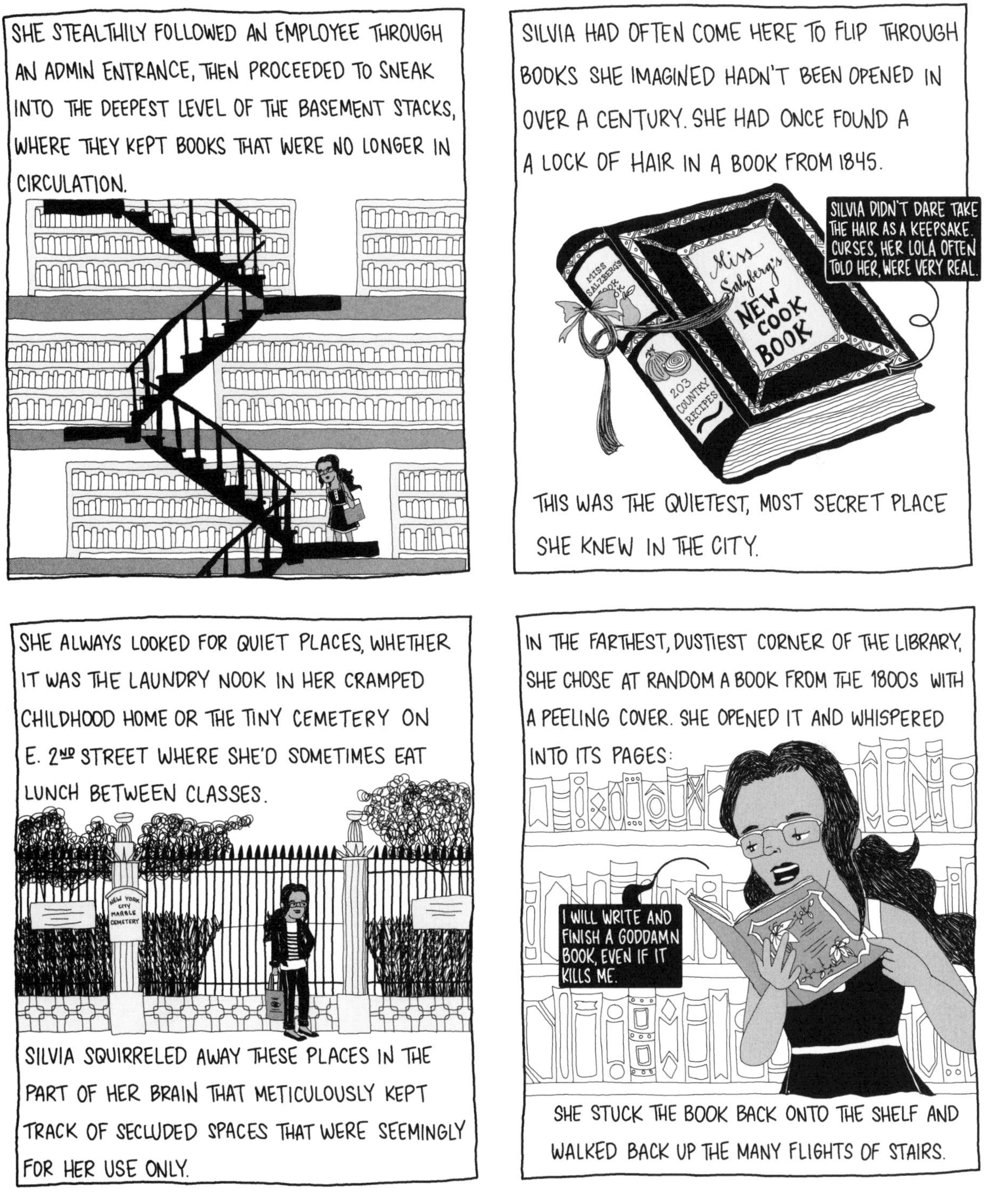
SHE STEALTHILY FOLLOWED AN EMPLOYEE THROUGH AN ADMIN ENTRANCE, THEN PROCEEDED TO SNEAK INTO THE DEEPEST LEVEL OF THE BASEMENT STACKS, WHERE THEY KEPT BOOKS THAT WERE NO LONGER IN CIRCULATION.
SILVIA HAD OFTEN COME HERE TO FLIP THROUGH BOOKS SHE IMAGINED HADN'T BEEN OPENED IN OVER A CENTURY. SHE HAD ONCE FOUND A A LOCK OF HAIR IN A BOOK FROM 1845.
Miss Salzberg's NEW COOK BOOK
MISS SALZBERG'S COOK BOOK
203 COUNTRY RECIPES
SILVIA DIDN'T DARE TAKE THE HAIR AS A KEEPSAKE. CURSES, HER LOLA OFTEN TOLD HER, WERE VERY REAL.
THIS WAS THE QUIETEST, MOST SECRET PLACE SHE KNEW IN THE CITY.
SHE ALWAYS LOOKED FOR QUIET PLACES, WHETHER IT WAS THE LAUNDRY NOOK IN HER CRAMPED CHILDHOOD HOME OR THE TINY CEMETERY ON E. 2ND STREET WHERE SHE'D SOMETIMES EAT LUNCH BETWEEN CLASSES.
NEW YORK CITY MARBLE CEMETERY
SILVIA SQUIRRELED AWAY THESE PLACES IN THE PART OF HER BRAIN THAT METICULOUSLY KEPT TRACK OF SECLUDED SPACES THAT WERE SEEMINGLY FOR HER USE ONLY.
IN THE FARTHEST, DUSTIEST CORNER OF THE LIBRARY, SHE CHOSE AT RANDOM A BOOK FROM THE 1800S WITH A PEELING COVER. SHE OPENED IT AND WHISPERED INTO ITS PAGES:
I WILL WRITE AND FINISH A GODDAMN BOOK, EVEN IF IT KILLS ME.
SHE STUCK THE BOOK BACK ONTO THE SHELF AND WALKED BACK UP THE MANY FLIGHTS OF STAIRS.

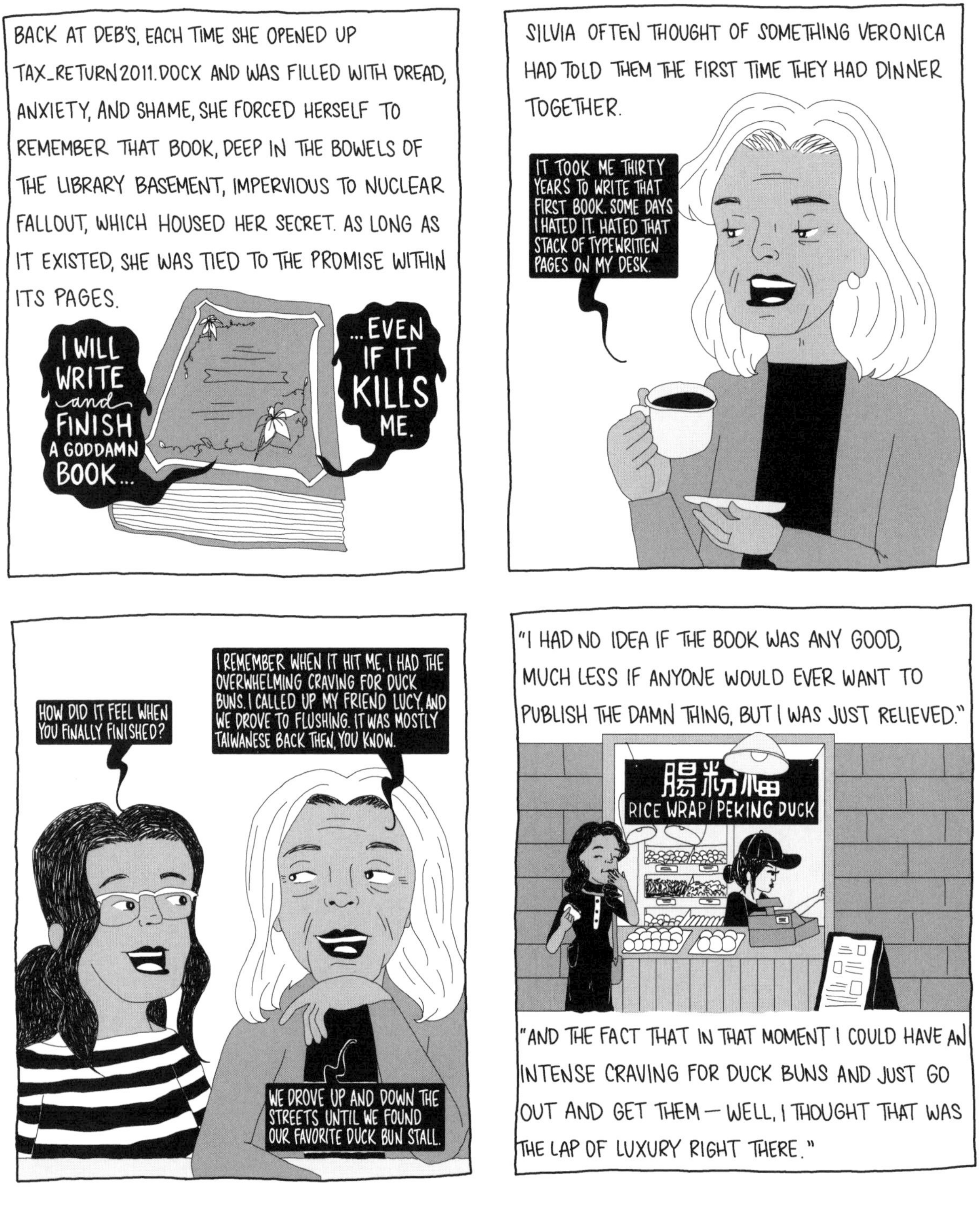
BACK AT DEB'S, EACH TIME SHE OPENED UP TAX_RETURN2011.DOCX AND WAS FILLED WITH DREAD, ANXIETY, AND SHAME, SHE FORCED HERSELF TO REMEMBER THAT BOOK, DEEP IN THE BOWELS OF THE LIBRARY BASEMENT, IMPERVIOUS TO NUCLEAR FALLOUT, WHICH HOUSED HER SECRET. AS LONG AS IT EXISTED, SHE WAS TIED TO THE PROMISE WITHIN ITS PAGES.
I WILL WRITE and FINISH A GODDAMN BOOK...
...EVEN IF IT KILLS ME.
SILVIA OFTEN THOUGHT OF SOMETHING VERONICA HAD TOLD THEM THE FIRST TIME THEY HAD DINNER TOGETHER.
IT TOOK ME THIRTY YEARS TO WRITE THAT FIRST BOOK. SOME DAYS I HATED IT. HATED THAT STACK OF TYPEWRITTEN PAGES ON MY DESK.
HOW DID IT FEEL WHEN YOU FINALLY FINISHED?
I REMEMBER WHEN IT HIT ME, I HAD THE OVERWHELMING CRAVING FOR DUCK BUNS. I CALLED UP MY FRIEND LUCY, AND WE DROVE TO FLUSHING. IT WAS MOSTLY TAIWANESE BACK THEN, YOU KNOW.
WE DROVE UP AND DOWN THE STREETS UNTIL WE FOUND OUR FAVORITE DUCK BUN STALL.
"I HAD NO IDEA IF THE BOOK WAS ANY GOOD, MUCH LESS IF ANYONE WOULD EVER WANT TO PUBLISH THE DAMN THING, BUT I WAS JUST RELIEVED."
腸粉檔
RICE WRAP / PEKING DUCK
"AND THE FACT THAT IN THAT MOMENT I COULD HAVE AN INTENSE CRAVING FOR DUCK BUNS AND JUST GO OUT AND GET THEM — WELL, I THOUGHT THAT WAS THE LAP OF LUXURY RIGHT THERE."

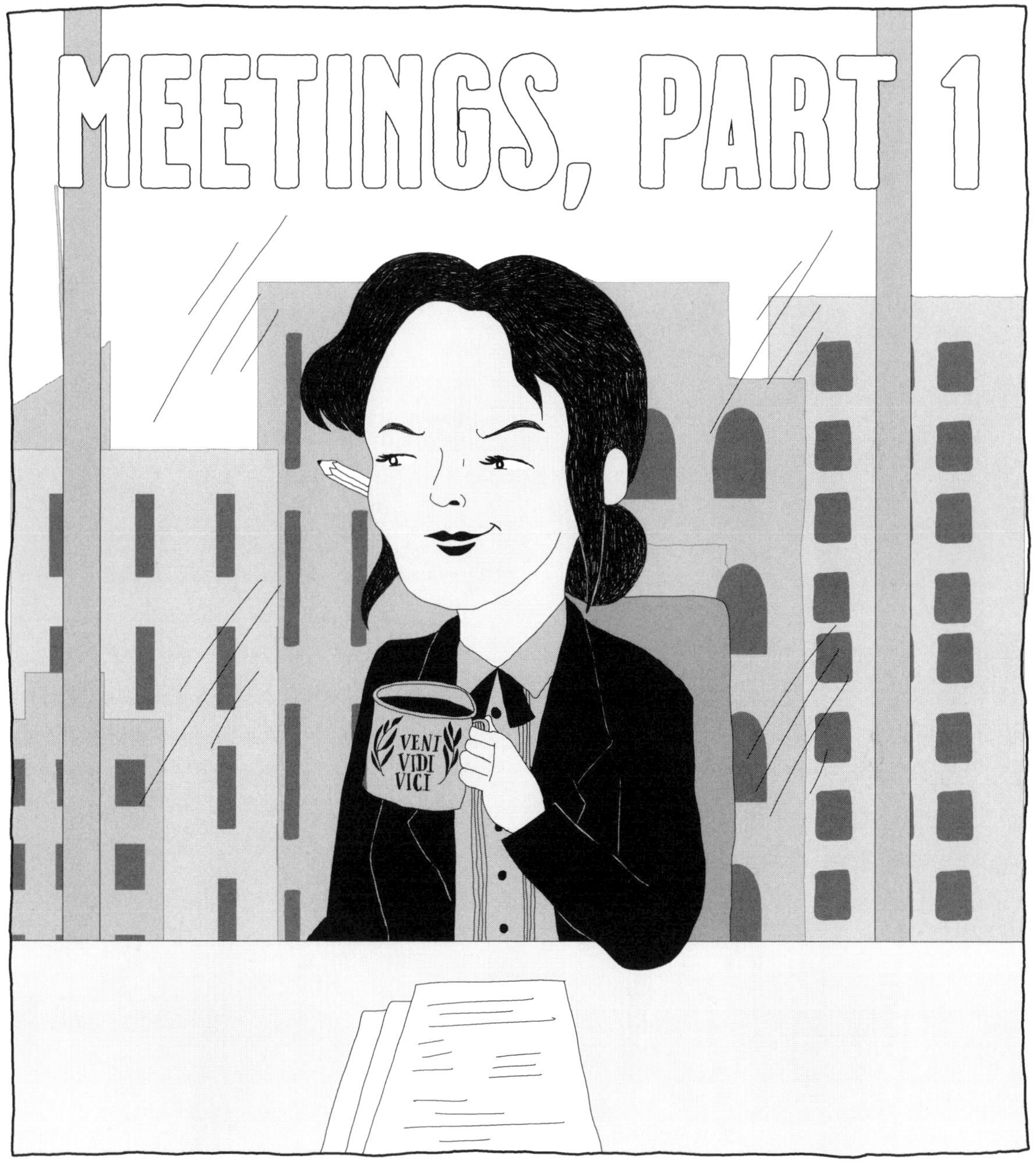
MEETINGS, PART 1
VENI
VIDI
VICI

NINA LOOKED FORWARD TO THURSDAY MORNINGS. SHE GOT TO THE OFFICE AT 7 A.M. TO PREPARE FOR THE WEEKLY EDITORIAL STATUS MEETING.

NINA DESCRIBES HER THURSDAY MEETING WARDROBE AS "CORPORATE ANNA KARINA."

SHIRIN DESCRIBES IT AS "UPPER EAST SIDE COLONEL SANDERS."

SHE PRINTED OUT DOUBLE-SIDED, COLLATED, STAPLED COPIES OF THE PRODUCTION SCHEDULE FOR EACH PERSON ATTENDING THE MEETING, ARRANGING THEM IN THE BIGGEST, WINDOW-LIT CONFERENCE ROOM.

SHE TRIPLE-CHECKED THE SCHEDULE TO MAKE SURE IT WAS UP-TO-DATE, RIGHT UP TO THE LAST EMAIL SHE RECEIVED FROM THE ART DIRECTOR AT 3 A.M. WHO WAS VACATIONING IN THE SEYCHELLES. SHE (TEMPORARILY) SWITCHED OVER FROM HER CUTESY DESK SUPPLIES TO HER SERIOUS, TAKE-NO-PRISONERS OFFICE SUPPLIES.

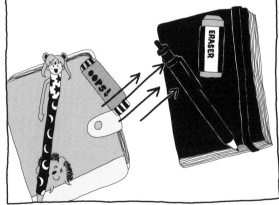

OOPS!

ERASER

BEFORE THE MEETING STARTED AT 9:15 A.M., NINA GRANTED EVERYONE 2-3 MINUTES OF MIND-NUMBING SMALL TALK BEFORE CUTTING THEM OFF WITH HER UPTIGHT SPELLING-BEE MODERATOR VOICE.

OKAY, FIRST TITLE!

SHE RAN THROUGH THE SCHEDULE, TAKING METICULOUS NOTES. CAROLYN ONLY SPOKE TO ASK PRODUCTION MANAGERS POINTED QUESTIONS ABOUT MISSED DEADLINES—JUST TO MAKE THEM SQUIRM.
SAY THAT AGAIN, PAM?
UH, THE AUTHOR NEEDS ANOTHER THREE MONTHS TO GO OVER THE REST OF THE COPYEDITS...
...BECAUSE OF HIS TENNIS ELBOW.

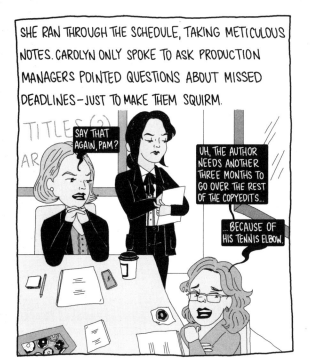

BY 10 A.M. THE MEETING WAS OVER, AND NINA BOUNDED BACK TO HER DESK, KEEN TO UPDATE THE PRODUCTION SCHEDULE AND UPDATE THE AGENDA FOR NEXT WEEK'S MEETING.
NINA'S PROFESSIONAL JOYS
INTIMIDATING COLLEAGUES
STOMPING UP AND DOWN HALLWAYS
DO NOT CROSS
BOSSING PEOPLE AROUND
MEETING DEADLINES
CONQUERING TO-DO LISTS
MAINTAINING AN UPWARD CAREER TRAJECTORY

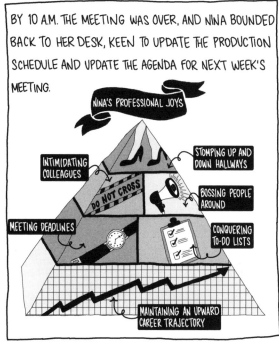

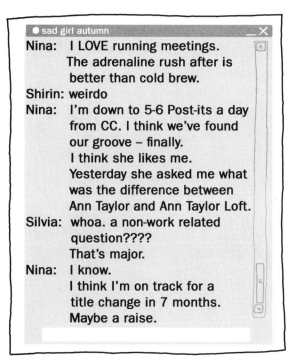

● sad girl autumn

Nina: I LOVE running meetings.
The adrenaline rush after is better than cold brew.
Shirin: weirdo
Nina: I'm down to 5-6 Post-its a day from CC. I think we've found our groove – finally.
I think she likes me.
Yesterday she asked me what was the difference between Ann Taylor and Ann Taylor Loft.
Silvia: whoa. a non-work related question????
That's major.
Nina: I know.
I think I'm on track for a title change in 7 months.
Maybe a raise.

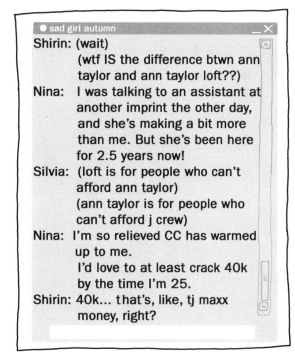

● sad girl autumn

Shirin: (wait)
(wtf IS the difference btwn ann taylor and ann taylor loft??)
Nina: I was talking to an assistant at another imprint the other day, and she's making a bit more than me. But she's been here for 2.5 years now!
Silvia: (loft is for people who can't afford ann taylor)
(ann taylor is for people who can't afford j crew)
Nina: I'm so relieved CC has warmed up to me.
I'd love to at least crack 40k by the time I'm 25.
Shirin: 40k... that's, like, tj maxx money, right?

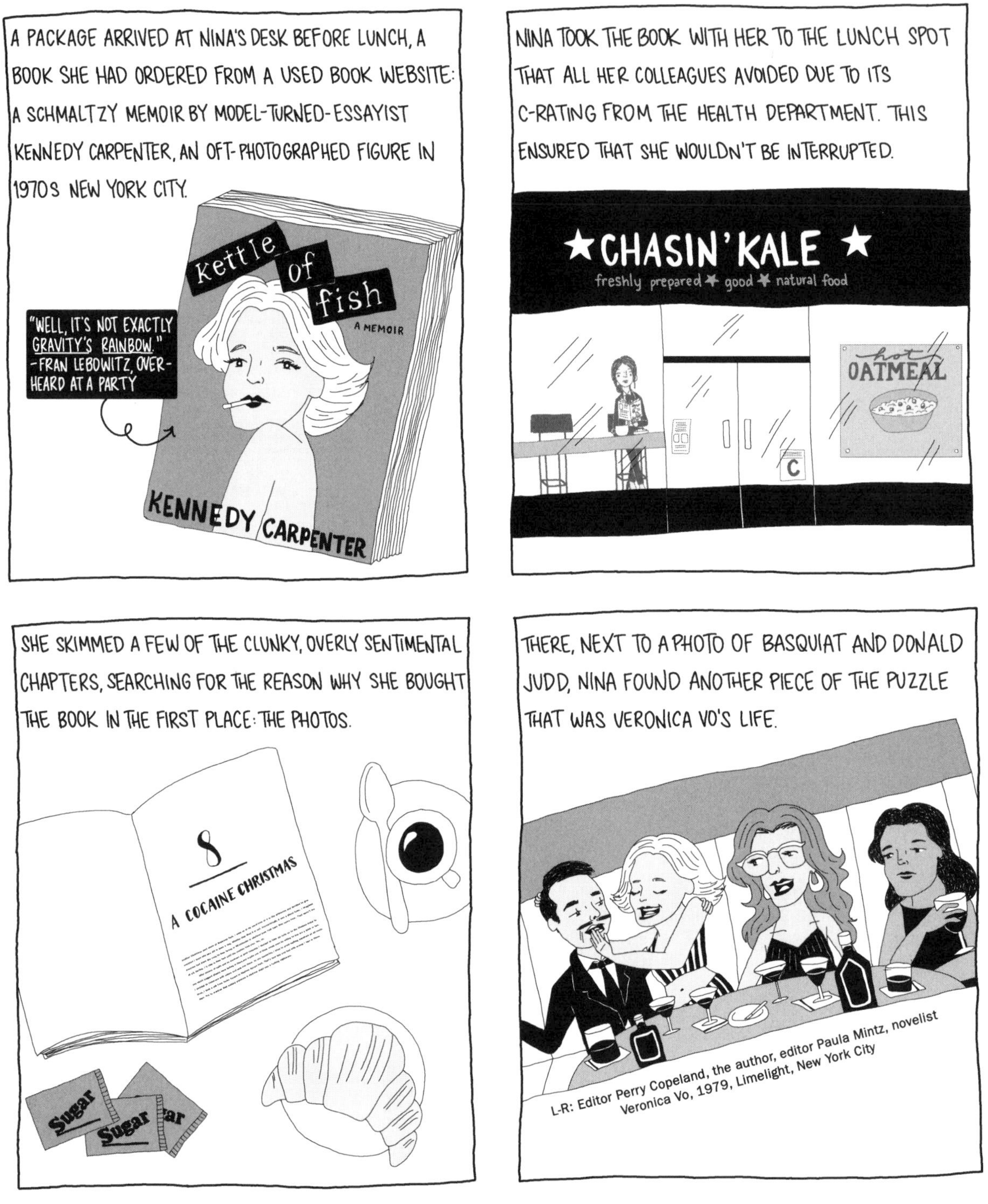
A PACKAGE ARRIVED AT NINA'S DESK BEFORE LUNCH, A BOOK SHE HAD ORDERED FROM A USED BOOK WEBSITE: A SCHMALTZY MEMOIR BY MODEL-TURNED-ESSAYIST KENNEDY CARPENTER, AN OFT-PHOTOGRAPHED FIGURE IN 1970S NEW YORK CITY.
kettle of fish
A MEMOIR
"WELL, IT'S NOT EXACTLY GRAVITY'S RAINBOW." -FRAN LEBOWITZ, OVERHEARD AT A PARTY
KENNEDY CARPENTER
NINA TOOK THE BOOK WITH HER TO THE LUNCH SPOT THAT ALL HER COLLEAGUES AVOIDED DUE TO ITS C-RATING FROM THE HEALTH DEPARTMENT. THIS ENSURED THAT SHE WOULDN'T BE INTERRUPTED.
★CHASIN' KALE★
freshly prepared ✶ good ✶ natural food
hot OATMEAL
C
SHE SKIMMED A FEW OF THE CLUNKY, OVERLY SENTIMENTAL CHAPTERS, SEARCHING FOR THE REASON WHY SHE BOUGHT THE BOOK IN THE FIRST PLACE: THE PHOTOS.
8
A COCAINE CHRISTMAS
Sugar
Sugar
THERE, NEXT TO A PHOTO OF BASQUIAT AND DONALD JUDD, NINA FOUND ANOTHER PIECE OF THE PUZZLE THAT WAS VERONICA VO'S LIFE.
L-R: Editor Perry Copeland, the author, editor Paula Mintz, novelist Veronica Vo, 1979, Limelight, New York City

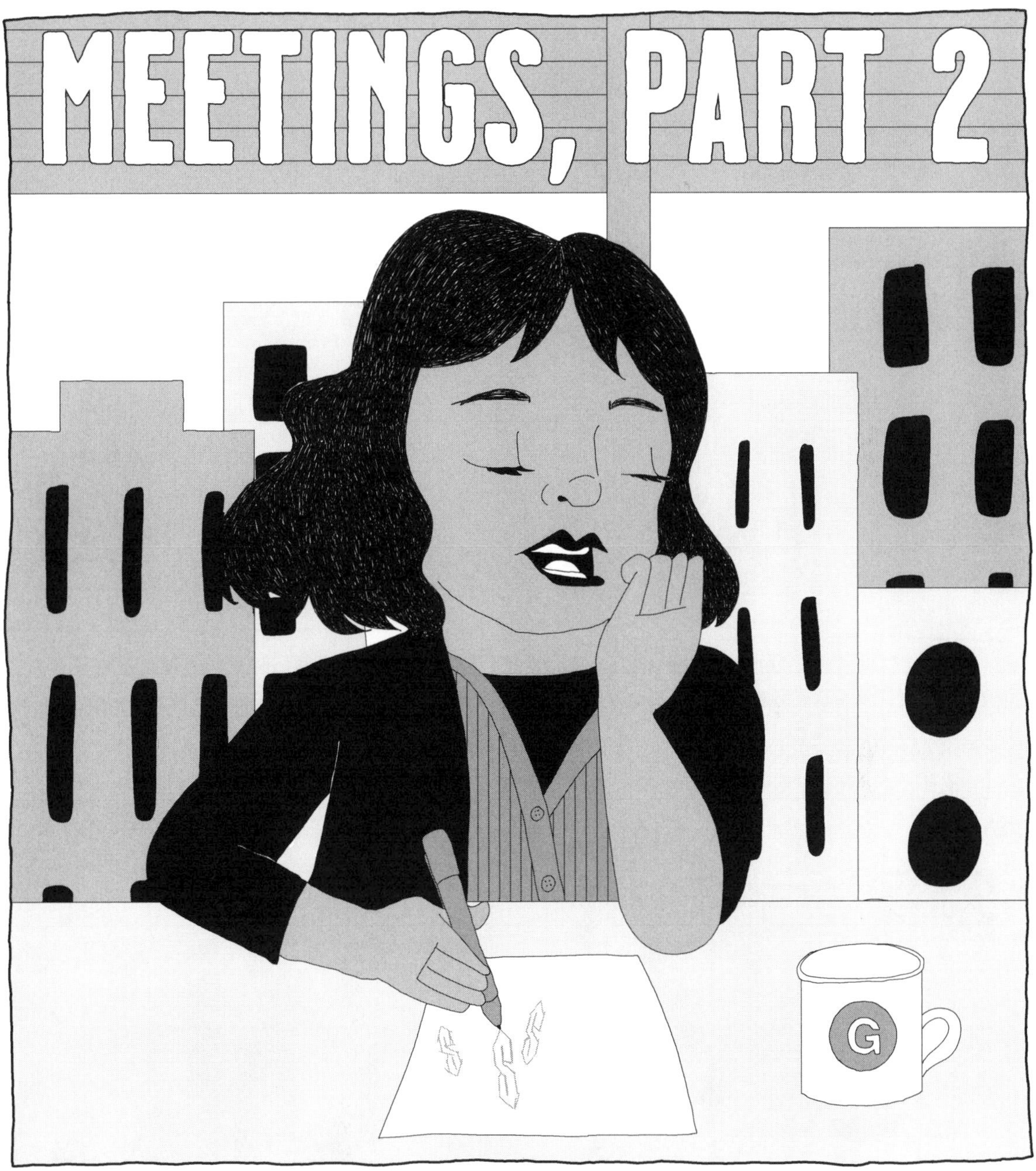
MEETINGS, PART 2
G

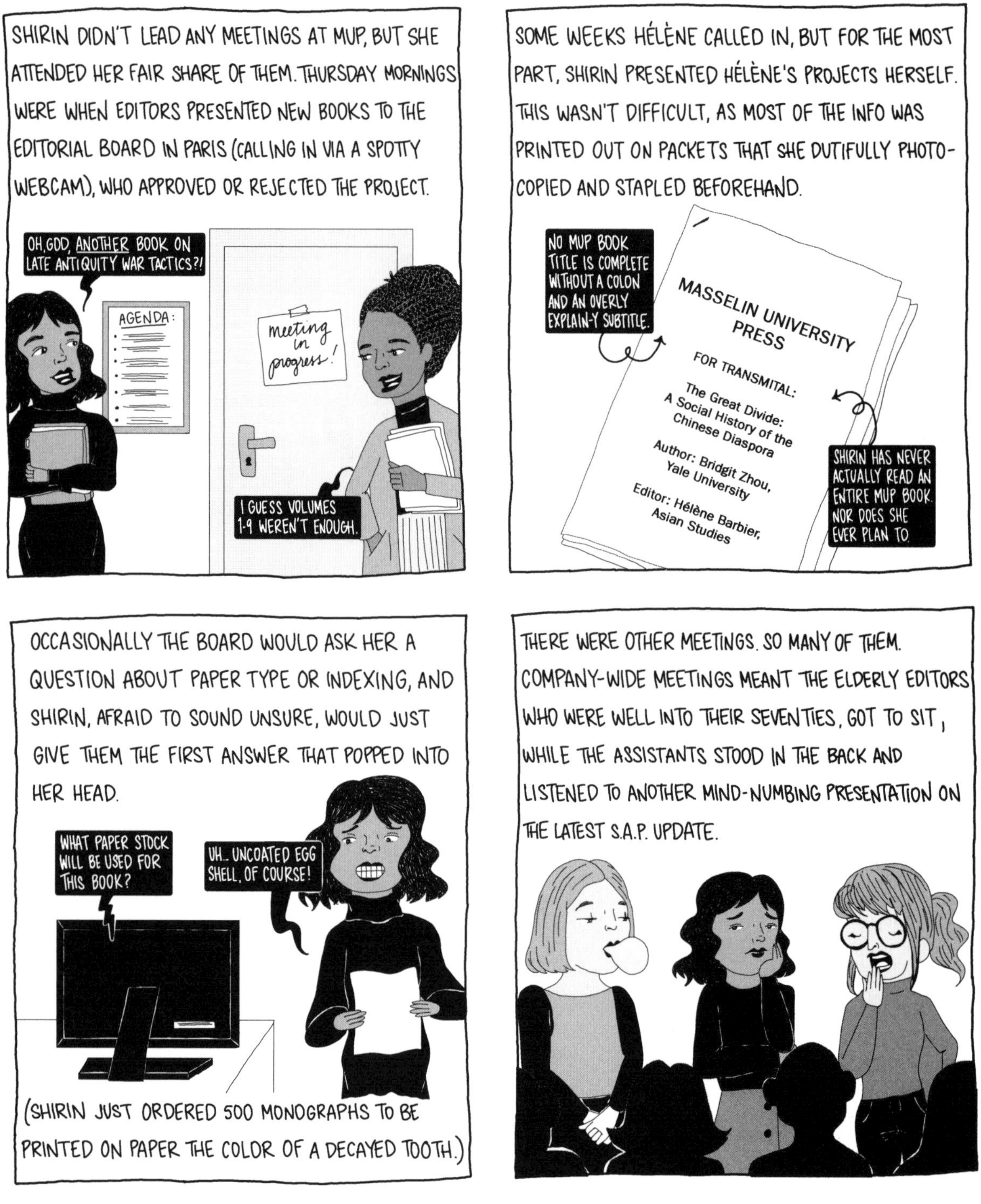
SHIRIN DIDN'T LEAD ANY MEETINGS AT MUP, BUT SHE ATTENDED HER FAIR SHARE OF THEM. THURSDAY MORNINGS WERE WHEN EDITORS PRESENTED NEW BOOKS TO THE EDITORIAL BOARD IN PARIS (CALLING IN VIA A SPOTTY WEBCAM), WHO APPROVED OR REJECTED THE PROJECT.
OH, GOD, ANOTHER BOOK ON LATE ANTIQUITY WAR TACTICS?!
AGENDA:
meeting in progress!
I GUESS VOLUMES 1-9 WEREN'T ENOUGH.
SOME WEEKS HÉLÈNE CALLED IN, BUT FOR THE MOST PART, SHIRIN PRESENTED HÉLÈNE'S PROJECTS HERSELF. THIS WASN'T DIFFICULT, AS MOST OF THE INFO WAS PRINTED OUT ON PACKETS THAT SHE DUTIFULLY PHOTOCOPIED AND STAPLED BEFOREHAND.
NO MUP BOOK TITLE IS COMPLETE WITHOUT A COLON AND AN OVERLY EXPLAIN-Y SUBTITLE.
MASSELIN UNIVERSITY PRESS
FOR TRANSMITAL:
The Great Divide: A Social History of the Chinese Diaspora
Author: Bridgit Zhou, Yale University
Editor: Hélène Barbier, Asian Studies
SHIRIN HAS NEVER ACTUALLY READ AN ENTIRE MUP BOOK. NOR DOES SHE EVER PLAN TO.
OCCASIONALLY THE BOARD WOULD ASK HER A QUESTION ABOUT PAPER TYPE OR INDEXING, AND SHIRIN, AFRAID TO SOUND UNSURE, WOULD JUST GIVE THEM THE FIRST ANSWER THAT POPPED INTO HER HEAD.
WHAT PAPER STOCK WILL BE USED FOR THIS BOOK?
UH... UNCOATED EGG SHELL, OF COURSE!
(SHIRIN JUST ORDERED 500 MONOGRAPHS TO BE PRINTED ON PAPER THE COLOR OF A DECAYED TOOTH.)
THERE WERE OTHER MEETINGS. SO MANY OF THEM. COMPANY-WIDE MEETINGS MEANT THE ELDERLY EDITORS WHO WERE WELL INTO THEIR SEVENTIES, GOT TO SIT, WHILE THE ASSISTANTS STOOD IN THE BACK AND LISTENED TO ANOTHER MIND-NUMBING PRESENTATION ON THE LATEST S.A.P. UPDATE.

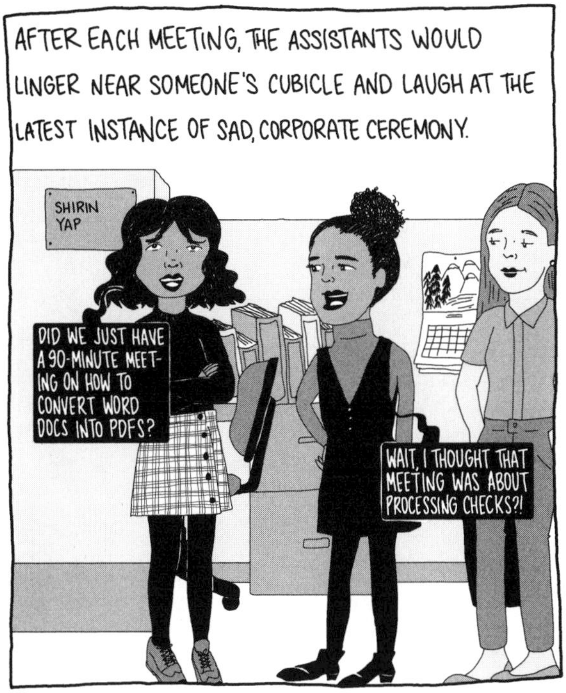
AFTER EACH MEETING, THE ASSISTANTS WOULD LINGER NEAR SOMEONE'S CUBICLE AND LAUGH AT THE LATEST INSTANCE OF SAD, CORPORATE CEREMONY.
SHIRIN YAP
DID WE JUST HAVE A 90-MINUTE MEETING ON HOW TO CONVERT WORD DOCS INTO PDFS?
WAIT, I THOUGHT THAT MEETING WAS ABOUT PROCESSING CHECKS?!

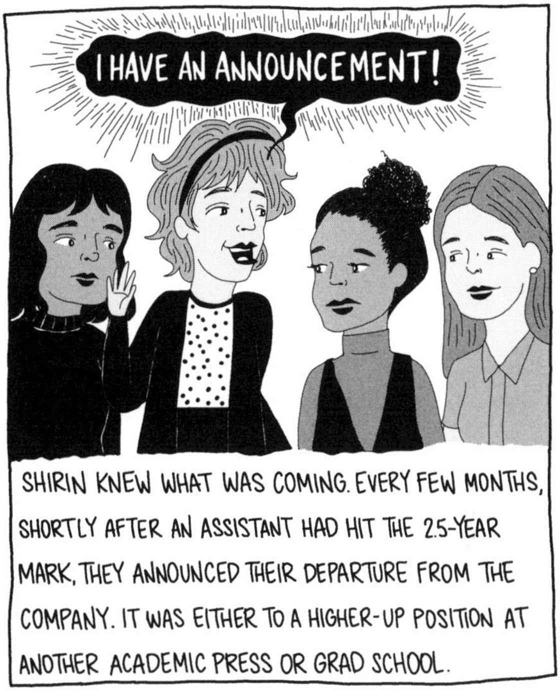
I HAVE AN ANNOUNCEMENT!
SHIRIN KNEW WHAT WAS COMING. EVERY FEW MONTHS, SHORTLY AFTER AN ASSISTANT HAD HIT THE 2.5-YEAR MARK, THEY ANNOUNCED THEIR DEPARTURE FROM THE COMPANY. IT WAS EITHER TO A HIGHER-UP POSITION AT ANOTHER ACADEMIC PRESS OR GRAD SCHOOL.

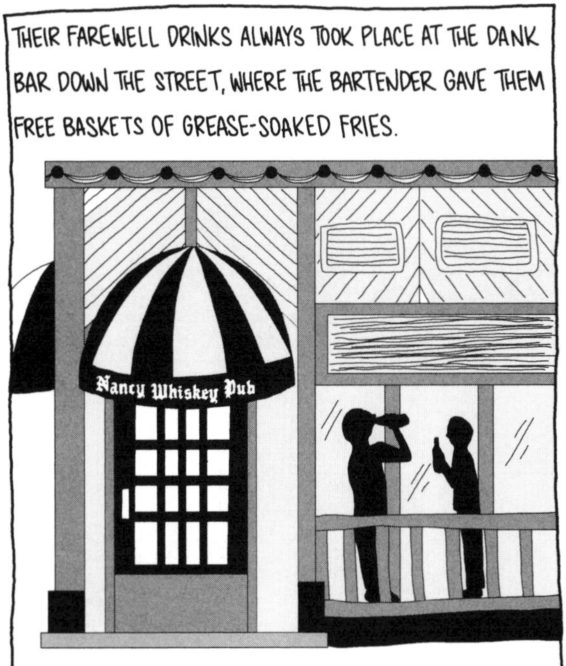
THEIR FAREWELL DRINKS ALWAYS TOOK PLACE AT THE DANK BAR DOWN THE STREET, WHERE THE BARTENDER GAVE THEM FREE BASKETS OF GREASE-SOAKED FRIES.
Nancy Whiskey Pub

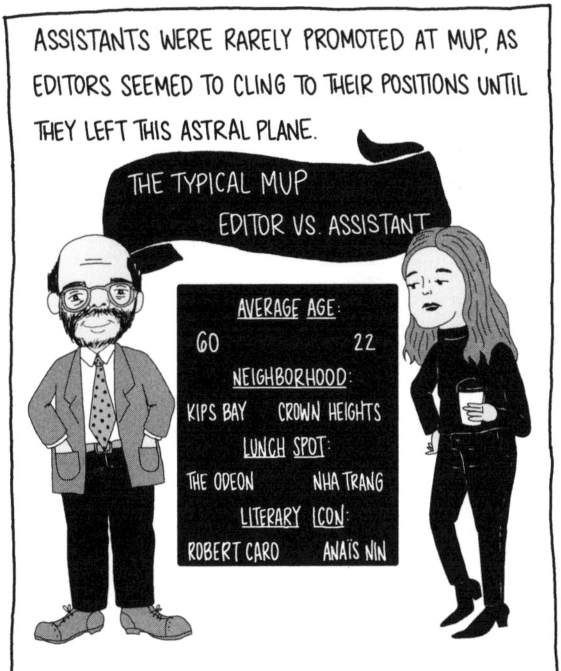
ASSISTANTS WERE RARELY PROMOTED AT MUP, AS EDITORS SEEMED TO CLING TO THEIR POSITIONS UNTIL THEY LEFT THIS ASTRAL PLANE.
THE TYPICAL MUP EDITOR VS. ASSISTANT
AVERAGE AGE:
60 22
NEIGHBORHOOD:
KIPS BAY CROWN HEIGHTS
LUNCH SPOT:
THE ODEON NHA TRANG
LITERARY ICON:
ROBERT CARO ANAÏS NIN

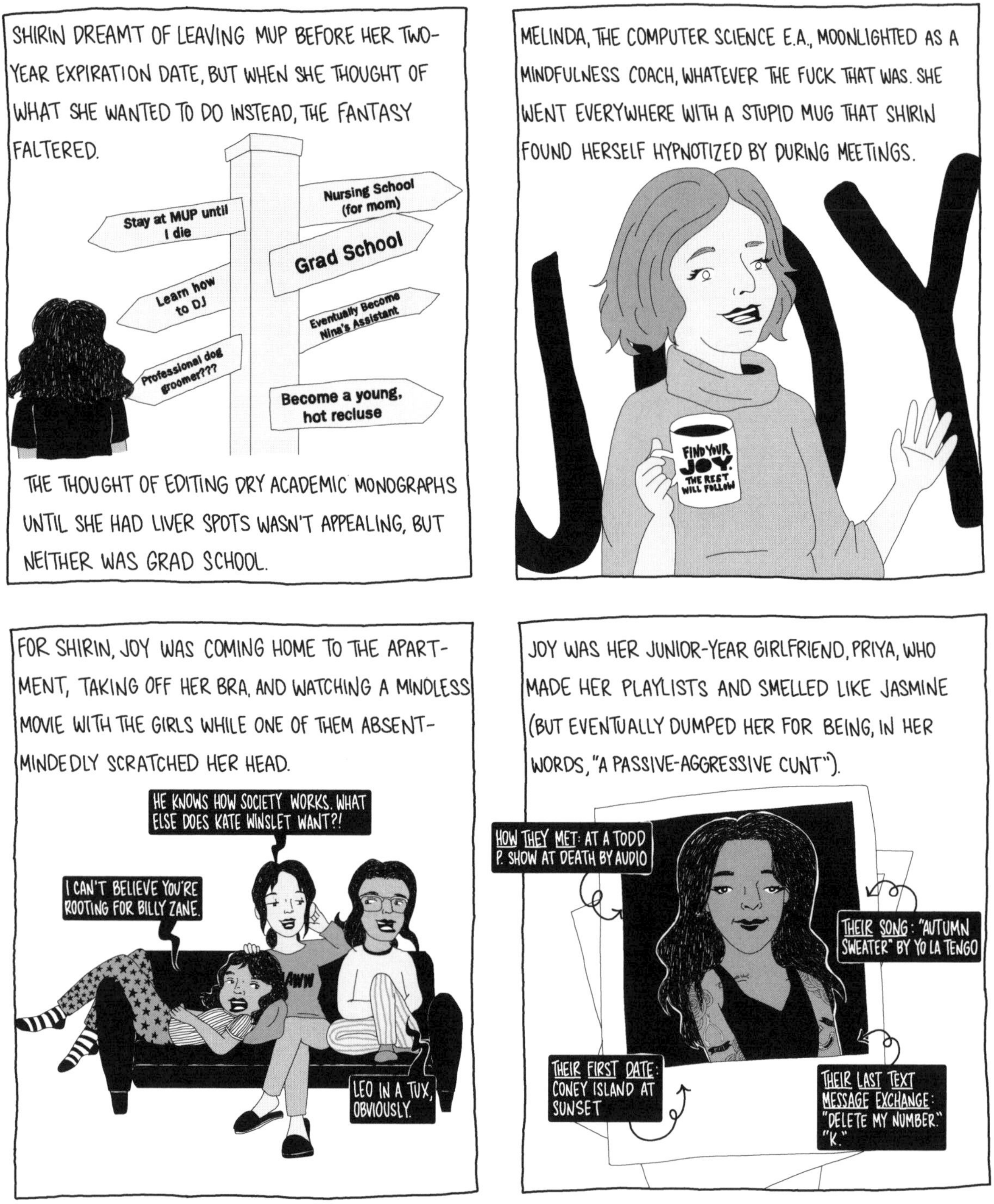
SHIRIN DREAMT OF LEAVING MUP BEFORE HER TWO-YEAR EXPIRATION DATE, BUT WHEN SHE THOUGHT OF WHAT SHE WANTED TO DO INSTEAD, THE FANTASY FALTERED.
Stay at MUP until I die
Nursing School (for mom)
Grad School
Learn how to DJ
Eventually Become Nina's Assistant
Professional dog groomer???
Become a young, hot recluse
THE THOUGHT OF EDITING DRY ACADEMIC MONOGRAPHS UNTIL SHE HAD LIVER SPOTS WASN'T APPEALING, BUT NEITHER WAS GRAD SCHOOL.
MELINDA, THE COMPUTER SCIENCE E.A., MOONLIGHTED AS A MINDFULNESS COACH, WHATEVER THE FUCK THAT WAS. SHE WENT EVERYWHERE WITH A STUPID MUG THAT SHIRIN FOUND HERSELF HYPNOTIZED BY DURING MEETINGS.
JOY
FIND YOUR JOY. THE REST WILL FOLLOW
FOR SHIRIN, JOY WAS COMING HOME TO THE APARTMENT, TAKING OFF HER BRA, AND WATCHING A MINDLESS MOVIE WITH THE GIRLS WHILE ONE OF THEM ABSENT-MINDEDLY SCRATCHED HER HEAD.
HE KNOWS HOW SOCIETY WORKS. WHAT ELSE DOES KATE WINSLET WANT?!
I CAN'T BELIEVE YOU'RE ROOTING FOR BILLY ZANE.
LEO IN A TUX, OBVIOUSLY.
JOY WAS HER JUNIOR-YEAR GIRLFRIEND, PRIYA, WHO MADE HER PLAYLISTS AND SMELLED LIKE JASMINE (BUT EVENTUALLY DUMPED HER FOR BEING, IN HER WORDS, "A PASSIVE-AGGRESSIVE CUNT").
HOW THEY MET: AT A TODD P. SHOW AT DEATH BY AUDIO
THEIR SONG: "AUTUMN SWEATER" BY YO LA TENGO
THEIR FIRST DATE: CONEY ISLAND AT SUNSET
THEIR LAST TEXT MESSAGE EXCHANGE: "DELETE MY NUMBER." "K."

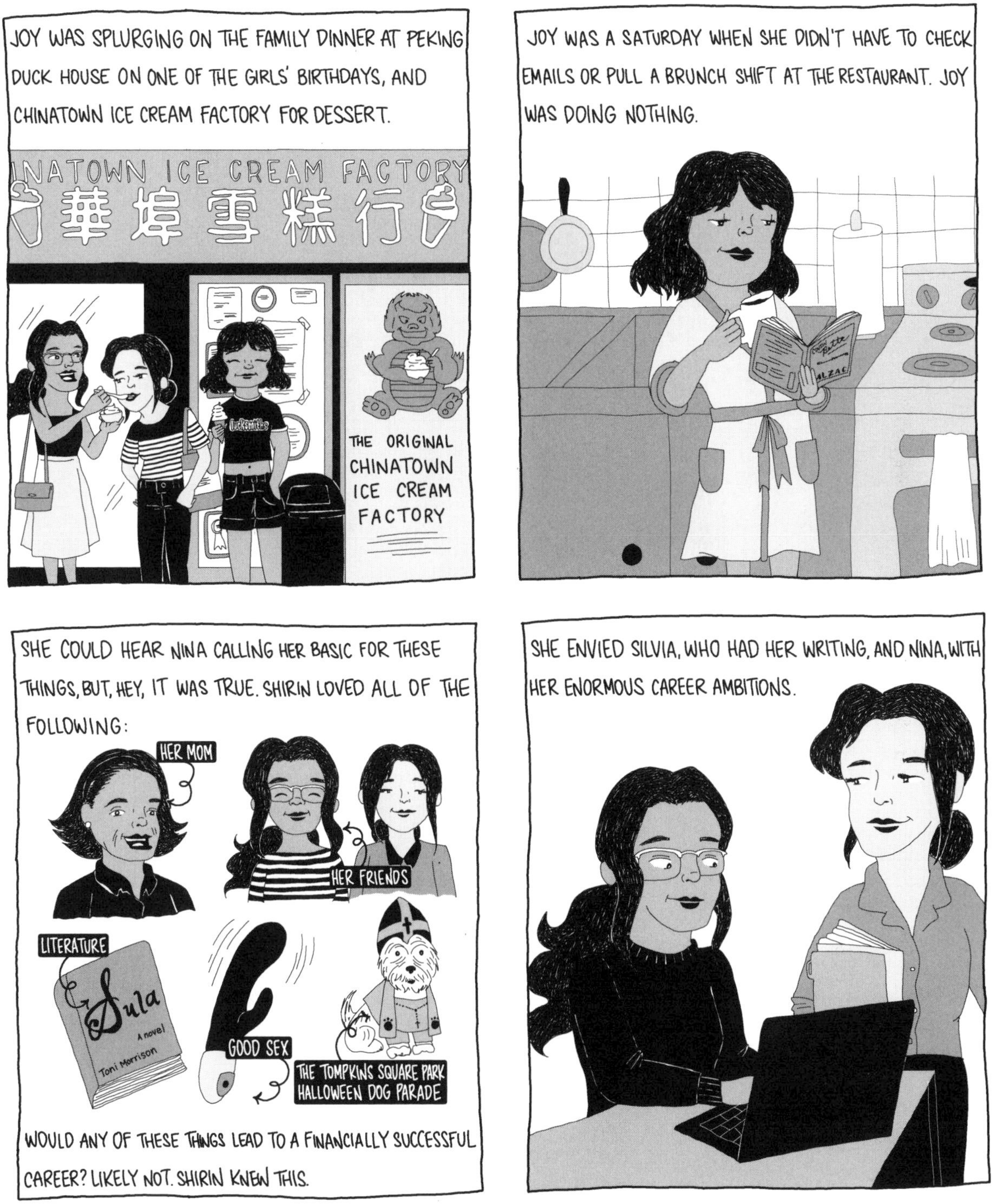
JOY WAS SPLURGING ON THE FAMILY DINNER AT PEKING DUCK HOUSE ON ONE OF THE GIRLS' BIRTHDAYS, AND CHINATOWN ICE CREAM FACTORY FOR DESSERT.
INATOWN ICE CREAM FACTORY
華埠雪糕行
lucksmiths
THE ORIGINAL CHINATOWN ICE CREAM FACTORY
JOY WAS A SATURDAY WHEN SHE DIDN'T HAVE TO CHECK EMAILS OR PULL A BRUNCH SHIFT AT THE RESTAURANT. JOY WAS DOING NOTHING.
SHE COULD HEAR NINA CALLING HER BASIC FOR THESE THINGS, BUT, HEY, IT WAS TRUE. SHIRIN LOVED ALL OF THE FOLLOWING:
HER MOM
HER FRIENDS
LITERATURE
Sula
A novel
Toni Morrison
GOOD SEX
THE TOMPKINS SQUARE PARK HALLOWEEN DOG PARADE
WOULD ANY OF THESE THINGS LEAD TO A FINANCIALLY SUCCESSFUL CAREER? LIKELY NOT. SHIRIN KNEW THIS.
SHE ENVIED SILVIA, WHO HAD HER WRITING, AND NINA, WITH HER ENORMOUS CAREER AMBITIONS.

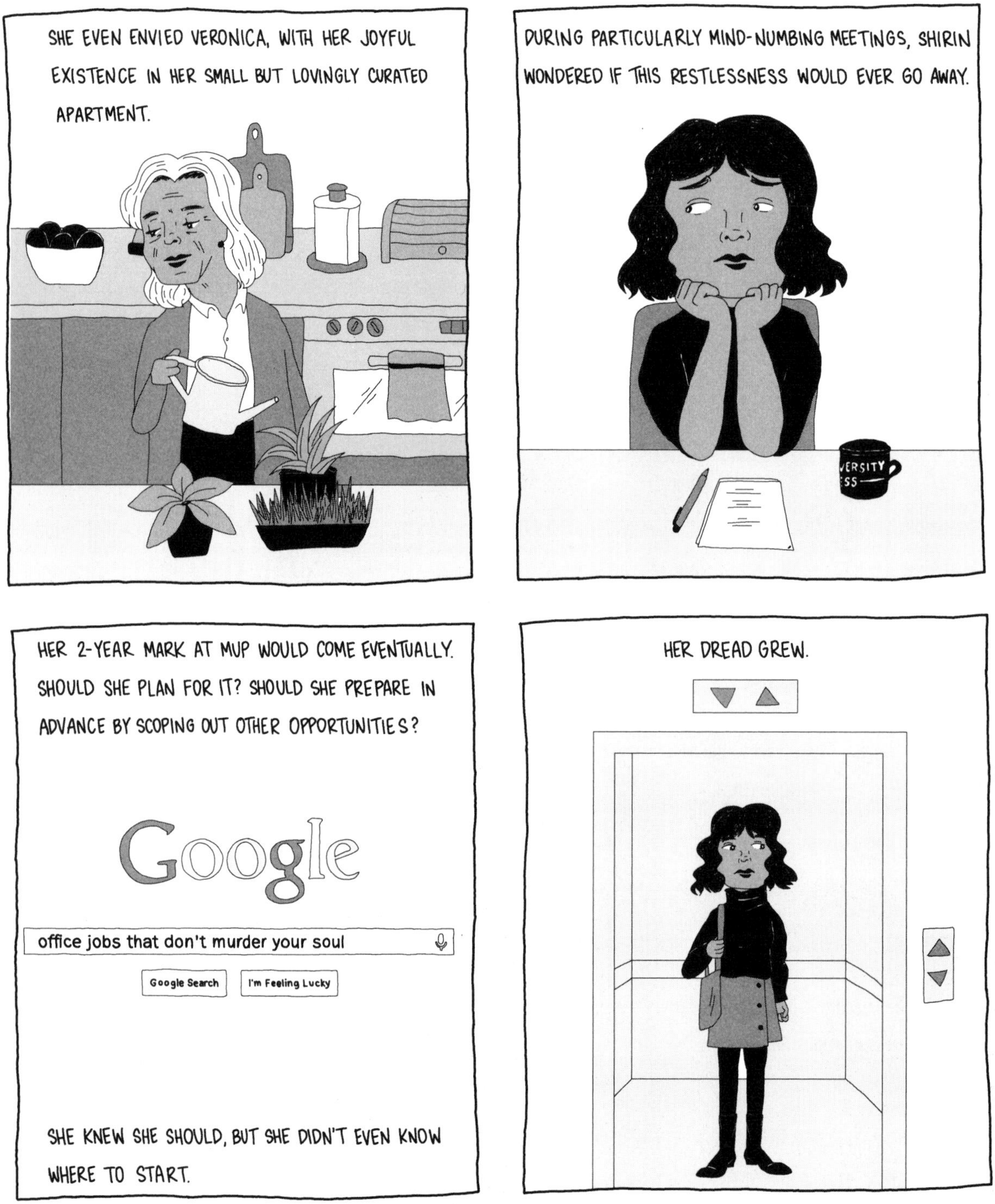
SHE EVEN ENVIED VERONICA, WITH HER JOYFUL EXISTENCE IN HER SMALL BUT LOVINGLY CURATED APARTMENT.
DURING PARTICULARLY MIND-NUMBING MEETINGS, SHIRIN WONDERED IF THIS RESTLESSNESS WOULD EVER GO AWAY.
HER 2-YEAR MARK AT MUP WOULD COME EVENTUALLY. SHOULD SHE PLAN FOR IT? SHOULD SHE PREPARE IN ADVANCE BY SCOPING OUT OTHER OPPORTUNITIES?
Google
office jobs that don't murder your soul
Google Search
I'm Feeling Lucky
SHE KNEW SHE SHOULD, BUT SHE DIDN'T EVEN KNOW WHERE TO START.
HER DREAD GREW.

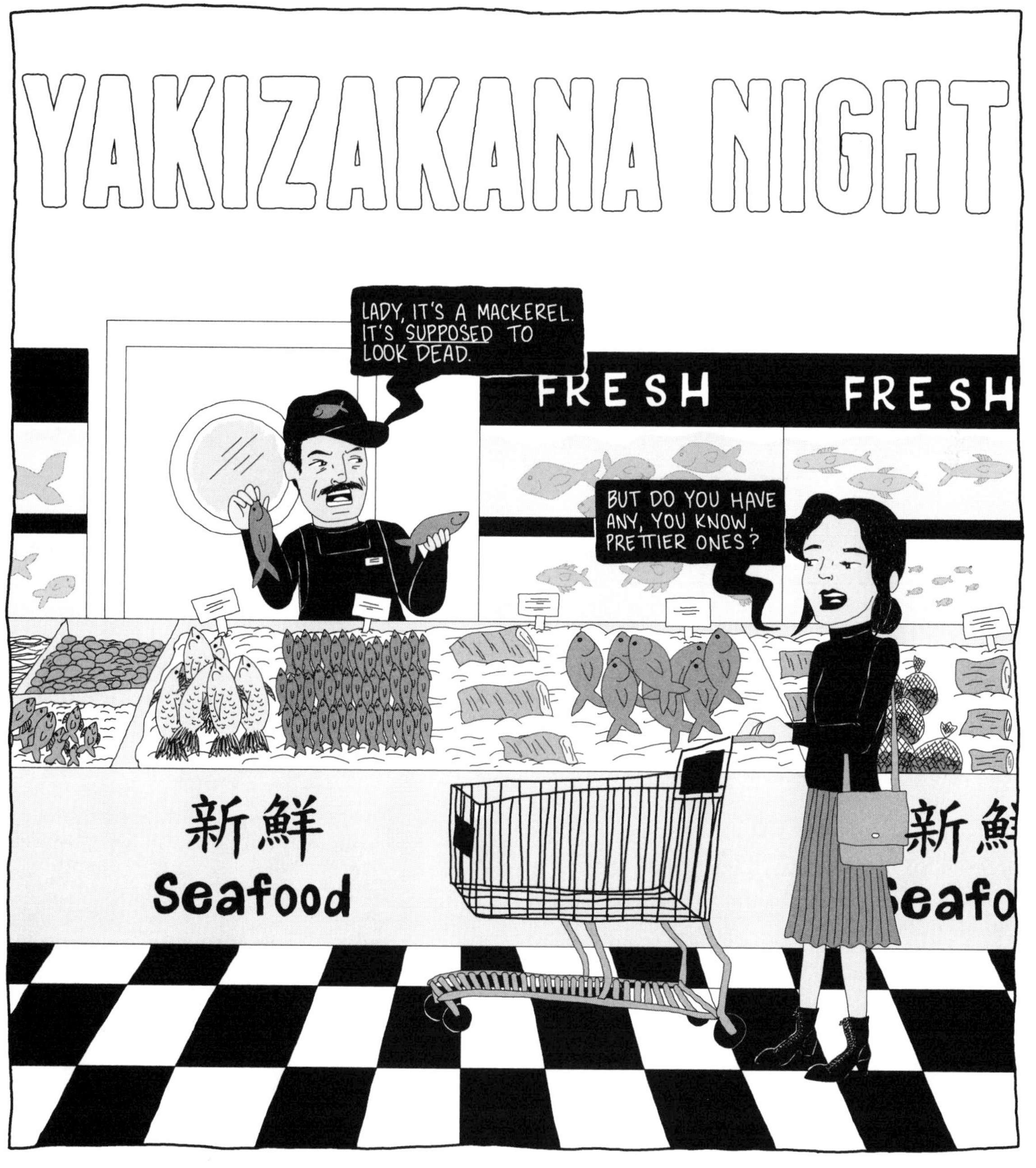
YAKIZAKANA NIGHT
LADY, IT'S A MACKEREL. IT'S SUPPOSED TO LOOK DEAD.
FRESH
FRESH
BUT DO YOU HAVE ANY, YOU KNOW, PRETTIER ONES?
新鮮
Seafood
新鮮
Seafo

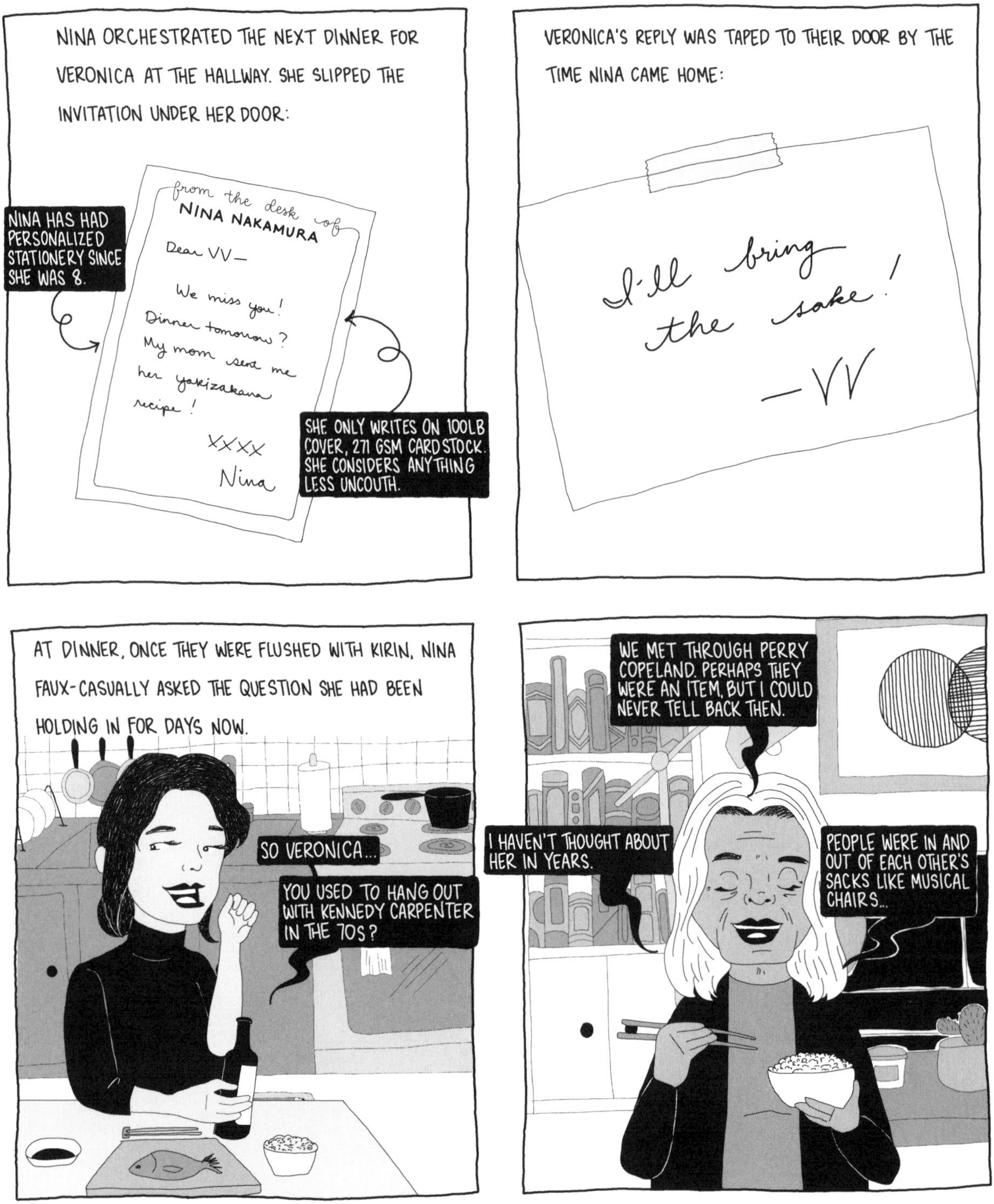
NINA ORCHESTRATED THE NEXT DINNER FOR VERONICA AT THE HALLWAY. SHE SLIPPED THE INVITATION UNDER HER DOOR:
NINA HAS HAD PERSONALIZED STATIONERY SINCE SHE WAS 8.
from the desk of NINA NAKAMURA
Dear VV—
We miss you! Dinner tomorrow? My mom sent me her yakizakana recipe!
XXXX
Nina
SHE ONLY WRITES ON 100LB COVER, 271 GSM CARD STOCK. SHE CONSIDERS ANYTHING LESS UNCOUTH.
VERONICA'S REPLY WAS TAPED TO THEIR DOOR BY THE TIME NINA CAME HOME:
I'll bring the sake!
—VV
AT DINNER, ONCE THEY WERE FLUSHED WITH KIRIN, NINA FAUX-CASUALLY ASKED THE QUESTION SHE HAD BEEN HOLDING IN FOR DAYS NOW.
SO VERONICA...
YOU USED TO HANG OUT WITH KENNEDY CARPENTER IN THE 70S?
I HAVEN'T THOUGHT ABOUT HER IN YEARS.
WE MET THROUGH PERRY COPELAND. PERHAPS THEY WERE AN ITEM, BUT I COULD NEVER TELL BACK THEN.
PEOPLE WERE IN AND OUT OF EACH OTHER'S SACKS LIKE MUSICAL CHAIRS...

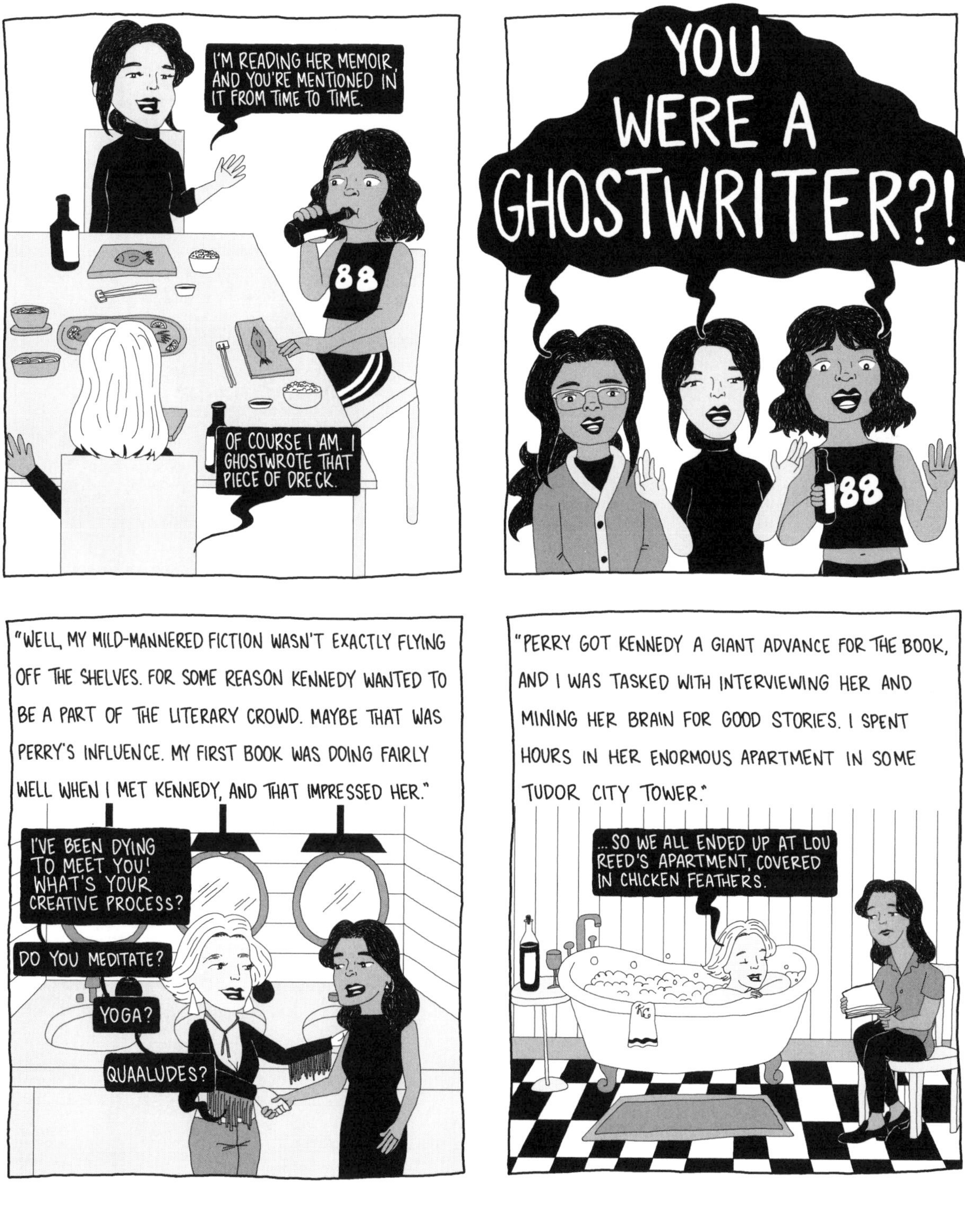
I'M READING HER MEMOIR, AND YOU'RE MENTIONED IN IT FROM TIME TO TIME.
OF COURSE I AM. I GHOSTWROTE THAT PIECE OF DRECK.
88
YOU WERE A GHOSTWRITER?!
88
"WELL, MY MILD-MANNERED FICTION WASN'T EXACTLY FLYING OFF THE SHELVES. FOR SOME REASON KENNEDY WANTED TO BE A PART OF THE LITERARY CROWD. MAYBE THAT WAS PERRY'S INFLUENCE. MY FIRST BOOK WAS DOING FAIRLY WELL WHEN I MET KENNEDY, AND THAT IMPRESSED HER."
I'VE BEEN DYING TO MEET YOU! WHAT'S YOUR CREATIVE PROCESS?
DO YOU MEDITATE?
YOGA?
QUAALUDES?
"PERRY GOT KENNEDY A GIANT ADVANCE FOR THE BOOK, AND I WAS TASKED WITH INTERVIEWING HER AND MINING HER BRAIN FOR GOOD STORIES. I SPENT HOURS IN HER ENORMOUS APARTMENT IN SOME TUDOR CITY TOWER."
...SO WE ALL ENDED UP AT LOU REED'S APARTMENT, COVERED IN CHICKEN FEATHERS.
KC

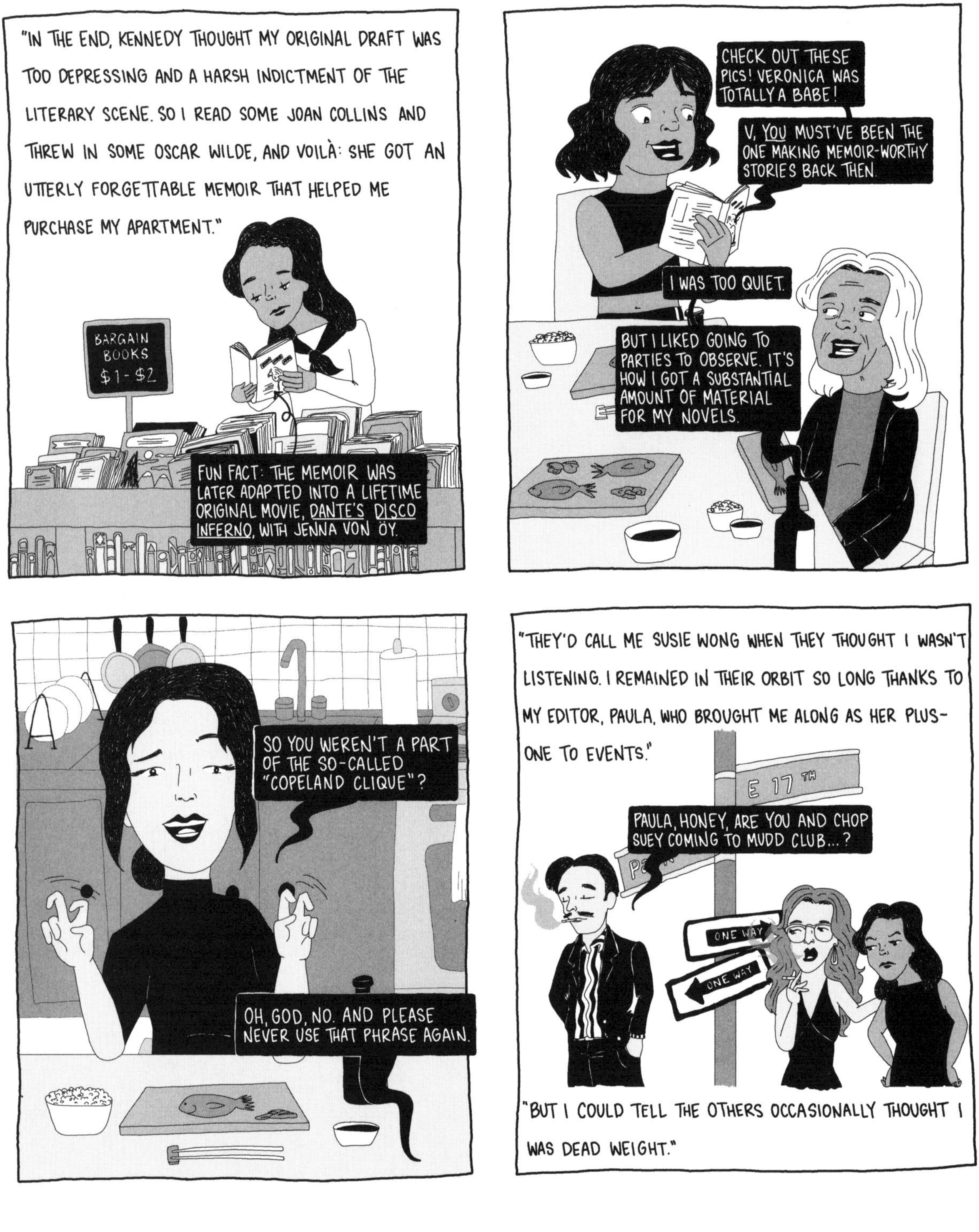
"IN THE END, KENNEDY THOUGHT MY ORIGINAL DRAFT WAS TOO DEPRESSING AND A HARSH INDICTMENT OF THE LITERARY SCENE. SO I READ SOME JOAN COLLINS AND THREW IN SOME OSCAR WILDE, AND VOILÀ: SHE GOT AN UTTERLY FORGETTABLE MEMOIR THAT HELPED ME PURCHASE MY APARTMENT."
BARGAIN BOOKS $1-$2
FUN FACT: THE MEMOIR WAS LATER ADAPTED INTO A LIFETIME ORIGINAL MOVIE, DANTE'S DISCO INFERNO, WITH JENNA VON ÖY.
CHECK OUT THESE PICS! VERONICA WAS TOTALLY A BABE!
V, YOU MUST'VE BEEN THE ONE MAKING MEMOIR-WORTHY STORIES BACK THEN.
I WAS TOO QUIET.
BUT I LIKED GOING TO PARTIES TO OBSERVE. IT'S HOW I GOT A SUBSTANTIAL AMOUNT OF MATERIAL FOR MY NOVELS.
SO YOU WEREN'T A PART OF THE SO-CALLED "COPELAND CLIQUE"?
OH, GOD, NO. AND PLEASE NEVER USE THAT PHRASE AGAIN.
"THEY'D CALL ME SUSIE WONG WHEN THEY THOUGHT I WASN'T LISTENING. I REMAINED IN THEIR ORBIT SO LONG THANKS TO MY EDITOR, PAULA, WHO BROUGHT ME ALONG AS HER PLUS-ONE TO EVENTS."
E 17TH
PAULA, HONEY, ARE YOU AND CHOP SUEY COMING TO MUDD CLUB...?
ONE WAY
ONE WAY
"BUT I COULD TELL THE OTHERS OCCASIONALLY THOUGHT I WAS DEAD WEIGHT."

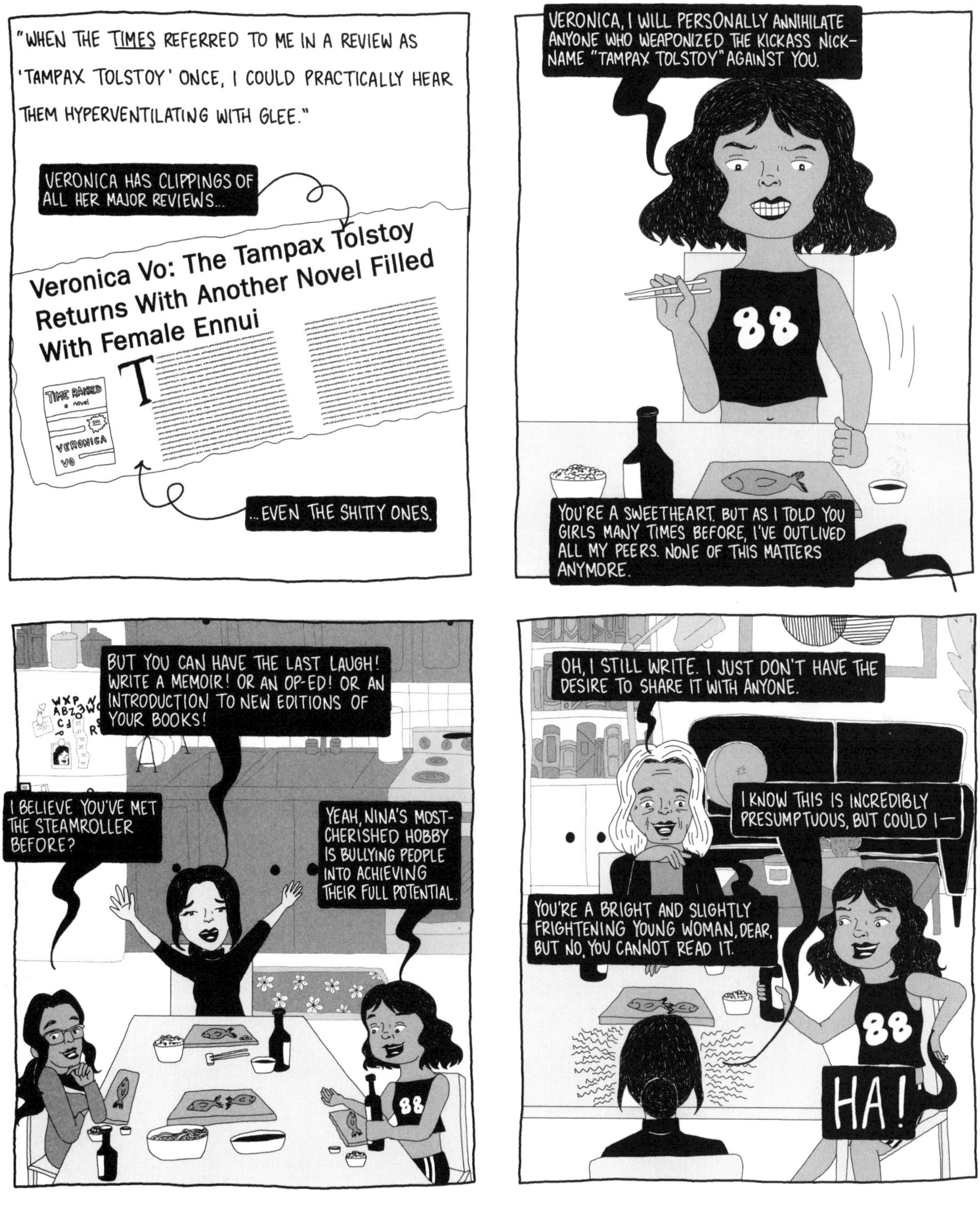
"WHEN THE TIMES REFERRED TO ME IN A REVIEW AS 'TAMPAX TOLSTOY' ONCE, I COULD PRACTICALLY HEAR THEM HYPERVENTILATING WITH GLEE."
VERONICA HAS CLIPPINGS OF ALL HER MAJOR REVIEWS...
Veronica Vo: The Tampax Tolstoy Returns With Another Novel Filled With Female Ennui
TIME RAISED
a novel
VERONICA VO
...EVEN THE SHITTY ONES.
VERONICA, I WILL PERSONALLY ANNIHILATE ANYONE WHO WEAPONIZED THE KICKASS NICKNAME "TAMPAX TOLSTOY" AGAINST YOU.
88
YOU'RE A SWEETHEART. BUT AS I TOLD YOU GIRLS MANY TIMES BEFORE, I'VE OUTLIVED ALL MY PEERS. NONE OF THIS MATTERS ANYMORE.
BUT YOU CAN HAVE THE LAST LAUGH! WRITE A MEMOIR! OR AN OP-ED! OR AN INTRODUCTION TO NEW EDITIONS OF YOUR BOOKS!
I BELIEVE YOU'VE MET THE STEAMROLLER BEFORE?
YEAH, NINA'S MOST-CHERISHED HOBBY IS BULLYING PEOPLE INTO ACHIEVING THEIR FULL POTENTIAL.
88
OH, I STILL WRITE. I JUST DON'T HAVE THE DESIRE TO SHARE IT WITH ANYONE.
I KNOW THIS IS INCREDIBLY PRESUMPTUOUS, BUT COULD I—
YOU'RE A BRIGHT AND SLIGHTLY FRIGHTENING YOUNG WOMAN, DEAR, BUT NO, YOU CANNOT READ IT.
88
HA!

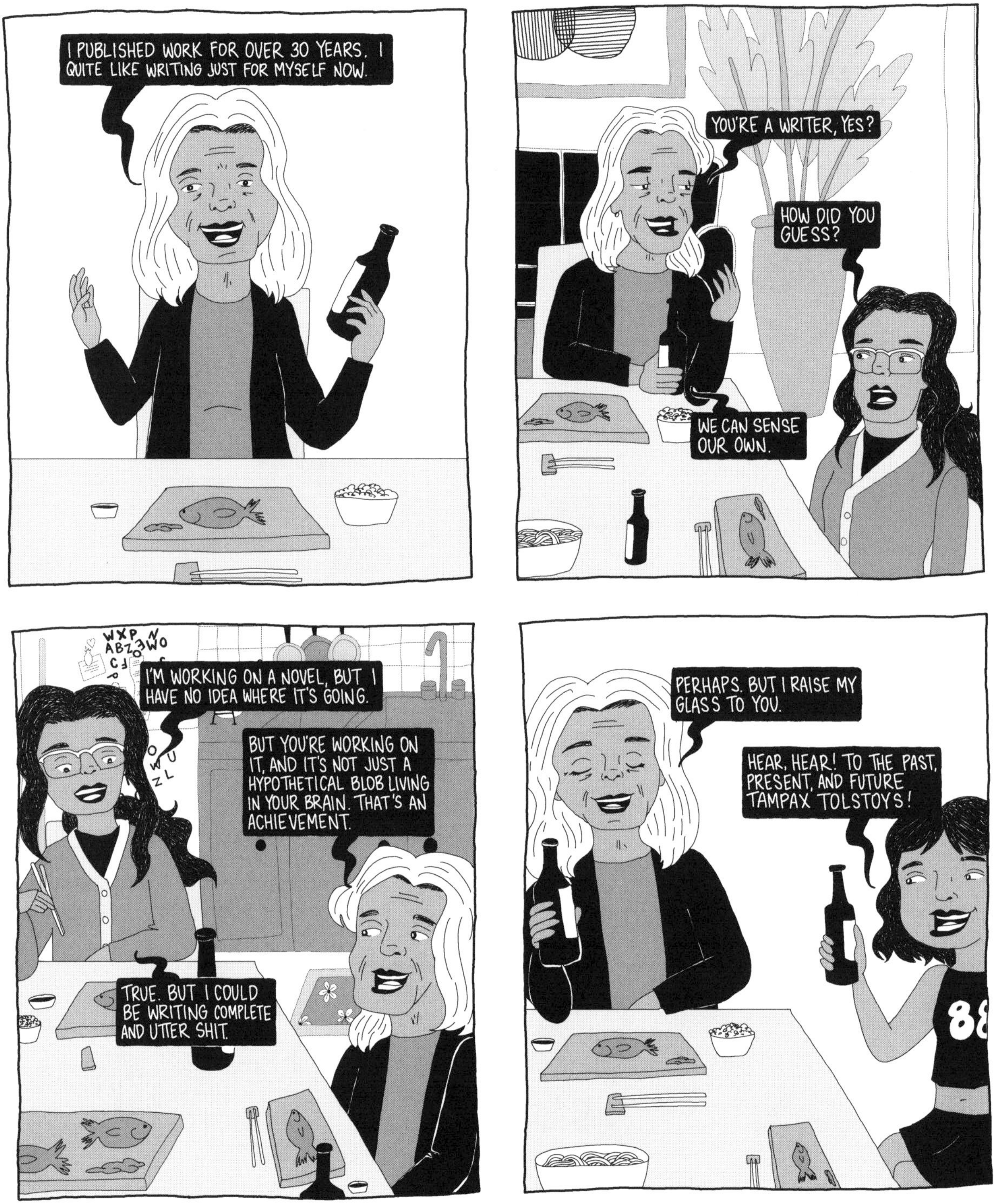
I PUBLISHED WORK FOR OVER 30 YEARS. I QUITE LIKE WRITING JUST FOR MYSELF NOW.
YOU'RE A WRITER, YES?
HOW DID YOU GUESS?
WE CAN SENSE OUR OWN.
I'M WORKING ON A NOVEL, BUT I HAVE NO IDEA WHERE IT'S GOING.
BUT YOU'RE WORKING ON IT, AND IT'S NOT JUST A HYPOTHETICAL BLOB LIVING IN YOUR BRAIN. THAT'S AN ACHIEVEMENT.
TRUE. BUT I COULD BE WRITING COMPLETE AND UTTER SHIT.
PERHAPS. BUT I RAISE MY GLASS TO YOU.
HEAR, HEAR! TO THE PAST, PRESENT, AND FUTURE TAMPAX TOLSTOYS!

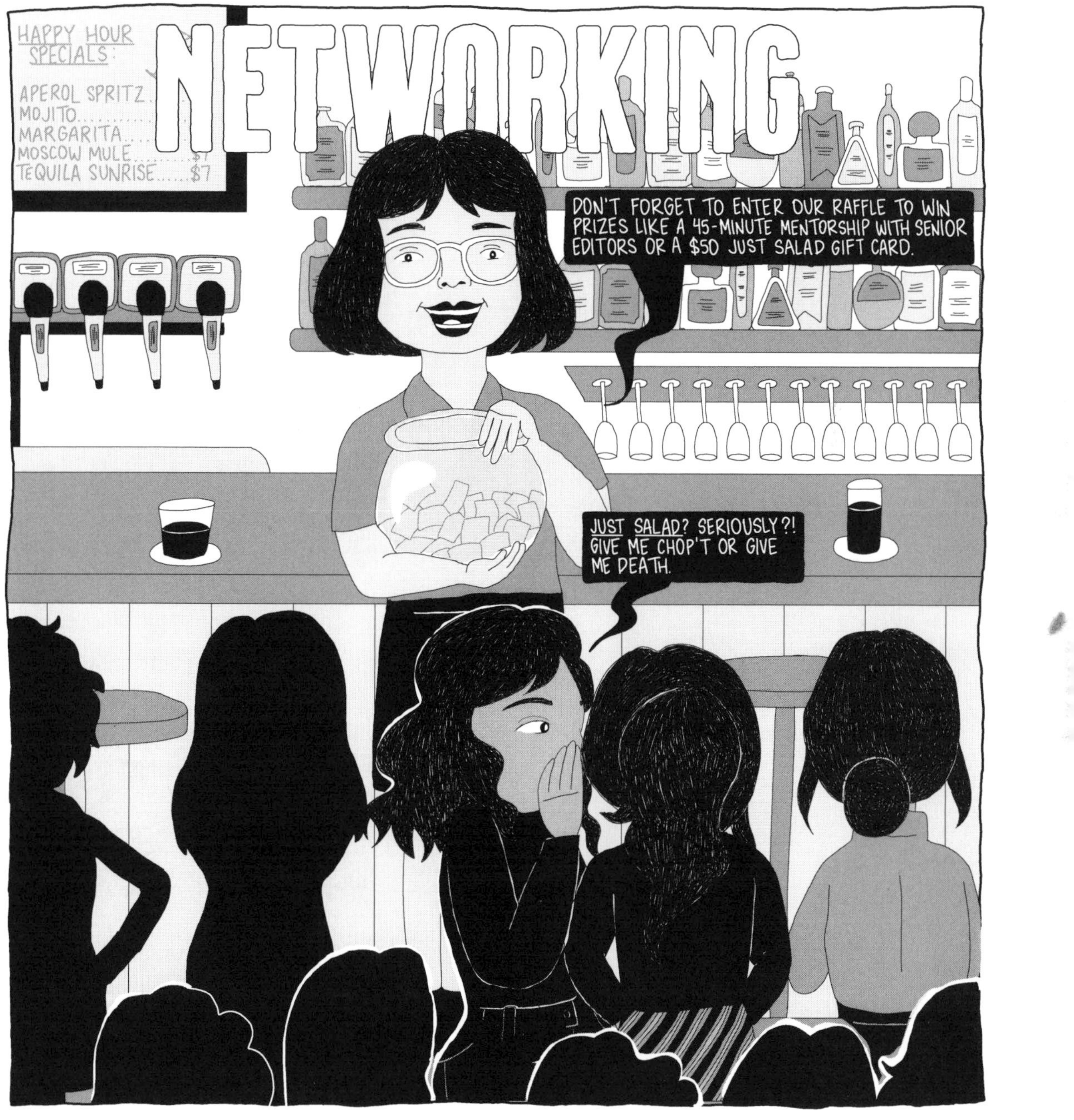
NETWORKING
HAPPY HOUR SPECIALS:
APEROL SPRITZ
MOJITO
MARGARITA
MOSCOW MULE
TEQUILA SUNRISE.....$7
DON'T FORGET TO ENTER OUR RAFFLE TO WIN PRIZES LIKE A 45-MINUTE MENTORSHIP WITH SENIOR EDITORS OR A $50 JUST SALAD GIFT CARD.
JUST SALAD? SERIOUSLY?! GIVE ME CHOP'T OR GIVE ME DEATH.

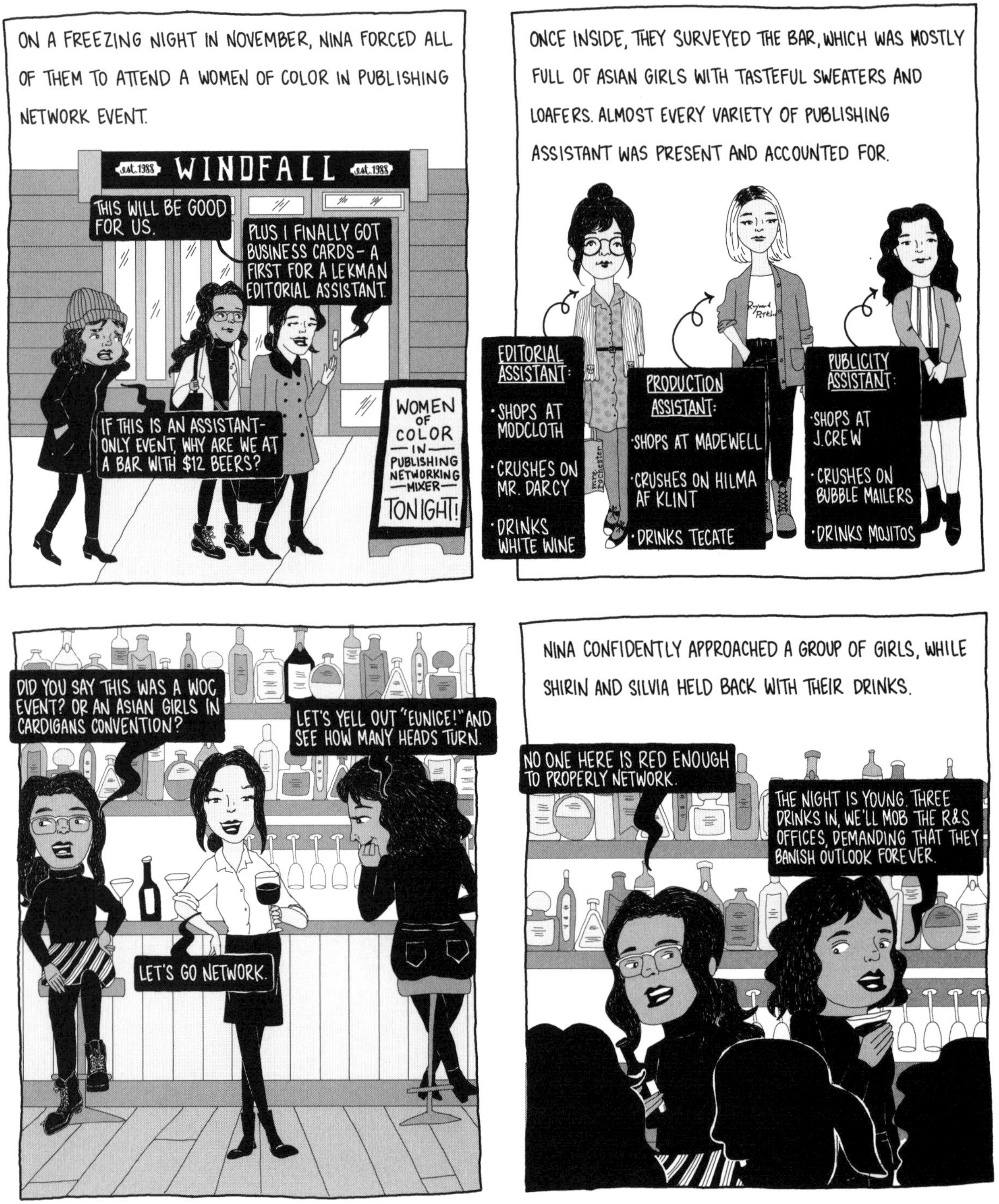

ON A FREEZING NIGHT IN NOVEMBER, NINA FORCED ALL OF THEM TO ATTEND A WOMEN OF COLOR IN PUBLISHING NETWORK EVENT.
est. 1988 WINDFALL est. 1988
THIS WILL BE GOOD FOR US.
PLUS I FINALLY GOT BUSINESS CARDS – A FIRST FOR A LEKMAN EDITORIAL ASSISTANT.
IF THIS IS AN ASSISTANT-ONLY EVENT, WHY ARE WE AT A BAR WITH $12 BEERS?
WOMEN OF COLOR IN PUBLISHING NETWORKING MIXER TONIGHT!
ONCE INSIDE, THEY SURVEYED THE BAR, WHICH WAS MOSTLY FULL OF ASIAN GIRLS WITH TASTEFUL SWEATERS AND LOAFERS. ALMOST EVERY VARIETY OF PUBLISHING ASSISTANT WAS PRESENT AND ACCOUNTED FOR.
EDITORIAL ASSISTANT: ·SHOPS AT MODCLOTH ·CRUSHES ON MR. DARCY ·DRINKS WHITE WINE
PRODUCTION ASSISTANT: ·SHOPS AT MADEWELL ·CRUSHES ON HILMA AF KLINT ·DRINKS TECATE
PUBLICITY ASSISTANT: ·SHOPS AT J.CREW ·CRUSHES ON BUBBLE MAILERS ·DRINKS MOJITOS
DID YOU SAY THIS WAS A WOC EVENT? OR AN ASIAN GIRLS IN CARDIGANS CONVENTION?
LET'S YELL OUT "EUNICE!" AND SEE HOW MANY HEADS TURN.
LET'S GO NETWORK.
NINA CONFIDENTLY APPROACHED A GROUP OF GIRLS, WHILE SHIRIN AND SILVIA HELD BACK WITH THEIR DRINKS.
NO ONE HERE IS RED ENOUGH TO PROPERLY NETWORK.
THE NIGHT IS YOUNG. THREE DRINKS IN, WE'LL MOB THE R&S OFFICES, DEMANDING THAT THEY BANISH OUTLOOK FOREVER.

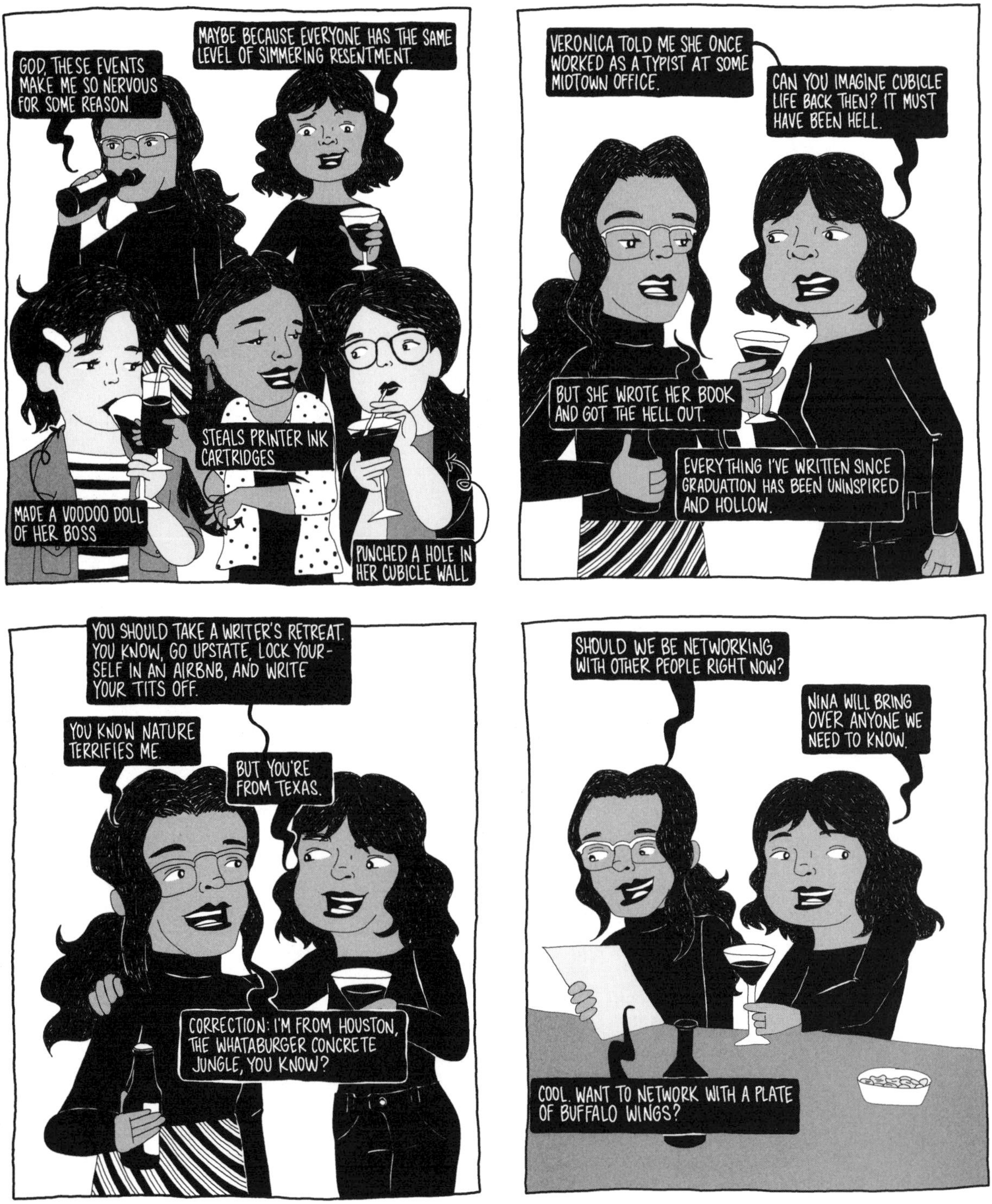
GOD, THESE EVENTS MAKE ME SO NERVOUS FOR SOME REASON.
MAYBE BECAUSE EVERYONE HAS THE SAME LEVEL OF SIMMERING RESENTMENT.
MADE A VOODOO DOLL OF HER BOSS
STEALS PRINTER INK CARTRIDGES
PUNCHED A HOLE IN HER CUBICLE WALL
VERONICA TOLD ME SHE ONCE WORKED AS A TYPIST AT SOME MIDTOWN OFFICE.
CAN YOU IMAGINE CUBICLE LIFE BACK THEN? IT MUST HAVE BEEN HELL.
BUT SHE WROTE HER BOOK AND GOT THE HELL OUT.
EVERYTHING I'VE WRITTEN SINCE GRADUATION HAS BEEN UNINSPIRED AND HOLLOW.
YOU SHOULD TAKE A WRITER'S RETREAT. YOU KNOW, GO UPSTATE, LOCK YOURSELF IN AN AIRBNB, AND WRITE YOUR TITS OFF.
YOU KNOW NATURE TERRIFIES ME.
BUT YOU'RE FROM TEXAS.
CORRECTION: I'M FROM HOUSTON, THE WHATABURGER CONCRETE JUNGLE, YOU KNOW?
SHOULD WE BE NETWORKING WITH OTHER PEOPLE RIGHT NOW?
NINA WILL BRING OVER ANYONE WE NEED TO KNOW.
COOL. WANT TO NETWORK WITH A PLATE OF BUFFALO WINGS?

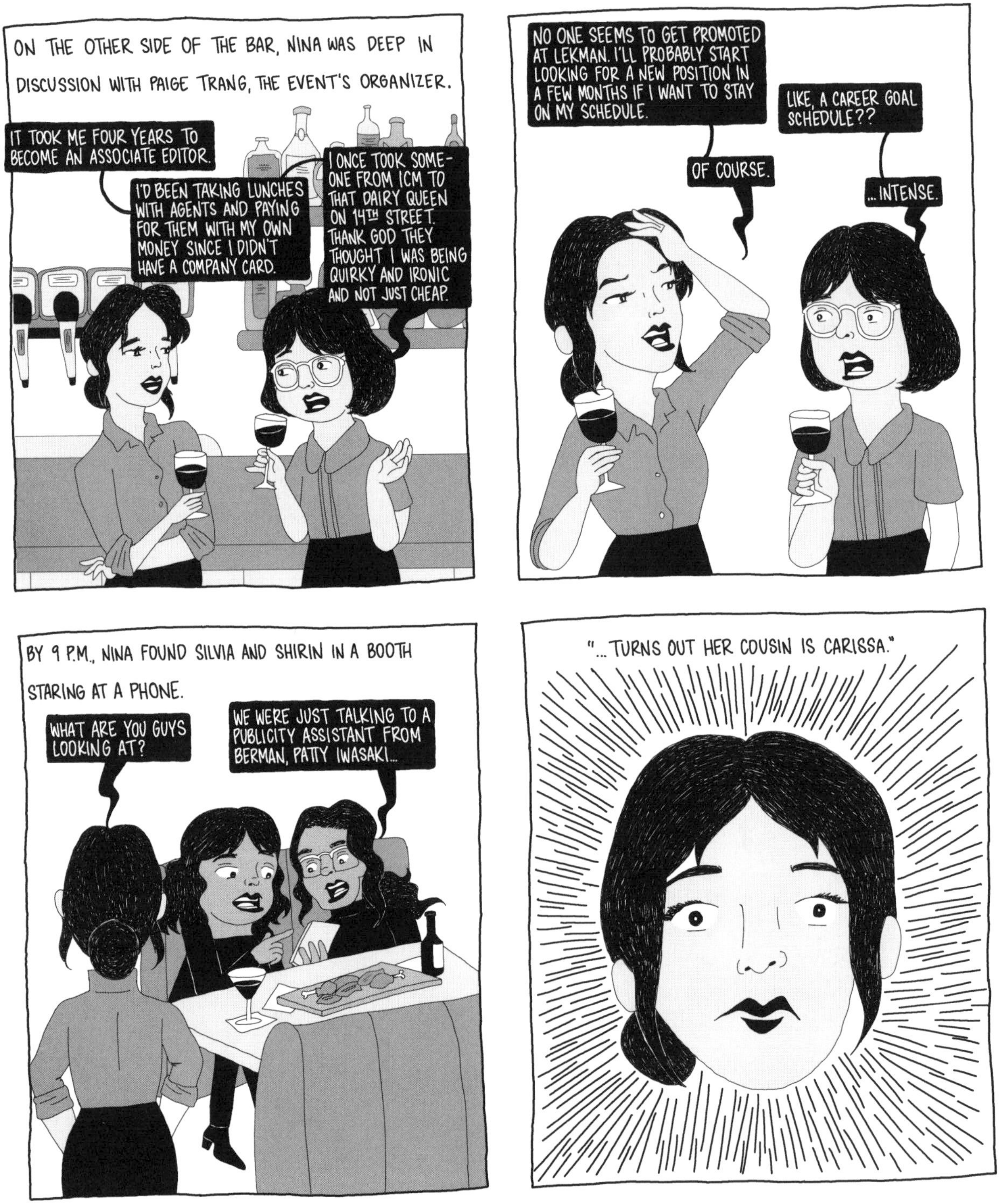

ON THE OTHER SIDE OF THE BAR, NINA WAS DEEP IN DISCUSSION WITH PAIGE TRANG, THE EVENT'S ORGANIZER.
IT TOOK ME FOUR YEARS TO BECOME AN ASSOCIATE EDITOR.
I'D BEEN TAKING LUNCHES WITH AGENTS AND PAYING FOR THEM WITH MY OWN MONEY SINCE I DIDN'T HAVE A COMPANY CARD.
I ONCE TOOK SOME-ONE FROM ICM TO THAT DAIRY QUEEN ON 14TH STREET. THANK GOD THEY THOUGHT I WAS BEING QUIRKY AND IRONIC AND NOT JUST CHEAP.
NO ONE SEEMS TO GET PROMOTED AT LEKMAN. I'LL PROBABLY START LOOKING FOR A NEW POSITION IN A FEW MONTHS IF I WANT TO STAY ON MY SCHEDULE.
LIKE, A CAREER GOAL SCHEDULE??
OF COURSE.
...INTENSE.
BY 9 P.M., NINA FOUND SILVIA AND SHIRIN IN A BOOTH STARING AT A PHONE.
WHAT ARE YOU GUYS LOOKING AT?
WE WERE JUST TALKING TO A PUBLICITY ASSISTANT FROM BERMAN, PATTY IWASAKI...
"...TURNS OUT HER COUSIN IS CARISSA."

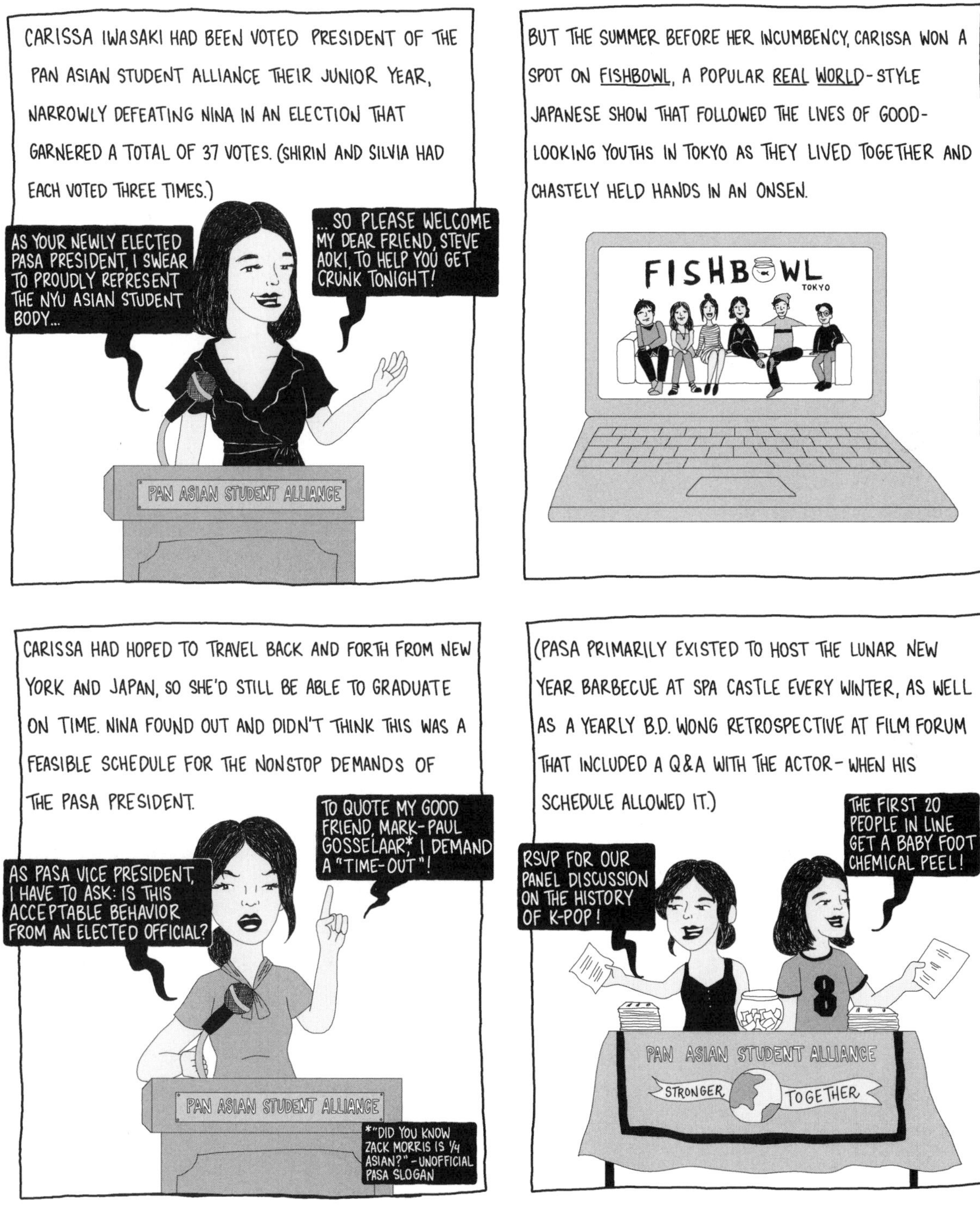
CARISSA IWASAKI HAD BEEN VOTED PRESIDENT OF THE PAN ASIAN STUDENT ALLIANCE THEIR JUNIOR YEAR, NARROWLY DEFEATING NINA IN AN ELECTION THAT GARNERED A TOTAL OF 37 VOTES. (SHIRIN AND SILVIA HAD EACH VOTED THREE TIMES.)
AS YOUR NEWLY ELECTED PASA PRESIDENT, I SWEAR TO PROUDLY REPRESENT THE NYU ASIAN STUDENT BODY...
... SO PLEASE WELCOME MY DEAR FRIEND, STEVE AOKI, TO HELP YOU GET CRUNK TONIGHT!
PAN ASIAN STUDENT ALLIANCE
BUT THE SUMMER BEFORE HER INCUMBENCY, CARISSA WON A SPOT ON FISHBOWL, A POPULAR REAL WORLD-STYLE JAPANESE SHOW THAT FOLLOWED THE LIVES OF GOOD-LOOKING YOUTHS IN TOKYO AS THEY LIVED TOGETHER AND CHASTELY HELD HANDS IN AN ONSEN.
FISHBOWL
TOKYO
CARISSA HAD HOPED TO TRAVEL BACK AND FORTH FROM NEW YORK AND JAPAN, SO SHE'D STILL BE ABLE TO GRADUATE ON TIME. NINA FOUND OUT AND DIDN'T THINK THIS WAS A FEASIBLE SCHEDULE FOR THE NONSTOP DEMANDS OF THE PASA PRESIDENT.
AS PASA VICE PRESIDENT, I HAVE TO ASK: IS THIS ACCEPTABLE BEHAVIOR FROM AN ELECTED OFFICIAL?
TO QUOTE MY GOOD FRIEND, MARK-PAUL GOSSELAAR,* I DEMAND A "TIME-OUT"!
PAN ASIAN STUDENT ALLIANCE
*"DID YOU KNOW ZACK MORRIS IS 1/4 ASIAN?" - UNOFFICIAL PASA SLOGAN
(PASA PRIMARILY EXISTED TO HOST THE LUNAR NEW YEAR BARBECUE AT SPA CASTLE EVERY WINTER, AS WELL AS A YEARLY B.D. WONG RETROSPECTIVE AT FILM FORUM THAT INCLUDED A Q&A WITH THE ACTOR- WHEN HIS SCHEDULE ALLOWED IT.)
RSVP FOR OUR PANEL DISCUSSION ON THE HISTORY OF K-POP!
THE FIRST 20 PEOPLE IN LINE GET A BABY FOOT CHEMICAL PEEL!
PAN ASIAN STUDENT ALLIANCE
STRONGER TOGETHER

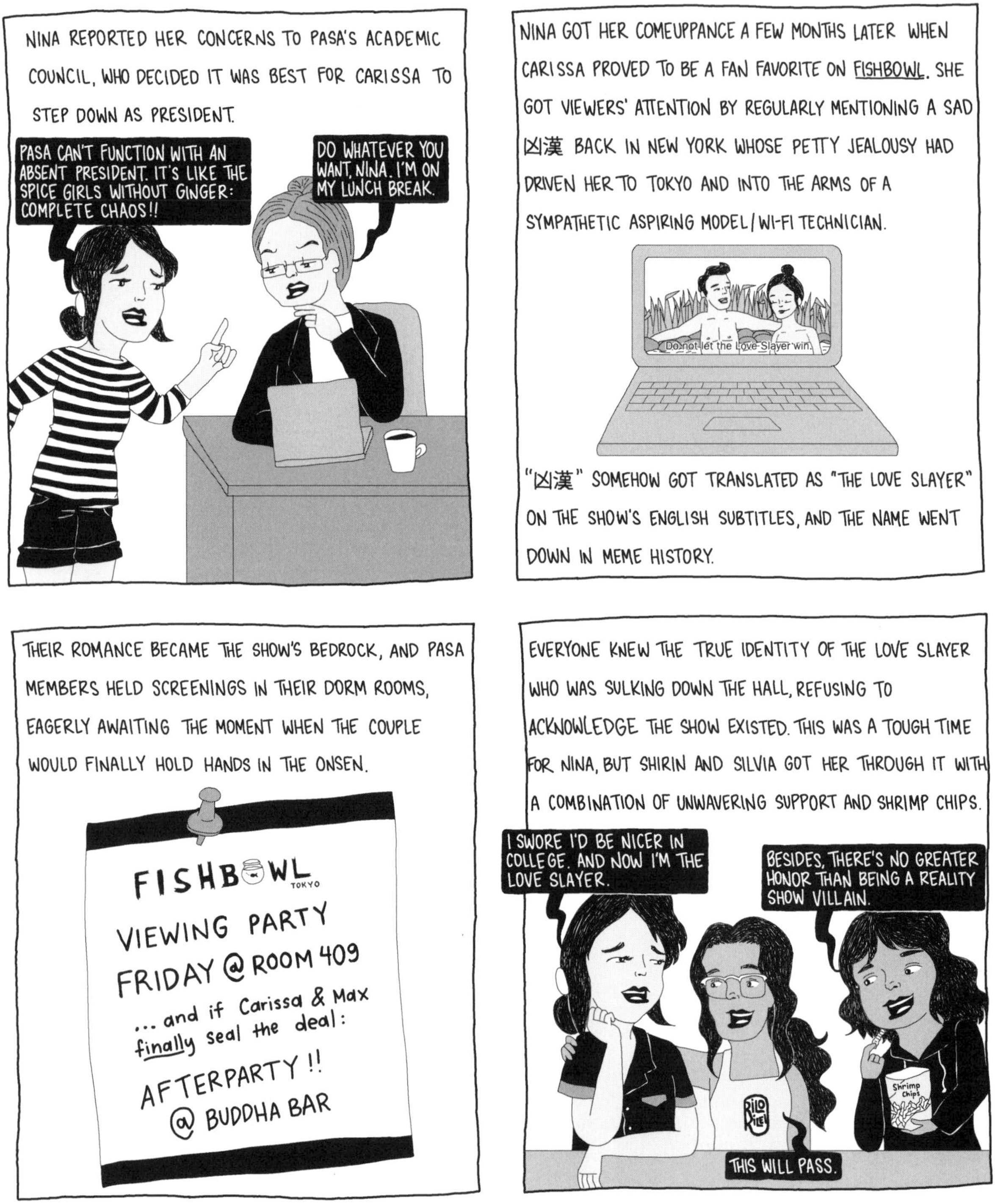
NINA REPORTED HER CONCERNS TO PASA'S ACADEMIC COUNCIL, WHO DECIDED IT WAS BEST FOR CARISSA TO STEP DOWN AS PRESIDENT.
PASA CAN'T FUNCTION WITH AN ABSENT PRESIDENT. IT'S LIKE THE SPICE GIRLS WITHOUT GINGER: COMPLETE CHAOS!!
DO WHATEVER YOU WANT, NINA. I'M ON MY LUNCH BREAK.
NINA GOT HER COMEUPPANCE A FEW MONTHS LATER WHEN CARISSA PROVED TO BE A FAN FAVORITE ON FISHBOWL. SHE GOT VIEWERS' ATTENTION BY REGULARLY MENTIONING A SAD 凶漢 BACK IN NEW YORK WHOSE PETTY JEALOUSY HAD DRIVEN HER TO TOKYO AND INTO THE ARMS OF A SYMPATHETIC ASPIRING MODEL/WI-FI TECHNICIAN.
Do not let the Love-Slayer win.
"凶漢" SOMEHOW GOT TRANSLATED AS "THE LOVE SLAYER" ON THE SHOW'S ENGLISH SUBTITLES, AND THE NAME WENT DOWN IN MEME HISTORY.
THEIR ROMANCE BECAME THE SHOW'S BEDROCK, AND PASA MEMBERS HELD SCREENINGS IN THEIR DORM ROOMS, EAGERLY AWAITING THE MOMENT WHEN THE COUPLE WOULD FINALLY HOLD HANDS IN THE ONSEN.
FISHBOWL TOKYO
VIEWING PARTY
FRIDAY @ ROOM 409
... and if Carissa & Max finally seal the deal:
AFTERPARTY !!
@ BUDDHA BAR
EVERYONE KNEW THE TRUE IDENTITY OF THE LOVE SLAYER WHO WAS SULKING DOWN THE HALL, REFUSING TO ACKNOWLEDGE THE SHOW EXISTED. THIS WAS A TOUGH TIME FOR NINA, BUT SHIRIN AND SILVIA GOT HER THROUGH IT WITH A COMBINATION OF UNWAVERING SUPPORT AND SHRIMP CHIPS.
I SWORE I'D BE NICER IN COLLEGE. AND NOW I'M THE LOVE SLAYER.
BESIDES, THERE'S NO GREATER HONOR THAN BEING A REALITY SHOW VILLAIN.
Shrimp Chips
THIS WILL PASS.

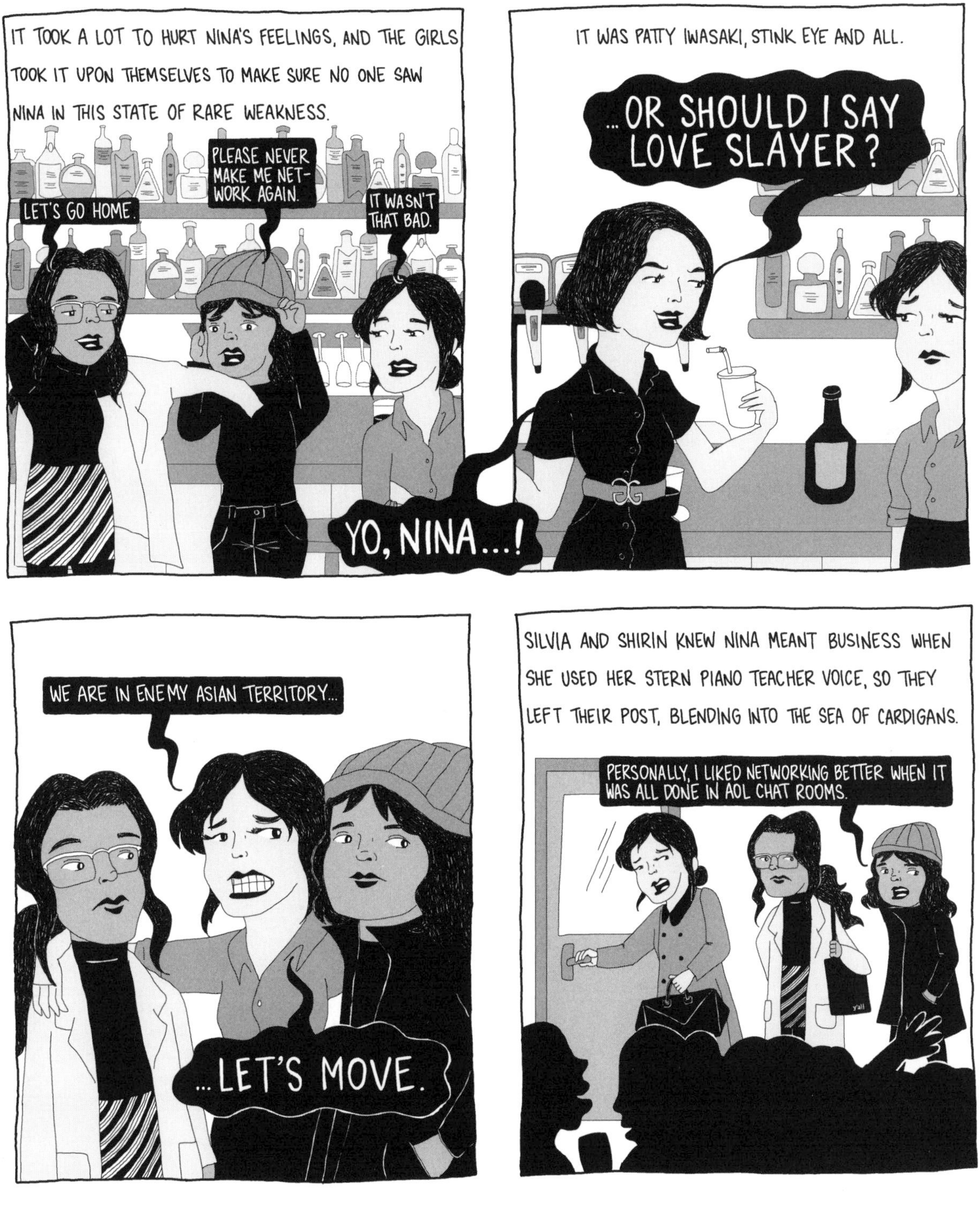

IT TOOK A LOT TO HURT NINA'S FEELINGS, AND THE GIRLS TOOK IT UPON THEMSELVES TO MAKE SURE NO ONE SAW NINA IN THIS STATE OF RARE WEAKNESS.
LET'S GO HOME.
PLEASE NEVER MAKE ME NET-WORK AGAIN.
IT WASN'T THAT BAD.
YO, NINA...!
IT WAS PATTY IWASAKI, STINK EYE AND ALL.
...OR SHOULD I SAY LOVE SLAYER?
WE ARE IN ENEMY ASIAN TERRITORY...
...LET'S MOVE.
SILVIA AND SHIRIN KNEW NINA MEANT BUSINESS WHEN SHE USED HER STERN PIANO TEACHER VOICE, SO THEY LEFT THEIR POST, BLENDING INTO THE SEA OF CARDIGANS.
PERSONALLY, I LIKED NETWORKING BETTER WHEN IT WAS ALL DONE IN AOL CHAT ROOMS.

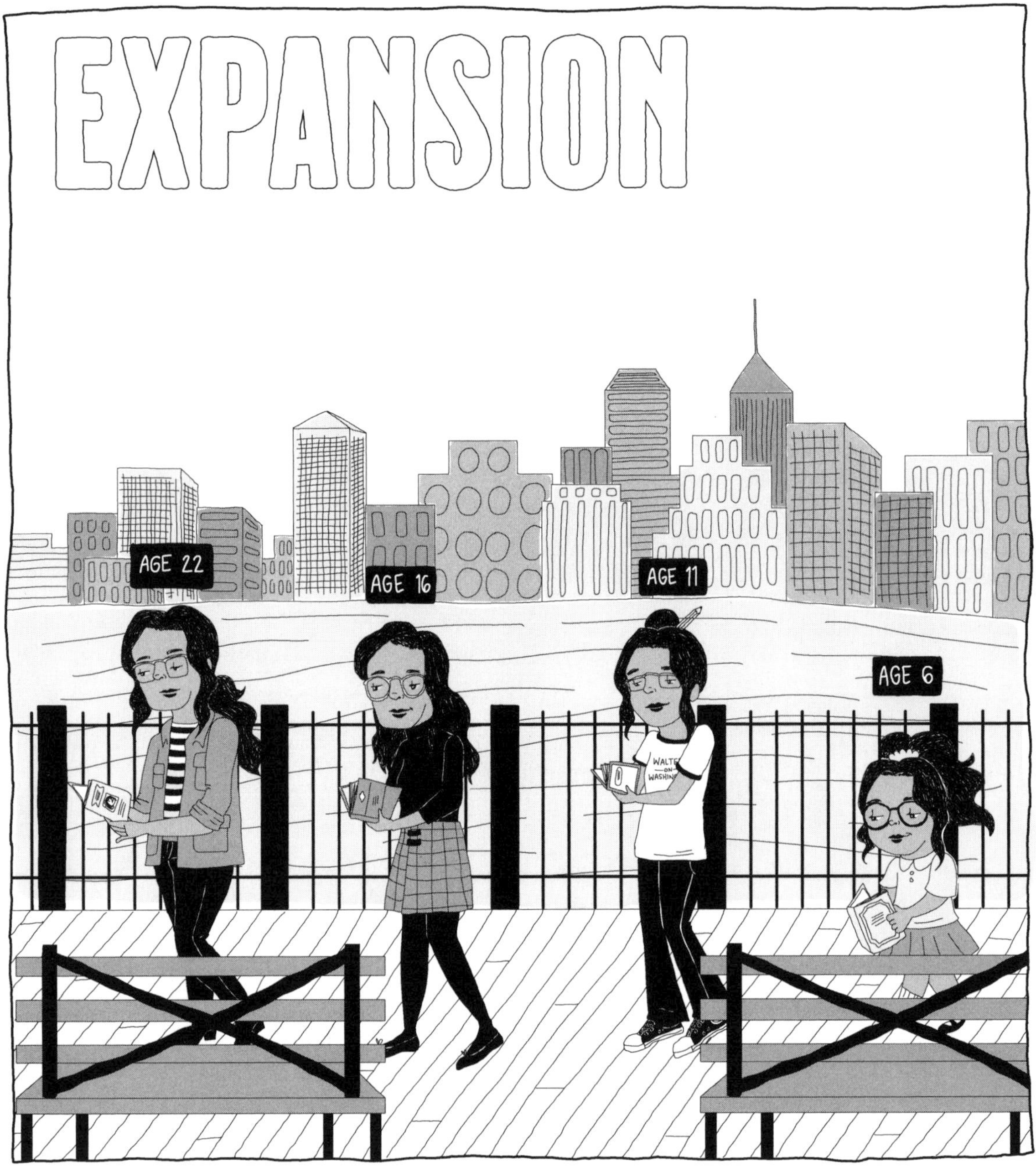
EXPANSION
AGE 22
AGE 16
AGE 11
AGE 6

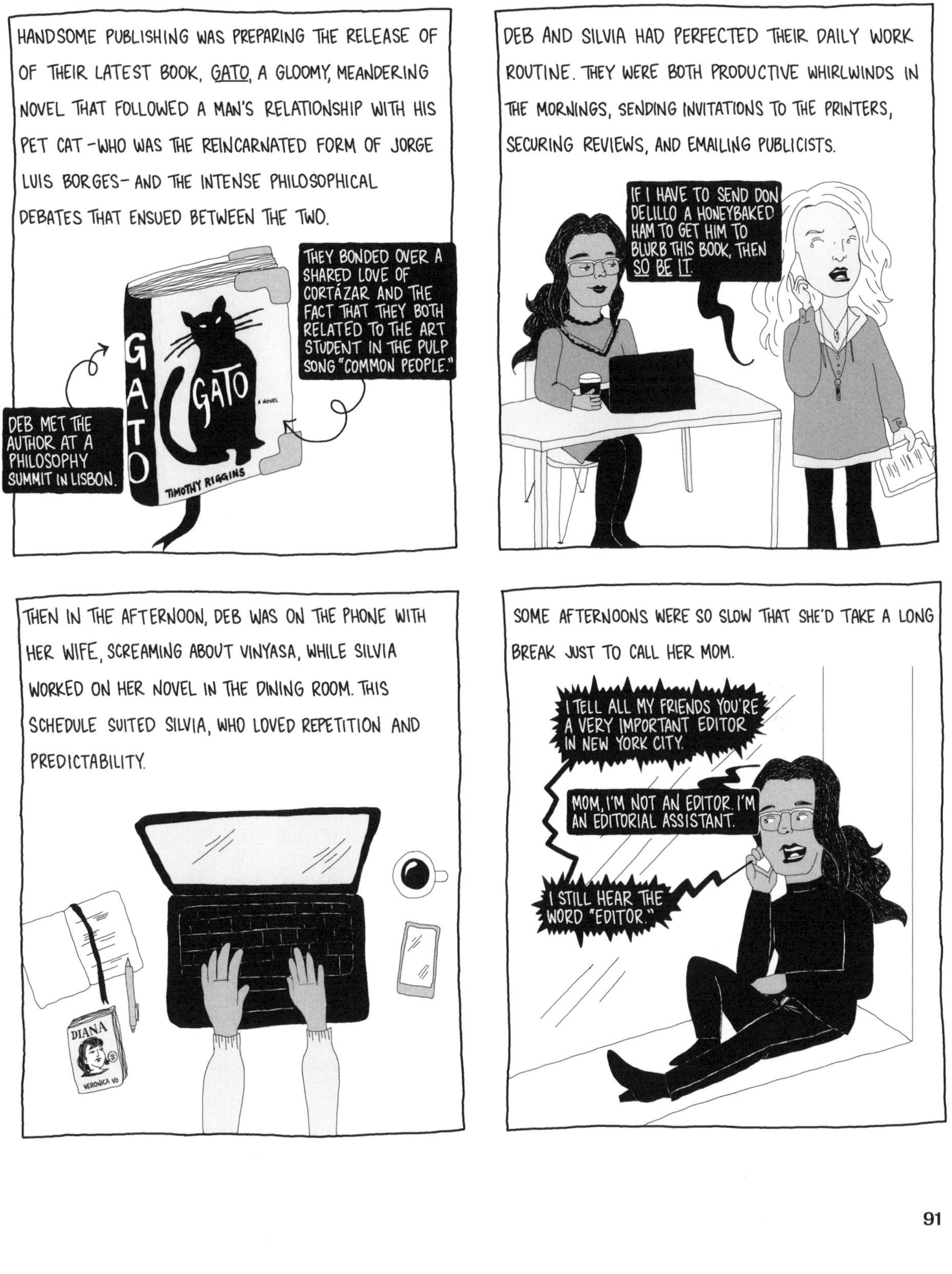
HANDSOME PUBLISHING WAS PREPARING THE RELEASE OF OF THEIR LATEST BOOK, GATO, A GLOOMY, MEANDERING NOVEL THAT FOLLOWED A MAN'S RELATIONSHIP WITH HIS PET CAT—WHO WAS THE REINCARNATED FORM OF JORGE LUIS BORGES—AND THE INTENSE PHILOSOPHICAL DEBATES THAT ENSUED BETWEEN THE TWO.
THEY BONDED OVER A SHARED LOVE OF CORTÁZAR AND THE FACT THAT THEY BOTH RELATED TO THE ART STUDENT IN THE PULP SONG "COMMON PEOPLE."
GATO
GATO
A NOVEL
TIMOTHY RIGGINS
DEB MET THE AUTHOR AT A PHILOSOPHY SUMMIT IN LISBON.
DEB AND SILVIA HAD PERFECTED THEIR DAILY WORK ROUTINE. THEY WERE BOTH PRODUCTIVE WHIRLWINDS IN THE MORNINGS, SENDING INVITATIONS TO THE PRINTERS, SECURING REVIEWS, AND EMAILING PUBLICISTS.
IF I HAVE TO SEND DON DELILLO A HONEYBAKED HAM TO GET HIM TO BLURB THIS BOOK, THEN SO BE IT.
THEN IN THE AFTERNOON, DEB WAS ON THE PHONE WITH HER WIFE, SCREAMING ABOUT VINYASA, WHILE SILVIA WORKED ON HER NOVEL IN THE DINING ROOM. THIS SCHEDULE SUITED SILVIA, WHO LOVED REPETITION AND PREDICTABILITY.
DIANA
VERONICA VO
SOME AFTERNOONS WERE SO SLOW THAT SHE'D TAKE A LONG BREAK JUST TO CALL HER MOM.
I TELL ALL MY FRIENDS YOU'RE A VERY IMPORTANT EDITOR IN NEW YORK CITY.
MOM, I'M NOT AN EDITOR. I'M AN EDITORIAL ASSISTANT.
I STILL HEAR THE WORD "EDITOR."

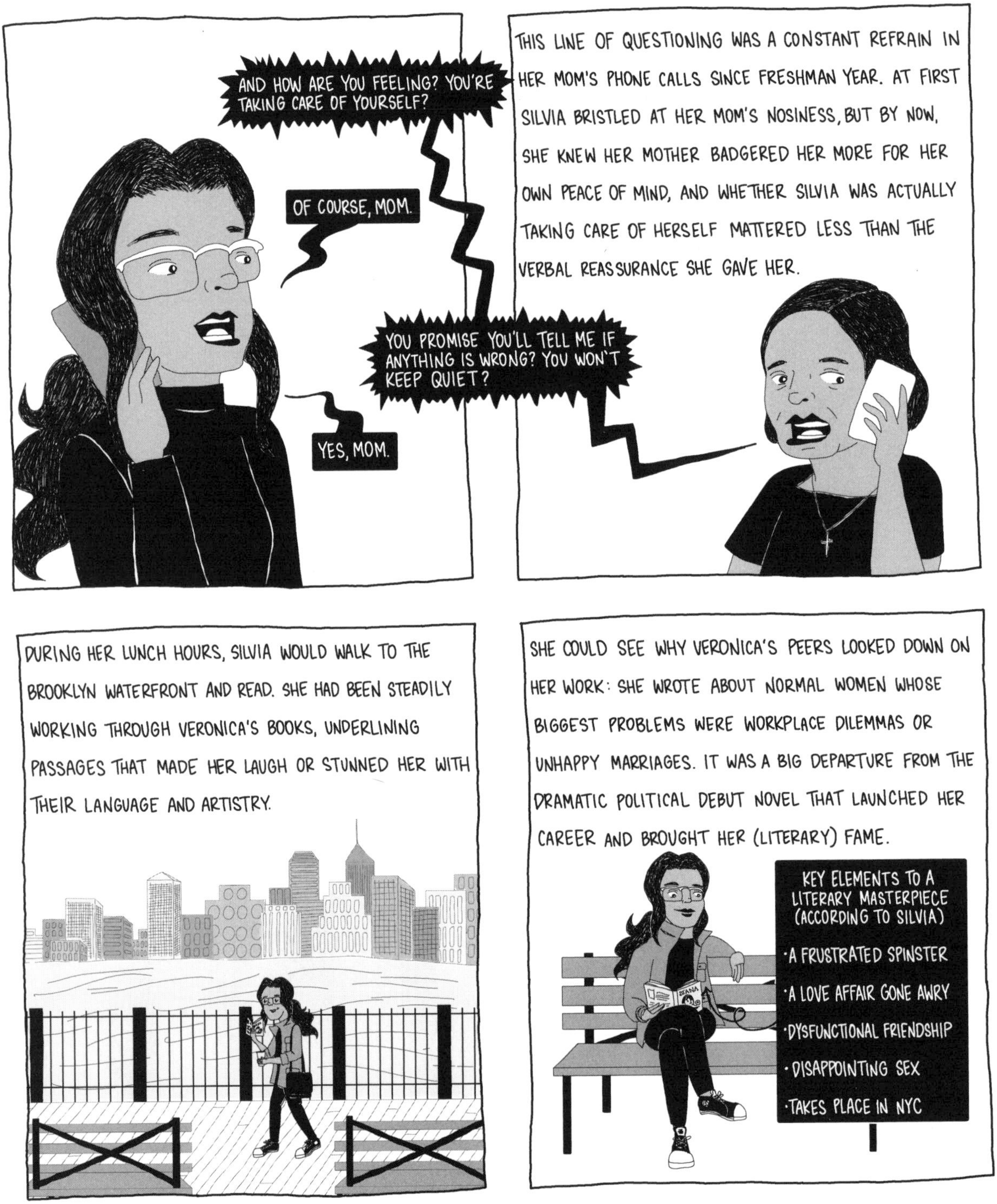
AND HOW ARE YOU FEELING? YOU'RE TAKING CARE OF YOURSELF?
OF COURSE, MOM.
YOU PROMISE YOU'LL TELL ME IF ANYTHING IS WRONG? YOU WON'T KEEP QUIET?
YES, MOM.
THIS LINE OF QUESTIONING WAS A CONSTANT REFRAIN IN HER MOM'S PHONE CALLS SINCE FRESHMAN YEAR. AT FIRST SILVIA BRISTLED AT HER MOM'S NOSINESS, BUT BY NOW, SHE KNEW HER MOTHER BADGERED HER MORE FOR HER OWN PEACE OF MIND, AND WHETHER SILVIA WAS ACTUALLY TAKING CARE OF HERSELF MATTERED LESS THAN THE VERBAL REASSURANCE SHE GAVE HER.
DURING HER LUNCH HOURS, SILVIA WOULD WALK TO THE BROOKLYN WATERFRONT AND READ. SHE HAD BEEN STEADILY WORKING THROUGH VERONICA'S BOOKS, UNDERLINING PASSAGES THAT MADE HER LAUGH OR STUNNED HER WITH THEIR LANGUAGE AND ARTISTRY.
SHE COULD SEE WHY VERONICA'S PEERS LOOKED DOWN ON HER WORK: SHE WROTE ABOUT NORMAL WOMEN WHOSE BIGGEST PROBLEMS WERE WORKPLACE DILEMMAS OR UNHAPPY MARRIAGES. IT WAS A BIG DEPARTURE FROM THE DRAMATIC POLITICAL DEBUT NOVEL THAT LAUNCHED HER CAREER AND BROUGHT HER (LITERARY) FAME.
KEY ELEMENTS TO A LITERARY MASTERPIECE (ACCORDING TO SILVIA)
·A FRUSTRATED SPINSTER
·A LOVE AFFAIR GONE AWRY
·DYSFUNCTIONAL FRIENDSHIP
·DISAPPOINTING SEX
·TAKES PLACE IN NYC

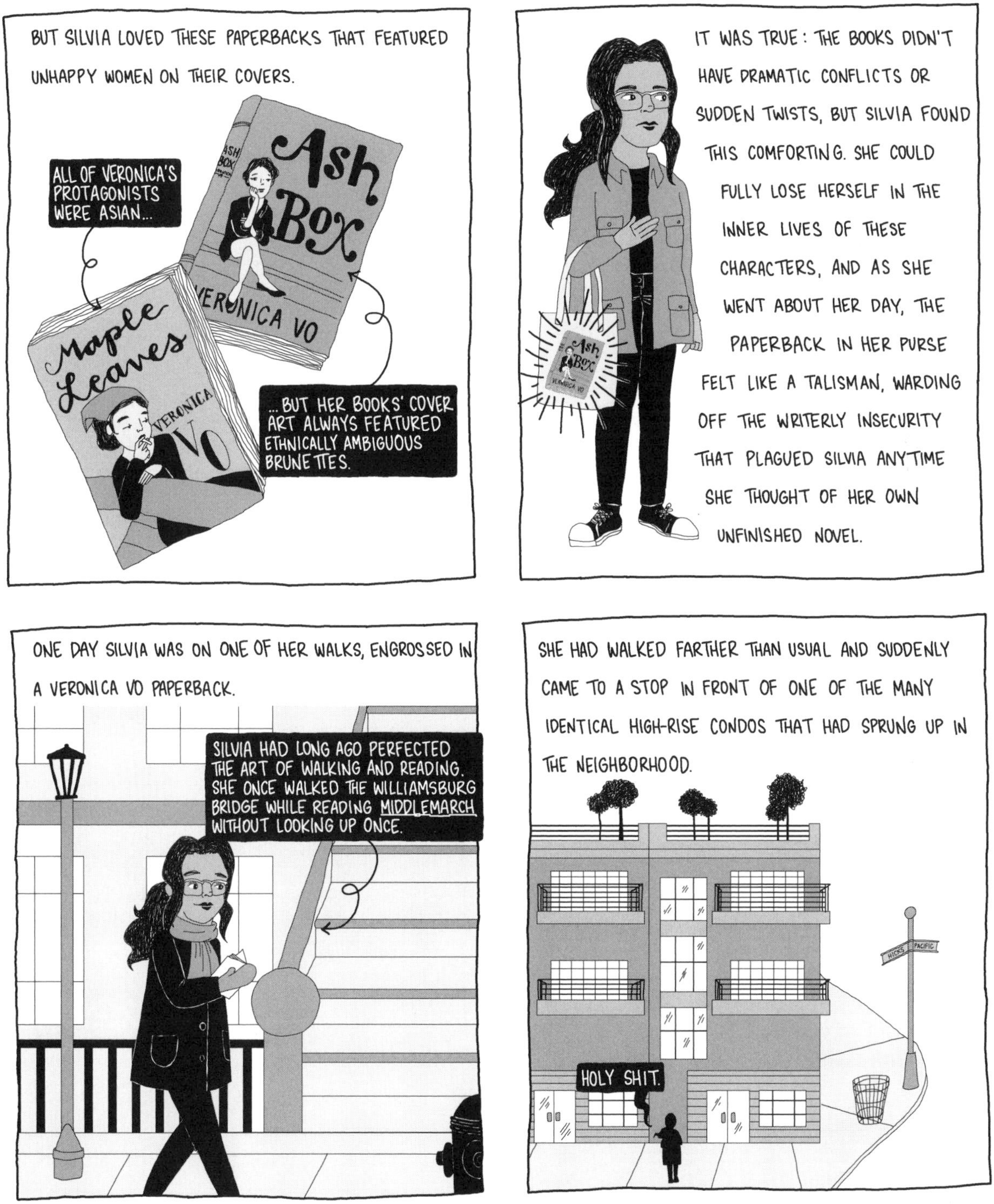
BUT SILVIA LOVED THESE PAPERBACKS THAT FEATURED UNHAPPY WOMEN ON THEIR COVERS.
ALL OF VERONICA'S PROTAGONISTS WERE ASIAN...
Ash Box
VERONICA VO
Maple Leaves
VERONICA VO
...BUT HER BOOKS' COVER ART ALWAYS FEATURED ETHNICALLY AMBIGUOUS BRUNETTES.
IT WAS TRUE: THE BOOKS DIDN'T HAVE DRAMATIC CONFLICTS OR SUDDEN TWISTS, BUT SILVIA FOUND THIS COMFORTING. SHE COULD FULLY LOSE HERSELF IN THE INNER LIVES OF THESE CHARACTERS, AND AS SHE WENT ABOUT HER DAY, THE PAPERBACK IN HER PURSE FELT LIKE A TALISMAN, WARDING OFF THE WRITERLY INSECURITY THAT PLAGUED SILVIA ANYTIME SHE THOUGHT OF HER OWN UNFINISHED NOVEL.
ONE DAY SILVIA WAS ON ONE OF HER WALKS, ENGROSSED IN A VERONICA VO PAPERBACK.
SILVIA HAD LONG AGO PERFECTED THE ART OF WALKING AND READING. SHE ONCE WALKED THE WILLIAMSBURG BRIDGE WHILE READING MIDDLEMARCH WITHOUT LOOKING UP ONCE.
SHE HAD WALKED FARTHER THAN USUAL AND SUDDENLY CAME TO A STOP IN FRONT OF ONE OF THE MANY IDENTICAL HIGH-RISE CONDOS THAT HAD SPRUNG UP IN THE NEIGHBORHOOD.
HICKS
PACIFIC
HOLY SHIT.

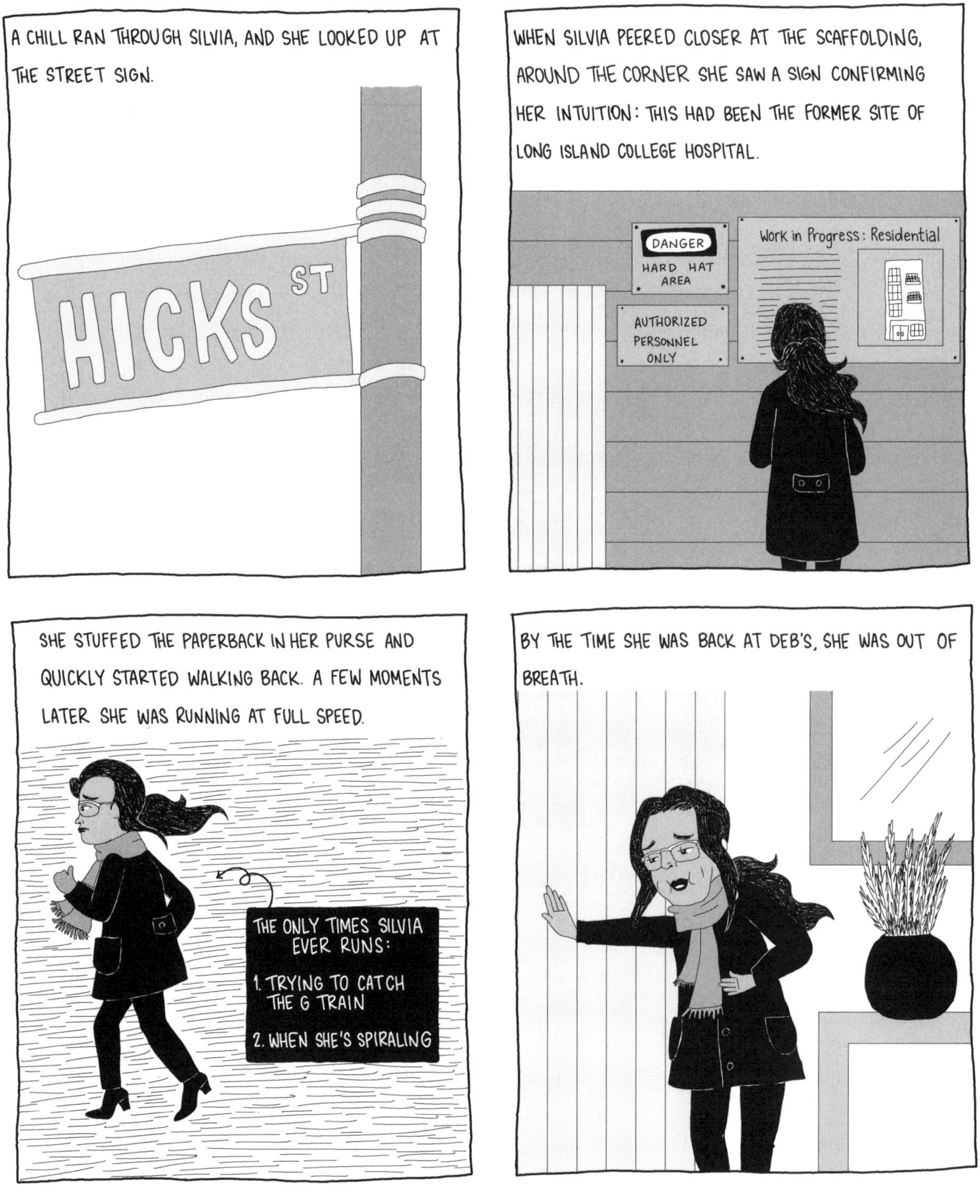
A CHILL RAN THROUGH SILVIA, AND SHE LOOKED UP AT THE STREET SIGN.
HICKS ST
WHEN SILVIA PEERED CLOSER AT THE SCAFFOLDING, AROUND THE CORNER SHE SAW A SIGN CONFIRMING HER INTUITION: THIS HAD BEEN THE FORMER SITE OF LONG ISLAND COLLEGE HOSPITAL.
DANGER
HARD HAT AREA
AUTHORIZED PERSONNEL ONLY
Work in Progress: Residential
SHE STUFFED THE PAPERBACK IN HER PURSE AND QUICKLY STARTED WALKING BACK. A FEW MOMENTS LATER SHE WAS RUNNING AT FULL SPEED.
THE ONLY TIMES SILVIA EVER RUNS:
1. TRYING TO CATCH THE G TRAIN
2. WHEN SHE'S SPIRALING
BY THE TIME SHE WAS BACK AT DEB'S, SHE WAS OUT OF BREATH.

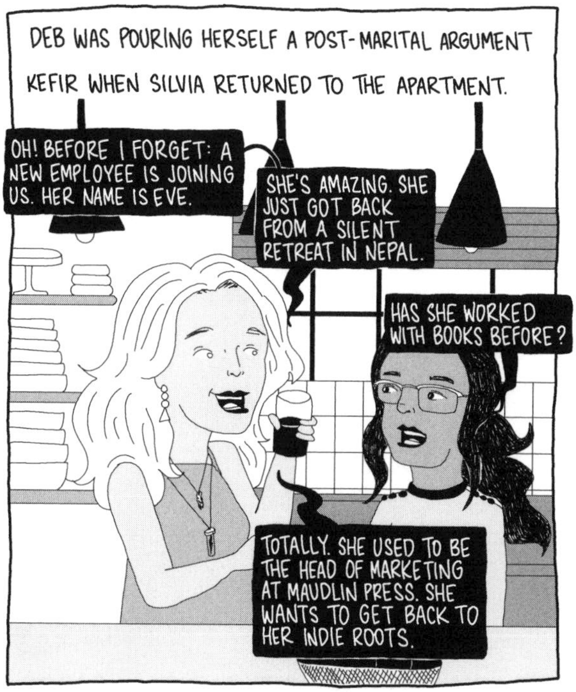
DEB WAS POURING HERSELF A POST-MARITAL ARGUMENT KEFIR WHEN SILVIA RETURNED TO THE APARTMENT.
OH! BEFORE I FORGET: A NEW EMPLOYEE IS JOINING US. HER NAME IS EVE.
SHE'S AMAZING. SHE JUST GOT BACK FROM A SILENT RETREAT IN NEPAL.
HAS SHE WORKED WITH BOOKS BEFORE?
TOTALLY. SHE USED TO BE THE HEAD OF MARKETING AT MAUDLIN PRESS. SHE WANTS TO GET BACK TO HER INDIE ROOTS.

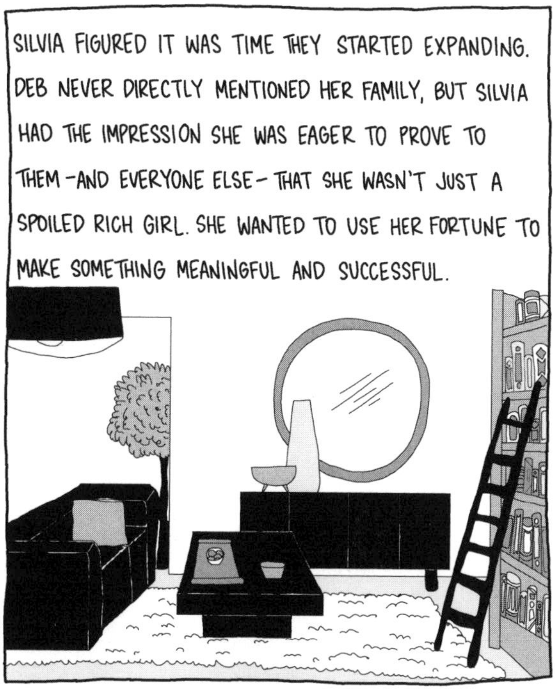
SILVIA FIGURED IT WAS TIME THEY STARTED EXPANDING. DEB NEVER DIRECTLY MENTIONED HER FAMILY, BUT SILVIA HAD THE IMPRESSION SHE WAS EAGER TO PROVE TO THEM—AND EVERYONE ELSE—THAT SHE WASN'T JUST A SPOILED RICH GIRL. SHE WANTED TO USE HER FORTUNE TO MAKE SOMETHING MEANINGFUL AND SUCCESSFUL.

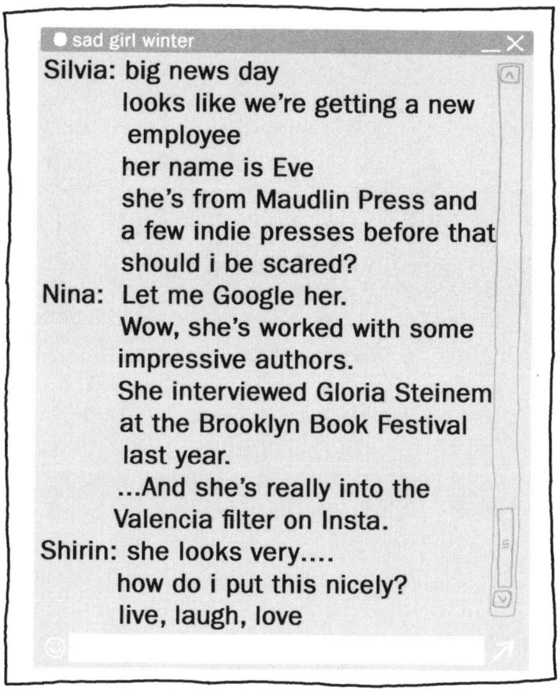
sad girl winter
Silvia: big news day
looks like we're getting a new employee
her name is Eve
she's from Maudlin Press and a few indie presses before that
should i be scared?
Nina: Let me Google her.
Wow, she's worked with some impressive authors.
She interviewed Gloria Steinem at the Brooklyn Book Festival last year.
...And she's really into the Valencia filter on Insta.
Shirin: she looks very....
how do i put this nicely?
live, laugh, love

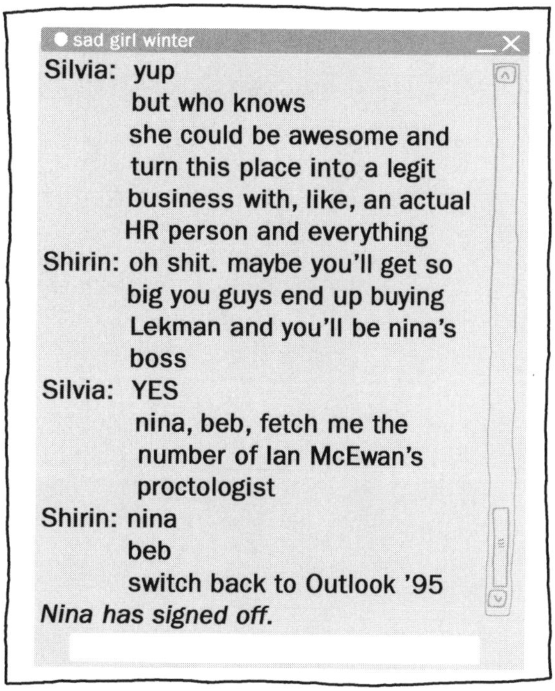
sad girl winter
Silvia: yup
but who knows
she could be awesome and turn this place into a legit business with, like, an actual HR person and everything
Shirin: oh shit. maybe you'll get so big you guys end up buying Lekman and you'll be nina's boss
Silvia: YES
nina, beb, fetch me the number of Ian McEwan's proctologist
Shirin: nina
beb
switch back to Outlook '95
Nina has signed off.

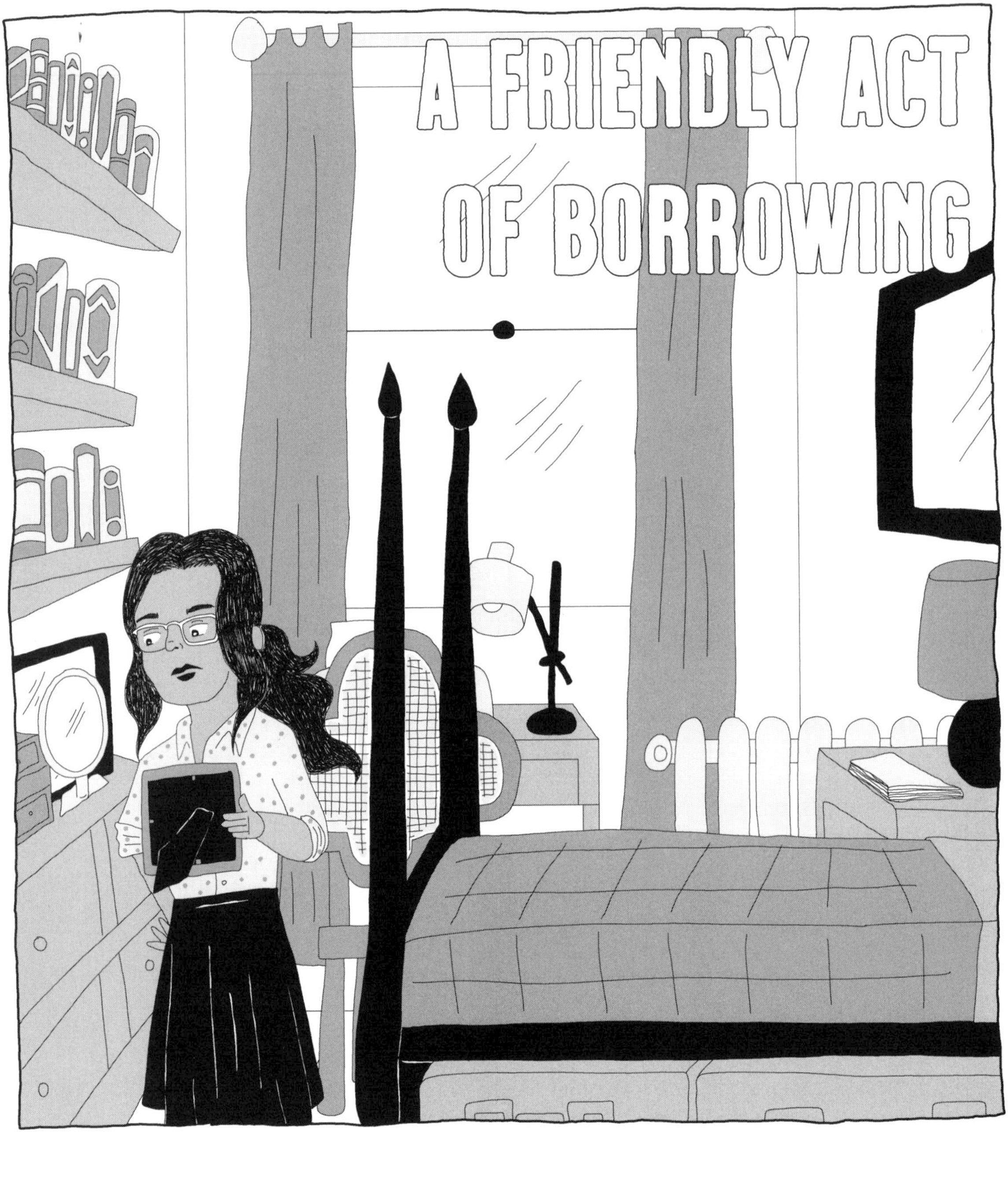
A FRIENDLY ACT
OF BORROWING

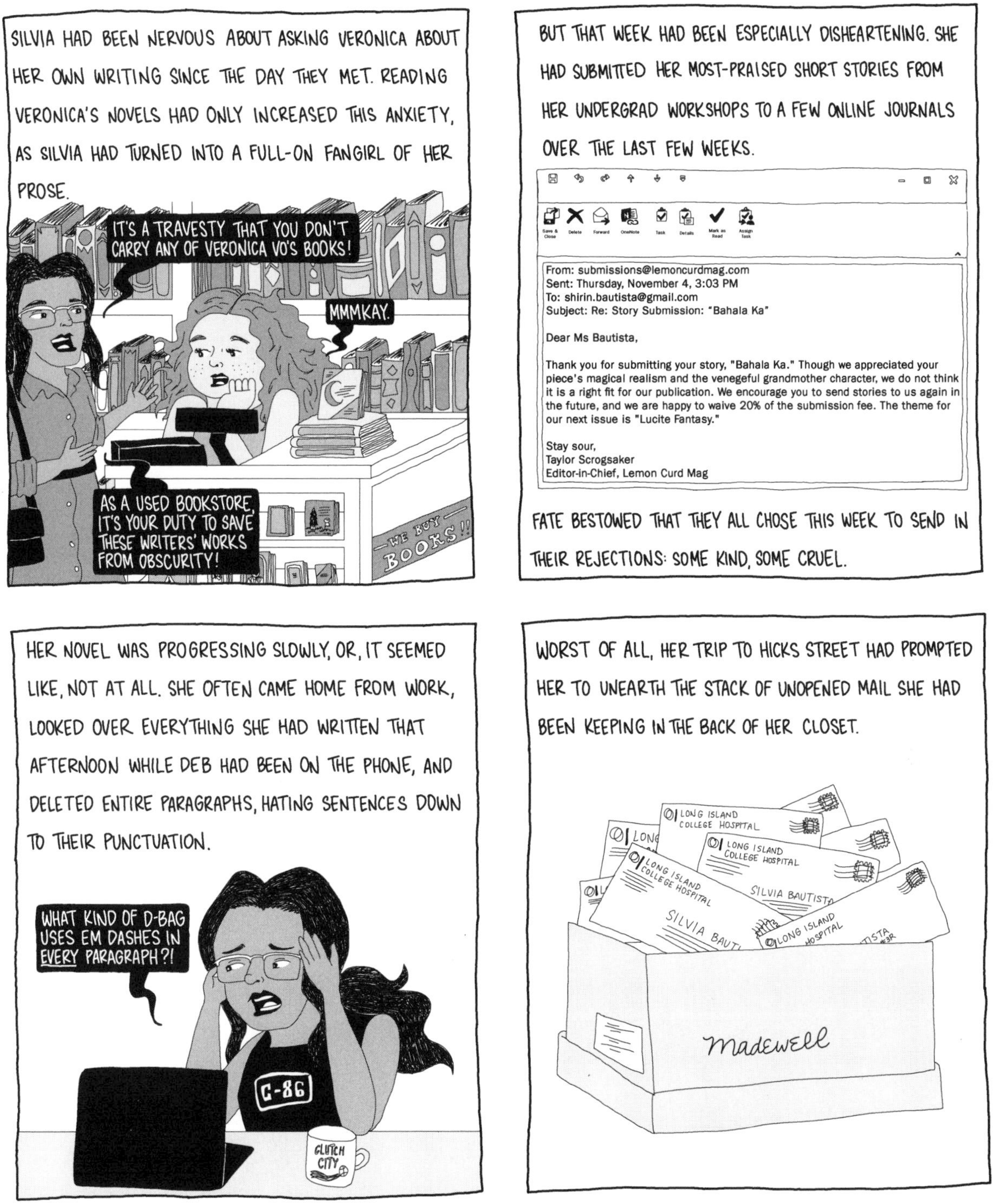
SILVIA HAD BEEN NERVOUS ABOUT ASKING VERONICA ABOUT HER OWN WRITING SINCE THE DAY THEY MET. READING VERONICA'S NOVELS HAD ONLY INCREASED THIS ANXIETY, AS SILVIA HAD TURNED INTO A FULL-ON FANGIRL OF HER PROSE.
IT'S A TRAVESTY THAT YOU DON'T CARRY ANY OF VERONICA VO'S BOOKS!
MMMKAY.
AS A USED BOOKSTORE, IT'S YOUR DUTY TO SAVE THESE WRITERS' WORKS FROM OBSCURITY!
WE BUY BOOKS!!
BUT THAT WEEK HAD BEEN ESPECIALLY DISHEARTENING. SHE HAD SUBMITTED HER MOST-PRAISED SHORT STORIES FROM HER UNDERGRAD WORKSHOPS TO A FEW ONLINE JOURNALS OVER THE LAST FEW WEEKS.
Save & Close
Delete
Forward
OneNote
Task
Details
Mark as Read
Assign Task
From: submissions@lemoncurdmag.com
Sent: Thursday, November 4, 3:03 PM
To: shirin.bautista@gmail.com
Subject: Re: Story Submission: "Bahala Ka"
Dear Ms Bautista,
Thank you for submitting your story, "Bahala Ka." Though we appreciated your piece's magical realism and the venegeful grandmother character, we do not think it is a right fit for our publication. We encourage you to send stories to us again in the future, and we are happy to waive 20% of the submission fee. The theme for our next issue is "Lucite Fantasy."
Stay sour,
Taylor Scrogsaker
Editor-in-Chief, Lemon Curd Mag
FATE BESTOWED THAT THEY ALL CHOSE THIS WEEK TO SEND IN THEIR REJECTIONS: SOME KIND, SOME CRUEL.
HER NOVEL WAS PROGRESSING SLOWLY, OR, IT SEEMED LIKE, NOT AT ALL. SHE OFTEN CAME HOME FROM WORK, LOOKED OVER EVERYTHING SHE HAD WRITTEN THAT AFTERNOON WHILE DEB HAD BEEN ON THE PHONE, AND DELETED ENTIRE PARAGRAPHS, HATING SENTENCES DOWN TO THEIR PUNCTUATION.
WHAT KIND OF D-BAG USES EM DASHES IN EVERY PARAGRAPH?!
C-86
CLUTCH CITY
WORST OF ALL, HER TRIP TO HICKS STREET HAD PROMPTED HER TO UNEARTH THE STACK OF UNOPENED MAIL SHE HAD BEEN KEEPING IN THE BACK OF HER CLOSET.
LONG ISLAND COLLEGE HOSPITAL
LONG ISLAND COLLEGE HOSPITAL
LONG ISLAND COLLEGE HOSPITAL
Madewell

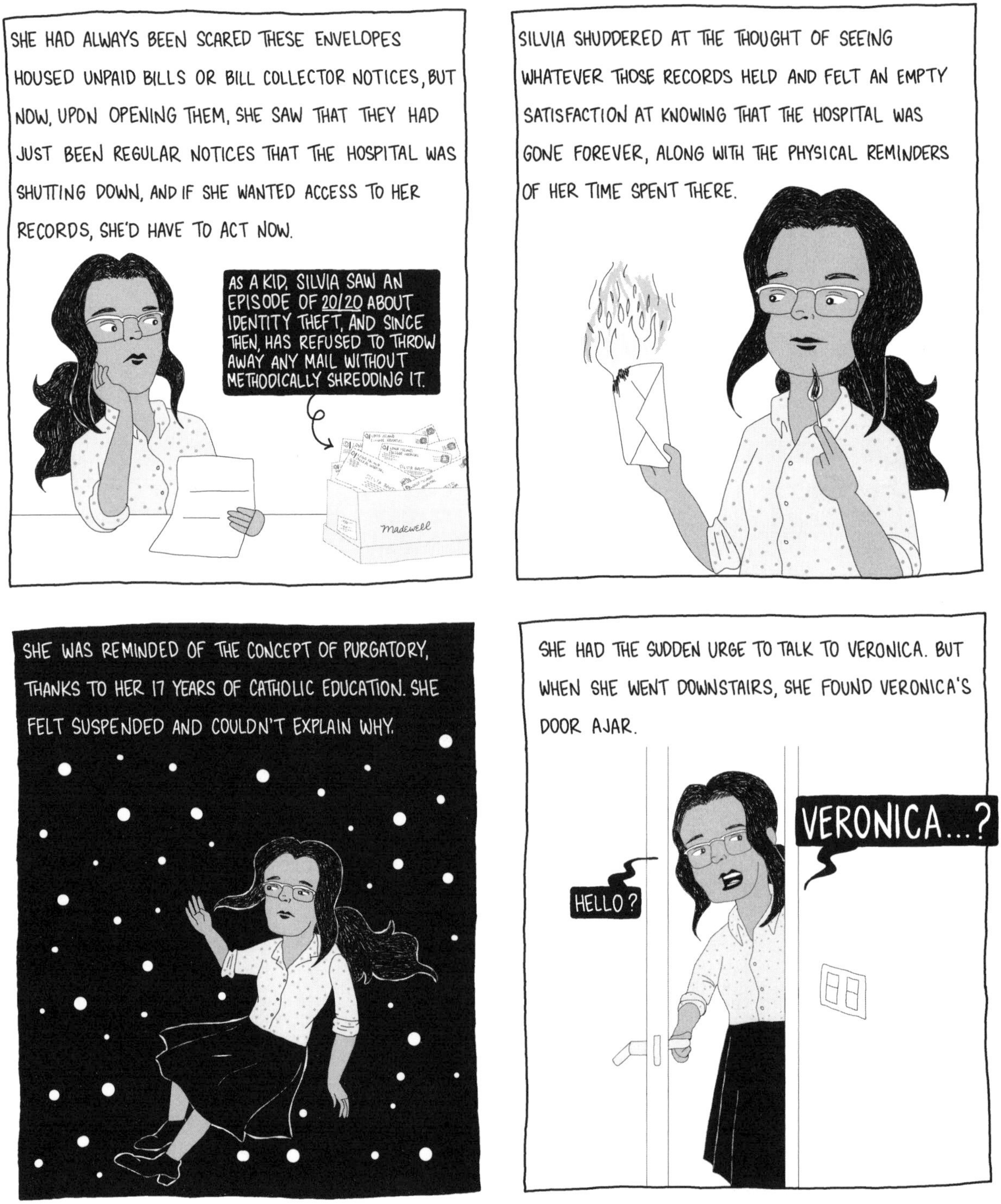
SHE HAD ALWAYS BEEN SCARED THESE ENVELOPES HOUSED UNPAID BILLS OR BILL COLLECTOR NOTICES, BUT NOW, UPON OPENING THEM, SHE SAW THAT THEY HAD JUST BEEN REGULAR NOTICES THAT THE HOSPITAL WAS SHUTTING DOWN, AND IF SHE WANTED ACCESS TO HER RECORDS, SHE'D HAVE TO ACT NOW.
AS A KID, SILVIA SAW AN EPISODE OF 20/20 ABOUT IDENTITY THEFT, AND SINCE THEN, HAS REFUSED TO THROW AWAY ANY MAIL WITHOUT METHODICALLY SHREDDING IT.
madewell
SILVIA SHUDDERED AT THE THOUGHT OF SEEING WHATEVER THOSE RECORDS HELD AND FELT AN EMPTY SATISFACTION AT KNOWING THAT THE HOSPITAL WAS GONE FOREVER, ALONG WITH THE PHYSICAL REMINDERS OF HER TIME SPENT THERE.
SHE WAS REMINDED OF THE CONCEPT OF PURGATORY, THANKS TO HER 17 YEARS OF CATHOLIC EDUCATION. SHE FELT SUSPENDED AND COULDN'T EXPLAIN WHY.
SHE HAD THE SUDDEN URGE TO TALK TO VERONICA. BUT WHEN SHE WENT DOWNSTAIRS, SHE FOUND VERONICA'S DOOR AJAR.
HELLO?
VERONICA...?

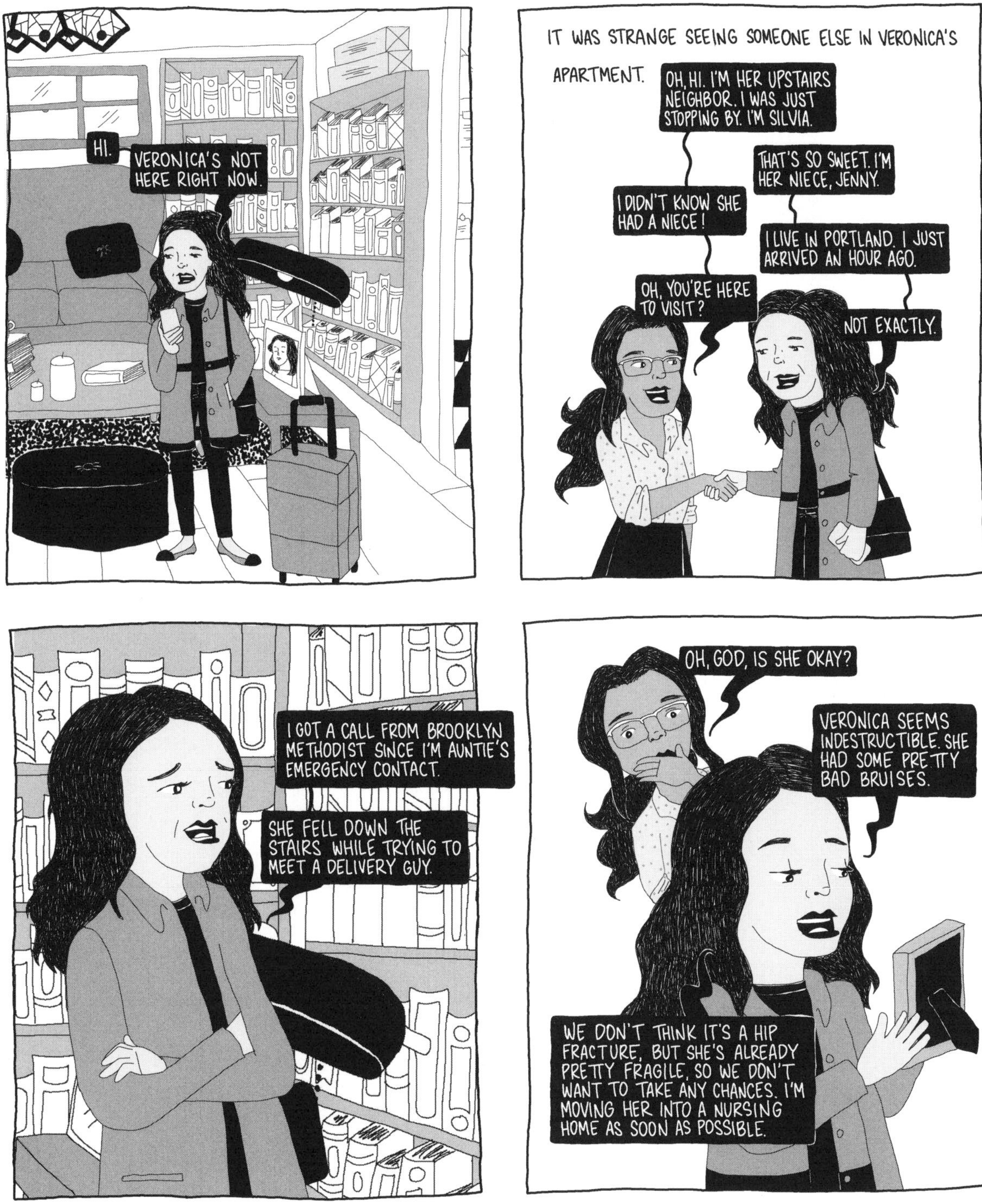
HI.
VERONICA'S NOT HERE RIGHT NOW.
IT WAS STRANGE SEEING SOMEONE ELSE IN VERONICA'S APARTMENT.
OH, HI. I'M HER UPSTAIRS NEIGHBOR. I WAS JUST STOPPING BY. I'M SILVIA.
THAT'S SO SWEET. I'M HER NIECE, JENNY.
I DIDN'T KNOW SHE HAD A NIECE!
I LIVE IN PORTLAND. I JUST ARRIVED AN HOUR AGO.
OH, YOU'RE HERE TO VISIT?
NOT EXACTLY.
I GOT A CALL FROM BROOKLYN METHODIST SINCE I'M AUNTIE'S EMERGENCY CONTACT.
SHE FELL DOWN THE STAIRS WHILE TRYING TO MEET A DELIVERY GUY.
OH, GOD, IS SHE OKAY?
VERONICA SEEMS INDESTRUCTIBLE. SHE HAD SOME PRETTY BAD BRUISES.
WE DON'T THINK IT'S A HIP FRACTURE, BUT SHE'S ALREADY PRETTY FRAGILE, SO WE DON'T WANT TO TAKE ANY CHANCES. I'M MOVING HER INTO A NURSING HOME AS SOON AS POSSIBLE.

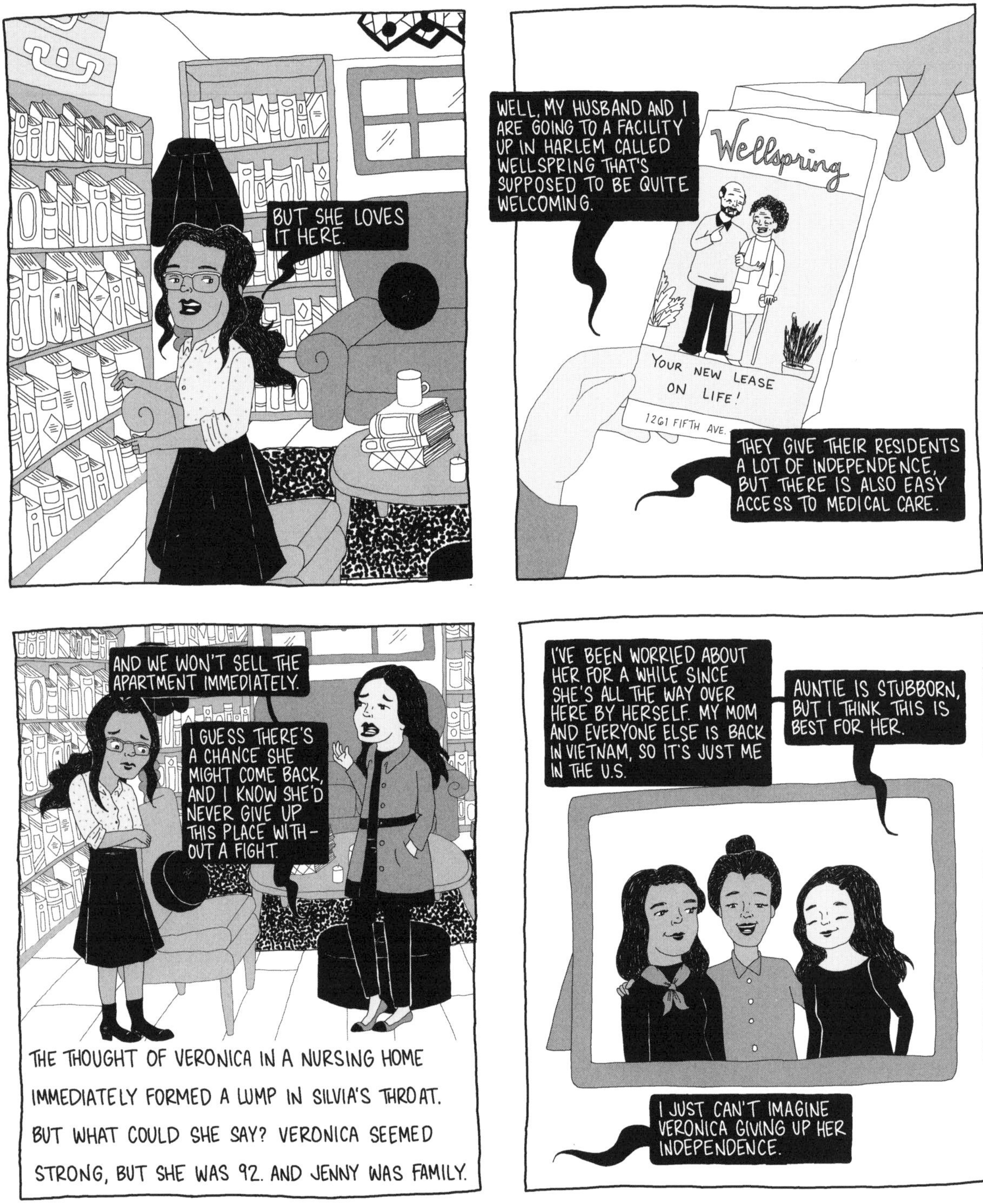
BUT SHE LOVES IT HERE.
WELL, MY HUSBAND AND I ARE GOING TO A FACILITY UP IN HARLEM CALLED WELLSPRING THAT'S SUPPOSED TO BE QUITE WELCOMING.
Wellspring
YOUR NEW LEASE ON LIFE!
1261 FIFTH AVE.
THEY GIVE THEIR RESIDENTS A LOT OF INDEPENDENCE, BUT THERE IS ALSO EASY ACCESS TO MEDICAL CARE.
AND WE WON'T SELL THE APARTMENT IMMEDIATELY.
I GUESS THERE'S A CHANCE SHE MIGHT COME BACK, AND I KNOW SHE'D NEVER GIVE UP THIS PLACE WITH-OUT A FIGHT.
THE THOUGHT OF VERONICA IN A NURSING HOME IMMEDIATELY FORMED A LUMP IN SILVIA'S THROAT. BUT WHAT COULD SHE SAY? VERONICA SEEMED STRONG, BUT SHE WAS 92. AND JENNY WAS FAMILY.
I'VE BEEN WORRIED ABOUT HER FOR A WHILE SINCE SHE'S ALL THE WAY OVER HERE BY HERSELF. MY MOM AND EVERYONE ELSE IS BACK IN VIETNAM, SO IT'S JUST ME IN THE U.S.
AUNTIE IS STUBBORN, BUT I THINK THIS IS BEST FOR HER.
I JUST CAN'T IMAGINE VERONICA GIVING UP HER INDEPENDENCE.

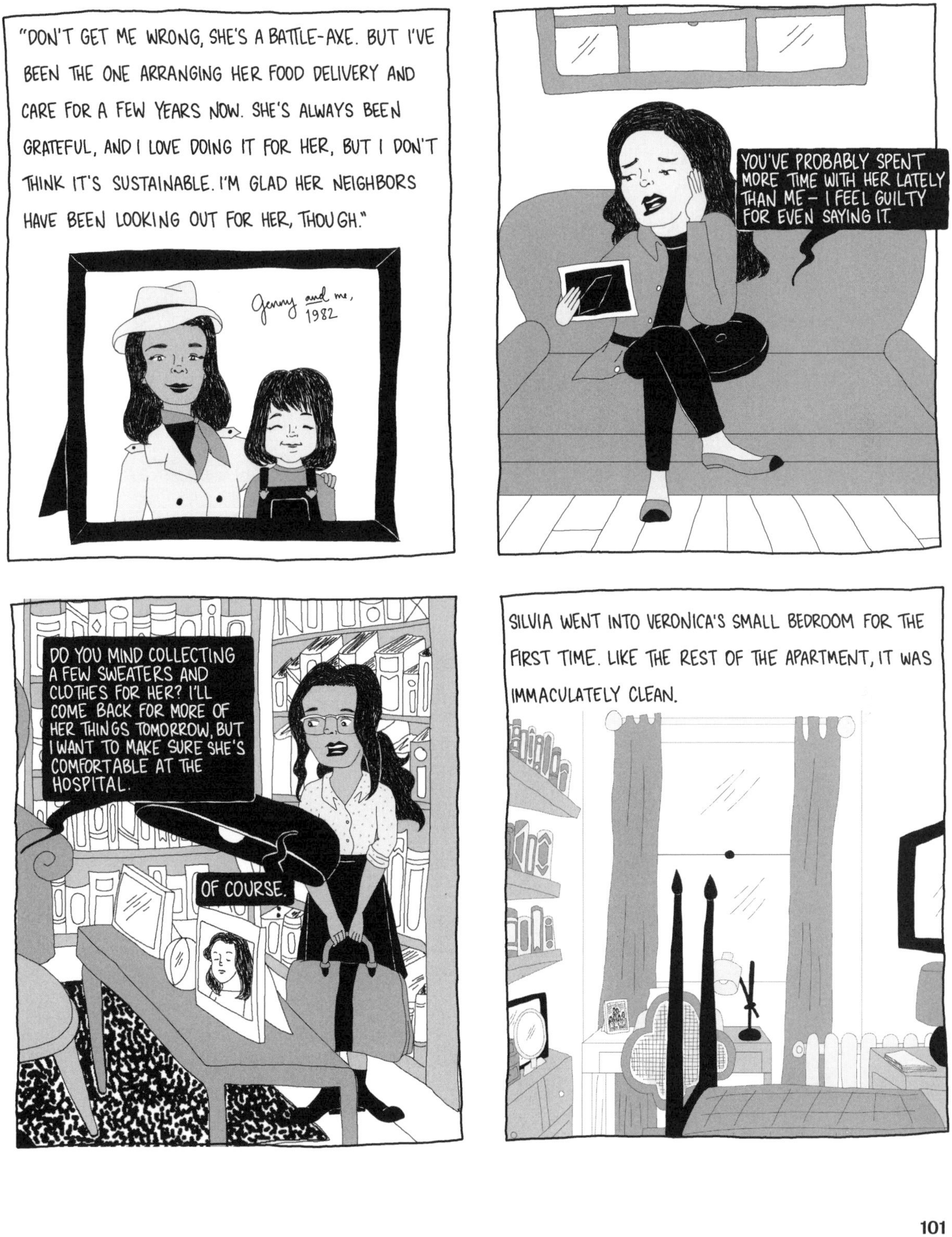
"DON'T GET ME WRONG, SHE'S A BATTLE-AXE. BUT I'VE BEEN THE ONE ARRANGING HER FOOD DELIVERY AND CARE FOR A FEW YEARS NOW. SHE'S ALWAYS BEEN GRATEFUL, AND I LOVE DOING IT FOR HER, BUT I DON'T THINK IT'S SUSTAINABLE. I'M GLAD HER NEIGHBORS HAVE BEEN LOOKING OUT FOR HER, THOUGH."
Genny and me, 1982
YOU'VE PROBABLY SPENT MORE TIME WITH HER LATELY THAN ME – I FEEL GUILTY FOR EVEN SAYING IT.
DO YOU MIND COLLECTING A FEW SWEATERS AND CLOTHES FOR HER? I'LL COME BACK FOR MORE OF HER THINGS TOMORROW, BUT I WANT TO MAKE SURE SHE'S COMFORTABLE AT THE HOSPITAL.
OF COURSE.
SILVIA WENT INTO VERONICA'S SMALL BEDROOM FOR THE FIRST TIME. LIKE THE REST OF THE APARTMENT, IT WAS IMMACULATELY CLEAN.

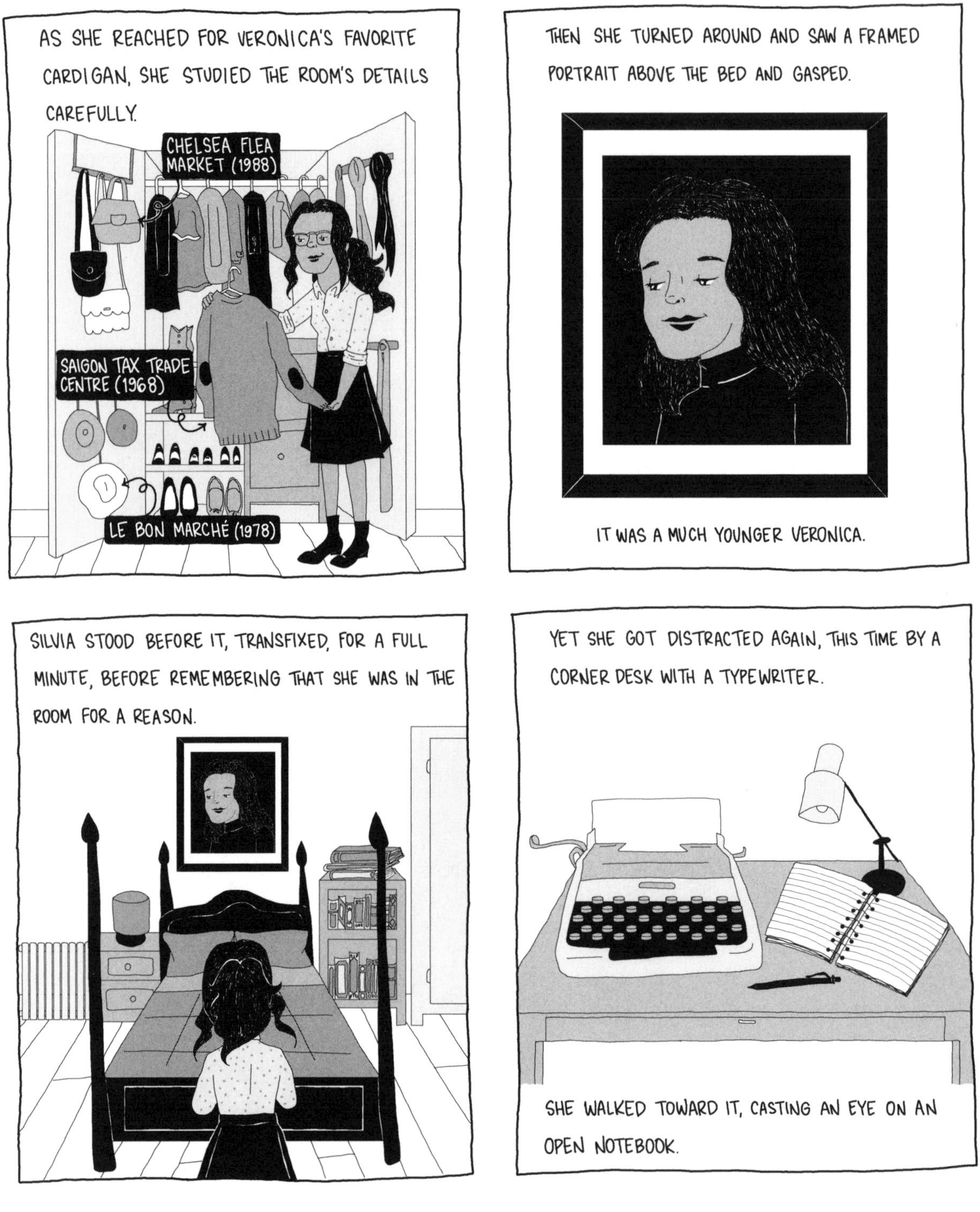
AS SHE REACHED FOR VERONICA'S FAVORITE CARDIGAN, SHE STUDIED THE ROOM'S DETAILS CAREFULLY.
CHELSEA FLEA MARKET (1988)
SAIGON TAX TRADE CENTRE (1968)
LE BON MARCHÉ (1978)
THEN SHE TURNED AROUND AND SAW A FRAMED PORTRAIT ABOVE THE BED AND GASPED.
IT WAS A MUCH YOUNGER VERONICA.
SILVIA STOOD BEFORE IT, TRANSFIXED, FOR A FULL MINUTE, BEFORE REMEMBERING THAT SHE WAS IN THE ROOM FOR A REASON.
YET SHE GOT DISTRACTED AGAIN, THIS TIME BY A CORNER DESK WITH A TYPEWRITER.
SHE WALKED TOWARD IT, CASTING AN EYE ON AN OPEN NOTEBOOK.

SHE SQUINTED TO READ THE LOOPY HANDWRITING.

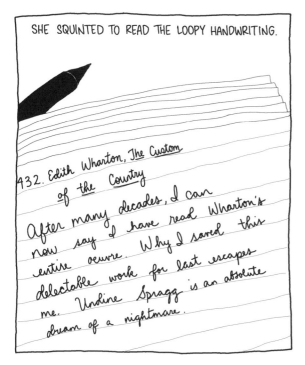

432. Edith Wharton, The Custom of the Country

After many decades, I can now say I have read Wharton's entire oeuvre. Why I saved this delectable work for last escapes me. Undine Spragg is an absolute dream of a nightmare.

THE NOTEBOOK WAS A READING LIST. SILVIA ALREADY FELT LIKE A CRIMINAL FOR SNOOPING, BUT AS SHE TIPPED THE NOTEBOOK INTO HER TOTE BAG, SHE CRINGED, WAITING FOR THE GOD FROM HER STAINED-GLASS CHURCH OR THOSE NIGHTS ON HICKS STREET TO STRIKE HER DOWN.

WHEN NO LIGHTNING BOLT CAME DOWN — OR EVEN THE SOUND OF JENNY'S FOOTSTEPS — SHE HUSTLED TO RETURN TO THE LIVING ROOM.

SHE COULDN'T LOOK JENNY IN THE EYE.

SEND MY LOVE TO VERONICA!

WE'LL VISIT HER AS SOON AS SHE'S READY FOR GUESTS!

THAT'S SO GREAT TO HEAR! I'VE ALWAYS BEEN WORRIED THAT SHE'S LONELY HERE.

BUT SILVIA DIDN'T HEAR HER. SHE WAS ALREADY OUT THE DOOR, SWEATING THROUGH HER J.CREW OUTLET BUTTON-DOWN.

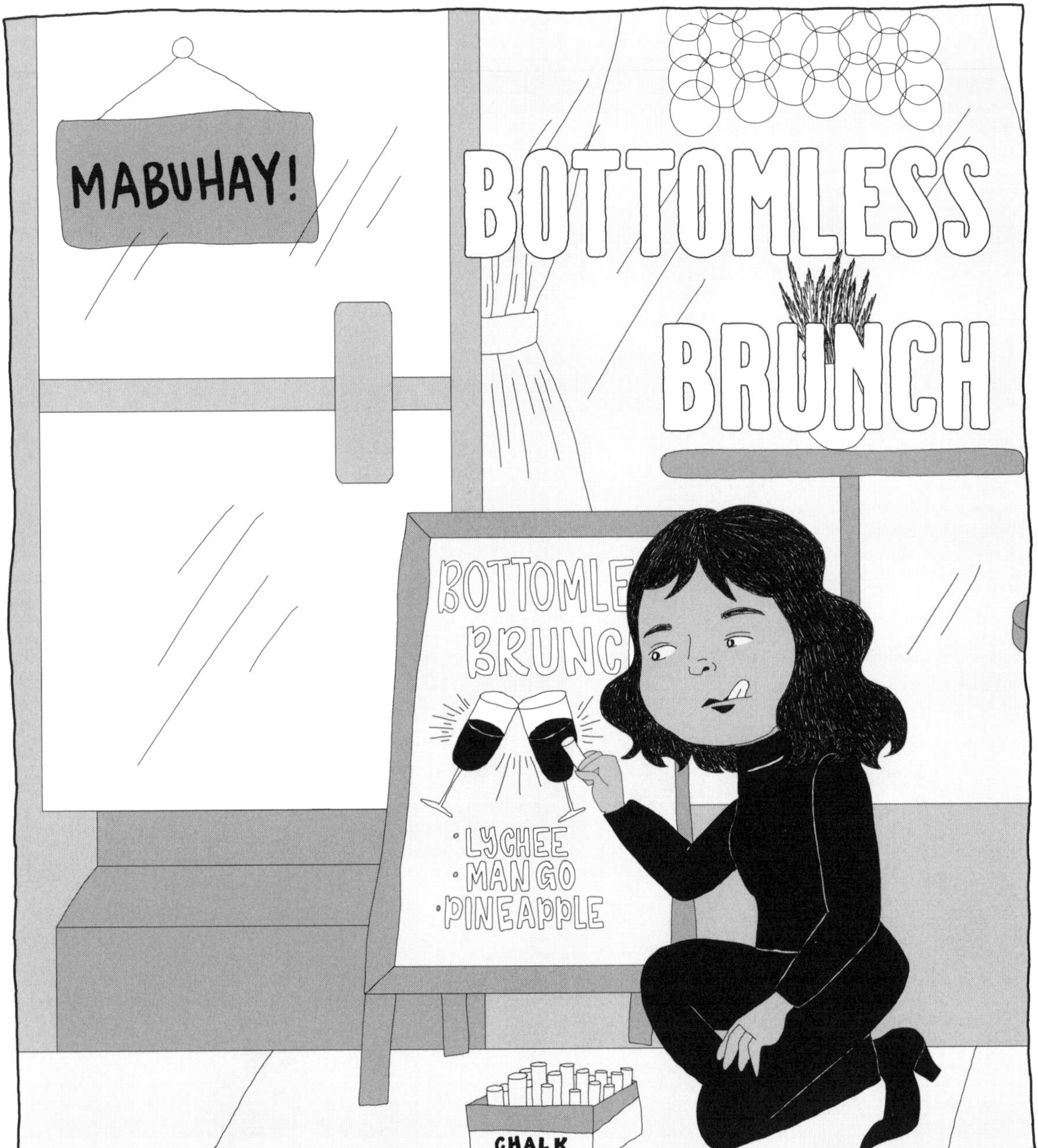
MABUHAY!
BOTTOMLESS
BRUNCH
BOTTOMLE
BRUNC
· LYCHEE
· MANGO
· PINEAPPLE
CHALK

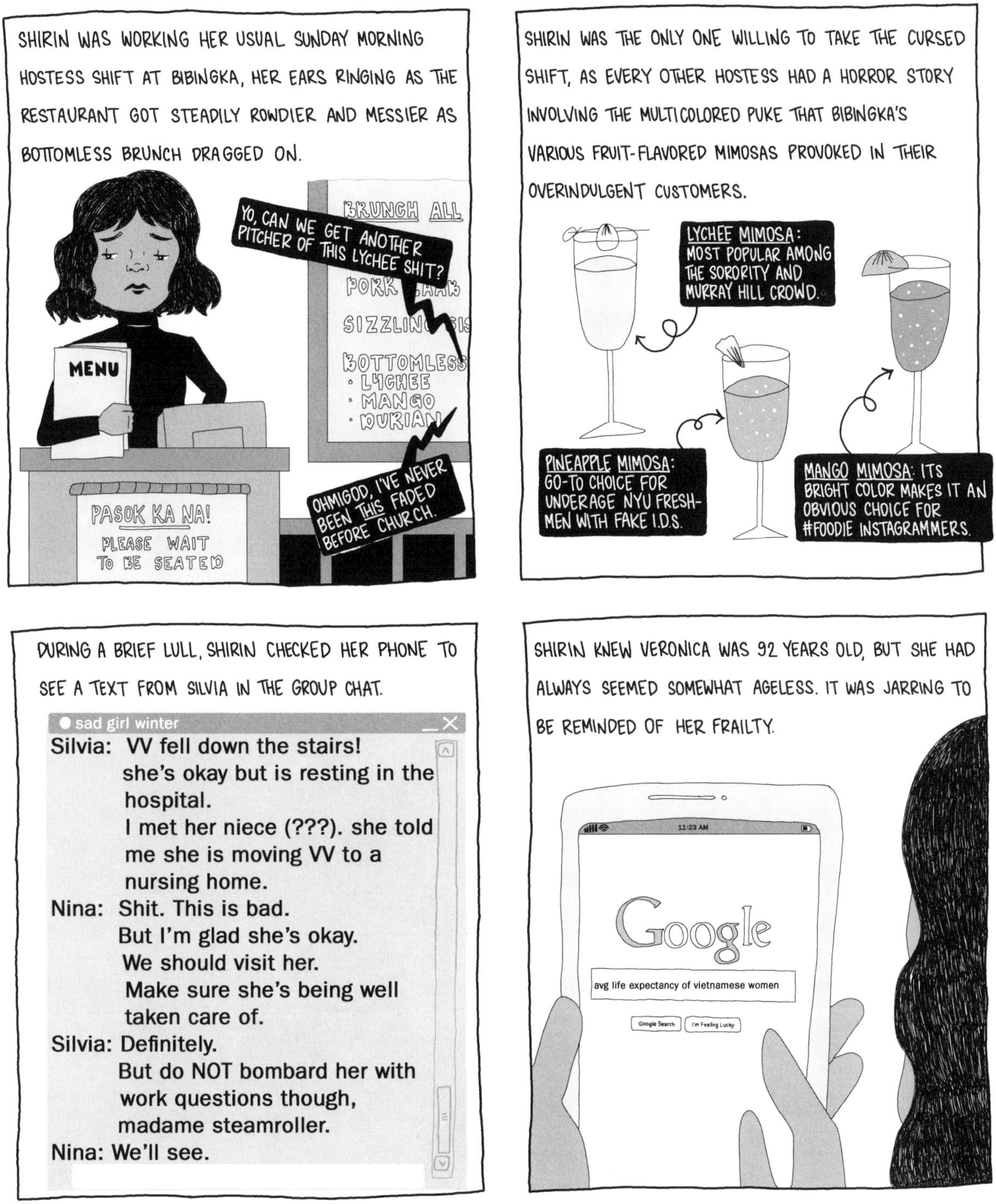
SHIRIN WAS WORKING HER USUAL SUNDAY MORNING HOSTESS SHIFT AT BIBINGKA, HER EARS RINGING AS THE RESTAURANT GOT STEADILY ROWDIER AND MESSIER AS BOTTOMLESS BRUNCH DRAGGED ON.
YO, CAN WE GET ANOTHER PITCHER OF THIS LYCHEE SHIT?
BRUNCH ALL
BOTTOMLESS
· LYCHEE
· MANGO
· DURIAN
MENU
PASOK KA NA!
PLEASE WAIT TO BE SEATED
OHMIGOD, I'VE NEVER BEEN THIS FADED BEFORE CHURCH.
SHIRIN WAS THE ONLY ONE WILLING TO TAKE THE CURSED SHIFT, AS EVERY OTHER HOSTESS HAD A HORROR STORY INVOLVING THE MULTICOLORED PUKE THAT BIBINGKA'S VARIOUS FRUIT-FLAVORED MIMOSAS PROVOKED IN THEIR OVERINDULGENT CUSTOMERS.
LYCHEE MIMOSA: MOST POPULAR AMONG THE SORORITY AND MURRAY HILL CROWD.
PINEAPPLE MIMOSA: GO-TO CHOICE FOR UNDERAGE NYU FRESHMEN WITH FAKE I.D.S.
MANGO MIMOSA: ITS BRIGHT COLOR MAKES IT AN OBVIOUS CHOICE FOR #FOODIE INSTAGRAMMERS.
DURING A BRIEF LULL, SHIRIN CHECKED HER PHONE TO SEE A TEXT FROM SILVIA IN THE GROUP CHAT.
sad girl winter
Silvia: VV fell down the stairs!
she's okay but is resting in the hospital.
I met her niece (???). she told me she is moving VV to a nursing home.
Nina: Shit. This is bad.
But I'm glad she's okay.
We should visit her.
Make sure she's being well taken care of.
Silvia: Definitely.
But do NOT bombard her with work questions though, madame steamroller.
Nina: We'll see.
SHIRIN KNEW VERONICA WAS 92 YEARS OLD, BUT SHE HAD ALWAYS SEEMED SOMEWHAT AGELESS. IT WAS JARRING TO BE REMINDED OF HER FRAILTY.
11:23 AM
Google
avg life expectancy of vietnamese women
Google Search
I'm Feeling Lucky

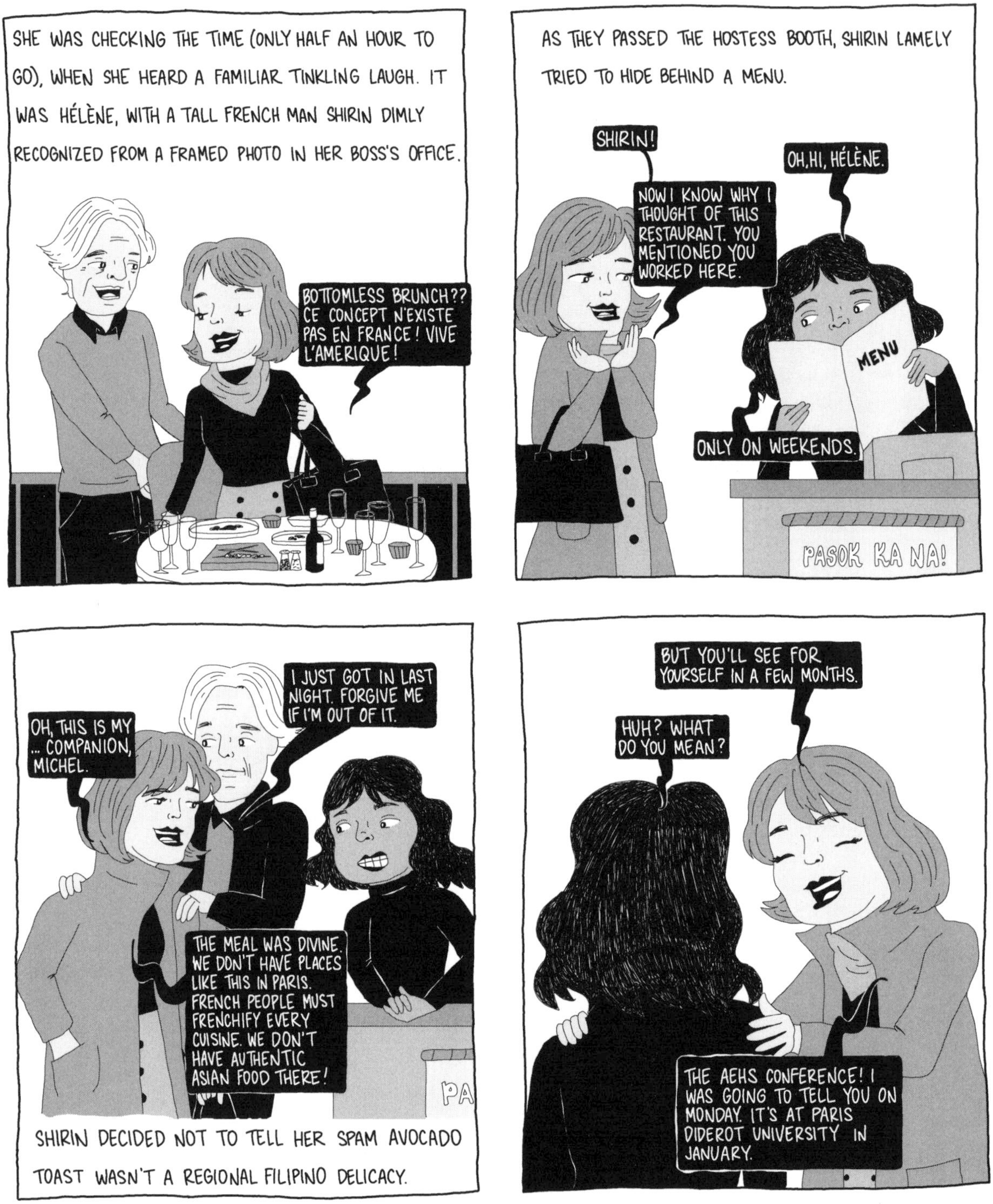
SHE WAS CHECKING THE TIME (ONLY HALF AN HOUR TO GO), WHEN SHE HEARD A FAMILIAR TINKLING LAUGH. IT WAS HÉLÈNE, WITH A TALL FRENCH MAN SHIRIN DIMLY RECOGNIZED FROM A FRAMED PHOTO IN HER BOSS'S OFFICE.
BOTTOMLESS BRUNCH?? CE CONCEPT N'EXISTE PAS EN FRANCE! VIVE L'AMERIQUE!
AS THEY PASSED THE HOSTESS BOOTH, SHIRIN LAMELY TRIED TO HIDE BEHIND A MENU.
SHIRIN!
OH, HI, HÉLÈNE.
NOW I KNOW WHY I THOUGHT OF THIS RESTAURANT. YOU MENTIONED YOU WORKED HERE.
MENU
ONLY ON WEEKENDS.
PASOK KA NA!
OH, THIS IS MY ... COMPANION, MICHEL.
I JUST GOT IN LAST NIGHT. FORGIVE ME IF I'M OUT OF IT.
THE MEAL WAS DIVINE. WE DON'T HAVE PLACES LIKE THIS IN PARIS. FRENCH PEOPLE MUST FRENCHIFY EVERY CUISINE. WE DON'T HAVE AUTHENTIC ASIAN FOOD THERE!
PA
SHIRIN DECIDED NOT TO TELL HER SPAM AVOCADO TOAST WASN'T A REGIONAL FILIPINO DELICACY.
BUT YOU'LL SEE FOR YOURSELF IN A FEW MONTHS.
HUH? WHAT DO YOU MEAN?
THE AEHS CONFERENCE! I WAS GOING TO TELL YOU ON MONDAY. IT'S AT PARIS DIDEROT UNIVERSITY IN JANUARY.

SHIRIN NO LONGER NEEDED THE ABBREVIATION PDF TO KNOW THAT AEHS STOOD FOR THE ASSOCIATION OF EASTERN HISTORY SCHOLARS. HÉLÈNE ACQUIRED THE MAJORITY OF HER NEW PROJECTS AT THEIR CONFERENCE.
AEHS
SPEAKER
ASSOCIATION OF EASTERN HISTORY SC
AEHS
AEHS
ASK ME ABOUT THE QING DYNASTY!
ASSOCIATION OF EASTERN HISTORY SCHOLARS
CONFERENCE PROGRAM
WAIT. I THOUGHT THE CONFERENCE WAS IN MADISON, WISCONSIN, LAST YEAR.
THEY WANTED SOMETHING A BIT MORE CONTINENTAL, I SUPPOSE?
I'VE ALREADY TOLD MY BOSS YOU'RE INDISPENSABLE, AND I NEED YOU THERE. WE USUALLY DON'T FLY OUT ASSISTANTS, BUT WE BOTH KNOW HOW MUCH I DEPEND ON YOU.
WELL, WE BETTER GO. I'LL SEE YOU TOMORROW, MON PETIT CHOU. WE'LL GO OVER ALL THE DETAILS.
ON Y VA?
BUT DON'T WORRY. IT'S ALL DECIDED. PARIS WILL BE OURS.
HÉLÈNE MARCHED OUT OF THE RESTAURANT, HUMMING SOMETHING SHIRIN ASSUMED WAS "LA MARSEILLAISE."
I GUESS I'M GOING TO PARIS.
PASOK KA NA!
PLEASE WAIT TO BE SEATED

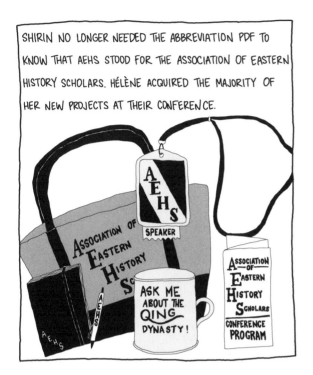

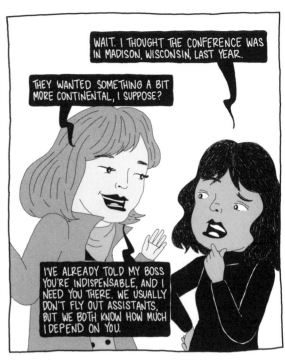

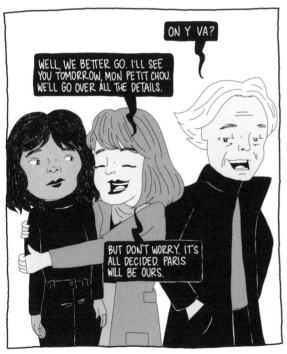

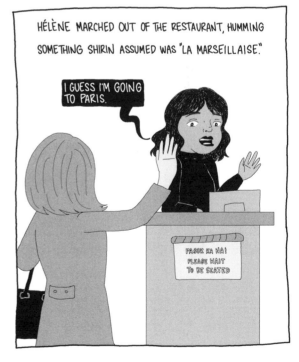

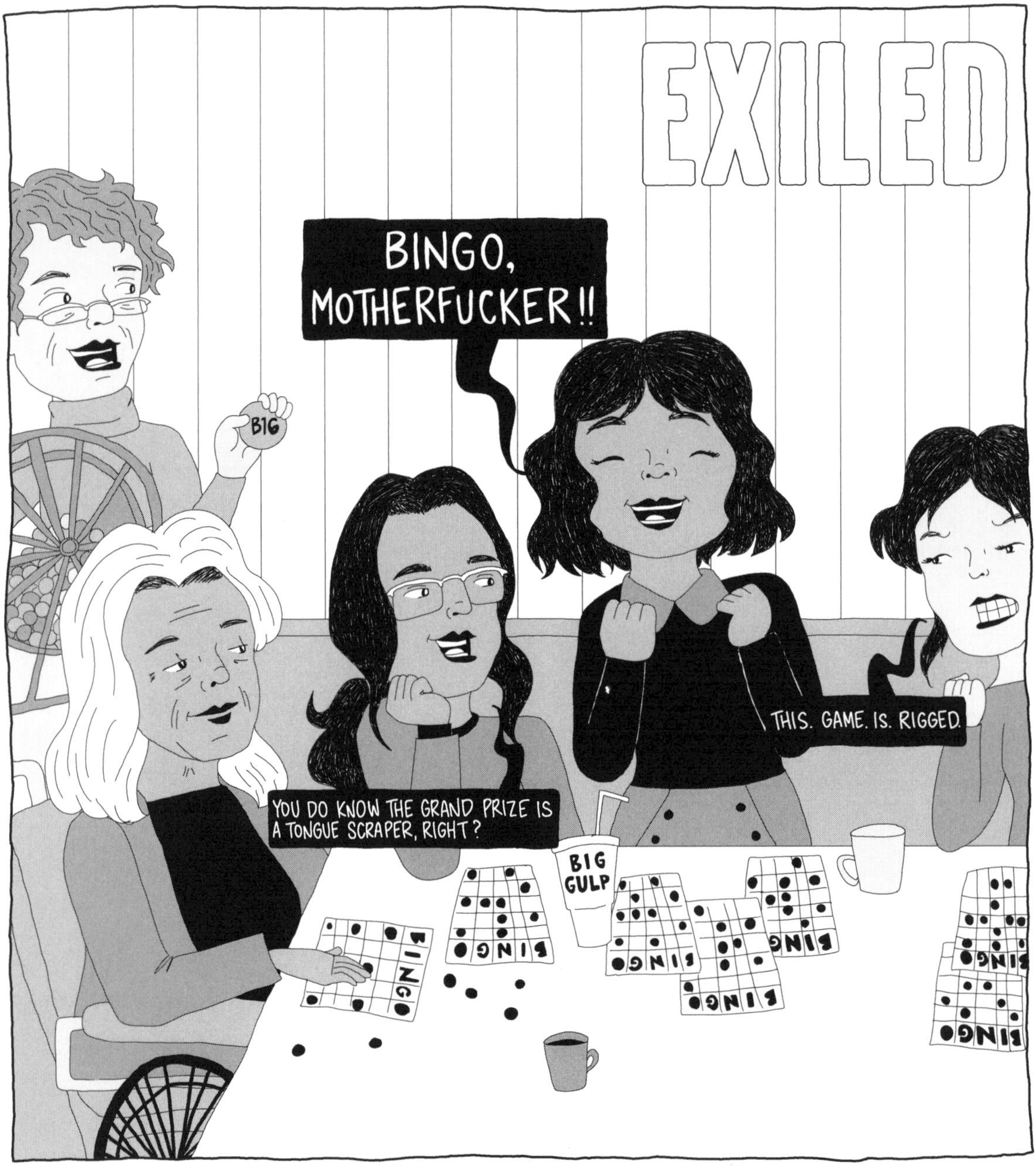
EXILED
BIG
BINGO, MOTHERFUCKER!!
THIS. GAME. IS. RIGGED.
YOU DO KNOW THE GRAND PRIZE IS A TONGUE SCRAPER, RIGHT?
BIG GULP
BINGO

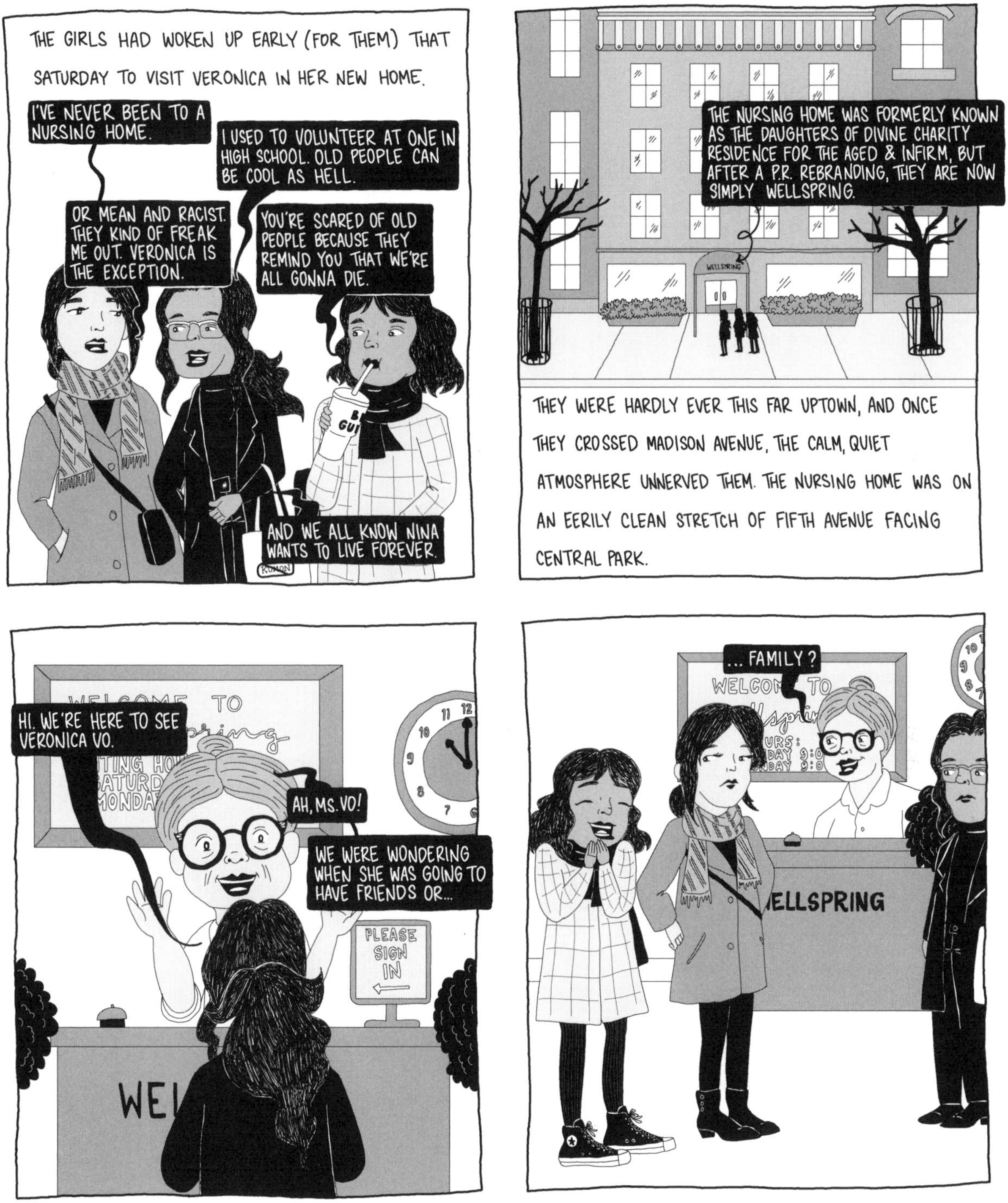
THE GIRLS HAD WOKEN UP EARLY (FOR THEM) THAT SATURDAY TO VISIT VERONICA IN HER NEW HOME.
I'VE NEVER BEEN TO A NURSING HOME.
I USED TO VOLUNTEER AT ONE IN HIGH SCHOOL. OLD PEOPLE CAN BE COOL AS HELL.
OR MEAN AND RACIST. THEY KIND OF FREAK ME OUT. VERONICA IS THE EXCEPTION.
YOU'RE SCARED OF OLD PEOPLE BECAUSE THEY REMIND YOU THAT WE'RE ALL GONNA DIE.
AND WE ALL KNOW NINA WANTS TO LIVE FOREVER.
THE NURSING HOME WAS FORMERLY KNOWN AS THE DAUGHTERS OF DIVINE CHARITY RESIDENCE FOR THE AGED & INFIRM, BUT AFTER A P.R. REBRANDING, THEY ARE NOW SIMPLY WELLSPRING.
THEY WERE HARDLY EVER THIS FAR UPTOWN, AND ONCE THEY CROSSED MADISON AVENUE, THE CALM, QUIET ATMOSPHERE UNNERVED THEM. THE NURSING HOME WAS ON AN EERILY CLEAN STRETCH OF FIFTH AVENUE FACING CENTRAL PARK.
HI. WE'RE HERE TO SEE VERONICA VO.
AH, MS. VO!
WE WERE WONDERING WHEN SHE WAS GOING TO HAVE FRIENDS OR...
PLEASE SIGN IN
... FAMILY?

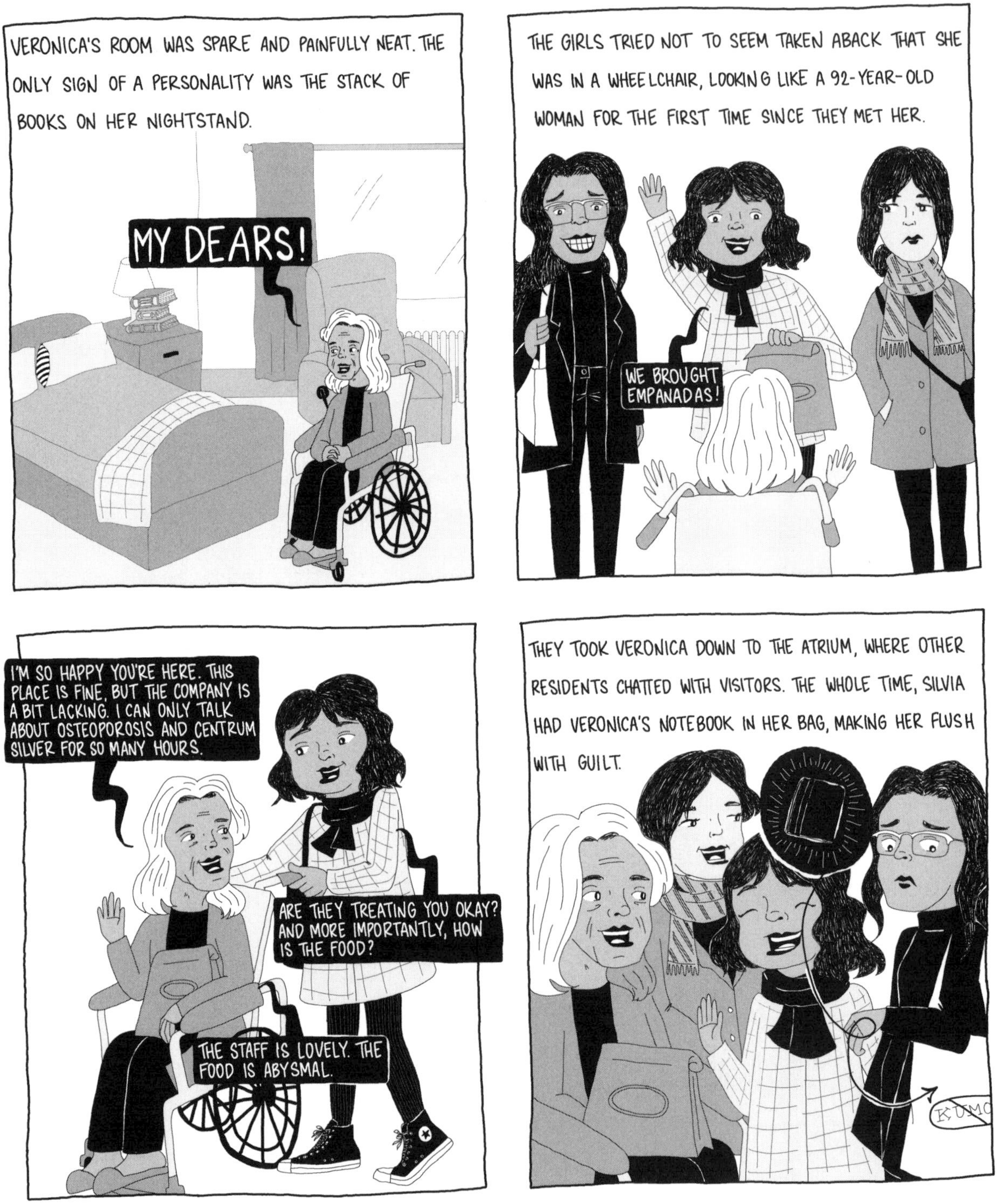
VERONICA'S ROOM WAS SPARE AND PAINFULLY NEAT. THE ONLY SIGN OF A PERSONALITY WAS THE STACK OF BOOKS ON HER NIGHTSTAND.
MY DEARS!
THE GIRLS TRIED NOT TO SEEM TAKEN ABACK THAT SHE WAS IN A WHEELCHAIR, LOOKING LIKE A 92-YEAR-OLD WOMAN FOR THE FIRST TIME SINCE THEY MET HER.
WE BROUGHT EMPANADAS!
I'M SO HAPPY YOU'RE HERE. THIS PLACE IS FINE, BUT THE COMPANY IS A BIT LACKING. I CAN ONLY TALK ABOUT OSTEOPOROSIS AND CENTRUM SILVER FOR SO MANY HOURS.
ARE THEY TREATING YOU OKAY? AND MORE IMPORTANTLY, HOW IS THE FOOD?
THE STAFF IS LOVELY. THE FOOD IS ABYSMAL.
THEY TOOK VERONICA DOWN TO THE ATRIUM, WHERE OTHER RESIDENTS CHATTED WITH VISITORS. THE WHOLE TIME, SILVIA HAD VERONICA'S NOTEBOOK IN HER BAG, MAKING HER FLUSH WITH GUILT.

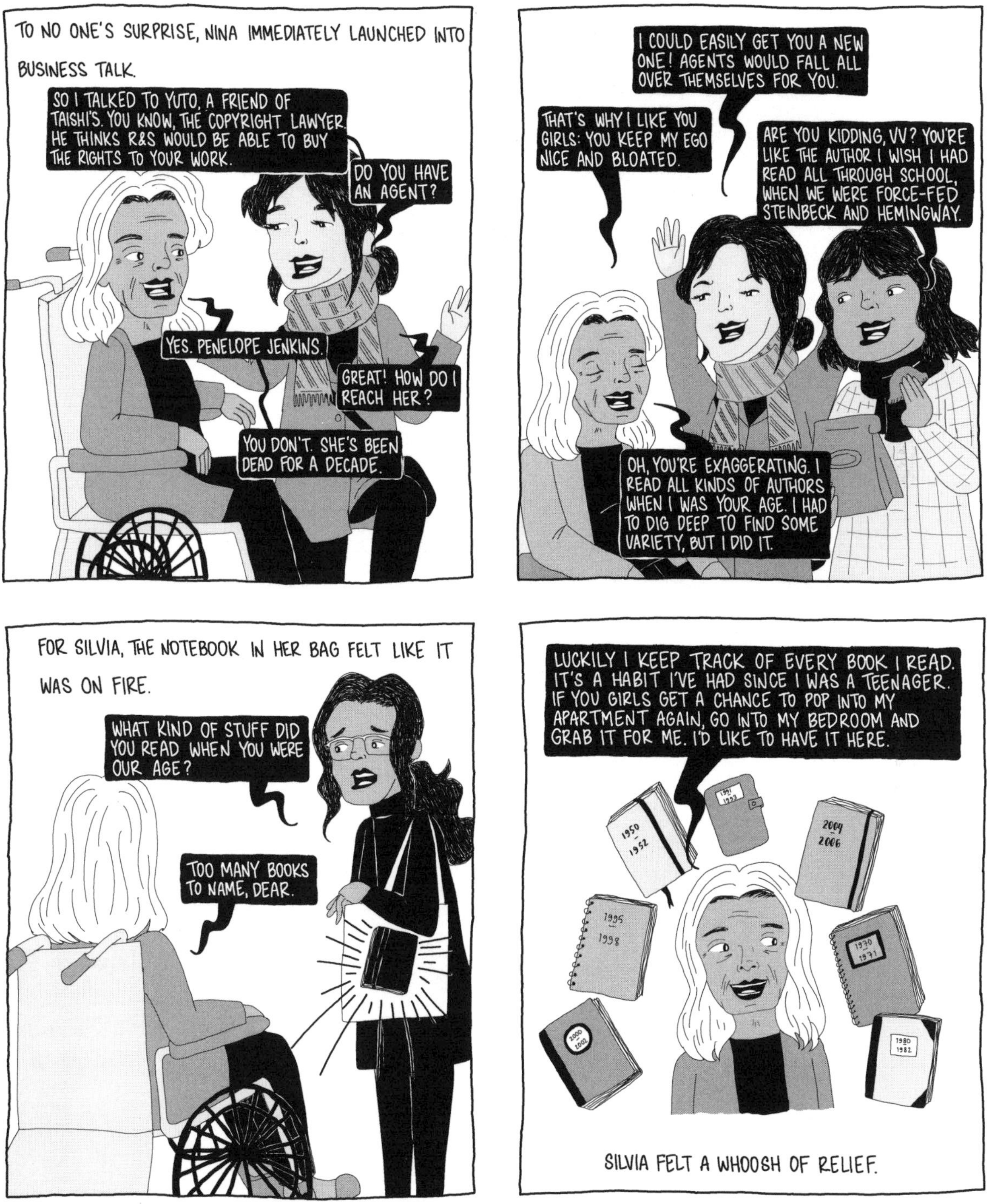
TO NO ONE'S SURPRISE, NINA IMMEDIATELY LAUNCHED INTO BUSINESS TALK.
SO I TALKED TO YUTO, A FRIEND OF TAISHI'S. YOU KNOW, THE COPYRIGHT LAWYER. HE THINKS R&S WOULD BE ABLE TO BUY THE RIGHTS TO YOUR WORK.
DO YOU HAVE AN AGENT?
YES. PENELOPE JENKINS.
GREAT! HOW DO I REACH HER?
YOU DON'T. SHE'S BEEN DEAD FOR A DECADE.
I COULD EASILY GET YOU A NEW ONE! AGENTS WOULD FALL ALL OVER THEMSELVES FOR YOU.
THAT'S WHY I LIKE YOU GIRLS: YOU KEEP MY EGO NICE AND BLOATED.
ARE YOU KIDDING, VV? YOU'RE LIKE THE AUTHOR I WISH I HAD READ ALL THROUGH SCHOOL, WHEN WE WERE FORCE-FED STEINBECK AND HEMINGWAY.
OH, YOU'RE EXAGGERATING. I READ ALL KINDS OF AUTHORS WHEN I WAS YOUR AGE. I HAD TO DIG DEEP TO FIND SOME VARIETY, BUT I DID IT.
FOR SILVIA, THE NOTEBOOK IN HER BAG FELT LIKE IT WAS ON FIRE.
WHAT KIND OF STUFF DID YOU READ WHEN YOU WERE OUR AGE?
TOO MANY BOOKS TO NAME, DEAR.
LUCKILY I KEEP TRACK OF EVERY BOOK I READ. IT'S A HABIT I'VE HAD SINCE I WAS A TEENAGER. IF YOU GIRLS GET A CHANCE TO POP INTO MY APARTMENT AGAIN, GO INTO MY BEDROOM AND GRAB IT FOR ME. I'D LIKE TO HAVE IT HERE.
1950 1952
2004 2006
1995 1998
2000 2002
1980 1982
SILVIA FELT A WHOOSH OF RELIEF.

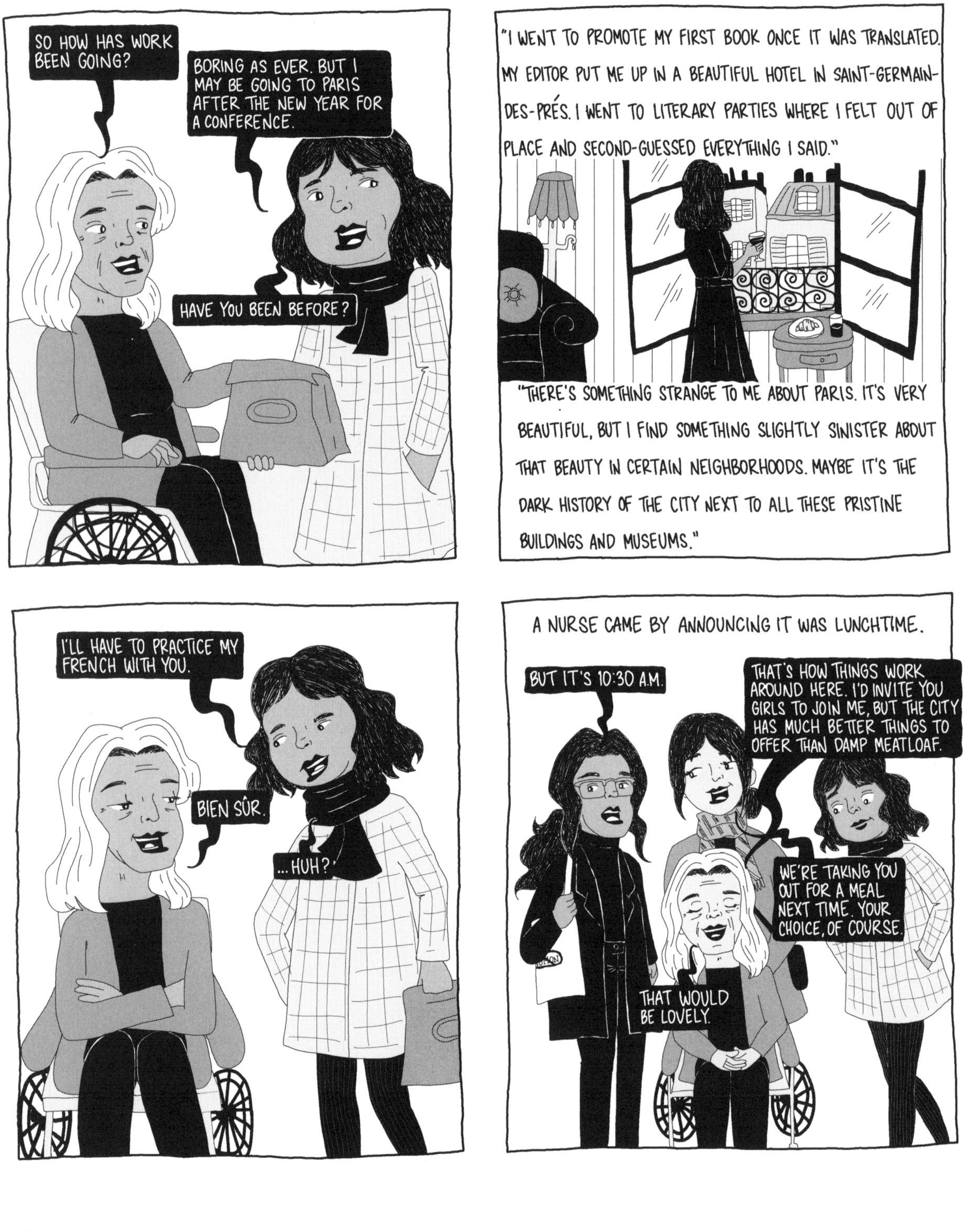
SO HOW HAS WORK BEEN GOING?
BORING AS EVER. BUT I MAY BE GOING TO PARIS AFTER THE NEW YEAR FOR A CONFERENCE.
HAVE YOU BEEN BEFORE?
"I WENT TO PROMOTE MY FIRST BOOK ONCE IT WAS TRANSLATED. MY EDITOR PUT ME UP IN A BEAUTIFUL HOTEL IN SAINT-GERMAIN-DES-PRÉS. I WENT TO LITERARY PARTIES WHERE I FELT OUT OF PLACE AND SECOND-GUESSED EVERYTHING I SAID."
"THERE'S SOMETHING STRANGE TO ME ABOUT PARIS. IT'S VERY BEAUTIFUL, BUT I FIND SOMETHING SLIGHTLY SINISTER ABOUT THAT BEAUTY IN CERTAIN NEIGHBORHOODS. MAYBE IT'S THE DARK HISTORY OF THE CITY NEXT TO ALL THESE PRISTINE BUILDINGS AND MUSEUMS."
I'LL HAVE TO PRACTICE MY FRENCH WITH YOU.
BIEN SÛR.
...HUH?
A NURSE CAME BY ANNOUNCING IT WAS LUNCHTIME.
BUT IT'S 10:30 A.M.
THAT'S HOW THINGS WORK AROUND HERE. I'D INVITE YOU GIRLS TO JOIN ME, BUT THE CITY HAS MUCH BETTER THINGS TO OFFER THAN DAMP MEATLOAF.
WE'RE TAKING YOU OUT FOR A MEAL NEXT TIME. YOUR CHOICE, OF COURSE.
THAT WOULD BE LOVELY.

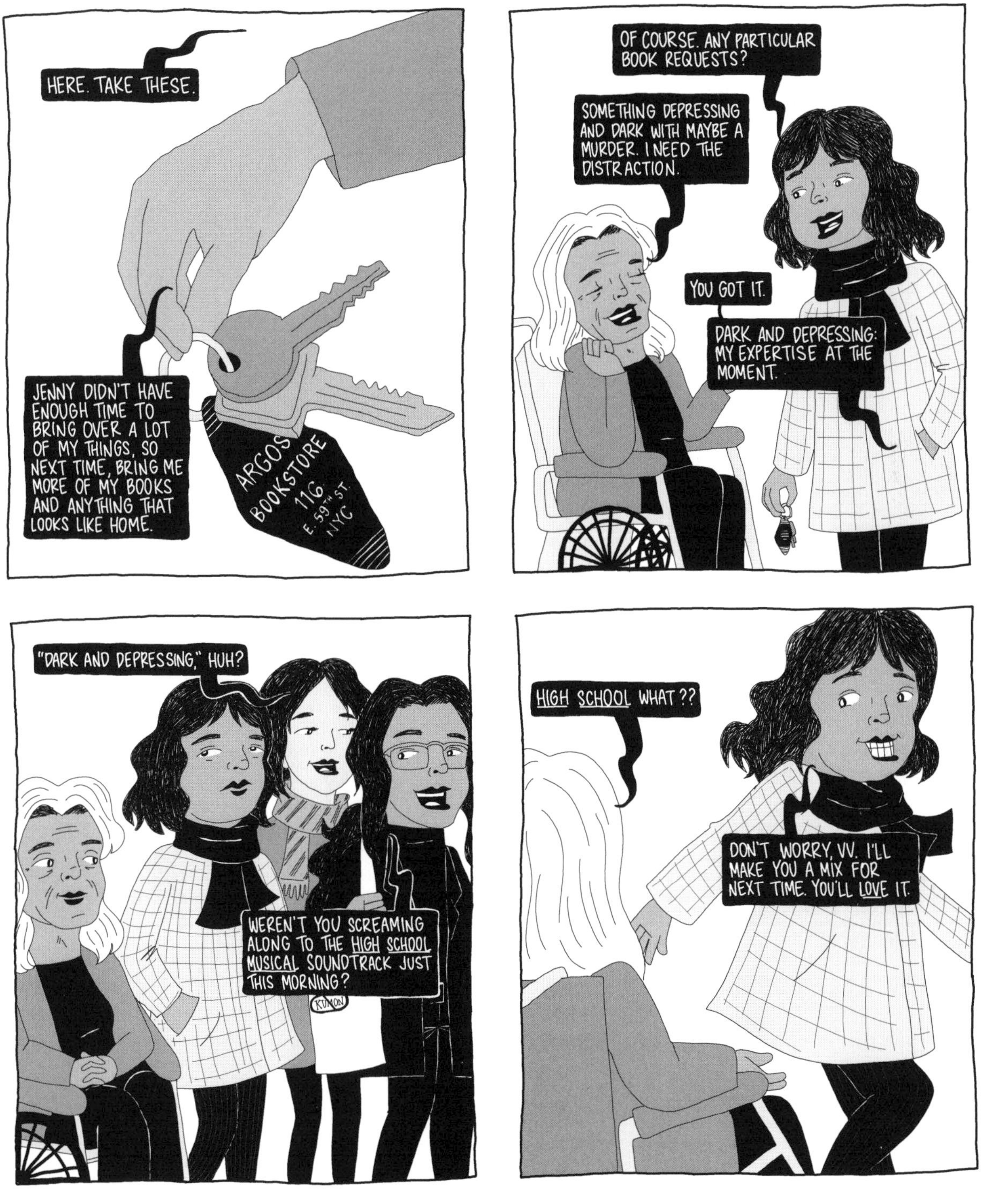
HERE. TAKE THESE.
JENNY DIDN'T HAVE ENOUGH TIME TO BRING OVER A LOT OF MY THINGS, SO NEXT TIME, BRING ME MORE OF MY BOOKS AND ANYTHING THAT LOOKS LIKE HOME.
ARGOS BOOKSTORE 116 E. 59TH ST. NYC
OF COURSE. ANY PARTICULAR BOOK REQUESTS?
SOMETHING DEPRESSING AND DARK WITH MAYBE A MURDER. I NEED THE DISTRACTION.
YOU GOT IT.
DARK AND DEPRESSING: MY EXPERTISE AT THE MOMENT.
"DARK AND DEPRESSING," HUH?
WEREN'T YOU SCREAMING ALONG TO THE HIGH SCHOOL MUSICAL SOUNDTRACK JUST THIS MORNING?
KUMON
HIGH SCHOOL WHAT??
DON'T WORRY, VV. I'LL MAKE YOU A MIX FOR NEXT TIME. YOU'LL LOVE IT.

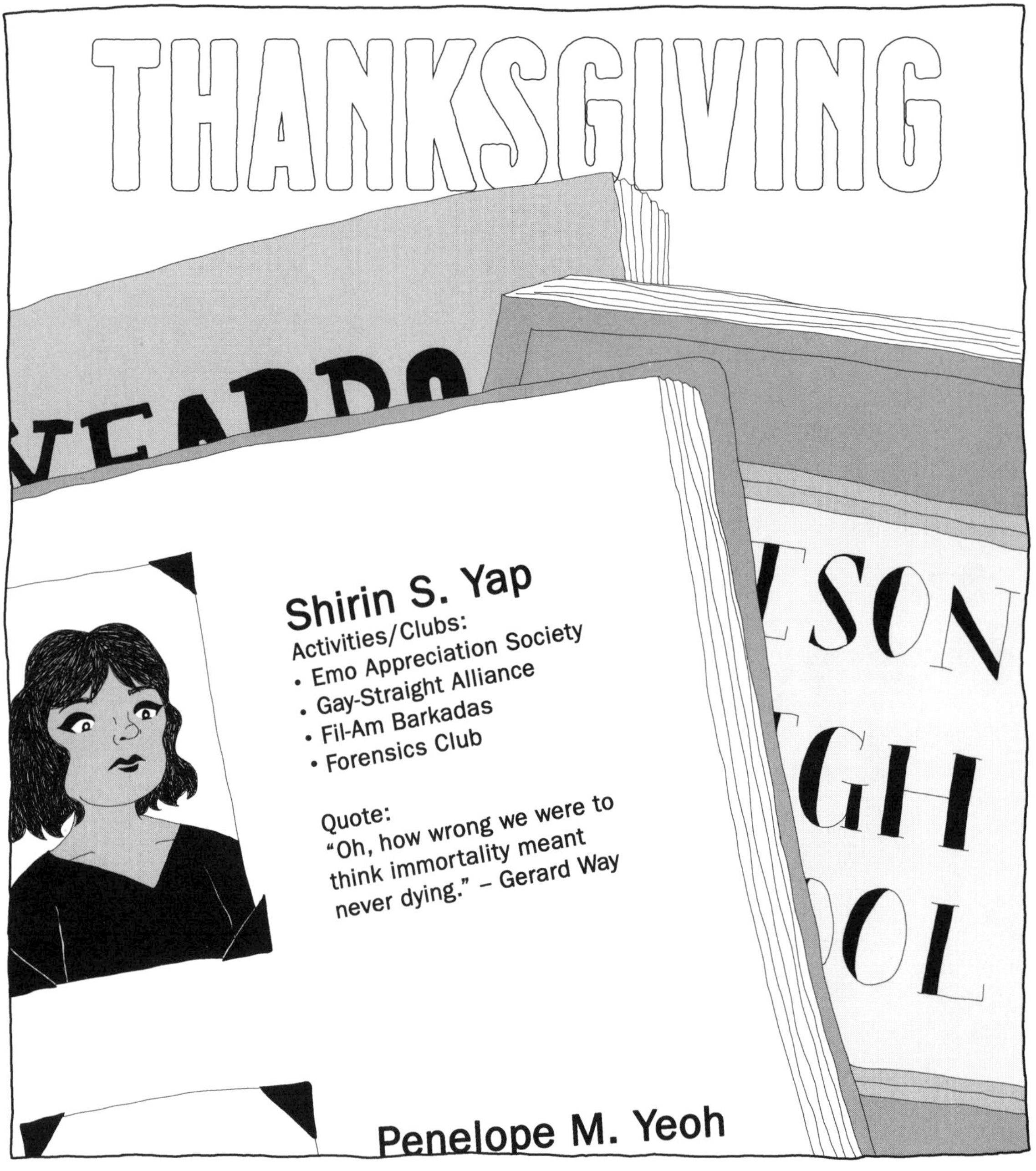
THANKSGIVING
Shirin S. Yap
Activities/Clubs:
• Emo Appreciation Society
• Gay-Straight Alliance
• Fil-Am Barkadas
• Forensics Club
Quote:
"Oh, how wrong we were to think immortality meant never dying." – Gerard Way
Penelope M. Yeoh

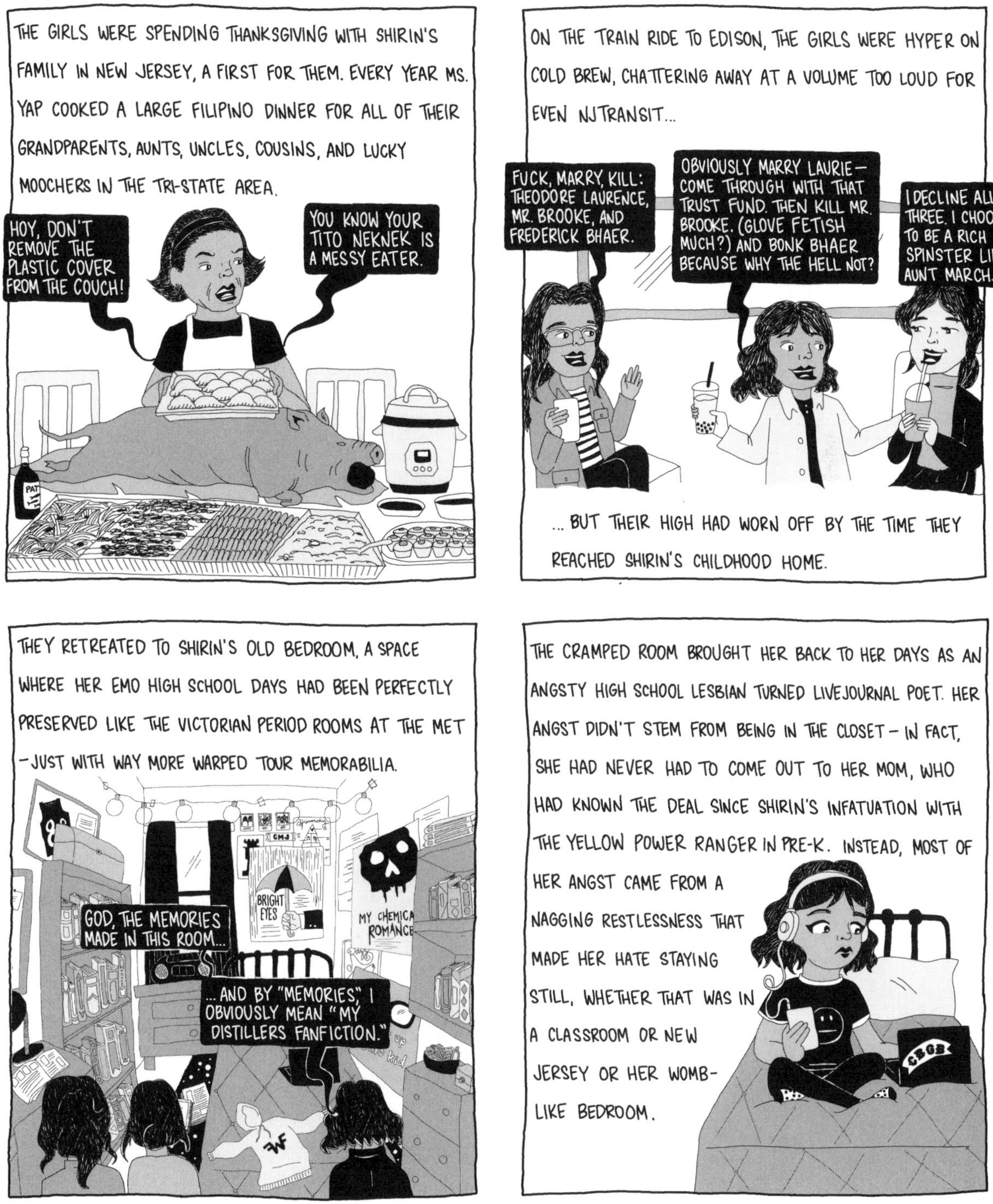
THE GIRLS WERE SPENDING THANKSGIVING WITH SHIRIN'S FAMILY IN NEW JERSEY, A FIRST FOR THEM. EVERY YEAR MS. YAP COOKED A LARGE FILIPINO DINNER FOR ALL OF THEIR GRANDPARENTS, AUNTS, UNCLES, COUSINS, AND LUCKY MOOCHERS IN THE TRI-STATE AREA.
HOY, DON'T REMOVE THE PLASTIC COVER FROM THE COUCH!
YOU KNOW YOUR TITO NEKNEK IS A MESSY EATER.
ON THE TRAIN RIDE TO EDISON, THE GIRLS WERE HYPER ON COLD BREW, CHATTERING AWAY AT A VOLUME TOO LOUD FOR EVEN NJTRANSIT...
FUCK, MARRY, KILL: THEODORE LAURENCE, MR. BROOKE, AND FREDERICK BHAER.
OBVIOUSLY MARRY LAURIE— COME THROUGH WITH THAT TRUST FUND. THEN KILL MR. BROOKE. (GLOVE FETISH MUCH?) AND BONK BHAER BECAUSE WHY THE HELL NOT?
I DECLINE ALL THREE. I CHOOSE TO BE A RICH SPINSTER LIKE AUNT MARCH.
... BUT THEIR HIGH HAD WORN OFF BY THE TIME THEY REACHED SHIRIN'S CHILDHOOD HOME.
THEY RETREATED TO SHIRIN'S OLD BEDROOM, A SPACE WHERE HER EMO HIGH SCHOOL DAYS HAD BEEN PERFECTLY PRESERVED LIKE THE VICTORIAN PERIOD ROOMS AT THE MET —JUST WITH WAY MORE WARPED TOUR MEMORABILIA.
BRIGHT EYES
GOD, THE MEMORIES MADE IN THIS ROOM...
... AND BY "MEMORIES," I OBVIOUSLY MEAN "MY DISTILLERS FANFICTION."
THE CRAMPED ROOM BROUGHT HER BACK TO HER DAYS AS AN ANGSTY HIGH SCHOOL LESBIAN TURNED LIVEJOURNAL POET. HER ANGST DIDN'T STEM FROM BEING IN THE CLOSET — IN FACT, SHE HAD NEVER HAD TO COME OUT TO HER MOM, WHO HAD KNOWN THE DEAL SINCE SHIRIN'S INFATUATION WITH THE YELLOW POWER RANGER IN PRE-K. INSTEAD, MOST OF HER ANGST CAME FROM A NAGGING RESTLESSNESS THAT MADE HER HATE STAYING STILL, WHETHER THAT WAS IN A CLASSROOM OR NEW JERSEY OR HER WOMB-LIKE BEDROOM.
CBGB

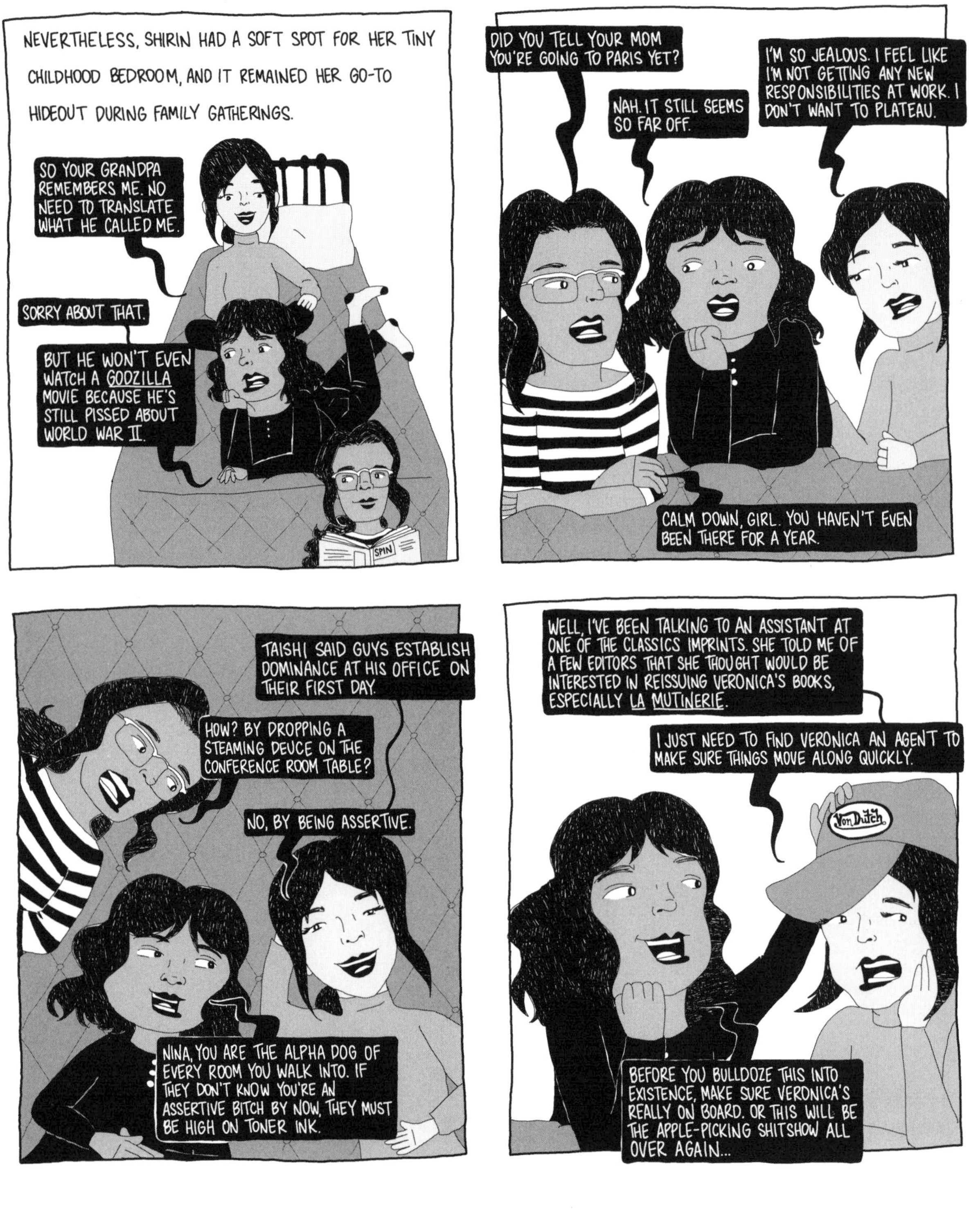

NEVERTHELESS, SHIRIN HAD A SOFT SPOT FOR HER TINY CHILDHOOD BEDROOM, AND IT REMAINED HER GO-TO HIDEOUT DURING FAMILY GATHERINGS.
SO YOUR GRANDPA REMEMBERS ME. NO NEED TO TRANSLATE WHAT HE CALLED ME.
SORRY ABOUT THAT.
BUT HE WON'T EVEN WATCH A GODZILLA MOVIE BECAUSE HE'S STILL PISSED ABOUT WORLD WAR II.
SPIN
DID YOU TELL YOUR MOM YOU'RE GOING TO PARIS YET?
NAH. IT STILL SEEMS SO FAR OFF.
I'M SO JEALOUS. I FEEL LIKE I'M NOT GETTING ANY NEW RESPONSIBILITIES AT WORK. I DON'T WANT TO PLATEAU.
CALM DOWN, GIRL. YOU HAVEN'T EVEN BEEN THERE FOR A YEAR.
TAISHI SAID GUYS ESTABLISH DOMINANCE AT HIS OFFICE ON THEIR FIRST DAY.
HOW? BY DROPPING A STEAMING DEUCE ON THE CONFERENCE ROOM TABLE?
NO, BY BEING ASSERTIVE.
NINA, YOU ARE THE ALPHA DOG OF EVERY ROOM YOU WALK INTO. IF THEY DON'T KNOW YOU'RE AN ASSERTIVE BITCH BY NOW, THEY MUST BE HIGH ON TONER INK.
WELL, I'VE BEEN TALKING TO AN ASSISTANT AT ONE OF THE CLASSICS IMPRINTS. SHE TOLD ME OF A FEW EDITORS THAT SHE THOUGHT WOULD BE INTERESTED IN REISSUING VERONICA'S BOOKS, ESPECIALLY LA MUTINERIE.
I JUST NEED TO FIND VERONICA AN AGENT TO MAKE SURE THINGS MOVE ALONG QUICKLY.
Von Dutch
BEFORE YOU BULLDOZE THIS INTO EXISTENCE, MAKE SURE VERONICA'S REALLY ON BOARD. OR THIS WILL BE THE APPLE-PICKING SHITSHOW ALL OVER AGAIN...

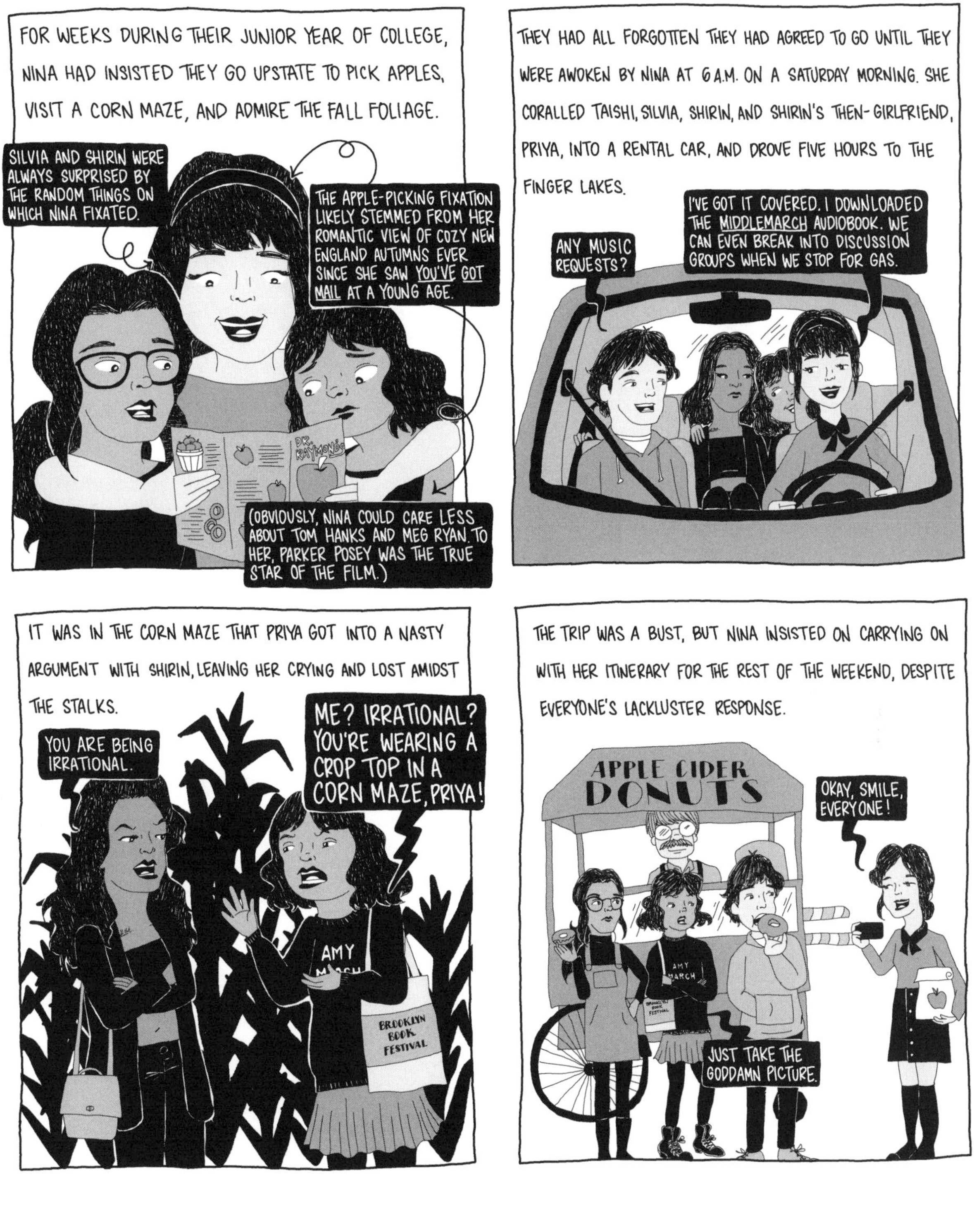
FOR WEEKS DURING THEIR JUNIOR YEAR OF COLLEGE, NINA HAD INSISTED THEY GO UPSTATE TO PICK APPLES, VISIT A CORN MAZE, AND ADMIRE THE FALL FOLIAGE.
SILVIA AND SHIRIN WERE ALWAYS SURPRISED BY THE RANDOM THINGS ON WHICH NINA FIXATED.
THE APPLE-PICKING FIXATION LIKELY STEMMED FROM HER ROMANTIC VIEW OF COZY NEW ENGLAND AUTUMNS EVER SINCE SHE SAW YOU'VE GOT MAIL AT A YOUNG AGE.
DR. RAYMOND'S
(OBVIOUSLY, NINA COULD CARE LESS ABOUT TOM HANKS AND MEG RYAN. TO HER, PARKER POSEY WAS THE TRUE STAR OF THE FILM.)
THEY HAD ALL FORGOTTEN THEY HAD AGREED TO GO UNTIL THEY WERE AWOKEN BY NINA AT 6 A.M. ON A SATURDAY MORNING. SHE CORALLED TAISHI, SILVIA, SHIRIN, AND SHIRIN'S THEN-GIRLFRIEND, PRIYA, INTO A RENTAL CAR, AND DROVE FIVE HOURS TO THE FINGER LAKES.
ANY MUSIC REQUESTS?
I'VE GOT IT COVERED. I DOWNLOADED THE MIDDLEMARCH AUDIOBOOK. WE CAN EVEN BREAK INTO DISCUSSION GROUPS WHEN WE STOP FOR GAS.
IT WAS IN THE CORN MAZE THAT PRIYA GOT INTO A NASTY ARGUMENT WITH SHIRIN, LEAVING HER CRYING AND LOST AMIDST THE STALKS.
YOU ARE BEING IRRATIONAL.
ME? IRRATIONAL? YOU'RE WEARING A CROP TOP IN A CORN MAZE, PRIYA!
AMY MARCH
BROOKLYN BOOK FESTIVAL
THE TRIP WAS A BUST, BUT NINA INSISTED ON CARRYING ON WITH HER ITINERARY FOR THE REST OF THE WEEKEND, DESPITE EVERYONE'S LACKLUSTER RESPONSE.
APPLE CIDER DONUTS
OKAY, SMILE, EVERYONE!
AMY MARCH
JUST TAKE THE GODDAMN PICTURE.

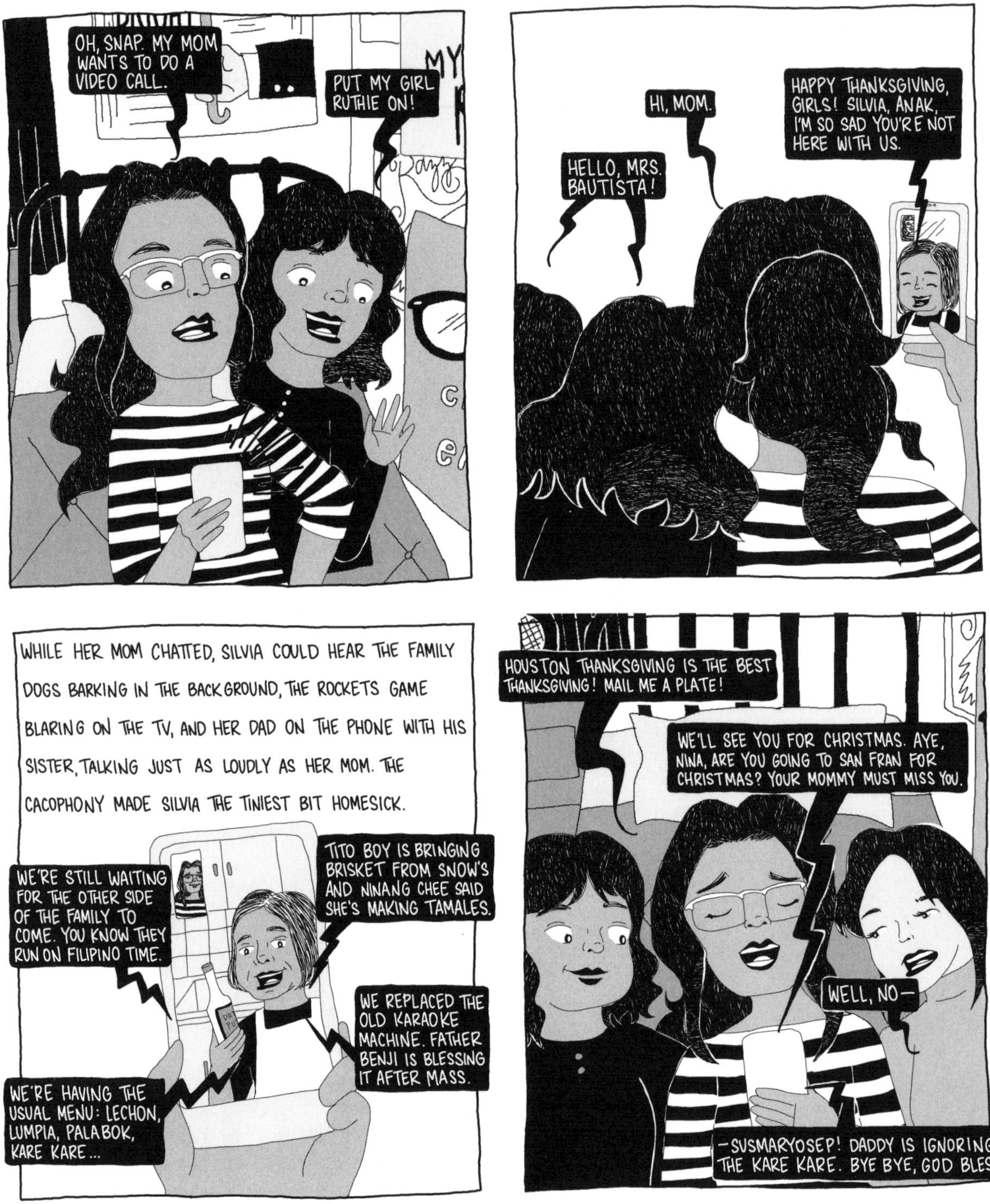
OH, SNAP. MY MOM WANTS TO DO A VIDEO CALL.
PUT MY GIRL RUTHIE ON!
HAPPY THANKSGIVING, GIRLS! SILVIA, ANAK, I'M SO SAD YOU'RE NOT HERE WITH US.
HI, MOM.
HELLO, MRS. BAUTISTA!
WHILE HER MOM CHATTED, SILVIA COULD HEAR THE FAMILY DOGS BARKING IN THE BACKGROUND, THE ROCKETS GAME BLARING ON THE TV, AND HER DAD ON THE PHONE WITH HIS SISTER, TALKING JUST AS LOUDLY AS HER MOM. THE CACOPHONY MADE SILVIA THE TINIEST BIT HOMESICK.
WE'RE STILL WAITING FOR THE OTHER SIDE OF THE FAMILY TO COME. YOU KNOW THEY RUN ON FILIPINO TIME.
TITO BOY IS BRINGING BRISKET FROM SNOW'S AND NINANG CHEE SAID SHE'S MAKING TAMALES.
WE REPLACED THE OLD KARAOKE MACHINE. FATHER BENJI IS BLESSING IT AFTER MASS.
WE'RE HAVING THE USUAL MENU: LECHON, LUMPIA, PALABOK, KARE KARE...
HOUSTON THANKSGIVING IS THE BEST THANKSGIVING! MAIL ME A PLATE!
WE'LL SEE YOU FOR CHRISTMAS. AYE, NINA, ARE YOU GOING TO SAN FRAN FOR CHRISTMAS? YOUR MOMMY MUST MISS YOU.
WELL, NO—
—SUSMARYOSEP! DADDY IS IGNORING THE KARE KARE. BYE BYE, GOD BLESS!

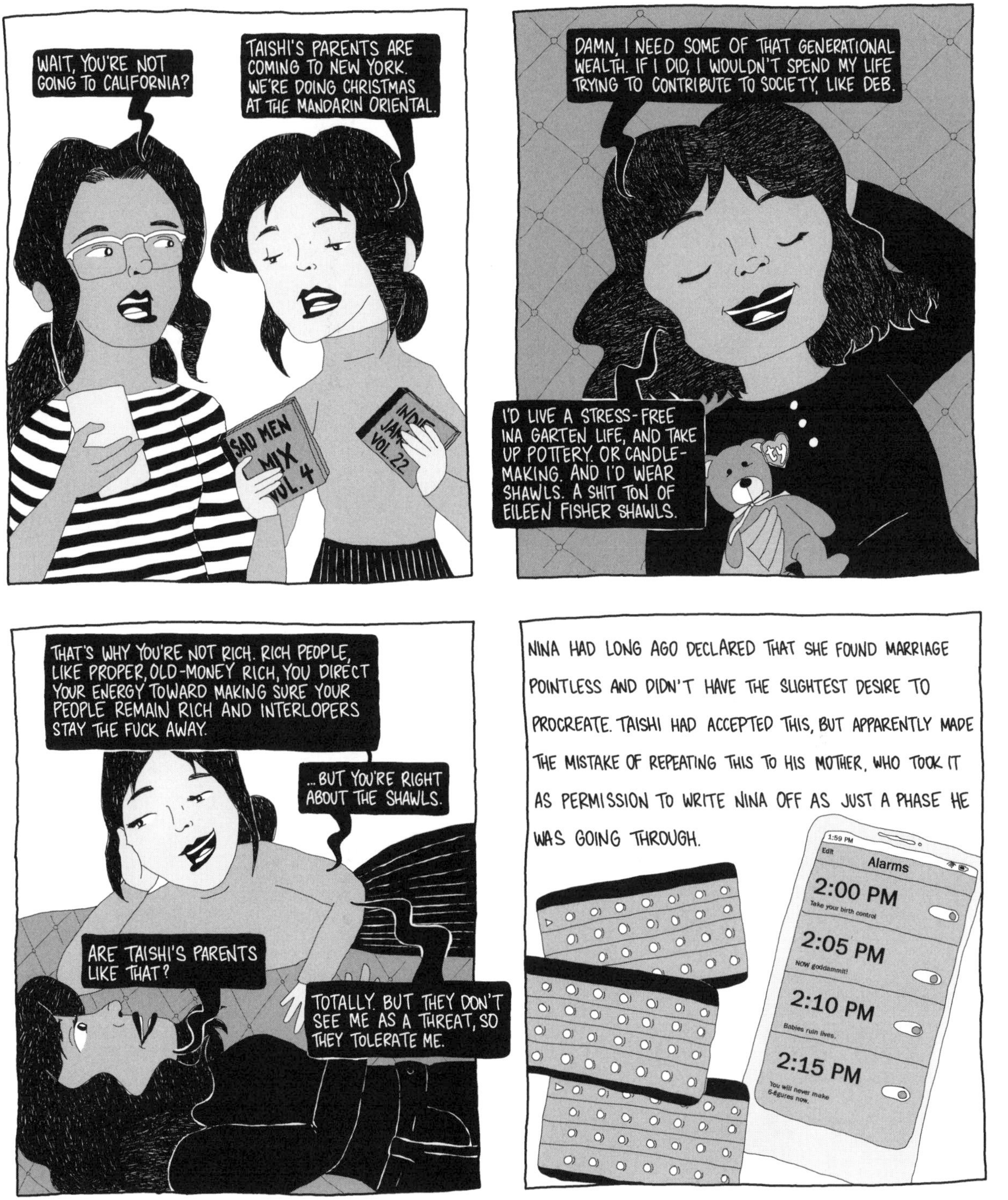
WAIT, YOU'RE NOT GOING TO CALIFORNIA?
TAISHI'S PARENTS ARE COMING TO NEW YORK. WE'RE DOING CHRISTMAS AT THE MANDARIN ORIENTAL.
SAD MEN MIX VOL. 4
INDIE JAMS VOL. 22
DAMN, I NEED SOME OF THAT GENERATIONAL WEALTH. IF I DID, I WOULDN'T SPEND MY LIFE TRYING TO CONTRIBUTE TO SOCIETY, LIKE DEB.
I'D LIVE A STRESS-FREE INA GARTEN LIFE, AND TAKE UP POTTERY. OR CANDLE-MAKING. AND I'D WEAR SHAWLS. A SHIT TON OF EILEEN FISHER SHAWLS.
ty
THAT'S WHY YOU'RE NOT RICH. RICH PEOPLE, LIKE PROPER, OLD-MONEY RICH, YOU DIRECT YOUR ENERGY TOWARD MAKING SURE YOUR PEOPLE REMAIN RICH AND INTERLOPERS STAY THE FUCK AWAY.
...BUT YOU'RE RIGHT ABOUT THE SHAWLS.
ARE TAISHI'S PARENTS LIKE THAT?
TOTALLY. BUT THEY DON'T SEE ME AS A THREAT, SO THEY TOLERATE ME.
NINA HAD LONG AGO DECLARED THAT SHE FOUND MARRIAGE POINTLESS AND DIDN'T HAVE THE SLIGHTEST DESIRE TO PROCREATE. TAISHI HAD ACCEPTED THIS, BUT APPARENTLY MADE THE MISTAKE OF REPEATING THIS TO HIS MOTHER, WHO TOOK IT AS PERMISSION TO WRITE NINA OFF AS JUST A PHASE HE WAS GOING THROUGH.
1:59 PM
Edit
Alarms
2:00 PM
Take your birth control
2:05 PM
NOW goddammit!
2:10 PM
Babies ruin lives.
2:15 PM
You will never make 6-figures now.

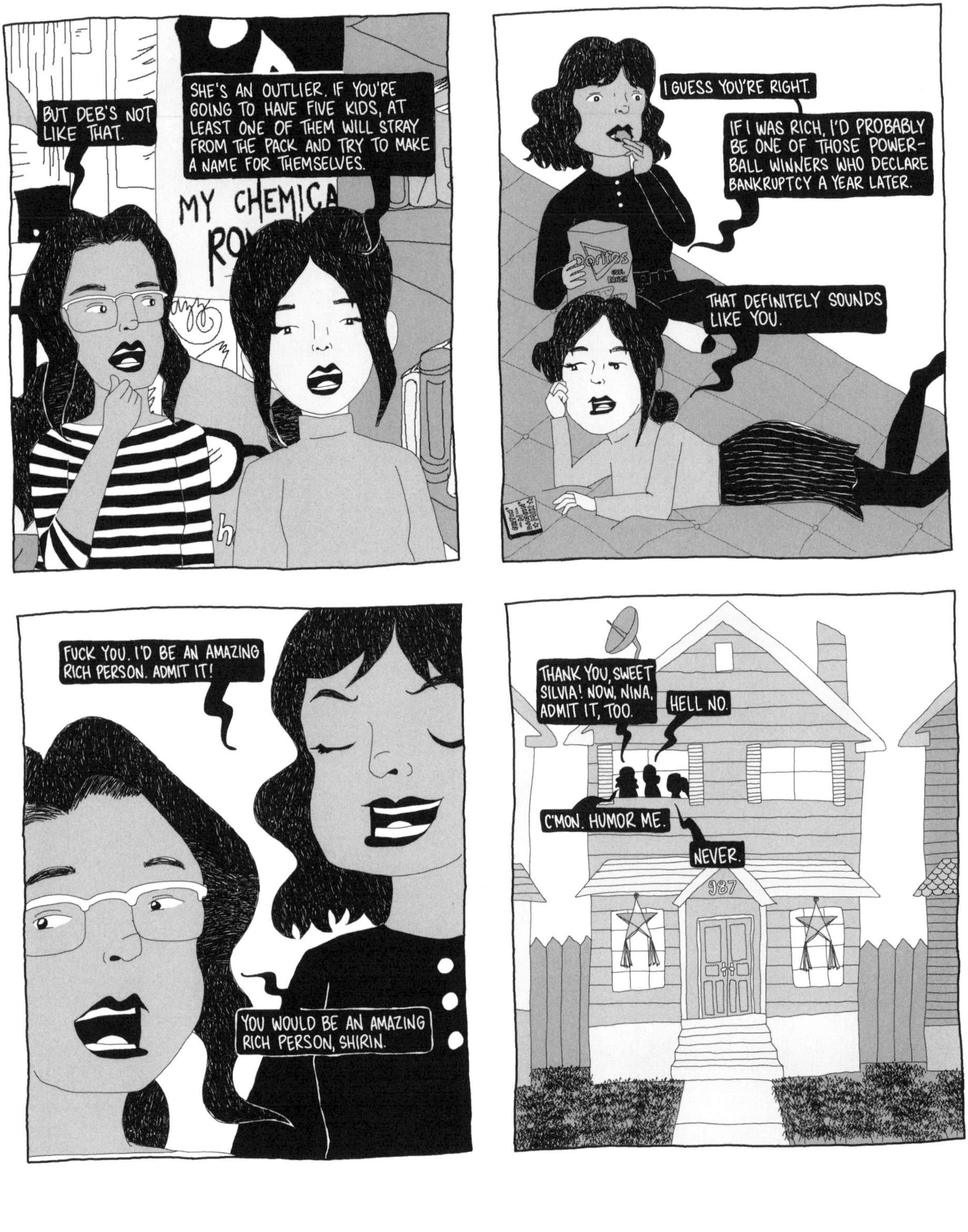
BUT DEB'S NOT LIKE THAT.
SHE'S AN OUTLIER. IF YOU'RE GOING TO HAVE FIVE KIDS, AT LEAST ONE OF THEM WILL STRAY FROM THE PACK AND TRY TO MAKE A NAME FOR THEMSELVES.
MY CHEMICA
I GUESS YOU'RE RIGHT.
IF I WAS RICH, I'D PROBABLY BE ONE OF THOSE POWER-BALL WINNERS WHO DECLARE BANKRUPTCY A YEAR LATER.
Doritos
THAT DEFINITELY SOUNDS LIKE YOU.
FUCK YOU. I'D BE AN AMAZING RICH PERSON. ADMIT IT!
YOU WOULD BE AN AMAZING RICH PERSON, SHIRIN.
THANK YOU, SWEET SILVIA! NOW, NINA, ADMIT IT, TOO.
HELL NO.
C'MON. HUMOR ME.
NEVER.
987

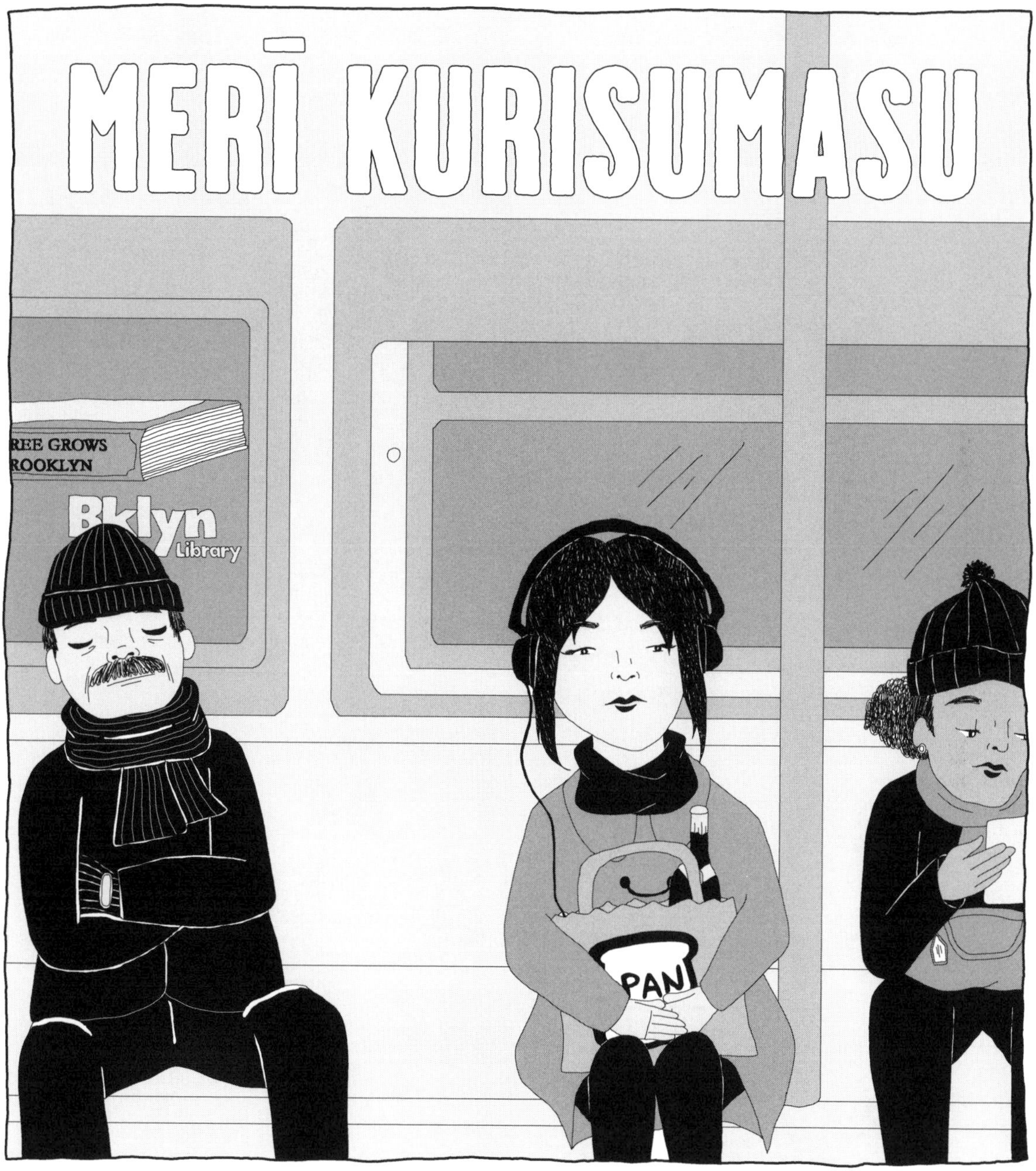
MERĪ KURISUMASU
REE GROWS
ROOKLYN
Bklyn
Library
PAN

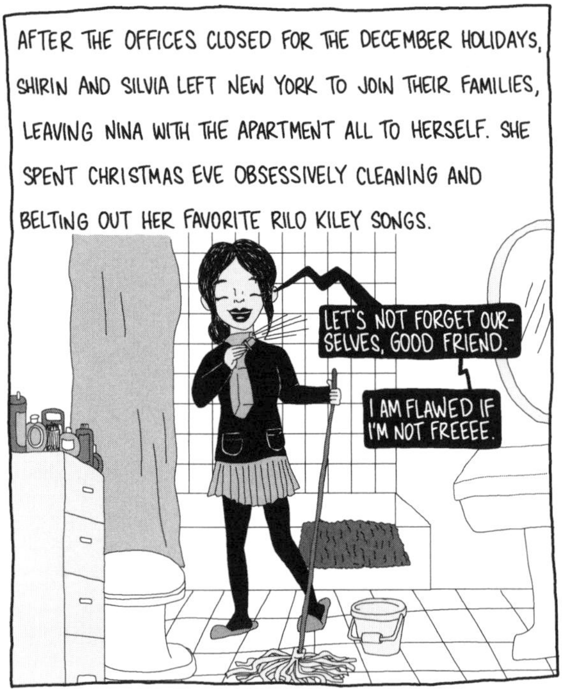
AFTER THE OFFICES CLOSED FOR THE DECEMBER HOLIDAYS, SHIRIN AND SILVIA LEFT NEW YORK TO JOIN THEIR FAMILIES, LEAVING NINA WITH THE APARTMENT ALL TO HERSELF. SHE SPENT CHRISTMAS EVE OBSESSIVELY CLEANING AND BELTING OUT HER FAVORITE RILO KILEY SONGS.
LET'S NOT FORGET OURSELVES, GOOD FRIEND.
I AM FLAWED IF I'M NOT FREEEE.

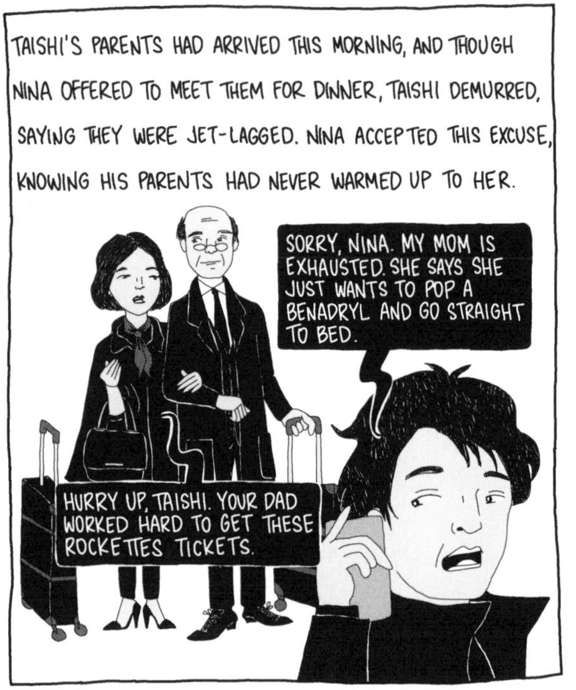
TAISHI'S PARENTS HAD ARRIVED THIS MORNING, AND THOUGH NINA OFFERED TO MEET THEM FOR DINNER, TAISHI DEMURRED, SAYING THEY WERE JET-LAGGED. NINA ACCEPTED THIS EXCUSE, KNOWING HIS PARENTS HAD NEVER WARMED UP TO HER.
SORRY, NINA. MY MOM IS EXHAUSTED. SHE SAYS SHE JUST WANTS TO POP A BENADRYL AND GO STRAIGHT TO BED.
HURRY UP, TAISHI. YOUR DAD WORKED HARD TO GET THESE ROCKETTES TICKETS.

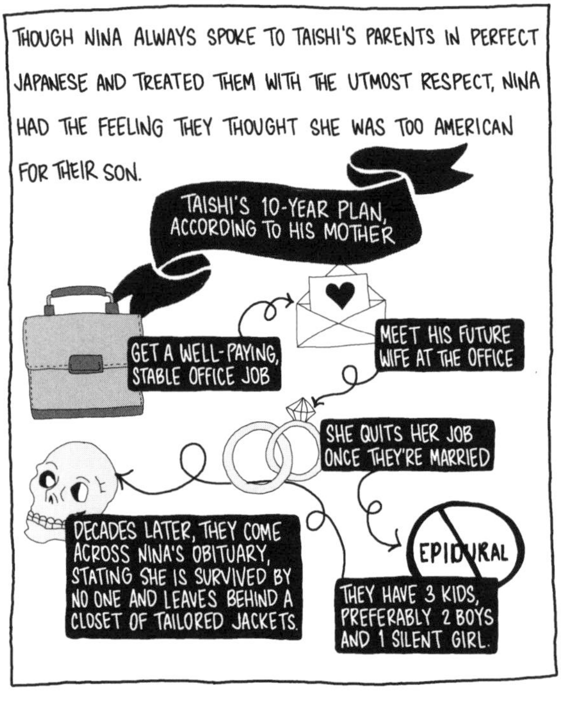
THOUGH NINA ALWAYS SPOKE TO TAISHI'S PARENTS IN PERFECT JAPANESE AND TREATED THEM WITH THE UTMOST RESPECT, NINA HAD THE FEELING THEY THOUGHT SHE WAS TOO AMERICAN FOR THEIR SON.
TAISHI'S 10-YEAR PLAN, ACCORDING TO HIS MOTHER
GET A WELL-PAYING, STABLE OFFICE JOB
MEET HIS FUTURE WIFE AT THE OFFICE
SHE QUITS HER JOB ONCE THEY'RE MARRIED
EPIDURAL
THEY HAVE 3 KIDS, PREFERABLY 2 BOYS AND 1 SILENT GIRL.
DECADES LATER, THEY COME ACROSS NINA'S OBITUARY, STATING SHE IS SURVIVED BY NO ONE AND LEAVES BEHIND A CLOSET OF TAILORED JACKETS.

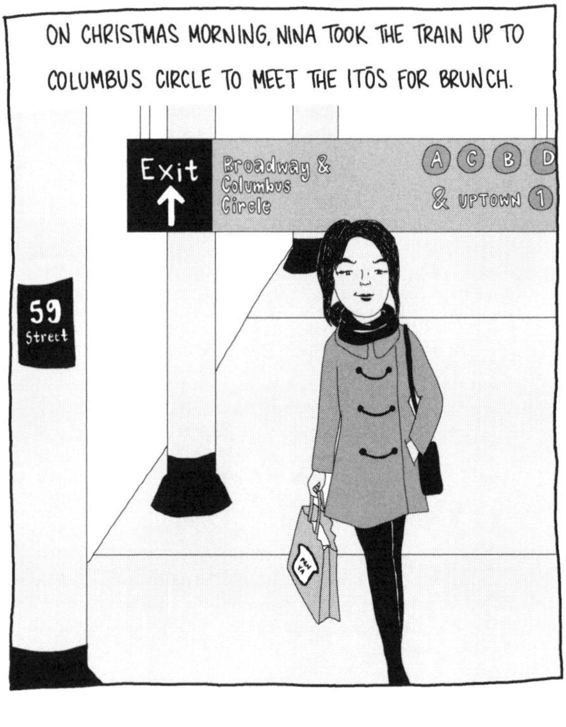
ON CHRISTMAS MORNING, NINA TOOK THE TRAIN UP TO COLUMBUS CIRCLE TO MEET THE ITŌS FOR BRUNCH.
Exit
Broadway & Columbus Circle
A C B D
& UPTOWN 1
59 Street

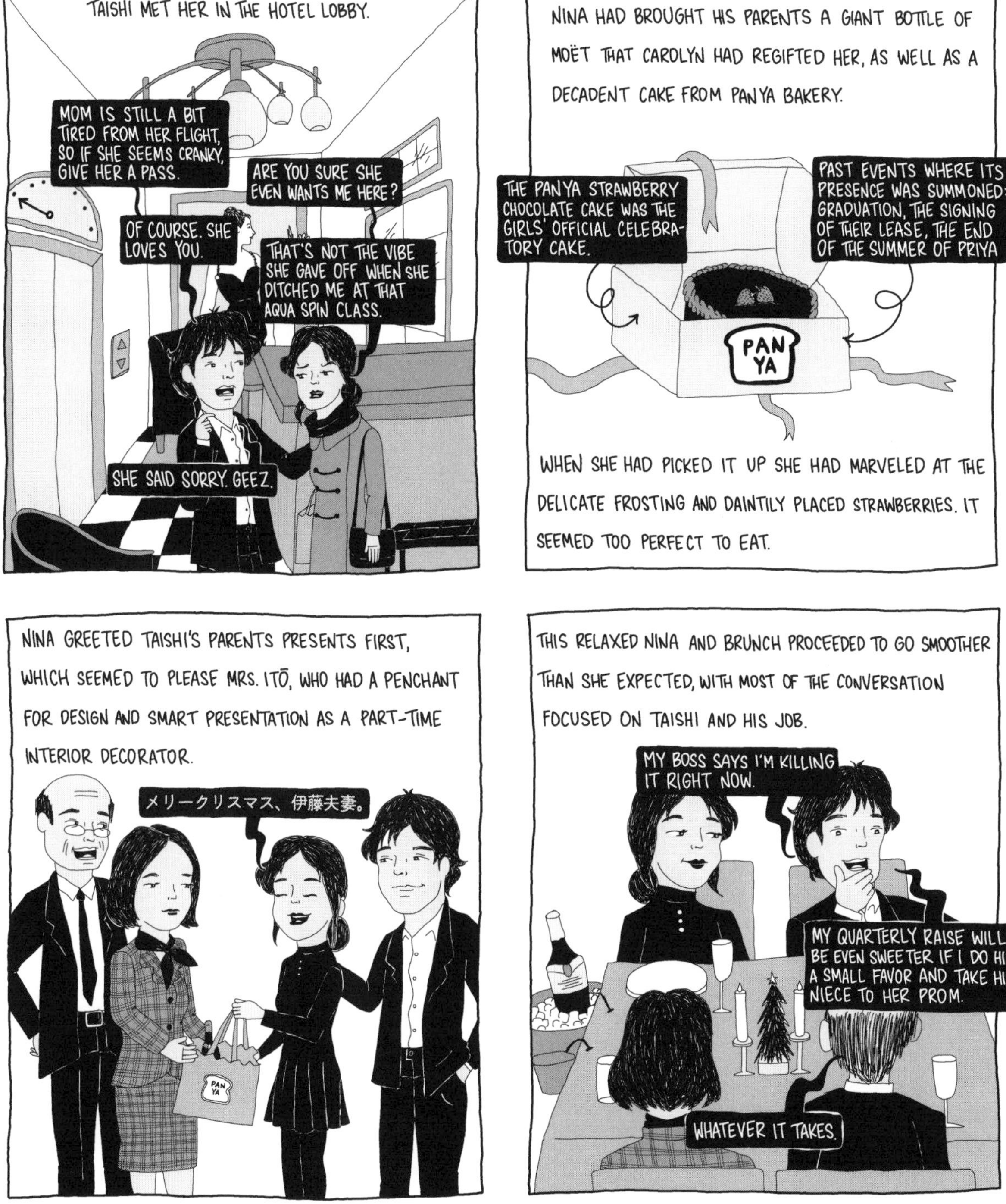
TAISHI MET HER IN THE HOTEL LOBBY.
MOM IS STILL A BIT TIRED FROM HER FLIGHT, SO IF SHE SEEMS CRANKY, GIVE HER A PASS.
ARE YOU SURE SHE EVEN WANTS ME HERE?
OF COURSE. SHE LOVES YOU.
THAT'S NOT THE VIBE SHE GAVE OFF WHEN SHE DITCHED ME AT THAT AQUA SPIN CLASS.
SHE SAID SORRY. GEEZ.
NINA HAD BROUGHT HIS PARENTS A GIANT BOTTLE OF MOËT THAT CAROLYN HAD REGIFTED HER, AS WELL AS A DECADENT CAKE FROM PANYA BAKERY.
THE PANYA STRAWBERRY CHOCOLATE CAKE WAS THE GIRLS' OFFICIAL CELEBRATORY CAKE.
PAST EVENTS WHERE ITS PRESENCE WAS SUMMONED: GRADUATION, THE SIGNING OF THEIR LEASE, THE END OF THE SUMMER OF PRIYA
PAN YA
WHEN SHE HAD PICKED IT UP SHE HAD MARVELED AT THE DELICATE FROSTING AND DAINTILY PLACED STRAWBERRIES. IT SEEMED TOO PERFECT TO EAT.
NINA GREETED TAISHI'S PARENTS PRESENTS FIRST, WHICH SEEMED TO PLEASE MRS. ITŌ, WHO HAD A PENCHANT FOR DESIGN AND SMART PRESENTATION AS A PART-TIME INTERIOR DECORATOR.
メリークリスマス、伊藤夫妻。
PAN YA
THIS RELAXED NINA AND BRUNCH PROCEEDED TO GO SMOOTHER THAN SHE EXPECTED, WITH MOST OF THE CONVERSATION FOCUSED ON TAISHI AND HIS JOB.
MY BOSS SAYS I'M KILLING IT RIGHT NOW.
MY QUARTERLY RAISE WILL BE EVEN SWEETER IF I DO HIM A SMALL FAVOR AND TAKE HIS NIECE TO HER PROM.
WHATEVER IT TAKES.

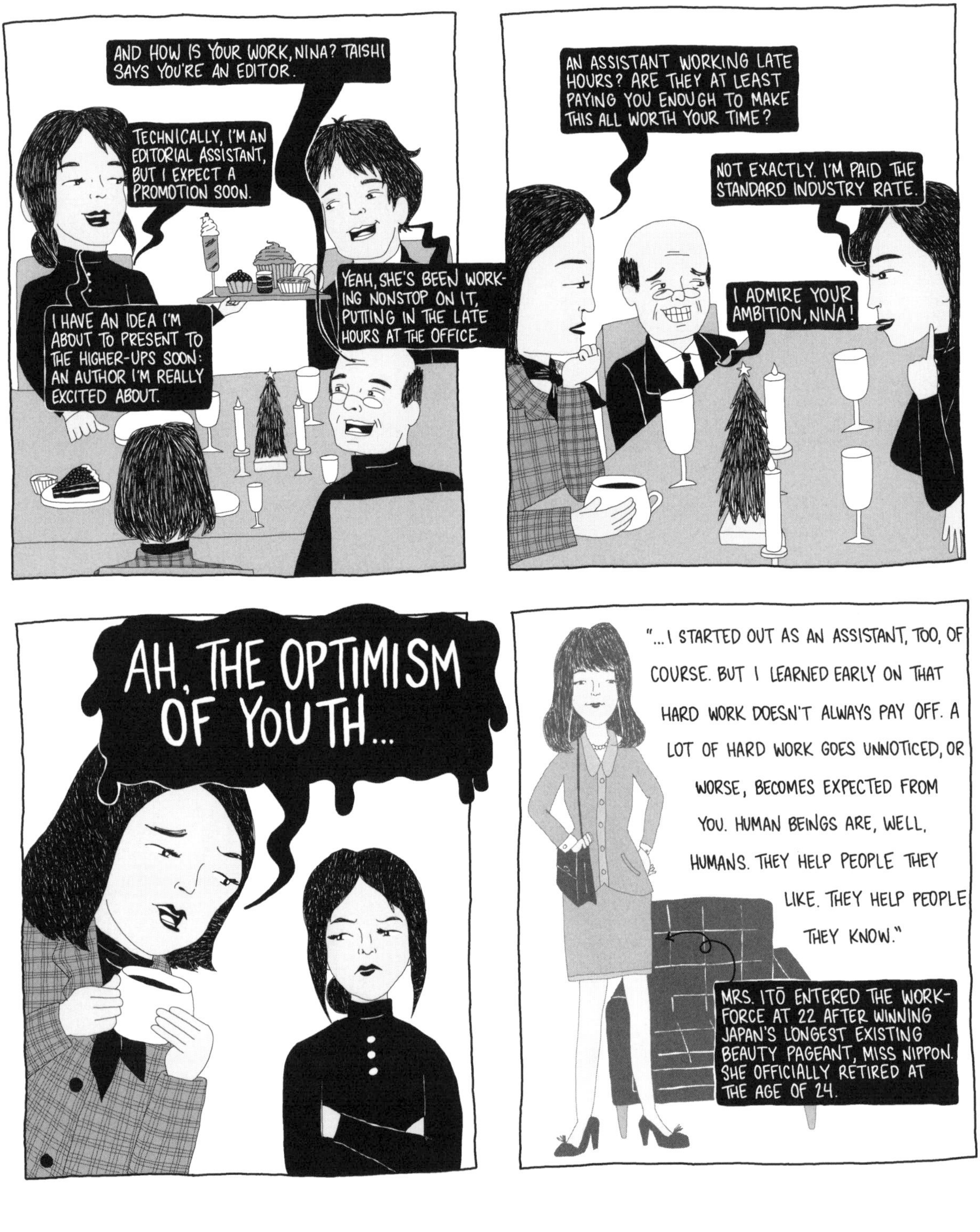

AND HOW IS YOUR WORK, NINA? TAISHI SAYS YOU'RE AN EDITOR.
TECHNICALLY, I'M AN EDITORIAL ASSISTANT, BUT I EXPECT A PROMOTION SOON.
I HAVE AN IDEA I'M ABOUT TO PRESENT TO THE HIGHER-UPS SOON: AN AUTHOR I'M REALLY EXCITED ABOUT.
YEAH, SHE'S BEEN WORKING NONSTOP ON IT, PUTTING IN THE LATE HOURS AT THE OFFICE.
AN ASSISTANT WORKING LATE HOURS? ARE THEY AT LEAST PAYING YOU ENOUGH TO MAKE THIS ALL WORTH YOUR TIME?
NOT EXACTLY. I'M PAID THE STANDARD INDUSTRY RATE.
I ADMIRE YOUR AMBITION, NINA!
AH, THE OPTIMISM OF YOUTH...
"...I STARTED OUT AS AN ASSISTANT, TOO, OF COURSE. BUT I LEARNED EARLY ON THAT HARD WORK DOESN'T ALWAYS PAY OFF. A LOT OF HARD WORK GOES UNNOTICED, OR WORSE, BECOMES EXPECTED FROM YOU. HUMAN BEINGS ARE, WELL, HUMANS. THEY HELP PEOPLE THEY LIKE. THEY HELP PEOPLE THEY KNOW."
MRS. ITŌ ENTERED THE WORKFORCE AT 22 AFTER WINNING JAPAN'S LONGEST EXISTING BEAUTY PAGEANT, MISS NIPPON. SHE OFFICIALLY RETIRED AT THE AGE OF 24.

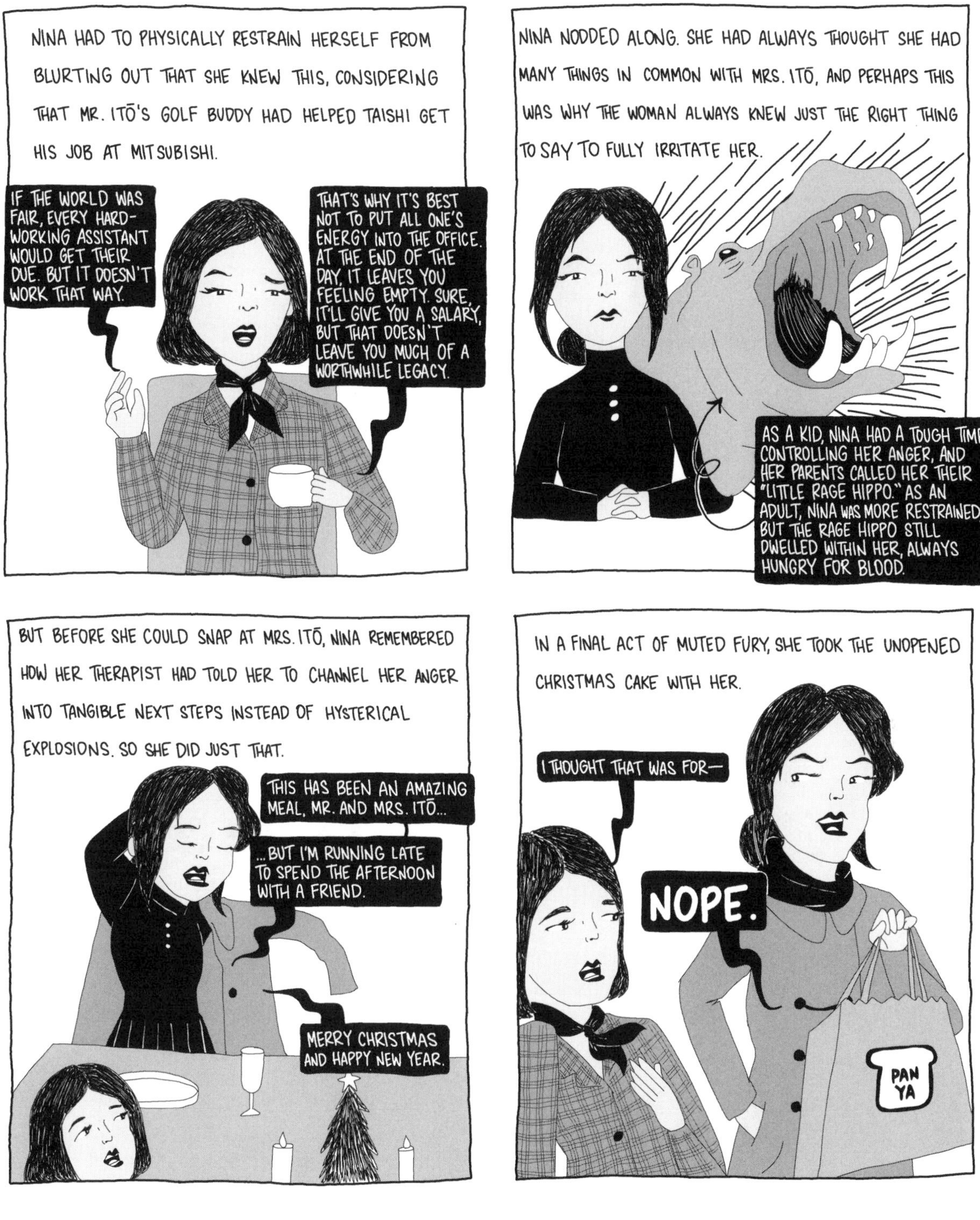
NINA HAD TO PHYSICALLY RESTRAIN HERSELF FROM BLURTING OUT THAT SHE KNEW THIS, CONSIDERING THAT MR. ITŌ'S GOLF BUDDY HAD HELPED TAISHI GET HIS JOB AT MITSUBISHI.
IF THE WORLD WAS FAIR, EVERY HARD-WORKING ASSISTANT WOULD GET THEIR DUE. BUT IT DOESN'T WORK THAT WAY.
THAT'S WHY IT'S BEST NOT TO PUT ALL ONE'S ENERGY INTO THE OFFICE. AT THE END OF THE DAY, IT LEAVES YOU FEELING EMPTY. SURE, IT'LL GIVE YOU A SALARY, BUT THAT DOESN'T LEAVE YOU MUCH OF A WORTHWHILE LEGACY.
NINA NODDED ALONG. SHE HAD ALWAYS THOUGHT SHE HAD MANY THINGS IN COMMON WITH MRS. ITŌ, AND PERHAPS THIS WAS WHY THE WOMAN ALWAYS KNEW JUST THE RIGHT THING TO SAY TO FULLY IRRITATE HER.
AS A KID, NINA HAD A TOUGH TIME CONTROLLING HER ANGER, AND HER PARENTS CALLED HER THEIR "LITTLE RAGE HIPPO." AS AN ADULT, NINA WAS MORE RESTRAINED, BUT THE RAGE HIPPO STILL DWELLED WITHIN HER, ALWAYS HUNGRY FOR BLOOD.
BUT BEFORE SHE COULD SNAP AT MRS. ITŌ, NINA REMEMBERED HOW HER THERAPIST HAD TOLD HER TO CHANNEL HER ANGER INTO TANGIBLE NEXT STEPS INSTEAD OF HYSTERICAL EXPLOSIONS. SO SHE DID JUST THAT.
THIS HAS BEEN AN AMAZING MEAL, MR. AND MRS. ITŌ...
...BUT I'M RUNNING LATE TO SPEND THE AFTERNOON WITH A FRIEND.
MERRY CHRISTMAS AND HAPPY NEW YEAR.
IN A FINAL ACT OF MUTED FURY, SHE TOOK THE UNOPENED CHRISTMAS CAKE WITH HER.
I THOUGHT THAT WAS FOR—
NOPE.
PAN YA

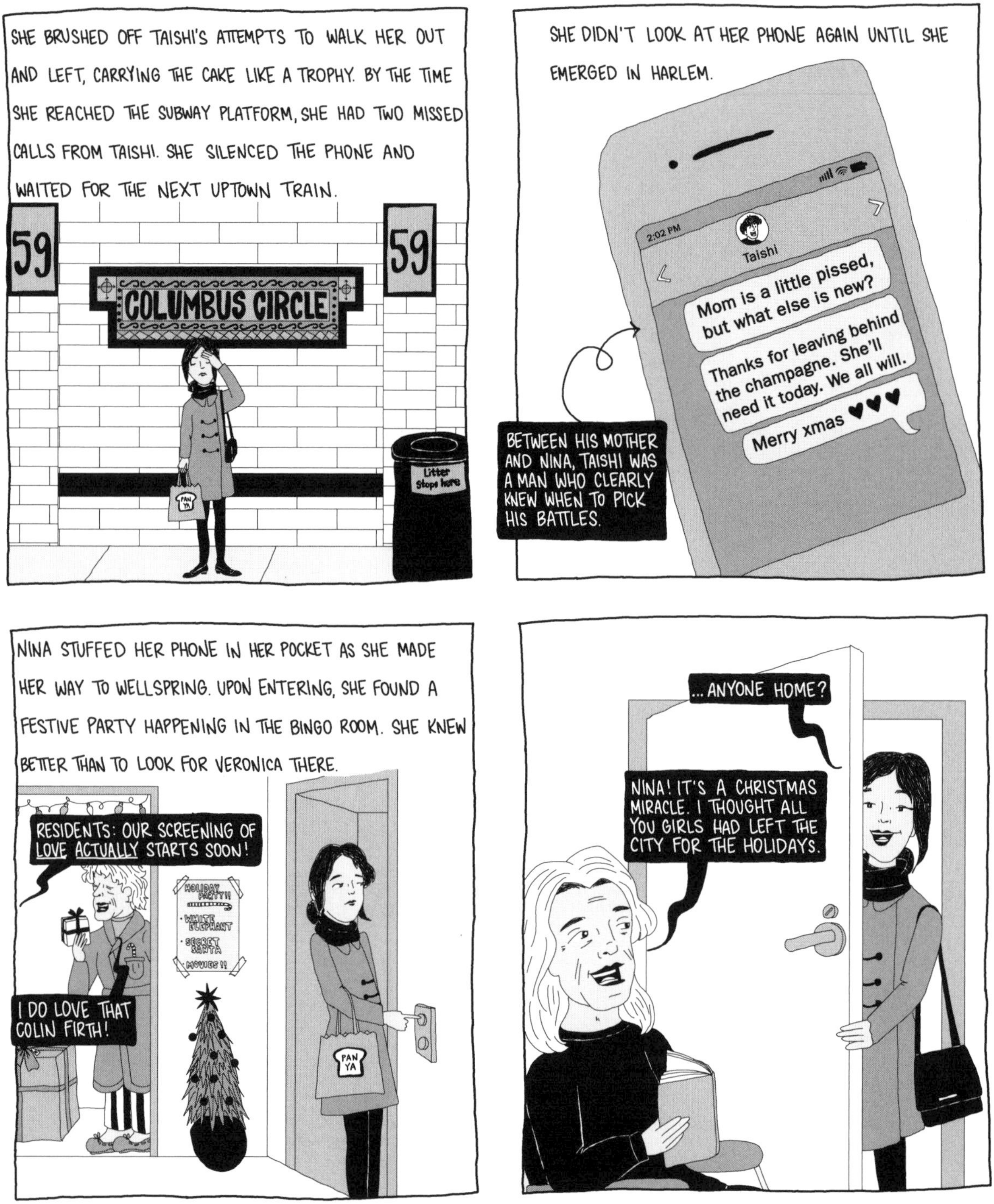
SHE BRUSHED OFF TAISHI'S ATTEMPTS TO WALK HER OUT AND LEFT, CARRYING THE CAKE LIKE A TROPHY. BY THE TIME SHE REACHED THE SUBWAY PLATFORM, SHE HAD TWO MISSED CALLS FROM TAISHI. SHE SILENCED THE PHONE AND WAITED FOR THE NEXT UPTOWN TRAIN.
59
COLUMBUS CIRCLE
59
PAN YA
Litter Stops here
SHE DIDN'T LOOK AT HER PHONE AGAIN UNTIL SHE EMERGED IN HARLEM.
2:02 PM
Taishi
Mom is a little pissed, but what else is new?
Thanks for leaving behind the champagne. She'll need it today. We all will.
Merry xmas ♥♥♥
BETWEEN HIS MOTHER AND NINA, TAISHI WAS A MAN WHO CLEARLY KNEW WHEN TO PICK HIS BATTLES.
NINA STUFFED HER PHONE IN HER POCKET AS SHE MADE HER WAY TO WELLSPRING. UPON ENTERING, SHE FOUND A FESTIVE PARTY HAPPENING IN THE BINGO ROOM. SHE KNEW BETTER THAN TO LOOK FOR VERONICA THERE.
RESIDENTS: OUR SCREENING OF LOVE ACTUALLY STARTS SOON!
HOLIDAY PARTY!!
WHITE ELEPHANT
SECRET SANTA
MOVIES!!
I DO LOVE THAT COLIN FIRTH!
PAN YA
...ANYONE HOME?
NINA! IT'S A CHRISTMAS MIRACLE. I THOUGHT ALL YOU GIRLS HAD LEFT THE CITY FOR THE HOLIDAYS.

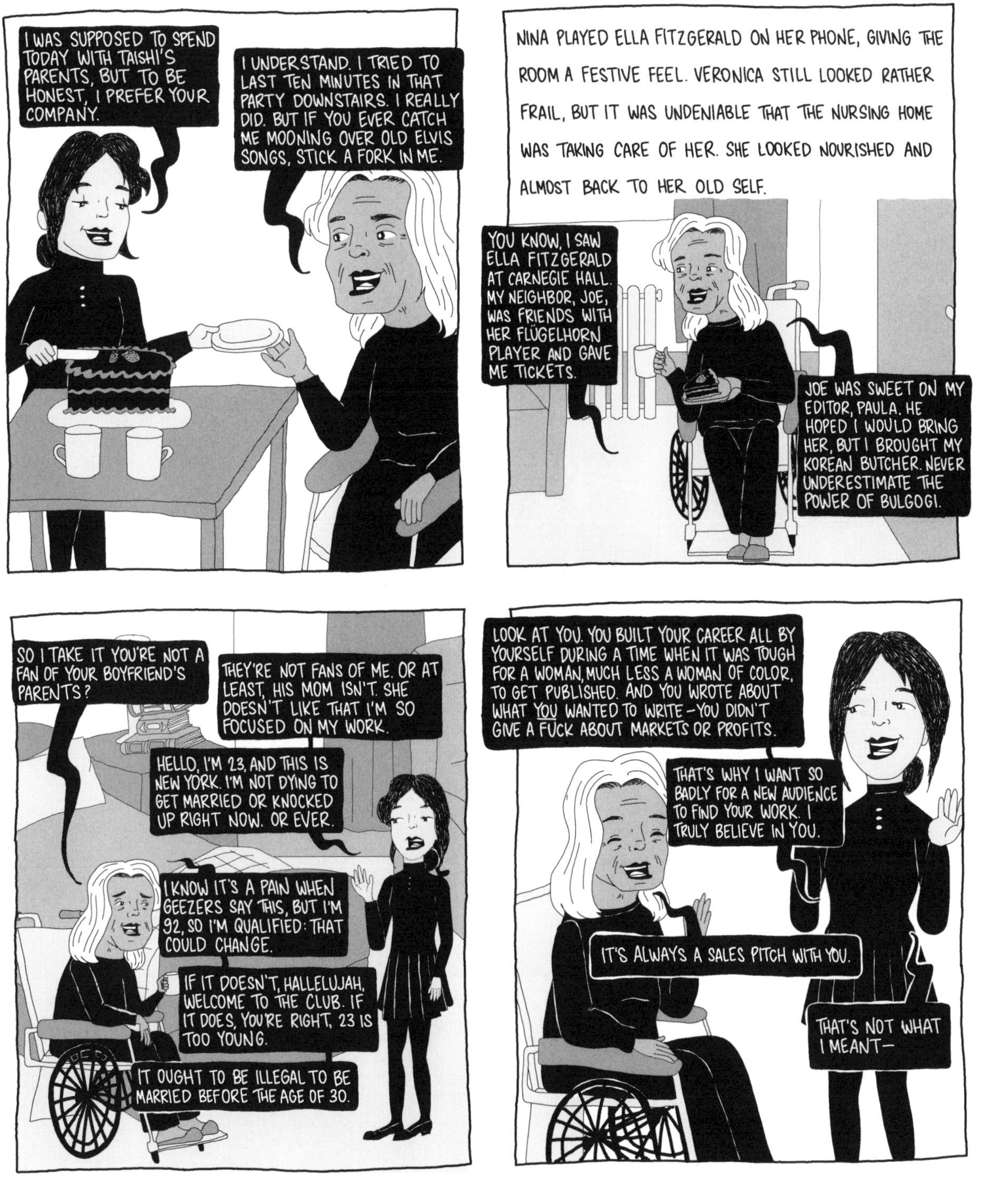
I WAS SUPPOSED TO SPEND TODAY WITH TAISHI'S PARENTS, BUT TO BE HONEST, I PREFER YOUR COMPANY.
I UNDERSTAND. I TRIED TO LAST TEN MINUTES IN THAT PARTY DOWNSTAIRS. I REALLY DID. BUT IF YOU EVER CATCH ME MOONING OVER OLD ELVIS SONGS, STICK A FORK IN ME.
NINA PLAYED ELLA FITZGERALD ON HER PHONE, GIVING THE ROOM A FESTIVE FEEL. VERONICA STILL LOOKED RATHER FRAIL, BUT IT WAS UNDENIABLE THAT THE NURSING HOME WAS TAKING CARE OF HER. SHE LOOKED NOURISHED AND ALMOST BACK TO HER OLD SELF.
YOU KNOW, I SAW ELLA FITZGERALD AT CARNEGIE HALL. MY NEIGHBOR, JOE, WAS FRIENDS WITH HER FLÜGELHORN PLAYER AND GAVE ME TICKETS.
JOE WAS SWEET ON MY EDITOR, PAULA. HE HOPED I WOULD BRING HER, BUT I BROUGHT MY KOREAN BUTCHER. NEVER UNDERESTIMATE THE POWER OF BULGOGI.
SO I TAKE IT YOU'RE NOT A FAN OF YOUR BOYFRIEND'S PARENTS?
THEY'RE NOT FANS OF ME. OR AT LEAST, HIS MOM ISN'T. SHE DOESN'T LIKE THAT I'M SO FOCUSED ON MY WORK.
HELLO, I'M 23, AND THIS IS NEW YORK. I'M NOT DYING TO GET MARRIED OR KNOCKED UP RIGHT NOW. OR EVER.
I KNOW IT'S A PAIN WHEN GEEZERS SAY THIS, BUT I'M 92, SO I'M QUALIFIED: THAT COULD CHANGE.
IF IT DOESN'T, HALLELUJAH, WELCOME TO THE CLUB. IF IT DOES, YOU'RE RIGHT, 23 IS TOO YOUNG.
IT OUGHT TO BE ILLEGAL TO BE MARRIED BEFORE THE AGE OF 30.
LOOK AT YOU. YOU BUILT YOUR CAREER ALL BY YOURSELF DURING A TIME WHEN IT WAS TOUGH FOR A WOMAN, MUCH LESS A WOMAN OF COLOR, TO GET PUBLISHED. AND YOU WROTE ABOUT WHAT YOU WANTED TO WRITE—YOU DIDN'T GIVE A FUCK ABOUT MARKETS OR PROFITS.
THAT'S WHY I WANT SO BADLY FOR A NEW AUDIENCE TO FIND YOUR WORK. I TRULY BELIEVE IN YOU.
IT'S ALWAYS A SALES PITCH WITH YOU.
THAT'S NOT WHAT I MEANT—

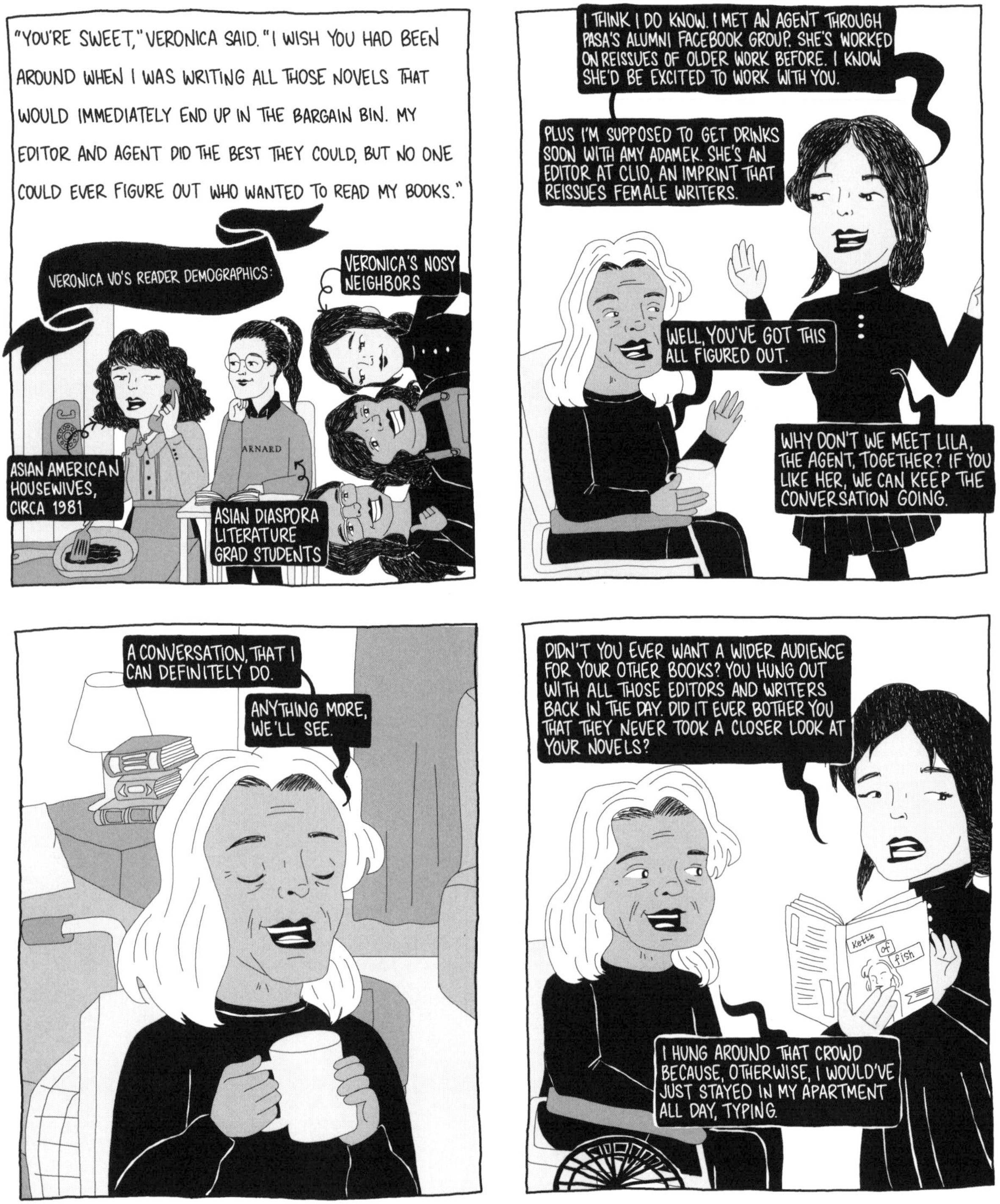
"YOU'RE SWEET," VERONICA SAID. "I WISH YOU HAD BEEN AROUND WHEN I WAS WRITING ALL THOSE NOVELS THAT WOULD IMMEDIATELY END UP IN THE BARGAIN BIN. MY EDITOR AND AGENT DID THE BEST THEY COULD, BUT NO ONE COULD EVER FIGURE OUT WHO WANTED TO READ MY BOOKS."
VERONICA VO'S READER DEMOGRAPHICS:
VERONICA'S NOSY NEIGHBORS
ASIAN AMERICAN HOUSEWIVES, CIRCA 1981
ARNARD
ASIAN DIASPORA LITERATURE GRAD STUDENTS
I THINK I DO KNOW. I MET AN AGENT THROUGH PASA'S ALUMNI FACEBOOK GROUP. SHE'S WORKED ON REISSUES OF OLDER WORK BEFORE. I KNOW SHE'D BE EXCITED TO WORK WITH YOU.
PLUS I'M SUPPOSED TO GET DRINKS SOON WITH AMY ADAMEK. SHE'S AN EDITOR AT CLIO, AN IMPRINT THAT REISSUES FEMALE WRITERS.
WELL, YOU'VE GOT THIS ALL FIGURED OUT.
WHY DON'T WE MEET LILA, THE AGENT, TOGETHER? IF YOU LIKE HER, WE CAN KEEP THE CONVERSATION GOING.
A CONVERSATION, THAT I CAN DEFINITELY DO.
ANYTHING MORE, WE'LL SEE.
DIDN'T YOU EVER WANT A WIDER AUDIENCE FOR YOUR OTHER BOOKS? YOU HUNG OUT WITH ALL THOSE EDITORS AND WRITERS BACK IN THE DAY. DID IT EVER BOTHER YOU THAT THEY NEVER TOOK A CLOSER LOOK AT YOUR NOVELS?
Kettle of fish
I HUNG AROUND THAT CROWD BECAUSE, OTHERWISE, I WOULD'VE JUST STAYED IN MY APARTMENT ALL DAY, TYPING.

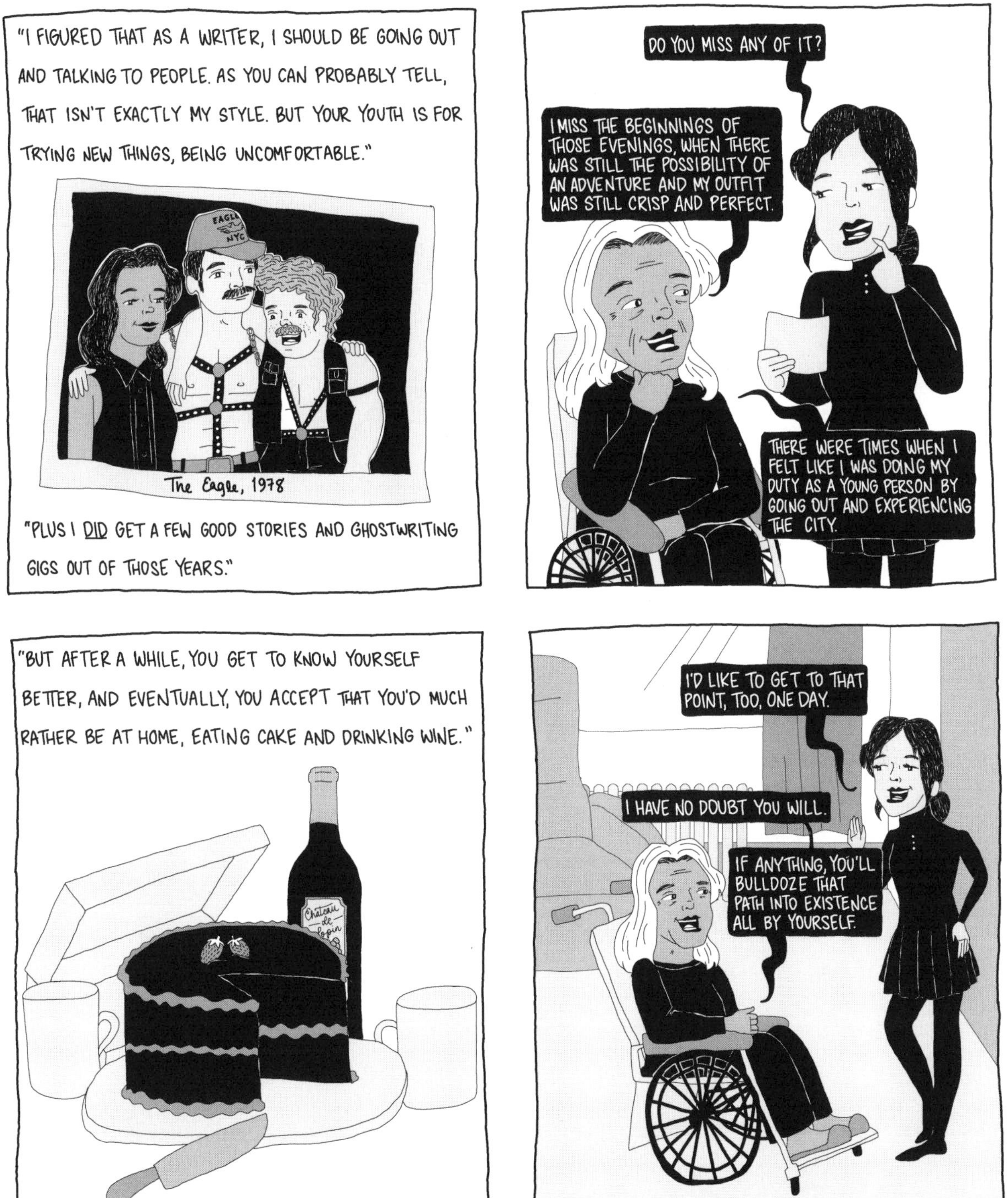
"I FIGURED THAT AS A WRITER, I SHOULD BE GOING OUT AND TALKING TO PEOPLE. AS YOU CAN PROBABLY TELL, THAT ISN'T EXACTLY MY STYLE. BUT YOUR YOUTH IS FOR TRYING NEW THINGS, BEING UNCOMFORTABLE."
The Eagle, 1978
"PLUS I DID GET A FEW GOOD STORIES AND GHOSTWRITING GIGS OUT OF THOSE YEARS."
DO YOU MISS ANY OF IT?
I MISS THE BEGINNINGS OF THOSE EVENINGS, WHEN THERE WAS STILL THE POSSIBILITY OF AN ADVENTURE AND MY OUTFIT WAS STILL CRISP AND PERFECT.
THERE WERE TIMES WHEN I FELT LIKE I WAS DOING MY DUTY AS A YOUNG PERSON BY GOING OUT AND EXPERIENCING THE CITY.
"BUT AFTER A WHILE, YOU GET TO KNOW YOURSELF BETTER, AND EVENTUALLY, YOU ACCEPT THAT YOU'D MUCH RATHER BE AT HOME, EATING CAKE AND DRINKING WINE."
I'D LIKE TO GET TO THAT POINT, TOO, ONE DAY.
I HAVE NO DOUBT YOU WILL.
IF ANYTHING, YOU'LL BULLDOZE THAT PATH INTO EXISTENCE ALL BY YOURSELF.

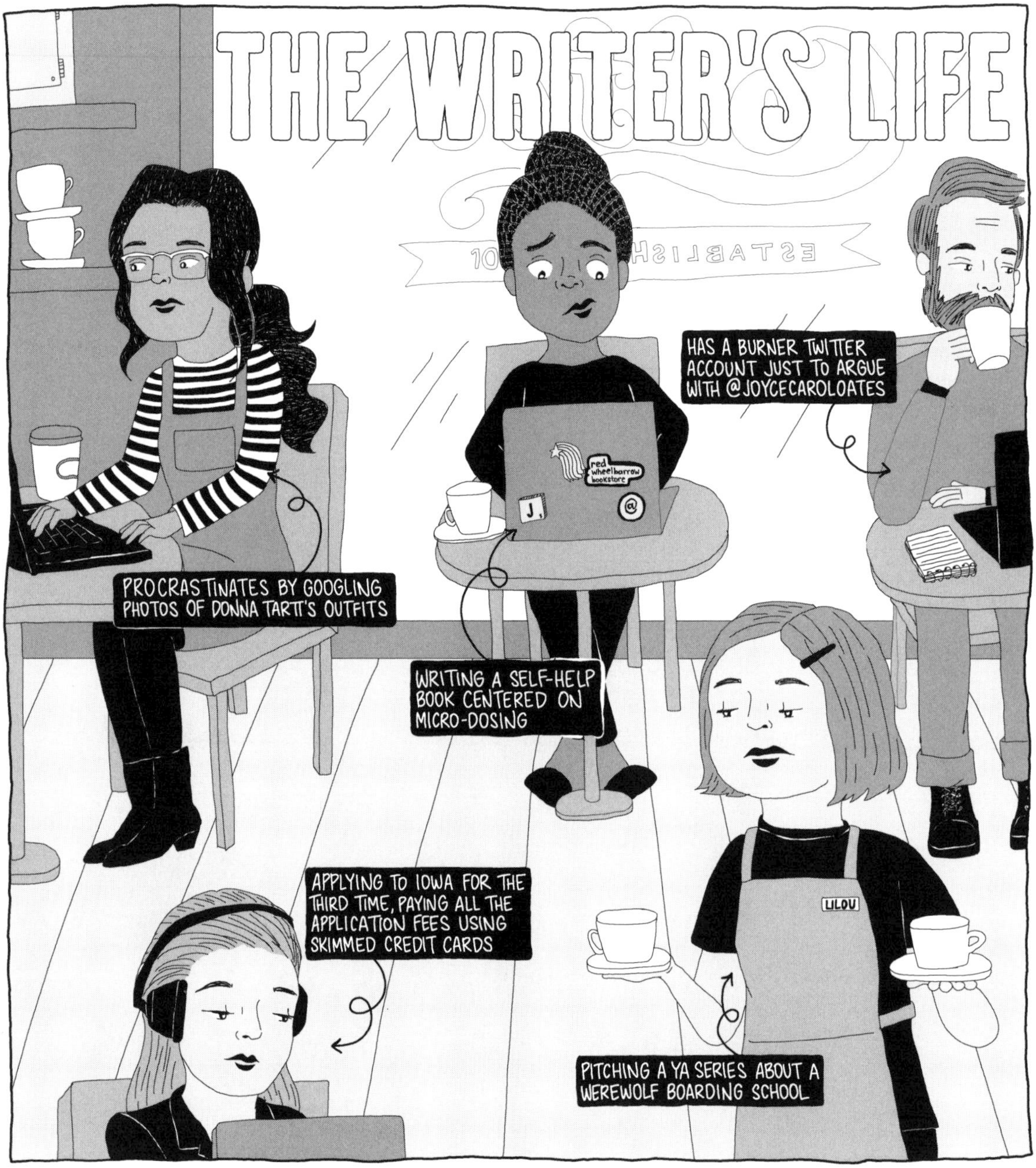
THE WRITER'S LIFE
PROCRASTINATES BY GOOGLING PHOTOS OF DONNA TARTT'S OUTFITS
red wheelbarrow bookstore
WRITING A SELF-HELP BOOK CENTERED ON MICRO-DOSING
HAS A BURNER TWITTER ACCOUNT JUST TO ARGUE WITH @JOYCECAROLOATES
APPLYING TO IOWA FOR THE THIRD TIME, PAYING ALL THE APPLICATION FEES USING SKIMMED CREDIT CARDS
LILOU
PITCHING A YA SERIES ABOUT A WEREWOLF BOARDING SCHOOL

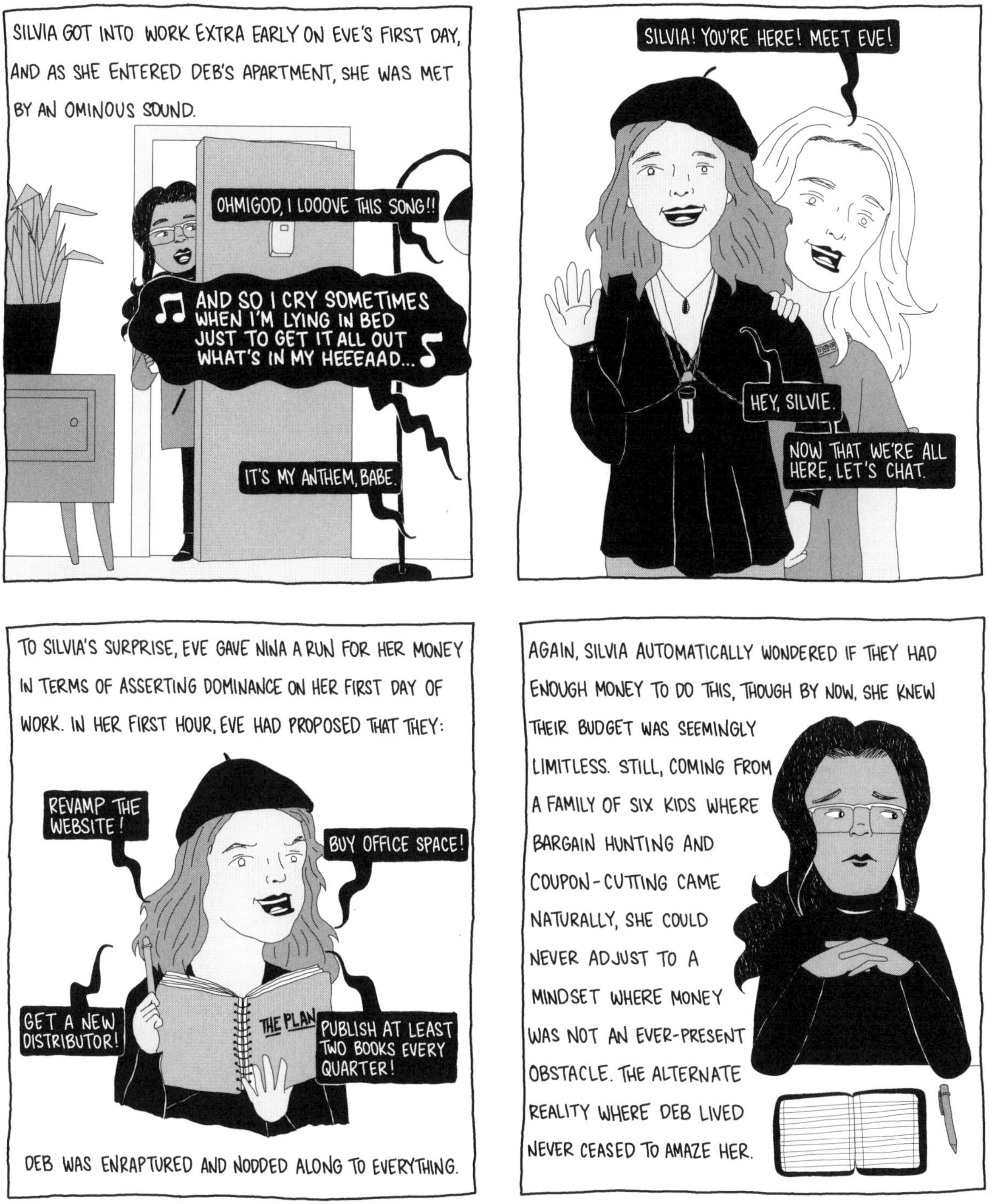
SILVIA GOT INTO WORK EXTRA EARLY ON EVE'S FIRST DAY, AND AS SHE ENTERED DEB'S APARTMENT, SHE WAS MET BY AN OMINOUS SOUND.
OHMIGOD, I LOOOVE THIS SONG!!
AND SO I CRY SOMETIMES WHEN I'M LYING IN BED JUST TO GET IT ALL OUT WHAT'S IN MY HEEEAAD...
IT'S MY ANTHEM, BABE.
SILVIA! YOU'RE HERE! MEET EVE!
HEY, SILVIE.
NOW THAT WE'RE ALL HERE, LET'S CHAT.
TO SILVIA'S SURPRISE, EVE GAVE NINA A RUN FOR HER MONEY IN TERMS OF ASSERTING DOMINANCE ON HER FIRST DAY OF WORK. IN HER FIRST HOUR, EVE HAD PROPOSED THAT THEY:
REVAMP THE WEBSITE!
BUY OFFICE SPACE!
GET A NEW DISTRIBUTOR!
THE PLAN
PUBLISH AT LEAST TWO BOOKS EVERY QUARTER!
DEB WAS ENRAPTURED AND NODDED ALONG TO EVERYTHING.
AGAIN, SILVIA AUTOMATICALLY WONDERED IF THEY HAD ENOUGH MONEY TO DO THIS, THOUGH BY NOW, SHE KNEW THEIR BUDGET WAS SEEMINGLY LIMITLESS. STILL, COMING FROM A FAMILY OF SIX KIDS WHERE BARGAIN HUNTING AND COUPON-CUTTING CAME NATURALLY, SHE COULD NEVER ADJUST TO A MINDSET WHERE MONEY WAS NOT AN EVER-PRESENT OBSTACLE. THE ALTERNATE REALITY WHERE DEB LIVED NEVER CEASED TO AMAZE HER.

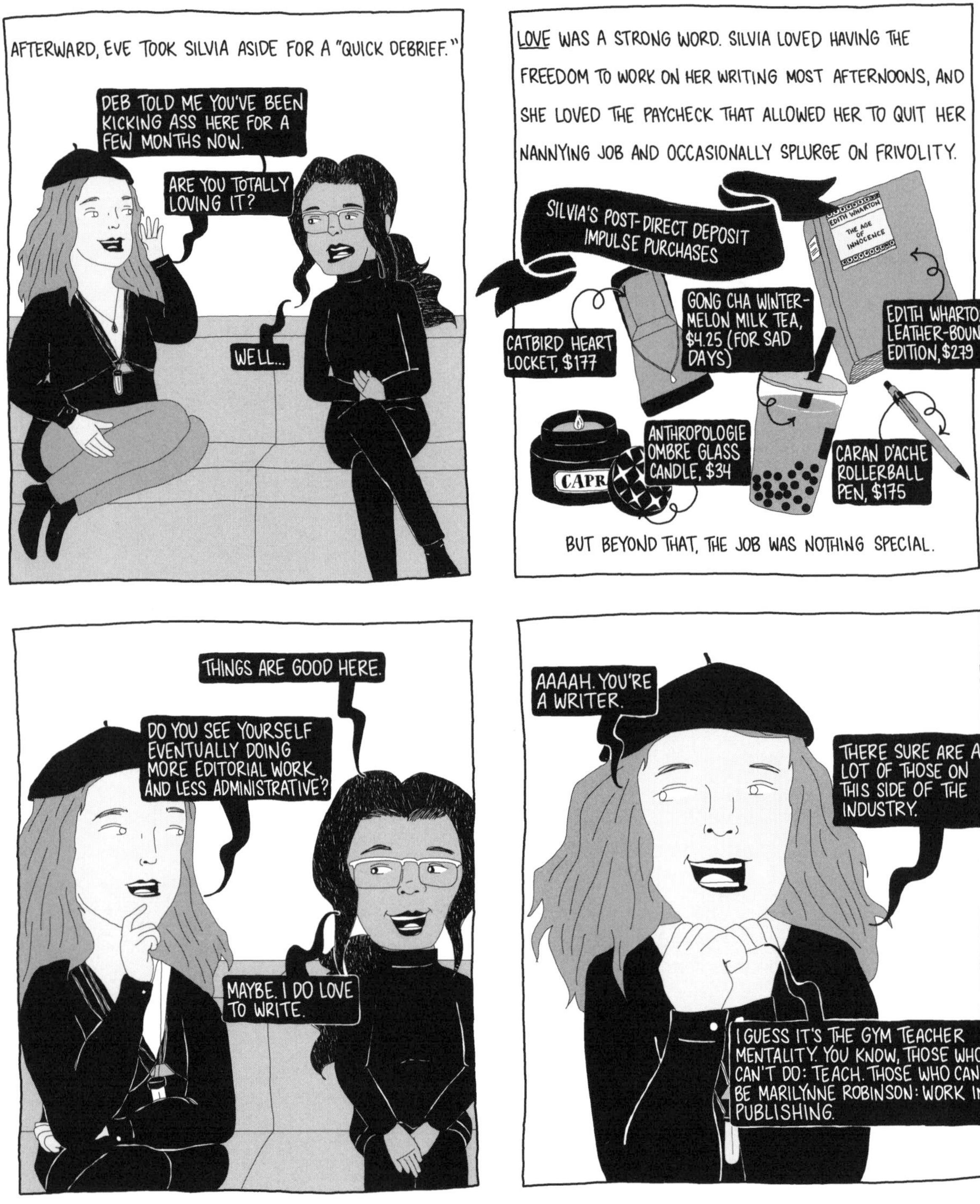
AFTERWARD, EVE TOOK SILVIA ASIDE FOR A "QUICK DEBRIEF."
DEB TOLD ME YOU'VE BEEN KICKING ASS HERE FOR A FEW MONTHS NOW.
ARE YOU TOTALLY LOVING IT?
WELL...
LOVE WAS A STRONG WORD. SILVIA LOVED HAVING THE FREEDOM TO WORK ON HER WRITING MOST AFTERNOONS, AND SHE LOVED THE PAYCHECK THAT ALLOWED HER TO QUIT HER NANNYING JOB AND OCCASIONALLY SPLURGE ON FRIVOLITY.
SILVIA'S POST-DIRECT DEPOSIT IMPULSE PURCHASES
CATBIRD HEART LOCKET, $177
GONG CHA WINTER-MELON MILK TEA, $4.25 (FOR SAD DAYS)
EDITH WHARTON THE AGE OF INNOCENCE
EDITH WHARTON LEATHER-BOUND EDITION, $279
CAPR
ANTHROPOLOGIE OMBRE GLASS CANDLE, $34
CARAN D'ACHE ROLLERBALL PEN, $175
BUT BEYOND THAT, THE JOB WAS NOTHING SPECIAL.
THINGS ARE GOOD HERE.
DO YOU SEE YOURSELF EVENTUALLY DOING MORE EDITORIAL WORK AND LESS ADMINISTRATIVE?
MAYBE. I DO LOVE TO WRITE.
AAAAH. YOU'RE A WRITER.
THERE SURE ARE A LOT OF THOSE ON THIS SIDE OF THE INDUSTRY.
I GUESS IT'S THE GYM TEACHER MENTALITY. YOU KNOW, THOSE WHO CAN'T DO: TEACH. THOSE WHO CAN'T BE MARILYNNE ROBINSON: WORK IN PUBLISHING.

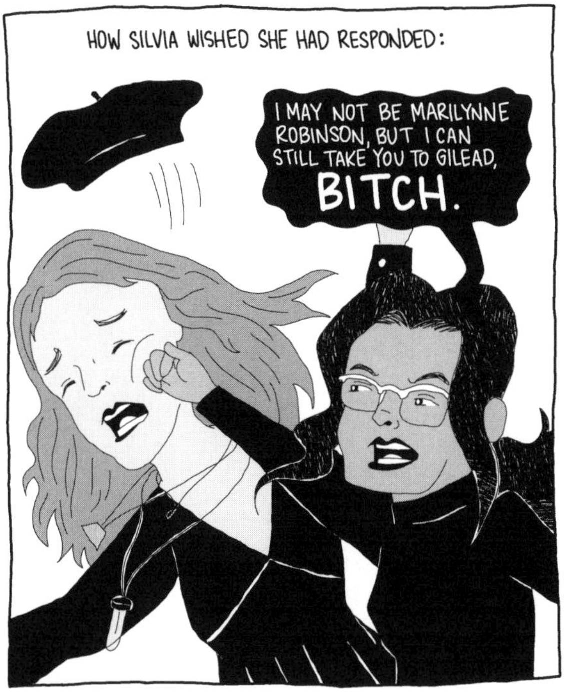
HOW SILVIA WISHED SHE HAD RESPONDED:
I MAY NOT BE MARILYNNE ROBINSON, BUT I CAN STILL TAKE YOU TO GILEAD, BITCH.

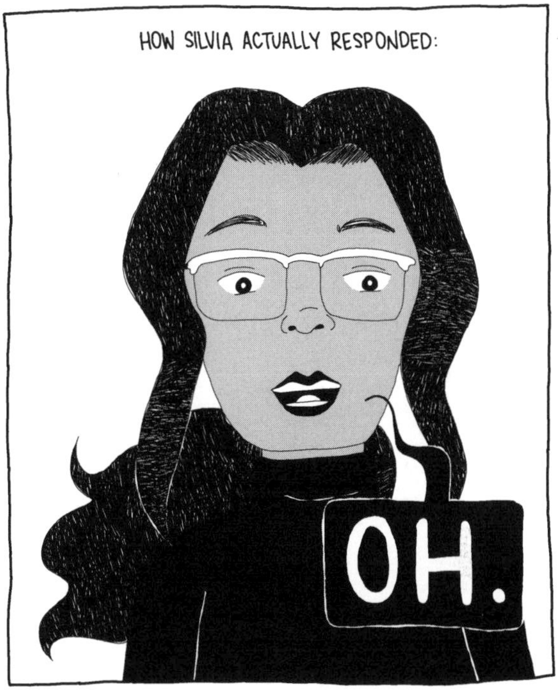
HOW SILVIA ACTUALLY RESPONDED:
OH.

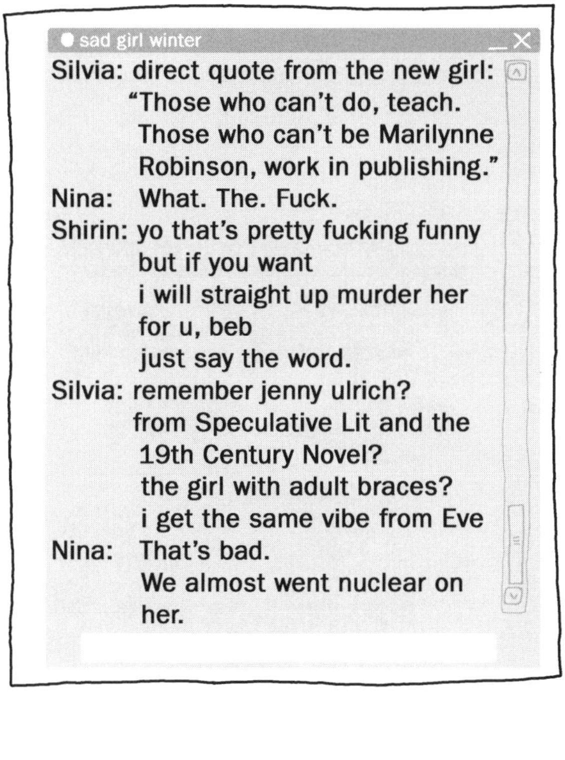
sad girl winter
Silvia: direct quote from the new girl:
"Those who can't do, teach.
Those who can't be Marilynne
Robinson, work in publishing."
Nina: What. The. Fuck.
Shirin: yo that's pretty fucking funny
but if you want
i will straight up murder her
for u, beb
just say the word.
Silvia: remember jenny ulrich?
from Speculative Lit and the
19th Century Novel?
the girl with adult braces?
i get the same vibe from Eve
Nina: That's bad.
We almost went nuclear on
her.

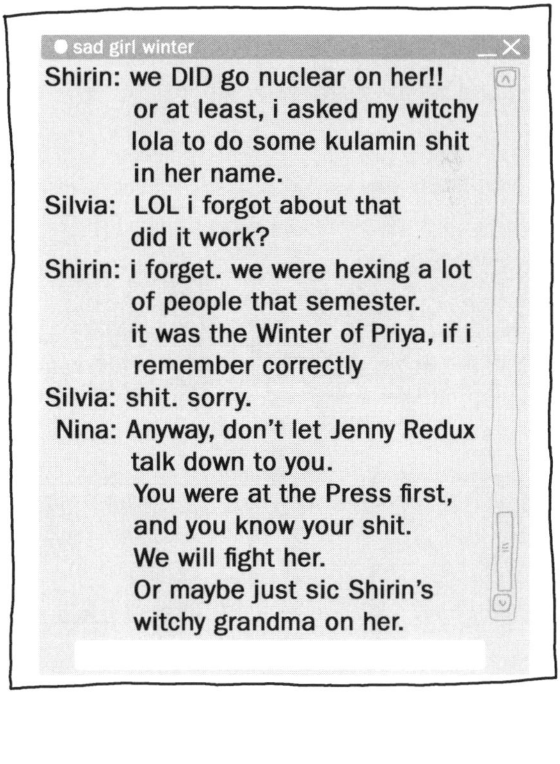
sad girl winter
Shirin: we DID go nuclear on her!!
or at least, i asked my witchy
lola to do some kulamin shit
in her name.
Silvia: LOL i forgot about that
did it work?
Shirin: i forget. we were hexing a lot
of people that semester.
it was the Winter of Priya, if i
remember correctly
Silvia: shit. sorry.
Nina: Anyway, don't let Jenny Redux
talk down to you.
You were at the Press first,
and you know your shit.
We will fight her.
Or maybe just sic Shirin's
witchy grandma on her.

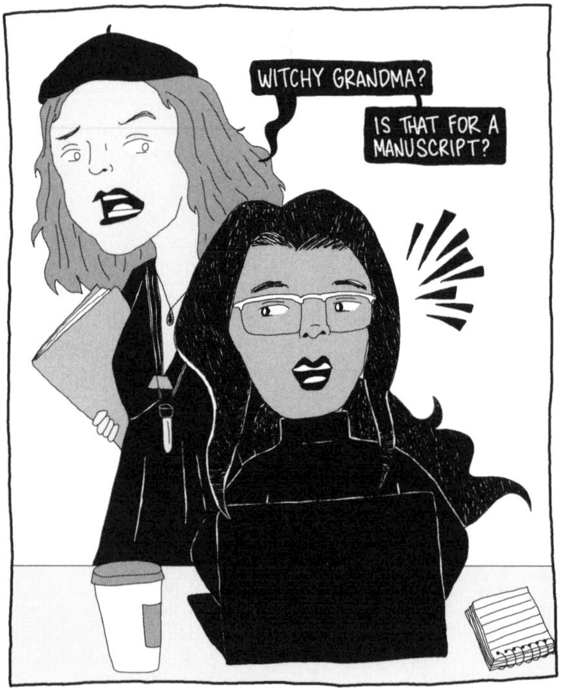
WITCHY GRANDMA?
IS THAT FOR A MANUSCRIPT?

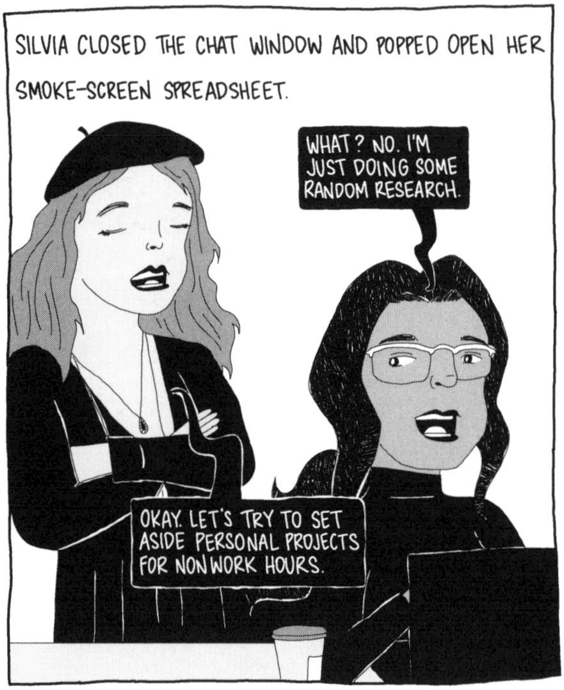
SILVIA CLOSED THE CHAT WINDOW AND POPPED OPEN HER SMOKE-SCREEN SPREADSHEET.
WHAT? NO. I'M JUST DOING SOME RANDOM RESEARCH.
OKAY. LET'S TRY TO SET ASIDE PERSONAL PROJECTS FOR NONWORK HOURS.

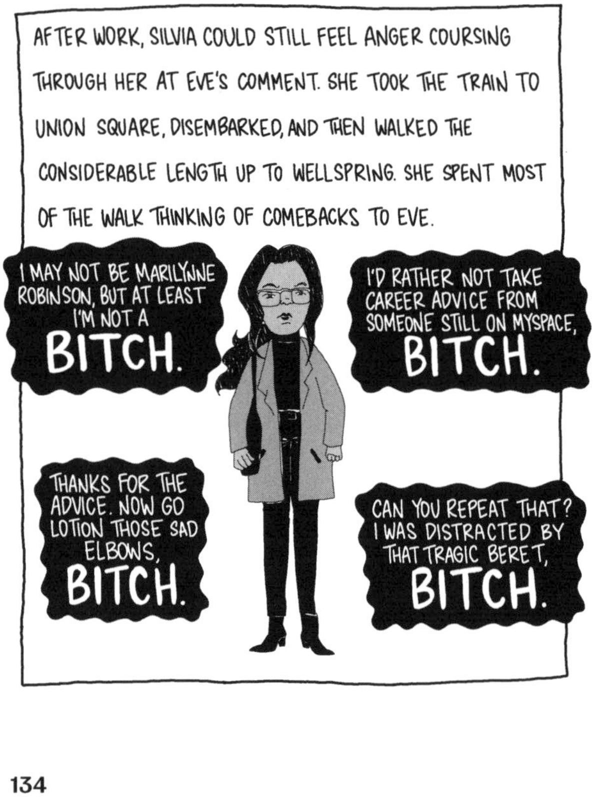
AFTER WORK, SILVIA COULD STILL FEEL ANGER COURSING THROUGH HER AT EVE'S COMMENT. SHE TOOK THE TRAIN TO UNION SQUARE, DISEMBARKED, AND THEN WALKED THE CONSIDERABLE LENGTH UP TO WELLSPRING. SHE SPENT MOST OF THE WALK THINKING OF COMEBACKS TO EVE.
I MAY NOT BE MARILYNNE ROBINSON, BUT AT LEAST I'M NOT A BITCH.
I'D RATHER NOT TAKE CAREER ADVICE FROM SOMEONE STILL ON MYSPACE, BITCH.
THANKS FOR THE ADVICE. NOW GO LOTION THOSE SAD ELBOWS, BITCH.
CAN YOU REPEAT THAT? I WAS DISTRACTED BY THAT TRAGIC BERET, BITCH.

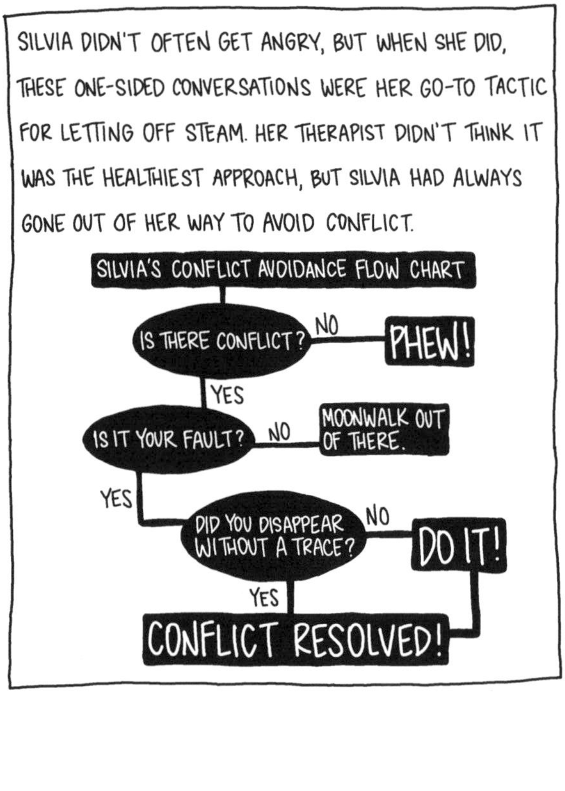
SILVIA DIDN'T OFTEN GET ANGRY, BUT WHEN SHE DID, THESE ONE-SIDED CONVERSATIONS WERE HER GO-TO TACTIC FOR LETTING OFF STEAM. HER THERAPIST DIDN'T THINK IT WAS THE HEALTHIEST APPROACH, BUT SILVIA HAD ALWAYS GONE OUT OF HER WAY TO AVOID CONFLICT.
SILVIA'S CONFLICT AVOIDANCE FLOW CHART
IS THERE CONFLICT?
NO
PHEW!
YES
IS IT YOUR FAULT?
NO
MOONWALK OUT OF THERE.
YES
DID YOU DISAPPEAR WITHOUT A TRACE?
NO
DO IT!
YES
CONFLICT RESOLVED!

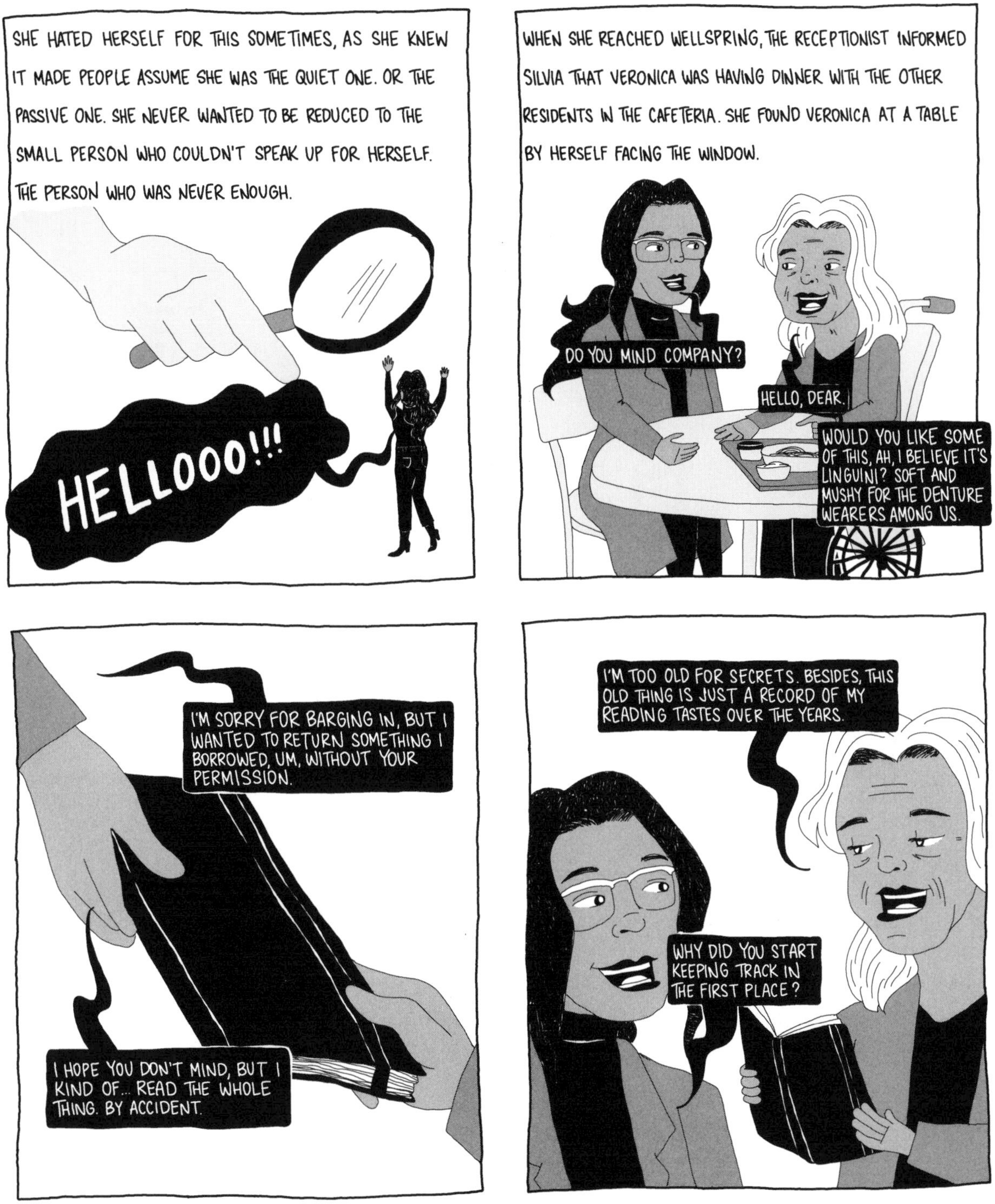
SHE HATED HERSELF FOR THIS SOMETIMES, AS SHE KNEW IT MADE PEOPLE ASSUME SHE WAS THE QUIET ONE. OR THE PASSIVE ONE. SHE NEVER WANTED TO BE REDUCED TO THE SMALL PERSON WHO COULDN'T SPEAK UP FOR HERSELF. THE PERSON WHO WAS NEVER ENOUGH.
HELLOOO!!!
WHEN SHE REACHED WELLSPRING, THE RECEPTIONIST INFORMED SILVIA THAT VERONICA WAS HAVING DINNER WITH THE OTHER RESIDENTS IN THE CAFETERIA. SHE FOUND VERONICA AT A TABLE BY HERSELF FACING THE WINDOW.
DO YOU MIND COMPANY?
HELLO, DEAR.
WOULD YOU LIKE SOME OF THIS, AH, I BELIEVE IT'S LINGUINI? SOFT AND MUSHY FOR THE DENTURE WEARERS AMONG US.
I'M SORRY FOR BARGING IN, BUT I WANTED TO RETURN SOMETHING I BORROWED, UM, WITHOUT YOUR PERMISSION.
I HOPE YOU DON'T MIND, BUT I KIND OF... READ THE WHOLE THING. BY ACCIDENT.
I'M TOO OLD FOR SECRETS. BESIDES, THIS OLD THING IS JUST A RECORD OF MY READING TASTES OVER THE YEARS.
WHY DID YOU START KEEPING TRACK IN THE FIRST PLACE?

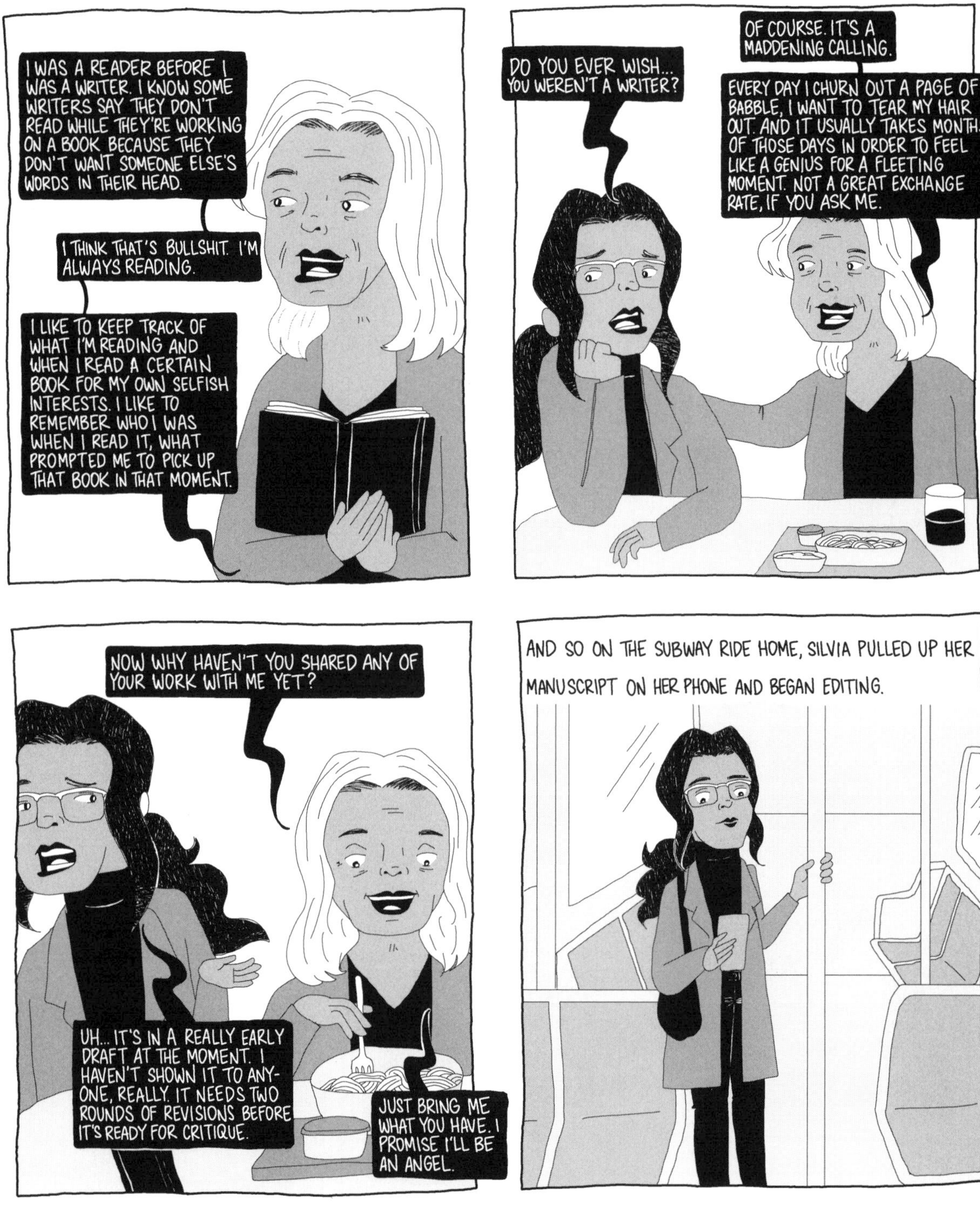
I WAS A READER BEFORE I WAS A WRITER. I KNOW SOME WRITERS SAY THEY DON'T READ WHILE THEY'RE WORKING ON A BOOK BECAUSE THEY DON'T WANT SOMEONE ELSE'S WORDS IN THEIR HEAD.
I THINK THAT'S BULLSHIT. I'M ALWAYS READING.
I LIKE TO KEEP TRACK OF WHAT I'M READING AND WHEN I READ A CERTAIN BOOK FOR MY OWN SELFISH INTERESTS. I LIKE TO REMEMBER WHO I WAS WHEN I READ IT, WHAT PROMPTED ME TO PICK UP THAT BOOK IN THAT MOMENT.
DO YOU EVER WISH... YOU WEREN'T A WRITER?
OF COURSE. IT'S A MADDENING CALLING.
EVERY DAY I CHURN OUT A PAGE OF BABBLE, I WANT TO TEAR MY HAIR OUT. AND IT USUALLY TAKES MONTHS OF THOSE DAYS IN ORDER TO FEEL LIKE A GENIUS FOR A FLEETING MOMENT. NOT A GREAT EXCHANGE RATE, IF YOU ASK ME.
NOW WHY HAVEN'T YOU SHARED ANY OF YOUR WORK WITH ME YET?
UH... IT'S IN A REALLY EARLY DRAFT AT THE MOMENT. I HAVEN'T SHOWN IT TO ANY-ONE, REALLY. IT NEEDS TWO ROUNDS OF REVISIONS BEFORE IT'S READY FOR CRITIQUE.
JUST BRING ME WHAT YOU HAVE. I PROMISE I'LL BE AN ANGEL.
AND SO ON THE SUBWAY RIDE HOME, SILVIA PULLED UP HER MANUSCRIPT ON HER PHONE AND BEGAN EDITING.

THE BALLAD OF MAGGIE LIERSON

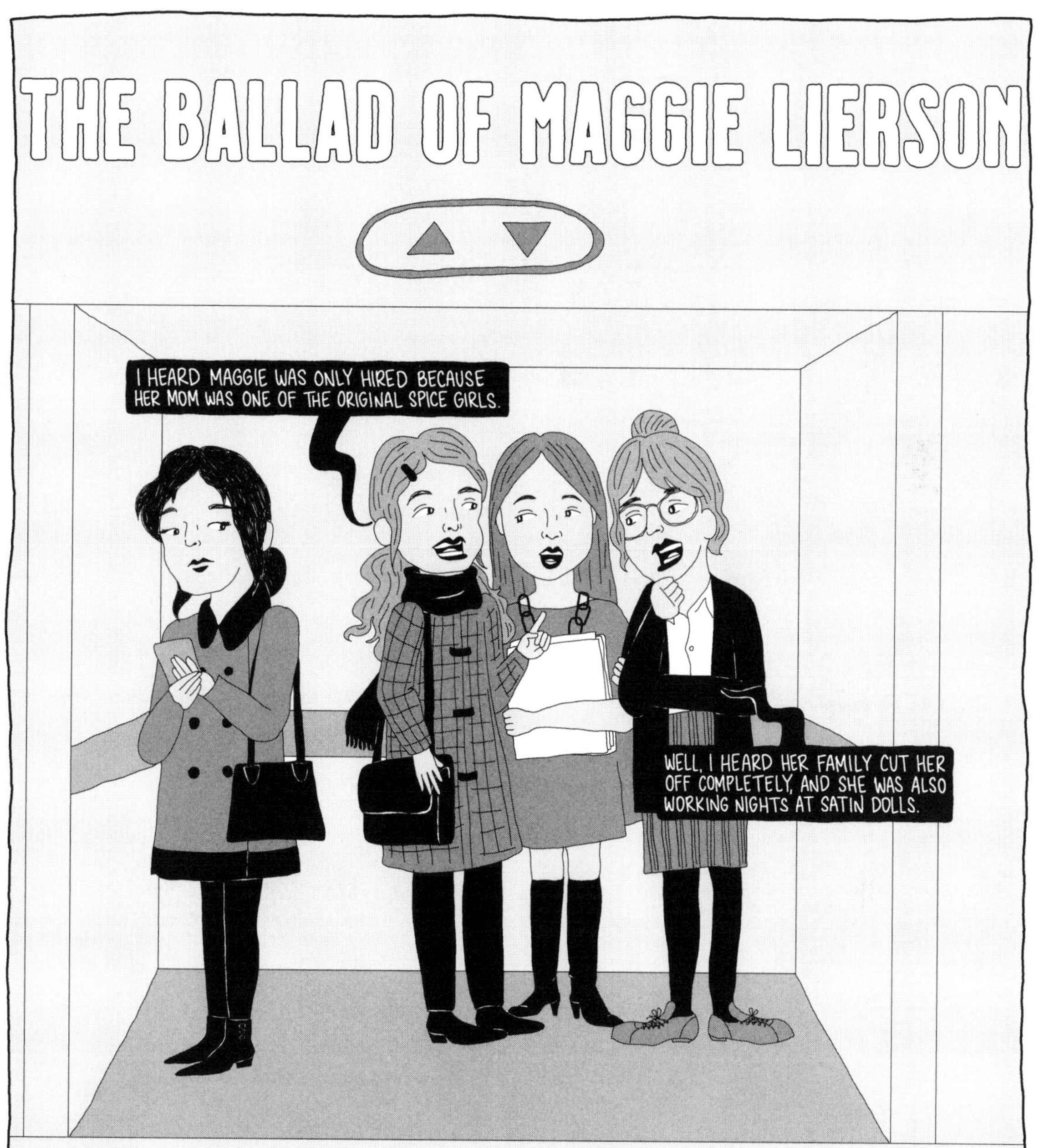
I HEARD MAGGIE WAS ONLY HIRED BECAUSE HER MOM WAS ONE OF THE ORIGINAL SPICE GIRLS.
WELL, I HEARD HER FAMILY CUT HER OFF COMPLETELY, AND SHE WAS ALSO WORKING NIGHTS AT SATIN DOLLS.

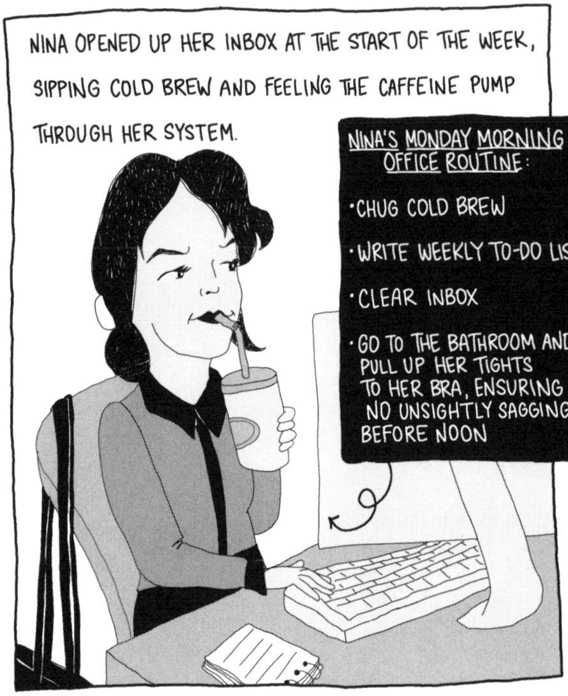
NINA OPENED UP HER INBOX AT THE START OF THE WEEK, SIPPING COLD BREW AND FEELING THE CAFFEINE PUMP THROUGH HER SYSTEM.
NINA'S MONDAY MORNING OFFICE ROUTINE:
•CHUG COLD BREW
•WRITE WEEKLY TO-DO LIST
•CLEAR INBOX
•GO TO THE BATHROOM AND PULL UP HER TIGHTS TO HER BRA, ENSURING NO UNSIGHTLY SAGGING BEFORE NOON

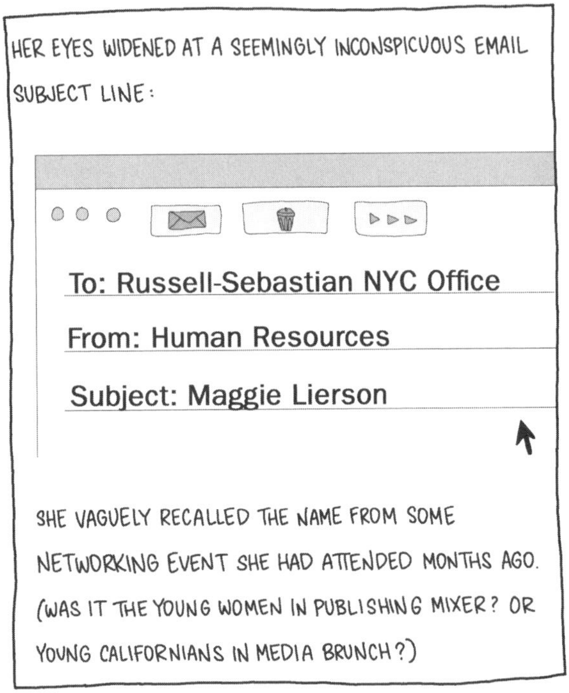
HER EYES WIDENED AT A SEEMINGLY INCONSPICUOUS EMAIL SUBJECT LINE:
To: Russell-Sebastian NYC Office
From: Human Resources
Subject: Maggie Lierson
SHE VAGUELY RECALLED THE NAME FROM SOME NETWORKING EVENT SHE HAD ATTENDED MONTHS AGO. (WAS IT THE YOUNG WOMEN IN PUBLISHING MIXER? OR YOUNG CALIFORNIANS IN MEDIA BRUNCH?)

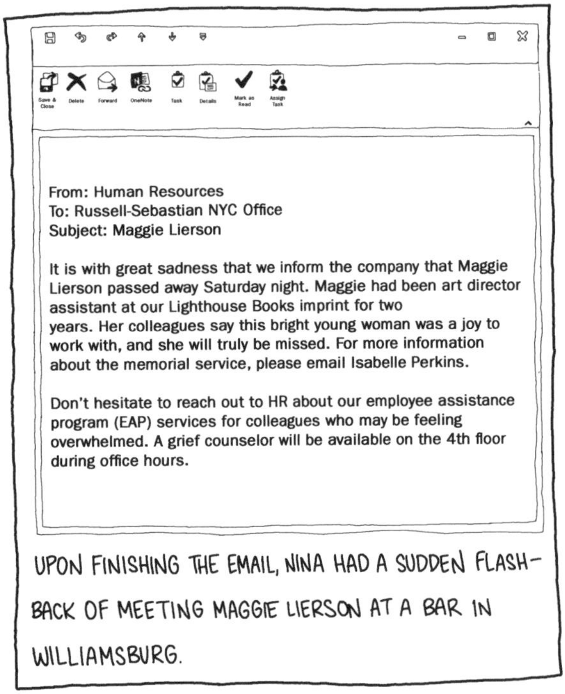
From: Human Resources
To: Russell-Sebastian NYC Office
Subject: Maggie Lierson
It is with great sadness that we inform the company that Maggie Lierson passed away Saturday night. Maggie had been art director assistant at our Lighthouse Books imprint for two years. Her colleagues say this bright young woman was a joy to work with, and she will truly be missed. For more information about the memorial service, please email Isabelle Perkins.
Don't hesitate to reach out to HR about our employee assistance program (EAP) services for colleagues who may be feeling overwhelmed. A grief counselor will be available on the 4th floor during office hours.
UPON FINISHING THE EMAIL, NINA HAD A SUDDEN FLASH-BACK OF MEETING MAGGIE LIERSON AT A BAR IN WILLIAMSBURG.

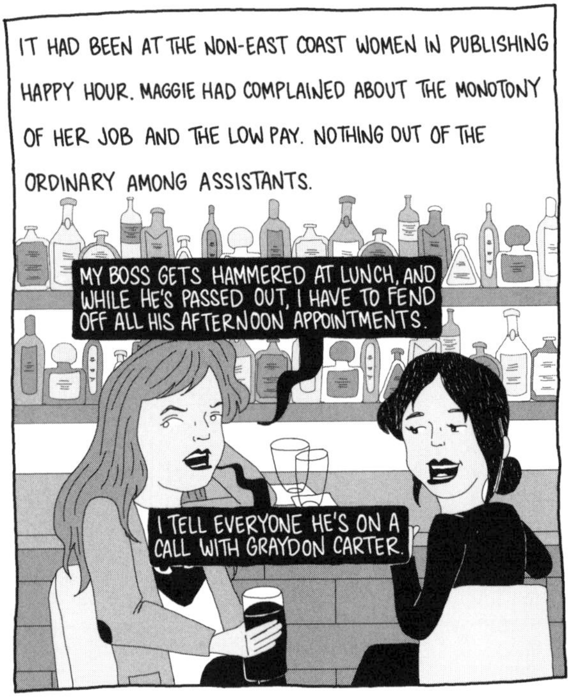
IT HAD BEEN AT THE NON-EAST COAST WOMEN IN PUBLISHING HAPPY HOUR. MAGGIE HAD COMPLAINED ABOUT THE MONOTONY OF HER JOB AND THE LOW PAY. NOTHING OUT OF THE ORDINARY AMONG ASSISTANTS.
MY BOSS GETS HAMMERED AT LUNCH, AND WHILE HE'S PASSED OUT, I HAVE TO FEND OFF ALL HIS AFTERNOON APPOINTMENTS.
I TELL EVERYONE HE'S ON A CALL WITH GRAYDON CARTER.

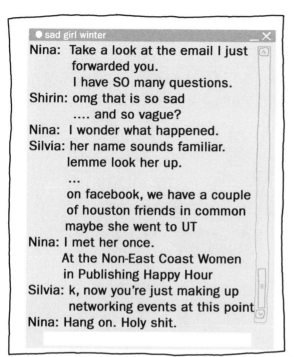

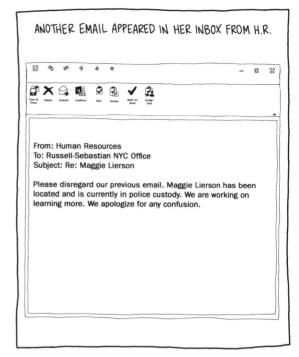

sad girl winter
Nina: Take a look at the email I just forwarded you.
I have SO many questions.
Shirin: omg that is so sad
.... and so vague?
Nina: I wonder what happened.
Silvia: her name sounds familiar.
lemme look her up.
...
on facebook, we have a couple of houston friends in common
maybe she went to UT
Nina: I met her once.
At the Non-East Coast Women in Publishing Happy Hour
Silvia: k, now you're just making up networking events at this point
Nina: Hang on. Holy shit.
ANOTHER EMAIL APPEARED IN HER INBOX FROM H.R.
From: Human Resources
To: Russell-Sebastian NYC Office
Subject: Re: Maggie Lierson
Please disregard our previous email. Maggie Lierson has been located and is currently in police custody. We are working on learning more. We apologize for any confusion.
sad girl winter
Nina: Okay. Check your email again.
Shirin: THIS IS BANANAS
so she's not dead?
did homegirl fake her own death?
why are the cops involved??
Nina: I have no clue.
Shirin: well, i am fully invested now and i do not plan to do a lick of work today during this IRL episode of Unsolved Mysteries
Silvia: see, this is why i need to work for a company with more than 3 people
we never get wild shit like this
Nina: If she fooled HR, Maggie must be a legit scammer.
Shirin: i bow down to my scam queen.
HR NEVER SENT A FOLLOW-UP EMAIL, SO NINA TOOK IT UPON HERSELF TO LEARN THE FULL STORY FROM GOSSIPING COLLEAGUES THROUGHOUT THE DAY.
I ONCE CAUGHT HER RAIDING THE KID LIT FLOOR, SAYING SHE WAS COLLECTING DONATIONS FOR AN ORPHANAGE.
BUT THEN I SAW MOST OF HER HAUL A WEEK LATER AT THE STRAND.
WHAT AN ODDBALL.

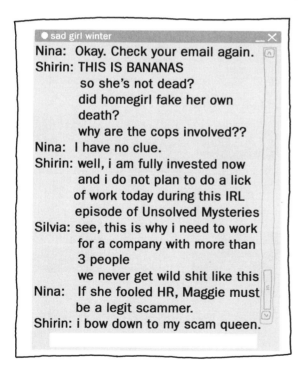

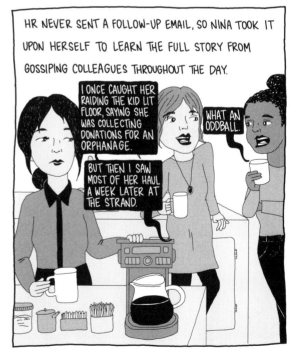

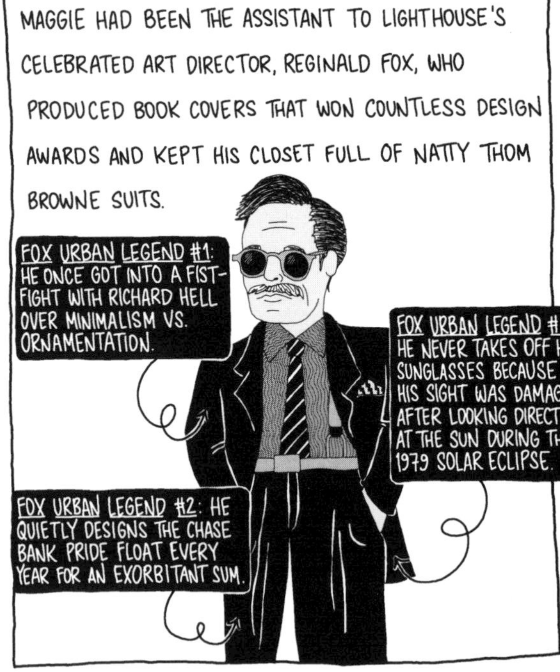
MAGGIE HAD BEEN THE ASSISTANT TO LIGHTHOUSE'S CELEBRATED ART DIRECTOR, REGINALD FOX, WHO PRODUCED BOOK COVERS THAT WON COUNTLESS DESIGN AWARDS AND KEPT HIS CLOSET FULL OF NATTY THOM BROWNE SUITS.
FOX URBAN LEGEND #1: HE ONCE GOT INTO A FIST-FIGHT WITH RICHARD HELL OVER MINIMALISM VS. ORNAMENTATION.
FOX URBAN LEGEND #3: HE NEVER TAKES OFF HIS SUNGLASSES BECAUSE HIS SIGHT WAS DAMAGED AFTER LOOKING DIRECTLY AT THE SUN DURING THE 1979 SOLAR ECLIPSE.
FOX URBAN LEGEND #2: HE QUIETLY DESIGNS THE CHASE BANK PRIDE FLOAT EVERY YEAR FOR AN EXORBITANT SUM.

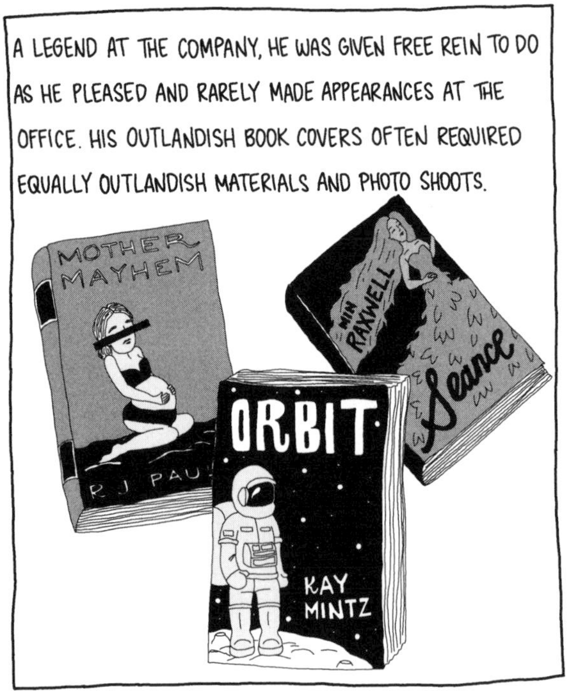
A LEGEND AT THE COMPANY, HE WAS GIVEN FREE REIN TO DO AS HE PLEASED AND RARELY MADE APPEARANCES AT THE OFFICE. HIS OUTLANDISH BOOK COVERS OFTEN REQUIRED EQUALLY OUTLANDISH MATERIALS AND PHOTO SHOOTS.
MOTHER MAYHEM
MIN RAXWELL
Seance
ORBIT
KAY MINTZ

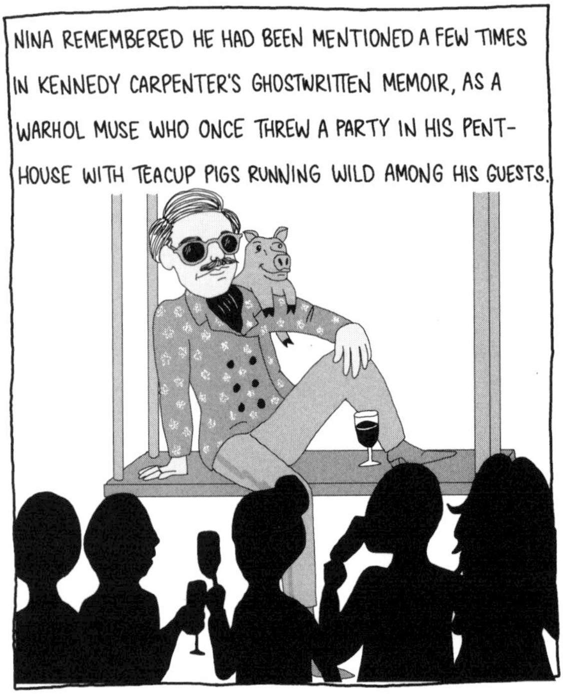
NINA REMEMBERED HE HAD BEEN MENTIONED A FEW TIMES IN KENNEDY CARPENTER'S GHOSTWRITTEN MEMOIR, AS A WARHOL MUSE WHO ONCE THREW A PARTY IN HIS PENT-HOUSE WITH TEACUP PIGS RUNNING WILD AMONG HIS GUESTS.

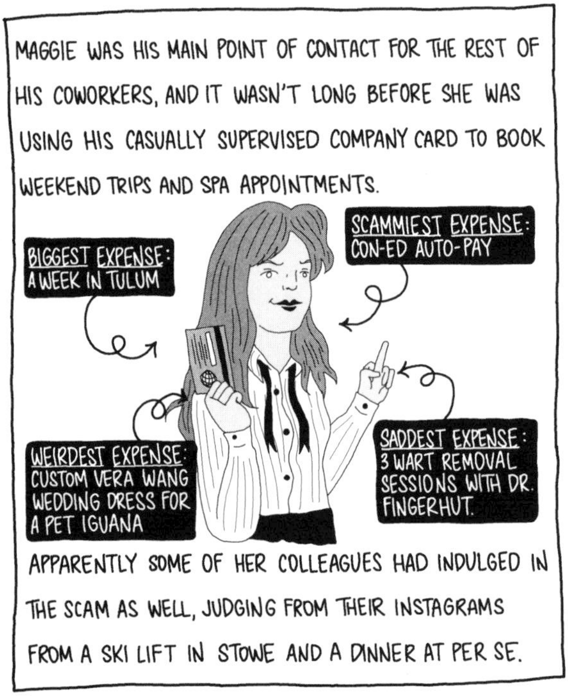
MAGGIE WAS HIS MAIN POINT OF CONTACT FOR THE REST OF HIS COWORKERS, AND IT WASN'T LONG BEFORE SHE WAS USING HIS CASUALLY SUPERVISED COMPANY CARD TO BOOK WEEKEND TRIPS AND SPA APPOINTMENTS.
BIGGEST EXPENSE: A WEEK IN TULUM
SCAMMIEST EXPENSE: CON-ED AUTO-PAY
WEIRDEST EXPENSE: CUSTOM VERA WANG WEDDING DRESS FOR A PET IGUANA
SADDEST EXPENSE: 3 WART REMOVAL SESSIONS WITH DR. FINGERHUT.
APPARENTLY SOME OF HER COLLEAGUES HAD INDULGED IN THE SCAM AS WELL, JUDGING FROM THEIR INSTAGRAMS FROM A SKI LIFT IN STOWE AND A DINNER AT PER SE.

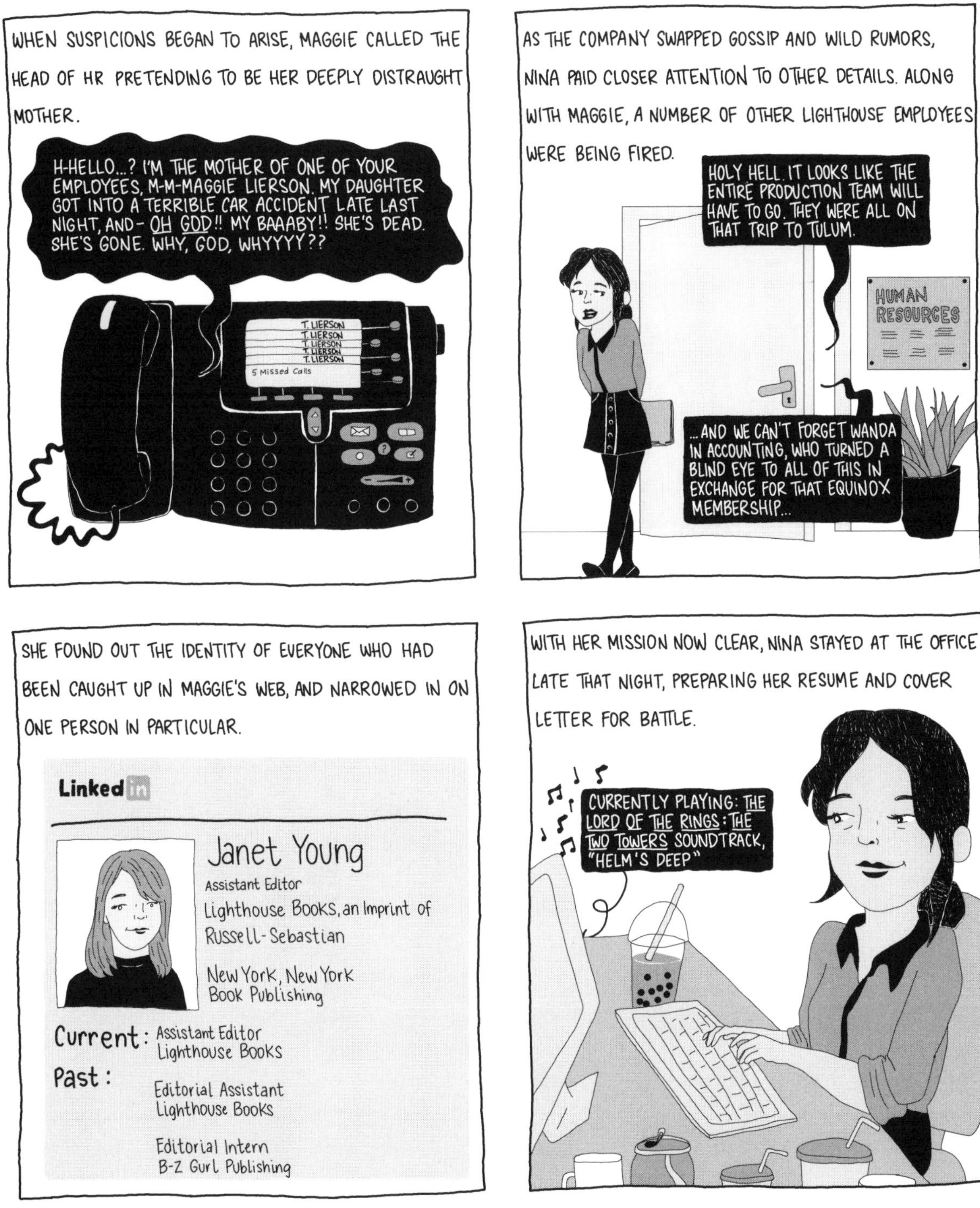
WHEN SUSPICIONS BEGAN TO ARISE, MAGGIE CALLED THE HEAD OF HR PRETENDING TO BE HER DEEPLY DISTRAUGHT MOTHER.
H-HELLO...? I'M THE MOTHER OF ONE OF YOUR EMPLOYEES, M-M-MAGGIE LIERSON. MY DAUGHTER GOT INTO A TERRIBLE CAR ACCIDENT LATE LAST NIGHT, AND- OH GOD!! MY BAAABY!! SHE'S DEAD. SHE'S GONE. WHY, GOD, WHYYYY??
T. LIERSON
T. LIERSON
T. LIERSON
T. LIERSON
T. LIERSON
5 Missed Calls
AS THE COMPANY SWAPPED GOSSIP AND WILD RUMORS, NINA PAID CLOSER ATTENTION TO OTHER DETAILS. ALONG WITH MAGGIE, A NUMBER OF OTHER LIGHTHOUSE EMPLOYEES WERE BEING FIRED.
HOLY HELL. IT LOOKS LIKE THE ENTIRE PRODUCTION TEAM WILL HAVE TO GO. THEY WERE ALL ON THAT TRIP TO TULUM.
HUMAN RESOURCES
...AND WE CAN'T FORGET WANDA IN ACCOUNTING, WHO TURNED A BLIND EYE TO ALL OF THIS IN EXCHANGE FOR THAT EQUINOX MEMBERSHIP...
SHE FOUND OUT THE IDENTITY OF EVERYONE WHO HAD BEEN CAUGHT UP IN MAGGIE'S WEB, AND NARROWED IN ON ONE PERSON IN PARTICULAR.
LinkedIn
Janet Young
Assistant Editor
Lighthouse Books, an Imprint of Russell-Sebastian
New York, New York
Book Publishing
Current: Assistant Editor Lighthouse Books
Past: Editorial Assistant Lighthouse Books
Editorial Intern B-Z Gurl Publishing
WITH HER MISSION NOW CLEAR, NINA STAYED AT THE OFFICE LATE THAT NIGHT, PREPARING HER RESUME AND COVER LETTER FOR BATTLE.
CURRENTLY PLAYING: THE LORD OF THE RINGS: THE TWO TOWERS SOUNDTRACK, "HELM'S DEEP"

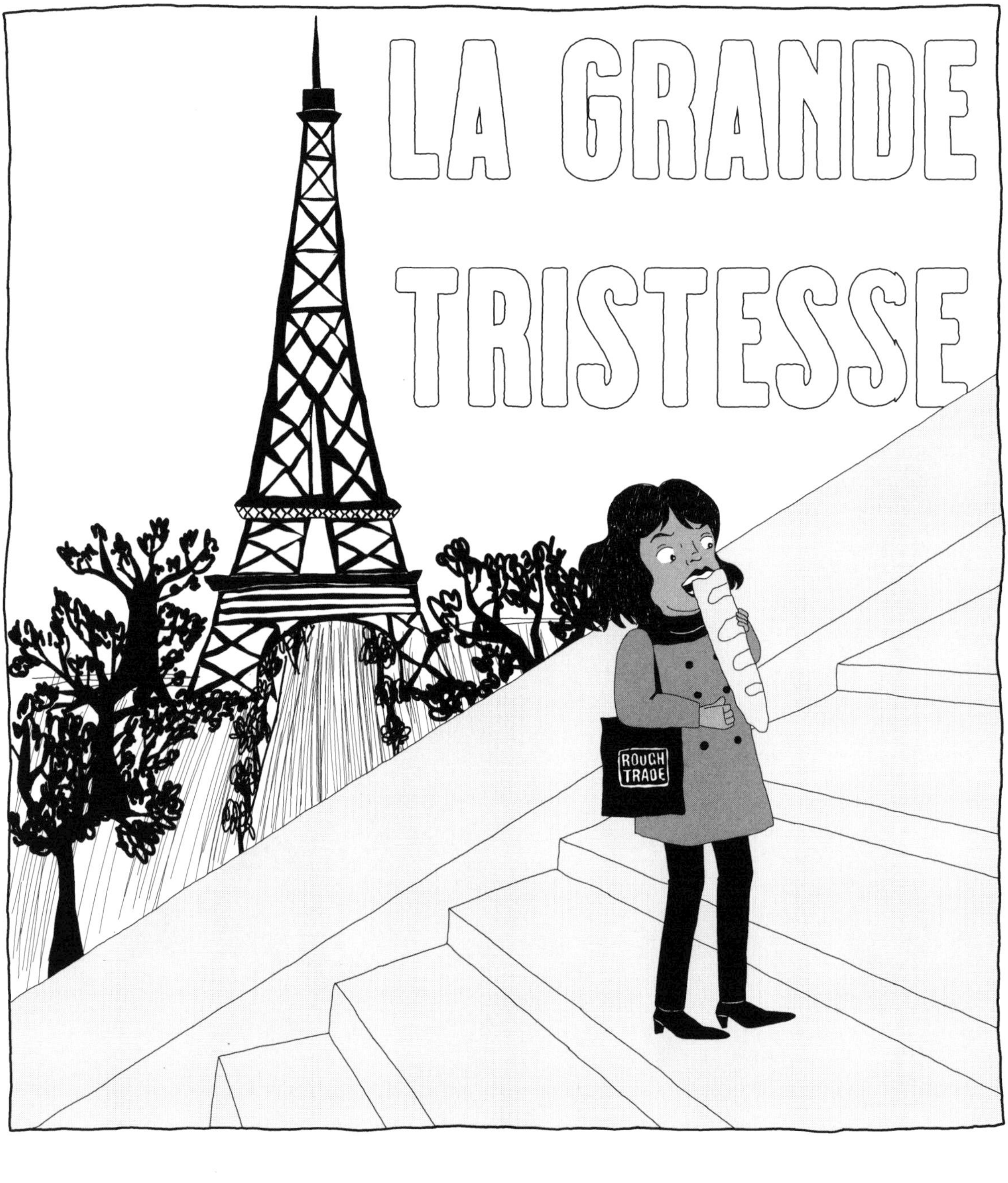
LA GRANDE
TRISTESSE
ROUGH
TRADE

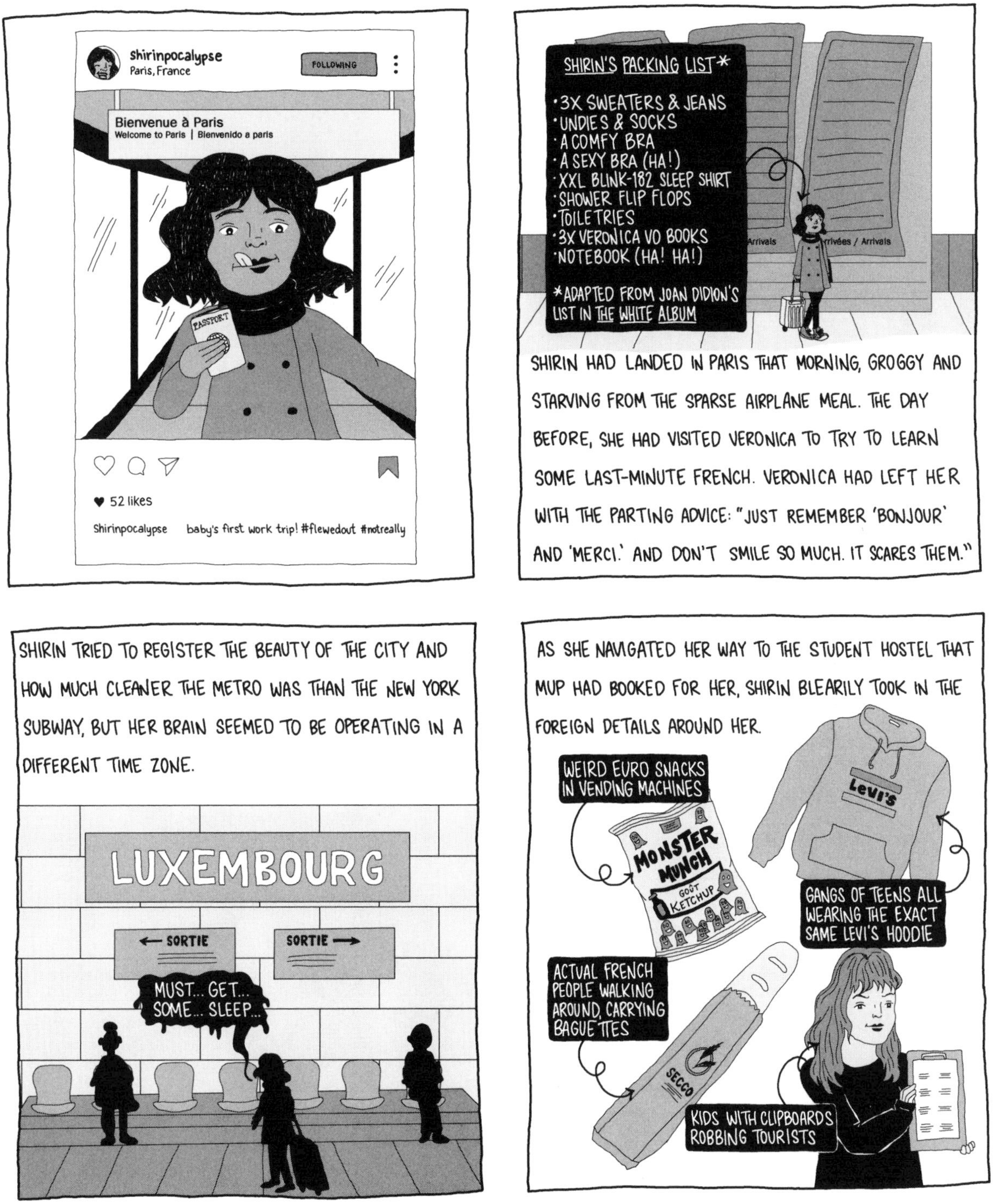
shirinpocalypse
Paris, France
FOLLOWING
Bienvenue à Paris
Welcome to Paris | Bienvenido a paris
PASSPORT
52 likes
Shirinpocalypse baby's first work trip! #flewedout #notreally
SHIRIN'S PACKING LIST*
•3X SWEATERS & JEANS
•UNDIES & SOCKS
•A COMFY BRA
•A SEXY BRA (HA!)
•XXL BLINK-182 SLEEP SHIRT
•SHOWER FLIP FLOPS
•TOILETRIES
•3X VERONICA VO BOOKS
•NOTEBOOK (HA! HA!)
*ADAPTED FROM JOAN DIDION'S LIST IN THE WHITE ALBUM
Arrivals
rivées / Arrivals
SHIRIN HAD LANDED IN PARIS THAT MORNING, GROGGY AND STARVING FROM THE SPARSE AIRPLANE MEAL. THE DAY BEFORE, SHE HAD VISITED VERONICA TO TRY TO LEARN SOME LAST-MINUTE FRENCH. VERONICA HAD LEFT HER WITH THE PARTING ADVICE: "JUST REMEMBER 'BONJOUR' AND 'MERCI.' AND DON'T SMILE SO MUCH. IT SCARES THEM."
SHIRIN TRIED TO REGISTER THE BEAUTY OF THE CITY AND HOW MUCH CLEANER THE METRO WAS THAN THE NEW YORK SUBWAY, BUT HER BRAIN SEEMED TO BE OPERATING IN A DIFFERENT TIME ZONE.
LUXEMBOURG
← SORTIE
SORTIE →
MUST... GET... SOME... SLEEP...
AS SHE NAVIGATED HER WAY TO THE STUDENT HOSTEL THAT MUP HAD BOOKED FOR HER, SHIRIN BLEARILY TOOK IN THE FOREIGN DETAILS AROUND HER.
WEIRD EURO SNACKS IN VENDING MACHINES
MONSTER MUNCH
GOÛT KETCHUP
LEVI'S
GANGS OF TEENS ALL WEARING THE EXACT SAME LEVI'S HOODIE
ACTUAL FRENCH PEOPLE WALKING AROUND, CARRYING BAGUETTES
SECCO
KIDS WITH CLIPBOARDS ROBBING TOURISTS

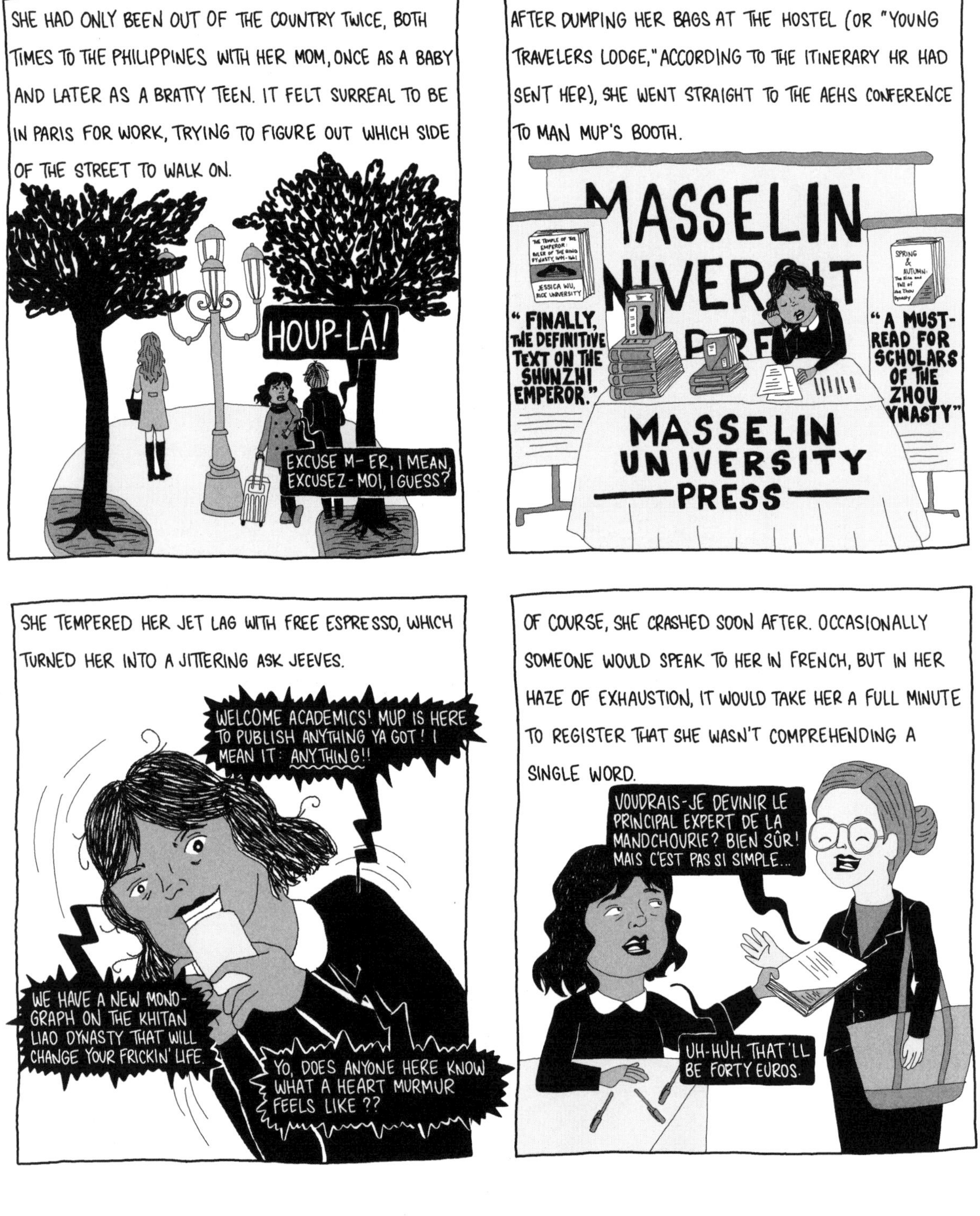
SHE HAD ONLY BEEN OUT OF THE COUNTRY TWICE, BOTH TIMES TO THE PHILIPPINES WITH HER MOM, ONCE AS A BABY AND LATER AS A BRATTY TEEN. IT FELT SURREAL TO BE IN PARIS FOR WORK, TRYING TO FIGURE OUT WHICH SIDE OF THE STREET TO WALK ON.
HOUP-LÀ!
EXCUSE M- ER, I MEAN, EXCUSEZ-MOI, I GUESS?
AFTER DUMPING HER BAGS AT THE HOSTEL (OR "YOUNG TRAVELERS LODGE," ACCORDING TO THE ITINERARY HR HAD SENT HER), SHE WENT STRAIGHT TO THE AEHS CONFERENCE TO MAN MUP'S BOOTH.
MASSELIN
"FINALLY, THE DEFINITIVE TEXT ON THE SHUNZHI EMPEROR."
"A MUST-READ FOR SCHOLARS OF THE ZHOU YNASTY"
MASSELIN UNIVERSITY PRESS
SHE TEMPERED HER JET LAG WITH FREE ESPRESSO, WHICH TURNED HER INTO A JITTERING ASK JEEVES.
WELCOME ACADEMICS! MUP IS HERE TO PUBLISH ANYTHING YA GOT! I MEAN IT: ANYTHING!!
WE HAVE A NEW MONOGRAPH ON THE KHITAN LIAO DYNASTY THAT WILL CHANGE YOUR FRICKIN' LIFE.
YO, DOES ANYONE HERE KNOW WHAT A HEART MURMUR FEELS LIKE??
OF COURSE, SHE CRASHED SOON AFTER. OCCASIONALLY SOMEONE WOULD SPEAK TO HER IN FRENCH, BUT IN HER HAZE OF EXHAUSTION, IT WOULD TAKE HER A FULL MINUTE TO REGISTER THAT SHE WASN'T COMPREHENDING A SINGLE WORD.
VOUDRAIS-JE DEVINIR LE PRINCIPAL EXPERT DE LA MANDCHOURIE? BIEN SÛR! MAIS C'EST PAS SI SIMPLE...
UH-HUH. THAT'LL BE FORTY EUROS.

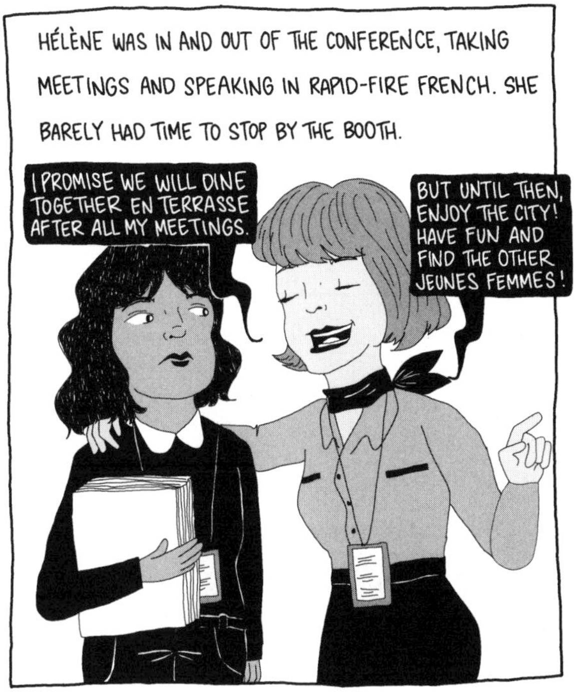
HÉLÈNE WAS IN AND OUT OF THE CONFERENCE, TAKING MEETINGS AND SPEAKING IN RAPID-FIRE FRENCH. SHE BARELY HAD TIME TO STOP BY THE BOOTH.
I PROMISE WE WILL DINE TOGETHER EN TERRASSE AFTER ALL MY MEETINGS.
BUT UNTIL THEN, ENJOY THE CITY! HAVE FUN AND FIND THE OTHER JEUNES FEMMES!

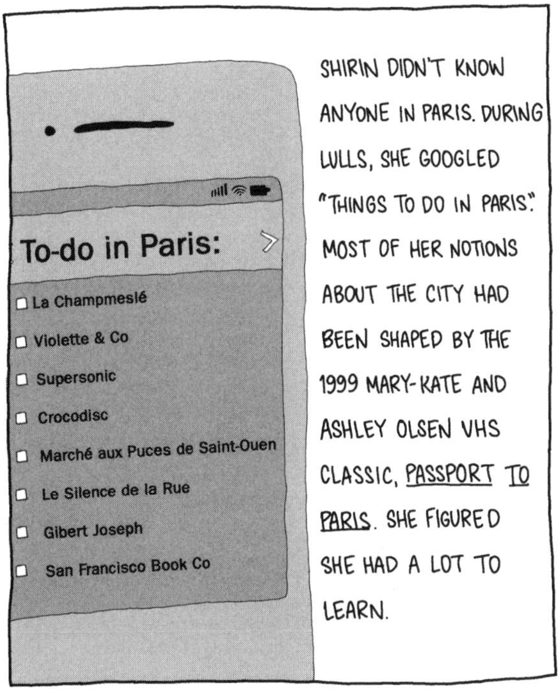
To-do in Paris:
La Champmeslé
Violette & Co
Supersonic
Crocodisc
Marché aux Puces de Saint-Ouen
Le Silence de la Rue
Gibert Joseph
San Francisco Book Co
SHIRIN DIDN'T KNOW ANYONE IN PARIS. DURING LULLS, SHE GOOGLED "THINGS TO DO IN PARIS." MOST OF HER NOTIONS ABOUT THE CITY HAD BEEN SHAPED BY THE 1999 MARY-KATE AND ASHLEY OLSEN VHS CLASSIC, PASSPORT TO PARIS. SHE FIGURED SHE HAD A LOT TO LEARN.

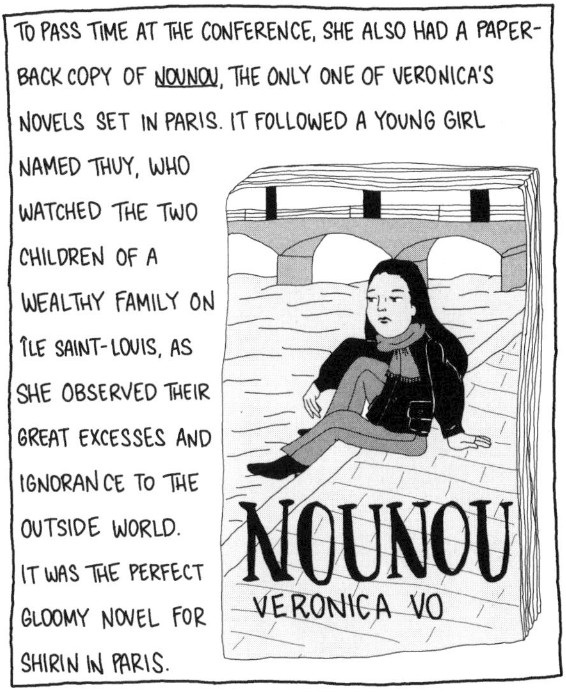
TO PASS TIME AT THE CONFERENCE, SHE ALSO HAD A PAPERBACK COPY OF NOUNOU, THE ONLY ONE OF VERONICA'S NOVELS SET IN PARIS. IT FOLLOWED A YOUNG GIRL NAMED THUY, WHO WATCHED THE TWO CHILDREN OF A WEALTHY FAMILY ON ÎLE SAINT-LOUIS, AS SHE OBSERVED THEIR GREAT EXCESSES AND IGNORANCE TO THE OUTSIDE WORLD. IT WAS THE PERFECT GLOOMY NOVEL FOR SHIRIN IN PARIS.
NOUNOU
VERONICA VO

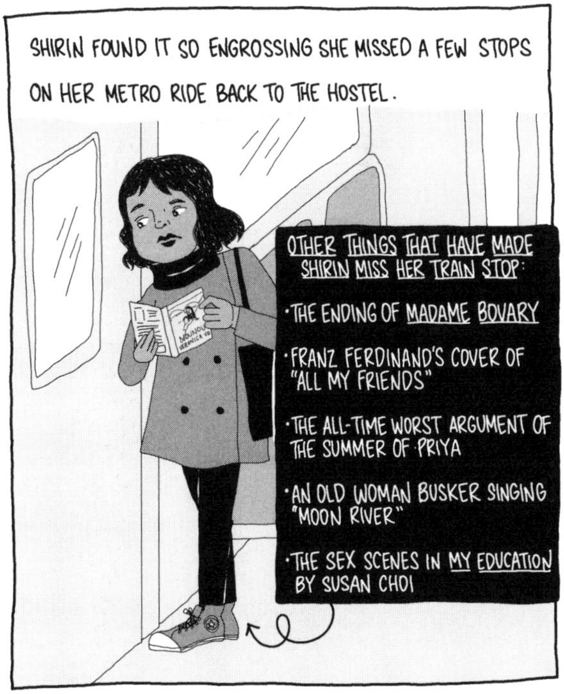
SHIRIN FOUND IT SO ENGROSSING SHE MISSED A FEW STOPS ON HER METRO RIDE BACK TO THE HOSTEL.
OTHER THINGS THAT HAVE MADE SHIRIN MISS HER TRAIN STOP:
·THE ENDING OF MADAME BOVARY
·FRANZ FERDINAND'S COVER OF "ALL MY FRIENDS"
·THE ALL-TIME WORST ARGUMENT OF THE SUMMER OF PRIYA
·AN OLD WOMAN BUSKER SINGING "MOON RIVER"
·THE SEX SCENES IN MY EDUCATION BY SUSAN CHOI

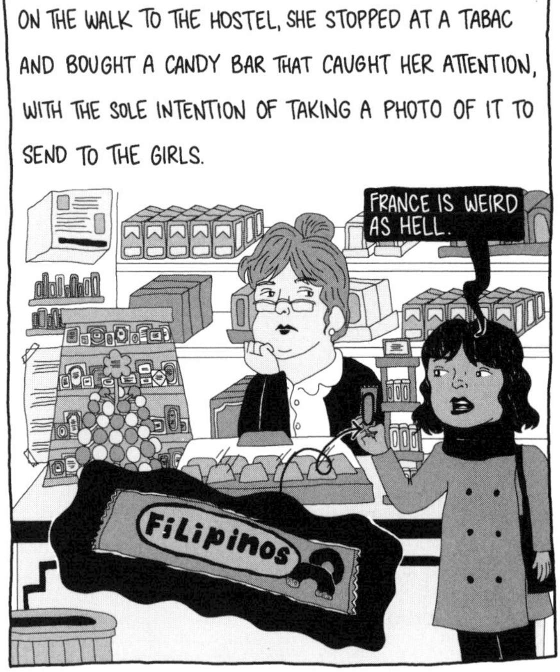
ON THE WALK TO THE HOSTEL, SHE STOPPED AT A TABAC AND BOUGHT A CANDY BAR THAT CAUGHT HER ATTENTION, WITH THE SOLE INTENTION OF TAKING A PHOTO OF IT TO SEND TO THE GIRLS.
FRANCE IS WEIRD AS HELL.
FiLipinos

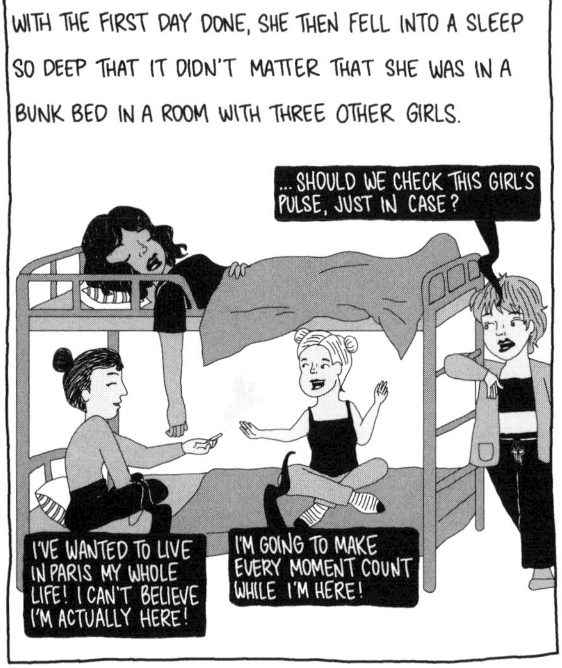
WITH THE FIRST DAY DONE, SHE THEN FELL INTO A SLEEP SO DEEP THAT IT DIDN'T MATTER THAT SHE WAS IN A BUNK BED IN A ROOM WITH THREE OTHER GIRLS.
... SHOULD WE CHECK THIS GIRL'S PULSE, JUST IN CASE?
I'VE WANTED TO LIVE IN PARIS MY WHOLE LIFE! I CAN'T BELIEVE I'M ACTUALLY HERE!
I'M GOING TO MAKE EVERY MOMENT COUNT WHILE I'M HERE!

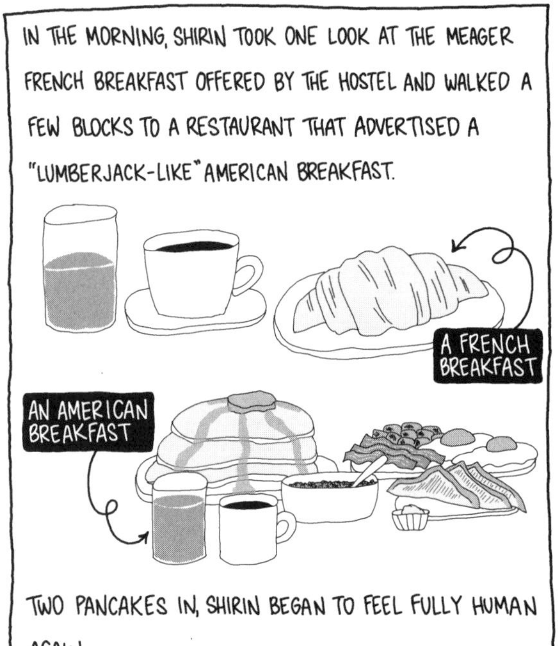
IN THE MORNING, SHIRIN TOOK ONE LOOK AT THE MEAGER FRENCH BREAKFAST OFFERED BY THE HOSTEL AND WALKED A FEW BLOCKS TO A RESTAURANT THAT ADVERTISED A "LUMBERJACK-LIKE" AMERICAN BREAKFAST.
A FRENCH BREAKFAST
AN AMERICAN BREAKFAST
TWO PANCAKES IN, SHIRIN BEGAN TO FEEL FULLY HUMAN AGAIN.

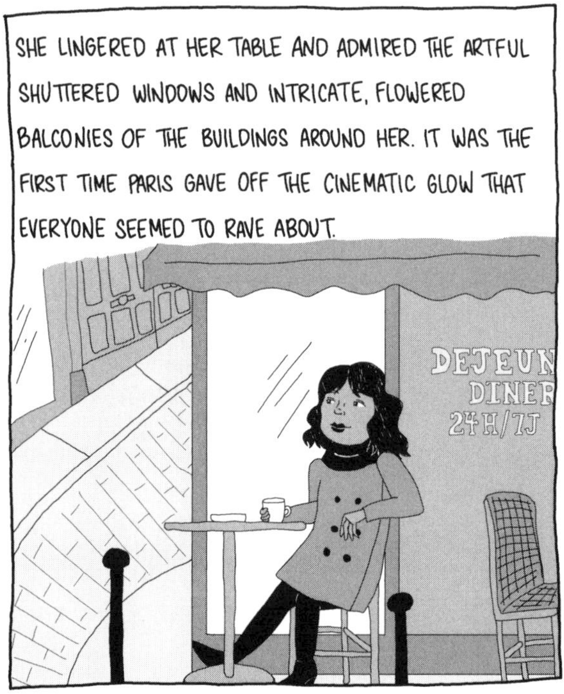
SHE LINGERED AT HER TABLE AND ADMIRED THE ARTFUL SHUTTERED WINDOWS AND INTRICATE, FLOWERED BALCONIES OF THE BUILDINGS AROUND HER. IT WAS THE FIRST TIME PARIS GAVE OFF THE CINEMATIC GLOW THAT EVERYONE SEEMED TO RAVE ABOUT.
DEJEUN
DINER
24H/7J

SHE STRUCK UP A CONVERSATION WITH A BACKPACKER FROM EDINBURGH WHO WAS SITTING NEARBY.

WE'RE HEADING TO MONT SAINT-MICHEL TODAY, BUT YOU SHOULD JOIN US AT THE HIGHLANDER LATER TONIGHT.

FOR SURE! I HAVEN'T DONE ANYTHING FUN OR FRENCH SINCE I'VE LANDED.

I DUNNO IF PARTYING WITH SCOTS COUNTS AS VERY FRENCH THOUGH...

ROUGH TRADE

IT WAS STRANGE BEING SIX HOURS AHEAD OF SILVIA AND NINA. EVEN IN THIS NEW, BEAUTIFUL CITY, THE DAYS DRAGGED ON IF SHE WASN'T ABLE TO TALK TO THEM REGULARLY.

SAN FRANCISCO BOOKS CO

[FRENCH LAUGHTER]

17

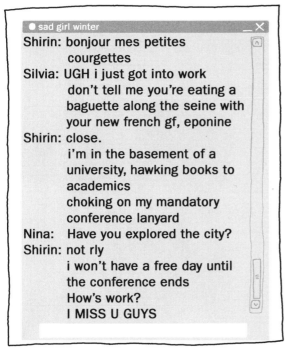

● sad girl winter ___ ✕

Shirin: bonjour mes petites
           courgettes
Silvia: UGH i just got into work
           don't tell me you're eating a
           baguette along the seine with
           your new french gf, eponine
Shirin: close.
           i'm in the basement of a
           university, hawking books to
           academics
           choking on my mandatory
           conference lanyard
Nina: Have you explored the city?
Shirin: not rly
           i won't have a free day until
           the conference ends
           How's work?
           I MISS U GUYS

● sad girl winter ___ ✕

Nina: My interview with the
          Lighthouse editor went well.
          The whole thing was more of just
          a gossip sesh really. She seems
          really cool.
          I also sent a set of VV's books
          to Lila, the agent. She loves
          them so far.
Shirin: look at u, making deals!!!
Silvia: you're not missing much here.
          the bros upstairs had a foam
          party on the roof last night
          so nina's ceiling began leaking
Nina: It was disgusting.
          I'm taking their next Blue Apron
          box as remuneration.
Shirin: i miss everything!!
Nina: Whatever, you're in Paris.

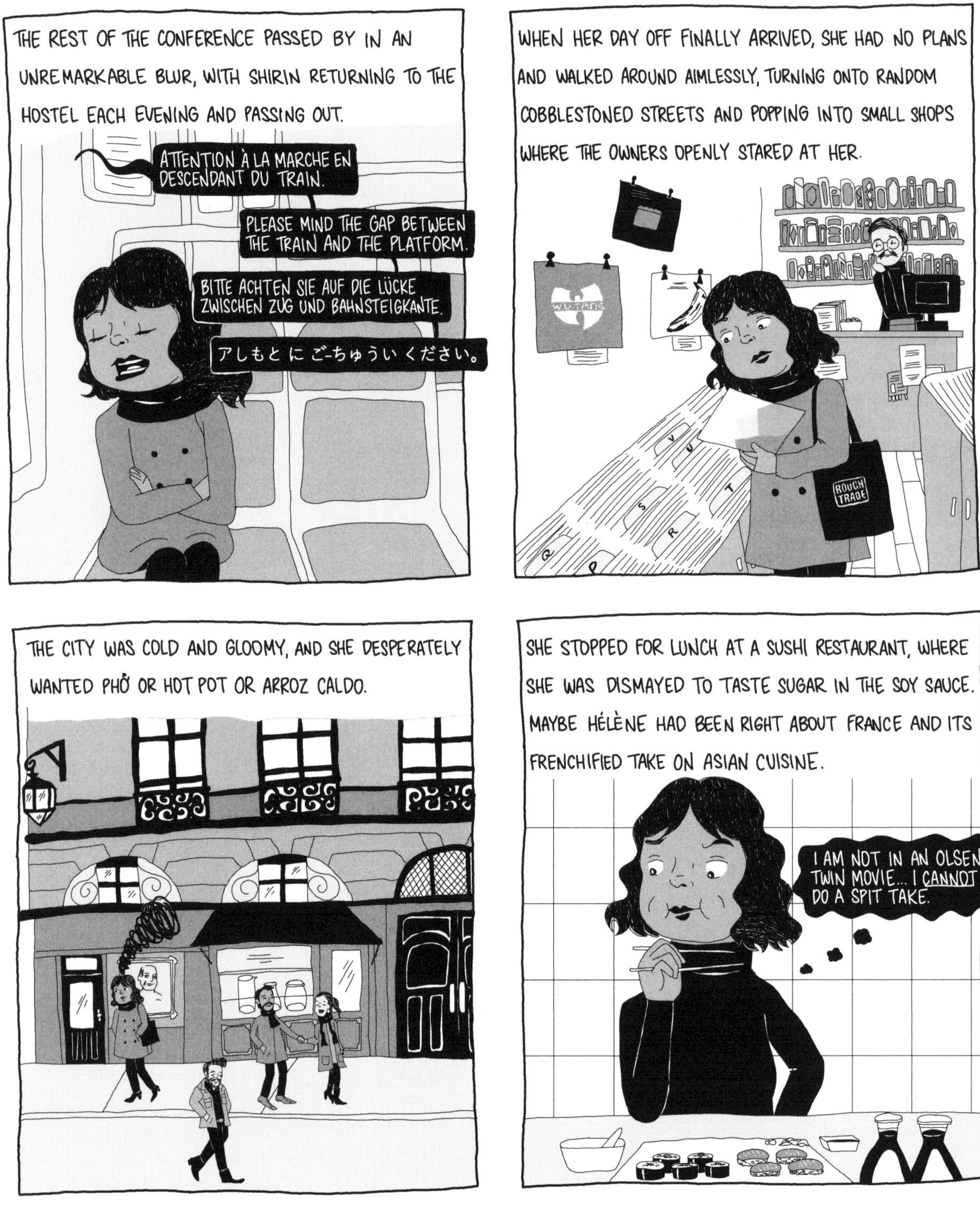
THE REST OF THE CONFERENCE PASSED BY IN AN UNREMARKABLE BLUR, WITH SHIRIN RETURNING TO THE HOSTEL EACH EVENING AND PASSING OUT.
ATTENTION À LA MARCHE EN DESCENDANT DU TRAIN.
PLEASE MIND THE GAP BETWEEN THE TRAIN AND THE PLATFORM.
BITTE ACHTEN SIE AUF DIE LÜCKE ZWISCHEN ZUG UND BAHNSTEIGKANTE.
アしもと に ごちゅうい ください。
WHEN HER DAY OFF FINALLY ARRIVED, SHE HAD NO PLANS AND WALKED AROUND AIMLESSLY, TURNING ONTO RANDOM COBBLESTONED STREETS AND POPPING INTO SMALL SHOPS WHERE THE OWNERS OPENLY STARED AT HER.
ROUGH TRADE
THE CITY WAS COLD AND GLOOMY, AND SHE DESPERATELY WANTED PHỞ OR HOT POT OR ARROZ CALDO.
SHE STOPPED FOR LUNCH AT A SUSHI RESTAURANT, WHERE SHE WAS DISMAYED TO TASTE SUGAR IN THE SOY SAUCE. MAYBE HÉLÈNE HAD BEEN RIGHT ABOUT FRANCE AND ITS FRENCHIFIED TAKE ON ASIAN CUISINE.
I AM NOT IN AN OLSEN TWIN MOVIE... I CANNOT DO A SPIT TAKE.

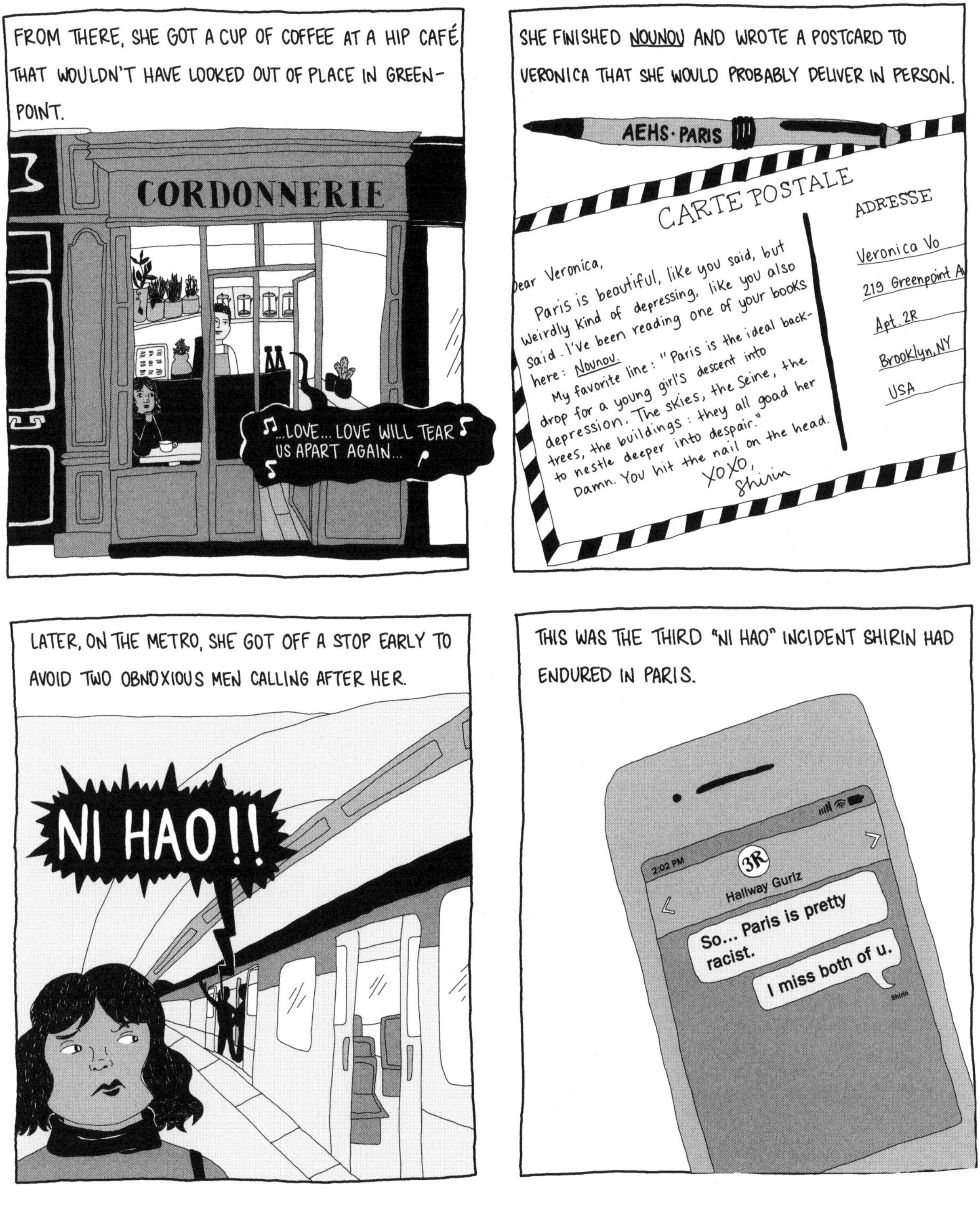
FROM THERE, SHE GOT A CUP OF COFFEE AT A HIP CAFÉ THAT WOULDN'T HAVE LOOKED OUT OF PLACE IN GREEN-POINT.
CORDONNERIE
...LOVE... LOVE WILL TEAR US APART AGAIN...
SHE FINISHED NOUNOU AND WROTE A POSTCARD TO VERONICA THAT SHE WOULD PROBABLY DELIVER IN PERSON.
AEHS · PARIS
CARTE POSTALE
Dear Veronica,
Paris is beautiful, like you said, but weirdly kind of depressing, like you also said. I've been reading one of your books here: Nounou.
My favorite line: "Paris is the ideal back-drop for a young girl's descent into depression. The skies, the Seine, the trees, the buildings: they all goad her to nestle deeper into despair."
Damn. You hit the nail on the head.
XOXO,
Shirin
ADRESSE
Veronica Vo
219 Greenpoint A
Apt. 2R
Brooklyn, NY
USA
LATER, ON THE METRO, SHE GOT OFF A STOP EARLY TO AVOID TWO OBNOXIOUS MEN CALLING AFTER HER.
NI HAO!!
THIS WAS THE THIRD "NI HAO" INCIDENT SHIRIN HAD ENDURED IN PARIS.
2:02 PM
3R
Hallway Gurlz
So... Paris is pretty racist.
I miss both of u.
Shirin

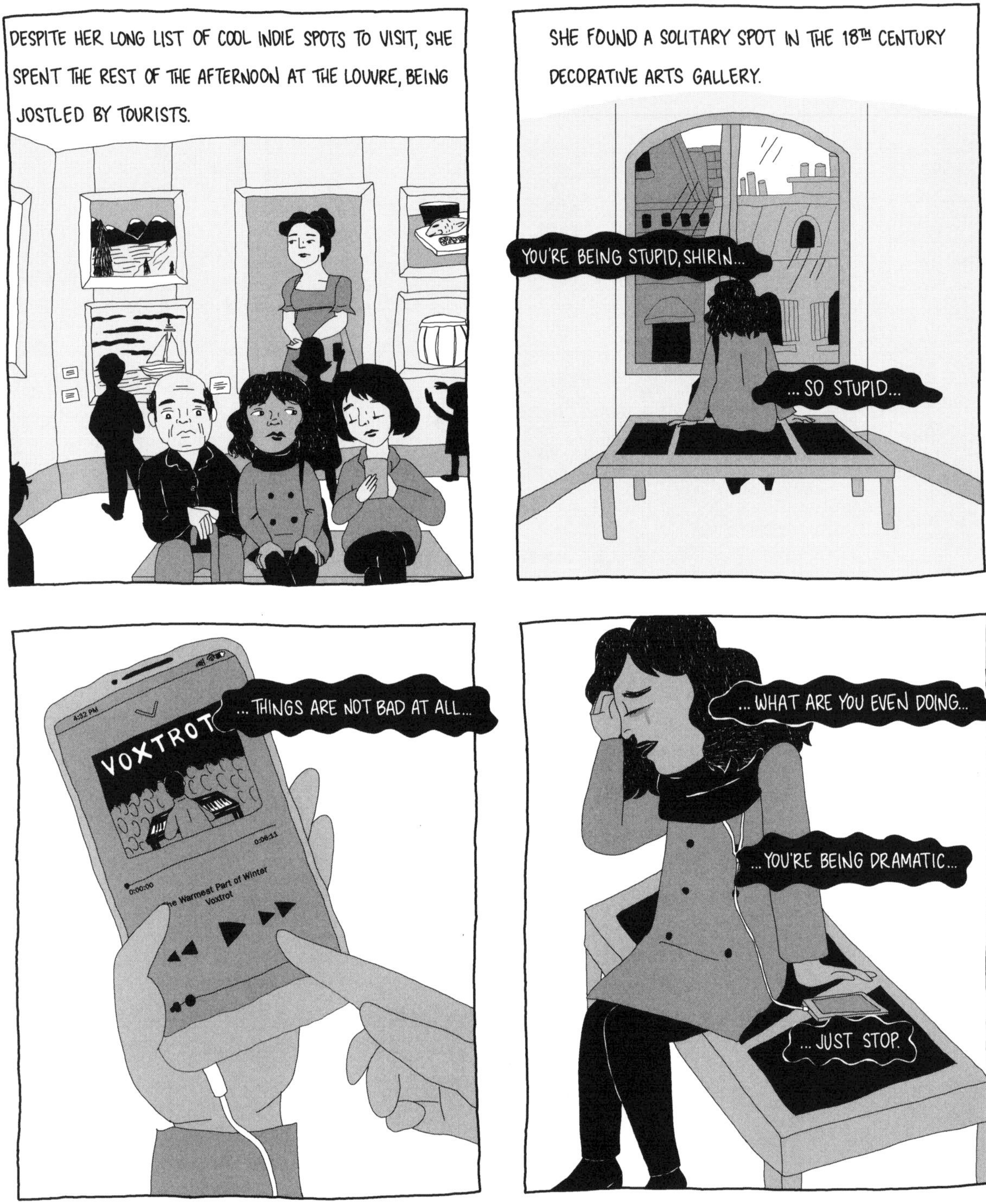
DESPITE HER LONG LIST OF COOL INDIE SPOTS TO VISIT, SHE SPENT THE REST OF THE AFTERNOON AT THE LOUVRE, BEING JOSTLED BY TOURISTS.
SHE FOUND A SOLITARY SPOT IN THE 18TH CENTURY DECORATIVE ARTS GALLERY.
YOU'RE BEING STUPID, SHIRIN...
... SO STUPID...
... THINGS ARE NOT BAD AT ALL...
VOXTROT
Voxtrot
... WHAT ARE YOU EVEN DOING...
... YOU'RE BEING DRAMATIC...
... JUST STOP.

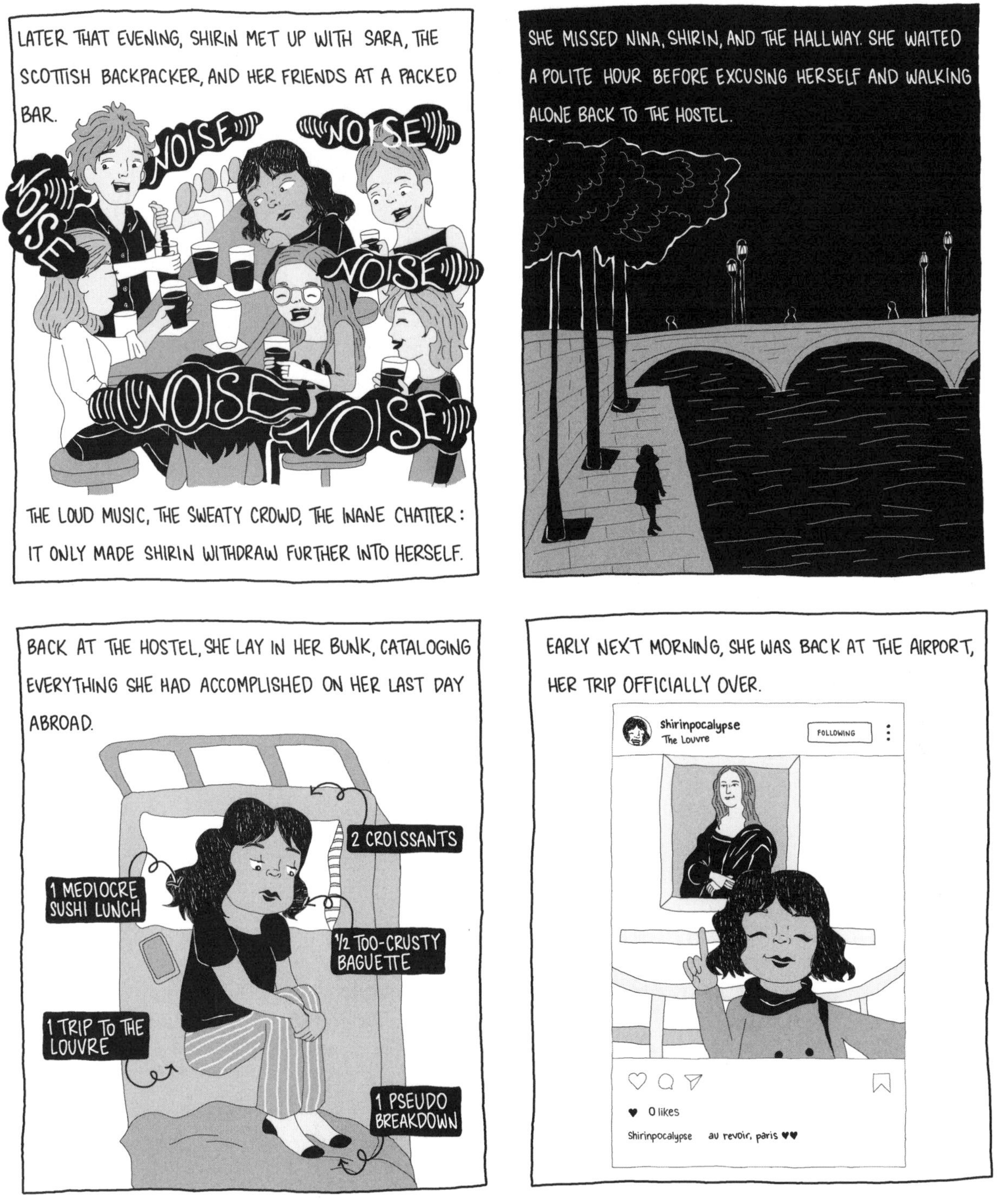
LATER THAT EVENING, SHIRIN MET UP WITH SARA, THE SCOTTISH BACKPACKER, AND HER FRIENDS AT A PACKED BAR.
NOISE
NOISE
NOISE
NOISE
NOISE
NOISE
THE LOUD MUSIC, THE SWEATY CROWD, THE INANE CHATTER: IT ONLY MADE SHIRIN WITHDRAW FURTHER INTO HERSELF.
SHE MISSED NINA, SHIRIN, AND THE HALLWAY. SHE WAITED A POLITE HOUR BEFORE EXCUSING HERSELF AND WALKING ALONE BACK TO THE HOSTEL.
BACK AT THE HOSTEL, SHE LAY IN HER BUNK, CATALOGING EVERYTHING SHE HAD ACCOMPLISHED ON HER LAST DAY ABROAD.
2 CROISSANTS
1 MEDIOCRE SUSHI LUNCH
1/2 TOO-CRUSTY BAGUETTE
1 TRIP TO THE LOUVRE
1 PSEUDO BREAKDOWN
EARLY NEXT MORNING, SHE WAS BACK AT THE AIRPORT, HER TRIP OFFICIALLY OVER.
shirinpocalypse
The Louvre
FOLLOWING
0 likes
Shirinpocalypse au revoir, paris ♥♥

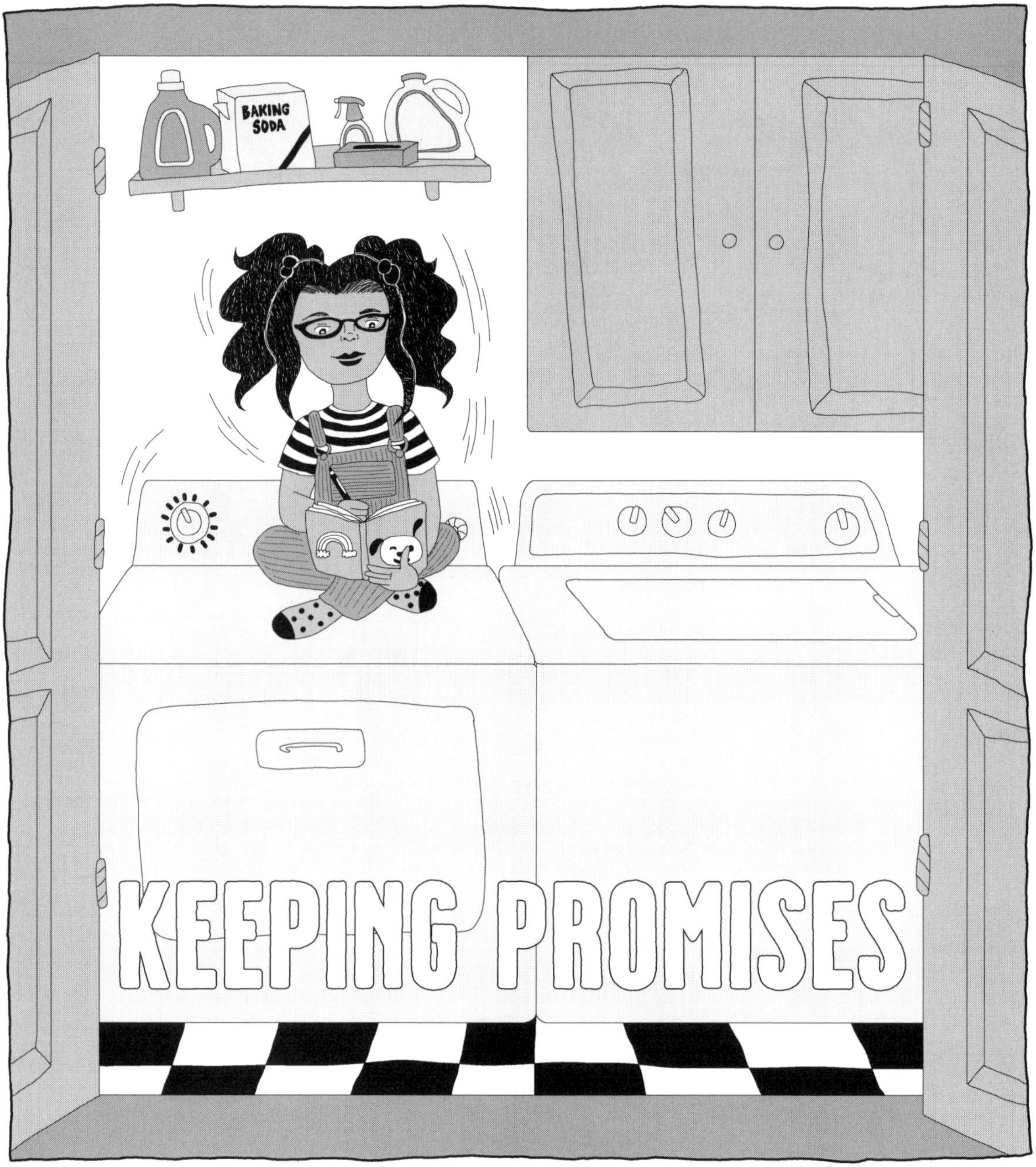
BAKING
SODA
KEEPING PROMISES

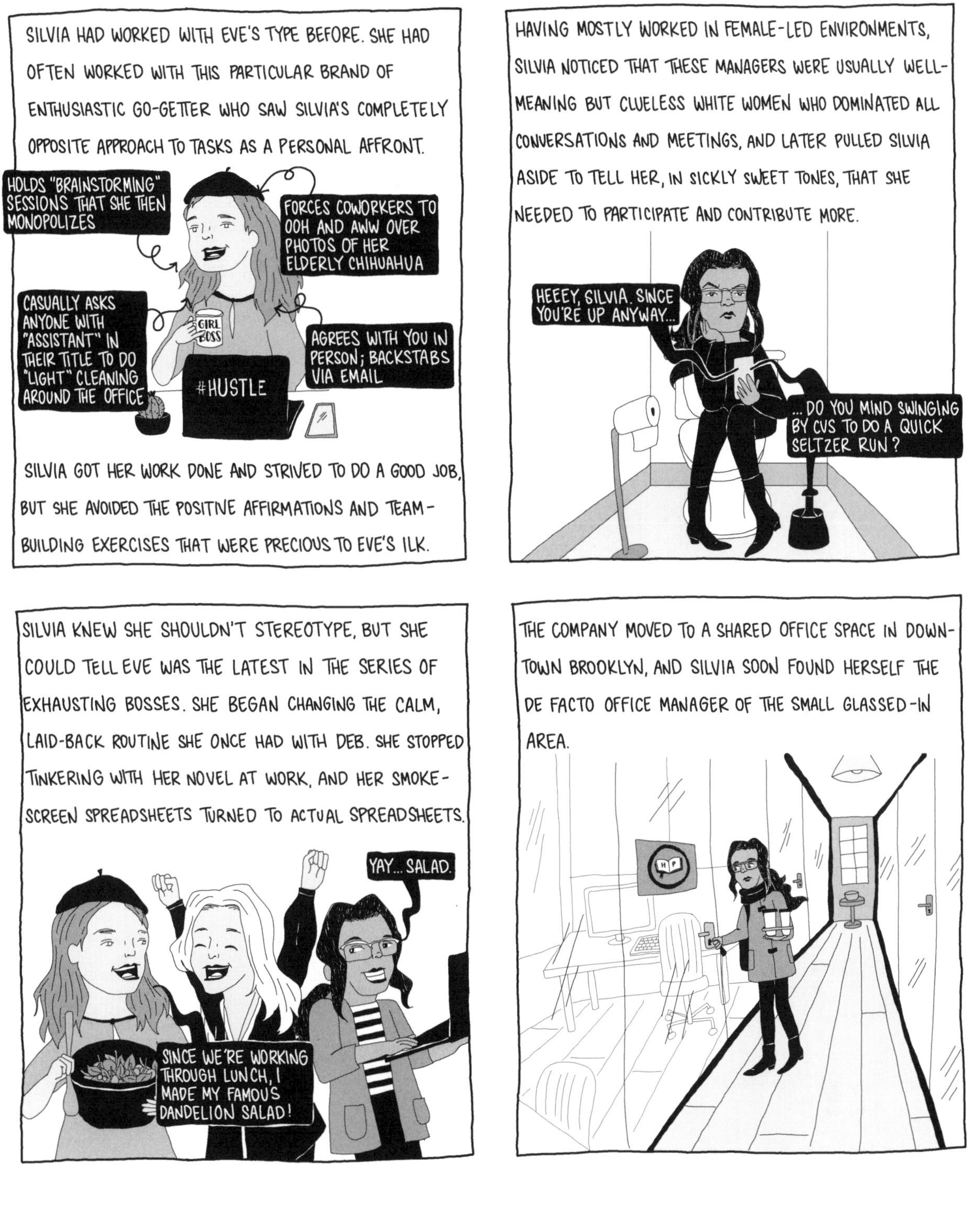
SILVIA HAD WORKED WITH EVE'S TYPE BEFORE. SHE HAD OFTEN WORKED WITH THIS PARTICULAR BRAND OF ENTHUSIASTIC GO-GETTER WHO SAW SILVIA'S COMPLETELY OPPOSITE APPROACH TO TASKS AS A PERSONAL AFFRONT.
HOLDS "BRAINSTORMING" SESSIONS THAT SHE THEN MONOPOLIZES
FORCES COWORKERS TO OOH AND AWW OVER PHOTOS OF HER ELDERLY CHIHUAHUA
CASUALLY ASKS ANYONE WITH "ASSISTANT" IN THEIR TITLE TO DO "LIGHT" CLEANING AROUND THE OFFICE
GIRL BOSS
AGREES WITH YOU IN PERSON; BACKSTABS VIA EMAIL
#HUSTLE
SILVIA GOT HER WORK DONE AND STRIVED TO DO A GOOD JOB, BUT SHE AVOIDED THE POSITIVE AFFIRMATIONS AND TEAM-BUILDING EXERCISES THAT WERE PRECIOUS TO EVE'S ILK.
HAVING MOSTLY WORKED IN FEMALE-LED ENVIRONMENTS, SILVIA NOTICED THAT THESE MANAGERS WERE USUALLY WELL-MEANING BUT CLUELESS WHITE WOMEN WHO DOMINATED ALL CONVERSATIONS AND MEETINGS, AND LATER PULLED SILVIA ASIDE TO TELL HER, IN SICKLY SWEET TONES, THAT SHE NEEDED TO PARTICIPATE AND CONTRIBUTE MORE.
HEEEY, SILVIA. SINCE YOU'RE UP ANYWAY...
... DO YOU MIND SWINGING BY CVS TO DO A QUICK SELTZER RUN?
SILVIA KNEW SHE SHOULDN'T STEREOTYPE, BUT SHE COULD TELL EVE WAS THE LATEST IN THE SERIES OF EXHAUSTING BOSSES. SHE BEGAN CHANGING THE CALM, LAID-BACK ROUTINE SHE ONCE HAD WITH DEB. SHE STOPPED TINKERING WITH HER NOVEL AT WORK, AND HER SMOKE-SCREEN SPREADSHEETS TURNED TO ACTUAL SPREADSHEETS.
YAY... SALAD.
SINCE WE'RE WORKING THROUGH LUNCH, I MADE MY FAMOUS DANDELION SALAD!
THE COMPANY MOVED TO A SHARED OFFICE SPACE IN DOWNTOWN BROOKLYN, AND SILVIA SOON FOUND HERSELF THE DE FACTO OFFICE MANAGER OF THE SMALL GLASSED-IN AREA.

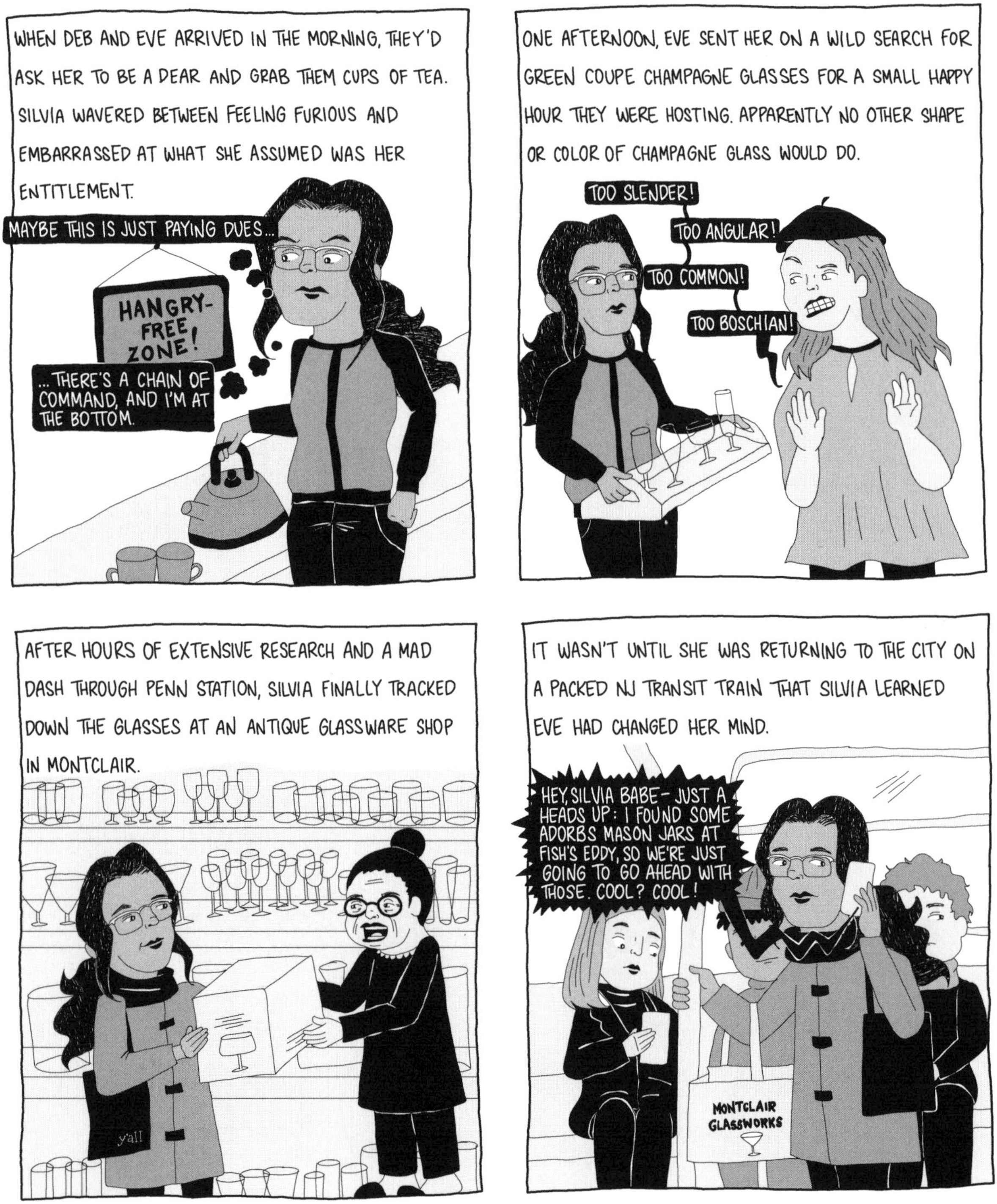
WHEN DEB AND EVE ARRIVED IN THE MORNING, THEY'D ASK HER TO BE A DEAR AND GRAB THEM CUPS OF TEA. SILVIA WAVERED BETWEEN FEELING FURIOUS AND EMBARRASSED AT WHAT SHE ASSUMED WAS HER ENTITLEMENT.
MAYBE THIS IS JUST PAYING DUES...
HANGRY-FREE ZONE!
... THERE'S A CHAIN OF COMMAND, AND I'M AT THE BOTTOM.
ONE AFTERNOON, EVE SENT HER ON A WILD SEARCH FOR GREEN COUPE CHAMPAGNE GLASSES FOR A SMALL HAPPY HOUR THEY WERE HOSTING. APPARENTLY NO OTHER SHAPE OR COLOR OF CHAMPAGNE GLASS WOULD DO.
TOO SLENDER!
TOO ANGULAR!
TOO COMMON!
TOO BOSCHIAN!
AFTER HOURS OF EXTENSIVE RESEARCH AND A MAD DASH THROUGH PENN STATION, SILVIA FINALLY TRACKED DOWN THE GLASSES AT AN ANTIQUE GLASSWARE SHOP IN MONTCLAIR.
y'all
IT WASN'T UNTIL SHE WAS RETURNING TO THE CITY ON A PACKED NJ TRANSIT TRAIN THAT SILVIA LEARNED EVE HAD CHANGED HER MIND.
HEY, SILVIA BABE— JUST A HEADS UP: I FOUND SOME ADORBS MASON JARS AT FISH'S EDDY, SO WE'RE JUST GOING TO GO AHEAD WITH THOSE. COOL? COOL!
MONTCLAIR GLASSWORKS

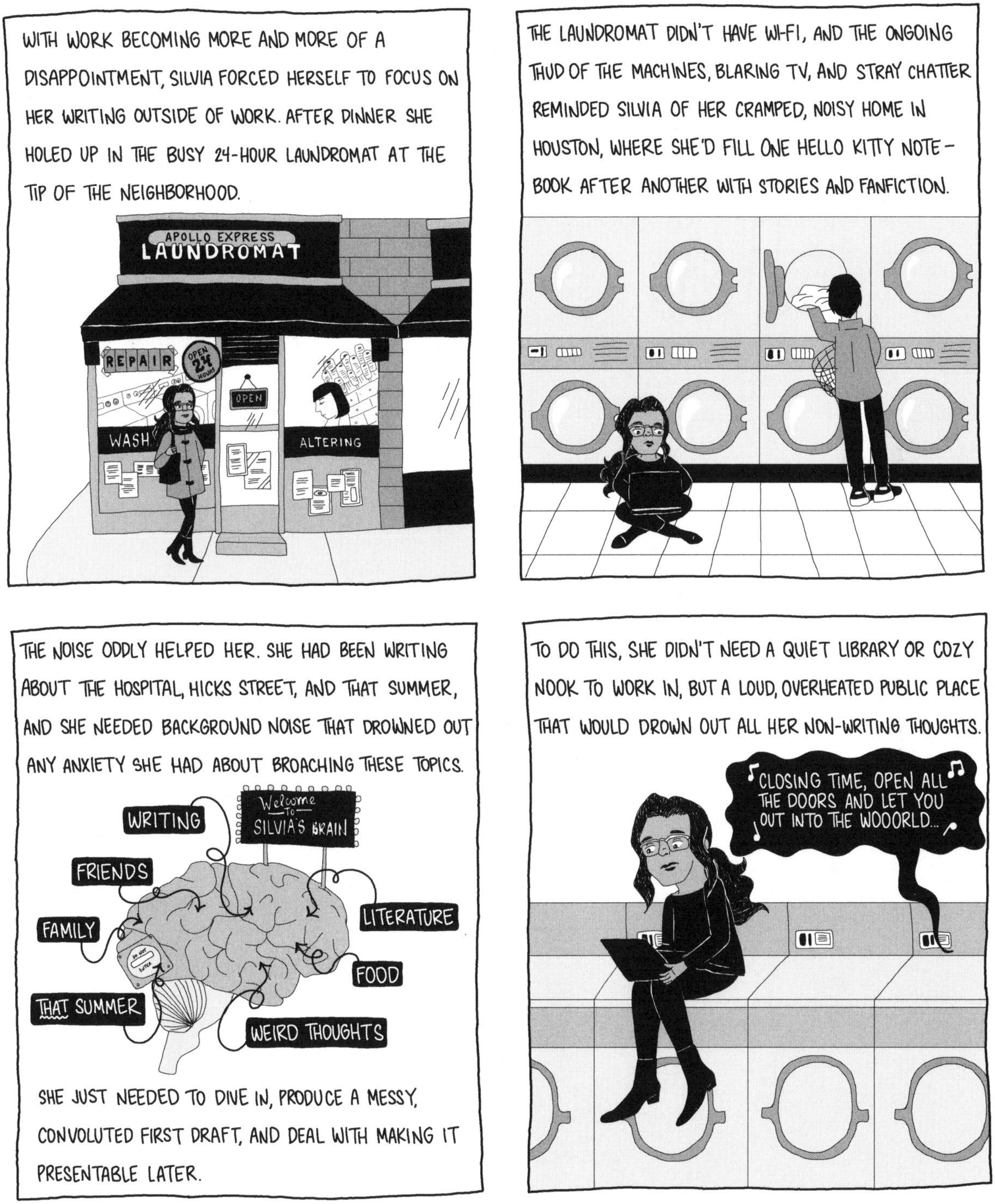
WITH WORK BECOMING MORE AND MORE OF A DISAPPOINTMENT, SILVIA FORCED HERSELF TO FOCUS ON HER WRITING OUTSIDE OF WORK. AFTER DINNER SHE HOLED UP IN THE BUSY 24-HOUR LAUNDROMAT AT THE TIP OF THE NEIGHBORHOOD.
APOLLO EXPRESS
LAUNDROMAT
REPAIR
OPEN 24 HOURS
OPEN
WASH
ALTERING
THE LAUNDROMAT DIDN'T HAVE WI-FI, AND THE ONGOING THUD OF THE MACHINES, BLARING TV, AND STRAY CHATTER REMINDED SILVIA OF HER CRAMPED, NOISY HOME IN HOUSTON, WHERE SHE'D FILL ONE HELLO KITTY NOTE-BOOK AFTER ANOTHER WITH STORIES AND FANFICTION.
THE NOISE ODDLY HELPED HER. SHE HAD BEEN WRITING ABOUT THE HOSPITAL, HICKS STREET, AND THAT SUMMER, AND SHE NEEDED BACKGROUND NOISE THAT DROWNED OUT ANY ANXIETY SHE HAD ABOUT BROACHING THESE TOPICS.
Welcome TO SILVIA'S BRAIN
WRITING
FRIENDS
FAMILY
THAT SUMMER
LITERATURE
FOOD
WEIRD THOUGHTS
SHE JUST NEEDED TO DIVE IN, PRODUCE A MESSY, CONVOLUTED FIRST DRAFT, AND DEAL WITH MAKING IT PRESENTABLE LATER.
TO DO THIS, SHE DIDN'T NEED A QUIET LIBRARY OR COZY NOOK TO WORK IN, BUT A LOUD, OVERHEATED PUBLIC PLACE THAT WOULD DROWN OUT ALL HER NON-WRITING THOUGHTS.
CLOSING TIME, OPEN ALL THE DOORS AND LET YOU OUT INTO THE WOOORLD...

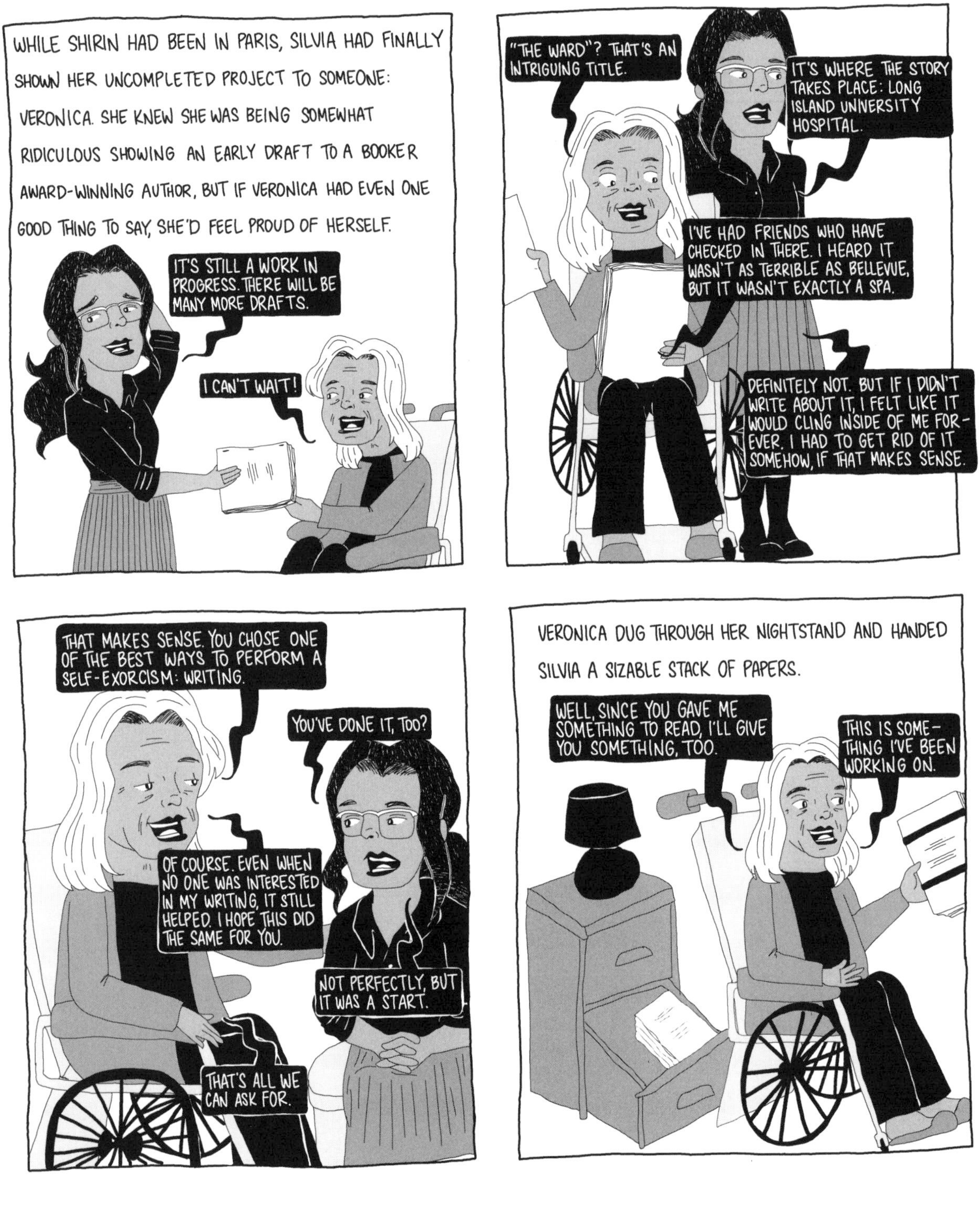
WHILE SHIRIN HAD BEEN IN PARIS, SILVIA HAD FINALLY SHOWN HER UNCOMPLETED PROJECT TO SOMEONE: VERONICA. SHE KNEW SHE WAS BEING SOMEWHAT RIDICULOUS SHOWING AN EARLY DRAFT TO A BOOKER AWARD-WINNING AUTHOR, BUT IF VERONICA HAD EVEN ONE GOOD THING TO SAY, SHE'D FEEL PROUD OF HERSELF.
IT'S STILL A WORK IN PROGRESS. THERE WILL BE MANY MORE DRAFTS.
I CAN'T WAIT!
"THE WARD"? THAT'S AN INTRIGUING TITLE.
IT'S WHERE THE STORY TAKES PLACE: LONG ISLAND UNIVERSITY HOSPITAL.
I'VE HAD FRIENDS WHO HAVE CHECKED IN THERE. I HEARD IT WASN'T AS TERRIBLE AS BELLEVUE, BUT IT WASN'T EXACTLY A SPA.
DEFINITELY NOT. BUT IF I DIDN'T WRITE ABOUT IT, I FELT LIKE IT WOULD CLING INSIDE OF ME FOR-EVER. I HAD TO GET RID OF IT SOMEHOW, IF THAT MAKES SENSE.
THAT MAKES SENSE. YOU CHOSE ONE OF THE BEST WAYS TO PERFORM A SELF-EXORCISM: WRITING.
YOU'VE DONE IT, TOO?
OF COURSE. EVEN WHEN NO ONE WAS INTERESTED IN MY WRITING, IT STILL HELPED. I HOPE THIS DID THE SAME FOR YOU.
NOT PERFECTLY, BUT IT WAS A START.
THAT'S ALL WE CAN ASK FOR.
VERONICA DUG THROUGH HER NIGHTSTAND AND HANDED SILVIA A SIZABLE STACK OF PAPERS.
WELL, SINCE YOU GAVE ME SOMETHING TO READ, I'LL GIVE YOU SOMETHING, TOO.
THIS IS SOME-THING I'VE BEEN WORKING ON.

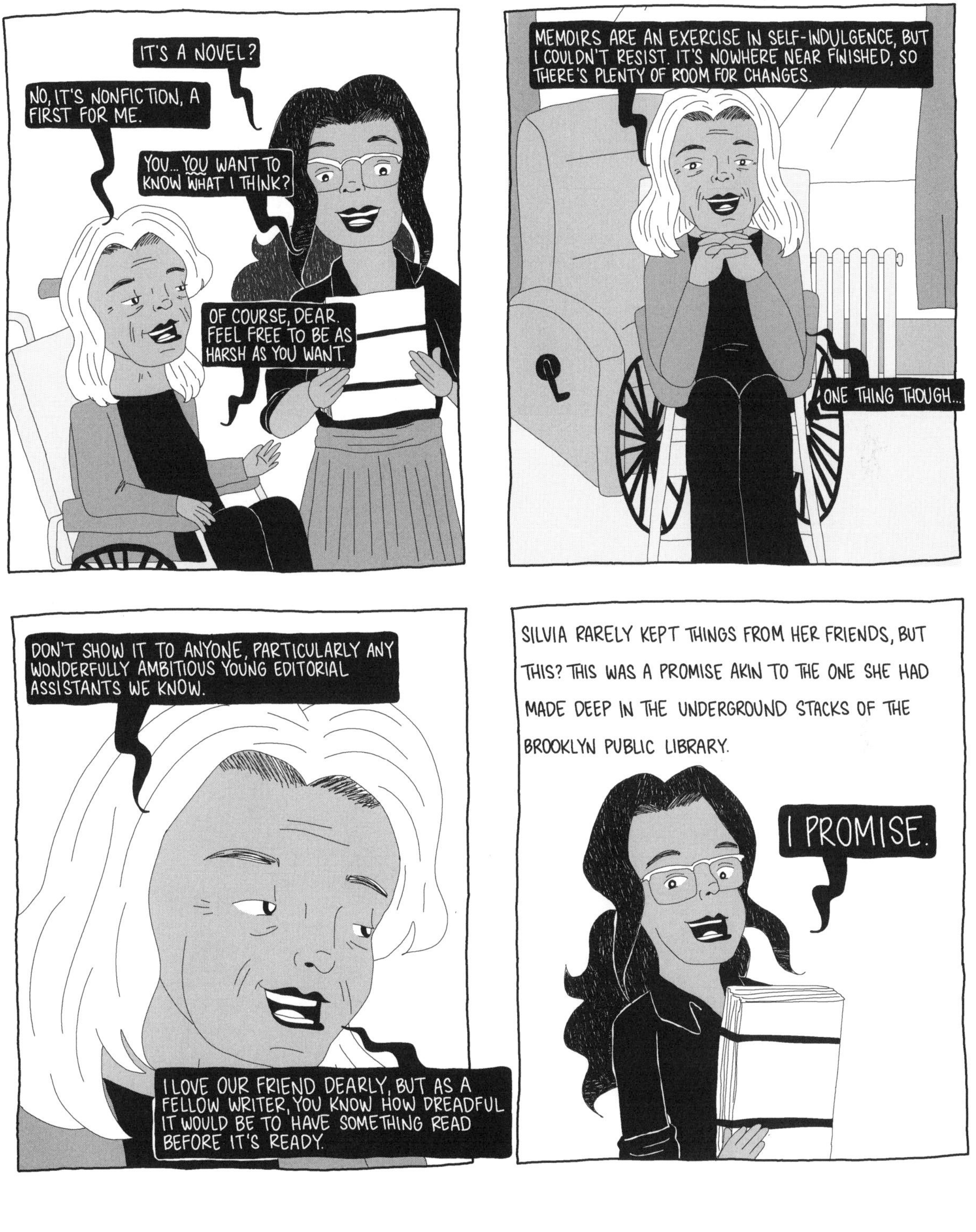
IT'S A NOVEL?
NO, IT'S NONFICTION, A FIRST FOR ME.
YOU... YOU WANT TO KNOW WHAT I THINK?
OF COURSE, DEAR. FEEL FREE TO BE AS HARSH AS YOU WANT.
MEMOIRS ARE AN EXERCISE IN SELF-INDULGENCE, BUT I COULDN'T RESIST. IT'S NOWHERE NEAR FINISHED, SO THERE'S PLENTY OF ROOM FOR CHANGES.
ONE THING THOUGH...
DON'T SHOW IT TO ANYONE, PARTICULARLY ANY WONDERFULLY AMBITIOUS YOUNG EDITORIAL ASSISTANTS WE KNOW.
I LOVE OUR FRIEND DEARLY, BUT AS A FELLOW WRITER, YOU KNOW HOW DREADFUL IT WOULD BE TO HAVE SOMETHING READ BEFORE IT'S READY.
SILVIA RARELY KEPT THINGS FROM HER FRIENDS, BUT THIS? THIS WAS A PROMISE AKIN TO THE ONE SHE HAD MADE DEEP IN THE UNDERGROUND STACKS OF THE BROOKLYN PUBLIC LIBRARY.
I PROMISE.

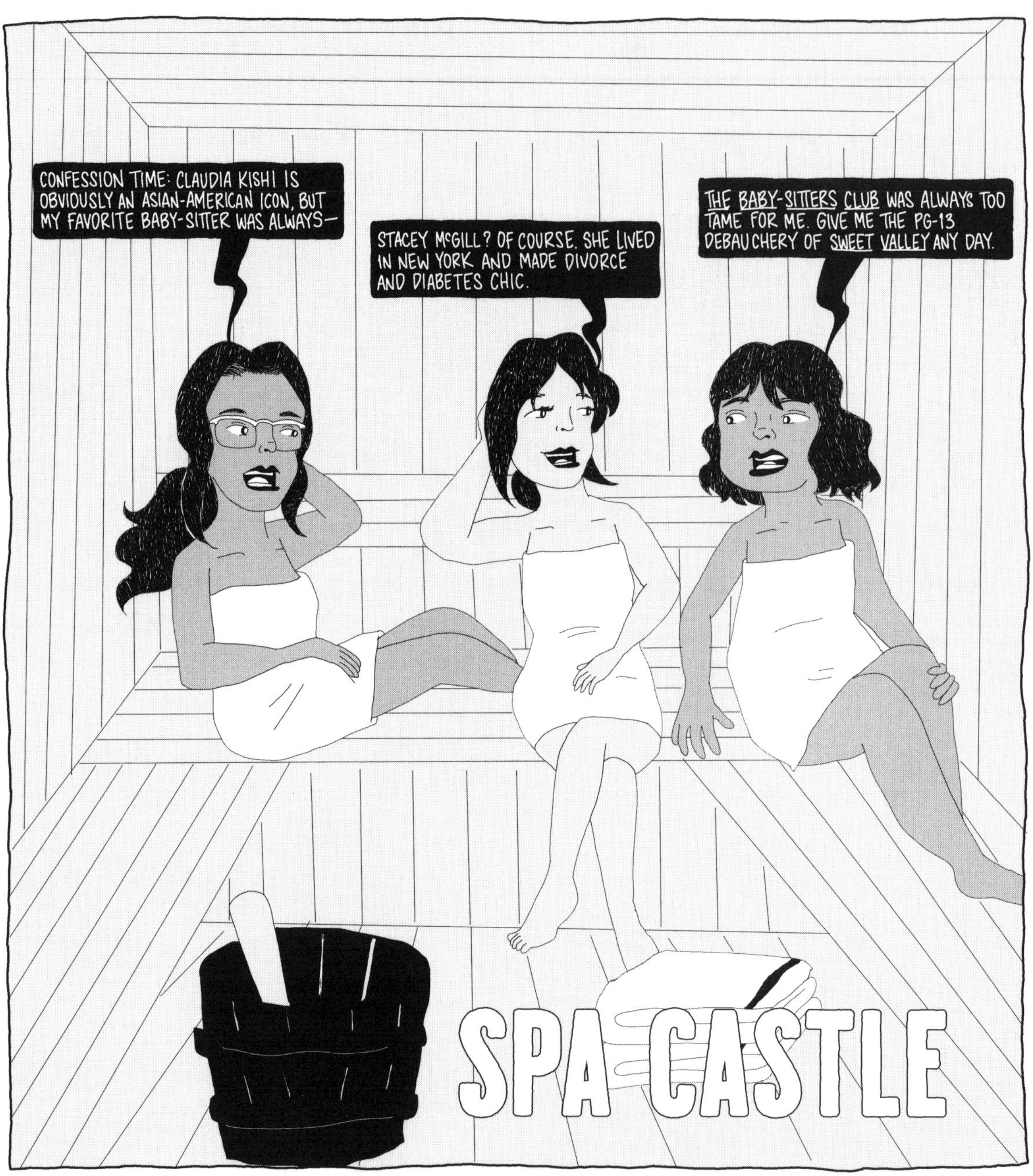
CONFESSION TIME: CLAUDIA KISHI IS OBVIOUSLY AN ASIAN-AMERICAN ICON, BUT MY FAVORITE BABY-SITTER WAS ALWAYS—
STACEY McGILL? OF COURSE. SHE LIVED IN NEW YORK AND MADE DIVORCE AND DIABETES CHIC.
THE BABY-SITTERS CLUB WAS ALWAYS TOO TAME FOR ME. GIVE ME THE PG-13 DEBAUCHERY OF SWEET VALLEY ANY DAY.
SPA CASTLE

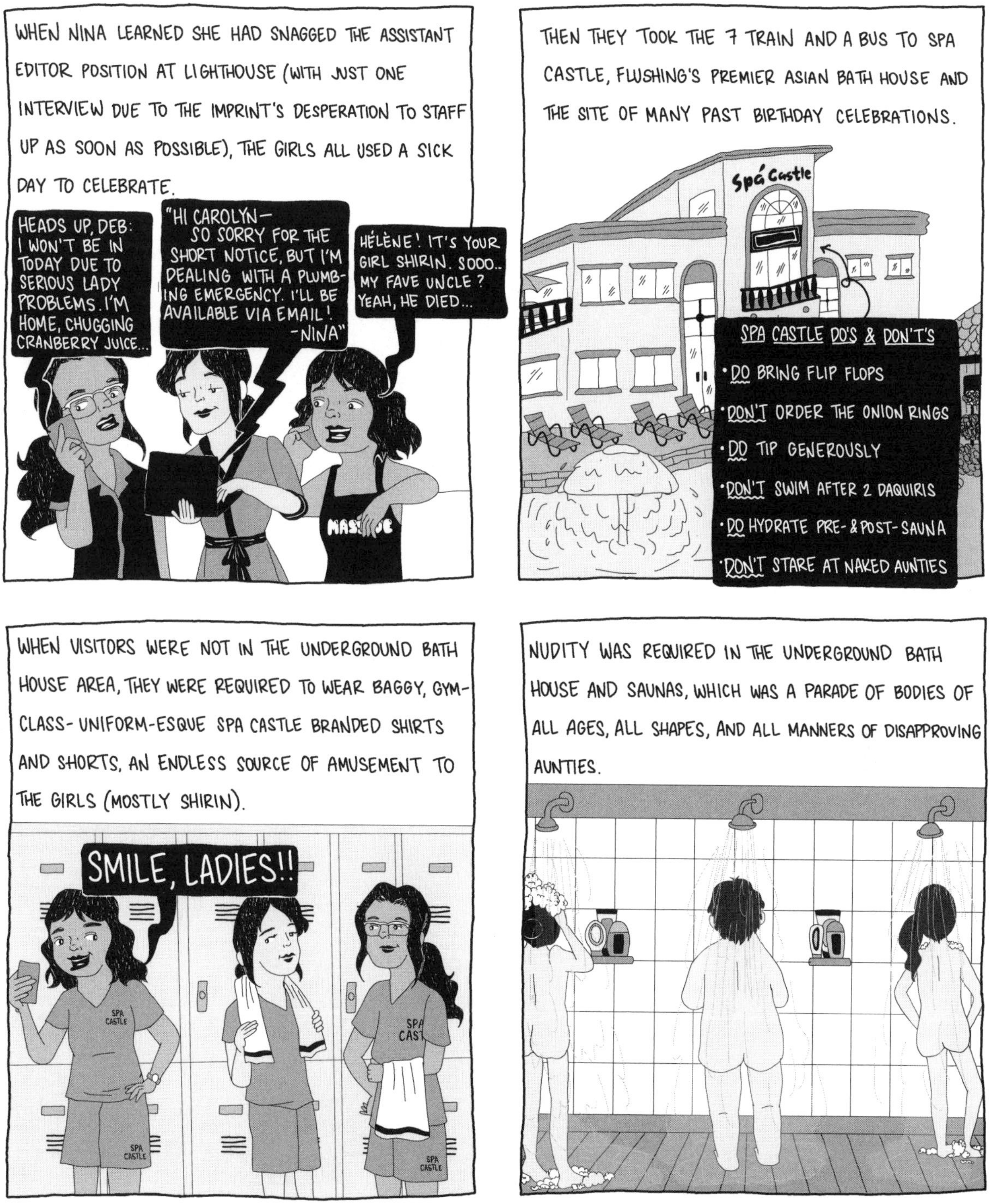
WHEN NINA LEARNED SHE HAD SNAGGED THE ASSISTANT EDITOR POSITION AT LIGHTHOUSE (WITH JUST ONE INTERVIEW DUE TO THE IMPRINT'S DESPERATION TO STAFF UP AS SOON AS POSSIBLE), THE GIRLS ALL USED A SICK DAY TO CELEBRATE.
HEADS UP, DEB: I WON'T BE IN TODAY DUE TO SERIOUS LADY PROBLEMS. I'M HOME, CHUGGING CRANBERRY JUICE...
"HI CAROLYN— SO SORRY FOR THE SHORT NOTICE, BUT I'M DEALING WITH A PLUMBING EMERGENCY. I'LL BE AVAILABLE VIA EMAIL! -NINA"
HÉLÈNE! IT'S YOUR GIRL SHIRIN. SOOO.. MY FAVE UNCLE? YEAH, HE DIED...
THEN THEY TOOK THE 7 TRAIN AND A BUS TO SPA CASTLE, FLUSHING'S PREMIER ASIAN BATH HOUSE AND THE SITE OF MANY PAST BIRTHDAY CELEBRATIONS.
Spá Castle
SPA CASTLE DO'S & DON'T'S
•DO BRING FLIP FLOPS
•DON'T ORDER THE ONION RINGS
•DO TIP GENEROUSLY
•DON'T SWIM AFTER 2 DAQUIRIS
•DO HYDRATE PRE- & POST-SAUNA
•DON'T STARE AT NAKED AUNTIES
WHEN VISITORS WERE NOT IN THE UNDERGROUND BATH HOUSE AREA, THEY WERE REQUIRED TO WEAR BAGGY, GYM-CLASS-UNIFORM-ESQUE SPA CASTLE BRANDED SHIRTS AND SHORTS, AN ENDLESS SOURCE OF AMUSEMENT TO THE GIRLS (MOSTLY SHIRIN).
SMILE, LADIES!!
SPA CASTLE
SPA CASTLE
NUDITY WAS REQUIRED IN THE UNDERGROUND BATH HOUSE AND SAUNAS, WHICH WAS A PARADE OF BODIES OF ALL AGES, ALL SHAPES, AND ALL MANNERS OF DISAPPROVING AUNTIES.

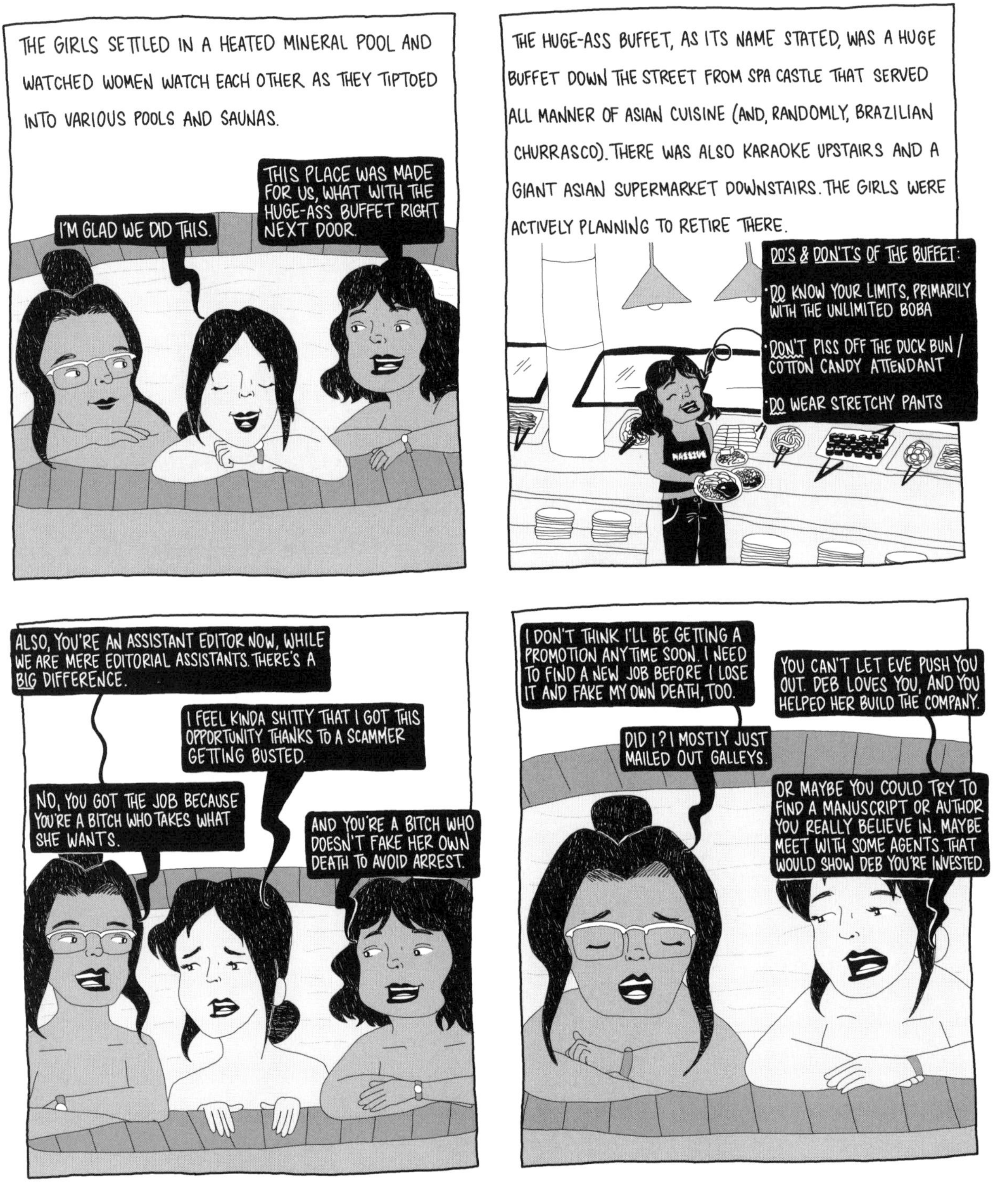
THE GIRLS SETTLED IN A HEATED MINERAL POOL AND WATCHED WOMEN WATCH EACH OTHER AS THEY TIPTOED INTO VARIOUS POOLS AND SAUNAS.
I'M GLAD WE DID THIS.
THIS PLACE WAS MADE FOR US, WHAT WITH THE HUGE-ASS BUFFET RIGHT NEXT DOOR.
THE HUGE-ASS BUFFET, AS ITS NAME STATED, WAS A HUGE BUFFET DOWN THE STREET FROM SPA CASTLE THAT SERVED ALL MANNER OF ASIAN CUISINE (AND, RANDOMLY, BRAZILIAN CHURRASCO). THERE WAS ALSO KARAOKE UPSTAIRS AND A GIANT ASIAN SUPERMARKET DOWNSTAIRS. THE GIRLS WERE ACTIVELY PLANNING TO RETIRE THERE.
DO'S & DON'T'S OF THE BUFFET:
· DO KNOW YOUR LIMITS, PRIMARILY WITH THE UNLIMITED BOBA
· DON'T PISS OFF THE DUCK BUN / COTTON CANDY ATTENDANT
· DO WEAR STRETCHY PANTS
MASSIVE
ALSO, YOU'RE AN ASSISTANT EDITOR NOW, WHILE WE ARE MERE EDITORIAL ASSISTANTS. THERE'S A BIG DIFFERENCE.
I FEEL KINDA SHITTY THAT I GOT THIS OPPORTUNITY THANKS TO A SCAMMER GETTING BUSTED.
NO, YOU GOT THE JOB BECAUSE YOU'RE A BITCH WHO TAKES WHAT SHE WANTS.
AND YOU'RE A BITCH WHO DOESN'T FAKE HER OWN DEATH TO AVOID ARREST.
I DON'T THINK I'LL BE GETTING A PROMOTION ANYTIME SOON. I NEED TO FIND A NEW JOB BEFORE I LOSE IT AND FAKE MY OWN DEATH, TOO.
YOU CAN'T LET EVE PUSH YOU OUT. DEB LOVES YOU, AND YOU HELPED HER BUILD THE COMPANY.
DID I? I MOSTLY JUST MAILED OUT GALLEYS.
OR MAYBE YOU COULD TRY TO FIND A MANUSCRIPT OR AUTHOR YOU REALLY BELIEVE IN. MAYBE MEET WITH SOME AGENTS. THAT WOULD SHOW DEB YOU'RE INVESTED.

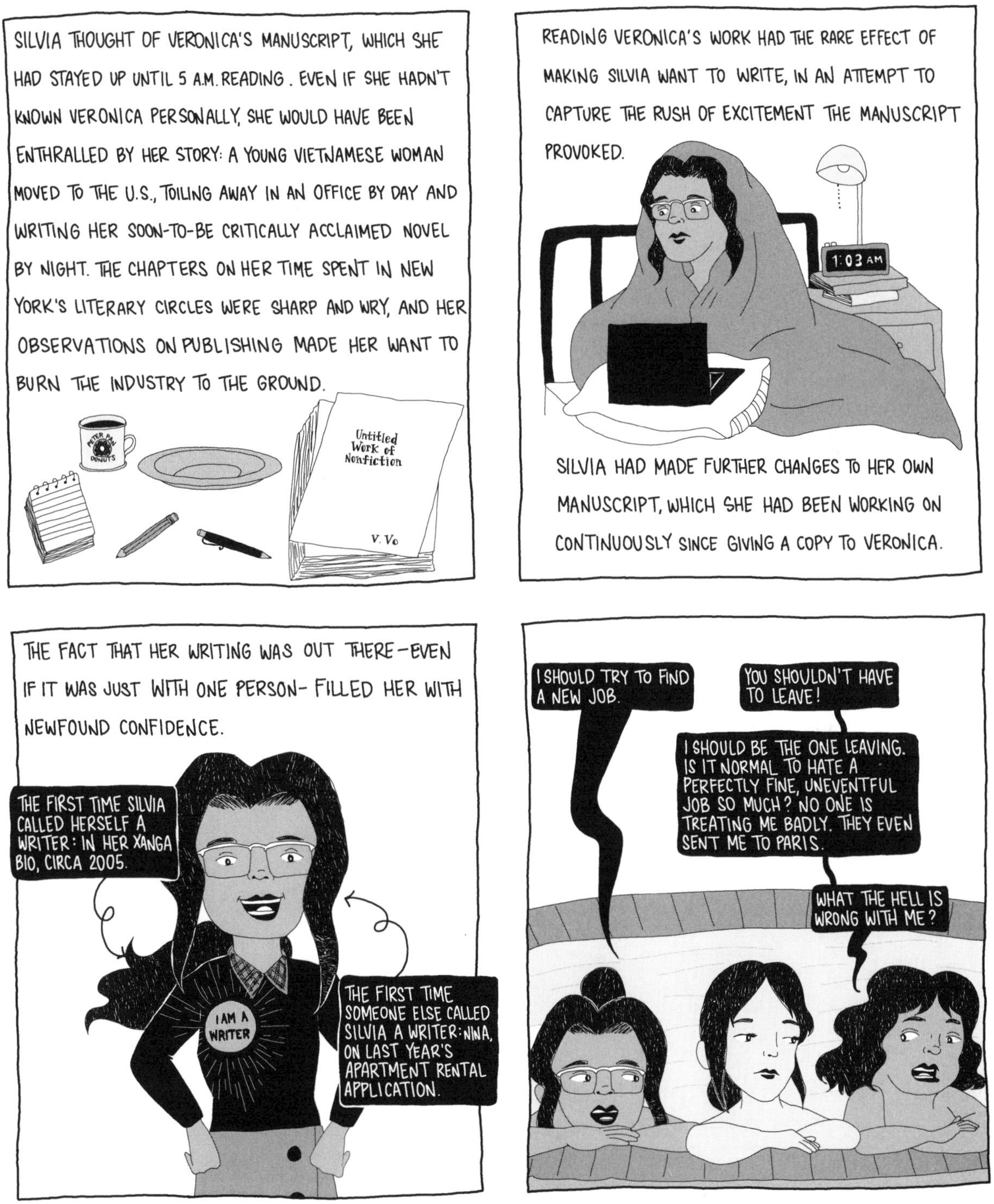
SILVIA THOUGHT OF VERONICA'S MANUSCRIPT, WHICH SHE HAD STAYED UP UNTIL 5 A.M. READING. EVEN IF SHE HADN'T KNOWN VERONICA PERSONALLY, SHE WOULD HAVE BEEN ENTHRALLED BY HER STORY: A YOUNG VIETNAMESE WOMAN MOVED TO THE U.S., TOILING AWAY IN AN OFFICE BY DAY AND WRITING HER SOON-TO-BE CRITICALLY ACCLAIMED NOVEL BY NIGHT. THE CHAPTERS ON HER TIME SPENT IN NEW YORK'S LITERARY CIRCLES WERE SHARP AND WRY, AND HER OBSERVATIONS ON PUBLISHING MADE HER WANT TO BURN THE INDUSTRY TO THE GROUND.
PETER PAN DONUTS
Untitled Work of Nonfiction
V. Vo
READING VERONICA'S WORK HAD THE RARE EFFECT OF MAKING SILVIA WANT TO WRITE, IN AN ATTEMPT TO CAPTURE THE RUSH OF EXCITEMENT THE MANUSCRIPT PROVOKED.
1:03 AM
SILVIA HAD MADE FURTHER CHANGES TO HER OWN MANUSCRIPT, WHICH SHE HAD BEEN WORKING ON CONTINUOUSLY SINCE GIVING A COPY TO VERONICA.
THE FACT THAT HER WRITING WAS OUT THERE—EVEN IF IT WAS JUST WITH ONE PERSON—FILLED HER WITH NEWFOUND CONFIDENCE.
THE FIRST TIME SILVIA CALLED HERSELF A WRITER: IN HER XANGA BIO, CIRCA 2005.
I AM A WRITER
THE FIRST TIME SOMEONE ELSE CALLED SILVIA A WRITER: NINA, ON LAST YEAR'S APARTMENT RENTAL APPLICATION.
I SHOULD TRY TO FIND A NEW JOB.
YOU SHOULDN'T HAVE TO LEAVE!
I SHOULD BE THE ONE LEAVING. IS IT NORMAL TO HATE A PERFECTLY FINE, UNEVENTFUL JOB SO MUCH? NO ONE IS TREATING ME BADLY. THEY EVEN SENT ME TO PARIS.
WHAT THE HELL IS WRONG WITH ME?

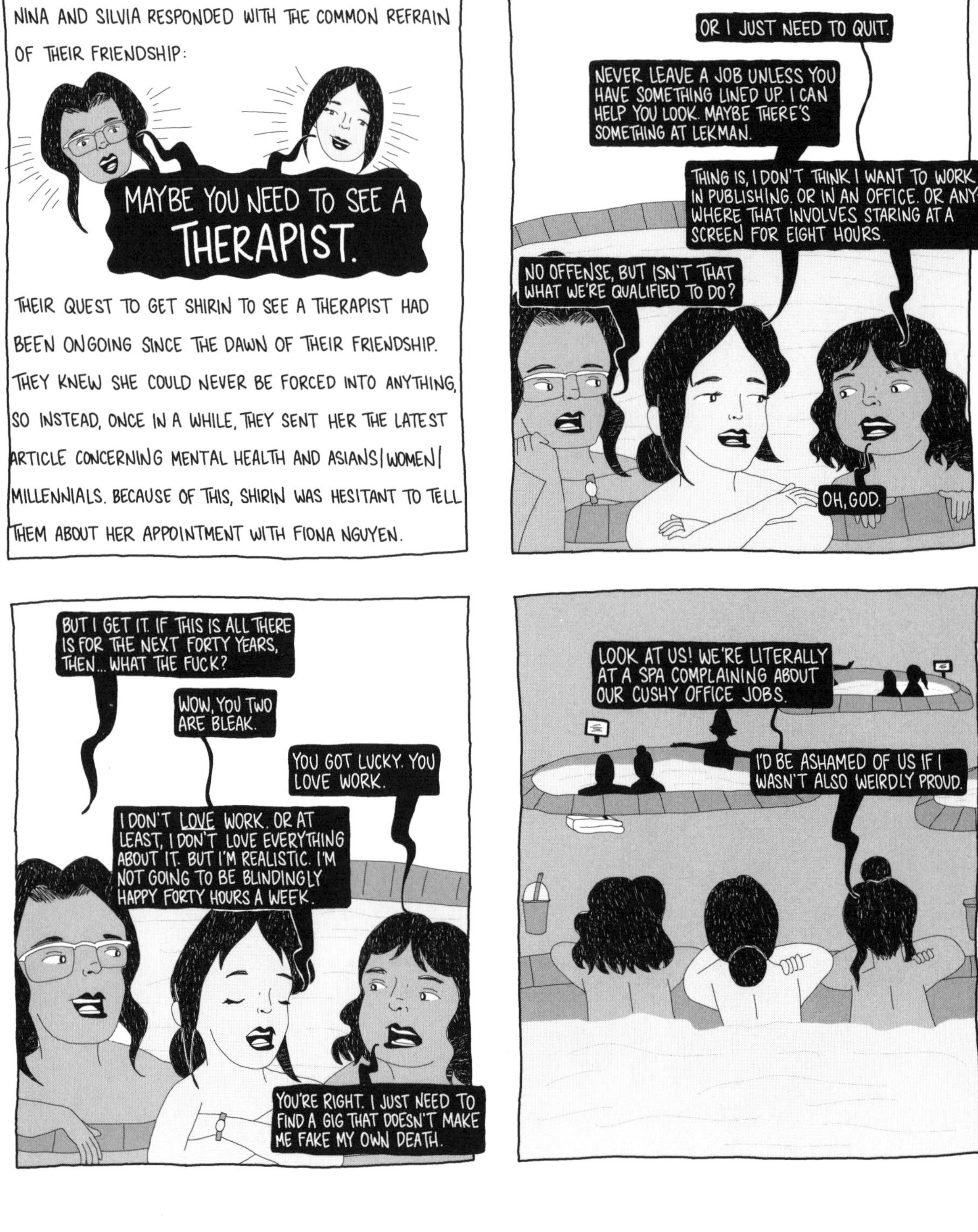
NINA AND SILVIA RESPONDED WITH THE COMMON REFRAIN OF THEIR FRIENDSHIP:
MAYBE YOU NEED TO SEE A THERAPIST.
THEIR QUEST TO GET SHIRIN TO SEE A THERAPIST HAD BEEN ONGOING SINCE THE DAWN OF THEIR FRIENDSHIP. THEY KNEW SHE COULD NEVER BE FORCED INTO ANYTHING, SO INSTEAD, ONCE IN A WHILE, THEY SENT HER THE LATEST ARTICLE CONCERNING MENTAL HEALTH AND ASIANS/WOMEN/MILLENNIALS. BECAUSE OF THIS, SHIRIN WAS HESITANT TO TELL THEM ABOUT HER APPOINTMENT WITH FIONA NGUYEN.
OR I JUST NEED TO QUIT.
NEVER LEAVE A JOB UNLESS YOU HAVE SOMETHING LINED UP. I CAN HELP YOU LOOK. MAYBE THERE'S SOMETHING AT LEKMAN.
THING IS, I DON'T THINK I WANT TO WORK IN PUBLISHING. OR IN AN OFFICE. OR ANYWHERE THAT INVOLVES STARING AT A SCREEN FOR EIGHT HOURS.
NO OFFENSE, BUT ISN'T THAT WHAT WE'RE QUALIFIED TO DO?
OH, GOD.
BUT I GET IT. IF THIS IS ALL THERE IS FOR THE NEXT FORTY YEARS, THEN... WHAT THE FUCK?
WOW, YOU TWO ARE BLEAK.
YOU GOT LUCKY. YOU LOVE WORK.
I DON'T LOVE WORK. OR AT LEAST, I DON'T LOVE EVERYTHING ABOUT IT. BUT I'M REALISTIC. I'M NOT GOING TO BE BLINDINGLY HAPPY FORTY HOURS A WEEK.
YOU'RE RIGHT. I JUST NEED TO FIND A GIG THAT DOESN'T MAKE ME FAKE MY OWN DEATH.
LOOK AT US! WE'RE LITERALLY AT A SPA COMPLAINING ABOUT OUR CUSHY OFFICE JOBS.
I'D BE ASHAMED OF US IF I WASN'T ALSO WEIRDLY PROUD.

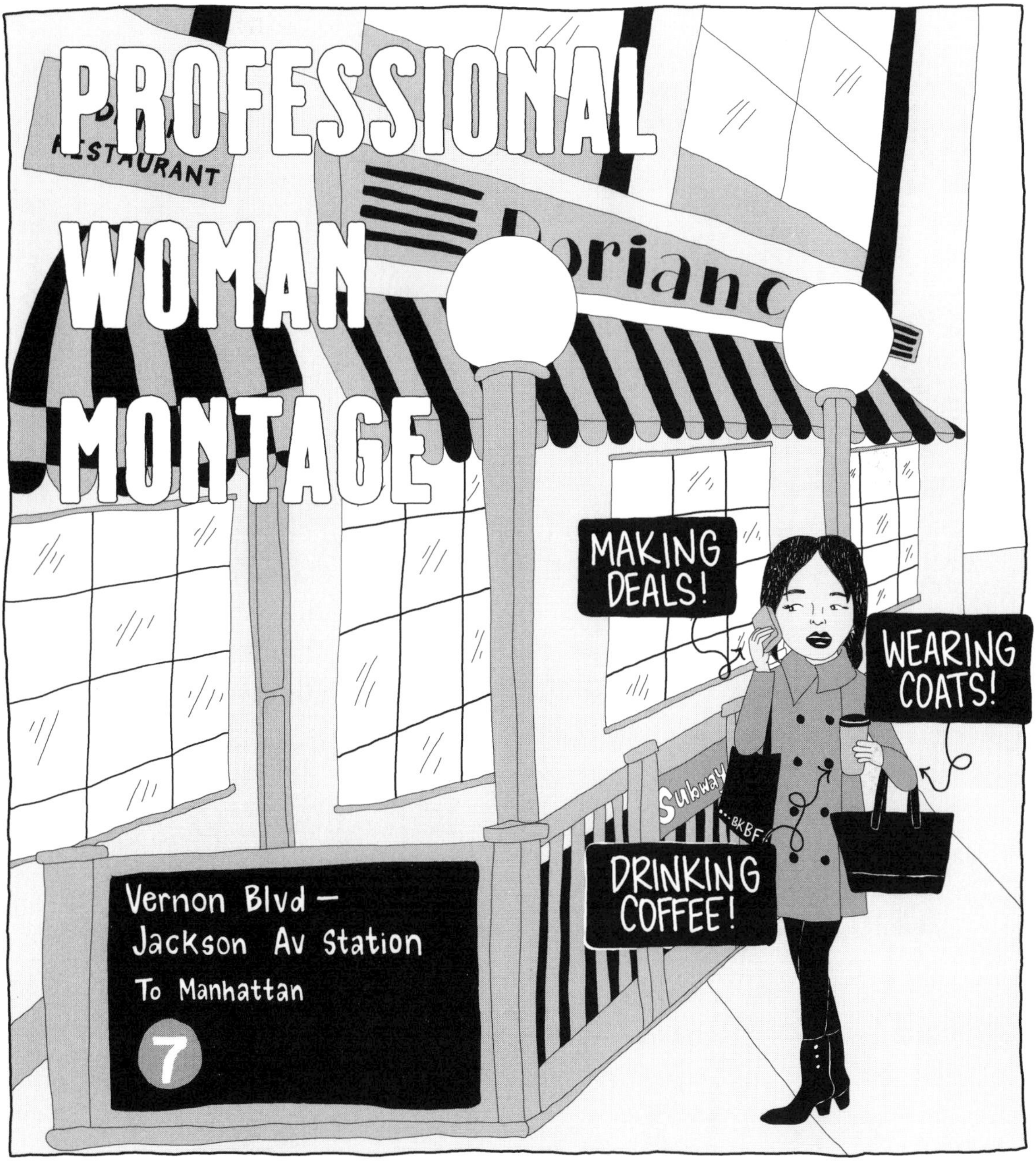
PROFESSIONAL WOMAN MONTAGE
MAKING DEALS!
WEARING COATS!
DRINKING COFFEE!
Subway
Vernon Blvd –
Jackson Av Station
To Manhattan
7

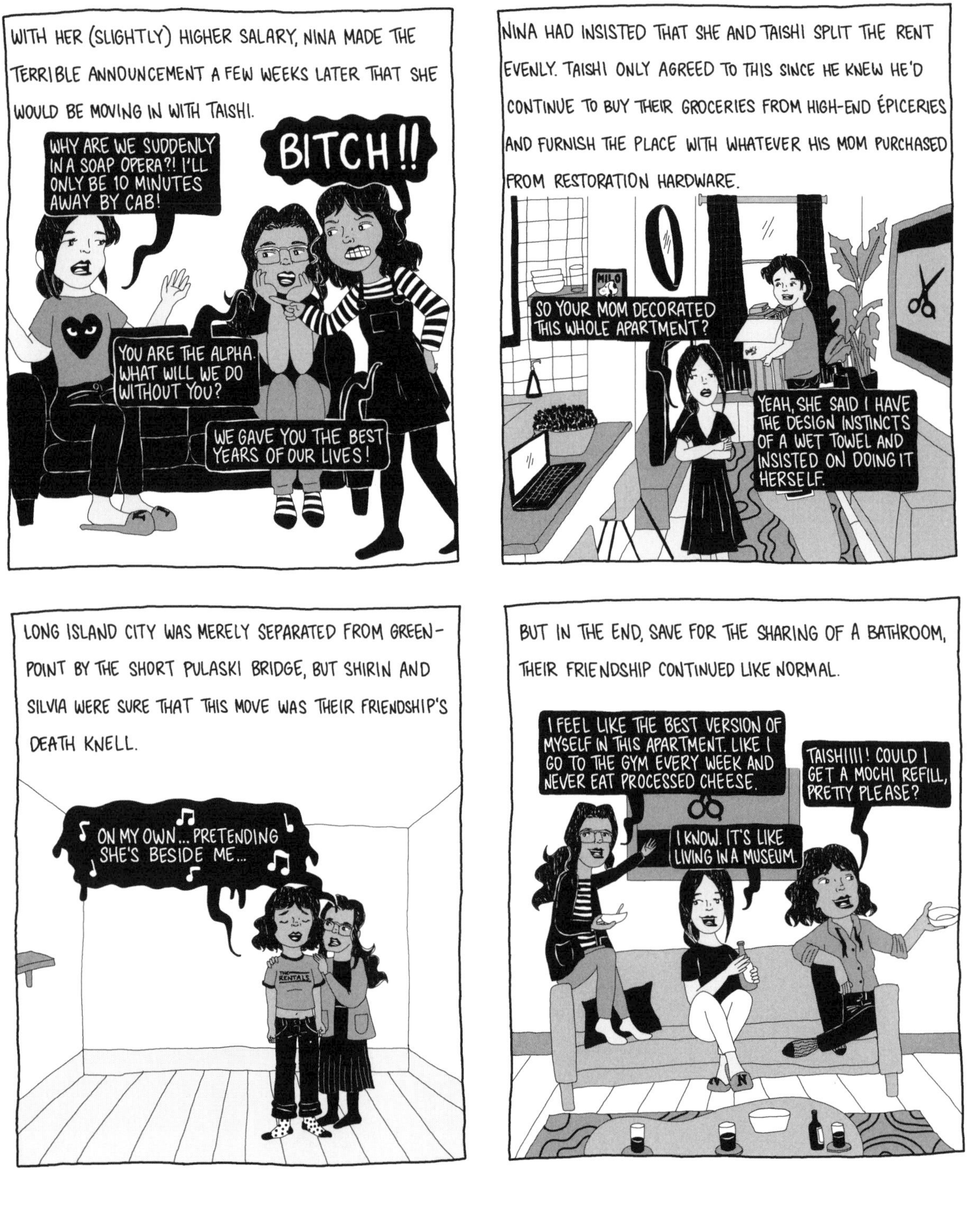
WITH HER (SLIGHTLY) HIGHER SALARY, NINA MADE THE TERRIBLE ANNOUNCEMENT A FEW WEEKS LATER THAT SHE WOULD BE MOVING IN WITH TAISHI.
WHY ARE WE SUDDENLY IN A SOAP OPERA?! I'LL ONLY BE 10 MINUTES AWAY BY CAB!
BITCH!!
YOU ARE THE ALPHA. WHAT WILL WE DO WITHOUT YOU?
WE GAVE YOU THE BEST YEARS OF OUR LIVES!
NINA HAD INSISTED THAT SHE AND TAISHI SPLIT THE RENT EVENLY. TAISHI ONLY AGREED TO THIS SINCE HE KNEW HE'D CONTINUE TO BUY THEIR GROCERIES FROM HIGH-END ÉPICERIES AND FURNISH THE PLACE WITH WHATEVER HIS MOM PURCHASED FROM RESTORATION HARDWARE.
MILO
SO YOUR MOM DECORATED THIS WHOLE APARTMENT?
YEAH, SHE SAID I HAVE THE DESIGN INSTINCTS OF A WET TOWEL AND INSISTED ON DOING IT HERSELF.
LONG ISLAND CITY WAS MERELY SEPARATED FROM GREEN-POINT BY THE SHORT PULASKI BRIDGE, BUT SHIRIN AND SILVIA WERE SURE THAT THIS MOVE WAS THEIR FRIENDSHIP'S DEATH KNELL.
ON MY OWN... PRETENDING SHE'S BESIDE ME...
THE RENTALS
BUT IN THE END, SAVE FOR THE SHARING OF A BATHROOM, THEIR FRIENDSHIP CONTINUED LIKE NORMAL.
I FEEL LIKE THE BEST VERSION OF MYSELF IN THIS APARTMENT. LIKE I GO TO THE GYM EVERY WEEK AND NEVER EAT PROCESSED CHEESE.
I KNOW. IT'S LIKE LIVING IN A MUSEUM.
TAISHIIII! COULD I GET A MOCHI REFILL, PRETTY PLEASE?

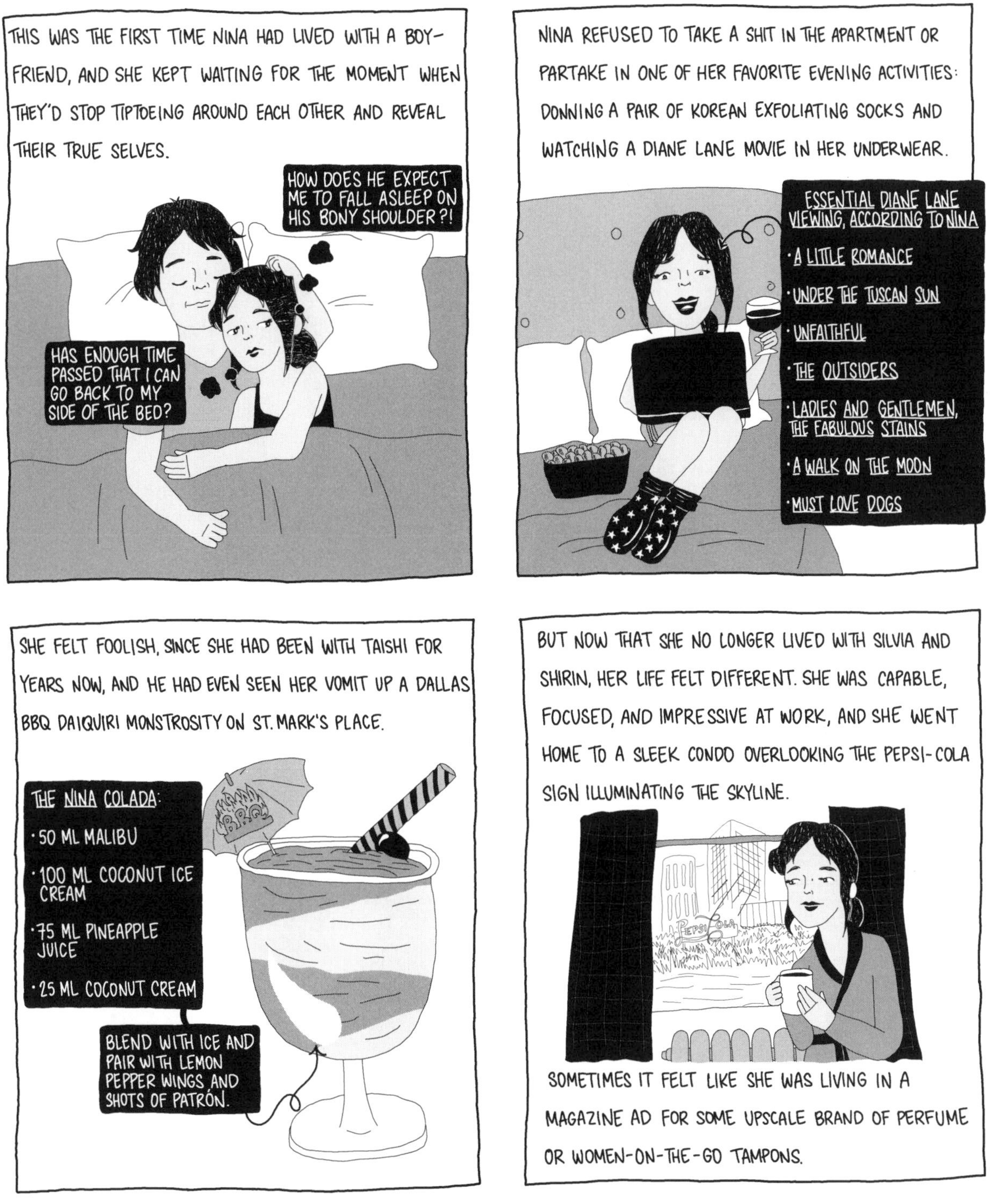
THIS WAS THE FIRST TIME NINA HAD LIVED WITH A BOY-FRIEND, AND SHE KEPT WAITING FOR THE MOMENT WHEN THEY'D STOP TIPTOEING AROUND EACH OTHER AND REVEAL THEIR TRUE SELVES.
HOW DOES HE EXPECT ME TO FALL ASLEEP ON HIS BONY SHOULDER?!
HAS ENOUGH TIME PASSED THAT I CAN GO BACK TO MY SIDE OF THE BED?
NINA REFUSED TO TAKE A SHIT IN THE APARTMENT OR PARTAKE IN ONE OF HER FAVORITE EVENING ACTIVITIES: DONNING A PAIR OF KOREAN EXFOLIATING SOCKS AND WATCHING A DIANE LANE MOVIE IN HER UNDERWEAR.
ESSENTIAL DIANE LANE VIEWING, ACCORDING TO NINA
· A LITTLE ROMANCE
· UNDER THE TUSCAN SUN
· UNFAITHFUL
· THE OUTSIDERS
· LADIES AND GENTLEMEN, THE FABULOUS STAINS
· A WALK ON THE MOON
· MUST LOVE DOGS
SHE FELT FOOLISH, SINCE SHE HAD BEEN WITH TAISHI FOR YEARS NOW, AND HE HAD EVEN SEEN HER VOMIT UP A DALLAS BBQ DAIQUIRI MONSTROSITY ON ST. MARK'S PLACE.
THE NINA COLADA:
· 50 ML MALIBU
· 100 ML COCONUT ICE CREAM
· 75 ML PINEAPPLE JUICE
· 25 ML COCONUT CREAM
BBQ
BLEND WITH ICE AND PAIR WITH LEMON PEPPER WINGS AND SHOTS OF PATRÓN.
BUT NOW THAT SHE NO LONGER LIVED WITH SILVIA AND SHIRIN, HER LIFE FELT DIFFERENT. SHE WAS CAPABLE, FOCUSED, AND IMPRESSIVE AT WORK, AND SHE WENT HOME TO A SLEEK CONDO OVERLOOKING THE PEPSI-COLA SIGN ILLUMINATING THE SKYLINE.
PEPSI-COLA
SOMETIMES IT FELT LIKE SHE WAS LIVING IN A MAGAZINE AD FOR SOME UPSCALE BRAND OF PERFUME OR WOMEN-ON-THE-GO TAMPONS.

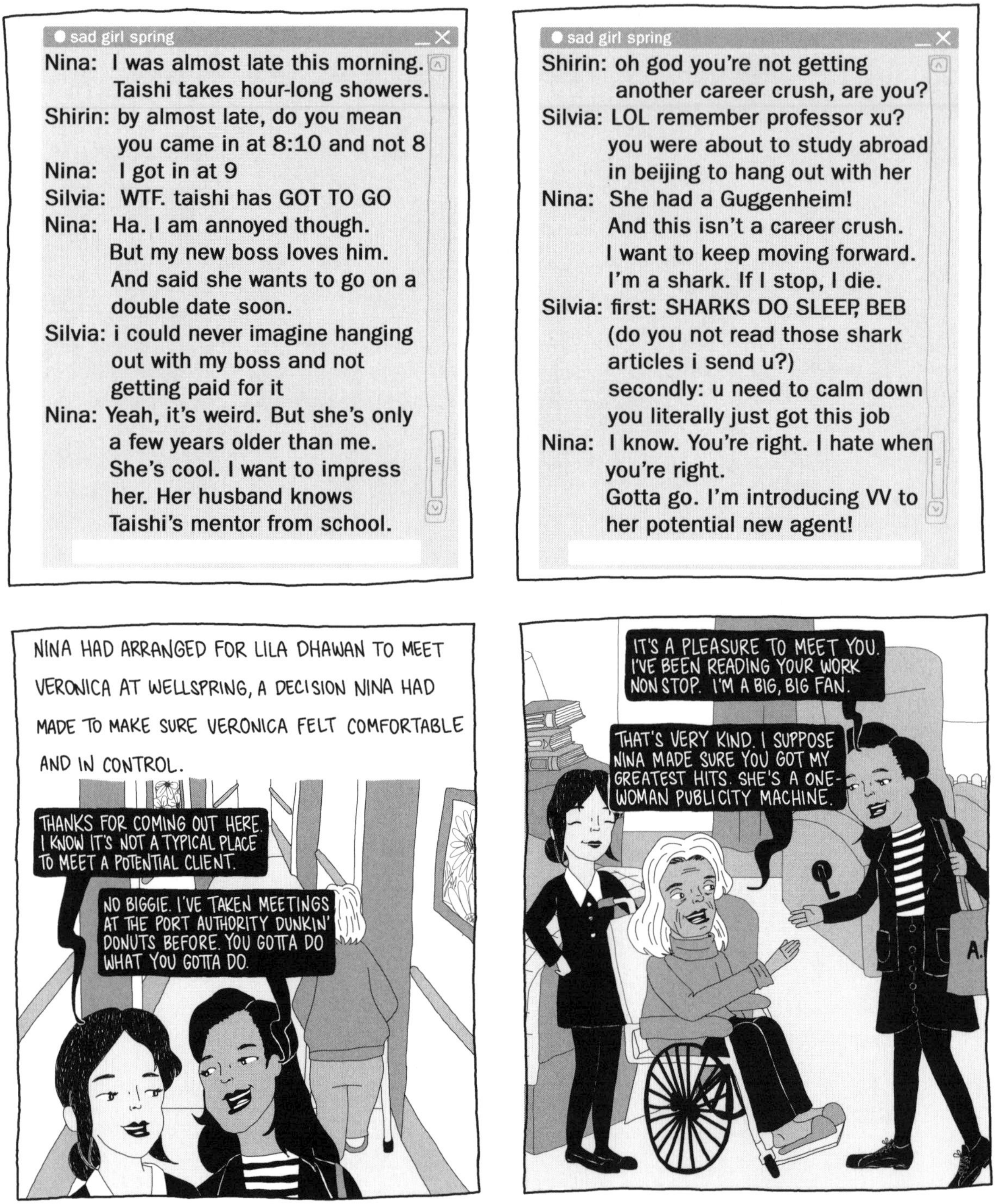
sad girl spring
Nina: I was almost late this morning. Taishi takes hour-long showers.
Shirin: by almost late, do you mean you came in at 8:10 and not 8
Nina: I got in at 9
Silvia: WTF. taishi has GOT TO GO
Nina: Ha. I am annoyed though. But my new boss loves him. And said she wants to go on a double date soon.
Silvia: i could never imagine hanging out with my boss and not getting paid for it
Nina: Yeah, it's weird. But she's only a few years older than me. She's cool. I want to impress her. Her husband knows Taishi's mentor from school.
sad girl spring
Shirin: oh god you're not getting another career crush, are you?
Silvia: LOL remember professor xu? you were about to study abroad in beijing to hang out with her
Nina: She had a Guggenheim! And this isn't a career crush. I want to keep moving forward. I'm a shark. If I stop, I die.
Silvia: first: SHARKS DO SLEEP, BEB (do you not read those shark articles i send u?) secondly: u need to calm down you literally just got this job
Nina: I know. You're right. I hate when you're right. Gotta go. I'm introducing VV to her potential new agent!
NINA HAD ARRANGED FOR LILA DHAWAN TO MEET VERONICA AT WELLSPRING, A DECISION NINA HAD MADE TO MAKE SURE VERONICA FELT COMFORTABLE AND IN CONTROL.
THANKS FOR COMING OUT HERE. I KNOW IT'S NOT A TYPICAL PLACE TO MEET A POTENTIAL CLIENT.
NO BIGGIE. I'VE TAKEN MEETINGS AT THE PORT AUTHORITY DUNKIN' DONUTS BEFORE. YOU GOTTA DO WHAT YOU GOTTA DO.
IT'S A PLEASURE TO MEET YOU. I'VE BEEN READING YOUR WORK NON STOP. I'M A BIG, BIG FAN.
THAT'S VERY KIND. I SUPPOSE NINA MADE SURE YOU GOT MY GREATEST HITS. SHE'S A ONE-WOMAN PUBLICITY MACHINE.

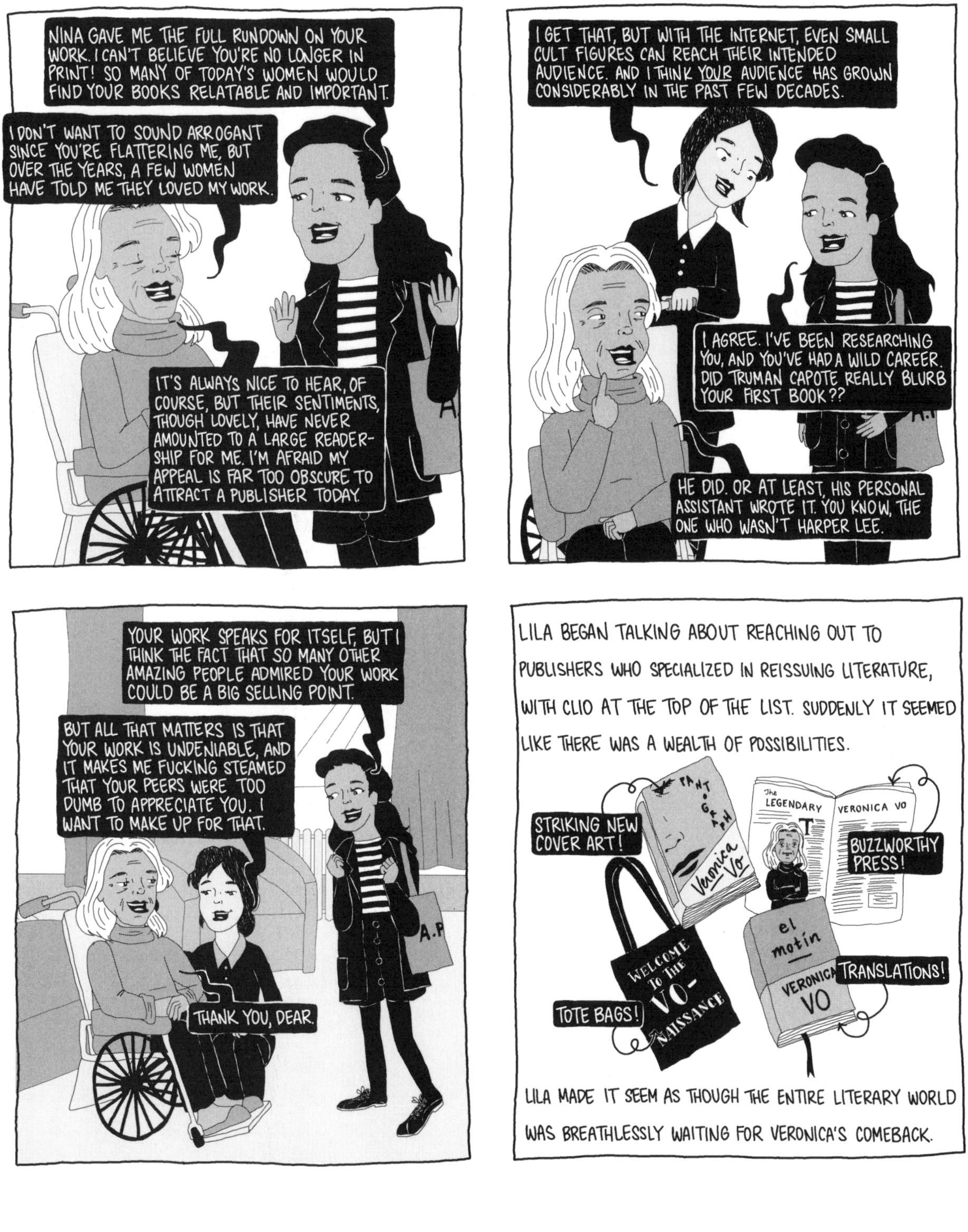
NINA GAVE ME THE FULL RUNDOWN ON YOUR WORK. I CAN'T BELIEVE YOU'RE NO LONGER IN PRINT! SO MANY OF TODAY'S WOMEN WOULD FIND YOUR BOOKS RELATABLE AND IMPORTANT.
I DON'T WANT TO SOUND ARROGANT SINCE YOU'RE FLATTERING ME, BUT OVER THE YEARS, A FEW WOMEN HAVE TOLD ME THEY LOVED MY WORK.
IT'S ALWAYS NICE TO HEAR, OF COURSE, BUT THEIR SENTIMENTS, THOUGH LOVELY, HAVE NEVER AMOUNTED TO A LARGE READERSHIP FOR ME. I'M AFRAID MY APPEAL IS FAR TOO OBSCURE TO ATTRACT A PUBLISHER TODAY.
A.P
I GET THAT, BUT WITH THE INTERNET, EVEN SMALL CULT FIGURES CAN REACH THEIR INTENDED AUDIENCE. AND I THINK YOUR AUDIENCE HAS GROWN CONSIDERABLY IN THE PAST FEW DECADES.
I AGREE. I'VE BEEN RESEARCHING YOU, AND YOU'VE HAD A WILD CAREER. DID TRUMAN CAPOTE REALLY BLURB YOUR FIRST BOOK??
HE DID. OR AT LEAST, HIS PERSONAL ASSISTANT WROTE IT. YOU KNOW, THE ONE WHO WASN'T HARPER LEE.
YOUR WORK SPEAKS FOR ITSELF, BUT I THINK THE FACT THAT SO MANY OTHER AMAZING PEOPLE ADMIRED YOUR WORK COULD BE A BIG SELLING POINT.
BUT ALL THAT MATTERS IS THAT YOUR WORK IS UNDENIABLE, AND IT MAKES ME FUCKING STEAMED THAT YOUR PEERS WERE TOO DUMB TO APPRECIATE YOU. I WANT TO MAKE UP FOR THAT.
A.P
THANK YOU, DEAR.
LILA BEGAN TALKING ABOUT REACHING OUT TO PUBLISHERS WHO SPECIALIZED IN REISSUING LITERATURE, WITH CLIO AT THE TOP OF THE LIST. SUDDENLY IT SEEMED LIKE THERE WAS A WEALTH OF POSSIBILITIES.
STRIKING NEW COVER ART!
Veronica Vo
The LEGENDARY
VERONICA VO
BUZZWORTHY PRESS!
el motín
VERONICA VO
TRANSLATIONS!
WELCOME TO THE VO-NAISSANCE
TOTE BAGS!
LILA MADE IT SEEM AS THOUGH THE ENTIRE LITERARY WORLD WAS BREATHLESSLY WAITING FOR VERONICA'S COMEBACK.

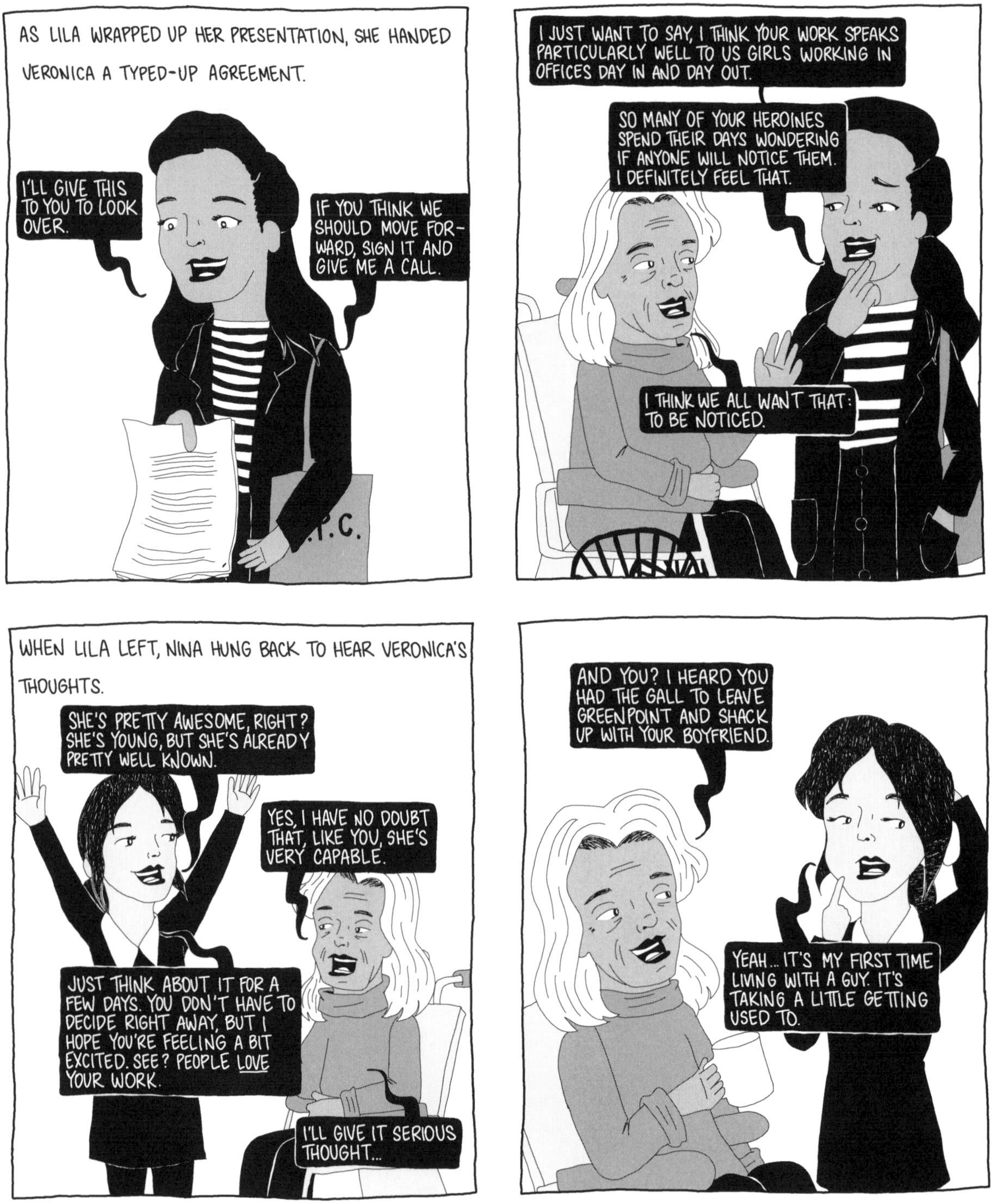
AS LILA WRAPPED UP HER PRESENTATION, SHE HANDED VERONICA A TYPED-UP AGREEMENT.
I'LL GIVE THIS TO YOU TO LOOK OVER.
IF YOU THINK WE SHOULD MOVE FORWARD, SIGN IT AND GIVE ME A CALL.
P.C.
I JUST WANT TO SAY, I THINK YOUR WORK SPEAKS PARTICULARLY WELL TO US GIRLS WORKING IN OFFICES DAY IN AND DAY OUT.
SO MANY OF YOUR HEROINES SPEND THEIR DAYS WONDERING IF ANYONE WILL NOTICE THEM. I DEFINITELY FEEL THAT.
I THINK WE ALL WANT THAT: TO BE NOTICED.
WHEN LILA LEFT, NINA HUNG BACK TO HEAR VERONICA'S THOUGHTS.
SHE'S PRETTY AWESOME, RIGHT? SHE'S YOUNG, BUT SHE'S ALREADY PRETTY WELL KNOWN.
YES, I HAVE NO DOUBT THAT, LIKE YOU, SHE'S VERY CAPABLE.
JUST THINK ABOUT IT FOR A FEW DAYS. YOU DON'T HAVE TO DECIDE RIGHT AWAY, BUT I HOPE YOU'RE FEELING A BIT EXCITED. SEE? PEOPLE LOVE YOUR WORK.
I'LL GIVE IT SERIOUS THOUGHT...
AND YOU? I HEARD YOU HAD THE GALL TO LEAVE GREENPOINT AND SHACK UP WITH YOUR BOYFRIEND.
YEAH... IT'S MY FIRST TIME LIVING WITH A GUY. IT'S TAKING A LITTLE GETTING USED TO.

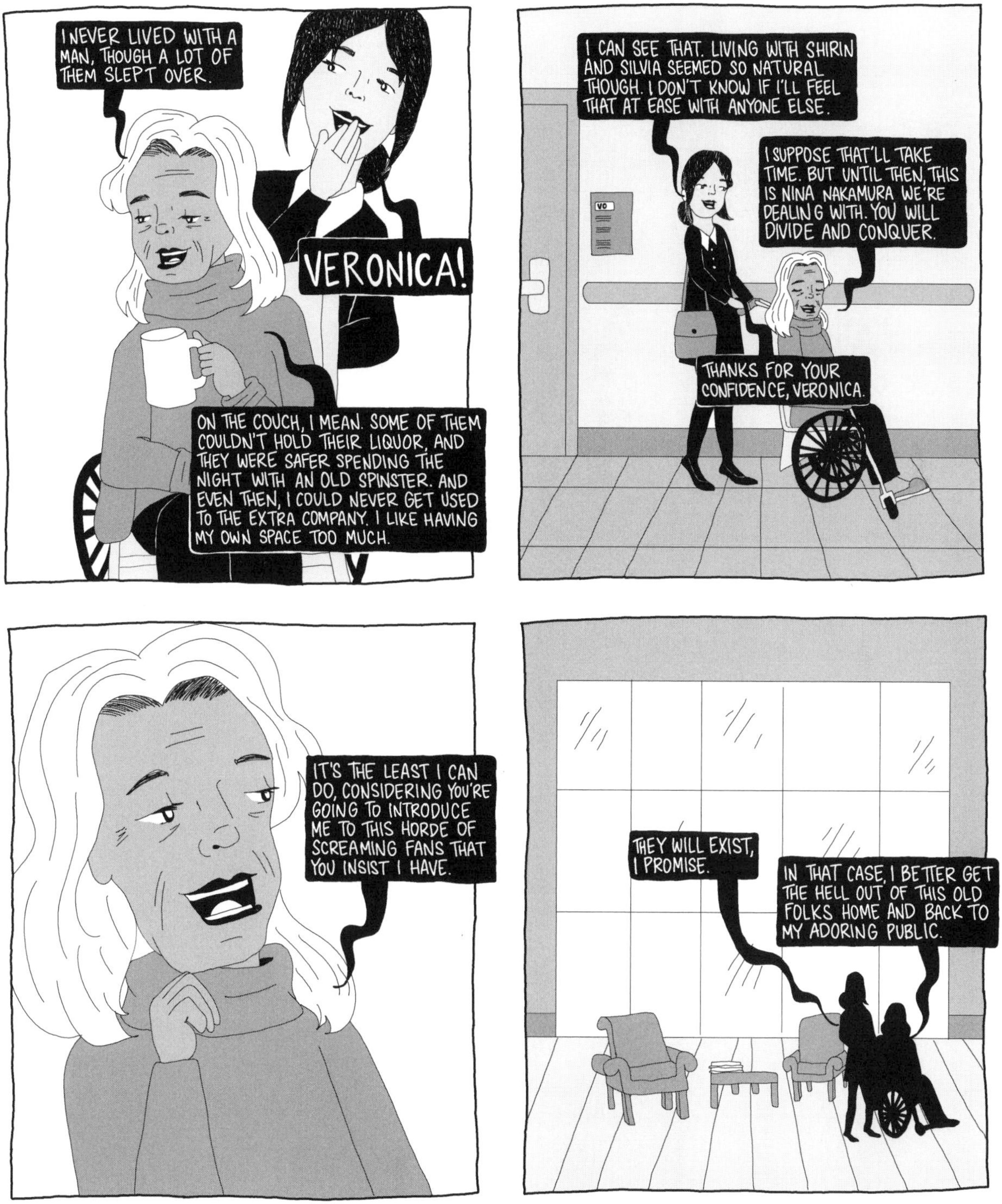
I NEVER LIVED WITH A MAN, THOUGH A LOT OF THEM SLEPT OVER.
VERONICA!
ON THE COUCH, I MEAN. SOME OF THEM COULDN'T HOLD THEIR LIQUOR, AND THEY WERE SAFER SPENDING THE NIGHT WITH AN OLD SPINSTER. AND EVEN THEN, I COULD NEVER GET USED TO THE EXTRA COMPANY. I LIKE HAVING MY OWN SPACE TOO MUCH.
I CAN SEE THAT. LIVING WITH SHIRIN AND SILVIA SEEMED SO NATURAL THOUGH. I DON'T KNOW IF I'LL FEEL THAT AT EASE WITH ANYONE ELSE.
I SUPPOSE THAT'LL TAKE TIME. BUT UNTIL THEN, THIS IS NINA NAKAMURA WE'RE DEALING WITH. YOU WILL DIVIDE AND CONQUER.
THANKS FOR YOUR CONFIDENCE, VERONICA.
IT'S THE LEAST I CAN DO, CONSIDERING YOU'RE GOING TO INTRODUCE ME TO THIS HORDE OF SCREAMING FANS THAT YOU INSIST I HAVE.
THEY WILL EXIST, I PROMISE.
IN THAT CASE, I BETTER GET THE HELL OUT OF THIS OLD FOLKS HOME AND BACK TO MY ADORING PUBLIC.

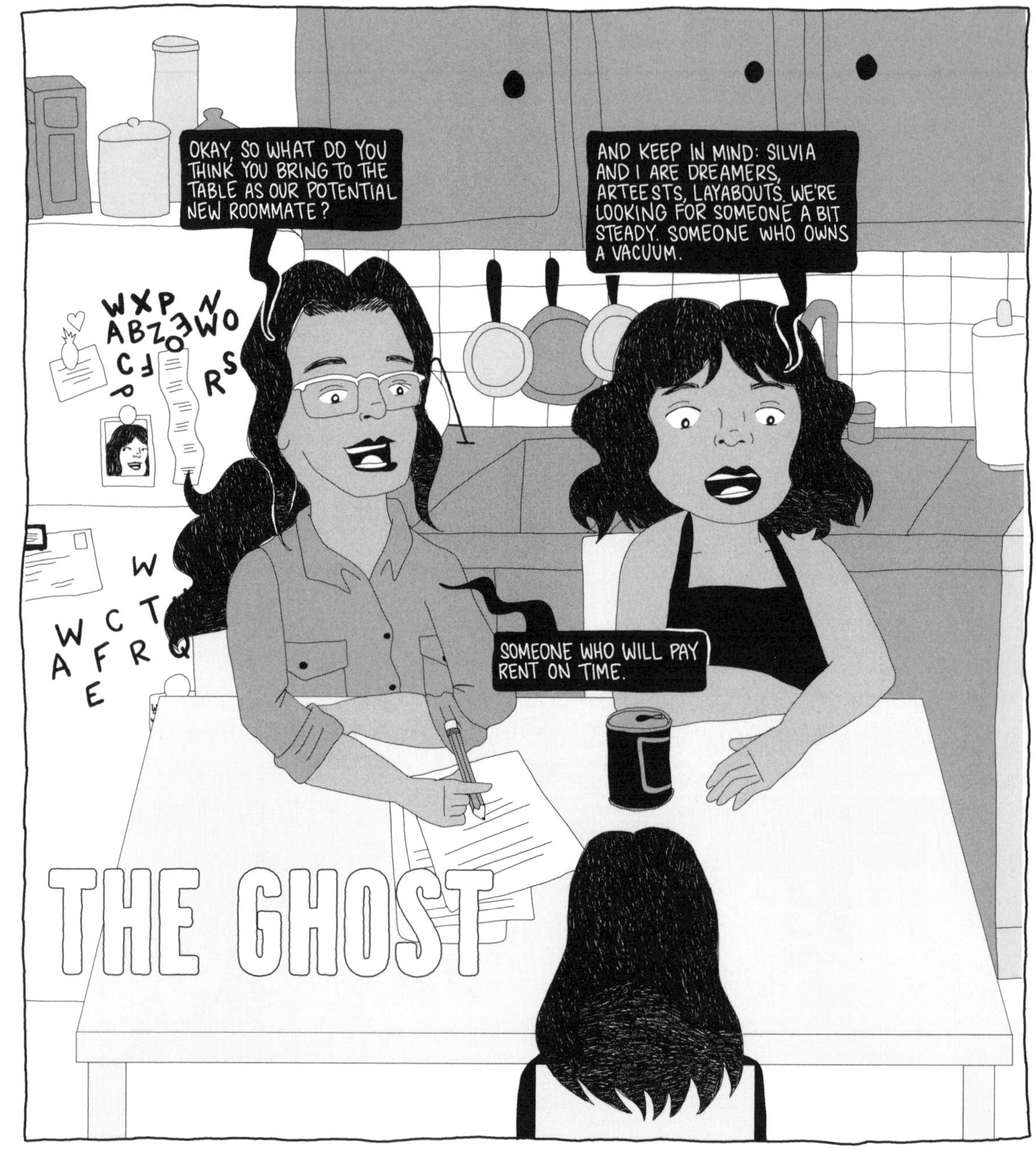
OKAY, SO WHAT DO YOU THINK YOU BRING TO THE TABLE AS OUR POTENTIAL NEW ROOMMATE?
AND KEEP IN MIND: SILVIA AND I ARE DREAMERS, ARTEESTS, LAYABOUTS. WE'RE LOOKING FOR SOMEONE A BIT STEADY. SOMEONE WHO OWNS A VACUUM.
SOMEONE WHO WILL PAY RENT ON TIME.
THE GHOST

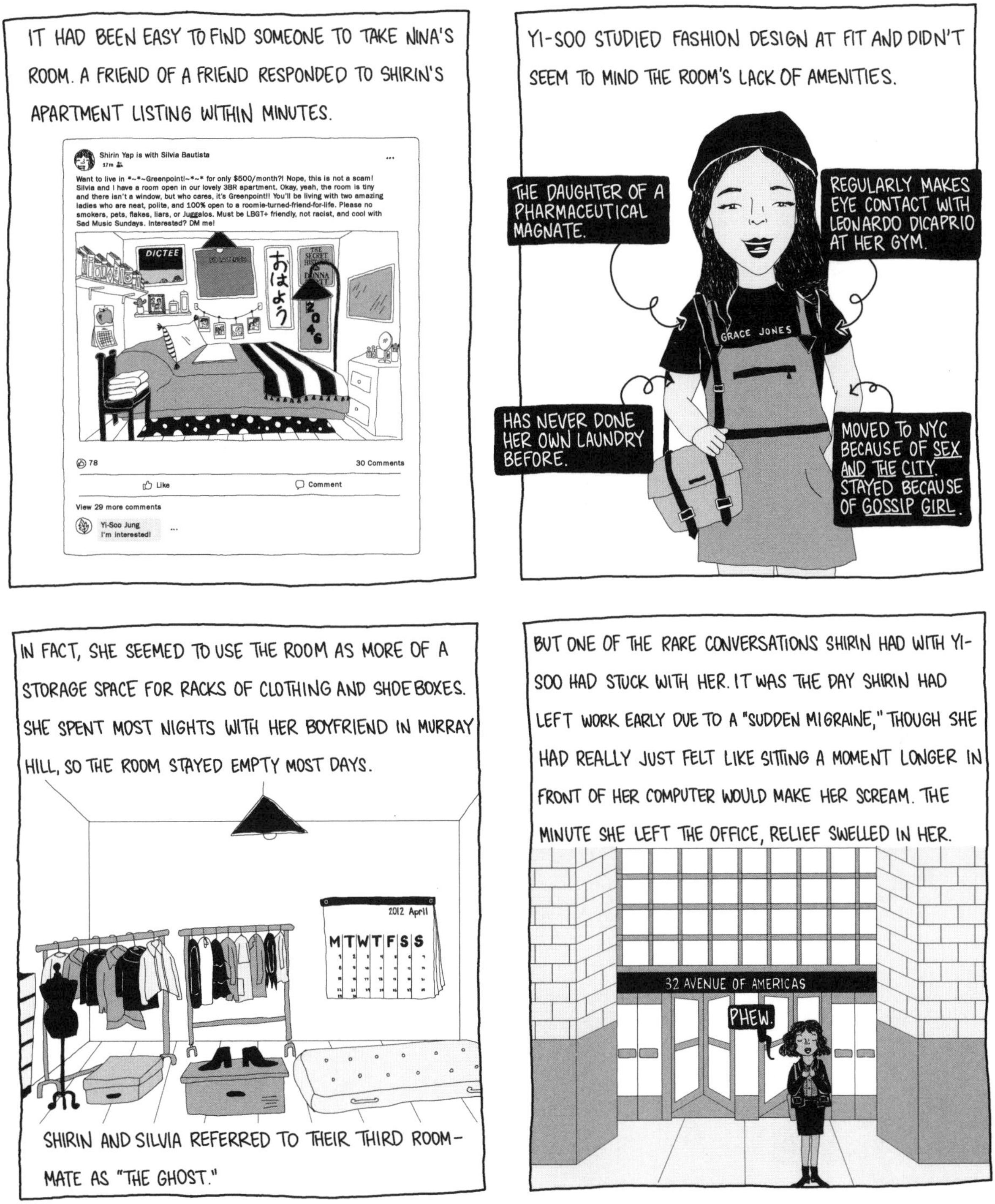
IT HAD BEEN EASY TO FIND SOMEONE TO TAKE NINA'S ROOM. A FRIEND OF A FRIEND RESPONDED TO SHIRIN'S APARTMENT LISTING WITHIN MINUTES.
Shirin Yap is with Silvia Bautista
17m
Want to live in *~*~Greenpoint!~*~* for only $500/month?! Nope, this is not a scam! Silvia and I have a room open in our lovely 3BR apartment. Okay, yeah, the room is tiny and there isn't a window, but who cares, it's Greenpoint!! You'll be living with two amazing ladies who are neat, polite, and 100% open to a roomie-turned-friend-for-life. Please no smokers, pets, flakes, liars, or Juggalos. Must be LBGT+ friendly, not racist, and cool with Sad Music Sundays. Interested? DM me!
DICTEE
THE SECRET HISTORY DONNA TARTT
おはよう
2046
78
30 Comments
Like
Comment
View 29 more comments
Yi-Soo Jung
I'm interested!
YI-SOO STUDIED FASHION DESIGN AT FIT AND DIDN'T SEEM TO MIND THE ROOM'S LACK OF AMENITIES.
THE DAUGHTER OF A PHARMACEUTICAL MAGNATE.
REGULARLY MAKES EYE CONTACT WITH LEONARDO DICAPRIO AT HER GYM.
GRACE JONES
HAS NEVER DONE HER OWN LAUNDRY BEFORE.
MOVED TO NYC BECAUSE OF SEX AND THE CITY. STAYED BECAUSE OF GOSSIP GIRL.
IN FACT, SHE SEEMED TO USE THE ROOM AS MORE OF A STORAGE SPACE FOR RACKS OF CLOTHING AND SHOEBOXES. SHE SPENT MOST NIGHTS WITH HER BOYFRIEND IN MURRAY HILL, SO THE ROOM STAYED EMPTY MOST DAYS.
2012 April
M T W T F S S
SHIRIN AND SILVIA REFERRED TO THEIR THIRD ROOMMATE AS "THE GHOST."
BUT ONE OF THE RARE CONVERSATIONS SHIRIN HAD WITH YI-SOO HAD STUCK WITH HER. IT WAS THE DAY SHIRIN HAD LEFT WORK EARLY DUE TO A "SUDDEN MIGRAINE," THOUGH SHE HAD REALLY JUST FELT LIKE SITTING A MOMENT LONGER IN FRONT OF HER COMPUTER WOULD MAKE HER SCREAM. THE MINUTE SHE LEFT THE OFFICE, RELIEF SWELLED IN HER.
32 AVENUE OF AMERICAS
PHEW.

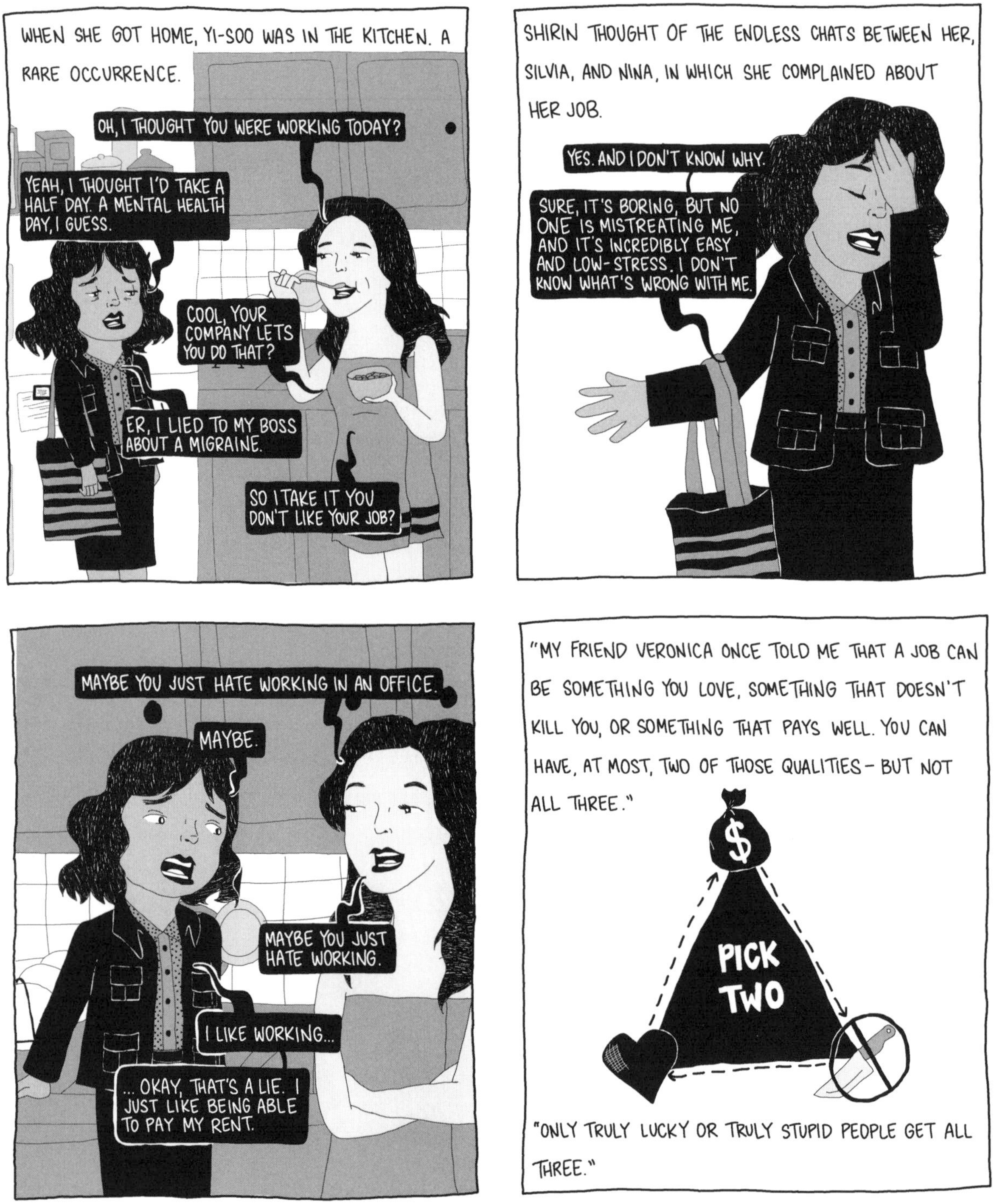
WHEN SHE GOT HOME, YI-SOO WAS IN THE KITCHEN. A RARE OCCURRENCE.
OH, I THOUGHT YOU WERE WORKING TODAY?
YEAH, I THOUGHT I'D TAKE A HALF DAY. A MENTAL HEALTH DAY, I GUESS.
COOL, YOUR COMPANY LETS YOU DO THAT?
ER, I LIED TO MY BOSS ABOUT A MIGRAINE.
SO I TAKE IT YOU DON'T LIKE YOUR JOB?
SHIRIN THOUGHT OF THE ENDLESS CHATS BETWEEN HER, SILVIA, AND NINA, IN WHICH SHE COMPLAINED ABOUT HER JOB.
YES. AND I DON'T KNOW WHY.
SURE, IT'S BORING, BUT NO ONE IS MISTREATING ME, AND IT'S INCREDIBLY EASY AND LOW-STRESS. I DON'T KNOW WHAT'S WRONG WITH ME.
MAYBE YOU JUST HATE WORKING IN AN OFFICE.
MAYBE.
MAYBE YOU JUST HATE WORKING.
I LIKE WORKING...
... OKAY, THAT'S A LIE. I JUST LIKE BEING ABLE TO PAY MY RENT.
"MY FRIEND VERONICA ONCE TOLD ME THAT A JOB CAN BE SOMETHING YOU LOVE, SOMETHING THAT DOESN'T KILL YOU, OR SOMETHING THAT PAYS WELL. YOU CAN HAVE, AT MOST, TWO OF THOSE QUALITIES – BUT NOT ALL THREE."
$
PICK TWO
"ONLY TRULY LUCKY OR TRULY STUPID PEOPLE GET ALL THREE."

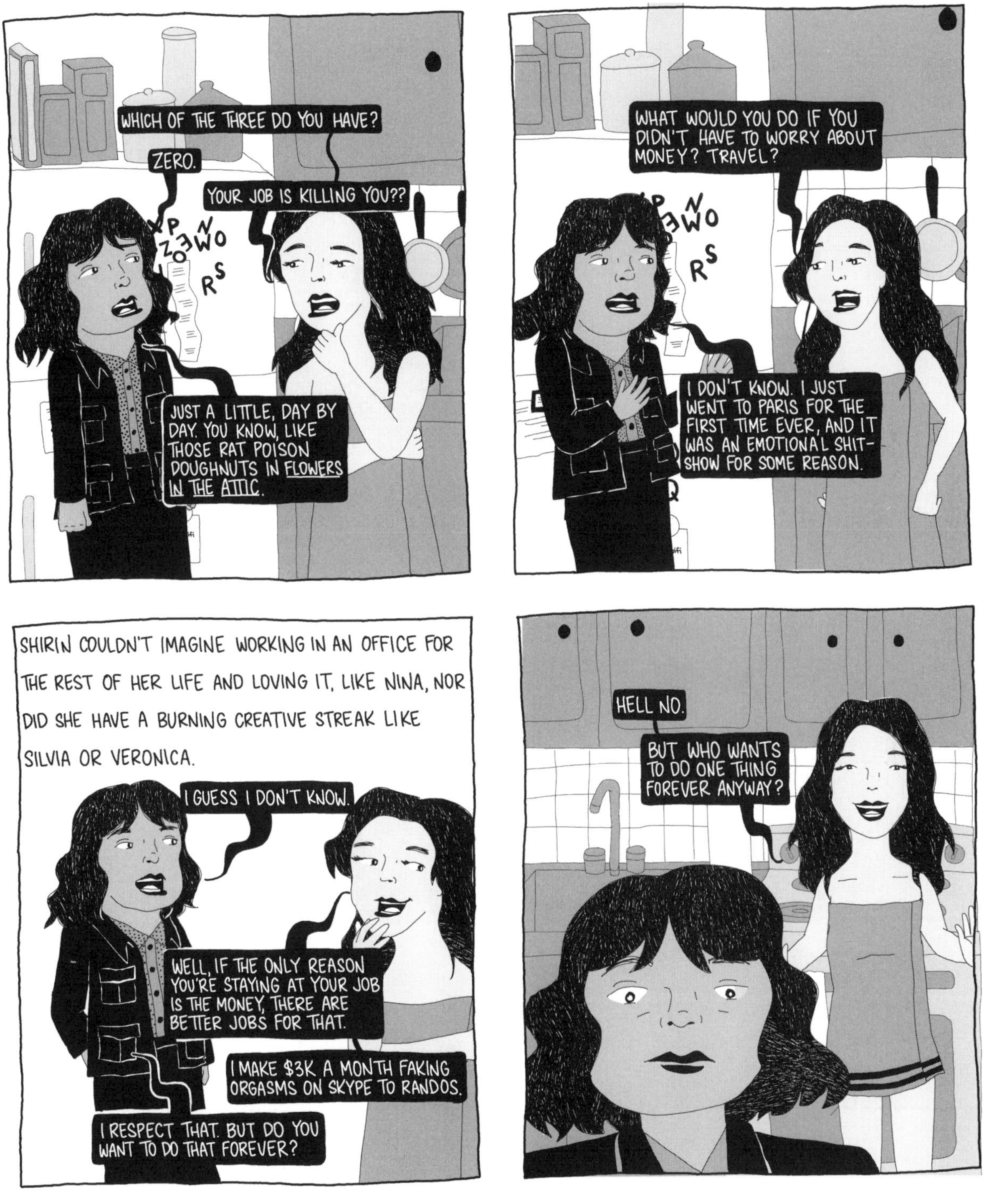
WHICH OF THE THREE DO YOU HAVE?
ZERO.
YOUR JOB IS KILLING YOU??
JUST A LITTLE, DAY BY DAY. YOU KNOW, LIKE THOSE RAT POISON DOUGHNUTS IN FLOWERS IN THE ATTIC.
WHAT WOULD YOU DO IF YOU DIDN'T HAVE TO WORRY ABOUT MONEY? TRAVEL?
I DON'T KNOW. I JUST WENT TO PARIS FOR THE FIRST TIME EVER, AND IT WAS AN EMOTIONAL SHIT-SHOW FOR SOME REASON.
SHIRIN COULDN'T IMAGINE WORKING IN AN OFFICE FOR THE REST OF HER LIFE AND LOVING IT, LIKE NINA, NOR DID SHE HAVE A BURNING CREATIVE STREAK LIKE SILVIA OR VERONICA.
I GUESS I DON'T KNOW.
WELL, IF THE ONLY REASON YOU'RE STAYING AT YOUR JOB IS THE MONEY, THERE ARE BETTER JOBS FOR THAT.
I MAKE $3K A MONTH FAKING ORGASMS ON SKYPE TO RANDOS.
I RESPECT THAT. BUT DO YOU WANT TO DO THAT FOREVER?
HELL NO.
BUT WHO WANTS TO DO ONE THING FOREVER ANYWAY?

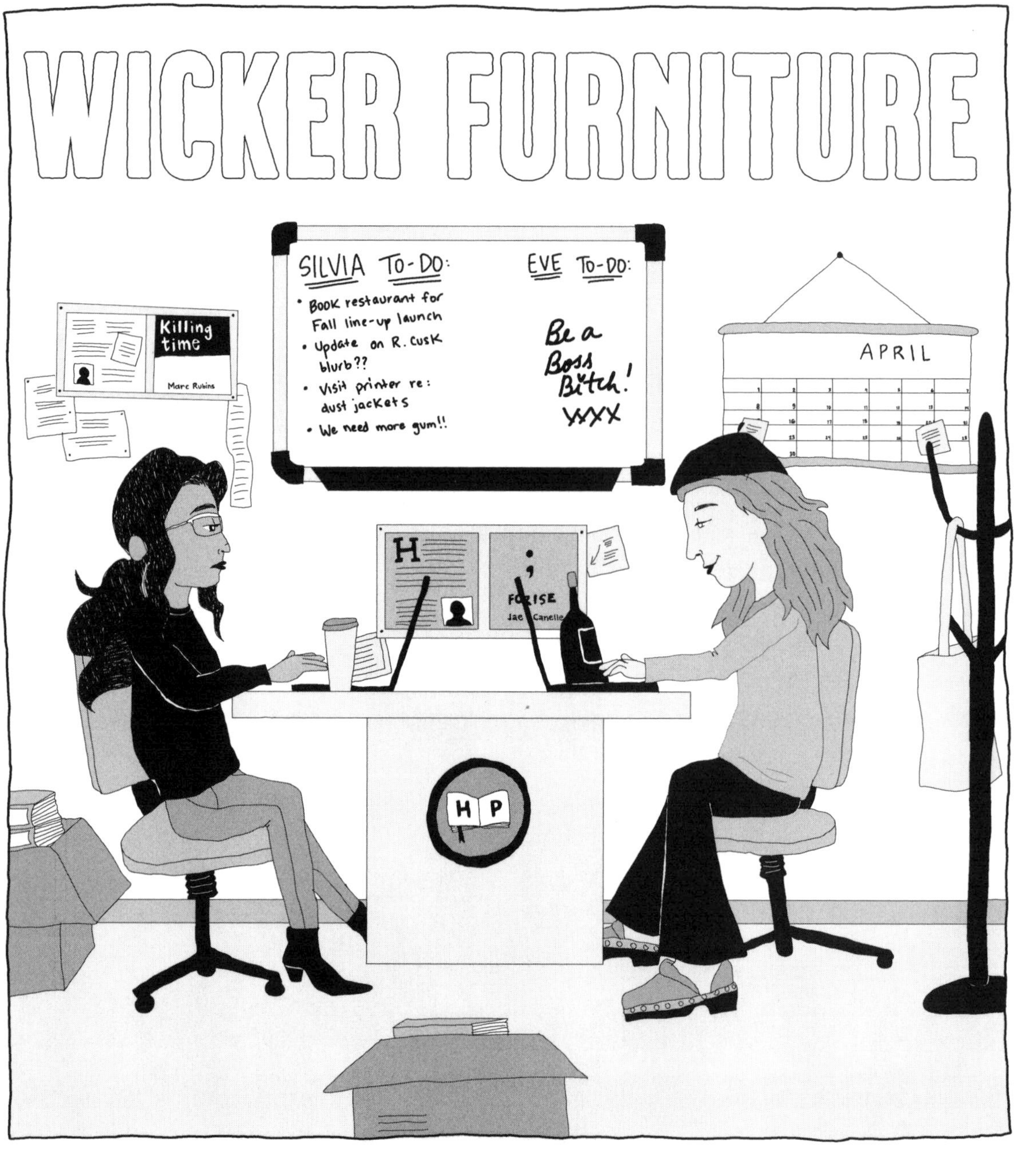
WICKER FURNITURE
SILVIA TO-DO:
• Book restaurant for Fall line-up launch
• Update on R. Cusk blurb??
• Visit printer re: dust jackets
• We need more gum!!
EVE TO-DO:
Be a Boss Bitch!
XXX
Killing time
Marc Rubins
APRIL
H P

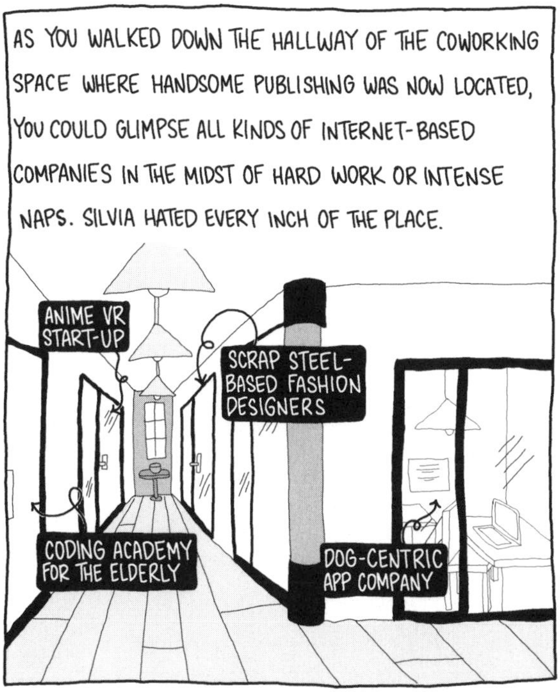
AS YOU WALKED DOWN THE HALLWAY OF THE COWORKING SPACE WHERE HANDSOME PUBLISHING WAS NOW LOCATED, YOU COULD GLIMPSE ALL KINDS OF INTERNET-BASED COMPANIES IN THE MIDST OF HARD WORK OR INTENSE NAPS. SILVIA HATED EVERY INCH OF THE PLACE.
ANIME VR START-UP
SCRAP STEEL-BASED FASHION DESIGNERS
CODING ACADEMY FOR THE ELDERLY
DOG-CENTRIC APP COMPANY

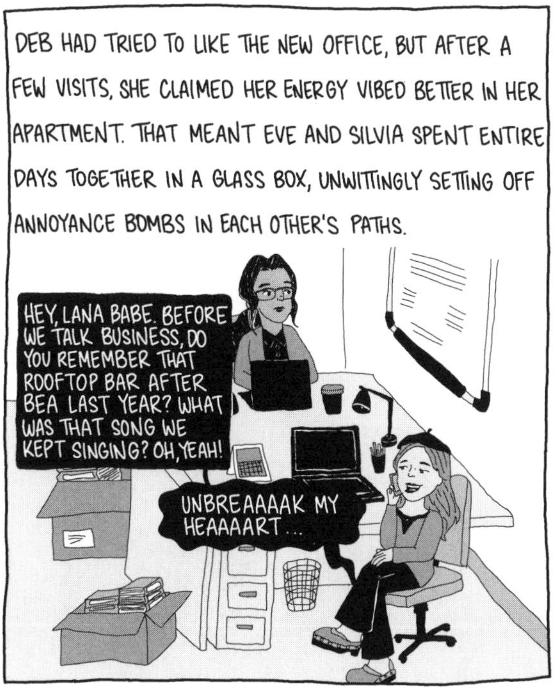
DEB HAD TRIED TO LIKE THE NEW OFFICE, BUT AFTER A FEW VISITS, SHE CLAIMED HER ENERGY VIBED BETTER IN HER APARTMENT. THAT MEANT EVE AND SILVIA SPENT ENTIRE DAYS TOGETHER IN A GLASS BOX, UNWITTINGLY SETTING OFF ANNOYANCE BOMBS IN EACH OTHER'S PATHS.
HEY, LANA BABE. BEFORE WE TALK BUSINESS, DO YOU REMEMBER THAT ROOFTOP BAR AFTER BEA LAST YEAR? WHAT WAS THAT SONG WE KEPT SINGING? OH, YEAH!
UNBREAAAAK MY HEAAAART...

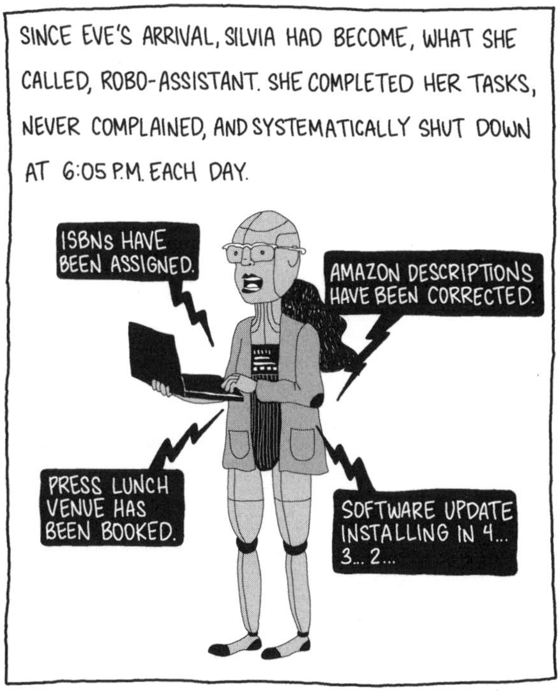
SINCE EVE'S ARRIVAL, SILVIA HAD BECOME, WHAT SHE CALLED, ROBO-ASSISTANT. SHE COMPLETED HER TASKS, NEVER COMPLAINED, AND SYSTEMATICALLY SHUT DOWN AT 6:05 P.M. EACH DAY.
ISBNs HAVE BEEN ASSIGNED.
AMAZON DESCRIPTIONS HAVE BEEN CORRECTED.
PRESS LUNCH VENUE HAS BEEN BOOKED.
SOFTWARE UPDATE INSTALLING IN 4... 3... 2...

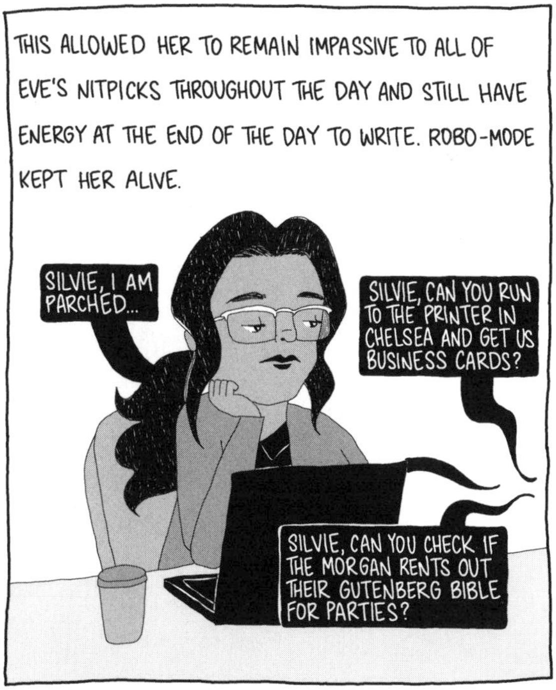
THIS ALLOWED HER TO REMAIN IMPASSIVE TO ALL OF EVE'S NITPICKS THROUGHOUT THE DAY AND STILL HAVE ENERGY AT THE END OF THE DAY TO WRITE. ROBO-MODE KEPT HER ALIVE.
SILVIE, I AM PARCHED...
SILVIE, CAN YOU RUN TO THE PRINTER IN CHELSEA AND GET US BUSINESS CARDS?
SILVIE, CAN YOU CHECK IF THE MORGAN RENTS OUT THEIR GUTENBERG BIBLE FOR PARTIES?

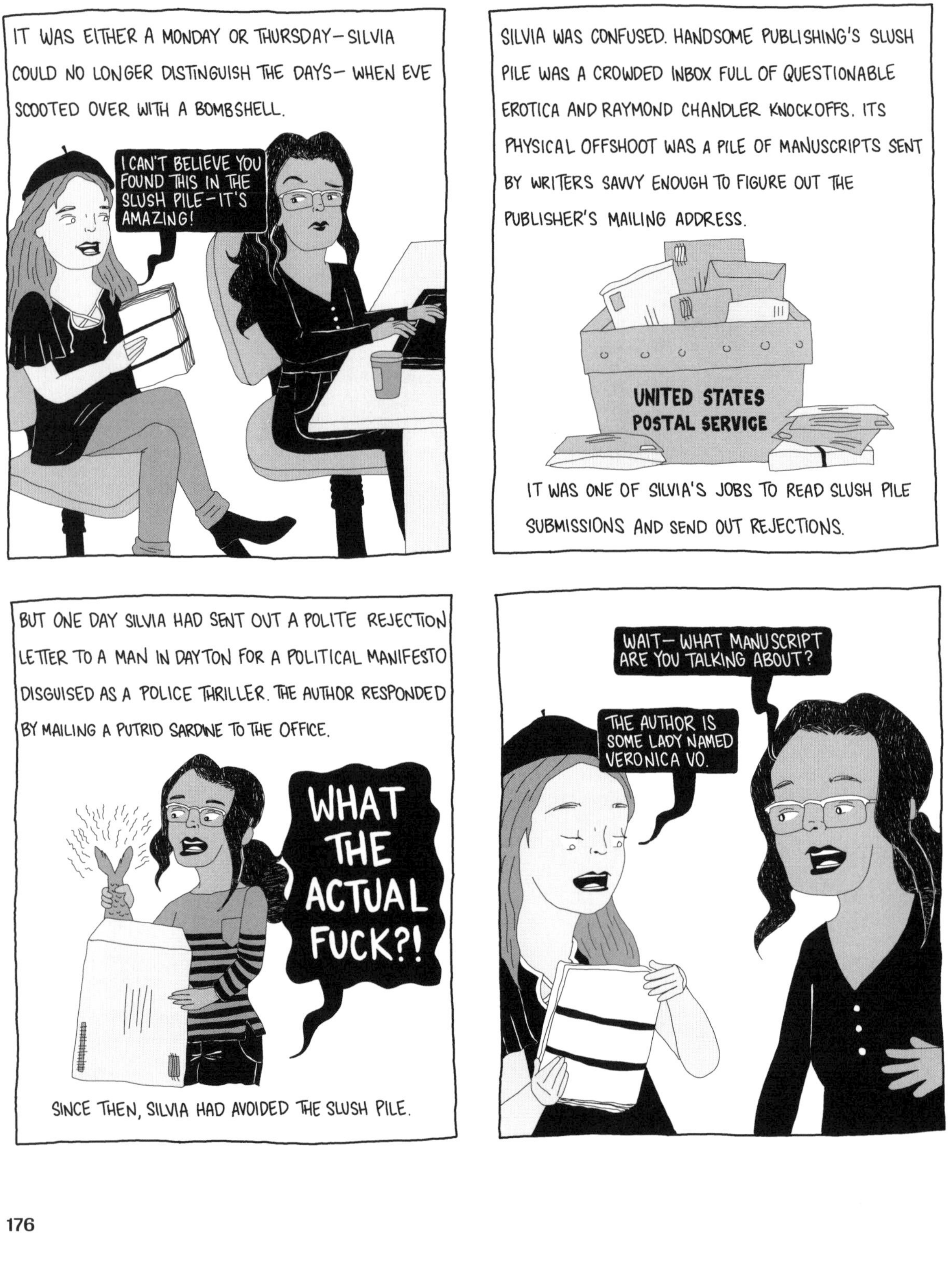
IT WAS EITHER A MONDAY OR THURSDAY—SILVIA COULD NO LONGER DISTINGUISH THE DAYS— WHEN EVE SCOOTED OVER WITH A BOMBSHELL.
I CAN'T BELIEVE YOU FOUND THIS IN THE SLUSH PILE—IT'S AMAZING!
SILVIA WAS CONFUSED. HANDSOME PUBLISHING'S SLUSH PILE WAS A CROWDED INBOX FULL OF QUESTIONABLE EROTICA AND RAYMOND CHANDLER KNOCKOFFS. ITS PHYSICAL OFFSHOOT WAS A PILE OF MANUSCRIPTS SENT BY WRITERS SAVVY ENOUGH TO FIGURE OUT THE PUBLISHER'S MAILING ADDRESS.
UNITED STATES POSTAL SERVICE
IT WAS ONE OF SILVIA'S JOBS TO READ SLUSH PILE SUBMISSIONS AND SEND OUT REJECTIONS.
BUT ONE DAY SILVIA HAD SENT OUT A POLITE REJECTION LETTER TO A MAN IN DAYTON FOR A POLITICAL MANIFESTO DISGUISED AS A POLICE THRILLER. THE AUTHOR RESPONDED BY MAILING A PUTRID SARDINE TO THE OFFICE.
WHAT THE ACTUAL FUCK?!
SINCE THEN, SILVIA HAD AVOIDED THE SLUSH PILE.
WAIT— WHAT MANUSCRIPT ARE YOU TALKING ABOUT?
THE AUTHOR IS SOME LADY NAMED VERONICA VO.

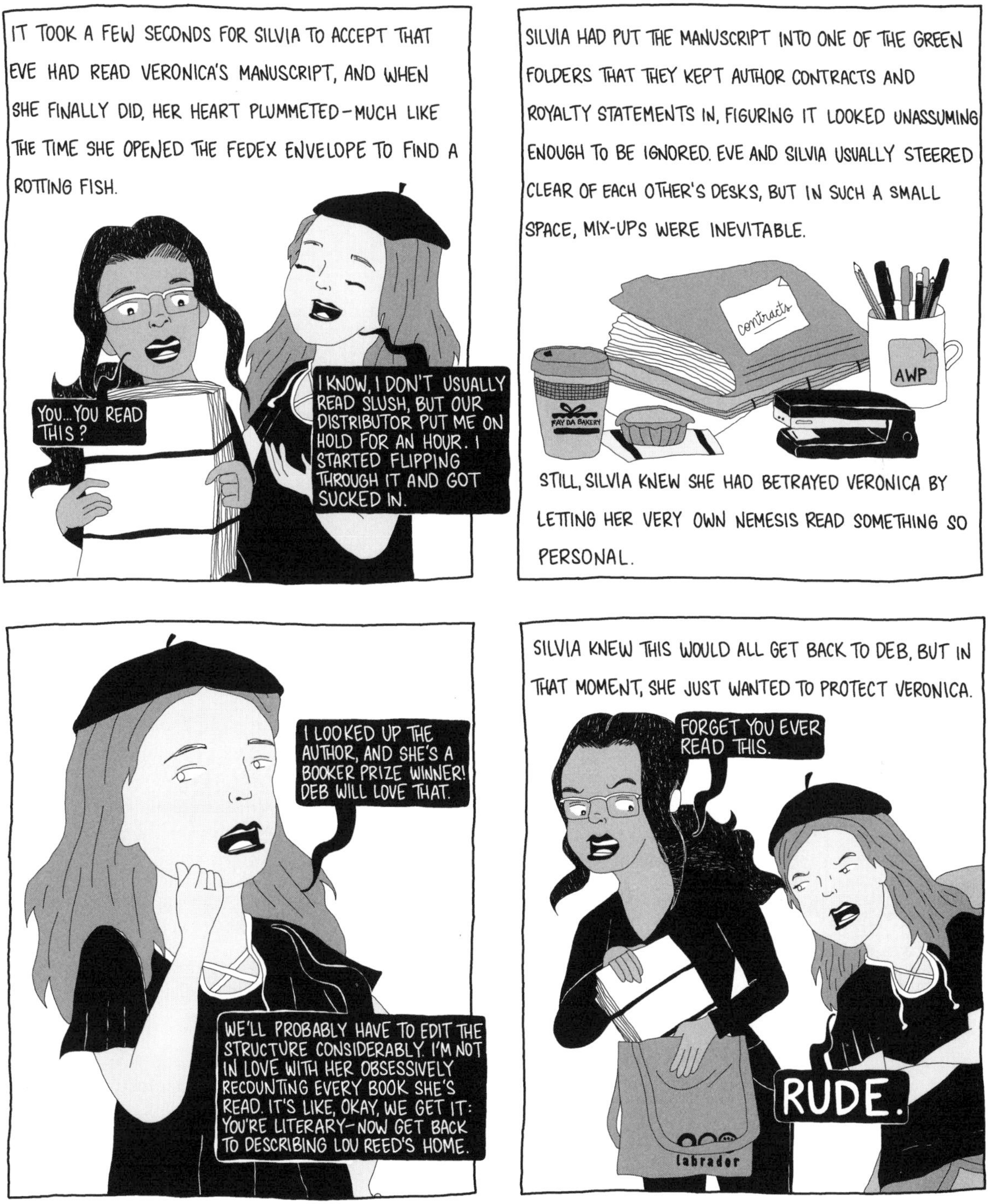
IT TOOK A FEW SECONDS FOR SILVIA TO ACCEPT THAT EVE HAD READ VERONICA'S MANUSCRIPT, AND WHEN SHE FINALLY DID, HER HEART PLUMMETED—MUCH LIKE THE TIME SHE OPENED THE FEDEX ENVELOPE TO FIND A ROTTING FISH.
YOU...YOU READ THIS?
I KNOW, I DON'T USUALLY READ SLUSH, BUT OUR DISTRIBUTOR PUT ME ON HOLD FOR AN HOUR. I STARTED FLIPPING THROUGH IT AND GOT SUCKED IN.
SILVIA HAD PUT THE MANUSCRIPT INTO ONE OF THE GREEN FOLDERS THAT THEY KEPT AUTHOR CONTRACTS AND ROYALTY STATEMENTS IN, FIGURING IT LOOKED UNASSUMING ENOUGH TO BE IGNORED. EVE AND SILVIA USUALLY STEERED CLEAR OF EACH OTHER'S DESKS, BUT IN SUCH A SMALL SPACE, MIX-UPS WERE INEVITABLE.
contracts
AWP
FAY DA BAKERY
STILL, SILVIA KNEW SHE HAD BETRAYED VERONICA BY LETTING HER VERY OWN NEMESIS READ SOMETHING SO PERSONAL.
I LOOKED UP THE AUTHOR, AND SHE'S A BOOKER PRIZE WINNER! DEB WILL LOVE THAT.
WE'LL PROBABLY HAVE TO EDIT THE STRUCTURE CONSIDERABLY. I'M NOT IN LOVE WITH HER OBSESSIVELY RECOUNTING EVERY BOOK SHE'S READ. IT'S LIKE, OKAY, WE GET IT: YOU'RE LITERARY—NOW GET BACK TO DESCRIBING LOU REED'S HOME.
SILVIA KNEW THIS WOULD ALL GET BACK TO DEB, BUT IN THAT MOMENT, SHE JUST WANTED TO PROTECT VERONICA.
FORGET YOU EVER READ THIS.
RUDE.
labrador

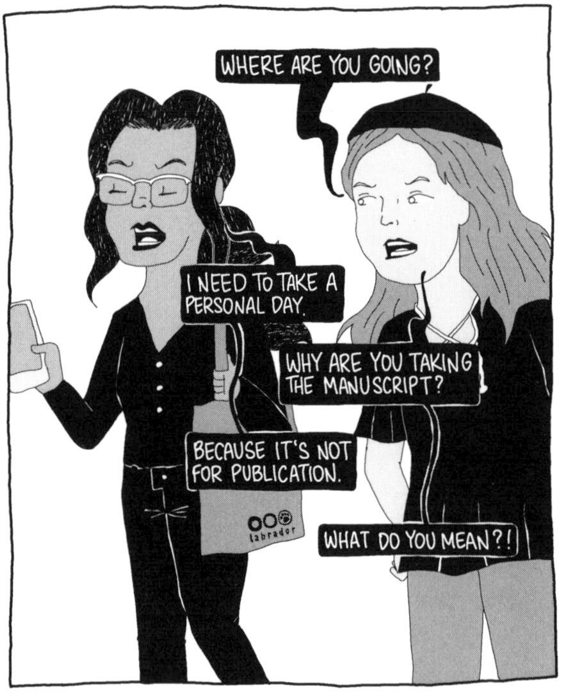
WHERE ARE YOU GOING?
I NEED TO TAKE A PERSONAL DAY.
WHY ARE YOU TAKING THE MANUSCRIPT?
BECAUSE IT'S NOT FOR PUBLICATION.
WHAT DO YOU MEAN?!

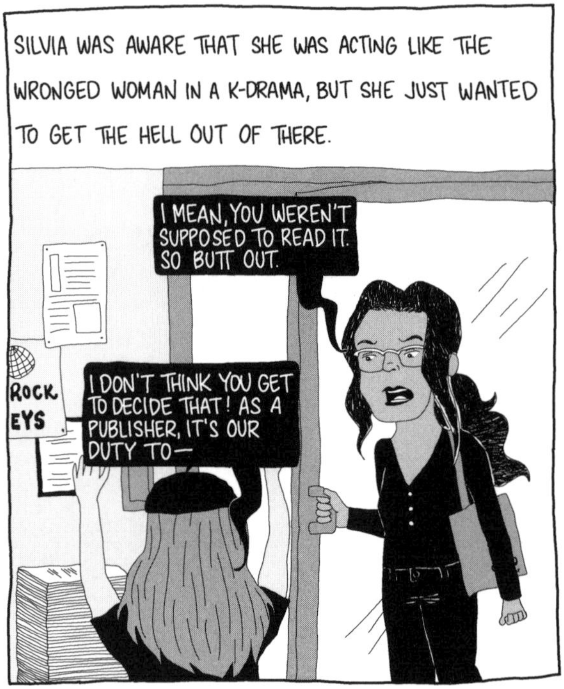
SILVIA WAS AWARE THAT SHE WAS ACTING LIKE THE WRONGED WOMAN IN A K-DRAMA, BUT SHE JUST WANTED TO GET THE HELL OUT OF THERE.
I MEAN, YOU WEREN'T SUPPOSED TO READ IT. SO BUTT OUT.
I DON'T THINK YOU GET TO DECIDE THAT! AS A PUBLISHER, IT'S OUR DUTY TO—

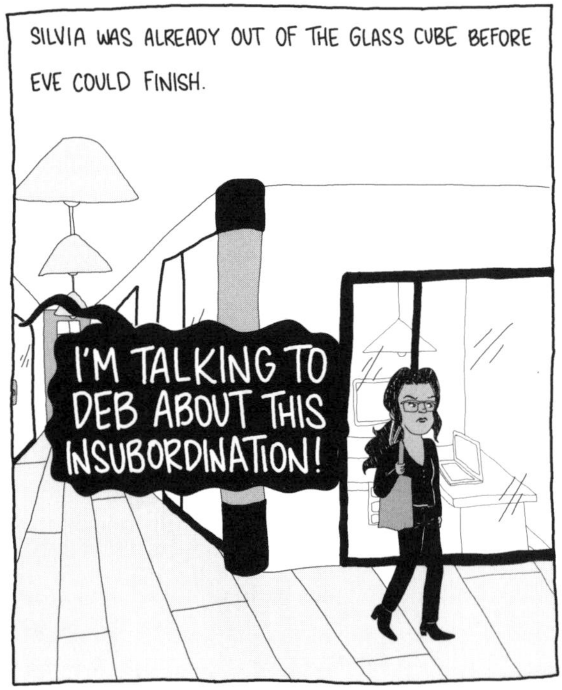
SILVIA WAS ALREADY OUT OF THE GLASS CUBE BEFORE EVE COULD FINISH.
I'M TALKING TO DEB ABOUT THIS INSUBORDINATION!

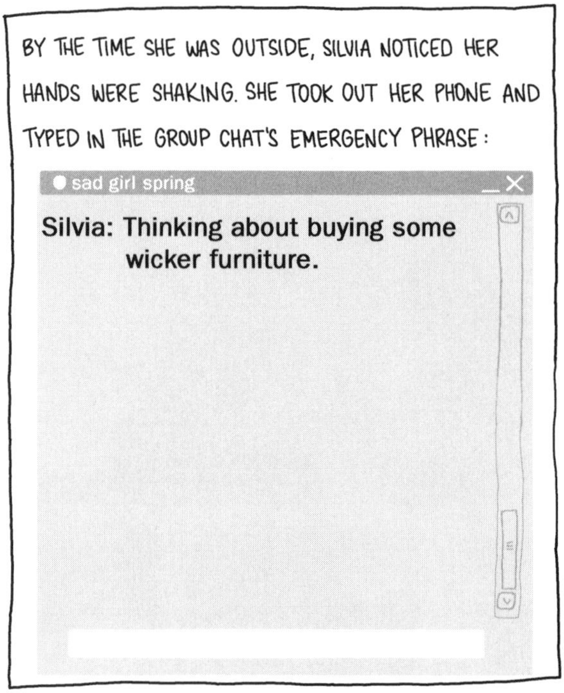
BY THE TIME SHE WAS OUTSIDE, SILVIA NOTICED HER HANDS WERE SHAKING. SHE TOOK OUT HER PHONE AND TYPED IN THE GROUP CHAT'S EMERGENCY PHRASE:
sad girl spring
Silvia: Thinking about buying some wicker furniture.

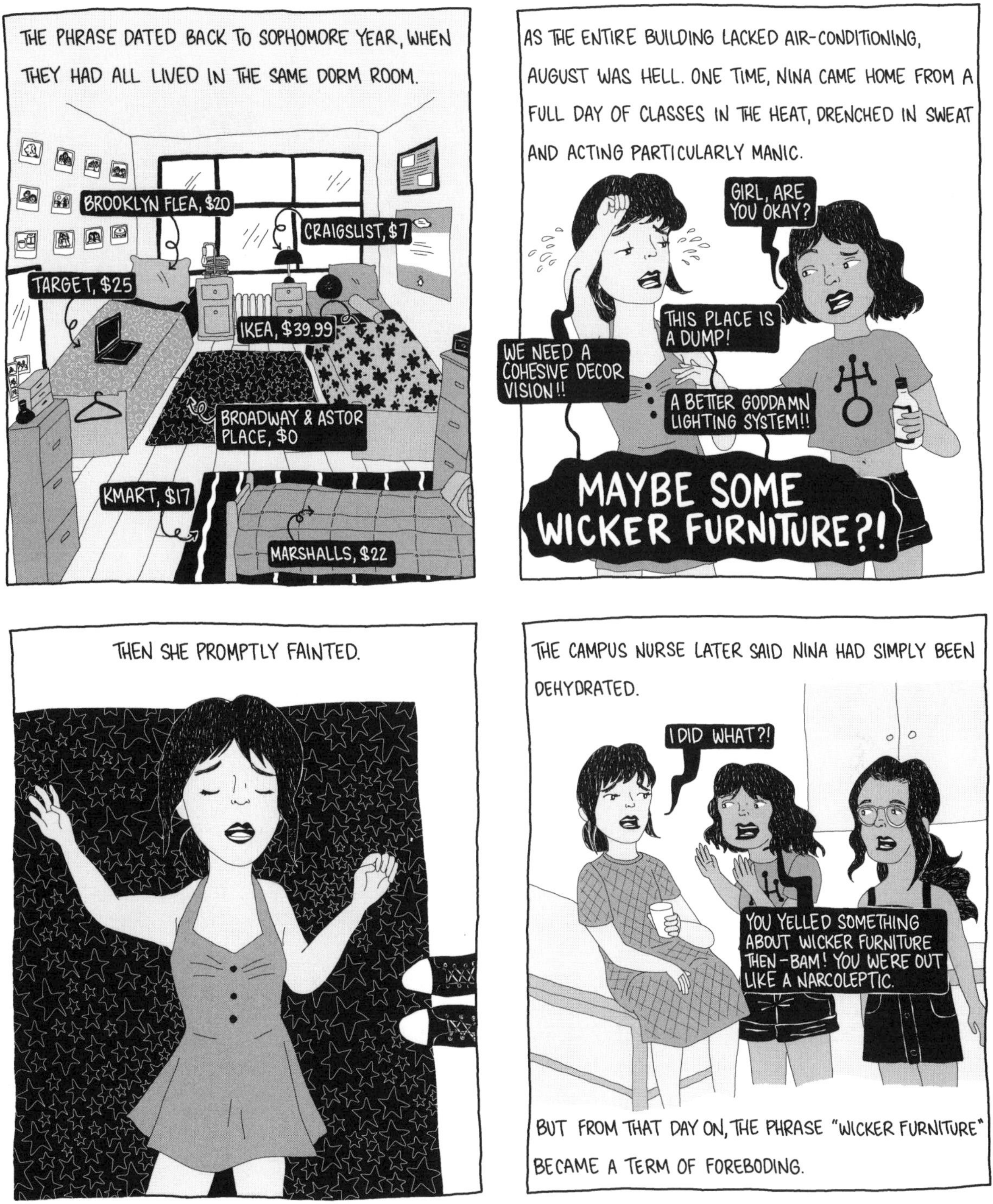
THE PHRASE DATED BACK TO SOPHOMORE YEAR, WHEN THEY HAD ALL LIVED IN THE SAME DORM ROOM.
BROOKLYN FLEA, $20
CRAIGSLIST, $7
TARGET, $25
IKEA, $39.99
BROADWAY & ASTOR PLACE, $0
KMART, $17
MARSHALLS, $22
AS THE ENTIRE BUILDING LACKED AIR-CONDITIONING, AUGUST WAS HELL. ONE TIME, NINA CAME HOME FROM A FULL DAY OF CLASSES IN THE HEAT, DRENCHED IN SWEAT AND ACTING PARTICULARLY MANIC.
GIRL, ARE YOU OKAY?
THIS PLACE IS A DUMP!
WE NEED A COHESIVE DECOR VISION!!
A BETTER GODDAMN LIGHTING SYSTEM!!
MAYBE SOME WICKER FURNITURE?!
THEN SHE PROMPTLY FAINTED.
THE CAMPUS NURSE LATER SAID NINA HAD SIMPLY BEEN DEHYDRATED.
I DID WHAT?!
YOU YELLED SOMETHING ABOUT WICKER FURNITURE THEN—BAM! YOU WERE OUT LIKE A NARCOLEPTIC.
BUT FROM THAT DAY ON, THE PHRASE "WICKER FURNITURE" BECAME A TERM OF FOREBODING.

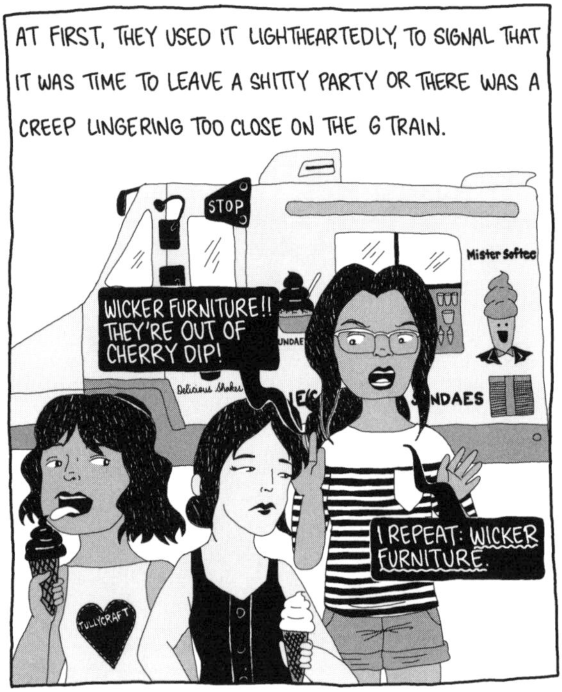
AT FIRST, THEY USED IT LIGHTHEARTEDLY, TO SIGNAL THAT IT WAS TIME TO LEAVE A SHITTY PARTY OR THERE WAS A CREEP LINGERING TOO CLOSE ON THE G TRAIN.
STOP
Mister Softee
WICKER FURNITURE!! THEY'RE OUT OF CHERRY DIP!
Delicious Shakes
I REPEAT: WICKER FURNITURE.
TULLYCRAFT

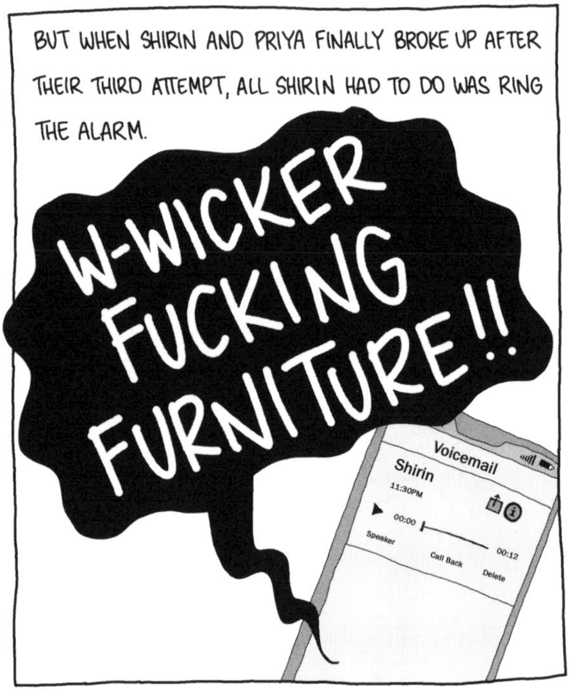
BUT WHEN SHIRIN AND PRIYA FINALLY BROKE UP AFTER THEIR THIRD ATTEMPT, ALL SHIRIN HAD TO DO WAS RING THE ALARM.
W-WICKER FUCKING FURNITURE!!
Voicemail
Shirin
11:30PM
00:00
00:12
Speaker
Call Back
Delete

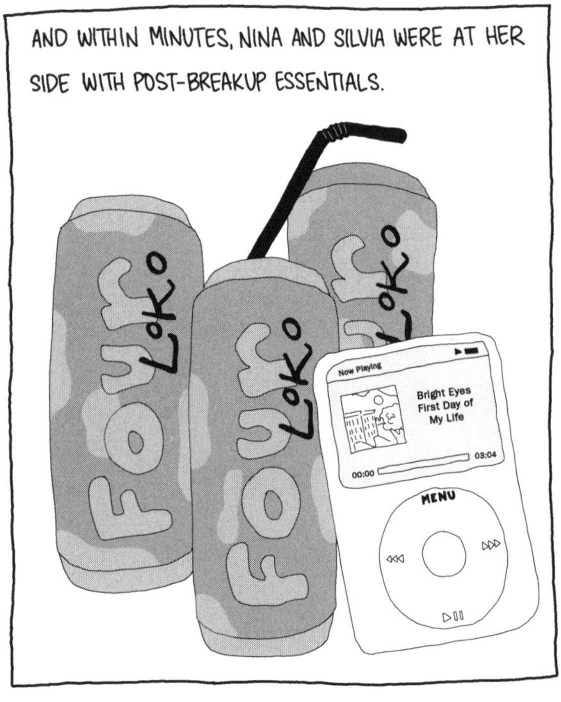
AND WITHIN MINUTES, NINA AND SILVIA WERE AT HER SIDE WITH POST-BREAKUP ESSENTIALS.
Four Loko
Four Loko
Four Loko
Now Playing
Bright Eyes
First Day of
My Life
00:00
03:04
MENU

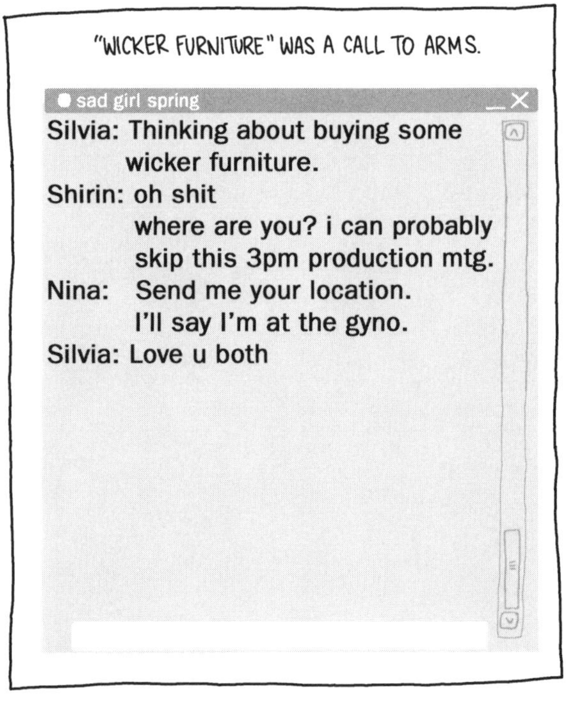
"WICKER FURNITURE" WAS A CALL TO ARMS.
sad girl spring
Silvia: Thinking about buying some wicker furniture.
Shirin: oh shit
where are you? i can probably skip this 3pm production mtg.
Nina: Send me your location.
I'll say I'm at the gyno.
Silvia: Love u both

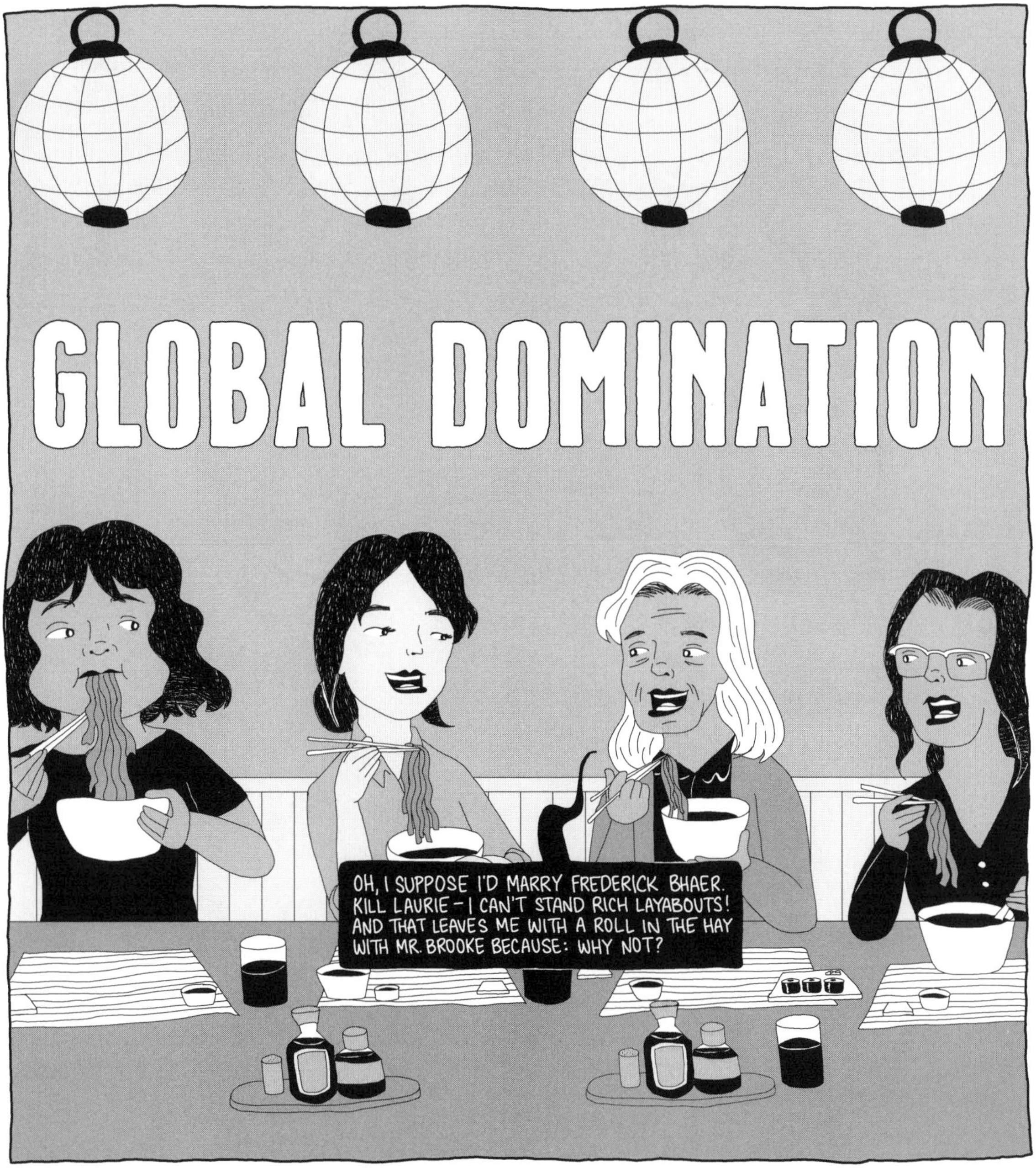
GLOBAL DOMINATION
OH, I SUPPOSE I'D MARRY FREDERICK BHAER. KILL LAURIE – I CAN'T STAND RICH LAYABOUTS! AND THAT LEAVES ME WITH A ROLL IN THE HAY WITH MR. BROOKE BECAUSE: WHY NOT?

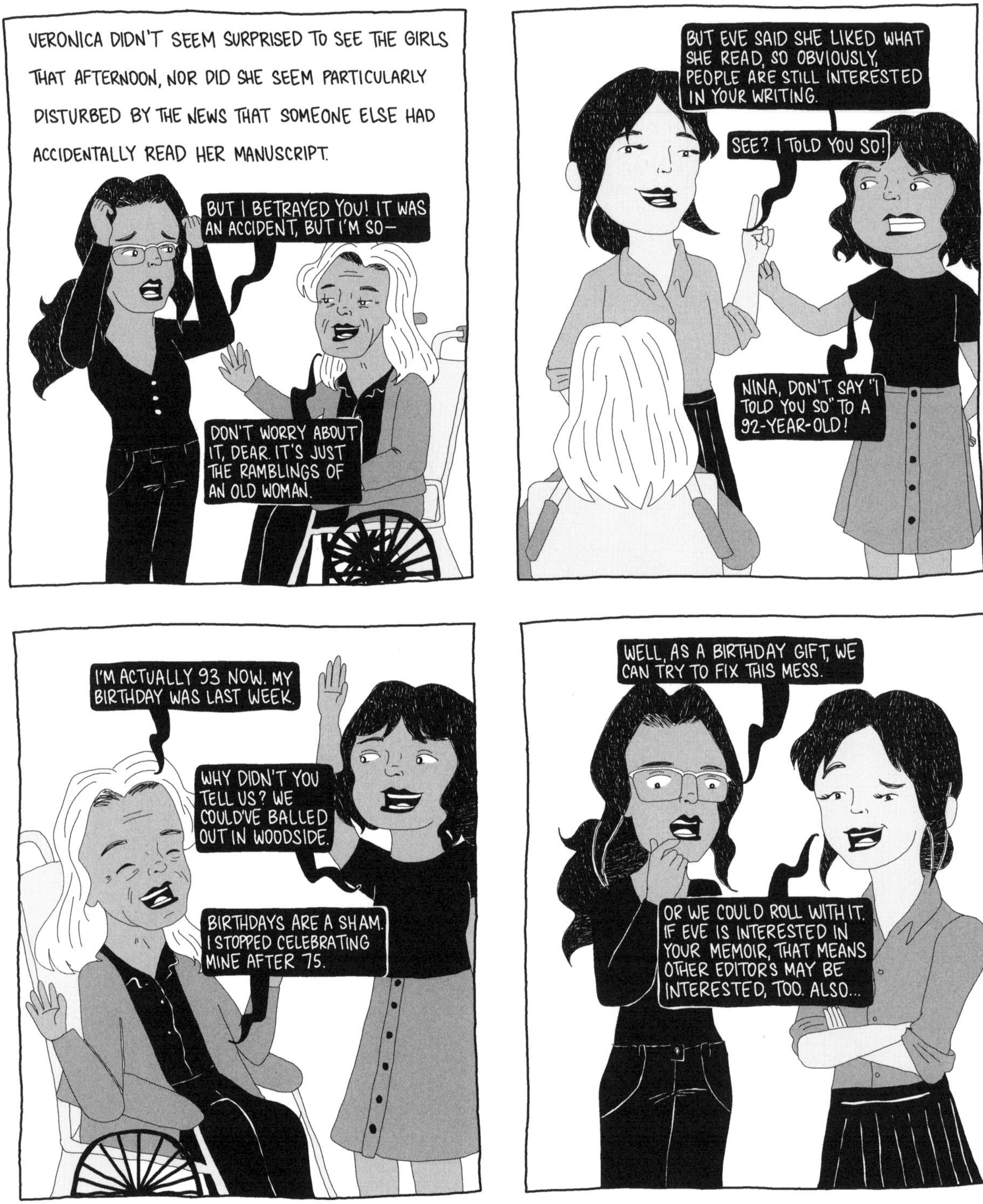
VERONICA DIDN'T SEEM SURPRISED TO SEE THE GIRLS THAT AFTERNOON, NOR DID SHE SEEM PARTICULARLY DISTURBED BY THE NEWS THAT SOMEONE ELSE HAD ACCIDENTALLY READ HER MANUSCRIPT.
BUT I BETRAYED YOU! IT WAS AN ACCIDENT, BUT I'M SO—
DON'T WORRY ABOUT IT, DEAR. IT'S JUST THE RAMBLINGS OF AN OLD WOMAN.
BUT EVE SAID SHE LIKED WHAT SHE READ, SO OBVIOUSLY, PEOPLE ARE STILL INTERESTED IN YOUR WRITING.
SEE? I TOLD YOU SO!
NINA, DON'T SAY "I TOLD YOU SO" TO A 92-YEAR-OLD!
I'M ACTUALLY 93 NOW. MY BIRTHDAY WAS LAST WEEK.
WHY DIDN'T YOU TELL US? WE COULD'VE BALLED OUT IN WOODSIDE.
BIRTHDAYS ARE A SHAM. I STOPPED CELEBRATING MINE AFTER 75.
WELL, AS A BIRTHDAY GIFT, WE CAN TRY TO FIX THIS MESS.
OR WE COULD ROLL WITH IT. IF EVE IS INTERESTED IN YOUR MEMOIR, THAT MEANS OTHER EDITORS MAY BE INTERESTED, TOO. ALSO...

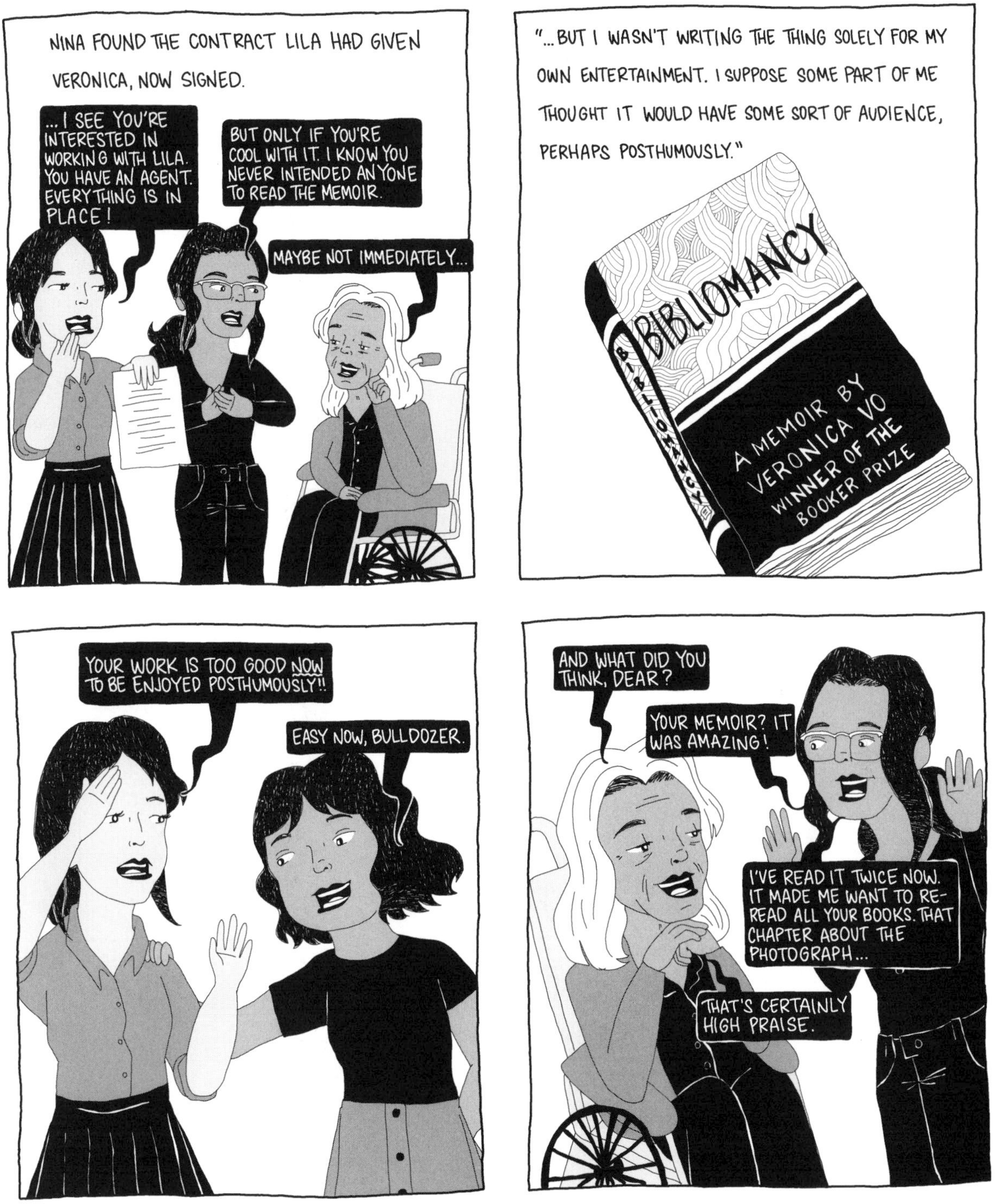
NINA FOUND THE CONTRACT LILA HAD GIVEN VERONICA, NOW SIGNED.
...I SEE YOU'RE INTERESTED IN WORKING WITH LILA. YOU HAVE AN AGENT. EVERYTHING IS IN PLACE!
BUT ONLY IF YOU'RE COOL WITH IT. I KNOW YOU NEVER INTENDED ANYONE TO READ THE MEMOIR.
MAYBE NOT IMMEDIATELY...
"...BUT I WASN'T WRITING THE THING SOLELY FOR MY OWN ENTERTAINMENT. I SUPPOSE SOME PART OF ME THOUGHT IT WOULD HAVE SOME SORT OF AUDIENCE, PERHAPS POSTHUMOUSLY."
BIBLIOMANCY
A MEMOIR BY VERONICA VO
WINNER OF THE BOOKER PRIZE
BIBLIOMANCY
YOUR WORK IS TOO GOOD NOW TO BE ENJOYED POSTHUMOUSLY!!
EASY NOW, BULLDOZER.
AND WHAT DID YOU THINK, DEAR?
YOUR MEMOIR? IT WAS AMAZING!
I'VE READ IT TWICE NOW. IT MADE ME WANT TO RE-READ ALL YOUR BOOKS. THAT CHAPTER ABOUT THE PHOTOGRAPH...
THAT'S CERTAINLY HIGH PRAISE.

WELL, I QUITE LIKED YOUR MANUSCRIPT, TOO.

WAIT, SILVIA, YOU FINISHED YOUR BOOK?!

THAT'S MAJOR. CAN WE READ IT?

IT'S JUST A DRAFT, GUYS.

YOU REALLY LIKED IT?

I DID. I HAVE DETAILED NOTES, WHICH I'M STILL WORKING ON, BUT OVERALL, I'M TRULY ENJOYING IT.

I CAN'T BELIEVE VERONICA VO LIKES MY WRITING.

THIS SEEMED TO PERK VERONICA UP.

NINA, TAKE THAT CONTRACT AND GIVE IT TO LILA. SHE CAN GO AHEAD AND HANDLE THE BUSINESS SIDE OF THINGS. I'M KEEPING MY EXPECTATIONS LOW, AND I EXPECT NOTHING TO COME FROM THIS, BUT YOU CAN ALL TRY.

FINALLY!!

WE WON'T LET YOU DOWN. YOU KNOW, LIGHTHOUSE PUBLISHED A FEW INTERESTING MEMOIRS LAST YEAR.

LIKE I SAID, I'M NOT EXPECTING ANYTHING. IF ANYTHING, MAYBE GETTING A NEW BOOK PUBLISHED WILL SHOW JENNY THAT I DON'T NEED TO BE IN THIS PLACE, AND GO BACK TO MY APARTMENT.

HONESTLY, THE FOOD HERE ALONE IS ENOUGH TO MAKE ME KEEL OVER, SPEAKING OF POSTHUMOUS FAME.

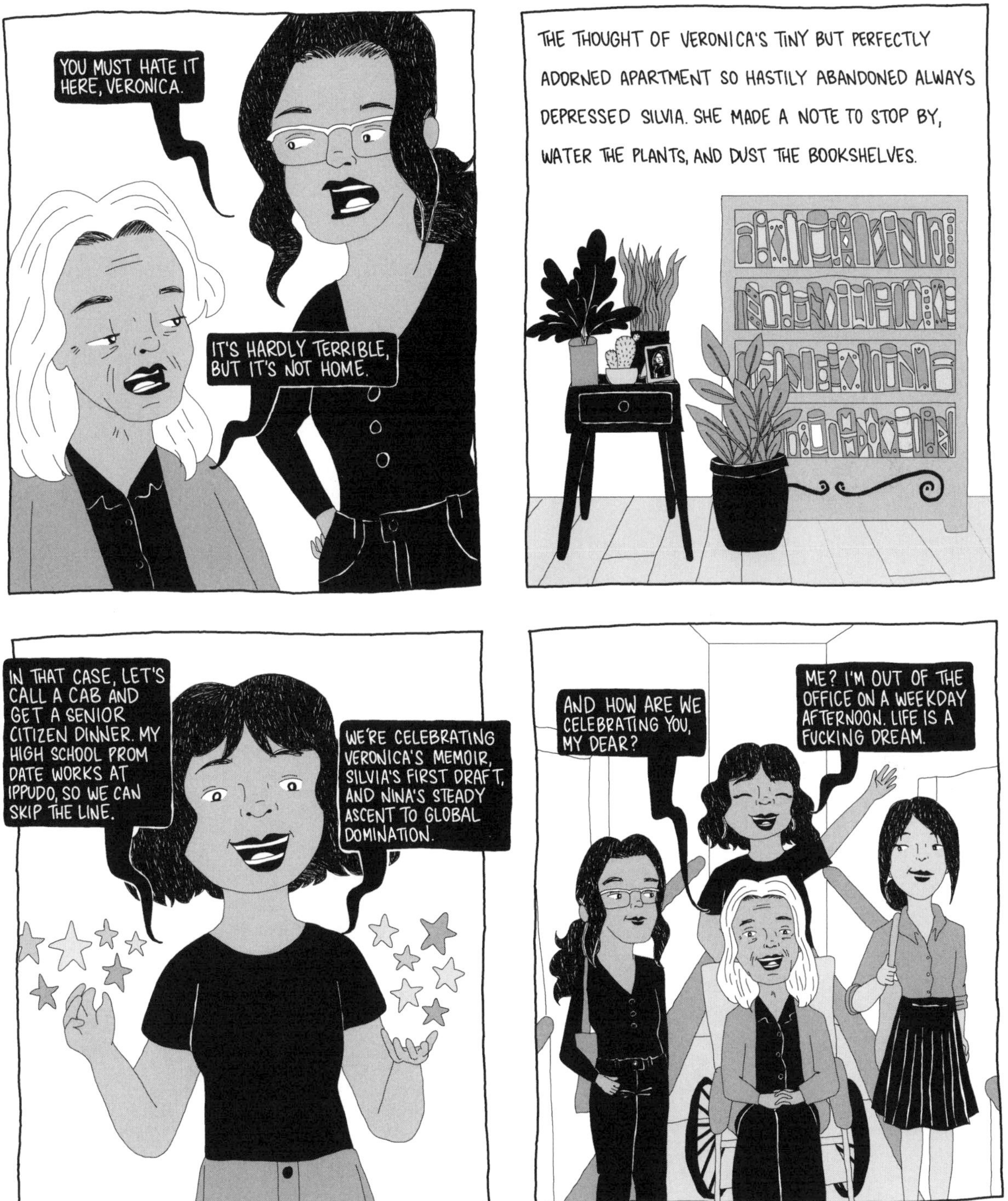
YOU MUST HATE IT HERE, VERONICA.
IT'S HARDLY TERRIBLE, BUT IT'S NOT HOME.
THE THOUGHT OF VERONICA'S TINY BUT PERFECTLY ADORNED APARTMENT SO HASTILY ABANDONED ALWAYS DEPRESSED SILVIA. SHE MADE A NOTE TO STOP BY, WATER THE PLANTS, AND DUST THE BOOKSHELVES.
IN THAT CASE, LET'S CALL A CAB AND GET A SENIOR CITIZEN DINNER. MY HIGH SCHOOL PROM DATE WORKS AT IPPUDO, SO WE CAN SKIP THE LINE.
WE'RE CELEBRATING VERONICA'S MEMOIR, SILVIA'S FIRST DRAFT, AND NINA'S STEADY ASCENT TO GLOBAL DOMINATION.
AND HOW ARE WE CELEBRATING YOU, MY DEAR?
ME? I'M OUT OF THE OFFICE ON A WEEKDAY AFTERNOON. LIFE IS A FUCKING DREAM.

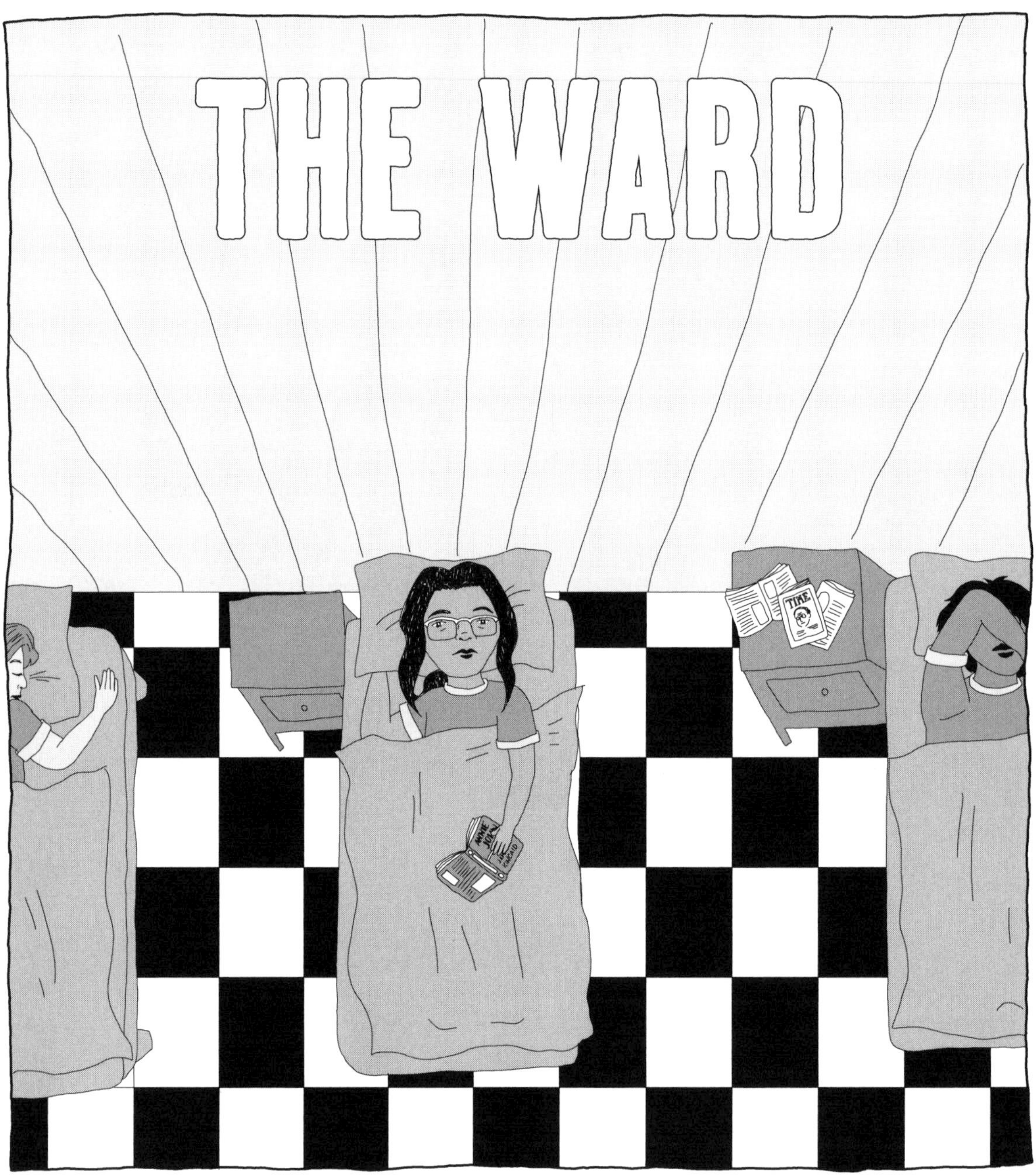
THE WARD
TIME

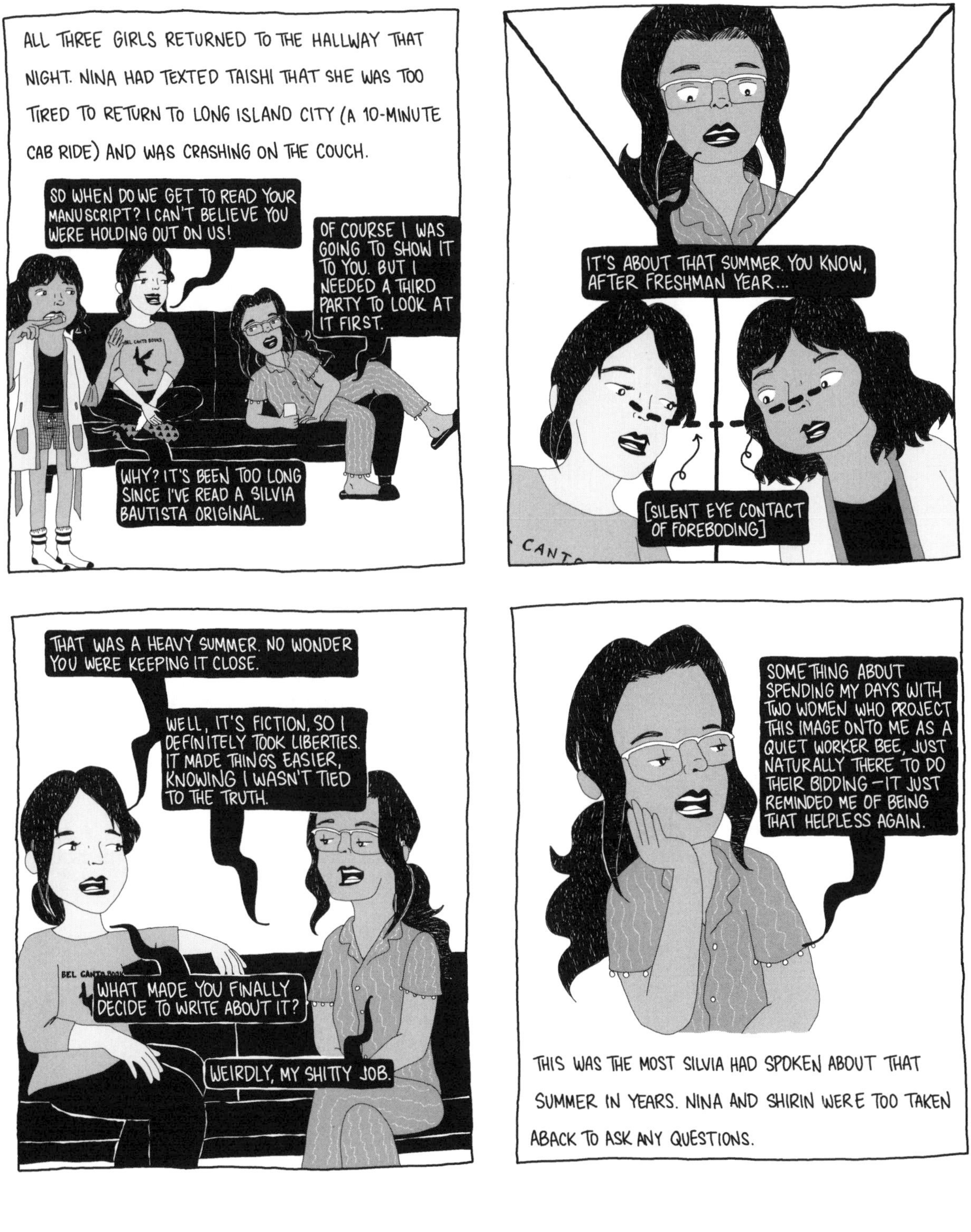
ALL THREE GIRLS RETURNED TO THE HALLWAY THAT NIGHT. NINA HAD TEXTED TAISHI THAT SHE WAS TOO TIRED TO RETURN TO LONG ISLAND CITY (A 10-MINUTE CAB RIDE) AND WAS CRASHING ON THE COUCH.
SO WHEN DO WE GET TO READ YOUR MANUSCRIPT? I CAN'T BELIEVE YOU WERE HOLDING OUT ON US!
OF COURSE I WAS GOING TO SHOW IT TO YOU. BUT I NEEDED A THIRD PARTY TO LOOK AT IT FIRST.
WHY? IT'S BEEN TOO LONG SINCE I'VE READ A SILVIA BAUTISTA ORIGINAL.
BEL CANTO BOOKS
IT'S ABOUT THAT SUMMER. YOU KNOW, AFTER FRESHMAN YEAR...
[SILENT EYE CONTACT OF FOREBODING]
THAT WAS A HEAVY SUMMER. NO WONDER YOU WERE KEEPING IT CLOSE.
WELL, IT'S FICTION, SO I DEFINITELY TOOK LIBERTIES. IT MADE THINGS EASIER, KNOWING I WASN'T TIED TO THE TRUTH.
WHAT MADE YOU FINALLY DECIDE TO WRITE ABOUT IT?
WEIRDLY, MY SHITTY JOB.
SOMETHING ABOUT SPENDING MY DAYS WITH TWO WOMEN WHO PROJECT THIS IMAGE ONTO ME AS A QUIET WORKER BEE, JUST NATURALLY THERE TO DO THEIR BIDDING—IT JUST REMINDED ME OF BEING THAT HELPLESS AGAIN.
THIS WAS THE MOST SILVIA HAD SPOKEN ABOUT THAT SUMMER IN YEARS. NINA AND SHIRIN WERE TOO TAKEN ABACK TO ASK ANY QUESTIONS.

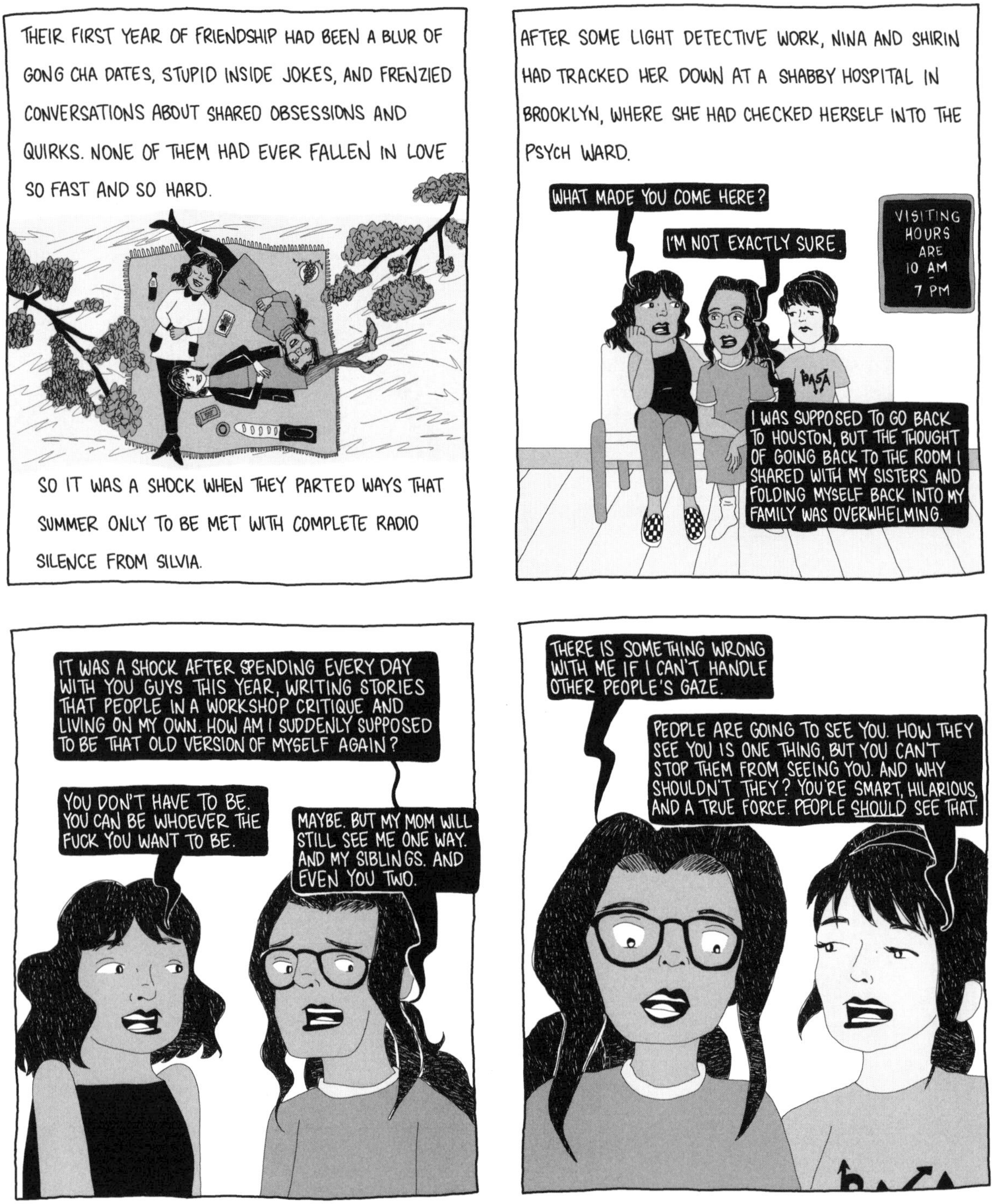
THEIR FIRST YEAR OF FRIENDSHIP HAD BEEN A BLUR OF GONG CHA DATES, STUPID INSIDE JOKES, AND FRENZIED CONVERSATIONS ABOUT SHARED OBSESSIONS AND QUIRKS. NONE OF THEM HAD EVER FALLEN IN LOVE SO FAST AND SO HARD.
SO IT WAS A SHOCK WHEN THEY PARTED WAYS THAT SUMMER ONLY TO BE MET WITH COMPLETE RADIO SILENCE FROM SILVIA.
AFTER SOME LIGHT DETECTIVE WORK, NINA AND SHIRIN HAD TRACKED HER DOWN AT A SHABBY HOSPITAL IN BROOKLYN, WHERE SHE HAD CHECKED HERSELF INTO THE PSYCH WARD.
WHAT MADE YOU COME HERE?
I'M NOT EXACTLY SURE.
VISITING HOURS ARE 10 AM - 7 PM
I WAS SUPPOSED TO GO BACK TO HOUSTON, BUT THE THOUGHT OF GOING BACK TO THE ROOM I SHARED WITH MY SISTERS AND FOLDING MYSELF BACK INTO MY FAMILY WAS OVERWHELMING.
IT WAS A SHOCK AFTER SPENDING EVERY DAY WITH YOU GUYS THIS YEAR, WRITING STORIES THAT PEOPLE IN A WORKSHOP CRITIQUE AND LIVING ON MY OWN. HOW AM I SUDDENLY SUPPOSED TO BE THAT OLD VERSION OF MYSELF AGAIN?
YOU DON'T HAVE TO BE. YOU CAN BE WHOEVER THE FUCK YOU WANT TO BE.
MAYBE. BUT MY MOM WILL STILL SEE ME ONE WAY. AND MY SIBLINGS. AND EVEN YOU TWO.
THERE IS SOMETHING WRONG WITH ME IF I CAN'T HANDLE OTHER PEOPLE'S GAZE.
PEOPLE ARE GOING TO SEE YOU. HOW THEY SEE YOU IS ONE THING, BUT YOU CAN'T STOP THEM FROM SEEING YOU. AND WHY SHOULDN'T THEY? YOU'RE SMART, HILARIOUS, AND A TRUE FORCE. PEOPLE SHOULD SEE THAT.

DAMN, NINA, THAT'S DEEP.

MY THERAPIST, FIONA NGUYEN, TOLD ME SOMETHING ALONG THOSE LINES.

WHEN WE GET YOU OUT OF HERE, I WILL HOOK YOU GUYS UP. I THINK SHE CAN HELP.

SILVIA HAD NEVER DETAILED THE REST OF HER STAY AT THE HOSPITAL WITH NINA AND SHIRIN, THOUGH SHE THOUGHT OFTEN OF THE STARKLY LIT HALLWAYS, BRUSQUE NURSES, AND THE NIGHTTIME MURMURINGS OF HER TRANSITORY ROOMMATES.

SHE HAD BEEN SCARED SHITLESS THE WHOLE TIME, WITH THE SAME REFRAIN LOOPING IN HER HEAD THE WHOLE TIME:

HOW DID I GET HERE?

TRASH

IT WASN'T UNTIL SHE MET WITH THE WARD'S MILD-MANNERED PSYCHIATRIST THAT SHE SIMPLY SAID THAT SHE'D LIKE TO LEAVE — AND TO HER SURPRISE, THEY ACQUIESCED.

YOU MEAN I CAN JUST... GO?

YOU AREN'T A DANGER TO YOURSELF OR ANY-ONE ELSE. I DON'T SEE WHY NOT.

AND JUST LIKE THAT, SHE HAD CHECKED OUT OF THE HOSPITAL WITH THE SAME EASE WITH WHICH SHE HAD CHECKED IN.

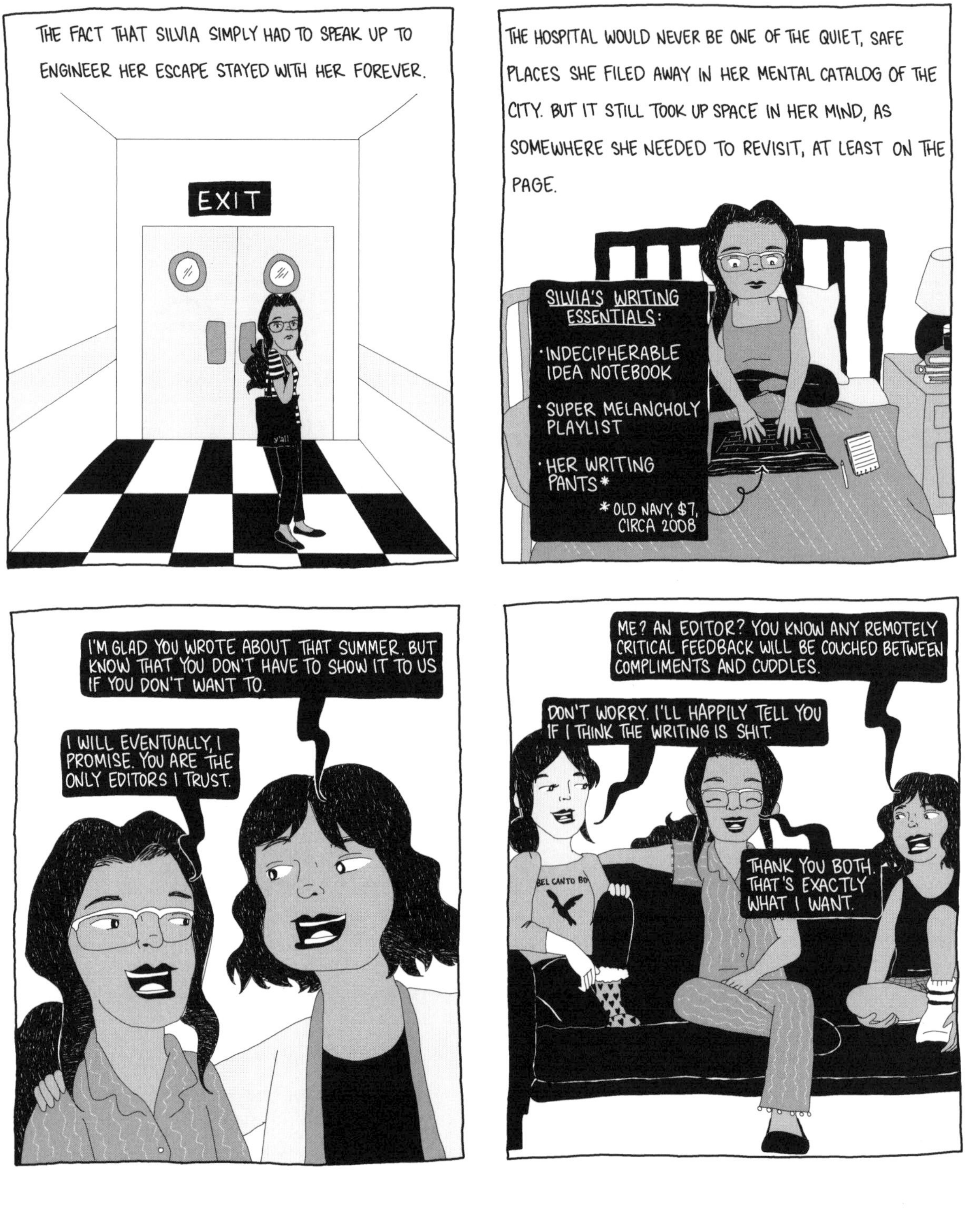
THE FACT THAT SILVIA SIMPLY HAD TO SPEAK UP TO ENGINEER HER ESCAPE STAYED WITH HER FOREVER.
EXIT
THE HOSPITAL WOULD NEVER BE ONE OF THE QUIET, SAFE PLACES SHE FILED AWAY IN HER MENTAL CATALOG OF THE CITY. BUT IT STILL TOOK UP SPACE IN HER MIND, AS SOMEWHERE SHE NEEDED TO REVISIT, AT LEAST ON THE PAGE.
SILVIA'S WRITING ESSENTIALS:
· INDECIPHERABLE IDEA NOTEBOOK
· SUPER MELANCHOLY PLAYLIST
· HER WRITING PANTS*
* OLD NAVY, $7, CIRCA 2008
I'M GLAD YOU WROTE ABOUT THAT SUMMER. BUT KNOW THAT YOU DON'T HAVE TO SHOW IT TO US IF YOU DON'T WANT TO.
I WILL EVENTUALLY, I PROMISE. YOU ARE THE ONLY EDITORS I TRUST.
ME? AN EDITOR? YOU KNOW ANY REMOTELY CRITICAL FEEDBACK WILL BE COUCHED BETWEEN COMPLIMENTS AND CUDDLES.
DON'T WORRY. I'LL HAPPILY TELL YOU IF I THINK THE WRITING IS SHIT.
THANK YOU BOTH. THAT'S EXACTLY WHAT I WANT.

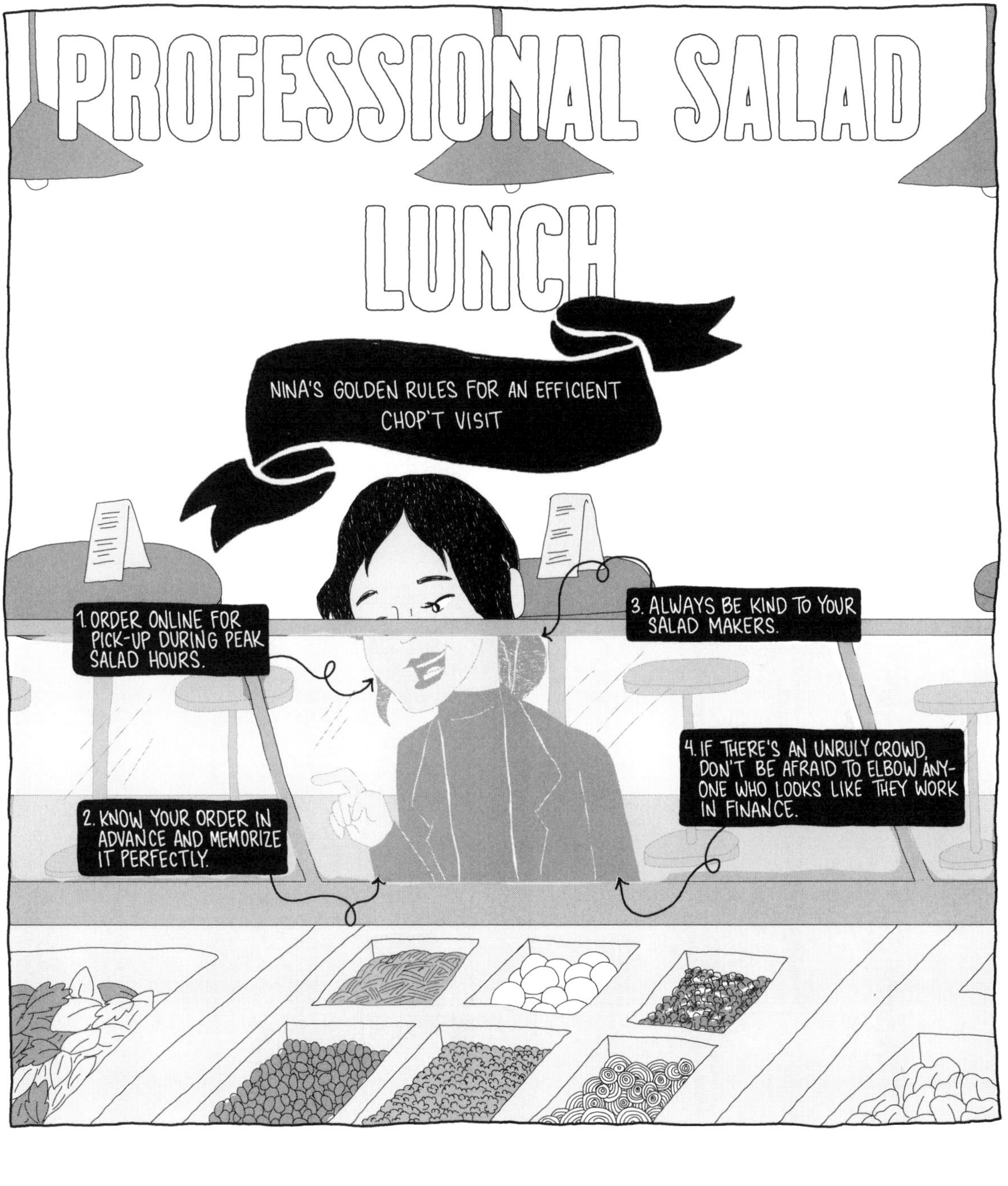
PROFESSIONAL SALAD LUNCH
NINA'S GOLDEN RULES FOR AN EFFICIENT CHOP'T VISIT
1. ORDER ONLINE FOR PICK-UP DURING PEAK SALAD HOURS.
2. KNOW YOUR ORDER IN ADVANCE AND MEMORIZE IT PERFECTLY.
3. ALWAYS BE KIND TO YOUR SALAD MAKERS.
4. IF THERE'S AN UNRULY CROWD, DON'T BE AFRAID TO ELBOW ANY-ONE WHO LOOKS LIKE THEY WORK IN FINANCE.

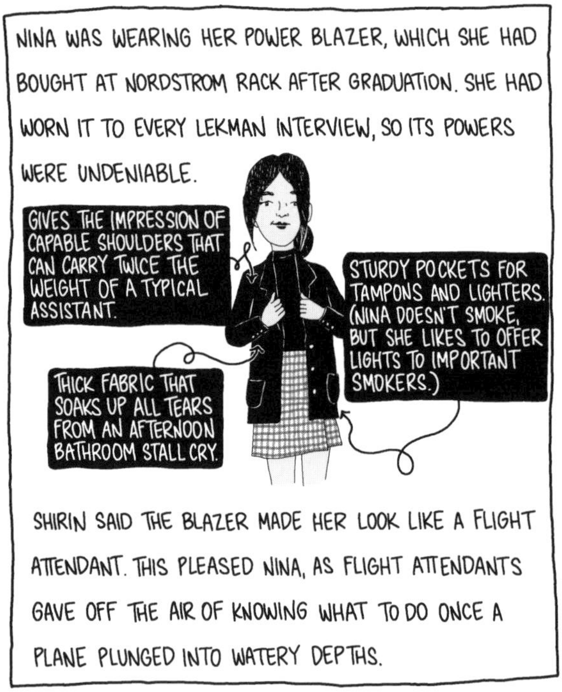
NINA WAS WEARING HER POWER BLAZER, WHICH SHE HAD BOUGHT AT NORDSTROM RACK AFTER GRADUATION. SHE HAD WORN IT TO EVERY LEKMAN INTERVIEW, SO ITS POWERS WERE UNDENIABLE.
GIVES THE IMPRESSION OF CAPABLE SHOULDERS THAT CAN CARRY TWICE THE WEIGHT OF A TYPICAL ASSISTANT.
STURDY POCKETS FOR TAMPONS AND LIGHTERS. (NINA DOESN'T SMOKE, BUT SHE LIKES TO OFFER LIGHTS TO IMPORTANT SMOKERS.)
THICK FABRIC THAT SOAKS UP ALL TEARS FROM AN AFTERNOON BATHROOM STALL CRY.
SHIRIN SAID THE BLAZER MADE HER LOOK LIKE A FLIGHT ATTENDANT. THIS PLEASED NINA, AS FLIGHT ATTENDANTS GAVE OFF THE AIR OF KNOWING WHAT TO DO ONCE A PLANE PLUNGED INTO WATERY DEPTHS.

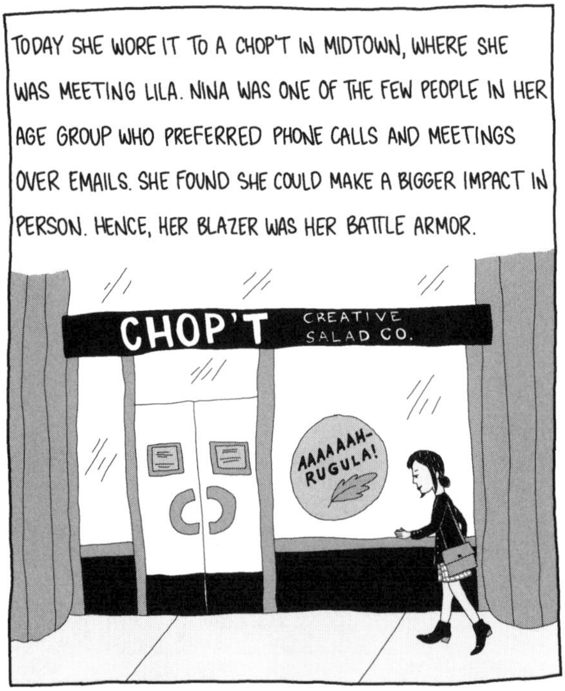
TODAY SHE WORE IT TO A CHOP'T IN MIDTOWN, WHERE SHE WAS MEETING LILA. NINA WAS ONE OF THE FEW PEOPLE IN HER AGE GROUP WHO PREFERRED PHONE CALLS AND MEETINGS OVER EMAILS. SHE FOUND SHE COULD MAKE A BIGGER IMPACT IN PERSON. HENCE, HER BLAZER WAS HER BATTLE ARMOR.
CHOP'T CREATIVE SALAD CO.
AAAAAAH-RUGULA!

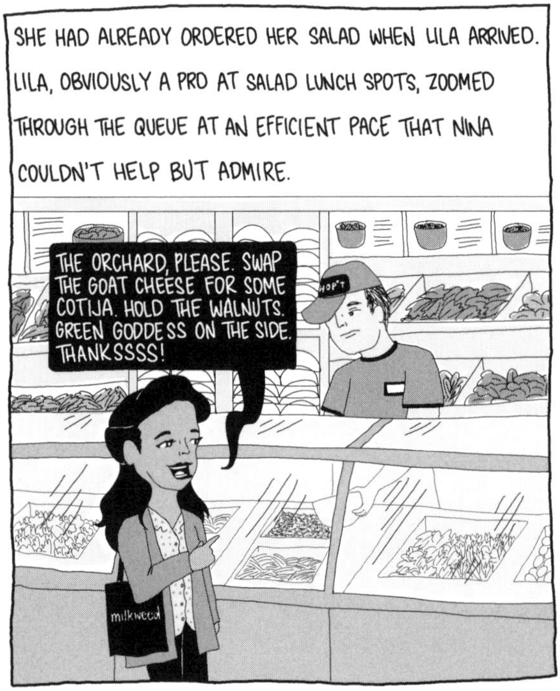
SHE HAD ALREADY ORDERED HER SALAD WHEN LILA ARRIVED. LILA, OBVIOUSLY A PRO AT SALAD LUNCH SPOTS, ZOOMED THROUGH THE QUEUE AT AN EFFICIENT PACE THAT NINA COULDN'T HELP BUT ADMIRE.
THE ORCHARD, PLEASE. SWAP THE GOAT CHEESE FOR SOME COTIJA. HOLD THE WALNUTS. GREEN GODDESS ON THE SIDE. THANKSSSS!
milkweed

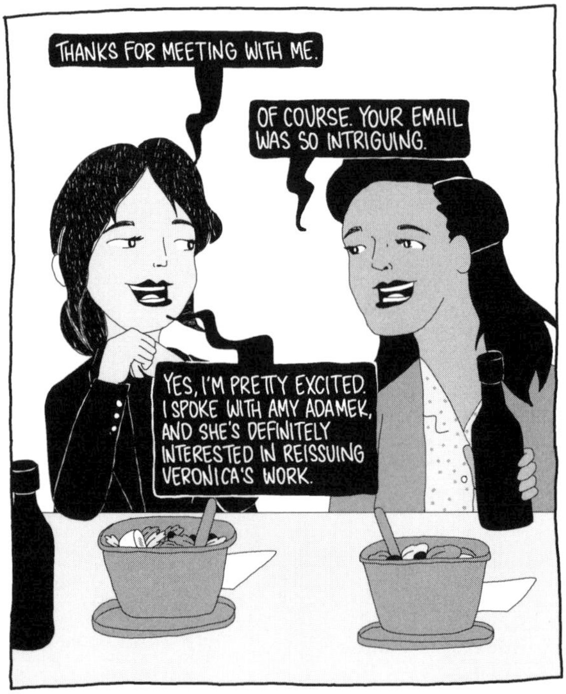
THANKS FOR MEETING WITH ME.
OF COURSE. YOUR EMAIL WAS SO INTRIGUING.
YES, I'M PRETTY EXCITED. I SPOKE WITH AMY ADAMEK, AND SHE'S DEFINITELY INTERESTED IN REISSUING VERONICA'S WORK.

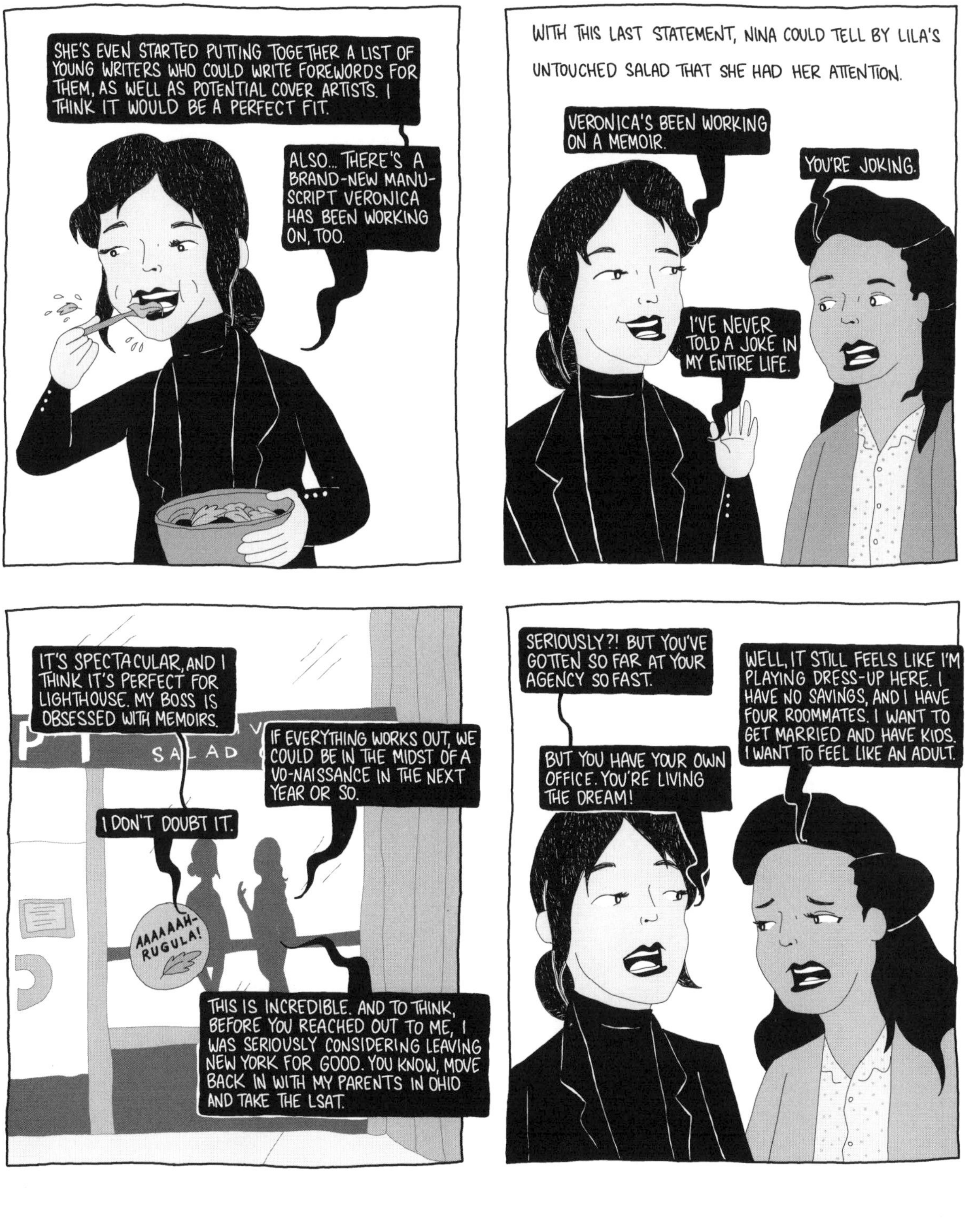
SHE'S EVEN STARTED PUTTING TOGETHER A LIST OF YOUNG WRITERS WHO COULD WRITE FOREWORDS FOR THEM, AS WELL AS POTENTIAL COVER ARTISTS. I THINK IT WOULD BE A PERFECT FIT.
ALSO... THERE'S A BRAND-NEW MANU-SCRIPT VERONICA HAS BEEN WORKING ON, TOO.
WITH THIS LAST STATEMENT, NINA COULD TELL BY LILA'S UNTOUCHED SALAD THAT SHE HAD HER ATTENTION.
VERONICA'S BEEN WORKING ON A MEMOIR.
YOU'RE JOKING.
I'VE NEVER TOLD A JOKE IN MY ENTIRE LIFE.
IT'S SPECTACULAR, AND I THINK IT'S PERFECT FOR LIGHTHOUSE. MY BOSS IS OBSESSED WITH MEMOIRS.
SALAD
I DON'T DOUBT IT.
IF EVERYTHING WORKS OUT, WE COULD BE IN THE MIDST OF A VO-NAISSANCE IN THE NEXT YEAR OR SO.
AAAAAAH-RUGULA!
THIS IS INCREDIBLE. AND TO THINK, BEFORE YOU REACHED OUT TO ME, I WAS SERIOUSLY CONSIDERING LEAVING NEW YORK FOR GOOD. YOU KNOW, MOVE BACK IN WITH MY PARENTS IN OHIO AND TAKE THE LSAT.
SERIOUSLY?! BUT YOU'VE GOTTEN SO FAR AT YOUR AGENCY SO FAST.
BUT YOU HAVE YOUR OWN OFFICE. YOU'RE LIVING THE DREAM!
WELL, IT STILL FEELS LIKE I'M PLAYING DRESS-UP HERE. I HAVE NO SAVINGS, AND I HAVE FOUR ROOMMATES. I WANT TO GET MARRIED AND HAVE KIDS. I WANT TO FEEL LIKE AN ADULT.

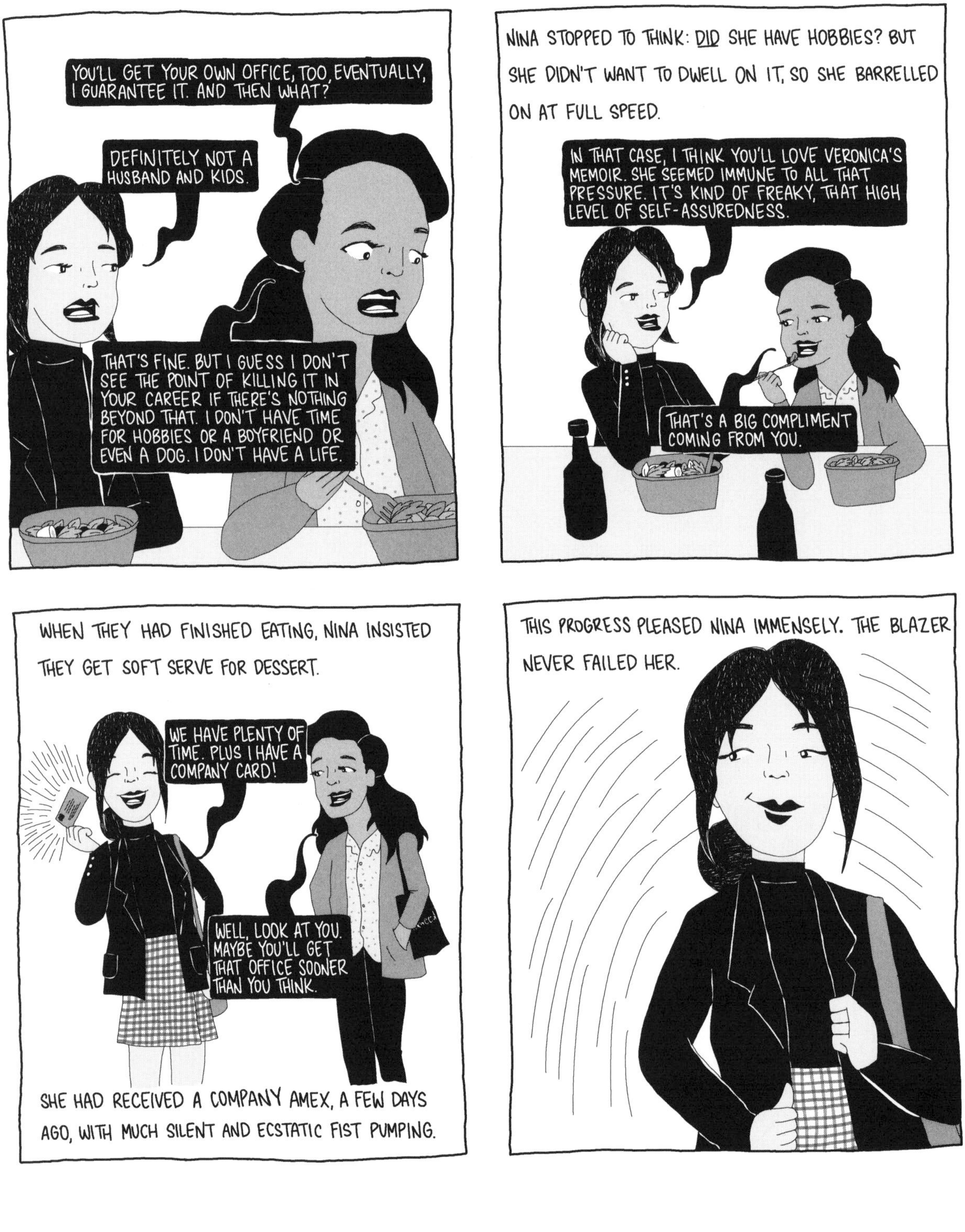
YOU'LL GET YOUR OWN OFFICE, TOO, EVENTUALLY, I GUARANTEE IT. AND THEN WHAT?
DEFINITELY NOT A HUSBAND AND KIDS.
THAT'S FINE. BUT I GUESS I DON'T SEE THE POINT OF KILLING IT IN YOUR CAREER IF THERE'S NOTHING BEYOND THAT. I DON'T HAVE TIME FOR HOBBIES OR A BOYFRIEND OR EVEN A DOG. I DON'T HAVE A LIFE.
NINA STOPPED TO THINK: DID SHE HAVE HOBBIES? BUT SHE DIDN'T WANT TO DWELL ON IT, SO SHE BARRELLED ON AT FULL SPEED.
IN THAT CASE, I THINK YOU'LL LOVE VERONICA'S MEMOIR. SHE SEEMED IMMUNE TO ALL THAT PRESSURE. IT'S KIND OF FREAKY, THAT HIGH LEVEL OF SELF-ASSUREDNESS.
THAT'S A BIG COMPLIMENT COMING FROM YOU.
WHEN THEY HAD FINISHED EATING, NINA INSISTED THEY GET SOFT SERVE FOR DESSERT.
WE HAVE PLENTY OF TIME. PLUS I HAVE A COMPANY CARD!
WELL, LOOK AT YOU. MAYBE YOU'LL GET THAT OFFICE SOONER THAN YOU THINK.
SHE HAD RECEIVED A COMPANY AMEX, A FEW DAYS AGO, WITH MUCH SILENT AND ECSTATIC FIST PUMPING.
THIS PROGRESS PLEASED NINA IMMENSELY. THE BLAZER NEVER FAILED HER.

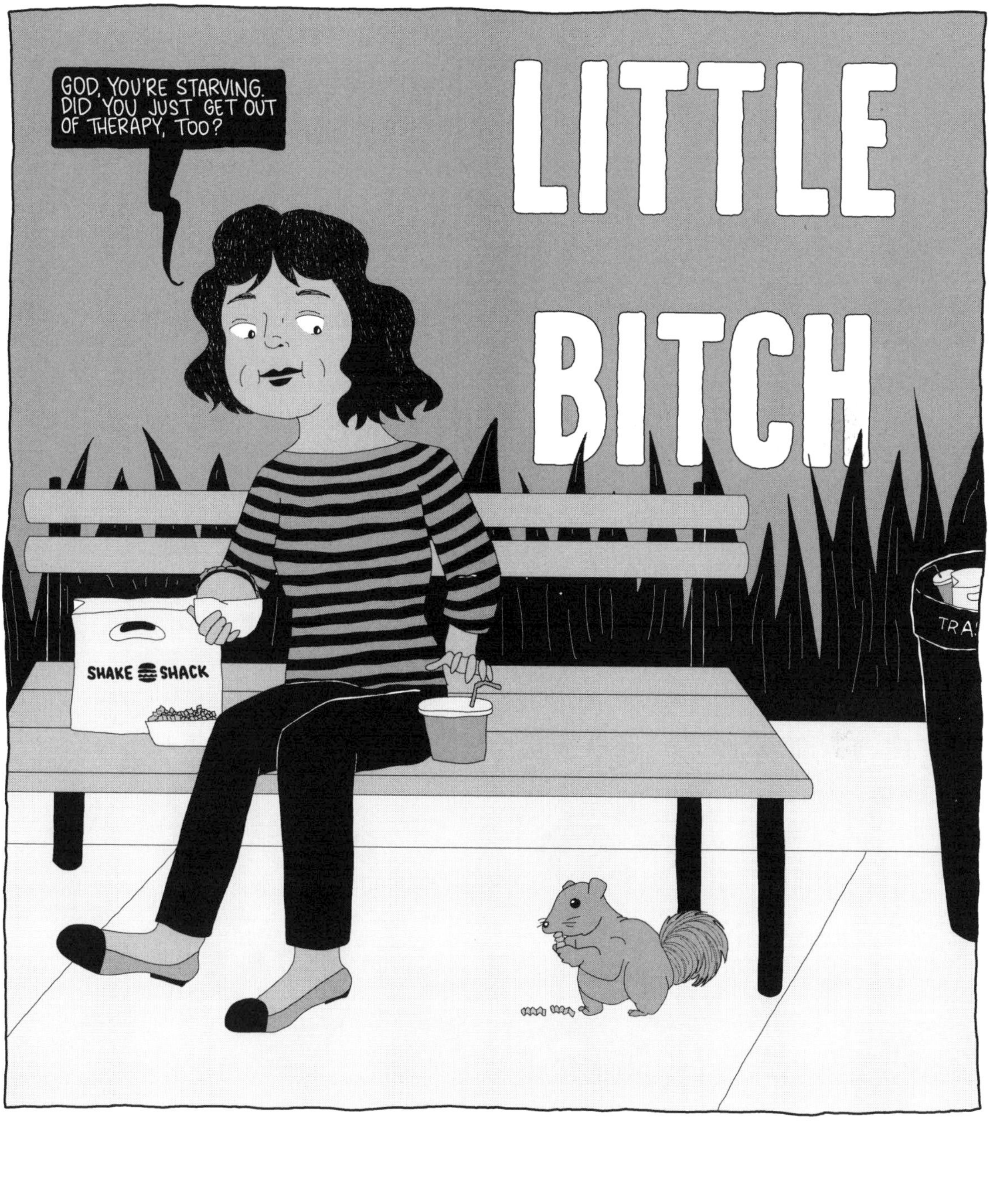
LITTLE BITCH
GOD, YOU'RE STARVING. DID YOU JUST GET OUT OF THERAPY, TOO?
SHAKE SHACK

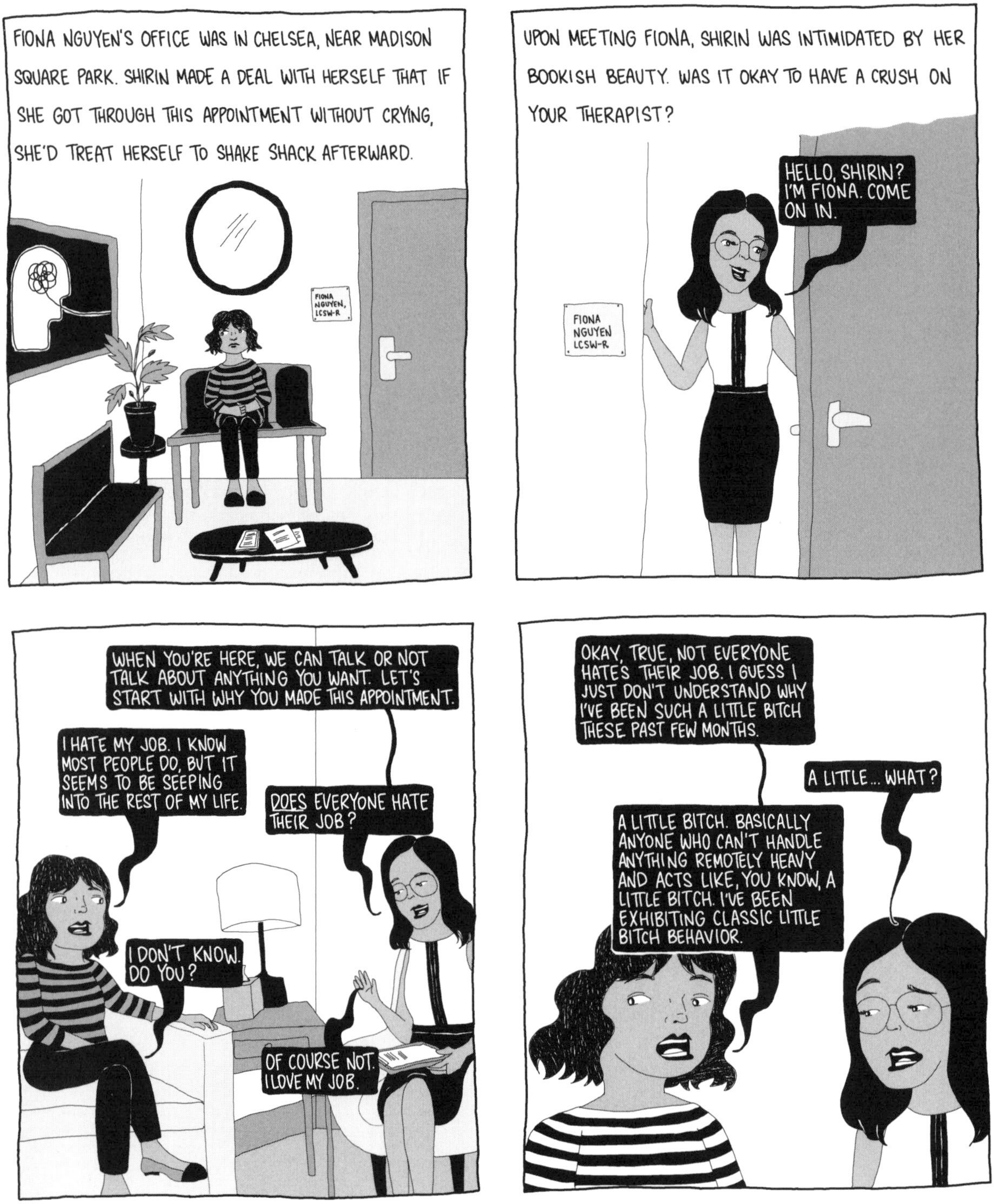
FIONA NGUYEN'S OFFICE WAS IN CHELSEA, NEAR MADISON SQUARE PARK. SHIRIN MADE A DEAL WITH HERSELF THAT IF SHE GOT THROUGH THIS APPOINTMENT WITHOUT CRYING, SHE'D TREAT HERSELF TO SHAKE SHACK AFTERWARD.
FIONA NGUYEN, LCSW-R
UPON MEETING FIONA, SHIRIN WAS INTIMIDATED BY HER BOOKISH BEAUTY. WAS IT OKAY TO HAVE A CRUSH ON YOUR THERAPIST?
HELLO, SHIRIN? I'M FIONA. COME ON IN.
FIONA NGUYEN LCSW-R
WHEN YOU'RE HERE, WE CAN TALK OR NOT TALK ABOUT ANYTHING YOU WANT. LET'S START WITH WHY YOU MADE THIS APPOINTMENT.
I HATE MY JOB. I KNOW MOST PEOPLE DO, BUT IT SEEMS TO BE SEEPING INTO THE REST OF MY LIFE.
DOES EVERYONE HATE THEIR JOB?
I DON'T KNOW. DO YOU?
OF COURSE NOT. I LOVE MY JOB.
OKAY, TRUE, NOT EVERYONE HATES THEIR JOB. I GUESS I JUST DON'T UNDERSTAND WHY I'VE BEEN SUCH A LITTLE BITCH THESE PAST FEW MONTHS.
A LITTLE... WHAT?
A LITTLE BITCH. BASICALLY ANYONE WHO CAN'T HANDLE ANYTHING REMOTELY HEAVY AND ACTS LIKE, YOU KNOW, A LITTLE BITCH. I'VE BEEN EXHIBITING CLASSIC LITTLE BITCH BEHAVIOR.

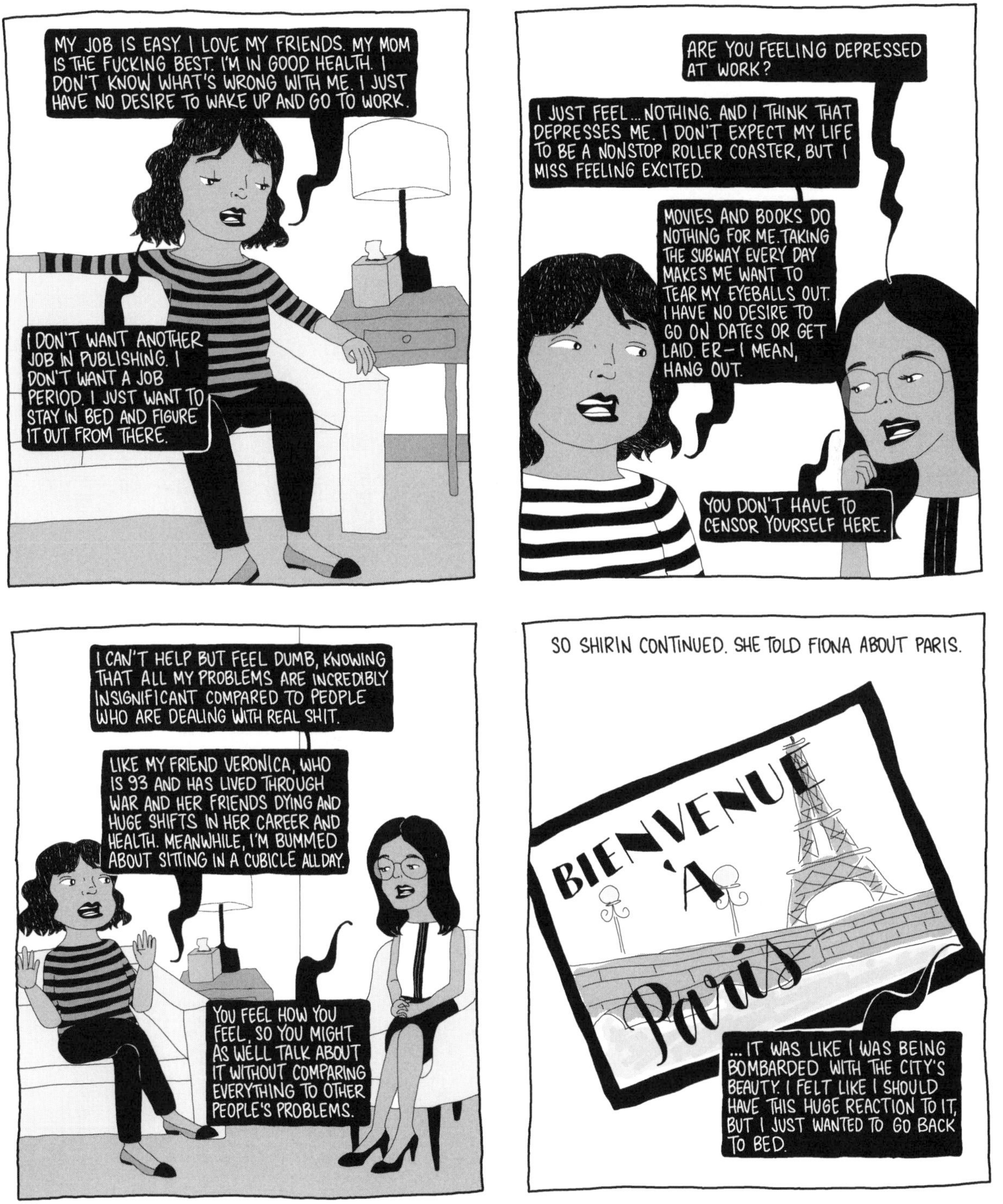
MY JOB IS EASY. I LOVE MY FRIENDS. MY MOM IS THE FUCKING BEST. I'M IN GOOD HEALTH. I DON'T KNOW WHAT'S WRONG WITH ME. I JUST HAVE NO DESIRE TO WAKE UP AND GO TO WORK.
I DON'T WANT ANOTHER JOB IN PUBLISHING. I DON'T WANT A JOB PERIOD. I JUST WANT TO STAY IN BED AND FIGURE IT OUT FROM THERE.
ARE YOU FEELING DEPRESSED AT WORK?
I JUST FEEL... NOTHING. AND I THINK THAT DEPRESSES ME. I DON'T EXPECT MY LIFE TO BE A NONSTOP ROLLER COASTER, BUT I MISS FEELING EXCITED.
MOVIES AND BOOKS DO NOTHING FOR ME. TAKING THE SUBWAY EVERY DAY MAKES ME WANT TO TEAR MY EYEBALLS OUT. I HAVE NO DESIRE TO GO ON DATES OR GET LAID. ER— I MEAN, HANG OUT.
YOU DON'T HAVE TO CENSOR YOURSELF HERE.
I CAN'T HELP BUT FEEL DUMB, KNOWING THAT ALL MY PROBLEMS ARE INCREDIBLY INSIGNIFICANT COMPARED TO PEOPLE WHO ARE DEALING WITH REAL SHIT.
LIKE MY FRIEND VERONICA, WHO IS 93 AND HAS LIVED THROUGH WAR AND HER FRIENDS DYING AND HUGE SHIFTS IN HER CAREER AND HEALTH. MEANWHILE, I'M BUMMED ABOUT SITTING IN A CUBICLE ALL DAY.
YOU FEEL HOW YOU FEEL, SO YOU MIGHT AS WELL TALK ABOUT IT WITHOUT COMPARING EVERYTHING TO OTHER PEOPLE'S PROBLEMS.
SO SHIRIN CONTINUED. SHE TOLD FIONA ABOUT PARIS.
BIENVENUE 'A Paris
...IT WAS LIKE I WAS BEING BOMBARDED WITH THE CITY'S BEAUTY. I FELT LIKE I SHOULD HAVE THIS HUGE REACTION TO IT, BUT I JUST WANTED TO GO BACK TO BED.

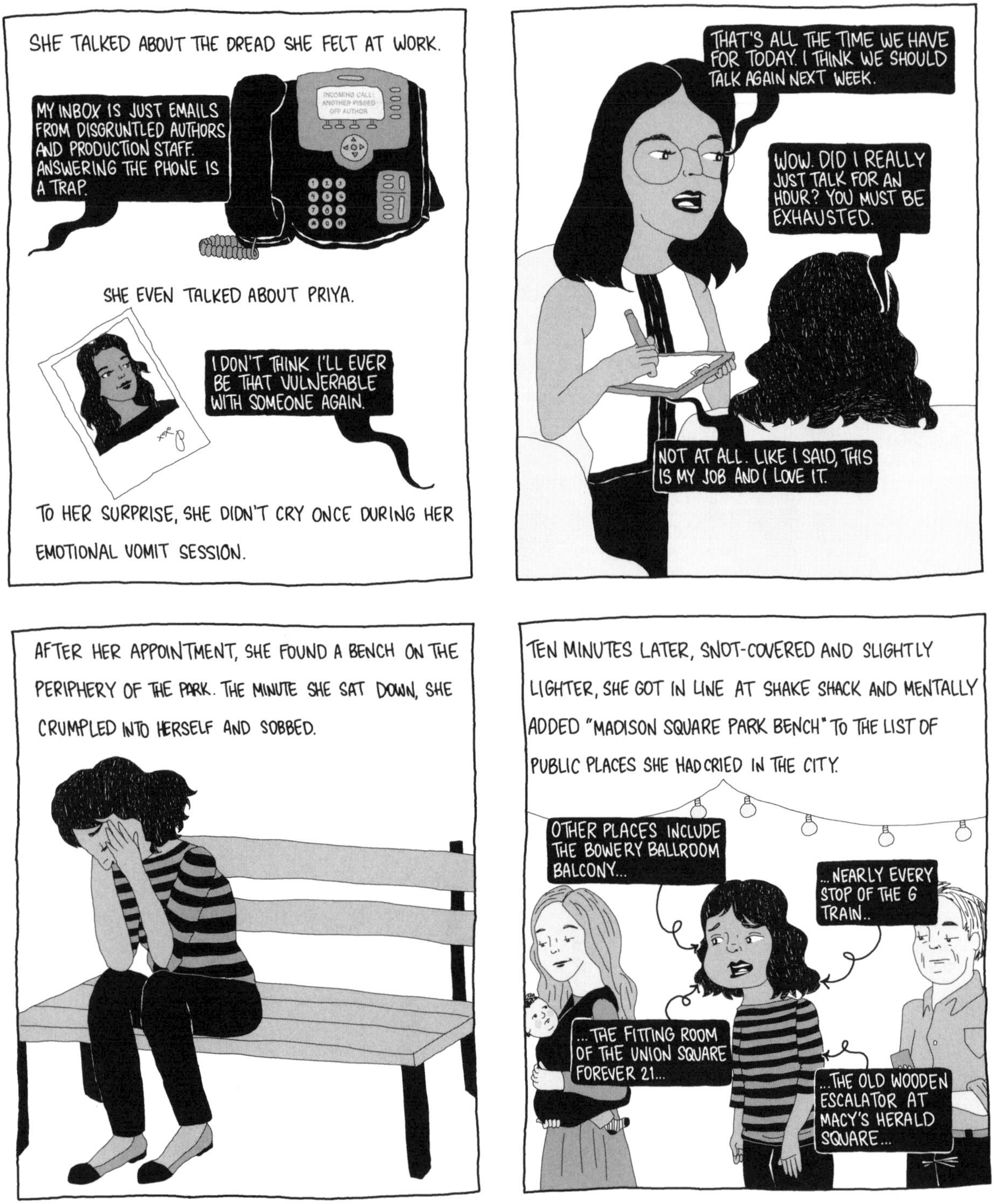

SHE TALKED ABOUT THE DREAD SHE FELT AT WORK.
MY INBOX IS JUST EMAILS FROM DISGRUNTLED AUTHORS AND PRODUCTION STAFF. ANSWERING THE PHONE IS A TRAP.
INCOMING CALL: ANOTHER PISSED OFF AUTHOR
SHE EVEN TALKED ABOUT PRIYA.
I DON'T THINK I'LL EVER BE THAT VULNERABLE WITH SOMEONE AGAIN.
TO HER SURPRISE, SHE DIDN'T CRY ONCE DURING HER EMOTIONAL VOMIT SESSION.
THAT'S ALL THE TIME WE HAVE FOR TODAY. I THINK WE SHOULD TALK AGAIN NEXT WEEK.
WOW. DID I REALLY JUST TALK FOR AN HOUR? YOU MUST BE EXHAUSTED.
NOT AT ALL. LIKE I SAID, THIS IS MY JOB AND I LOVE IT.
AFTER HER APPOINTMENT, SHE FOUND A BENCH ON THE PERIPHERY OF THE PARK. THE MINUTE SHE SAT DOWN, SHE CRUMPLED INTO HERSELF AND SOBBED.
TEN MINUTES LATER, SNOT-COVERED AND SLIGHTLY LIGHTER, SHE GOT IN LINE AT SHAKE SHACK AND MENTALLY ADDED "MADISON SQUARE PARK BENCH" TO THE LIST OF PUBLIC PLACES SHE HAD CRIED IN THE CITY.
OTHER PLACES INCLUDE THE BOWERY BALLROOM BALCONY...
...NEARLY EVERY STOP OF THE G TRAIN..
...THE FITTING ROOM OF THE UNION SQUARE FOREVER 21...
...THE OLD WOODEN ESCALATOR AT MACY'S HERALD SQUARE...

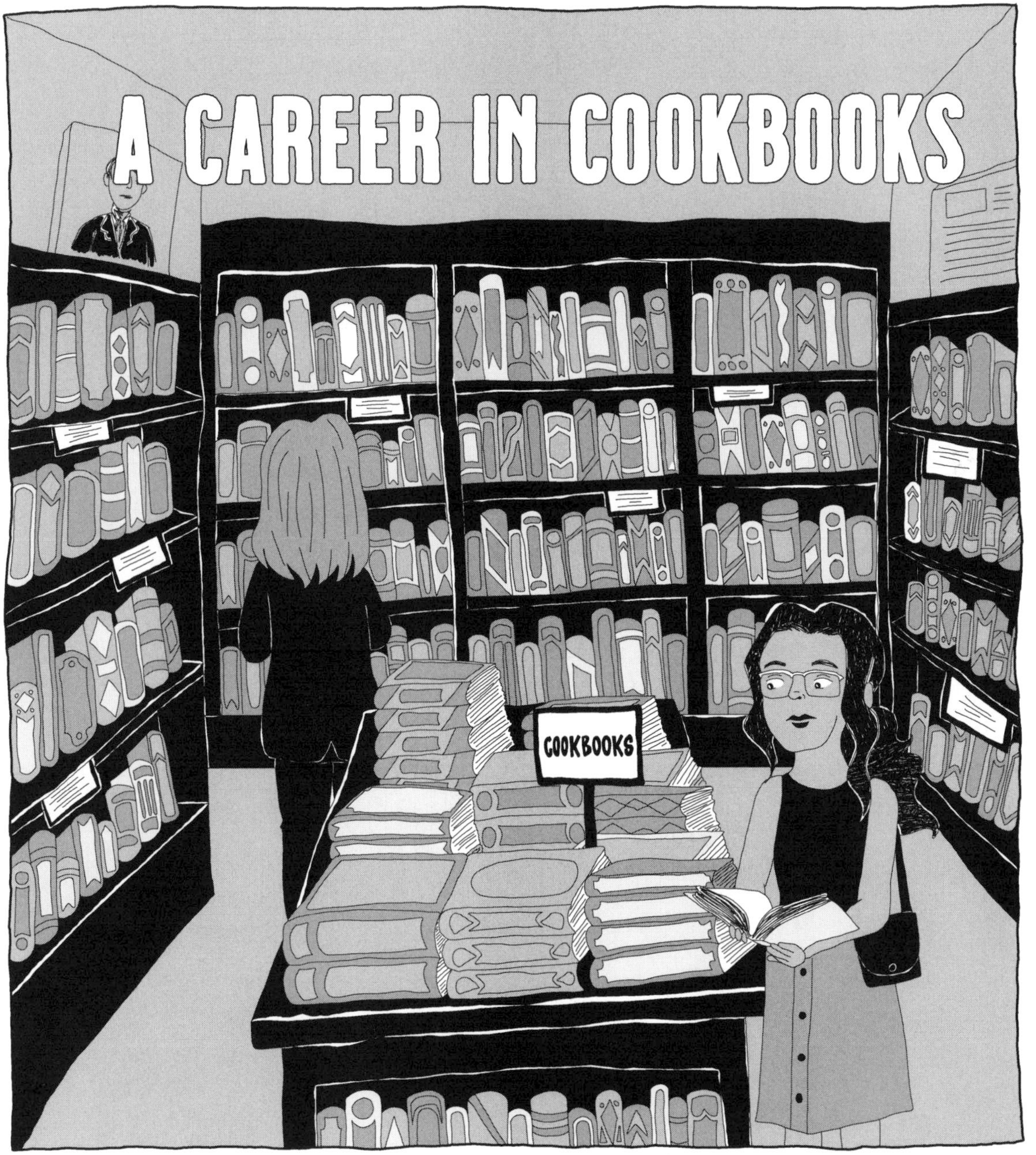
A CAREER IN COOKBOOKS
COOKBOOKS

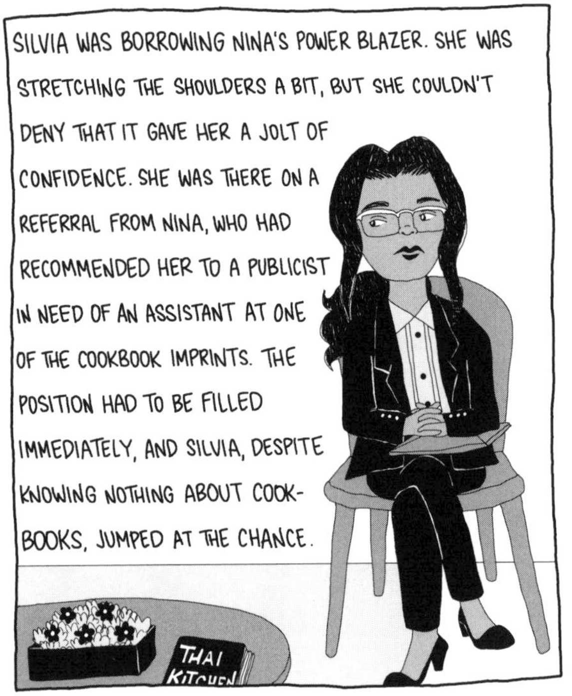
SILVIA WAS BORROWING NINA'S POWER BLAZER. SHE WAS STRETCHING THE SHOULDERS A BIT, BUT SHE COULDN'T DENY THAT IT GAVE HER A JOLT OF CONFIDENCE. SHE WAS THERE ON A REFERRAL FROM NINA, WHO HAD RECOMMENDED HER TO A PUBLICIST IN NEED OF AN ASSISTANT AT ONE OF THE COOKBOOK IMPRINTS. THE POSITION HAD TO BE FILLED IMMEDIATELY, AND SILVIA, DESPITE KNOWING NOTHING ABOUT COOK-BOOKS, JUMPED AT THE CHANCE.
THAI KITCHEN

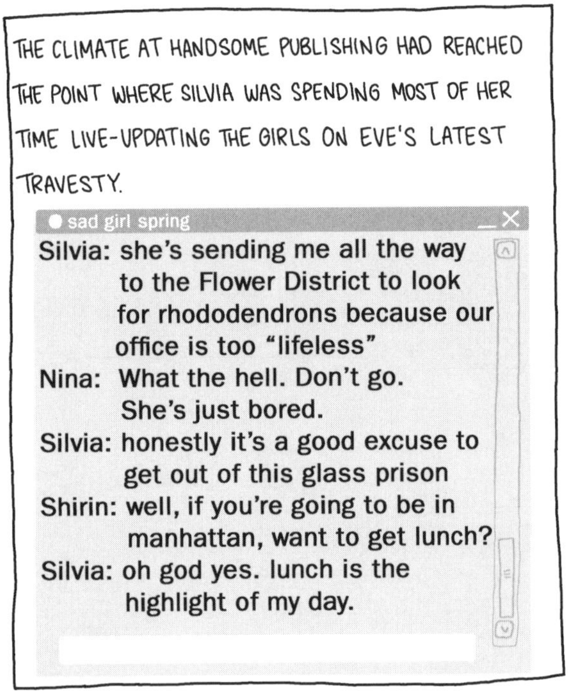
THE CLIMATE AT HANDSOME PUBLISHING HAD REACHED THE POINT WHERE SILVIA WAS SPENDING MOST OF HER TIME LIVE-UPDATING THE GIRLS ON EVE'S LATEST TRAVESTY.
sad girl spring
Silvia: she's sending me all the way to the Flower District to look for rhododendrons because our office is too "lifeless"
Nina: What the hell. Don't go. She's just bored.
Silvia: honestly it's a good excuse to get out of this glass prison
Shirin: well, if you're going to be in manhattan, want to get lunch?
Silvia: oh god yes. lunch is the highlight of my day.

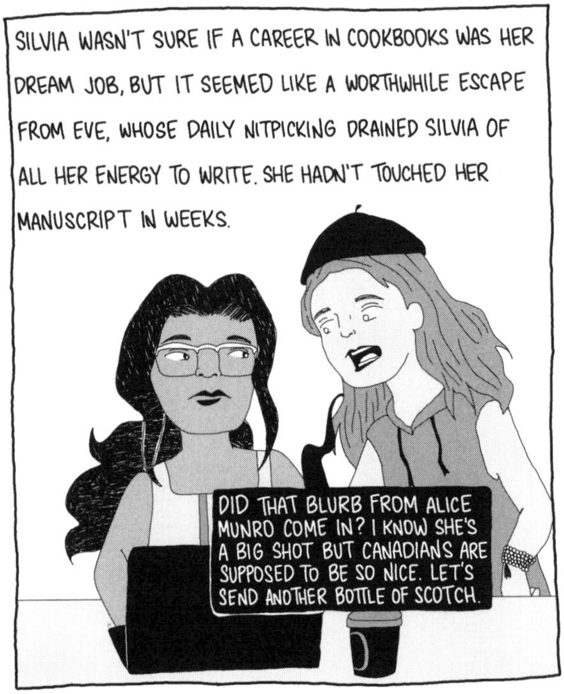
SILVIA WASN'T SURE IF A CAREER IN COOKBOOKS WAS HER DREAM JOB, BUT IT SEEMED LIKE A WORTHWHILE ESCAPE FROM EVE, WHOSE DAILY NITPICKING DRAINED SILVIA OF ALL HER ENERGY TO WRITE. SHE HADN'T TOUCHED HER MANUSCRIPT IN WEEKS.
DID THAT BLURB FROM ALICE MUNRO COME IN? I KNOW SHE'S A BIG SHOT BUT CANADIANS ARE SUPPOSED TO BE SO NICE. LET'S SEND ANOTHER BOTTLE OF SCOTCH.

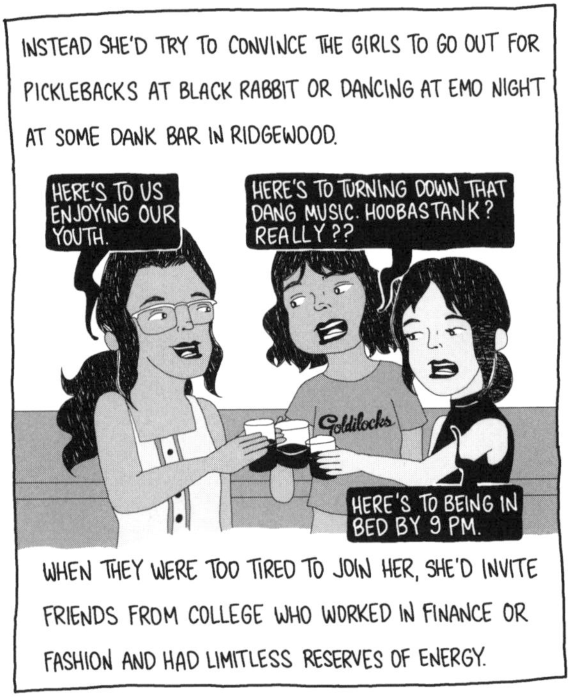
INSTEAD SHE'D TRY TO CONVINCE THE GIRLS TO GO OUT FOR PICKLEBACKS AT BLACK RABBIT OR DANCING AT EMO NIGHT AT SOME DANK BAR IN RIDGEWOOD.
HERE'S TO US ENJOYING OUR YOUTH.
HERE'S TO TURNING DOWN THAT DANG MUSIC. HOOBASTANK? REALLY??
Goldilocks
HERE'S TO BEING IN BED BY 9 PM.
WHEN THEY WERE TOO TIRED TO JOIN HER, SHE'D INVITE FRIENDS FROM COLLEGE WHO WORKED IN FINANCE OR FASHION AND HAD LIMITLESS RESERVES OF ENERGY.

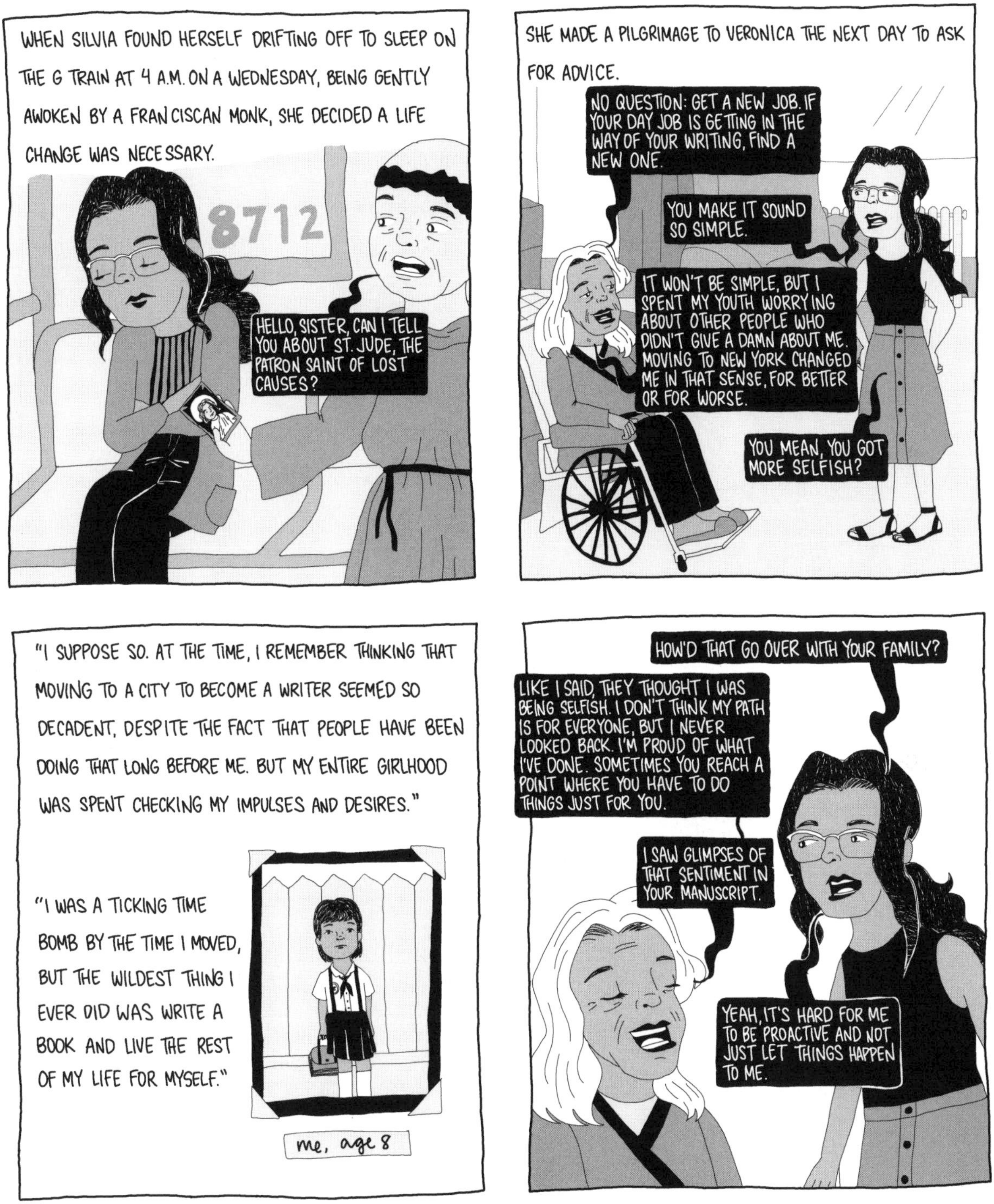
WHEN SILVIA FOUND HERSELF DRIFTING OFF TO SLEEP ON THE G TRAIN AT 4 A.M. ON A WEDNESDAY, BEING GENTLY AWOKEN BY A FRANCISCAN MONK, SHE DECIDED A LIFE CHANGE WAS NECESSARY.
8712
HELLO, SISTER, CAN I TELL YOU ABOUT ST. JUDE, THE PATRON SAINT OF LOST CAUSES?
SHE MADE A PILGRIMAGE TO VERONICA THE NEXT DAY TO ASK FOR ADVICE.
NO QUESTION: GET A NEW JOB. IF YOUR DAY JOB IS GETTING IN THE WAY OF YOUR WRITING, FIND A NEW ONE.
YOU MAKE IT SOUND SO SIMPLE.
IT WON'T BE SIMPLE, BUT I SPENT MY YOUTH WORRYING ABOUT OTHER PEOPLE WHO DIDN'T GIVE A DAMN ABOUT ME. MOVING TO NEW YORK CHANGED ME IN THAT SENSE, FOR BETTER OR FOR WORSE.
YOU MEAN, YOU GOT MORE SELFISH?
"I SUPPOSE SO. AT THE TIME, I REMEMBER THINKING THAT MOVING TO A CITY TO BECOME A WRITER SEEMED SO DECADENT, DESPITE THE FACT THAT PEOPLE HAVE BEEN DOING THAT LONG BEFORE ME. BUT MY ENTIRE GIRLHOOD WAS SPENT CHECKING MY IMPULSES AND DESIRES."
"I WAS A TICKING TIME BOMB BY THE TIME I MOVED, BUT THE WILDEST THING I EVER DID WAS WRITE A BOOK AND LIVE THE REST OF MY LIFE FOR MYSELF."
me, age 8
HOW'D THAT GO OVER WITH YOUR FAMILY?
LIKE I SAID, THEY THOUGHT I WAS BEING SELFISH. I DON'T THINK MY PATH IS FOR EVERYONE, BUT I NEVER LOOKED BACK. I'M PROUD OF WHAT I'VE DONE. SOMETIMES YOU REACH A POINT WHERE YOU HAVE TO DO THINGS JUST FOR YOU.
I SAW GLIMPSES OF THAT SENTIMENT IN YOUR MANUSCRIPT.
YEAH, IT'S HARD FOR ME TO BE PROACTIVE AND NOT JUST LET THINGS HAPPEN TO ME.

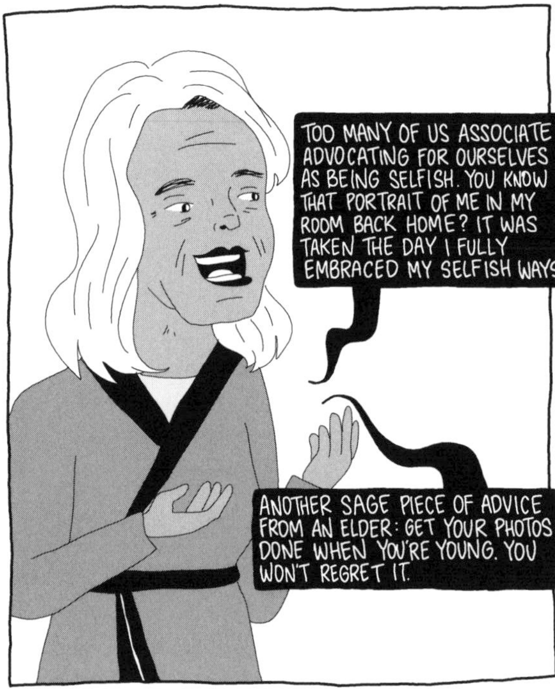
TOO MANY OF US ASSOCIATE ADVOCATING FOR OURSELVES AS BEING SELFISH. YOU KNOW THAT PORTRAIT OF ME IN MY ROOM BACK HOME? IT WAS TAKEN THE DAY I FULLY EMBRACED MY SELFISH WAYS.
ANOTHER SAGE PIECE OF ADVICE FROM AN ELDER: GET YOUR PHOTOS DONE WHEN YOU'RE YOUNG. YOU WON'T REGRET IT.

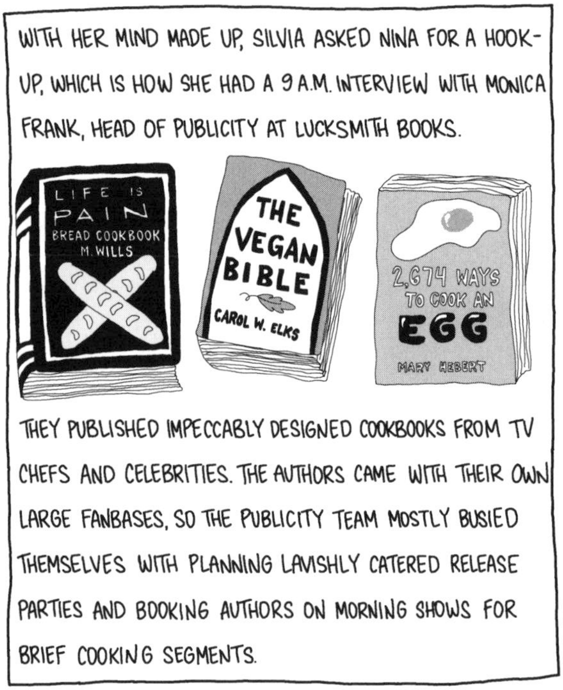
WITH HER MIND MADE UP, SILVIA ASKED NINA FOR A HOOK-UP, WHICH IS HOW SHE HAD A 9 A.M. INTERVIEW WITH MONICA FRANK, HEAD OF PUBLICITY AT LUCKSMITH BOOKS.
LIFE IS PAIN
BREAD COOKBOOK
M. WILLS
THE VEGAN BIBLE
CAROL W. ELKS
2,674 WAYS TO COOK AN EGG
MARY HEBERT
THEY PUBLISHED IMPECCABLY DESIGNED COOKBOOKS FROM TV CHEFS AND CELEBRITIES. THE AUTHORS CAME WITH THEIR OWN LARGE FANBASES, SO THE PUBLICITY TEAM MOSTLY BUSIED THEMSELVES WITH PLANNING LAVISHLY CATERED RELEASE PARTIES AND BOOKING AUTHORS ON MORNING SHOWS FOR BRIEF COOKING SEGMENTS.

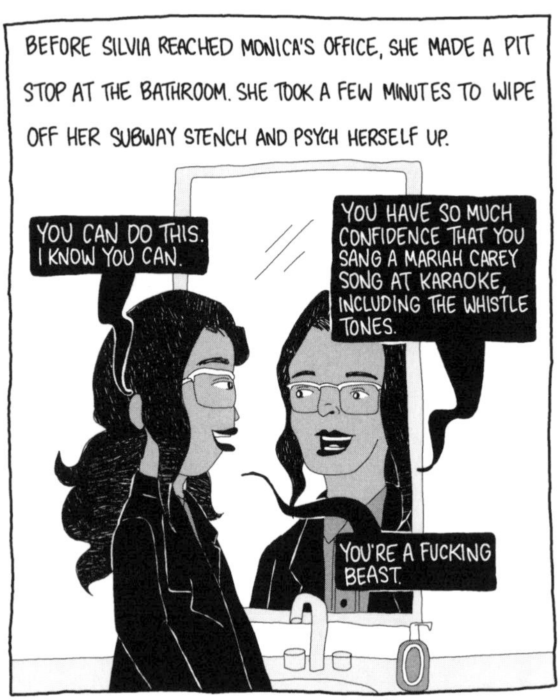
BEFORE SILVIA REACHED MONICA'S OFFICE, SHE MADE A PIT STOP AT THE BATHROOM. SHE TOOK A FEW MINUTES TO WIPE OFF HER SUBWAY STENCH AND PSYCH HERSELF UP.
YOU CAN DO THIS. I KNOW YOU CAN.
YOU HAVE SO MUCH CONFIDENCE THAT YOU SANG A MARIAH CAREY SONG AT KARAOKE, INCLUDING THE WHISTLE TONES.
YOU'RE A FUCKING BEAST.

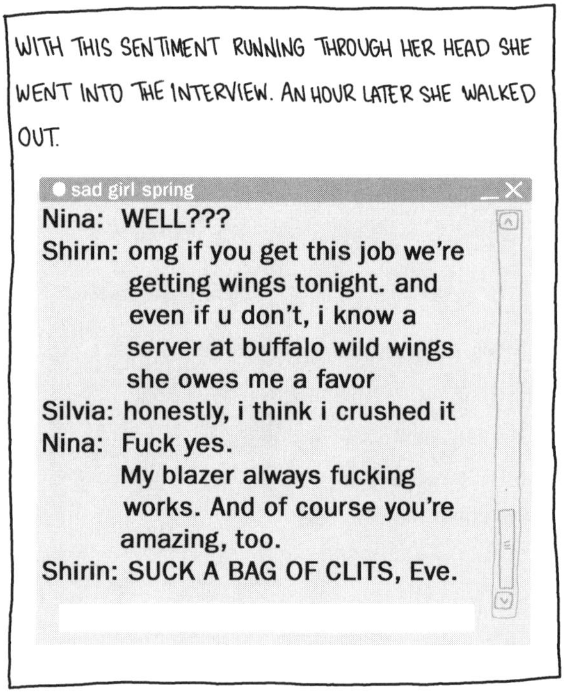
WITH THIS SENTIMENT RUNNING THROUGH HER HEAD SHE WENT INTO THE INTERVIEW. AN HOUR LATER SHE WALKED OUT.
sad girl spring
Nina: WELL???
Shirin: omg if you get this job we're getting wings tonight. and even if u don't, i know a server at buffalo wild wings she owes me a favor
Silvia: honestly, i think i crushed it
Nina: Fuck yes.
My blazer always fucking works. And of course you're amazing, too.
Shirin: SUCK A BAG OF CLITS, Eve.

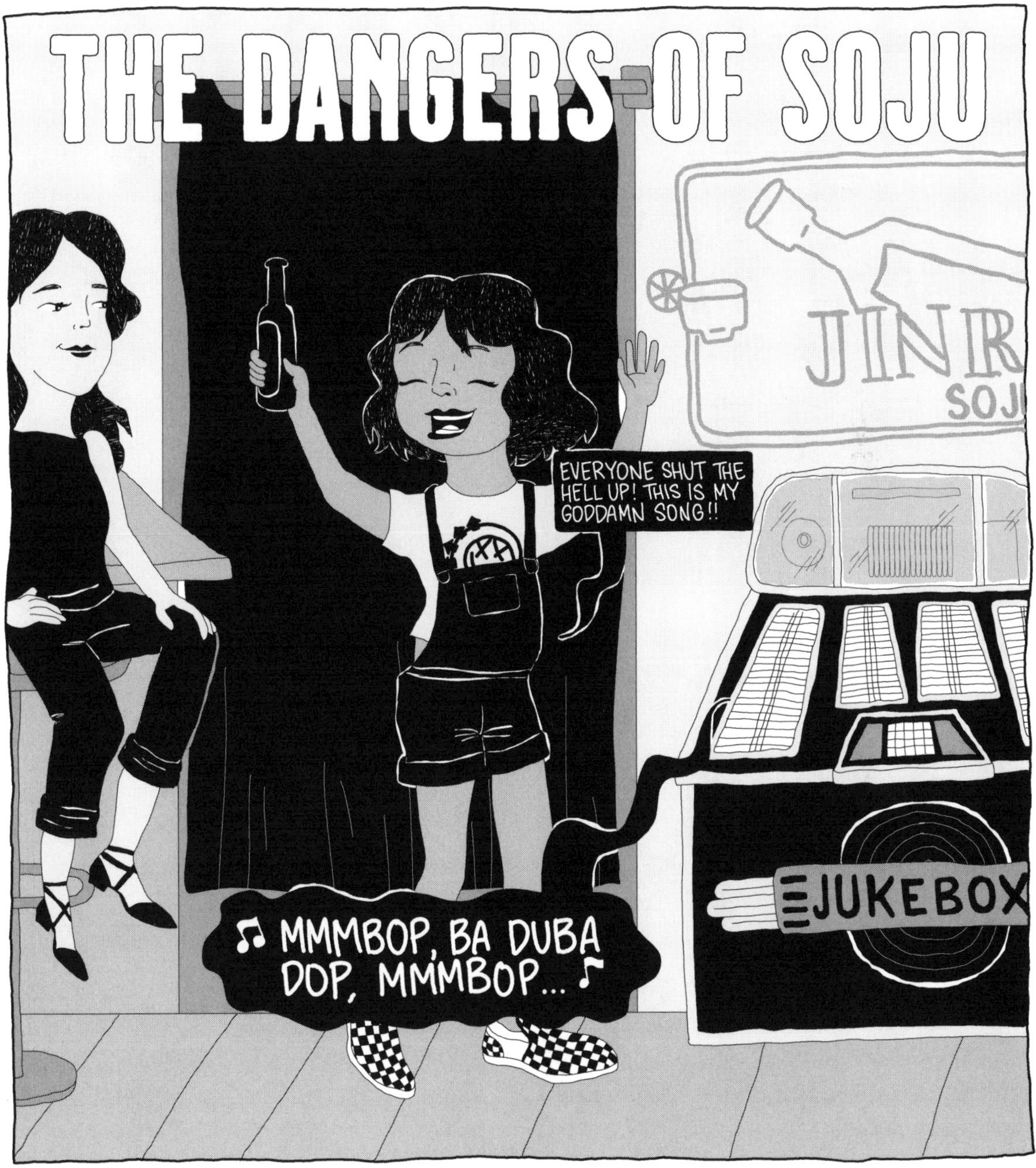
THE DANGERS OF SOJU
JINR
SOJU
EVERYONE SHUT THE HELL UP! THIS IS MY GODDAMN SONG!!
JUKEBOX
MMMBOP, BA DUBA DOP, MMMBOP...

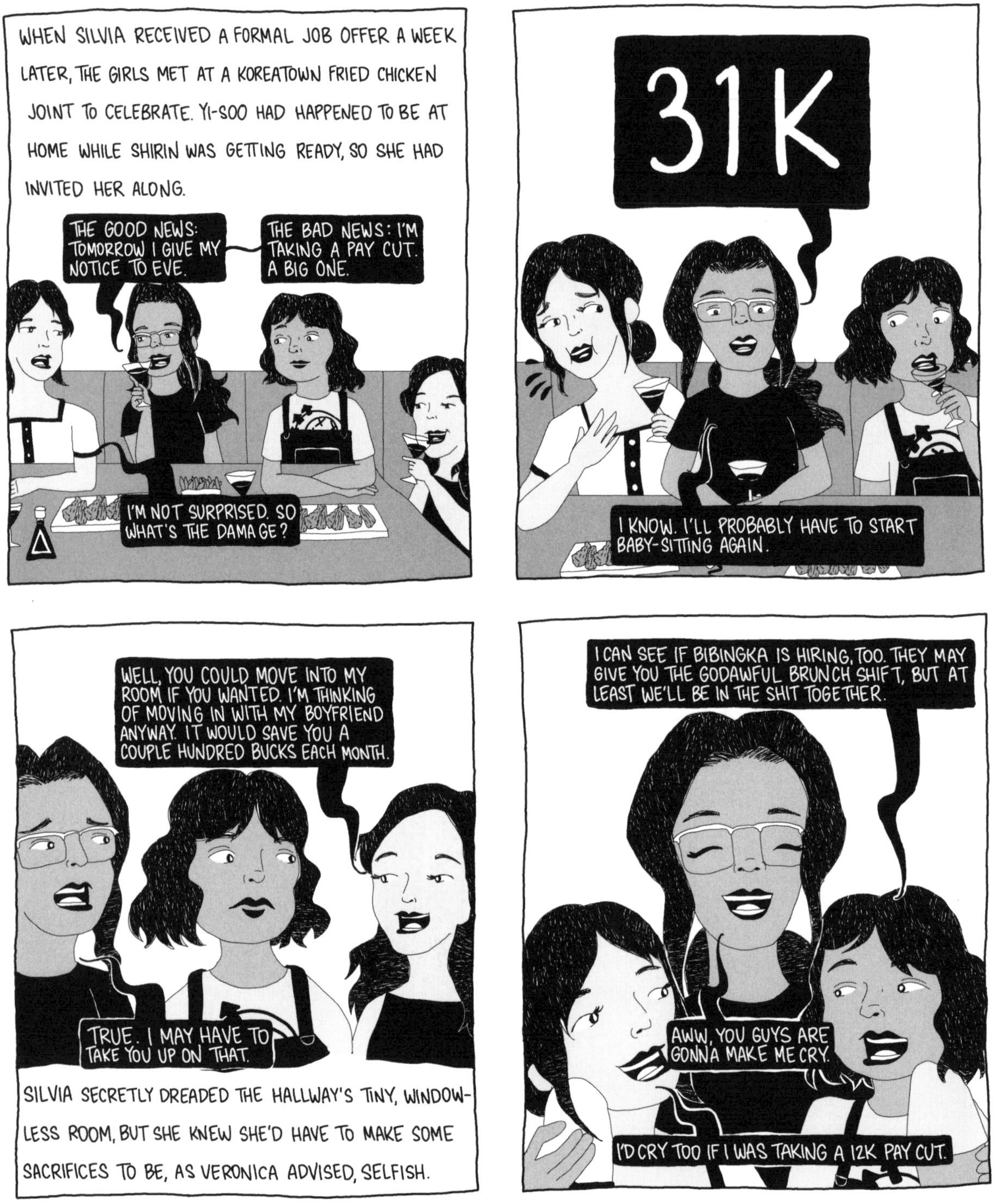
WHEN SILVIA RECEIVED A FORMAL JOB OFFER A WEEK LATER, THE GIRLS MET AT A KOREATOWN FRIED CHICKEN JOINT TO CELEBRATE. YI-SOO HAD HAPPENED TO BE AT HOME WHILE SHIRIN WAS GETTING READY, SO SHE HAD INVITED HER ALONG.
THE GOOD NEWS: TOMORROW I GIVE MY NOTICE TO EVE.
THE BAD NEWS: I'M TAKING A PAY CUT. A BIG ONE.
I'M NOT SURPRISED. SO WHAT'S THE DAMAGE?
31K
I KNOW. I'LL PROBABLY HAVE TO START BABY-SITTING AGAIN.
WELL, YOU COULD MOVE INTO MY ROOM IF YOU WANTED. I'M THINKING OF MOVING IN WITH MY BOYFRIEND ANYWAY. IT WOULD SAVE YOU A COUPLE HUNDRED BUCKS EACH MONTH.
TRUE. I MAY HAVE TO TAKE YOU UP ON THAT.
SILVIA SECRETLY DREADED THE HALLWAY'S TINY, WINDOWLESS ROOM, BUT SHE KNEW SHE'D HAVE TO MAKE SOME SACRIFICES TO BE, AS VERONICA ADVISED, SELFISH.
I CAN SEE IF BIBINGKA IS HIRING, TOO. THEY MAY GIVE YOU THE GODAWFUL BRUNCH SHIFT, BUT AT LEAST WE'LL BE IN THE SHIT TOGETHER.
AWW, YOU GUYS ARE GONNA MAKE ME CRY.
I'D CRY TOO IF I WAS TAKING A 12K PAY CUT.

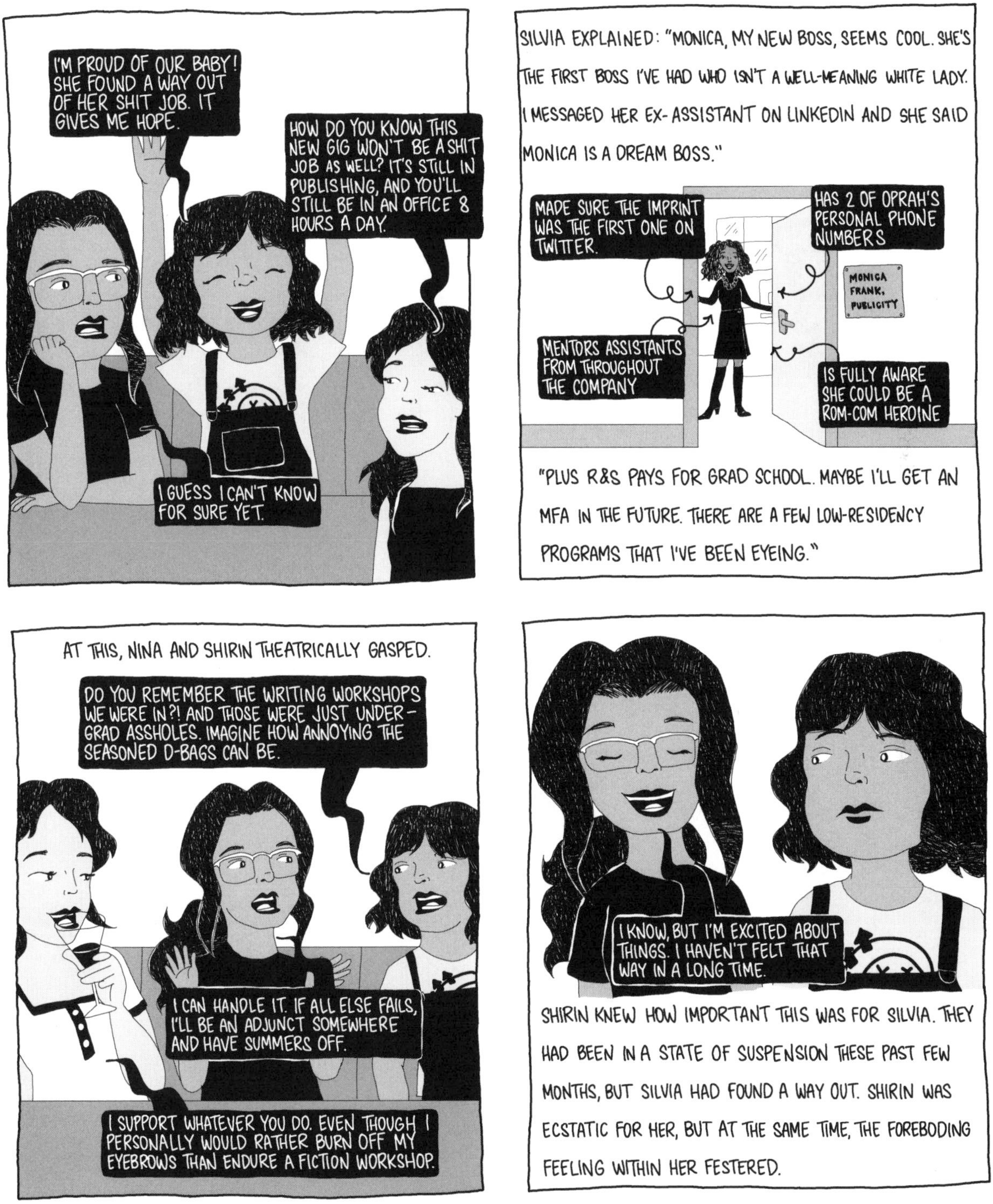
I'M PROUD OF OUR BABY! SHE FOUND A WAY OUT OF HER SHIT JOB. IT GIVES ME HOPE.
HOW DO YOU KNOW THIS NEW GIG WON'T BE A SHIT JOB AS WELL? IT'S STILL IN PUBLISHING, AND YOU'LL STILL BE IN AN OFFICE 8 HOURS A DAY.
I GUESS I CAN'T KNOW FOR SURE YET.
SILVIA EXPLAINED: "MONICA, MY NEW BOSS, SEEMS COOL. SHE'S THE FIRST BOSS I'VE HAD WHO ISN'T A WELL-MEANING WHITE LADY. I MESSAGED HER EX-ASSISTANT ON LINKEDIN AND SHE SAID MONICA IS A DREAM BOSS."
MADE SURE THE IMPRINT WAS THE FIRST ONE ON TWITTER.
HAS 2 OF OPRAH'S PERSONAL PHONE NUMBERS
MONICA FRANK, PUBLICITY
MENTORS ASSISTANTS FROM THROUGHOUT THE COMPANY
IS FULLY AWARE SHE COULD BE A ROM-COM HEROINE
"PLUS R&S PAYS FOR GRAD SCHOOL. MAYBE I'LL GET AN MFA IN THE FUTURE. THERE ARE A FEW LOW-RESIDENCY PROGRAMS THAT I'VE BEEN EYEING."
AT THIS, NINA AND SHIRIN THEATRICALLY GASPED.
DO YOU REMEMBER THE WRITING WORKSHOPS WE WERE IN?! AND THOSE WERE JUST UNDER-GRAD ASSHOLES. IMAGINE HOW ANNOYING THE SEASONED D-BAGS CAN BE.
I CAN HANDLE IT. IF ALL ELSE FAILS, I'LL BE AN ADJUNCT SOMEWHERE AND HAVE SUMMERS OFF.
I SUPPORT WHATEVER YOU DO. EVEN THOUGH I PERSONALLY WOULD RATHER BURN OFF MY EYEBROWS THAN ENDURE A FICTION WORKSHOP.
I KNOW, BUT I'M EXCITED ABOUT THINGS. I HAVEN'T FELT THAT WAY IN A LONG TIME.
SHIRIN KNEW HOW IMPORTANT THIS WAS FOR SILVIA. THEY HAD BEEN IN A STATE OF SUSPENSION THESE PAST FEW MONTHS, BUT SILVIA HAD FOUND A WAY OUT. SHIRIN WAS ECSTATIC FOR HER, BUT AT THE SAME TIME, THE FOREBODING FEELING WITHIN HER FESTERED.

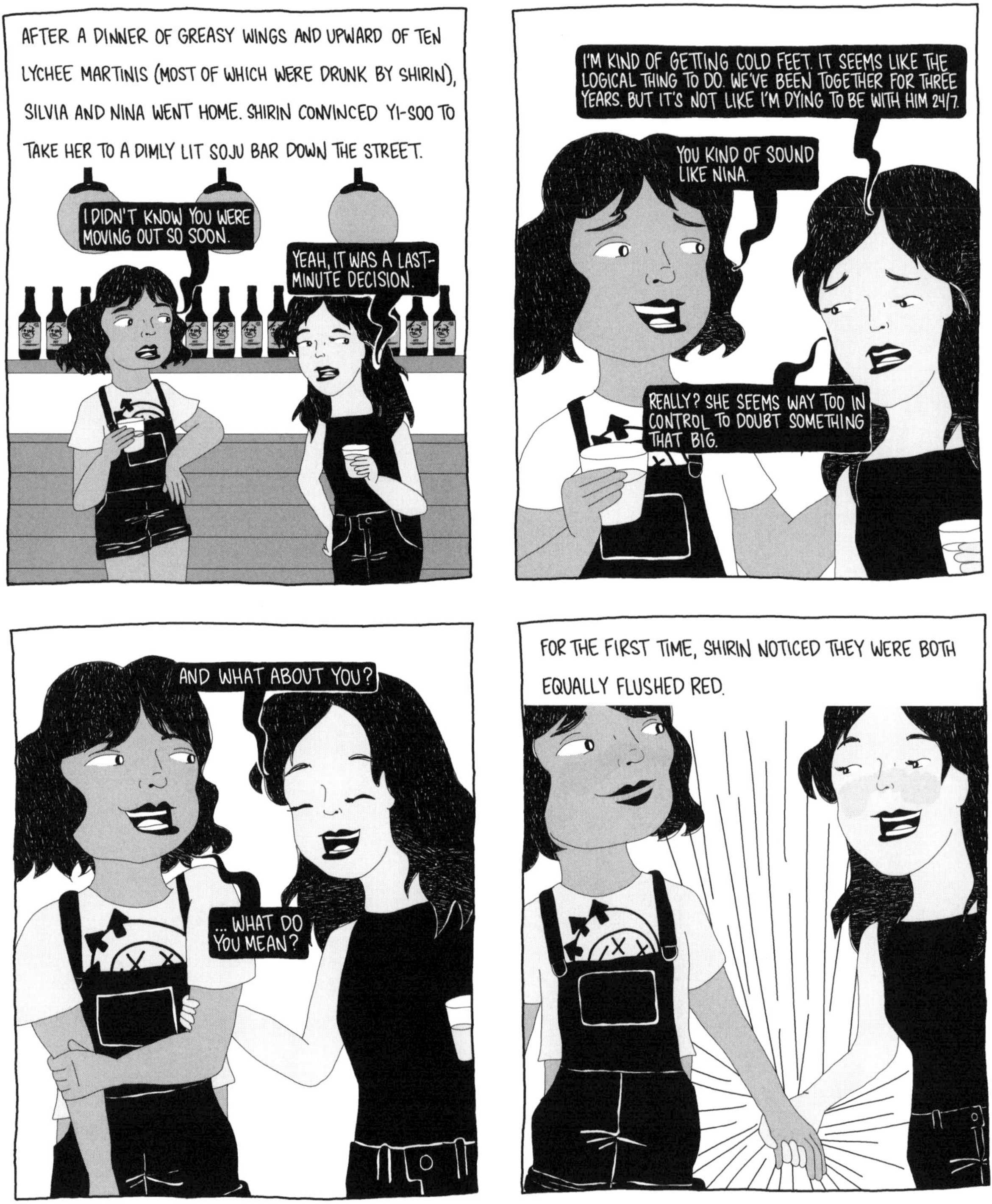
AFTER A DINNER OF GREASY WINGS AND UPWARD OF TEN LYCHEE MARTINIS (MOST OF WHICH WERE DRUNK BY SHIRIN), SILVIA AND NINA WENT HOME. SHIRIN CONVINCED YI-SOO TO TAKE HER TO A DIMLY LIT SOJU BAR DOWN THE STREET.
I DIDN'T KNOW YOU WERE MOVING OUT SO SOON.
YEAH, IT WAS A LAST-MINUTE DECISION.
I'M KIND OF GETTING COLD FEET. IT SEEMS LIKE THE LOGICAL THING TO DO. WE'VE BEEN TOGETHER FOR THREE YEARS. BUT IT'S NOT LIKE I'M DYING TO BE WITH HIM 24/7.
YOU KIND OF SOUND LIKE NINA.
REALLY? SHE SEEMS WAY TOO IN CONTROL TO DOUBT SOMETHING THAT BIG.
AND WHAT ABOUT YOU?
... WHAT DO YOU MEAN?
FOR THE FIRST TIME, SHIRIN NOTICED THEY WERE BOTH EQUALLY FLUSHED RED.

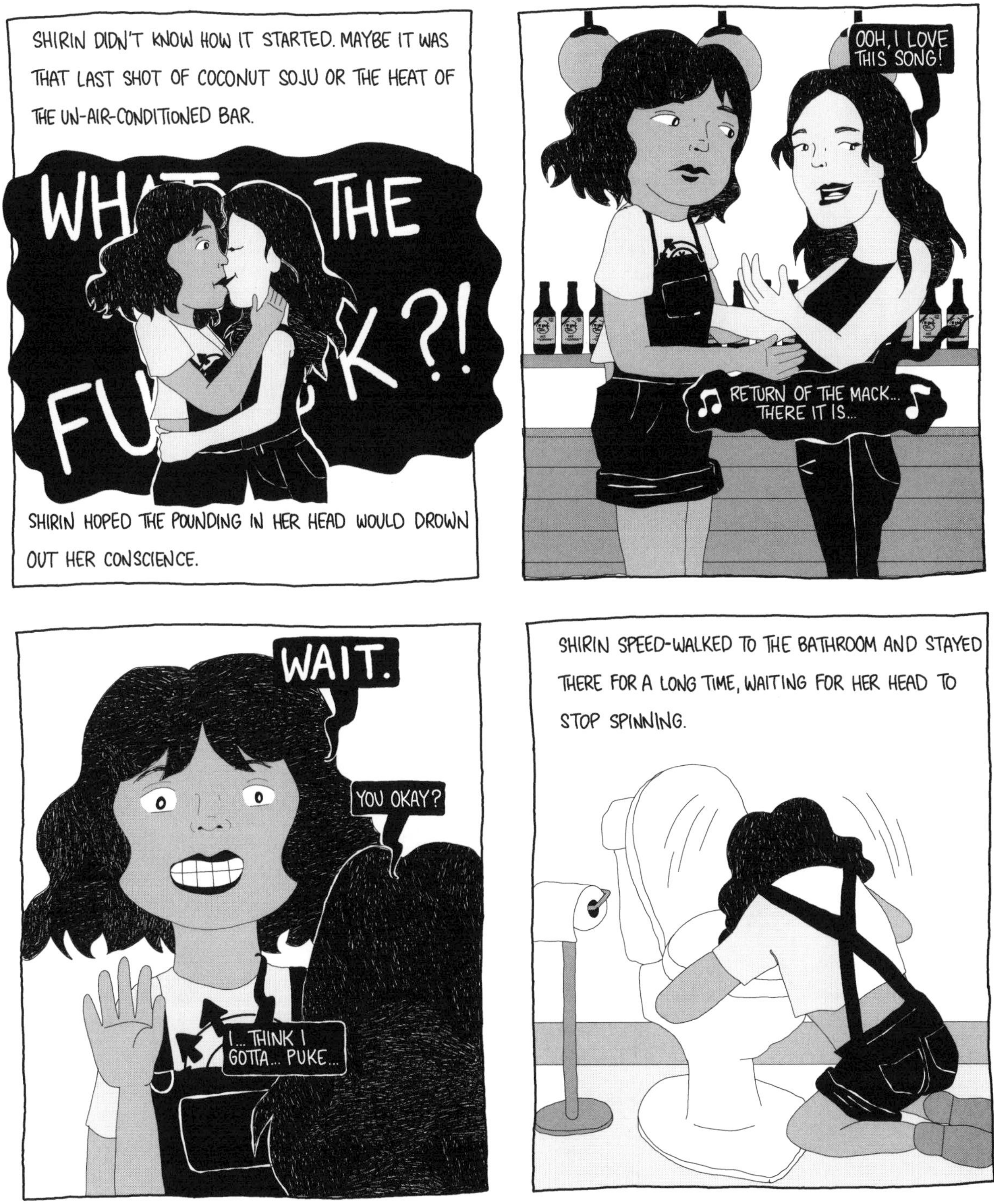
SHIRIN DIDN'T KNOW HOW IT STARTED. MAYBE IT WAS THAT LAST SHOT OF COCONUT SOJU OR THE HEAT OF THE UN-AIR-CONDITIONED BAR.
SHIRIN HOPED THE POUNDING IN HER HEAD WOULD DROWN OUT HER CONSCIENCE.
OOH, I LOVE THIS SONG!
RETURN OF THE MACK... THERE IT IS...
WAIT.
YOU OKAY?
I... THINK I GOTTA... PUKE...
SHIRIN SPEED-WALKED TO THE BATHROOM AND STAYED THERE FOR A LONG TIME, WAITING FOR HER HEAD TO STOP SPINNING.

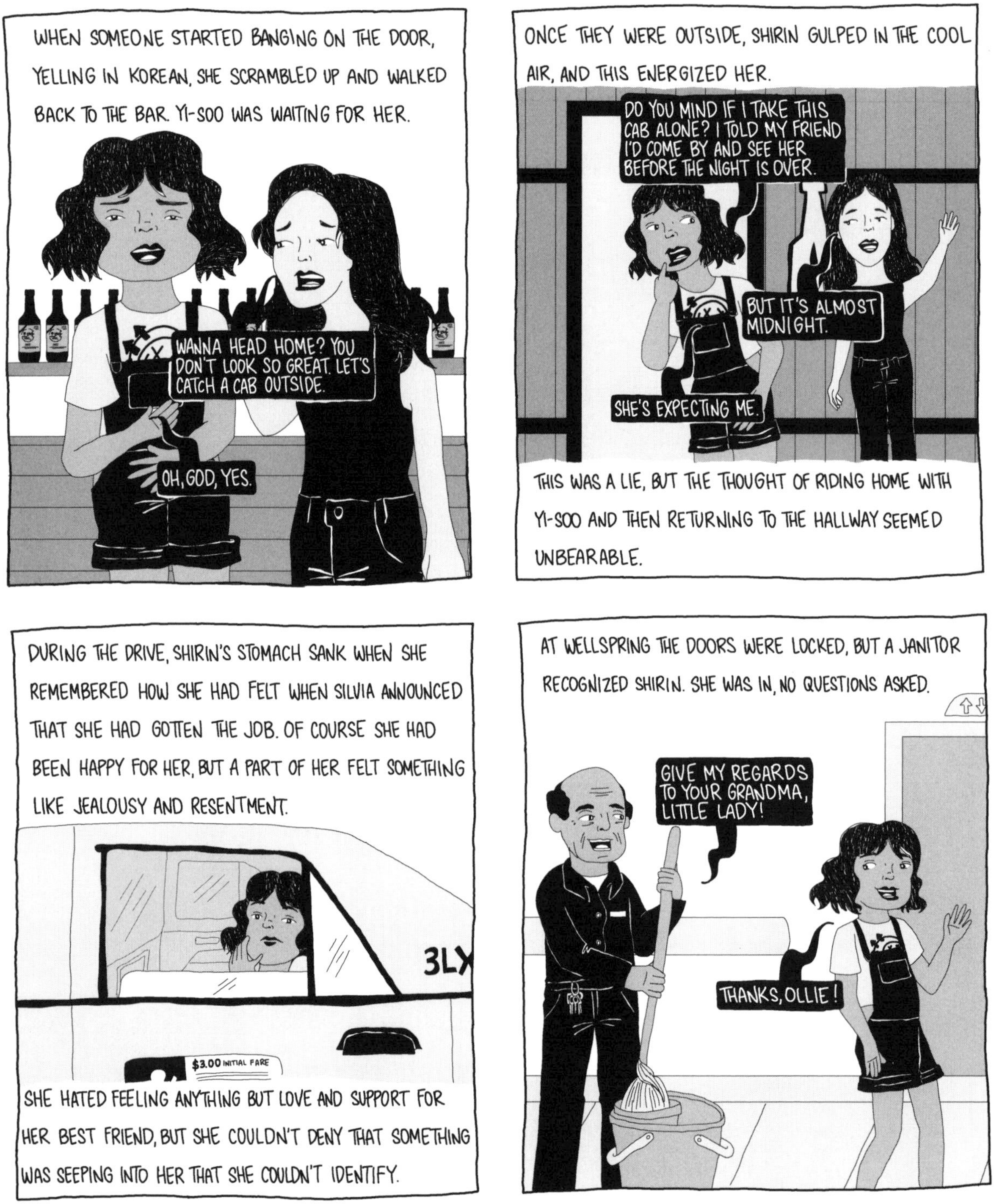
WHEN SOMEONE STARTED BANGING ON THE DOOR, YELLING IN KOREAN, SHE SCRAMBLED UP AND WALKED BACK TO THE BAR. YI-SOO WAS WAITING FOR HER.
WANNA HEAD HOME? YOU DON'T LOOK SO GREAT. LET'S CATCH A CAB OUTSIDE.
OH, GOD, YES.
ONCE THEY WERE OUTSIDE, SHIRIN GULPED IN THE COOL AIR, AND THIS ENERGIZED HER.
DO YOU MIND IF I TAKE THIS CAB ALONE? I TOLD MY FRIEND I'D COME BY AND SEE HER BEFORE THE NIGHT IS OVER.
BUT IT'S ALMOST MIDNIGHT.
SHE'S EXPECTING ME.
THIS WAS A LIE, BUT THE THOUGHT OF RIDING HOME WITH YI-SOO AND THEN RETURNING TO THE HALLWAY SEEMED UNBEARABLE.
DURING THE DRIVE, SHIRIN'S STOMACH SANK WHEN SHE REMEMBERED HOW SHE HAD FELT WHEN SILVIA ANNOUNCED THAT SHE HAD GOTTEN THE JOB. OF COURSE SHE HAD BEEN HAPPY FOR HER, BUT A PART OF HER FELT SOMETHING LIKE JEALOUSY AND RESENTMENT.
3LX
$3.00 INITIAL FARE
SHE HATED FEELING ANYTHING BUT LOVE AND SUPPORT FOR HER BEST FRIEND, BUT SHE COULDN'T DENY THAT SOMETHING WAS SEEPING INTO HER THAT SHE COULDN'T IDENTIFY.
AT WELLSPRING THE DOORS WERE LOCKED, BUT A JANITOR RECOGNIZED SHIRIN. SHE WAS IN, NO QUESTIONS ASKED.
GIVE MY REGARDS TO YOUR GRANDMA, LITTLE LADY!
THANKS, OLLIE!

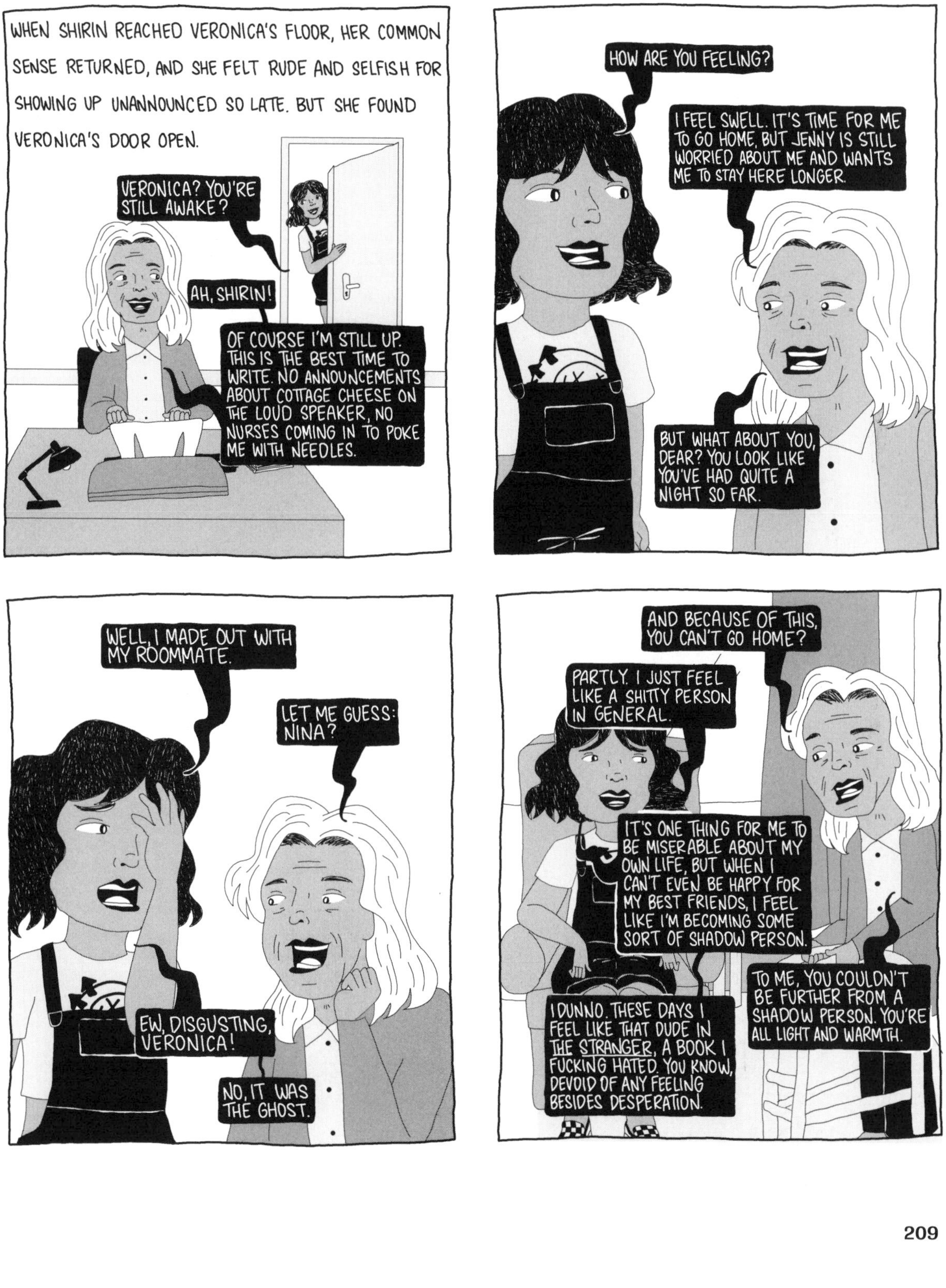
WHEN SHIRIN REACHED VERONICA'S FLOOR, HER COMMON SENSE RETURNED, AND SHE FELT RUDE AND SELFISH FOR SHOWING UP UNANNOUNCED SO LATE. BUT SHE FOUND VERONICA'S DOOR OPEN.
VERONICA? YOU'RE STILL AWAKE?
AH, SHIRIN!
OF COURSE I'M STILL UP. THIS IS THE BEST TIME TO WRITE. NO ANNOUNCEMENTS ABOUT COTTAGE CHEESE ON THE LOUD SPEAKER, NO NURSES COMING IN TO POKE ME WITH NEEDLES.
HOW ARE YOU FEELING?
I FEEL SWELL. IT'S TIME FOR ME TO GO HOME, BUT JENNY IS STILL WORRIED ABOUT ME AND WANTS ME TO STAY HERE LONGER.
BUT WHAT ABOUT YOU, DEAR? YOU LOOK LIKE YOU'VE HAD QUITE A NIGHT SO FAR.
WELL, I MADE OUT WITH MY ROOMMATE.
LET ME GUESS: NINA?
EW, DISGUSTING, VERONICA!
NO, IT WAS THE GHOST.
AND BECAUSE OF THIS, YOU CAN'T GO HOME?
PARTLY. I JUST FEEL LIKE A SHITTY PERSON IN GENERAL.
IT'S ONE THING FOR ME TO BE MISERABLE ABOUT MY OWN LIFE, BUT WHEN I CAN'T EVEN BE HAPPY FOR MY BEST FRIENDS, I FEEL LIKE I'M BECOMING SOME SORT OF SHADOW PERSON.
I DUNNO. THESE DAYS I FEEL LIKE THAT DUDE IN THE STRANGER, A BOOK I FUCKING HATED. YOU KNOW, DEVOID OF ANY FEELING BESIDES DESPERATION.
TO ME, YOU COULDN'T BE FURTHER FROM A SHADOW PERSON. YOU'RE ALL LIGHT AND WARMTH.

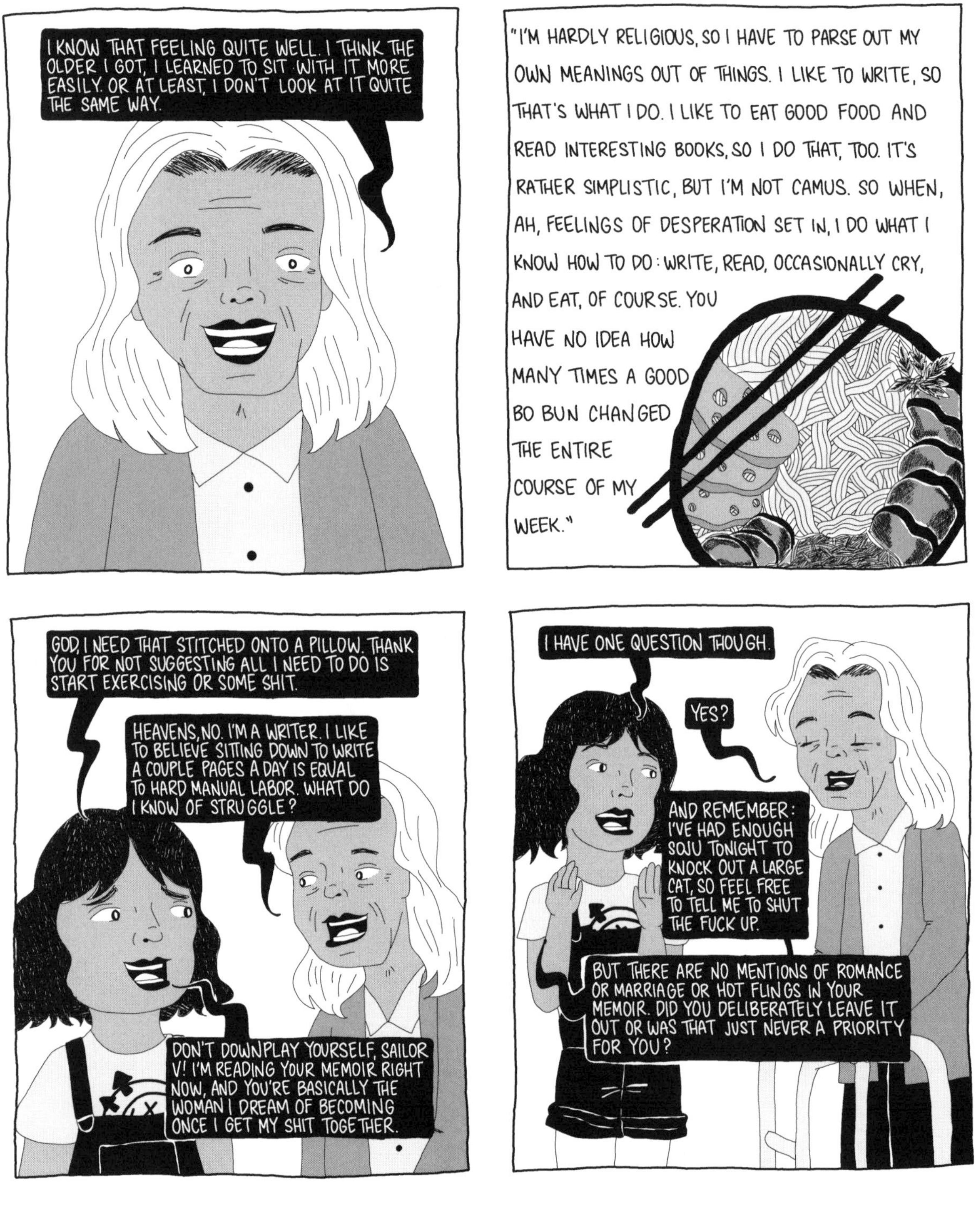
I KNOW THAT FEELING QUITE WELL. I THINK THE OLDER I GOT, I LEARNED TO SIT WITH IT MORE EASILY. OR AT LEAST, I DON'T LOOK AT IT QUITE THE SAME WAY.
"I'M HARDLY RELIGIOUS, SO I HAVE TO PARSE OUT MY OWN MEANINGS OUT OF THINGS. I LIKE TO WRITE, SO THAT'S WHAT I DO. I LIKE TO EAT GOOD FOOD AND READ INTERESTING BOOKS, SO I DO THAT, TOO. IT'S RATHER SIMPLISTIC, BUT I'M NOT CAMUS. SO WHEN, AH, FEELINGS OF DESPERATION SET IN, I DO WHAT I KNOW HOW TO DO: WRITE, READ, OCCASIONALLY CRY, AND EAT, OF COURSE. YOU HAVE NO IDEA HOW MANY TIMES A GOOD BO BUN CHANGED THE ENTIRE COURSE OF MY WEEK."
GOD, I NEED THAT STITCHED ONTO A PILLOW. THANK YOU FOR NOT SUGGESTING ALL I NEED TO DO IS START EXERCISING OR SOME SHIT.
HEAVENS, NO. I'M A WRITER. I LIKE TO BELIEVE SITTING DOWN TO WRITE A COUPLE PAGES A DAY IS EQUAL TO HARD MANUAL LABOR. WHAT DO I KNOW OF STRUGGLE?
DON'T DOWNPLAY YOURSELF, SAILOR V! I'M READING YOUR MEMOIR RIGHT NOW, AND YOU'RE BASICALLY THE WOMAN I DREAM OF BECOMING ONCE I GET MY SHIT TOGETHER.
I HAVE ONE QUESTION THOUGH.
YES?
AND REMEMBER: I'VE HAD ENOUGH SOJU TONIGHT TO KNOCK OUT A LARGE CAT, SO FEEL FREE TO TELL ME TO SHUT THE FUCK UP.
BUT THERE ARE NO MENTIONS OF ROMANCE OR MARRIAGE OR HOT FLINGS IN YOUR MEMOIR. DID YOU DELIBERATELY LEAVE IT OUT OR WAS THAT JUST NEVER A PRIORITY FOR YOU?

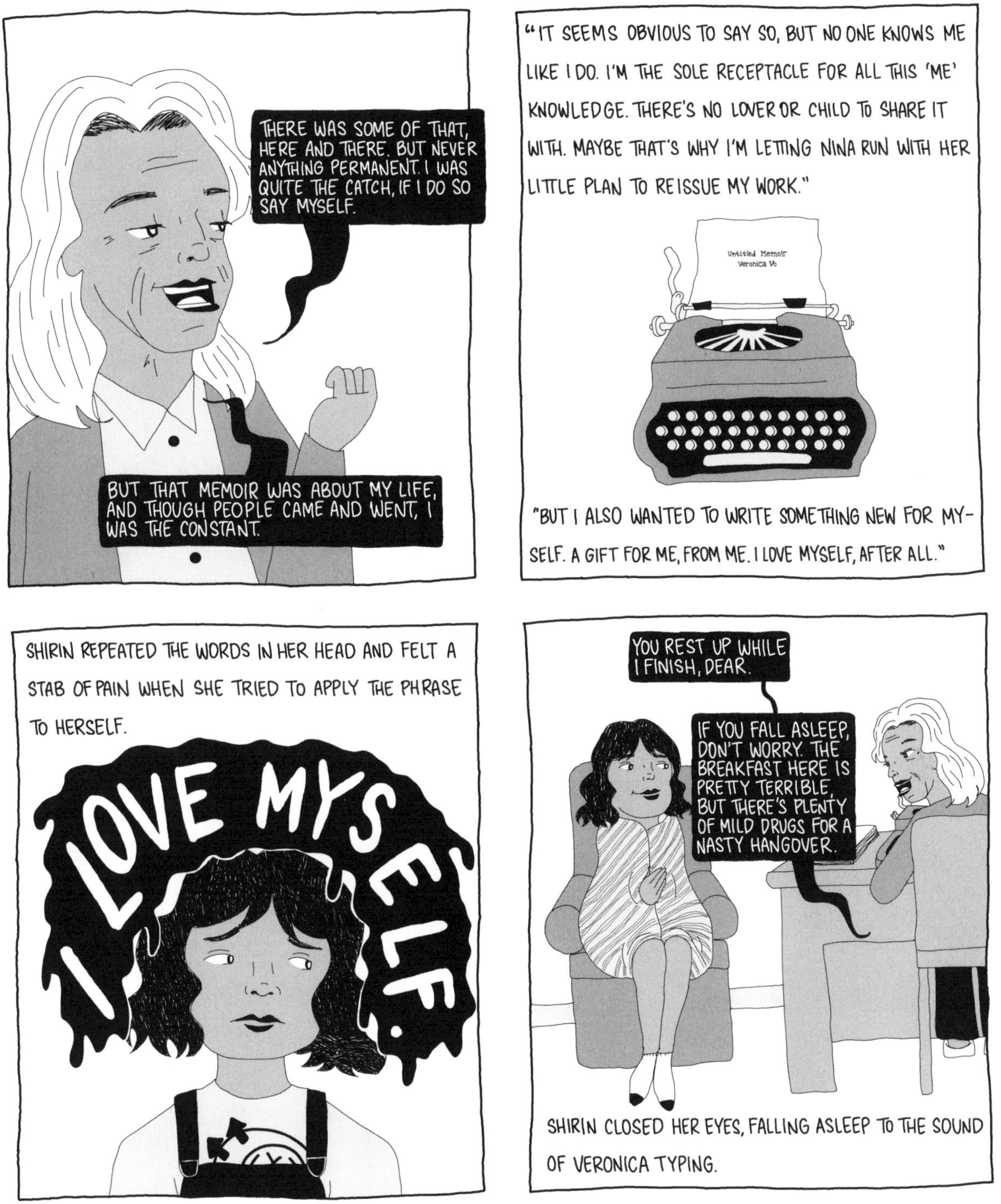
THERE WAS SOME OF THAT, HERE AND THERE. BUT NEVER ANYTHING PERMANENT. I WAS QUITE THE CATCH, IF I DO SO SAY MYSELF.
BUT THAT MEMOIR WAS ABOUT MY LIFE, AND THOUGH PEOPLE CAME AND WENT, I WAS THE CONSTANT.
"IT SEEMS OBVIOUS TO SAY SO, BUT NO ONE KNOWS ME LIKE I DO. I'M THE SOLE RECEPTACLE FOR ALL THIS 'ME' KNOWLEDGE. THERE'S NO LOVER OR CHILD TO SHARE IT WITH. MAYBE THAT'S WHY I'M LETTING NINA RUN WITH HER LITTLE PLAN TO REISSUE MY WORK."
Untitled Memoir
Veronica Vo
"BUT I ALSO WANTED TO WRITE SOMETHING NEW FOR MYSELF. A GIFT FOR ME, FROM ME. I LOVE MYSELF, AFTER ALL."
SHIRIN REPEATED THE WORDS IN HER HEAD AND FELT A STAB OF PAIN WHEN SHE TRIED TO APPLY THE PHRASE TO HERSELF.
I LOVE MYSELF.
YOU REST UP WHILE I FINISH, DEAR.
IF YOU FALL ASLEEP, DON'T WORRY. THE BREAKFAST HERE IS PRETTY TERRIBLE, BUT THERE'S PLENTY OF MILD DRUGS FOR A NASTY HANGOVER.
SHIRIN CLOSED HER EYES, FALLING ASLEEP TO THE SOUND OF VERONICA TYPING.

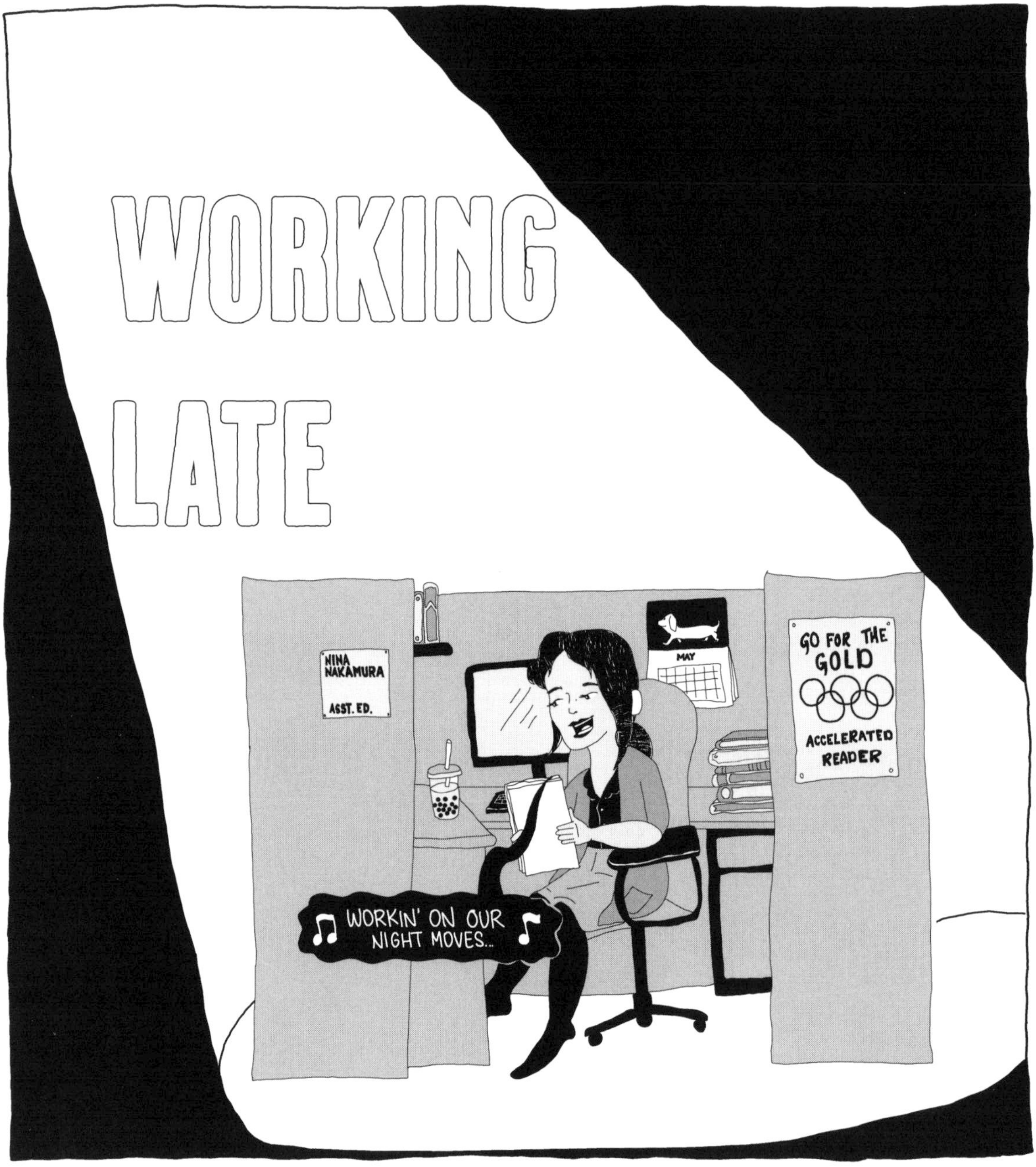
WORKING
LATE
NINA NAKAMURA
ASST. ED.
MAY
GO FOR THE GOLD
ACCELERATED READER
WORKIN' ON OUR NIGHT MOVES...

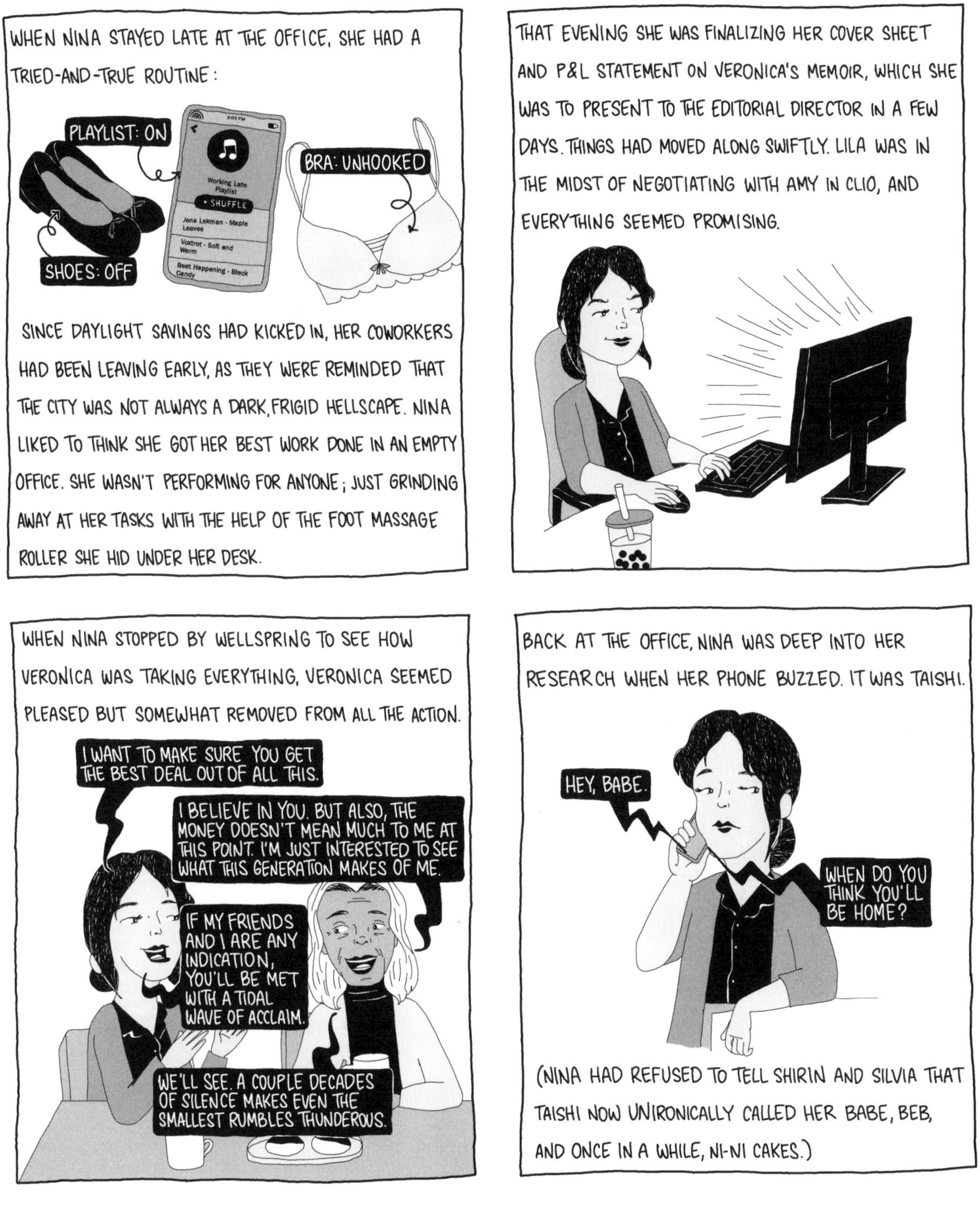
WHEN NINA STAYED LATE AT THE OFFICE, SHE HAD A TRIED-AND-TRUE ROUTINE:
PLAYLIST: ON
Working Late Playlist
SHUFFLE
Jens Lekman - Maple Leaves
Voxtrot - Soft and Warm
BRA: UNHOOKED
SHOES: OFF
SINCE DAYLIGHT SAVINGS HAD KICKED IN, HER COWORKERS HAD BEEN LEAVING EARLY, AS THEY WERE REMINDED THAT THE CITY WAS NOT ALWAYS A DARK, FRIGID HELLSCAPE. NINA LIKED TO THINK SHE GOT HER BEST WORK DONE IN AN EMPTY OFFICE. SHE WASN'T PERFORMING FOR ANYONE; JUST GRINDING AWAY AT HER TASKS WITH THE HELP OF THE FOOT MASSAGE ROLLER SHE HID UNDER HER DESK.
THAT EVENING SHE WAS FINALIZING HER COVER SHEET AND P&L STATEMENT ON VERONICA'S MEMOIR, WHICH SHE WAS TO PRESENT TO THE EDITORIAL DIRECTOR IN A FEW DAYS. THINGS HAD MOVED ALONG SWIFTLY. LILA WAS IN THE MIDST OF NEGOTIATING WITH AMY IN CLIO, AND EVERYTHING SEEMED PROMISING.
WHEN NINA STOPPED BY WELLSPRING TO SEE HOW VERONICA WAS TAKING EVERYTHING, VERONICA SEEMED PLEASED BUT SOMEWHAT REMOVED FROM ALL THE ACTION.
I WANT TO MAKE SURE YOU GET THE BEST DEAL OUT OF ALL THIS.
I BELIEVE IN YOU. BUT ALSO, THE MONEY DOESN'T MEAN MUCH TO ME AT THIS POINT. I'M JUST INTERESTED TO SEE WHAT THIS GENERATION MAKES OF ME.
IF MY FRIENDS AND I ARE ANY INDICATION, YOU'LL BE MET WITH A TIDAL WAVE OF ACCLAIM.
WE'LL SEE. A COUPLE DECADES OF SILENCE MAKES EVEN THE SMALLEST RUMBLES THUNDEROUS.
BACK AT THE OFFICE, NINA WAS DEEP INTO HER RESEARCH WHEN HER PHONE BUZZED. IT WAS TAISHI.
HEY, BABE.
WHEN DO YOU THINK YOU'LL BE HOME?
(NINA HAD REFUSED TO TELL SHIRIN AND SILVIA THAT TAISHI NOW UNIRONICALLY CALLED HER BABE, BEB, AND ONCE IN A WHILE, NI-NI CAKES.)

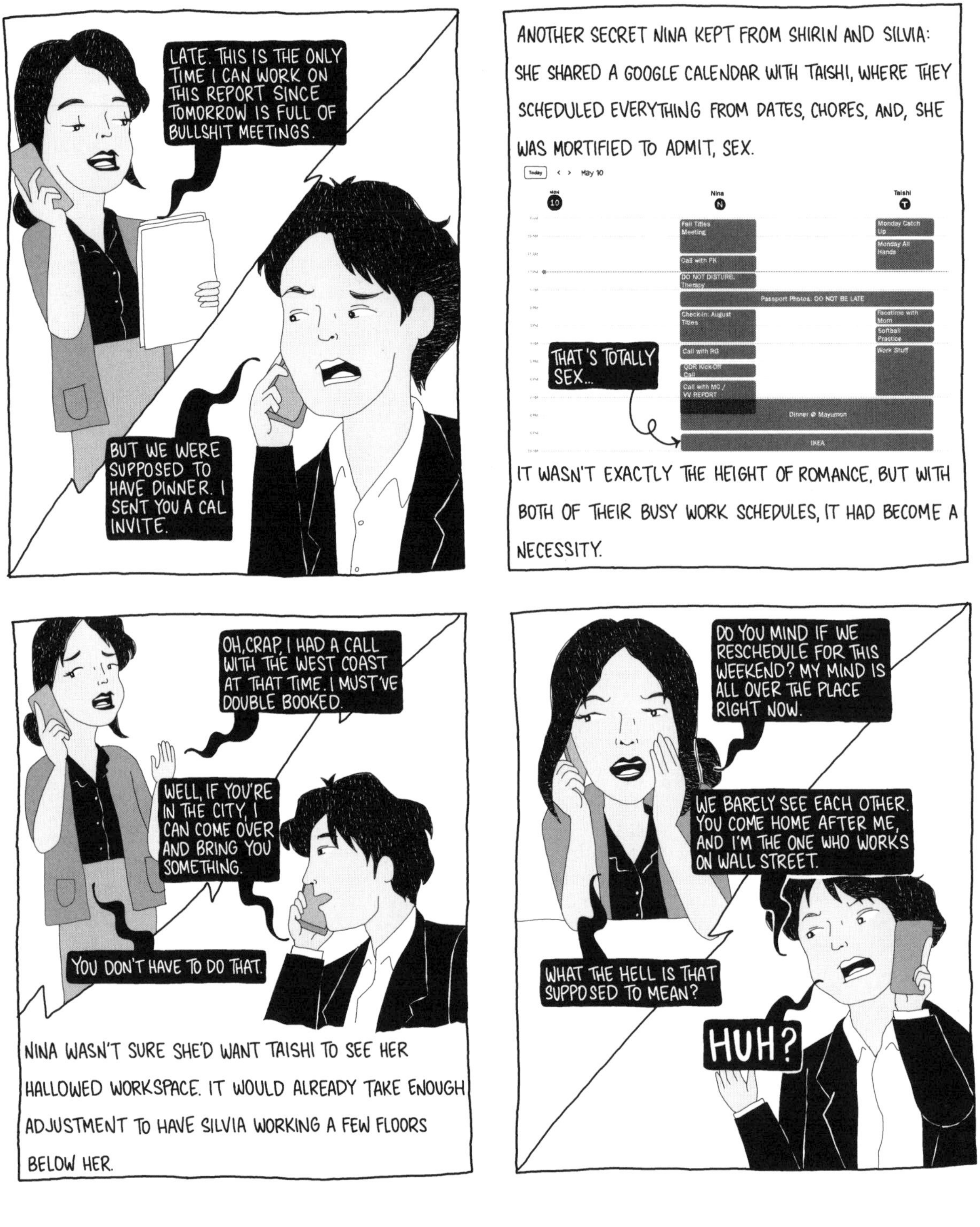
LATE. THIS IS THE ONLY TIME I CAN WORK ON THIS REPORT SINCE TOMORROW IS FULL OF BULLSHIT MEETINGS.
BUT WE WERE SUPPOSED TO HAVE DINNER. I SENT YOU A CAL INVITE.
ANOTHER SECRET NINA KEPT FROM SHIRIN AND SILVIA: SHE SHARED A GOOGLE CALENDAR WITH TAISHI, WHERE THEY SCHEDULED EVERYTHING FROM DATES, CHORES, AND, SHE WAS MORTIFIED TO ADMIT, SEX.
Today
May 10
MON
10
Nina
Taishi
Fall Titles Meeting
Call with PK
DO NOT DISTURB: Therapy
Monday Catch Up
Monday All Hands
Passport Photos: DO NOT BE LATE
Check-In: August Titles
Facetime with Mom
Softball Practice
Call with RG
QDR Kick-Off Call
Call with MC / VV REPORT
Work Stuff
Dinner @ Mayumon
IKEA
THAT'S TOTALLY SEX...
IT WASN'T EXACTLY THE HEIGHT OF ROMANCE, BUT WITH BOTH OF THEIR BUSY WORK SCHEDULES, IT HAD BECOME A NECESSITY.
OH, CRAP, I HAD A CALL WITH THE WEST COAST AT THAT TIME. I MUST'VE DOUBLE BOOKED.
WELL, IF YOU'RE IN THE CITY, I CAN COME OVER AND BRING YOU SOMETHING.
YOU DON'T HAVE TO DO THAT.
NINA WASN'T SURE SHE'D WANT TAISHI TO SEE HER HALLOWED WORKSPACE. IT WOULD ALREADY TAKE ENOUGH ADJUSTMENT TO HAVE SILVIA WORKING A FEW FLOORS BELOW HER.
DO YOU MIND IF WE RESCHEDULE FOR THIS WEEKEND? MY MIND IS ALL OVER THE PLACE RIGHT NOW.
WE BARELY SEE EACH OTHER. YOU COME HOME AFTER ME, AND I'M THE ONE WHO WORKS ON WALL STREET.
WHAT THE HELL IS THAT SUPPOSED TO MEAN?
HUH?

NINA KNEW SHE WAS PICKING A FIGHT, BUT SHE COULDN'T STOP HERSELF.

ARE YOU IMPLYING THAT JUST BECAUSE I WORK WITH BOOKS AND NOT FINANCE, I SHOULDN'T GIVE A SHIT ABOUT MY JOB?

WHERE THE HELL DID YOU COME UP WITH THAT? I JUST WANTED TO HAVE DINNER WITH YOU TONIGHT.

I TOLD YOU: I'M BUSY.

FINE. I'M GOING OUT WITH COWORKERS TONIGHT THEN.

SHE HUNG UP AND TRIED TO GET BACK TO WORK.

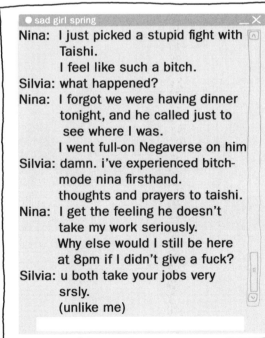

● sad girl spring

Nina: I just picked a stupid fight with Taishi.
I feel like such a bitch.
Silvia: what happened?
Nina: I forgot we were having dinner tonight, and he called just to see where I was.
I went full-on Negaverse on him
Silvia: damn. i've experienced bitch-mode nina firsthand.
thoughts and prayers to taishi.
Nina: I get the feeling he doesn't take my work seriously.
Why else would I still be here at 8pm if I didn't give a fuck?
Silvia: u both take your jobs very srsly.
(unlike me)

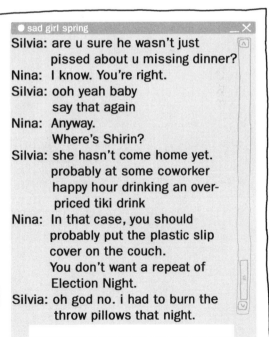

● sad girl spring

Silvia: are u sure he wasn't just pissed about u missing dinner?
Nina: I know. You're right.
Silvia: ooh yeah baby
say that again
Nina: Anyway.
Where's Shirin?
Silvia: she hasn't come home yet.
probably at some coworker happy hour drinking an over-priced tiki drink
Nina: In that case, you should probably put the plastic slip cover on the couch.
You don't want a repeat of Election Night.
Silvia: oh god no. i had to burn the throw pillows that night.

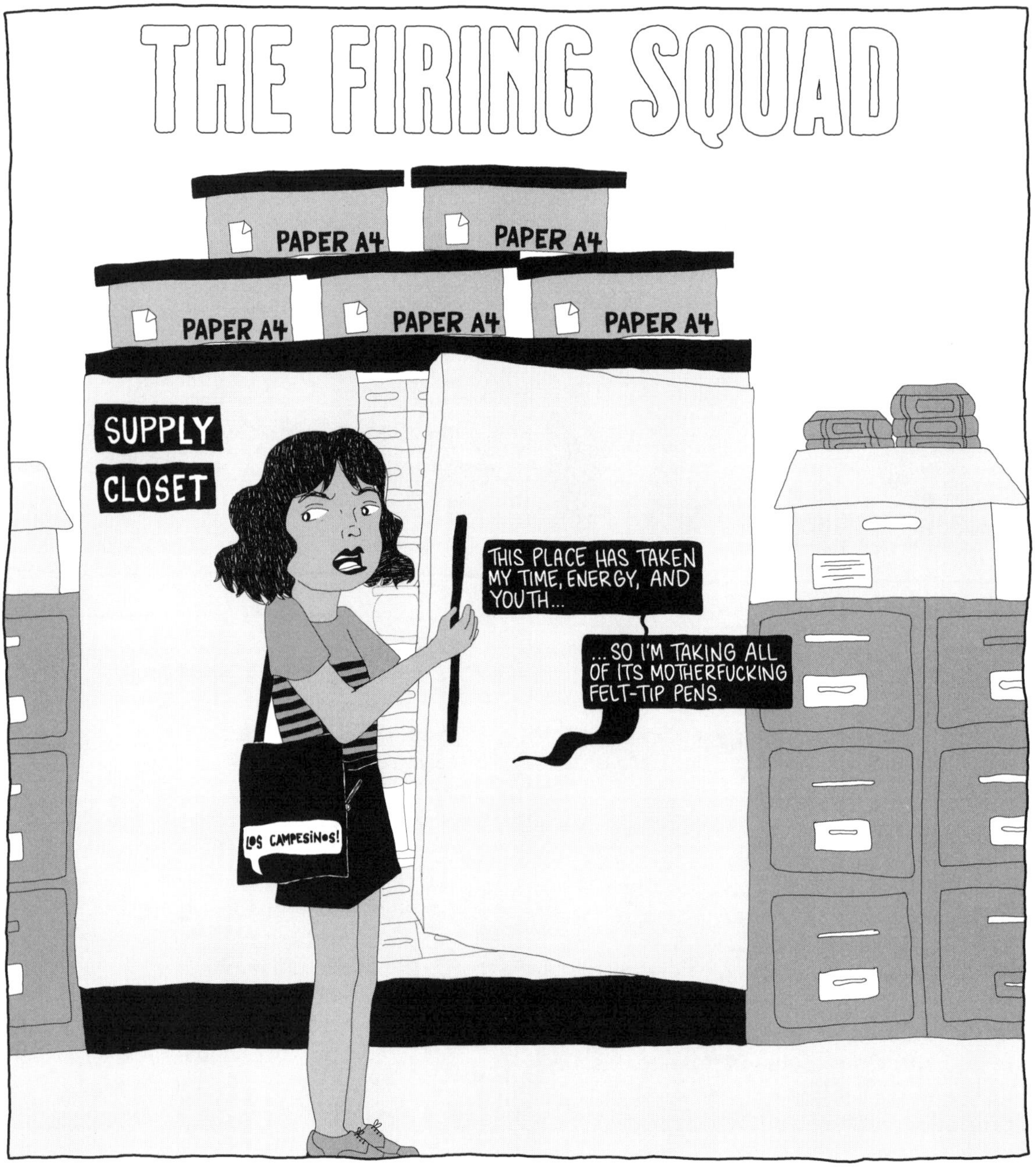
THE FIRING SQUAD
PAPER A4
PAPER A4
PAPER A4
PAPER A4
PAPER A4
SUPPLY
CLOSET
THIS PLACE HAS TAKEN MY TIME, ENERGY, AND YOUTH...
...SO I'M TAKING ALL OF ITS MOTHERFUCKING FELT-TIP PENS.
LOS CAMPESINOS!

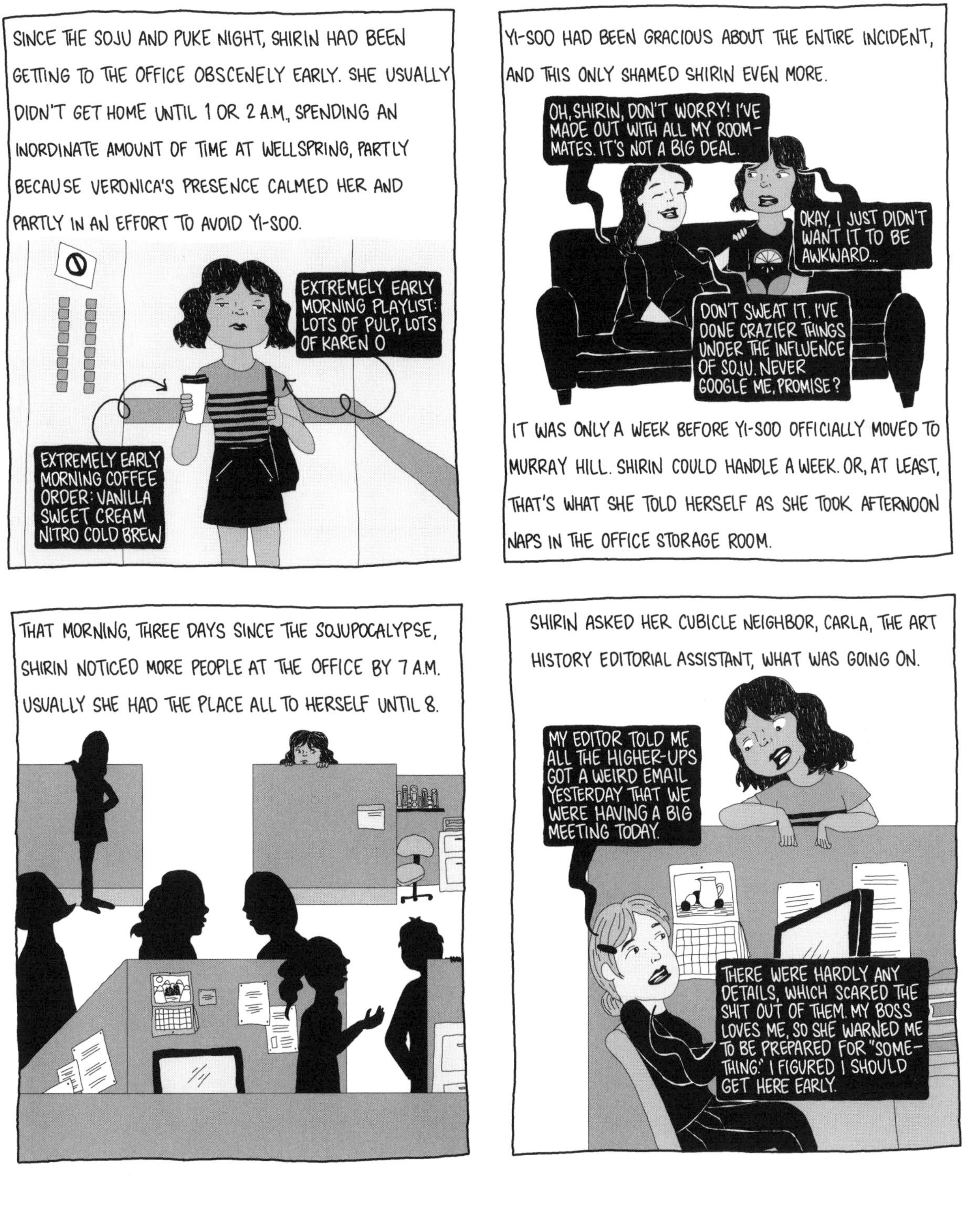
SINCE THE SOJU AND PUKE NIGHT, SHIRIN HAD BEEN GETTING TO THE OFFICE OBSCENELY EARLY. SHE USUALLY DIDN'T GET HOME UNTIL 1 OR 2 A.M., SPENDING AN INORDINATE AMOUNT OF TIME AT WELLSPRING, PARTLY BECAUSE VERONICA'S PRESENCE CALMED HER AND PARTLY IN AN EFFORT TO AVOID YI-SOO.
EXTREMELY EARLY MORNING PLAYLIST: LOTS OF PULP, LOTS OF KAREN O
EXTREMELY EARLY MORNING COFFEE ORDER: VANILLA SWEET CREAM NITRO COLD BREW
YI-SOO HAD BEEN GRACIOUS ABOUT THE ENTIRE INCIDENT, AND THIS ONLY SHAMED SHIRIN EVEN MORE.
OH, SHIRIN, DON'T WORRY! I'VE MADE OUT WITH ALL MY ROOMMATES. IT'S NOT A BIG DEAL.
OKAY, I JUST DIDN'T WANT IT TO BE AWKWARD...
DON'T SWEAT IT. I'VE DONE CRAZIER THINGS UNDER THE INFLUENCE OF SOJU. NEVER GOOGLE ME, PROMISE?
IT WAS ONLY A WEEK BEFORE YI-SOO OFFICIALLY MOVED TO MURRAY HILL. SHIRIN COULD HANDLE A WEEK. OR, AT LEAST, THAT'S WHAT SHE TOLD HERSELF AS SHE TOOK AFTERNOON NAPS IN THE OFFICE STORAGE ROOM.
THAT MORNING, THREE DAYS SINCE THE SOJUPOCALYPSE, SHIRIN NOTICED MORE PEOPLE AT THE OFFICE BY 7 A.M. USUALLY SHE HAD THE PLACE ALL TO HERSELF UNTIL 8.
SHIRIN ASKED HER CUBICLE NEIGHBOR, CARLA, THE ART HISTORY EDITORIAL ASSISTANT, WHAT WAS GOING ON.
MY EDITOR TOLD ME ALL THE HIGHER-UPS GOT A WEIRD EMAIL YESTERDAY THAT WE WERE HAVING A BIG MEETING TODAY.
THERE WERE HARDLY ANY DETAILS, WHICH SCARED THE SHIT OUT OF THEM. MY BOSS LOVES ME, SO SHE WARNED ME TO BE PREPARED FOR "SOMETHING." I FIGURED I SHOULD GET HERE EARLY.

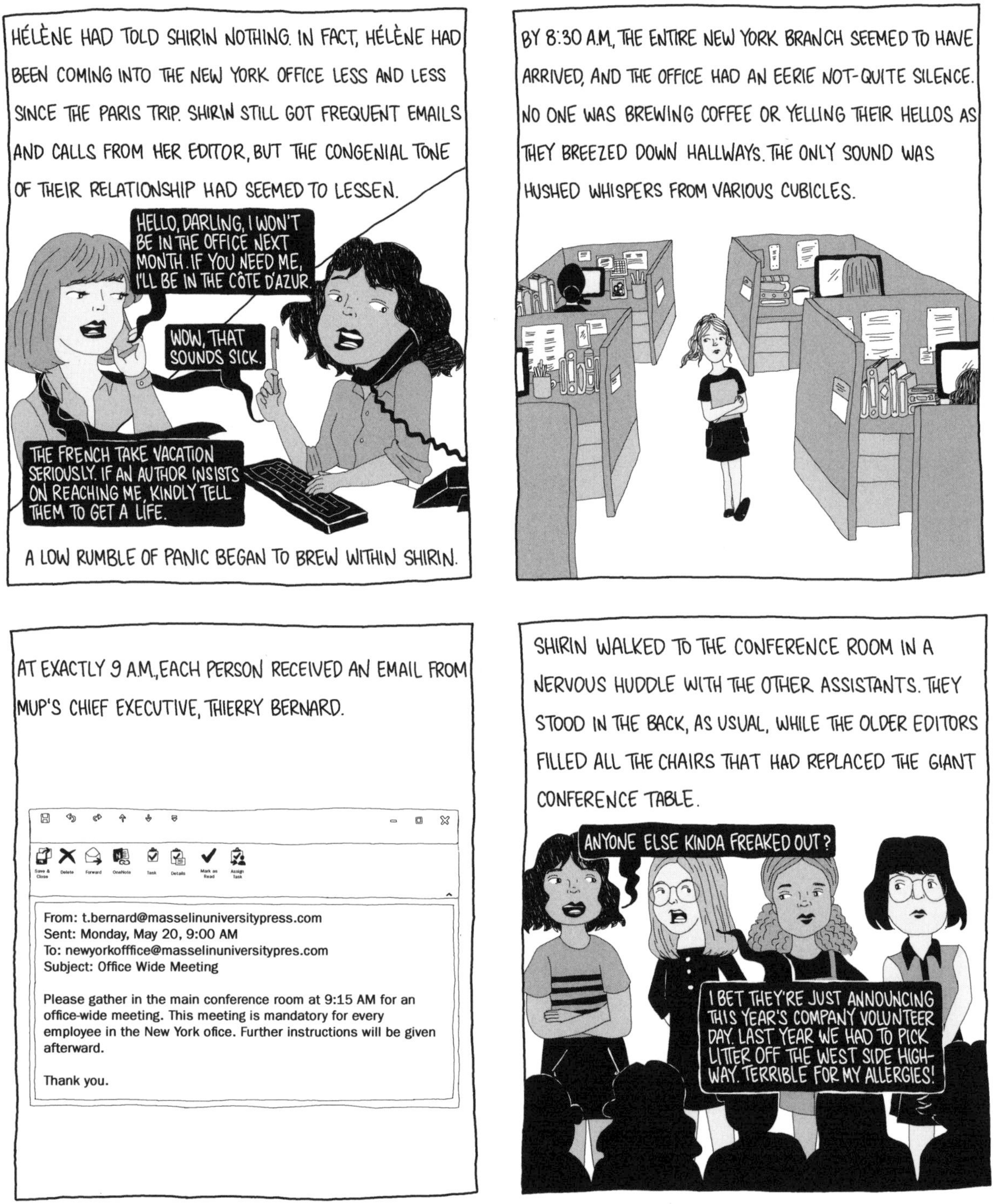
HÉLÈNE HAD TOLD SHIRIN NOTHING. IN FACT, HÉLÈNE HAD BEEN COMING INTO THE NEW YORK OFFICE LESS AND LESS SINCE THE PARIS TRIP. SHIRIN STILL GOT FREQUENT EMAILS AND CALLS FROM HER EDITOR, BUT THE CONGENIAL TONE OF THEIR RELATIONSHIP HAD SEEMED TO LESSEN.
HELLO, DARLING, I WON'T BE IN THE OFFICE NEXT MONTH. IF YOU NEED ME, I'LL BE IN THE CÔTE D'AZUR.
WOW, THAT SOUNDS SICK.
THE FRENCH TAKE VACATION SERIOUSLY. IF AN AUTHOR INSISTS ON REACHING ME, KINDLY TELL THEM TO GET A LIFE.
A LOW RUMBLE OF PANIC BEGAN TO BREW WITHIN SHIRIN.
BY 8:30 A.M., THE ENTIRE NEW YORK BRANCH SEEMED TO HAVE ARRIVED, AND THE OFFICE HAD AN EERIE NOT-QUITE SILENCE. NO ONE WAS BREWING COFFEE OR YELLING THEIR HELLOS AS THEY BREEZED DOWN HALLWAYS. THE ONLY SOUND WAS HUSHED WHISPERS FROM VARIOUS CUBICLES.
AT EXACTLY 9 A.M., EACH PERSON RECEIVED AN EMAIL FROM MUP'S CHIEF EXECUTIVE, THIERRY BERNARD.
Save & Close
Delete
Forward
OneNote
Task
Details
Mark as Read
Assign Task
From: t.bernard@masselinuniversitypress.com
Sent: Monday, May 20, 9:00 AM
To: newyorkofffice@masselinuniversitypres.com
Subject: Office Wide Meeting
Please gather in the main conference room at 9:15 AM for an office-wide meeting. This meeting is mandatory for every employee in the New York ofice. Further instructions will be given afterward.
Thank you.
SHIRIN WALKED TO THE CONFERENCE ROOM IN A NERVOUS HUDDLE WITH THE OTHER ASSISTANTS. THEY STOOD IN THE BACK, AS USUAL, WHILE THE OLDER EDITORS FILLED ALL THE CHAIRS THAT HAD REPLACED THE GIANT CONFERENCE TABLE.
ANYONE ELSE KINDA FREAKED OUT?
I BET THEY'RE JUST ANNOUNCING THIS YEAR'S COMPANY VOLUNTEER DAY. LAST YEAR WE HAD TO PICK LITTER OFF THE WEST SIDE HIGHWAY. TERRIBLE FOR MY ALLERGIES!

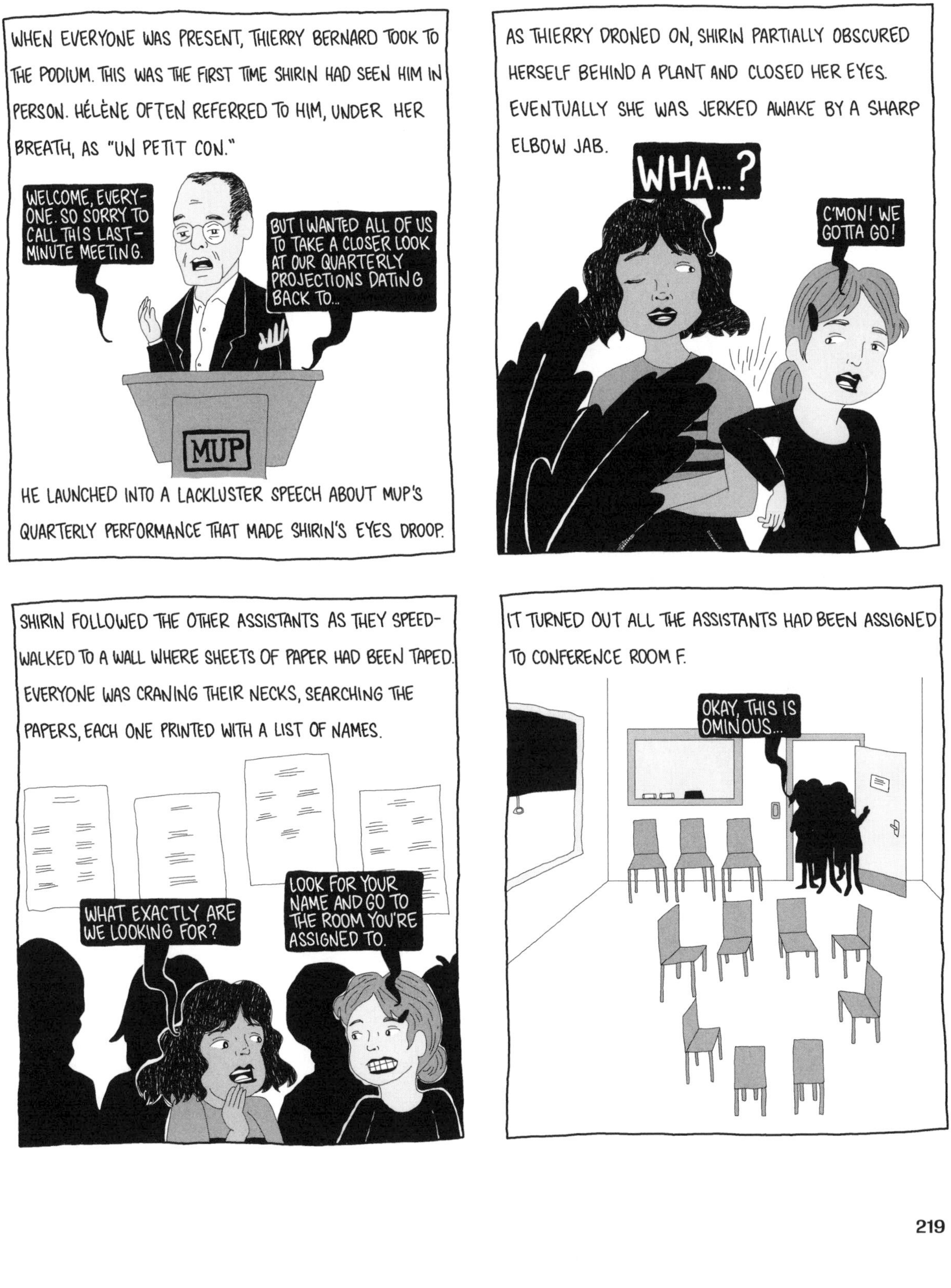
WHEN EVERYONE WAS PRESENT, THIERRY BERNARD TOOK TO THE PODIUM. THIS WAS THE FIRST TIME SHIRIN HAD SEEN HIM IN PERSON. HÉLÈNE OFTEN REFERRED TO HIM, UNDER HER BREATH, AS "UN PETIT CON."
WELCOME, EVERYONE. SO SORRY TO CALL THIS LAST-MINUTE MEETING.
BUT I WANTED ALL OF US TO TAKE A CLOSER LOOK AT OUR QUARTERLY PROJECTIONS DATING BACK TO...
MUP
HE LAUNCHED INTO A LACKLUSTER SPEECH ABOUT MUP'S QUARTERLY PERFORMANCE THAT MADE SHIRIN'S EYES DROOP.
AS THIERRY DRONED ON, SHIRIN PARTIALLY OBSCURED HERSELF BEHIND A PLANT AND CLOSED HER EYES. EVENTUALLY SHE WAS JERKED AWAKE BY A SHARP ELBOW JAB.
WHA...?
C'MON! WE GOTTA GO!
SHIRIN FOLLOWED THE OTHER ASSISTANTS AS THEY SPEED-WALKED TO A WALL WHERE SHEETS OF PAPER HAD BEEN TAPED. EVERYONE WAS CRANING THEIR NECKS, SEARCHING THE PAPERS, EACH ONE PRINTED WITH A LIST OF NAMES.
WHAT EXACTLY ARE WE LOOKING FOR?
LOOK FOR YOUR NAME AND GO TO THE ROOM YOU'RE ASSIGNED TO.
IT TURNED OUT ALL THE ASSISTANTS HAD BEEN ASSIGNED TO CONFERENCE ROOM F.
OKAY, THIS IS OMINOUS...

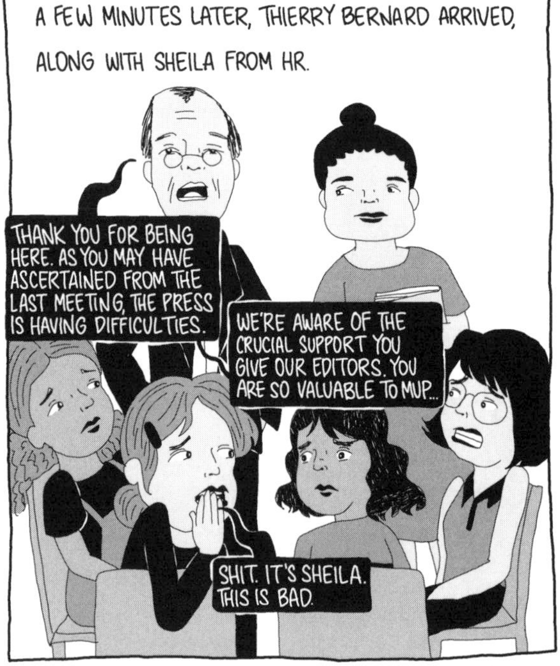
A FEW MINUTES LATER, THIERRY BERNARD ARRIVED, ALONG WITH SHEILA FROM HR.
THANK YOU FOR BEING HERE. AS YOU MAY HAVE ASCERTAINED FROM THE LAST MEETING, THE PRESS IS HAVING DIFFICULTIES.
WE'RE AWARE OF THE CRUCIAL SUPPORT YOU GIVE OUR EDITORS. YOU ARE SO VALUABLE TO MUP...
SHIT. IT'S SHEILA. THIS IS BAD.

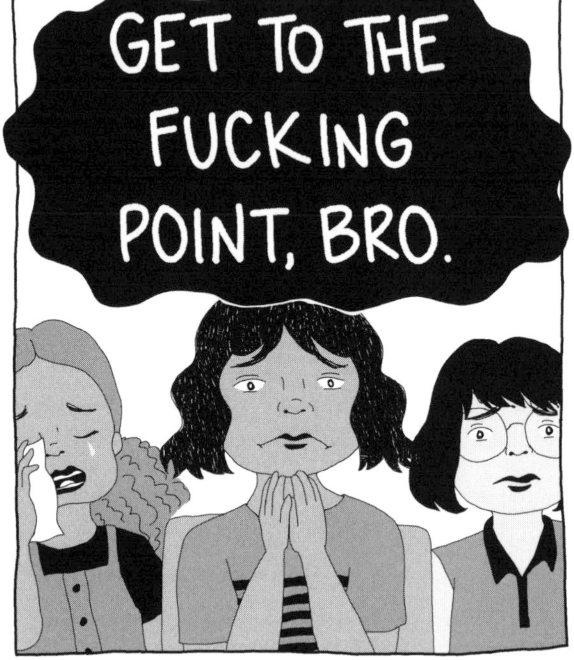
GET TO THE FUCKING POINT, BRO.

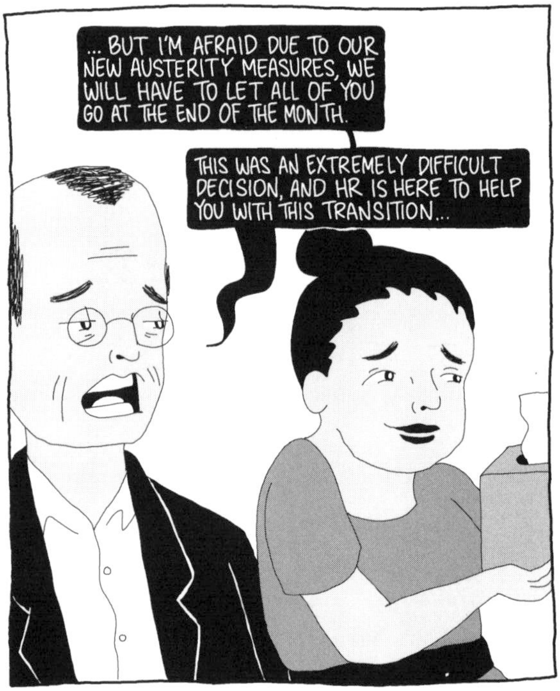
... BUT I'M AFRAID DUE TO OUR NEW AUSTERITY MEASURES, WE WILL HAVE TO LET ALL OF YOU GO AT THE END OF THE MONTH.
THIS WAS AN EXTREMELY DIFFICULT DECISION, AND HR IS HERE TO HELP YOU WITH THIS TRANSITION...

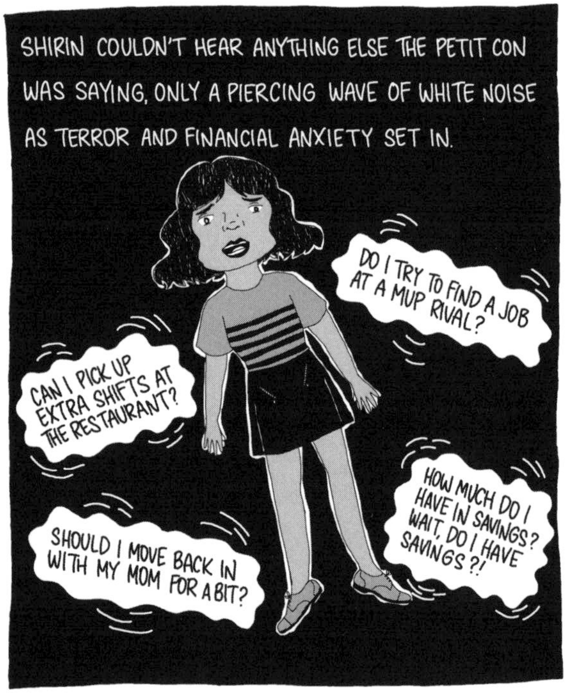
SHIRIN COULDN'T HEAR ANYTHING ELSE THE PETIT CON WAS SAYING, ONLY A PIERCING WAVE OF WHITE NOISE AS TERROR AND FINANCIAL ANXIETY SET IN.
DO I TRY TO FIND A JOB AT A MUP RIVAL?
CAN I PICK UP EXTRA SHIFTS AT THE RESTAURANT?
HOW MUCH DO I HAVE IN SAVINGS? WAIT, DO I HAVE SAVINGS?!
SHOULD I MOVE BACK IN WITH MY MOM FOR A BIT?

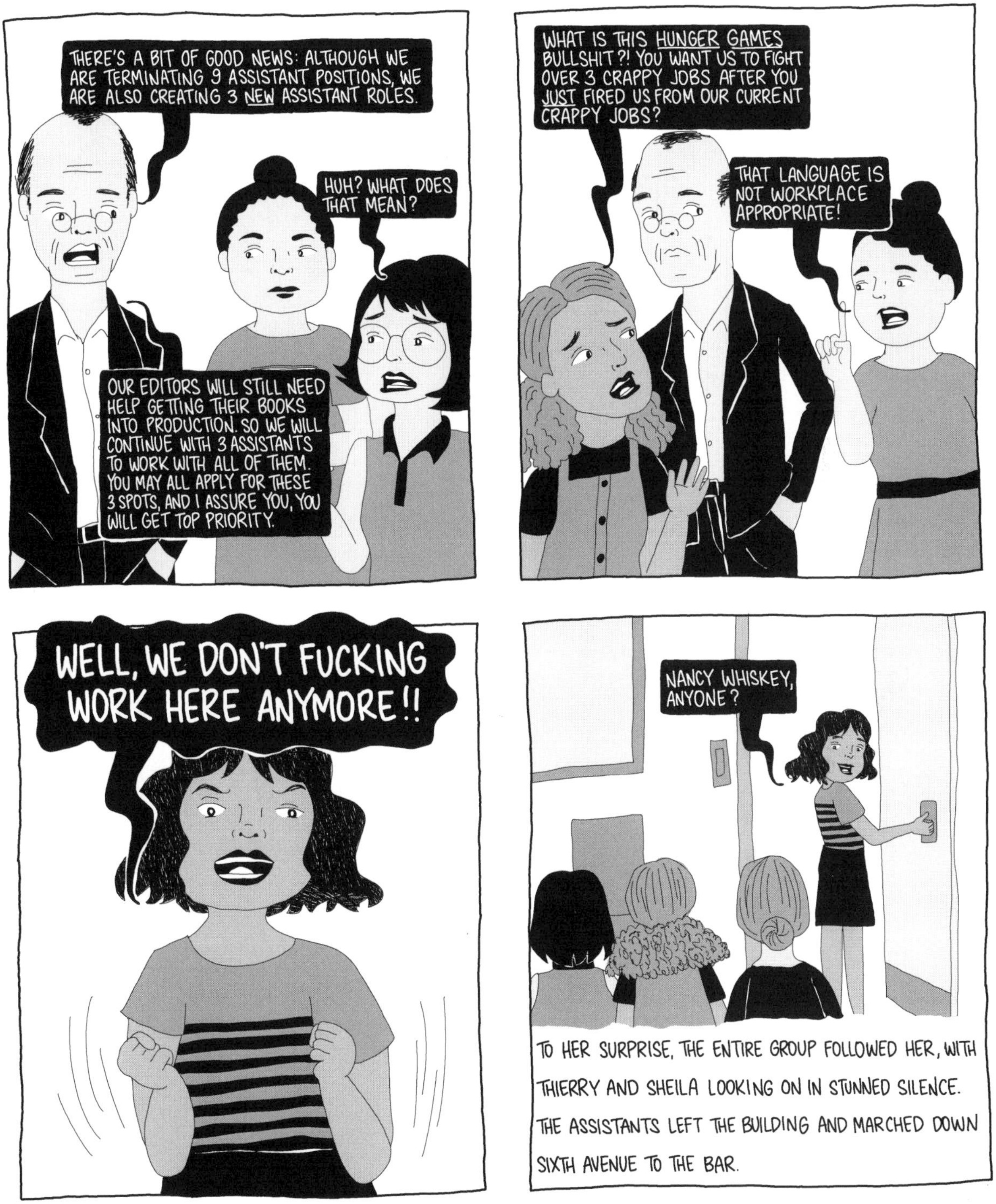
THERE'S A BIT OF GOOD NEWS: ALTHOUGH WE ARE TERMINATING 9 ASSISTANT POSITIONS, WE ARE ALSO CREATING 3 NEW ASSISTANT ROLES.
HUH? WHAT DOES THAT MEAN?
OUR EDITORS WILL STILL NEED HELP GETTING THEIR BOOKS INTO PRODUCTION. SO WE WILL CONTINUE WITH 3 ASSISTANTS TO WORK WITH ALL OF THEM. YOU MAY ALL APPLY FOR THESE 3 SPOTS, AND I ASSURE YOU, YOU WILL GET TOP PRIORITY.
WHAT IS THIS HUNGER GAMES BULLSHIT?! YOU WANT US TO FIGHT OVER 3 CRAPPY JOBS AFTER YOU JUST FIRED US FROM OUR CURRENT CRAPPY JOBS?
THAT LANGUAGE IS NOT WORKPLACE APPROPRIATE!
WELL, WE DON'T FUCKING WORK HERE ANYMORE!!
NANCY WHISKEY, ANYONE?
TO HER SURPRISE, THE ENTIRE GROUP FOLLOWED HER, WITH THIERRY AND SHEILA LOOKING ON IN STUNNED SILENCE. THE ASSISTANTS LEFT THE BUILDING AND MARCHED DOWN SIXTH AVENUE TO THE BAR.

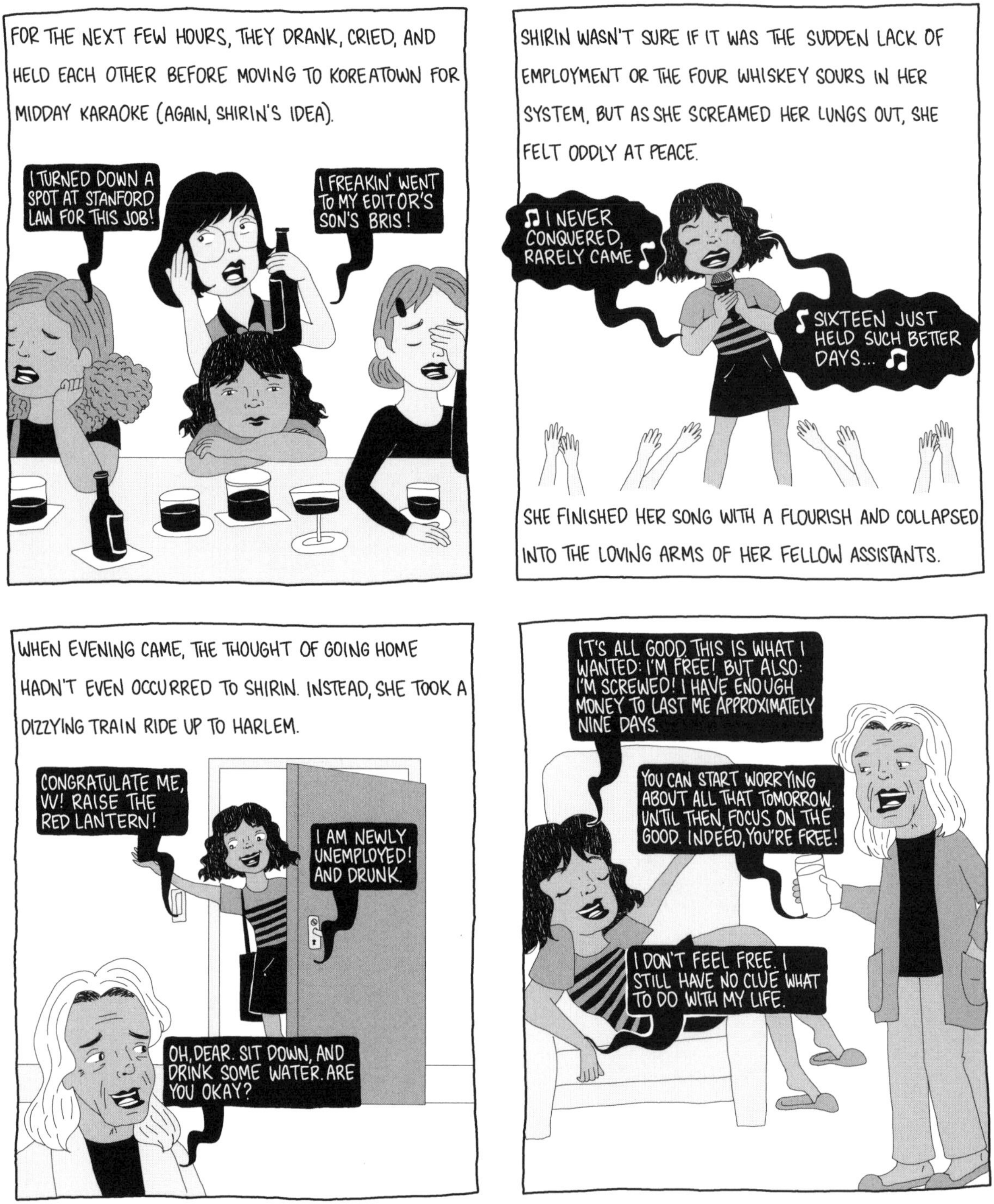
FOR THE NEXT FEW HOURS, THEY DRANK, CRIED, AND HELD EACH OTHER BEFORE MOVING TO KOREATOWN FOR MIDDAY KARAOKE (AGAIN, SHIRIN'S IDEA).
I TURNED DOWN A SPOT AT STANFORD LAW FOR THIS JOB!
I FREAKIN' WENT TO MY EDITOR'S SON'S BRIS!
SHIRIN WASN'T SURE IF IT WAS THE SUDDEN LACK OF EMPLOYMENT OR THE FOUR WHISKEY SOURS IN HER SYSTEM, BUT AS SHE SCREAMED HER LUNGS OUT, SHE FELT ODDLY AT PEACE.
♫ I NEVER CONQUERED, RARELY CAME ♪
♪ SIXTEEN JUST HELD SUCH BETTER DAYS... ♫
SHE FINISHED HER SONG WITH A FLOURISH AND COLLAPSED INTO THE LOVING ARMS OF HER FELLOW ASSISTANTS.
WHEN EVENING CAME, THE THOUGHT OF GOING HOME HADN'T EVEN OCCURRED TO SHIRIN. INSTEAD, SHE TOOK A DIZZYING TRAIN RIDE UP TO HARLEM.
CONGRATULATE ME, VV! RAISE THE RED LANTERN!
I AM NEWLY UNEMPLOYED! AND DRUNK.
OH, DEAR. SIT DOWN, AND DRINK SOME WATER. ARE YOU OKAY?
IT'S ALL GOOD. THIS IS WHAT I WANTED: I'M FREE! BUT ALSO: I'M SCREWED! I HAVE ENOUGH MONEY TO LAST ME APPROXIMATELY NINE DAYS.
YOU CAN START WORRYING ABOUT ALL THAT TOMORROW. UNTIL THEN, FOCUS ON THE GOOD. INDEED, YOU'RE FREE!
I DON'T FEEL FREE. I STILL HAVE NO CLUE WHAT TO DO WITH MY LIFE.

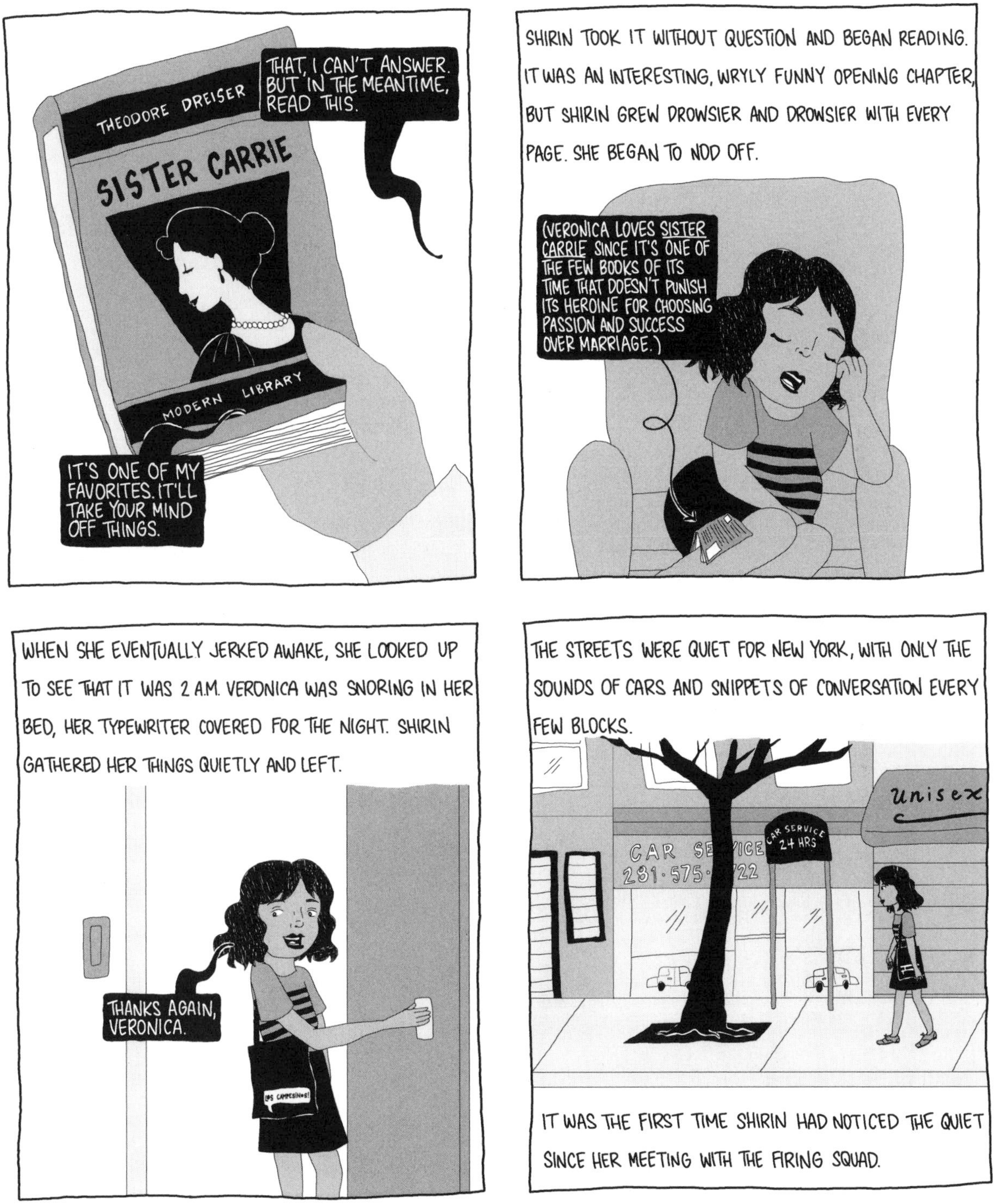
THAT, I CAN'T ANSWER. BUT IN THE MEANTIME, READ THIS.
THEODORE DREISER
SISTER CARRIE
MODERN LIBRARY
IT'S ONE OF MY FAVORITES. IT'LL TAKE YOUR MIND OFF THINGS.
SHIRIN TOOK IT WITHOUT QUESTION AND BEGAN READING. IT WAS AN INTERESTING, WRYLY FUNNY OPENING CHAPTER, BUT SHIRIN GREW DROWSIER AND DROWSIER WITH EVERY PAGE. SHE BEGAN TO NOD OFF.
(VERONICA LOVES SISTER CARRIE SINCE IT'S ONE OF THE FEW BOOKS OF ITS TIME THAT DOESN'T PUNISH ITS HEROINE FOR CHOOSING PASSION AND SUCCESS OVER MARRIAGE.)
WHEN SHE EVENTUALLY JERKED AWAKE, SHE LOOKED UP TO SEE THAT IT WAS 2 A.M. VERONICA WAS SNORING IN HER BED, HER TYPEWRITER COVERED FOR THE NIGHT. SHIRIN GATHERED HER THINGS QUIETLY AND LEFT.
THANKS AGAIN, VERONICA.
LOS CAMPESINOS!
THE STREETS WERE QUIET FOR NEW YORK, WITH ONLY THE SOUNDS OF CARS AND SNIPPETS OF CONVERSATION EVERY FEW BLOCKS.
unisex
CAR SERVICE 24 HRS
IT WAS THE FIRST TIME SHIRIN HAD NOTICED THE QUIET SINCE HER MEETING WITH THE FIRING SQUAD.

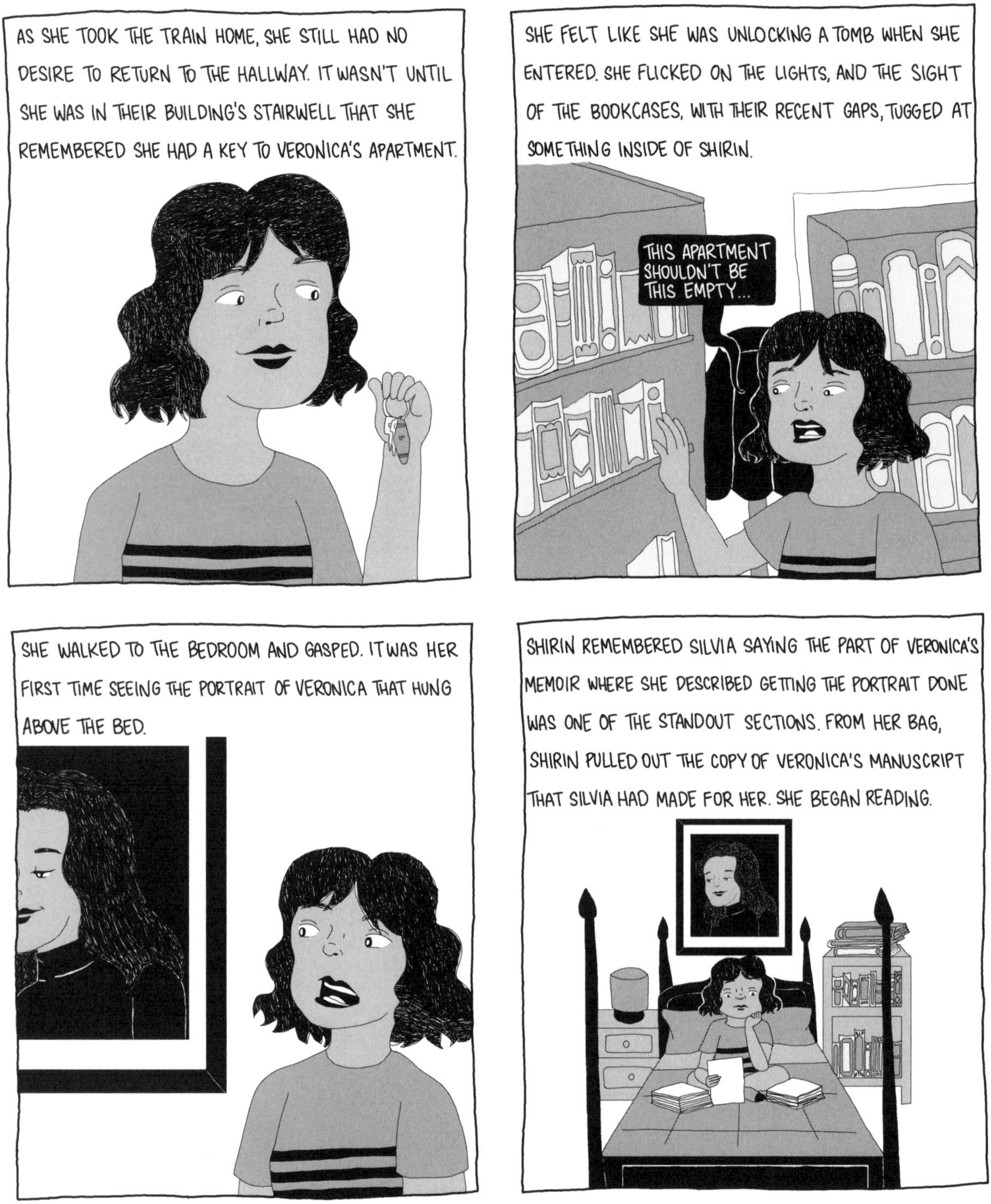
AS SHE TOOK THE TRAIN HOME, SHE STILL HAD NO DESIRE TO RETURN TO THE HALLWAY. IT WASN'T UNTIL SHE WAS IN THEIR BUILDING'S STAIRWELL THAT SHE REMEMBERED SHE HAD A KEY TO VERONICA'S APARTMENT.
SHE FELT LIKE SHE WAS UNLOCKING A TOMB WHEN SHE ENTERED. SHE FLICKED ON THE LIGHTS, AND THE SIGHT OF THE BOOKCASES, WITH THEIR RECENT GAPS, TUGGED AT SOMETHING INSIDE OF SHIRIN.
THIS APARTMENT SHOULDN'T BE THIS EMPTY...
SHE WALKED TO THE BEDROOM AND GASPED. IT WAS HER FIRST TIME SEEING THE PORTRAIT OF VERONICA THAT HUNG ABOVE THE BED.
SHIRIN REMEMBERED SILVIA SAYING THE PART OF VERONICA'S MEMOIR WHERE SHE DESCRIBED GETTING THE PORTRAIT DONE WAS ONE OF THE STANDOUT SECTIONS. FROM HER BAG, SHIRIN PULLED OUT THE COPY OF VERONICA'S MANUSCRIPT THAT SILVIA HAD MADE FOR HER. SHE BEGAN READING.

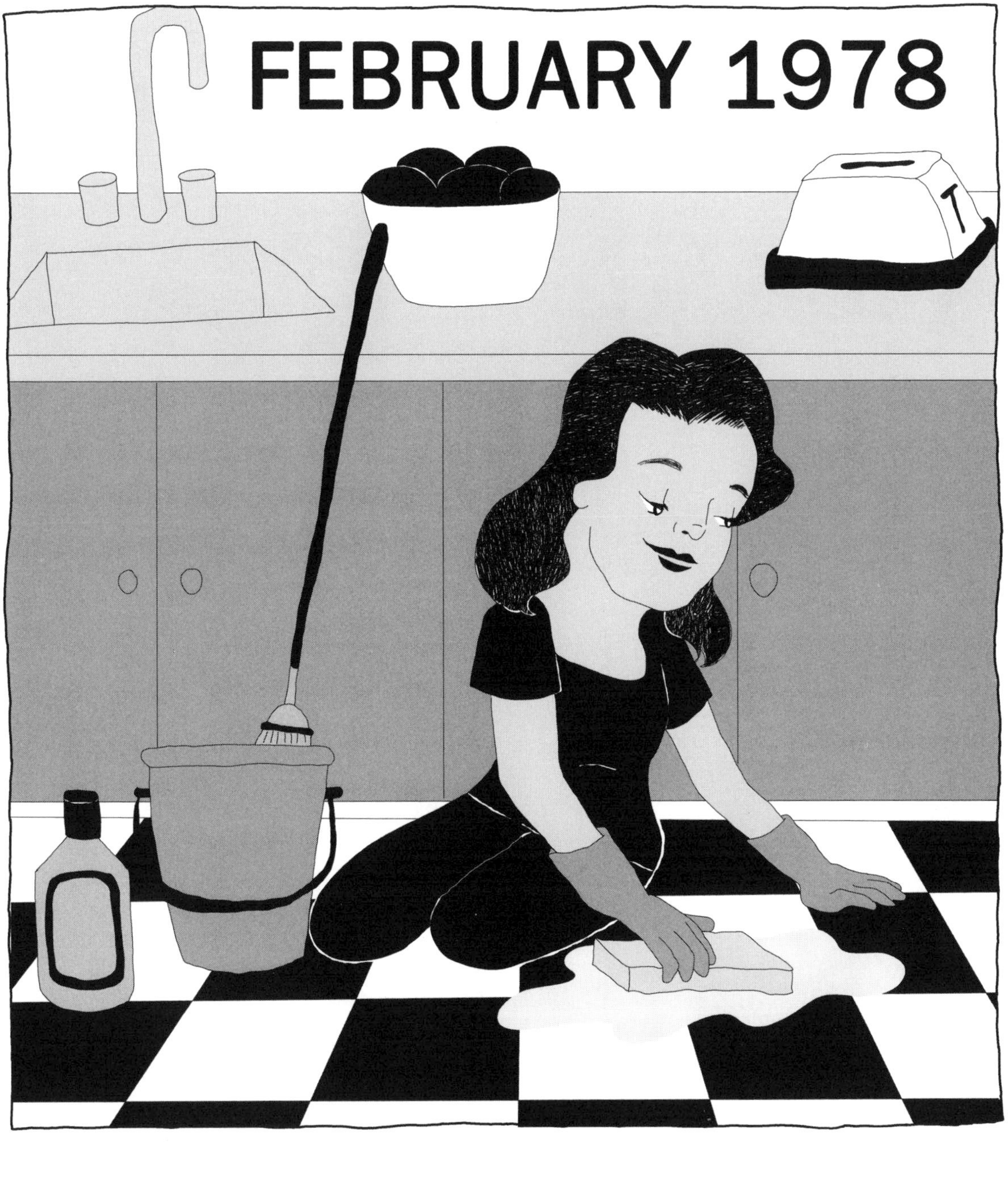
FEBRUARY 1978

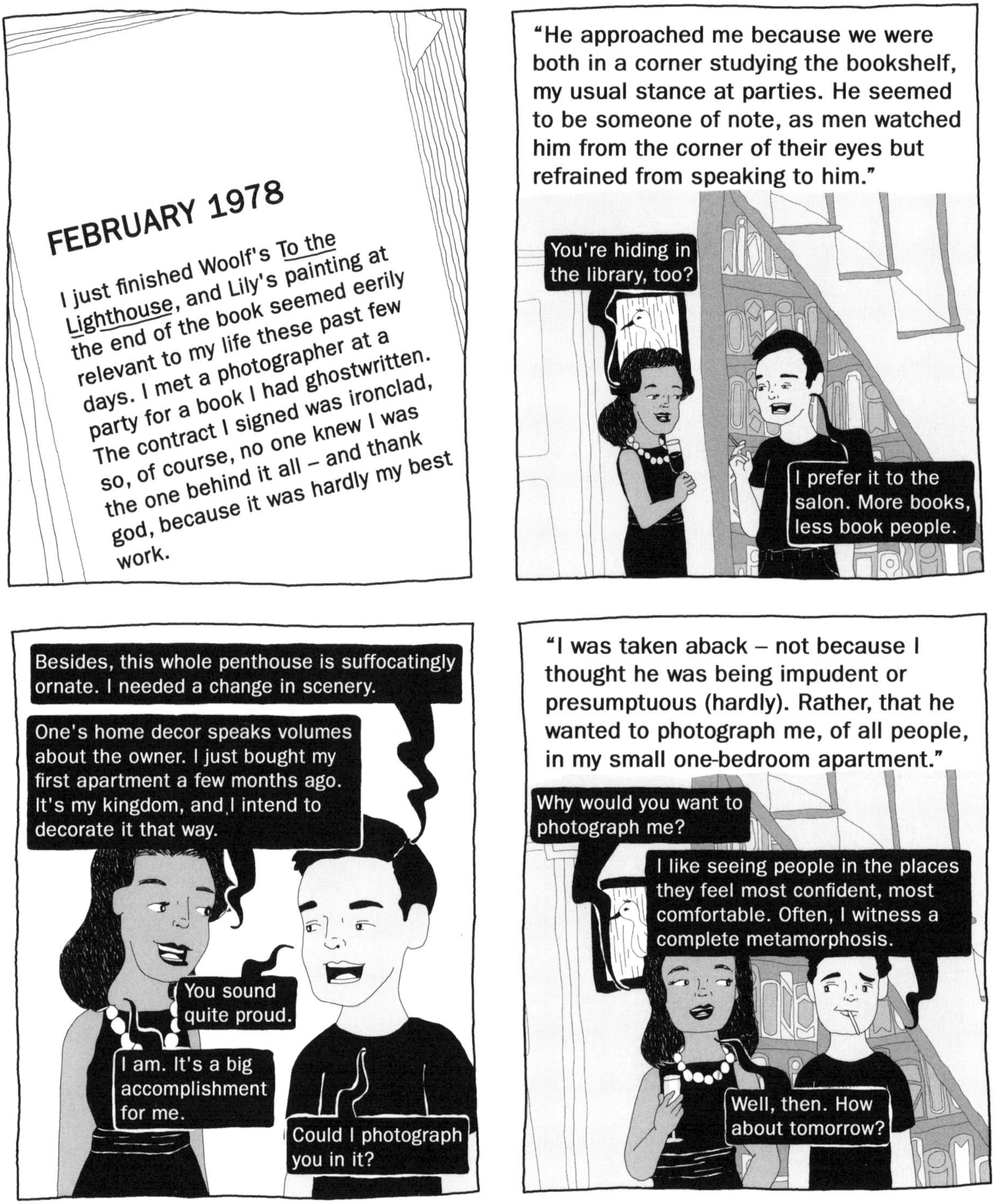
FEBRUARY 1978
I just finished Woolf's To the Lighthouse, and Lily's painting at the end of the book seemed eerily relevant to my life these past few days. I met a photographer at a party for a book I had ghostwritten. The contract I signed was ironclad, so, of course, no one knew I was the one behind it all – and thank god, because it was hardly my best work.
"He approached me because we were both in a corner studying the bookshelf, my usual stance at parties. He seemed to be someone of note, as men watched him from the corner of their eyes but refrained from speaking to him."
You're hiding in the library, too?
I prefer it to the salon. More books, less book people.
Besides, this whole penthouse is suffocatingly ornate. I needed a change in scenery.
One's home decor speaks volumes about the owner. I just bought my first apartment a few months ago. It's my kingdom, and I intend to decorate it that way.
You sound quite proud.
I am. It's a big accomplishment for me.
Could I photograph you in it?
"I was taken aback – not because I thought he was being impudent or presumptuous (hardly). Rather, that he wanted to photograph me, of all people, in my small one-bedroom apartment."
Why would you want to photograph me?
I like seeing people in the places they feel most confident, most comfortable. Often, I witness a complete metamorphosis.
Well, then. How about tomorrow?

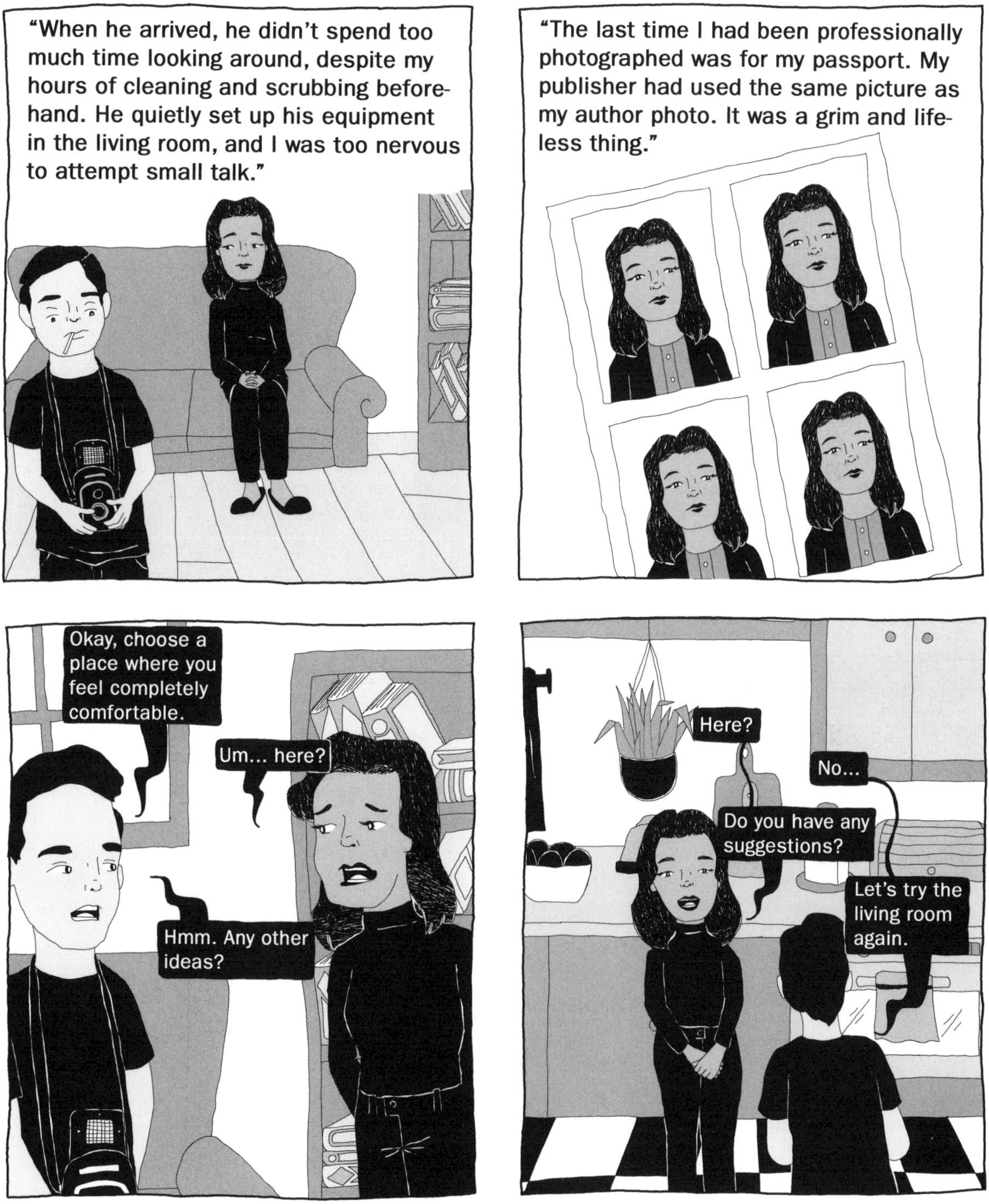
"When he arrived, he didn't spend too much time looking around, despite my hours of cleaning and scrubbing beforehand. He quietly set up his equipment in the living room, and I was too nervous to attempt small talk."
"The last time I had been professionally photographed was for my passport. My publisher had used the same picture as my author photo. It was a grim and lifeless thing."
Okay, choose a place where you feel completely comfortable.
Um... here?
Hmm. Any other ideas?
Here?
No...
Do you have any suggestions?
Let's try the living room again.

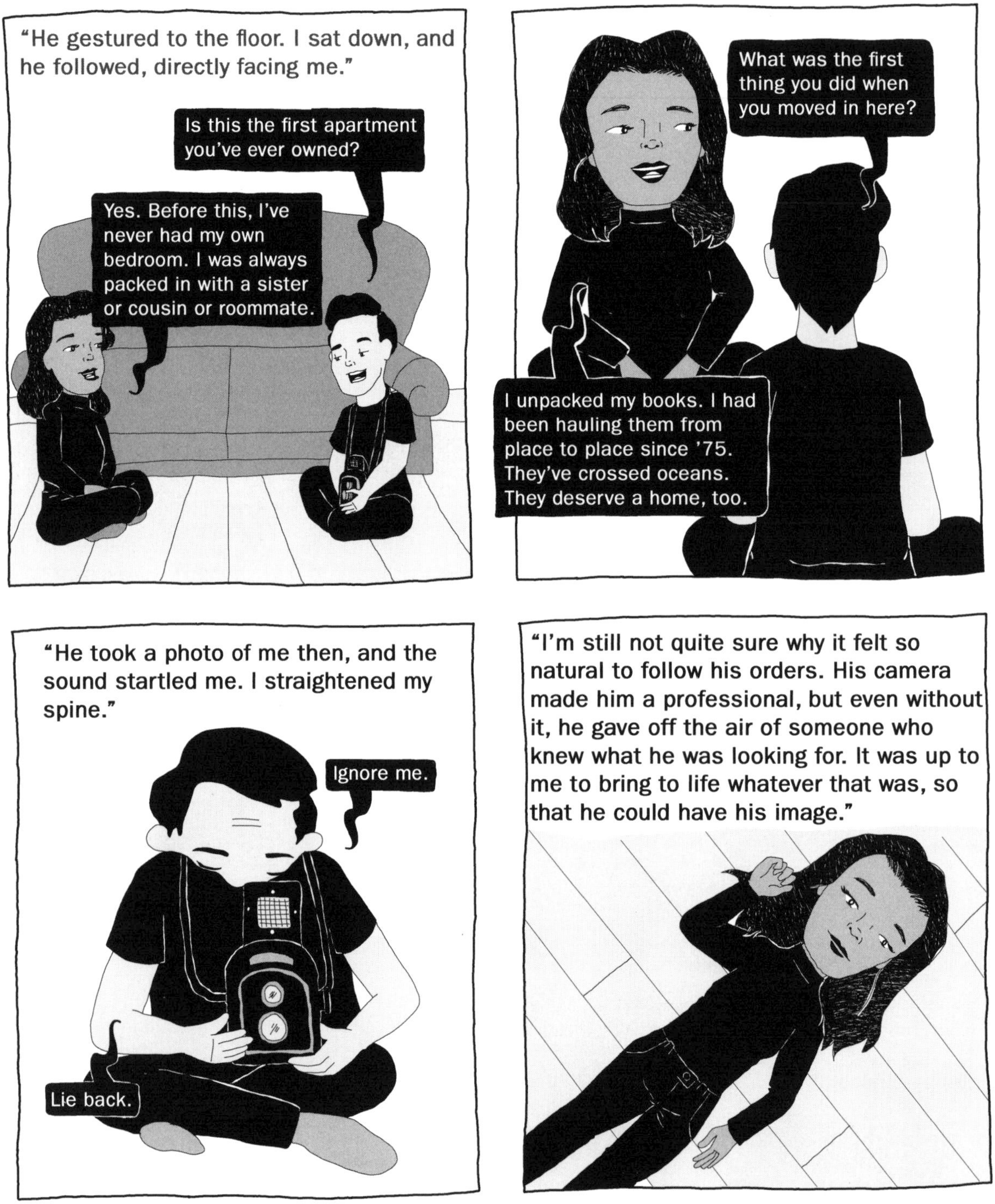
"He gestured to the floor. I sat down, and he followed, directly facing me."
Is this the first apartment you've ever owned?
Yes. Before this, I've never had my own bedroom. I was always packed in with a sister or cousin or roommate.
What was the first thing you did when you moved in here?
I unpacked my books. I had been hauling them from place to place since '75. They've crossed oceans. They deserve a home, too.
"He took a photo of me then, and the sound startled me. I straightened my spine."
Ignore me.
Lie back.
"I'm still not quite sure why it felt so natural to follow his orders. His camera made him a professional, but even without it, he gave off the air of someone who knew what he was looking for. It was up to me to bring to life whatever that was, so that he could have his image."

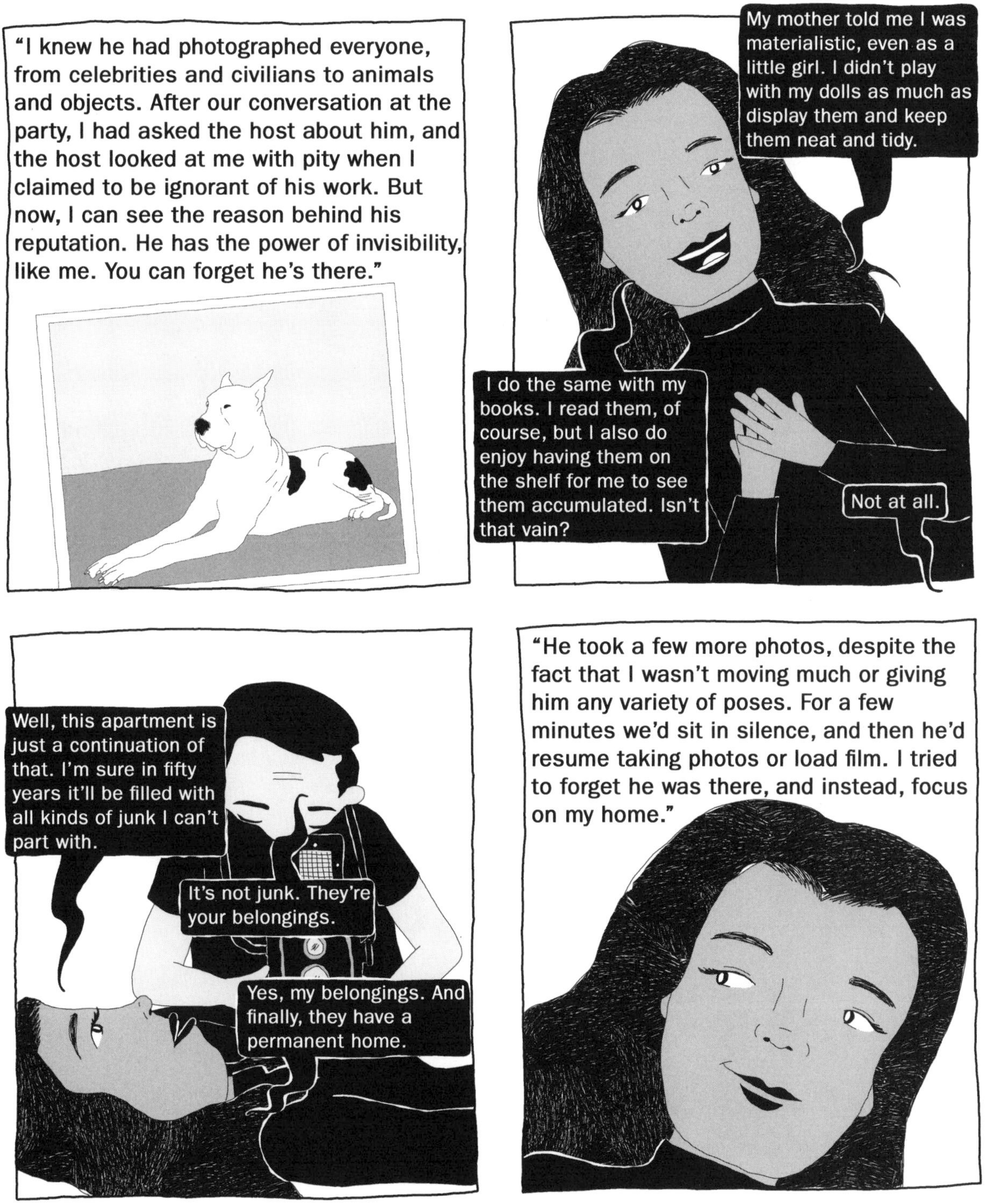
"I knew he had photographed everyone, from celebrities and civilians to animals and objects. After our conversation at the party, I had asked the host about him, and the host looked at me with pity when I claimed to be ignorant of his work. But now, I can see the reason behind his reputation. He has the power of invisibility, like me. You can forget he's there."
My mother told me I was materialistic, even as a little girl. I didn't play with my dolls as much as display them and keep them neat and tidy.
I do the same with my books. I read them, of course, but I also do enjoy having them on the shelf for me to see them accumulated. Isn't that vain?
Not at all.
Well, this apartment is just a continuation of that. I'm sure in fifty years it'll be filled with all kinds of junk I can't part with.
It's not junk. They're your belongings.
Yes, my belongings. And finally, they have a permanent home.
"He took a few more photos, despite the fact that I wasn't moving much or giving him any variety of poses. For a few minutes we'd sit in silence, and then he'd resume taking photos or load film. I tried to forget he was there, and instead, focus on my home."

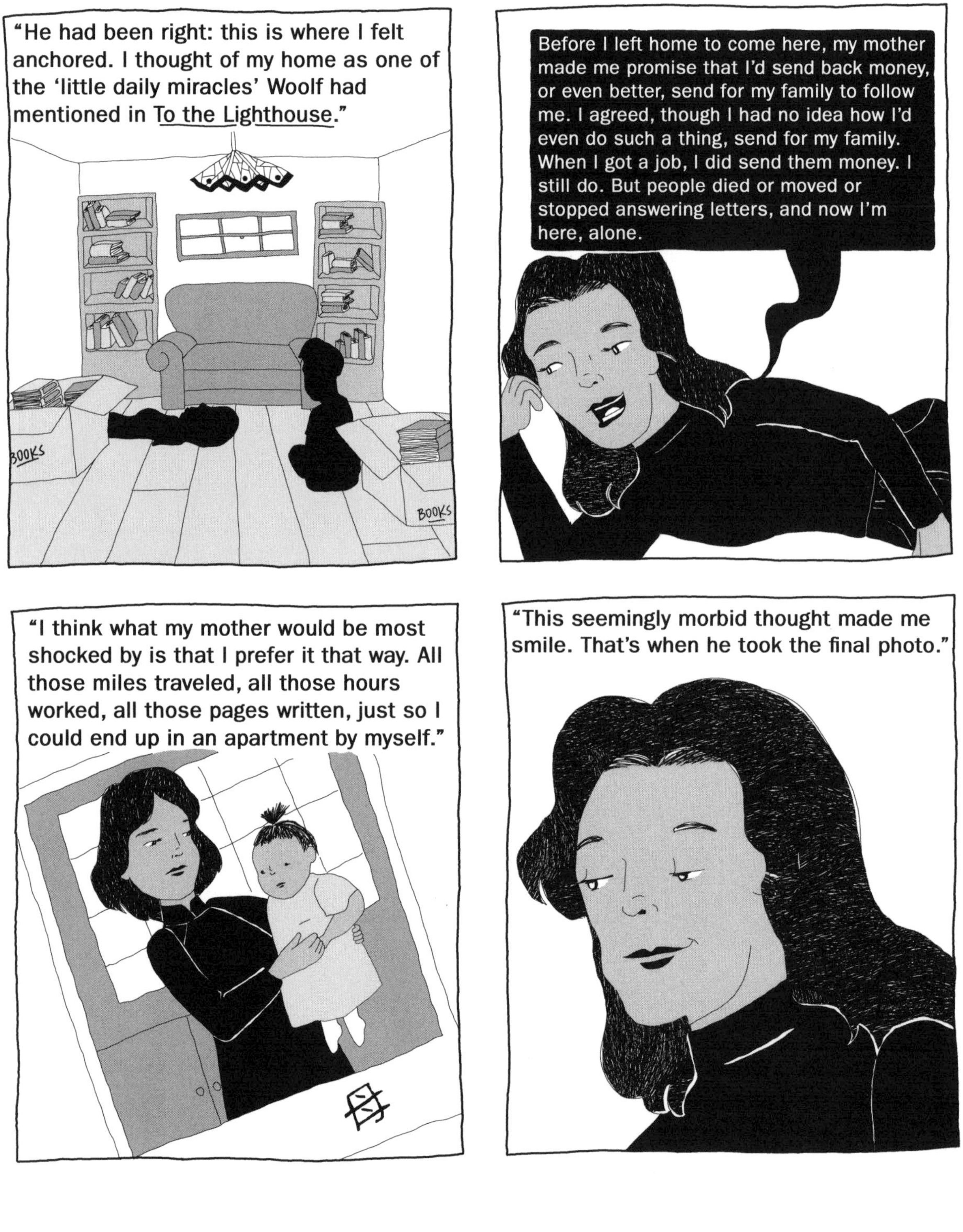
"He had been right: this is where I felt anchored. I thought of my home as one of the 'little daily miracles' Woolf had mentioned in To the Lighthouse."
BOOKS
BOOKS
Before I left home to come here, my mother made me promise that I'd send back money, or even better, send for my family to follow me. I agreed, though I had no idea how I'd even do such a thing, send for my family. When I got a job, I did send them money. I still do. But people died or moved or stopped answering letters, and now I'm here, alone.
"I think what my mother would be most shocked by is that I prefer it that way. All those miles traveled, all those hours worked, all those pages written, just so I could end up in an apartment by myself."
"This seemingly morbid thought made me smile. That's when he took the final photo."

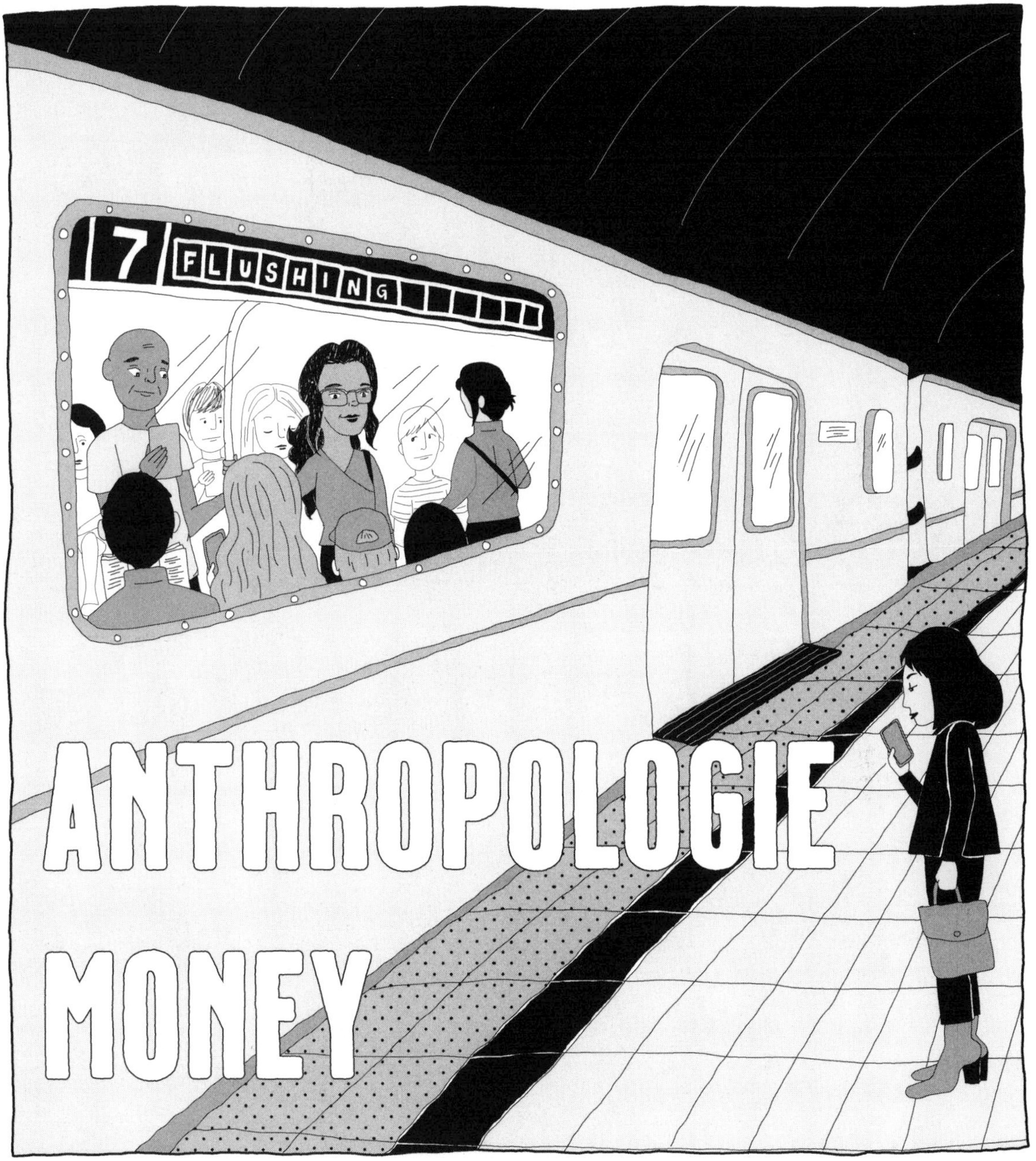
7
FLUSHING
ANTHROPOLOGIE
MONEY

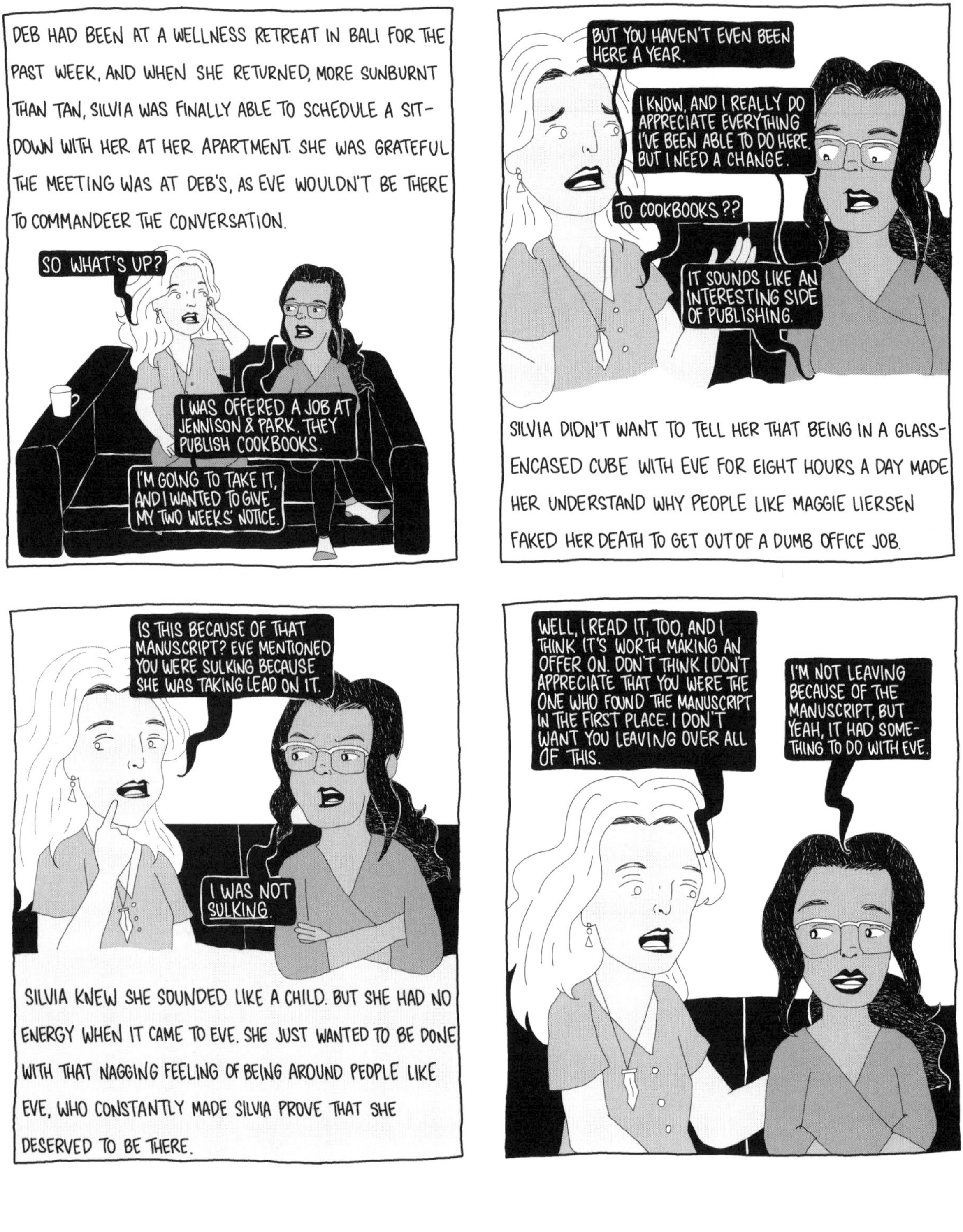
DEB HAD BEEN AT A WELLNESS RETREAT IN BALI FOR THE PAST WEEK, AND WHEN SHE RETURNED, MORE SUNBURNT THAN TAN, SILVIA WAS FINALLY ABLE TO SCHEDULE A SIT-DOWN WITH HER AT HER APARTMENT. SHE WAS GRATEFUL THE MEETING WAS AT DEB'S, AS EVE WOULDN'T BE THERE TO COMMANDEER THE CONVERSATION.
SO WHAT'S UP?
I WAS OFFERED A JOB AT JENNISON & PARK. THEY PUBLISH COOKBOOKS.
I'M GOING TO TAKE IT, AND I WANTED TO GIVE MY TWO WEEKS' NOTICE.
BUT YOU HAVEN'T EVEN BEEN HERE A YEAR.
I KNOW, AND I REALLY DO APPRECIATE EVERYTHING I'VE BEEN ABLE TO DO HERE. BUT I NEED A CHANGE.
TO COOKBOOKS??
IT SOUNDS LIKE AN INTERESTING SIDE OF PUBLISHING.
SILVIA DIDN'T WANT TO TELL HER THAT BEING IN A GLASS-ENCASED CUBE WITH EVE FOR EIGHT HOURS A DAY MADE HER UNDERSTAND WHY PEOPLE LIKE MAGGIE LIERSEN FAKED HER DEATH TO GET OUT OF A DUMB OFFICE JOB.
IS THIS BECAUSE OF THAT MANUSCRIPT? EVE MENTIONED YOU WERE SULKING BECAUSE SHE WAS TAKING LEAD ON IT.
I WAS NOT SULKING.
SILVIA KNEW SHE SOUNDED LIKE A CHILD. BUT SHE HAD NO ENERGY WHEN IT CAME TO EVE. SHE JUST WANTED TO BE DONE WITH THAT NAGGING FEELING OF BEING AROUND PEOPLE LIKE EVE, WHO CONSTANTLY MADE SILVIA PROVE THAT SHE DESERVED TO BE THERE.
WELL, I READ IT, TOO, AND I THINK IT'S WORTH MAKING AN OFFER ON. DON'T THINK I DON'T APPRECIATE THAT YOU WERE THE ONE WHO FOUND THE MANUSCRIPT IN THE FIRST PLACE. I DON'T WANT YOU LEAVING OVER ALL OF THIS.
I'M NOT LEAVING BECAUSE OF THE MANUSCRIPT, BUT YEAH, IT HAD SOME-THING TO DO WITH EVE.

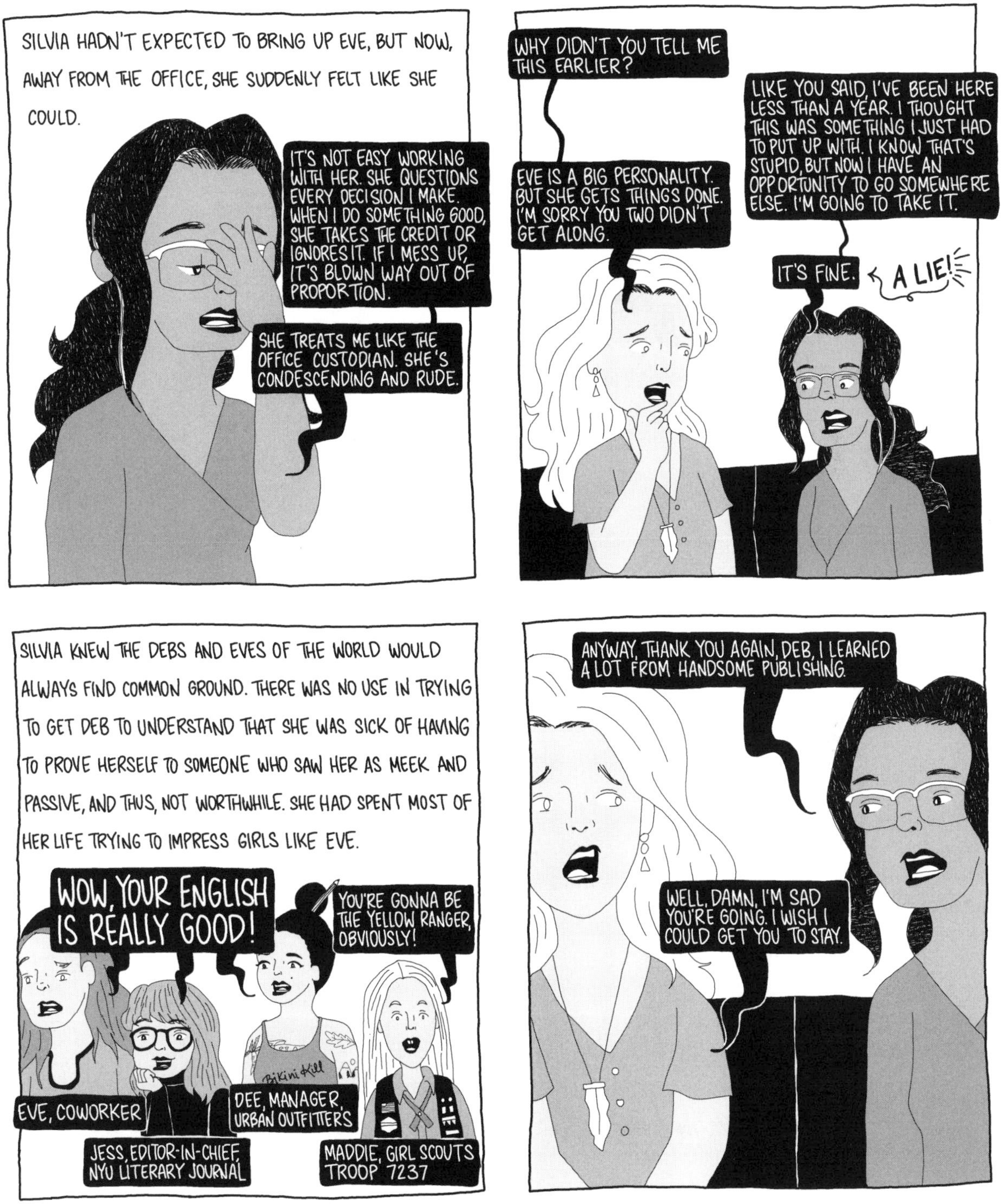

SILVIA HADN'T EXPECTED TO BRING UP EVE, BUT NOW, AWAY FROM THE OFFICE, SHE SUDDENLY FELT LIKE SHE COULD.
IT'S NOT EASY WORKING WITH HER. SHE QUESTIONS EVERY DECISION I MAKE. WHEN I DO SOMETHING GOOD, SHE TAKES THE CREDIT OR IGNORES IT. IF I MESS UP, IT'S BLOWN WAY OUT OF PROPORTION.
SHE TREATS ME LIKE THE OFFICE CUSTODIAN. SHE'S CONDESCENDING AND RUDE.
WHY DIDN'T YOU TELL ME THIS EARLIER?
LIKE YOU SAID, I'VE BEEN HERE LESS THAN A YEAR. I THOUGHT THIS WAS SOMETHING I JUST HAD TO PUT UP WITH. I KNOW THAT'S STUPID, BUT NOW I HAVE AN OPPORTUNITY TO GO SOMEWHERE ELSE. I'M GOING TO TAKE IT.
EVE IS A BIG PERSONALITY. BUT SHE GETS THINGS DONE. I'M SORRY YOU TWO DIDN'T GET ALONG.
IT'S FINE.
A LIE!
SILVIA KNEW THE DEBS AND EVES OF THE WORLD WOULD ALWAYS FIND COMMON GROUND. THERE WAS NO USE IN TRYING TO GET DEB TO UNDERSTAND THAT SHE WAS SICK OF HAVING TO PROVE HERSELF TO SOMEONE WHO SAW HER AS MEEK AND PASSIVE, AND THUS, NOT WORTHWHILE. SHE HAD SPENT MOST OF HER LIFE TRYING TO IMPRESS GIRLS LIKE EVE.
WOW, YOUR ENGLISH IS REALLY GOOD!
YOU'RE GONNA BE THE YELLOW RANGER, OBVIOUSLY!
Bikini Kill
EVE, COWORKER
JESS, EDITOR-IN-CHIEF, NYU LITERARY JOURNAL
DEE, MANAGER, URBAN OUTFITTER'S
MADDIE, GIRL SCOUTS TROOP 7237
ANYWAY, THANK YOU AGAIN, DEB, I LEARNED A LOT FROM HANDSOME PUBLISHING.
WELL, DAMN, I'M SAD YOU'RE GOING. I WISH I COULD GET YOU TO STAY.

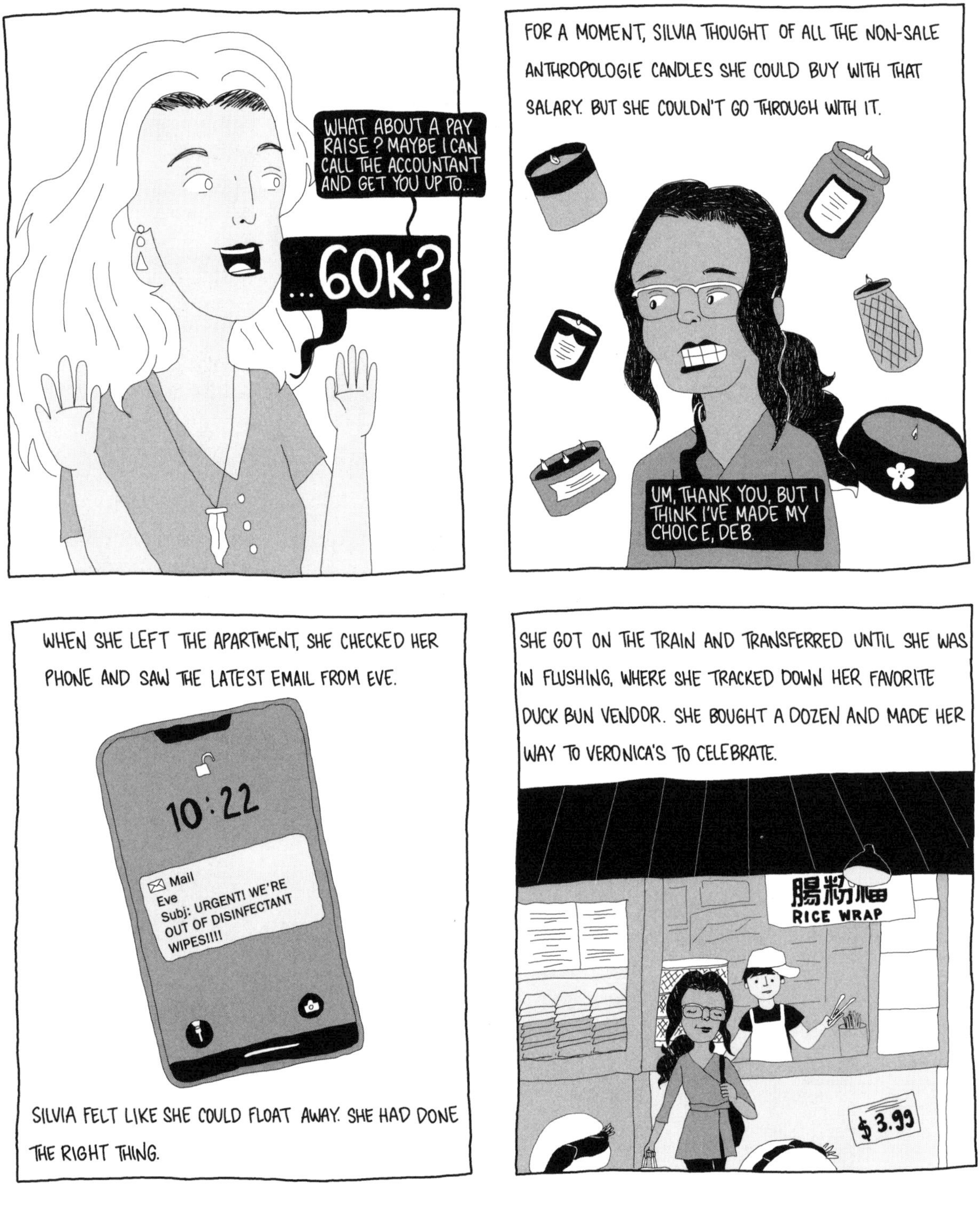
WHAT ABOUT A PAY RAISE? MAYBE I CAN CALL THE ACCOUNTANT AND GET YOU UP TO...
...60K?
FOR A MOMENT, SILVIA THOUGHT OF ALL THE NON-SALE ANTHROPOLOGIE CANDLES SHE COULD BUY WITH THAT SALARY. BUT SHE COULDN'T GO THROUGH WITH IT.
UM, THANK YOU, BUT I THINK I'VE MADE MY CHOICE, DEB.
WHEN SHE LEFT THE APARTMENT, SHE CHECKED HER PHONE AND SAW THE LATEST EMAIL FROM EVE.
10:22
Mail
Eve
Subj: URGENT! WE'RE OUT OF DISINFECTANT WIPES!!!!
SILVIA FELT LIKE SHE COULD FLOAT AWAY. SHE HAD DONE THE RIGHT THING.
SHE GOT ON THE TRAIN AND TRANSFERRED UNTIL SHE WAS IN FLUSHING, WHERE SHE TRACKED DOWN HER FAVORITE DUCK BUN VENDOR. SHE BOUGHT A DOZEN AND MADE HER WAY TO VERONICA'S TO CELEBRATE.
腸粉
RICE WRAP
$ 3.99

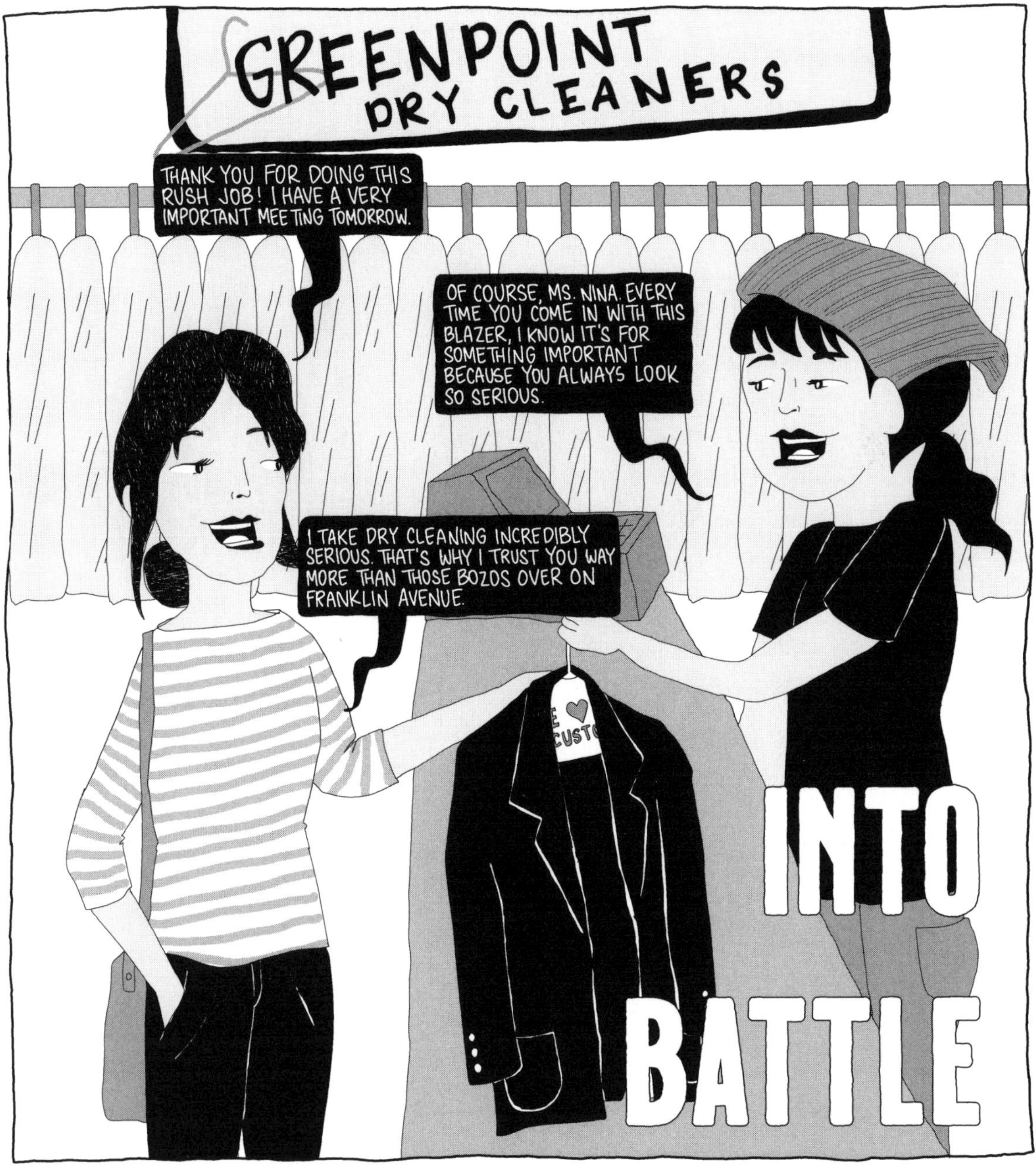
GREENPOINT DRY CLEANERS
THANK YOU FOR DOING THIS RUSH JOB! I HAVE A VERY IMPORTANT MEETING TOMORROW.
OF COURSE, MS. NINA. EVERY TIME YOU COME IN WITH THIS BLAZER, I KNOW IT'S FOR SOMETHING IMPORTANT BECAUSE YOU ALWAYS LOOK SO SERIOUS.
I TAKE DRY CLEANING INCREDIBLY SERIOUS. THAT'S WHY I TRUST YOU WAY MORE THAN THOSE BOZOS OVER ON FRANKLIN AVENUE.
INTO BATTLE

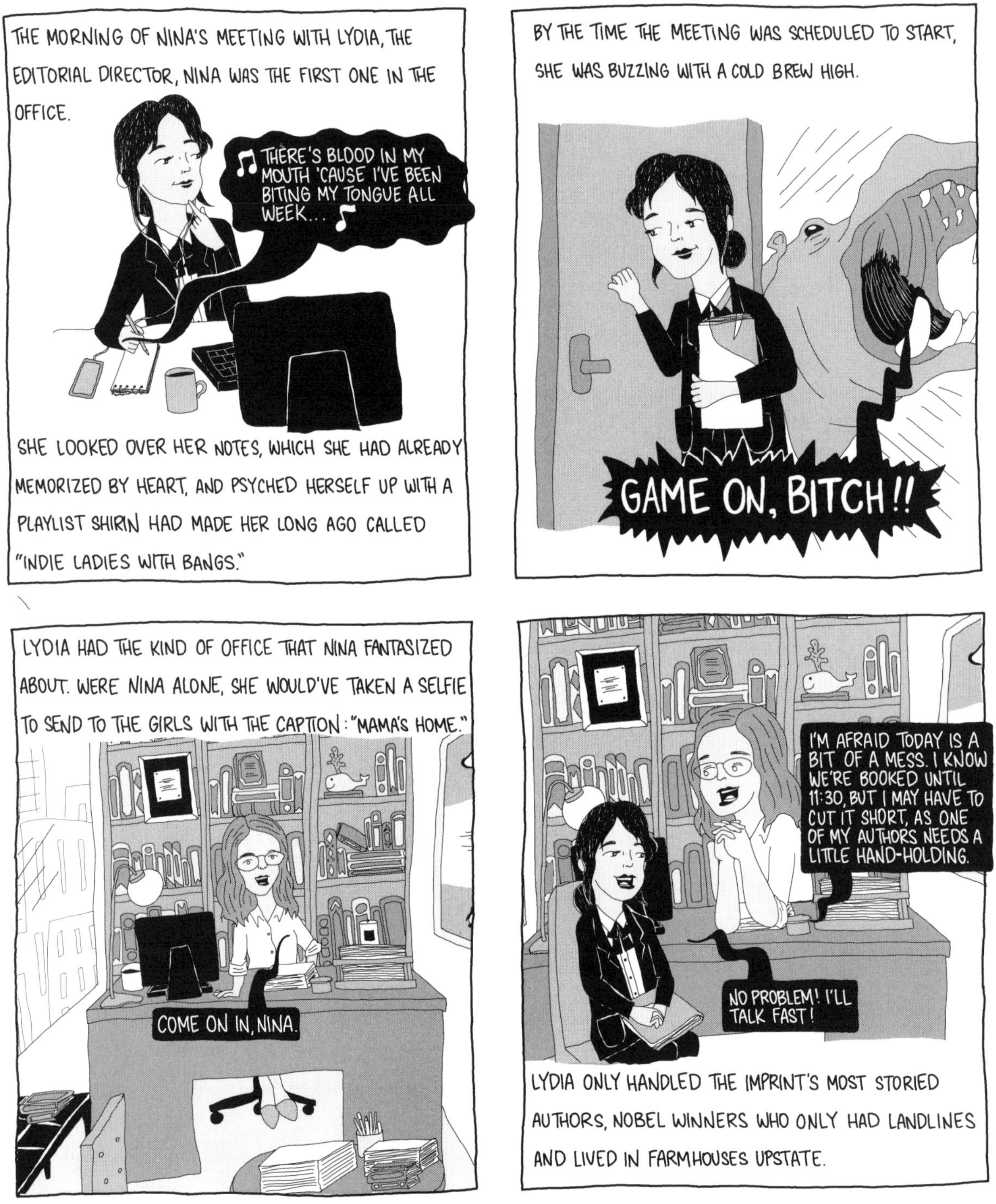
THE MORNING OF NINA'S MEETING WITH LYDIA, THE EDITORIAL DIRECTOR, NINA WAS THE FIRST ONE IN THE OFFICE.
THERE'S BLOOD IN MY MOUTH 'CAUSE I'VE BEEN BITING MY TONGUE ALL WEEK...
SHE LOOKED OVER HER NOTES, WHICH SHE HAD ALREADY MEMORIZED BY HEART, AND PSYCHED HERSELF UP WITH A PLAYLIST SHIRIN HAD MADE HER LONG AGO CALLED "INDIE LADIES WITH BANGS."
BY THE TIME THE MEETING WAS SCHEDULED TO START, SHE WAS BUZZING WITH A COLD BREW HIGH.
GAME ON, BITCH!!
LYDIA HAD THE KIND OF OFFICE THAT NINA FANTASIZED ABOUT. WERE NINA ALONE, SHE WOULD'VE TAKEN A SELFIE TO SEND TO THE GIRLS WITH THE CAPTION: "MAMA'S HOME."
COME ON IN, NINA.
I'M AFRAID TODAY IS A BIT OF A MESS. I KNOW WE'RE BOOKED UNTIL 11:30, BUT I MAY HAVE TO CUT IT SHORT, AS ONE OF MY AUTHORS NEEDS A LITTLE HAND-HOLDING.
NO PROBLEM! I'LL TALK FAST!
LYDIA ONLY HANDLED THE IMPRINT'S MOST STORIED AUTHORS, NOBEL WINNERS WHO ONLY HAD LANDLINES AND LIVED IN FARMHOUSES UPSTATE.

SO I SENT YOU THE MANUSCRIPT AND P&L, AND AS YOU CAN SEE, VERONICA VO HAS A LEGACY OF—

YES, I READ ALL OF IT JUST THIS MORNING.

THE— THE WHOLE MANUSCRIPT?

MOST OF IT. IT'S BEAUTIFULLY WRITTEN, AND I CAN UNDERSTAND THE FASCINATION WITH HER LIFE. THAT WHOLE CROWD FROM THE '70S AND '80S HAVE BEEN BACK SINCE PATTI SMITH'S BOOK.

EXACTLY! I LOVE ALL THOSE MEMOIRS FROM THAT ERA, BUT I'VE ALWAYS CRAVED A PERSPECTIVE FROM SOMEONE, YOU KNOW, A BIT OTHER.

VERONICA WAS AN INSIDER IN TERMS OF BEING A PUBLISHED AUTHOR, BUT SHE HAD TO PUT UP WITH SEXISM, RACISM, XENOPHOBIA—

TO NINA'S DISAPPOINTMENT, SHE SAW LYDIA GLANCE AT HER PHONE, AS IF WILLING IT TO RING.

SHE HAS A GREAT STORY, BUT WHO IS VERONICA VO TO TODAY'S AUDIENCE?

SHE WON THE BOOKER AND DISAPPEARED. HOW WILL WE MAKE READERS CARE?

SHE'S A LIVING LEGEND. THE ASIAN AMERICAN CANON NEEDS HER— OR RATHER, THE AMERICAN CANON. WE HAVE A CHANCE TO RE-INTRODUCE HER TO A NEW AUDIENCE, NOT JUST BY RE-ISSUING HER BOOKS, BUT ALSO—

RE-INTRODUCE? RE-ISSUE?

THIS WAS THE THIRD TIME LYDIA HAD INTERRUPTED, AND DESPITE NINA'S AWE AT HER POSITION AS EDITORIAL DIRECTOR, NINA COULDN'T DENY THAT IT WAS PISSING HER OFF.

YOU SEE, THIS IS NOT MS. VO'S FIRST GO AT THIS. SHE HAD HER CHANCE, AND I THINK SHE DID AN ADMIRABLE JOB. SHE WON THE BOOKER, AND I'M SURE THAT BOOK IS STILL TAUGHT IN ASIAN LIT COURSES, AS IT SHOULD BE.

SHE'S WRITTEN SO MANY MORE BOOKS THOUGH, AND THEY'RE ALL AMAZING.

WHAT PART OF "LIVING LEGEND" DO YOU NOT FUCKING UNDERSTAND?!

237

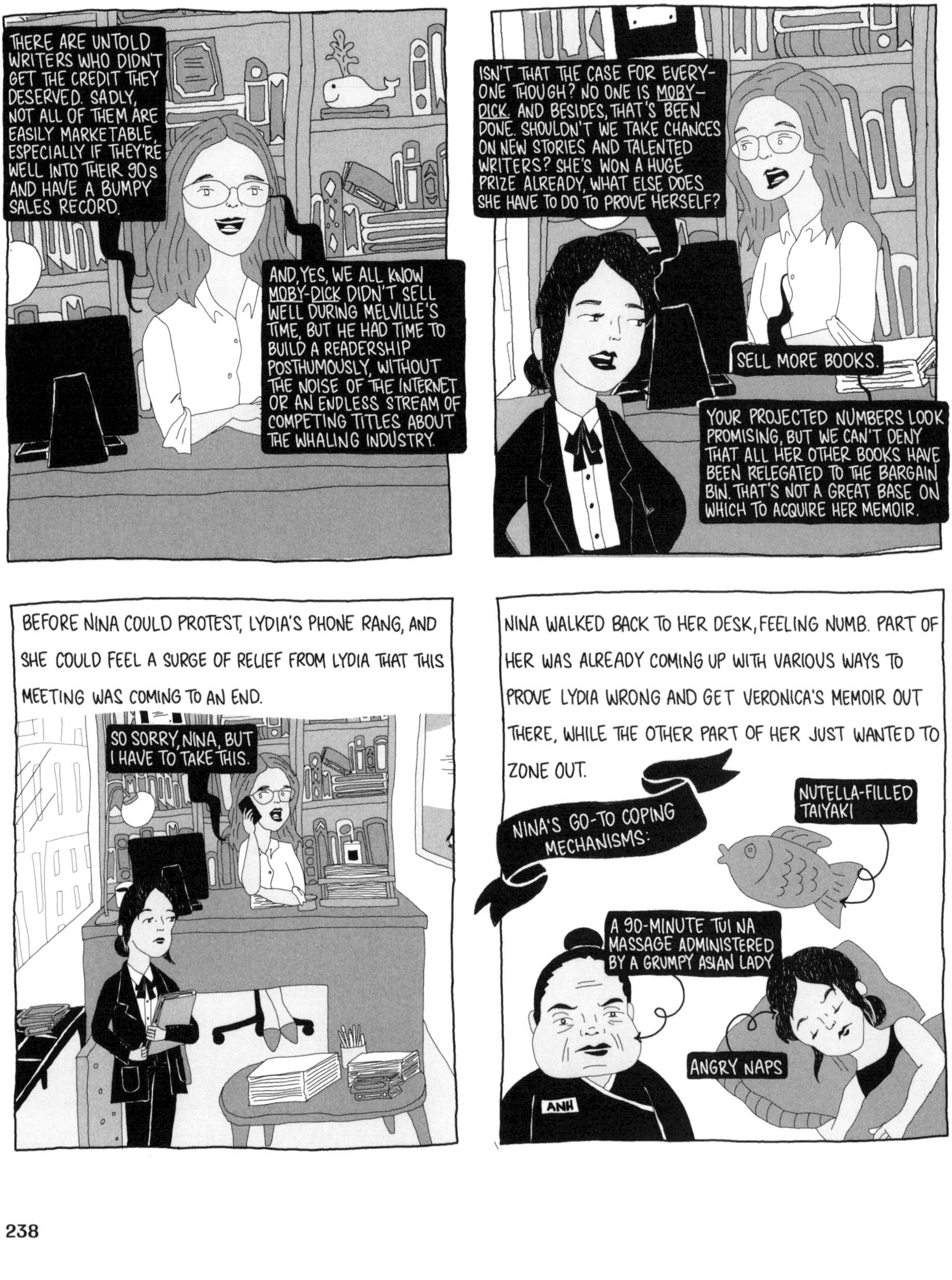
THERE ARE UNTOLD WRITERS WHO DIDN'T GET THE CREDIT THEY DESERVED. SADLY, NOT ALL OF THEM ARE EASILY MARKETABLE, ESPECIALLY IF THEY'RE WELL INTO THEIR 90s AND HAVE A BUMPY SALES RECORD.
AND, YES, WE ALL KNOW MOBY-DICK DIDN'T SELL WELL DURING MELVILLE'S TIME, BUT HE HAD TIME TO BUILD A READERSHIP POSTHUMOUSLY, WITHOUT THE NOISE OF THE INTERNET OR AN ENDLESS STREAM OF COMPETING TITLES ABOUT THE WHALING INDUSTRY.
ISN'T THAT THE CASE FOR EVERYONE THOUGH? NO ONE IS MOBY-DICK. AND BESIDES, THAT'S BEEN DONE. SHOULDN'T WE TAKE CHANCES ON NEW STORIES AND TALENTED WRITERS? SHE'S WON A HUGE PRIZE ALREADY, WHAT ELSE DOES SHE HAVE TO DO TO PROVE HERSELF?
SELL MORE BOOKS.
YOUR PROJECTED NUMBERS LOOK PROMISING, BUT WE CAN'T DENY THAT ALL HER OTHER BOOKS HAVE BEEN RELEGATED TO THE BARGAIN BIN. THAT'S NOT A GREAT BASE ON WHICH TO ACQUIRE HER MEMOIR.
BEFORE NINA COULD PROTEST, LYDIA'S PHONE RANG, AND SHE COULD FEEL A SURGE OF RELIEF FROM LYDIA THAT THIS MEETING WAS COMING TO AN END.
SO SORRY, NINA, BUT I HAVE TO TAKE THIS.
NINA WALKED BACK TO HER DESK, FEELING NUMB. PART OF HER WAS ALREADY COMING UP WITH VARIOUS WAYS TO PROVE LYDIA WRONG AND GET VERONICA'S MEMOIR OUT THERE, WHILE THE OTHER PART OF HER JUST WANTED TO ZONE OUT.
NINA'S GO-TO COPING MECHANISMS:
NUTELLA-FILLED TAIYAKI
A 90-MINUTE TUI NA MASSAGE ADMINISTERED BY A GRUMPY ASIAN LADY
ANH
ANGRY NAPS

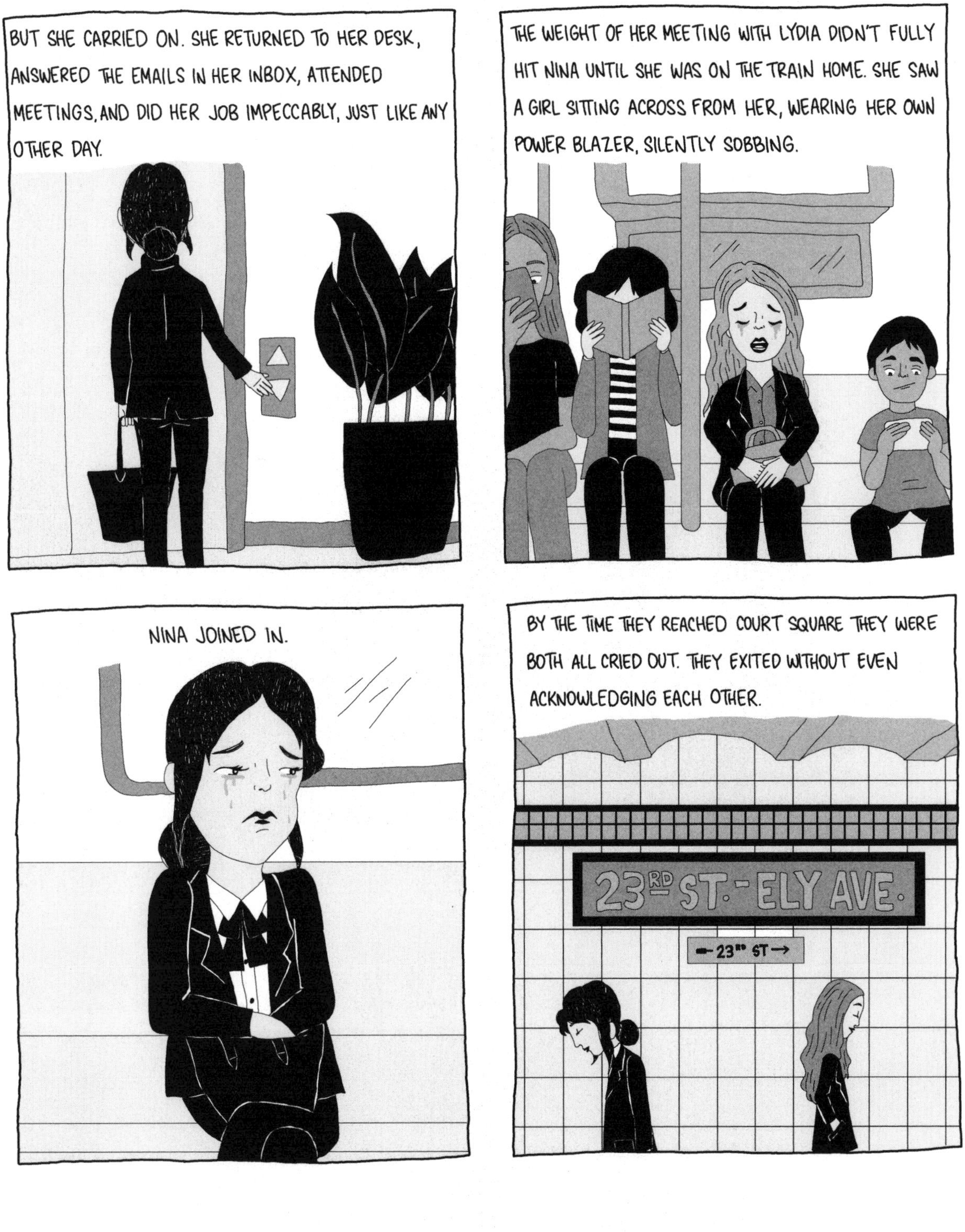
BUT SHE CARRIED ON. SHE RETURNED TO HER DESK, ANSWERED THE EMAILS IN HER INBOX, ATTENDED MEETINGS, AND DID HER JOB IMPECCABLY, JUST LIKE ANY OTHER DAY.
THE WEIGHT OF HER MEETING WITH LYDIA DIDN'T FULLY HIT NINA UNTIL SHE WAS ON THE TRAIN HOME. SHE SAW A GIRL SITTING ACROSS FROM HER, WEARING HER OWN POWER BLAZER, SILENTLY SOBBING.
NINA JOINED IN.
BY THE TIME THEY REACHED COURT SQUARE THEY WERE BOTH ALL CRIED OUT. THEY EXITED WITHOUT EVEN ACKNOWLEDGING EACH OTHER.
23RD ST. - ELY AVE.
23RD ST

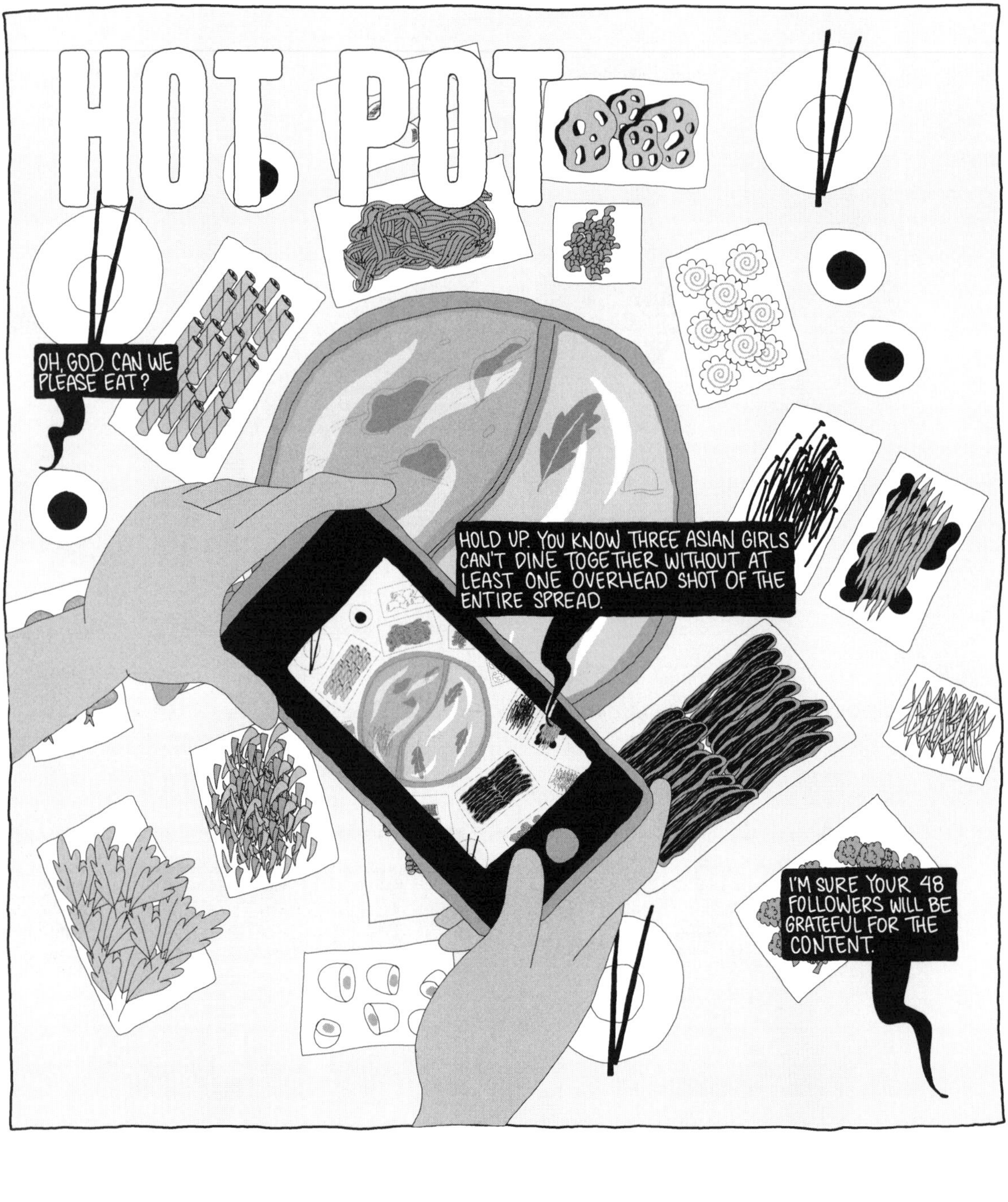
HOT POT
OH, GOD. CAN WE PLEASE EAT?
HOLD UP. YOU KNOW THREE ASIAN GIRLS CAN'T DINE TOGETHER WITHOUT AT LEAST ONE OVERHEAD SHOT OF THE ENTIRE SPREAD.
I'M SURE YOUR 48 FOLLOWERS WILL BE GRATEFUL FOR THE CONTENT.

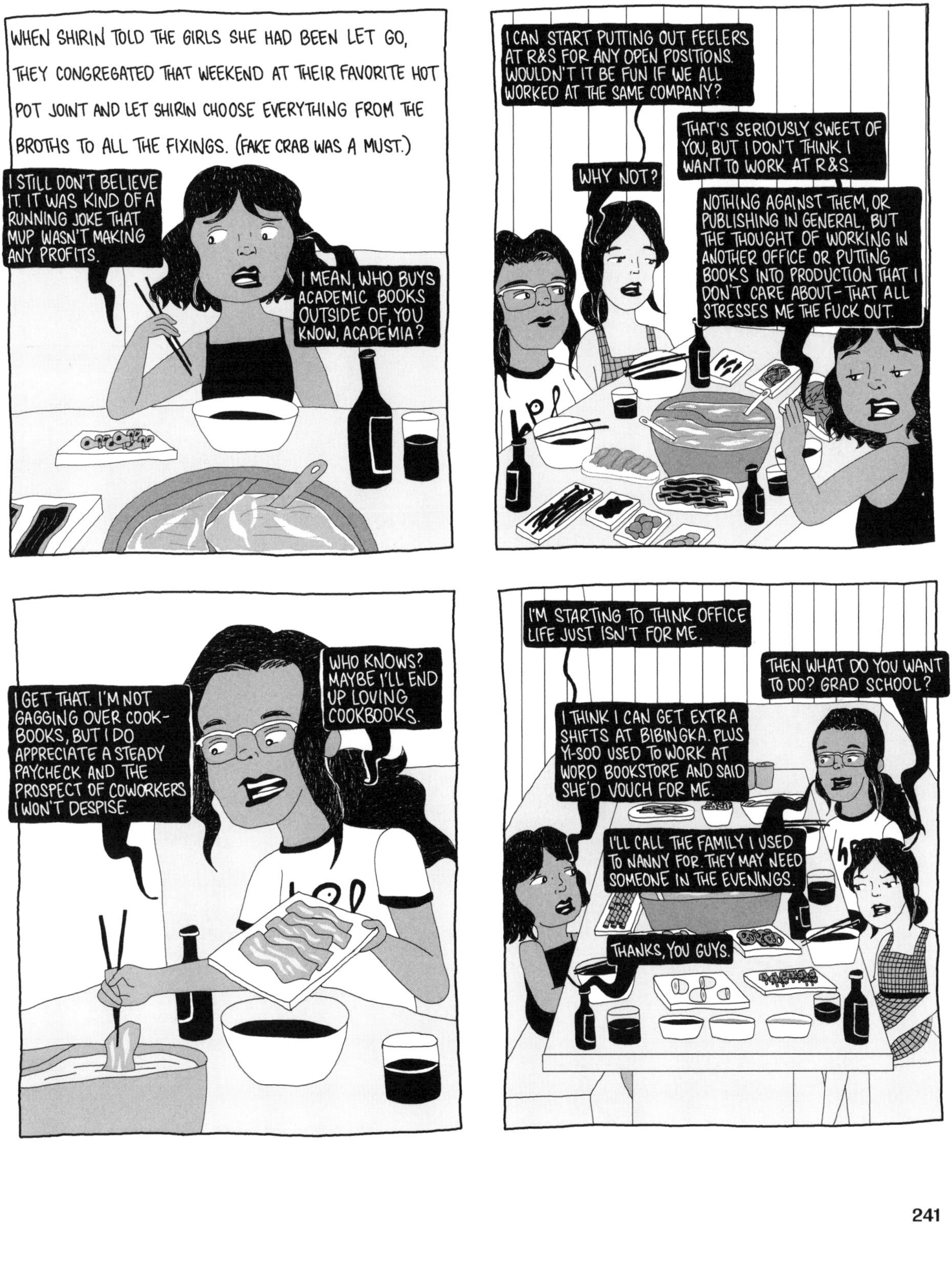

WHEN SHIRIN TOLD THE GIRLS SHE HAD BEEN LET GO, THEY CONGREGATED THAT WEEKEND AT THEIR FAVORITE HOT POT JOINT AND LET SHIRIN CHOOSE EVERYTHING FROM THE BROTHS TO ALL THE FIXINGS. (FAKE CRAB WAS A MUST.)
I STILL DON'T BELIEVE IT. IT WAS KIND OF A RUNNING JOKE THAT MUP WASN'T MAKING ANY PROFITS.
I MEAN, WHO BUYS ACADEMIC BOOKS OUTSIDE OF, YOU KNOW, ACADEMIA?
I CAN START PUTTING OUT FEELERS AT R&S FOR ANY OPEN POSITIONS. WOULDN'T IT BE FUN IF WE ALL WORKED AT THE SAME COMPANY?
THAT'S SERIOUSLY SWEET OF YOU, BUT I DON'T THINK I WANT TO WORK AT R&S.
WHY NOT?
NOTHING AGAINST THEM, OR PUBLISHING IN GENERAL, BUT THE THOUGHT OF WORKING IN ANOTHER OFFICE OR PUTTING BOOKS INTO PRODUCTION THAT I DON'T CARE ABOUT- THAT ALL STRESSES ME THE FUCK OUT.
I GET THAT. I'M NOT GAGGING OVER COOK-BOOKS, BUT I DO APPRECIATE A STEADY PAYCHECK AND THE PROSPECT OF COWORKERS I WON'T DESPISE.
WHO KNOWS? MAYBE I'LL END UP LOVING COOKBOOKS.
I'M STARTING TO THINK OFFICE LIFE JUST ISN'T FOR ME.
THEN WHAT DO YOU WANT TO DO? GRAD SCHOOL?
I THINK I CAN GET EXTRA SHIFTS AT BIBINGKA. PLUS YI-SOO USED TO WORK AT WORD BOOKSTORE AND SAID SHE'D VOUCH FOR ME.
I'LL CALL THE FAMILY I USED TO NANNY FOR. THEY MAY NEED SOMEONE IN THE EVENINGS.
THANKS, YOU GUYS.

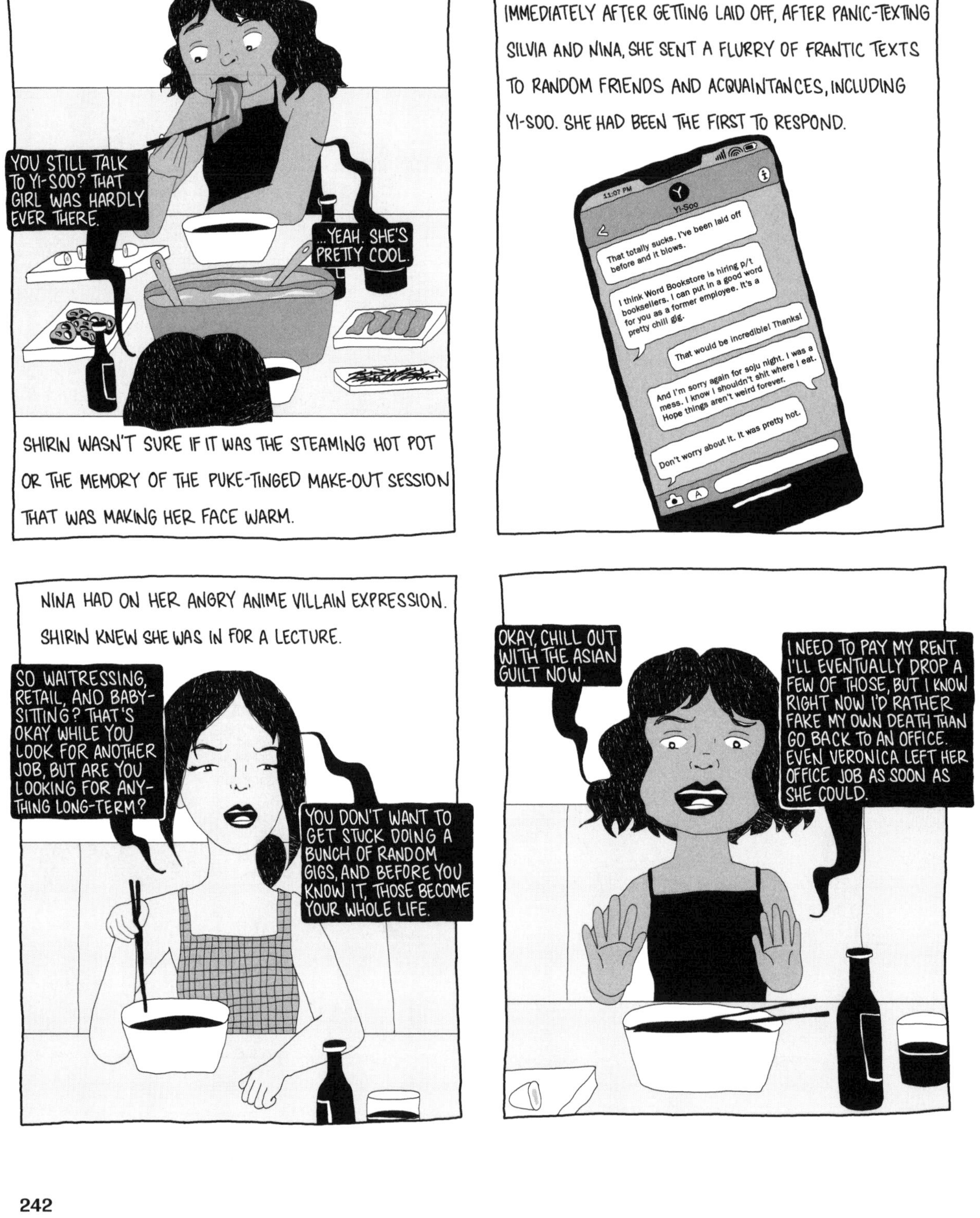
YOU STILL TALK TO YI-SOO? THAT GIRL WAS HARDLY EVER THERE.
...YEAH. SHE'S PRETTY COOL.
SHIRIN WASN'T SURE IF IT WAS THE STEAMING HOT POT OR THE MEMORY OF THE PUKE-TINGED MAKE-OUT SESSION THAT WAS MAKING HER FACE WARM.
IMMEDIATELY AFTER GETTING LAID OFF, AFTER PANIC-TEXTING SILVIA AND NINA, SHE SENT A FLURRY OF FRANTIC TEXTS TO RANDOM FRIENDS AND ACQUAINTANCES, INCLUDING YI-SOO. SHE HAD BEEN THE FIRST TO RESPOND.
11:07 PM
Yi-Soo
That totally sucks. I've been laid off before and it blows.
I think Word Bookstore is hiring p/t booksellers. I can put in a good word for you as a former employee. It's a pretty chill gig.
That would be incredible! Thanks!
And I'm sorry again for soju night. I was a mess. I know I shouldn't shit where I eat. Hope things aren't weird forever.
Don't worry about it. It was pretty hot.
NINA HAD ON HER ANGRY ANIME VILLAIN EXPRESSION. SHIRIN KNEW SHE WAS IN FOR A LECTURE.
SO WAITRESSING, RETAIL, AND BABY-SITTING? THAT'S OKAY WHILE YOU LOOK FOR ANOTHER JOB, BUT ARE YOU LOOKING FOR ANY-THING LONG-TERM?
YOU DON'T WANT TO GET STUCK DOING A BUNCH OF RANDOM GIGS, AND BEFORE YOU KNOW IT, THOSE BECOME YOUR WHOLE LIFE.
OKAY, CHILL OUT WITH THE ASIAN GUILT NOW.
I NEED TO PAY MY RENT. I'LL EVENTUALLY DROP A FEW OF THOSE, BUT I KNOW RIGHT NOW I'D RATHER FAKE MY OWN DEATH THAN GO BACK TO AN OFFICE. EVEN VERONICA LEFT HER OFFICE JOB AS SOON AS SHE COULD.

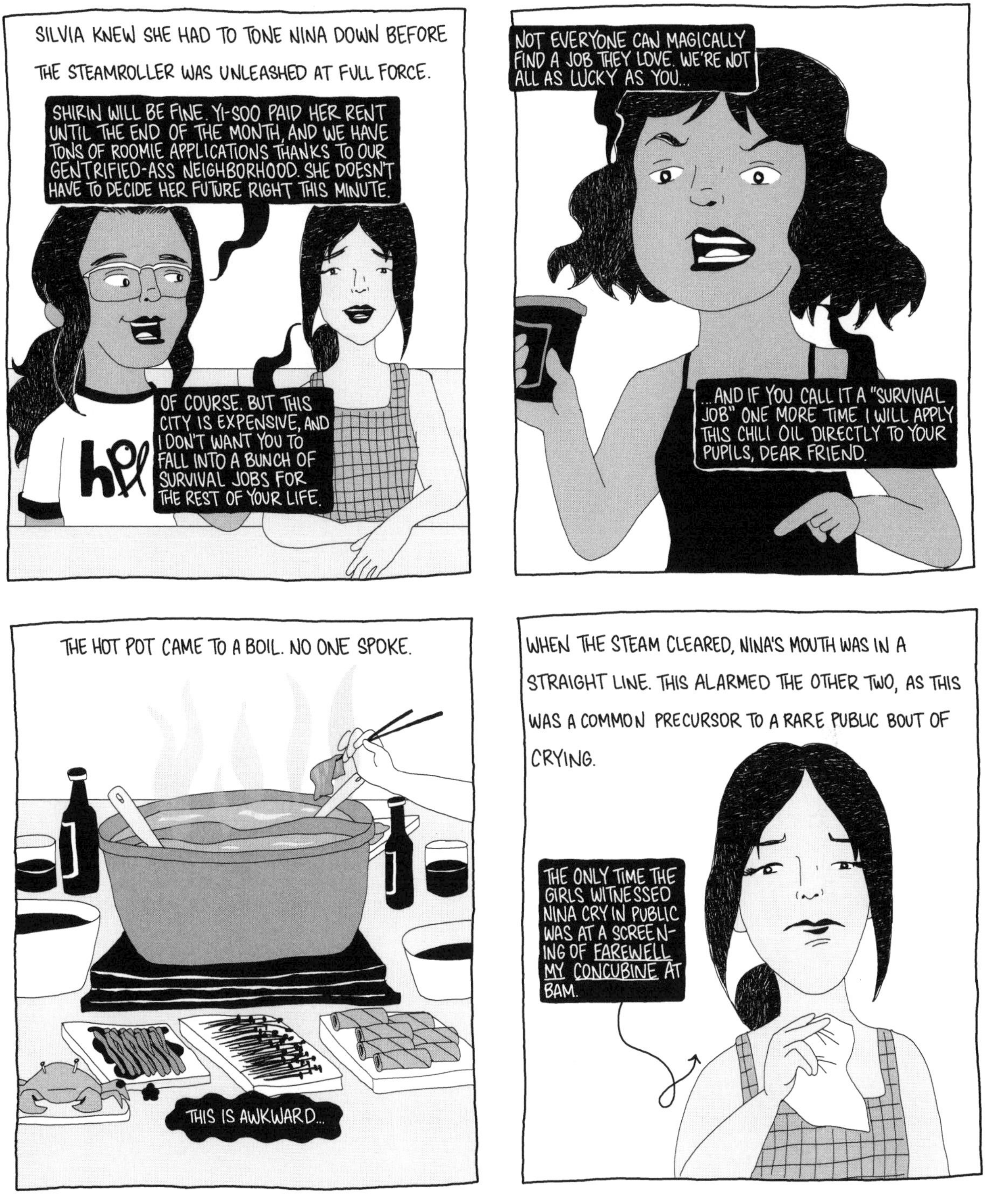
SILVIA KNEW SHE HAD TO TONE NINA DOWN BEFORE THE STEAMROLLER WAS UNLEASHED AT FULL FORCE.
SHIRIN WILL BE FINE. YI-SOO PAID HER RENT UNTIL THE END OF THE MONTH, AND WE HAVE TONS OF ROOMIE APPLICATIONS THANKS TO OUR GENTRIFIED-ASS NEIGHBORHOOD. SHE DOESN'T HAVE TO DECIDE HER FUTURE RIGHT THIS MINUTE.
OF COURSE. BUT THIS CITY IS EXPENSIVE, AND I DON'T WANT YOU TO FALL INTO A BUNCH OF SURVIVAL JOBS FOR THE REST OF YOUR LIFE.
NOT EVERYONE CAN MAGICALLY FIND A JOB THEY LOVE. WE'RE NOT ALL AS LUCKY AS YOU...
...AND IF YOU CALL IT A "SURVIVAL JOB" ONE MORE TIME I WILL APPLY THIS CHILI OIL DIRECTLY TO YOUR PUPILS, DEAR FRIEND.
THE HOT POT CAME TO A BOIL. NO ONE SPOKE.
THIS IS AWKWARD...
WHEN THE STEAM CLEARED, NINA'S MOUTH WAS IN A STRAIGHT LINE. THIS ALARMED THE OTHER TWO, AS THIS WAS A COMMON PRECURSOR TO A RARE PUBLIC BOUT OF CRYING.
THE ONLY TIME THE GIRLS WITNESSED NINA CRY IN PUBLIC WAS AT A SCREENING OF FAREWELL MY CONCUBINE AT BAM.

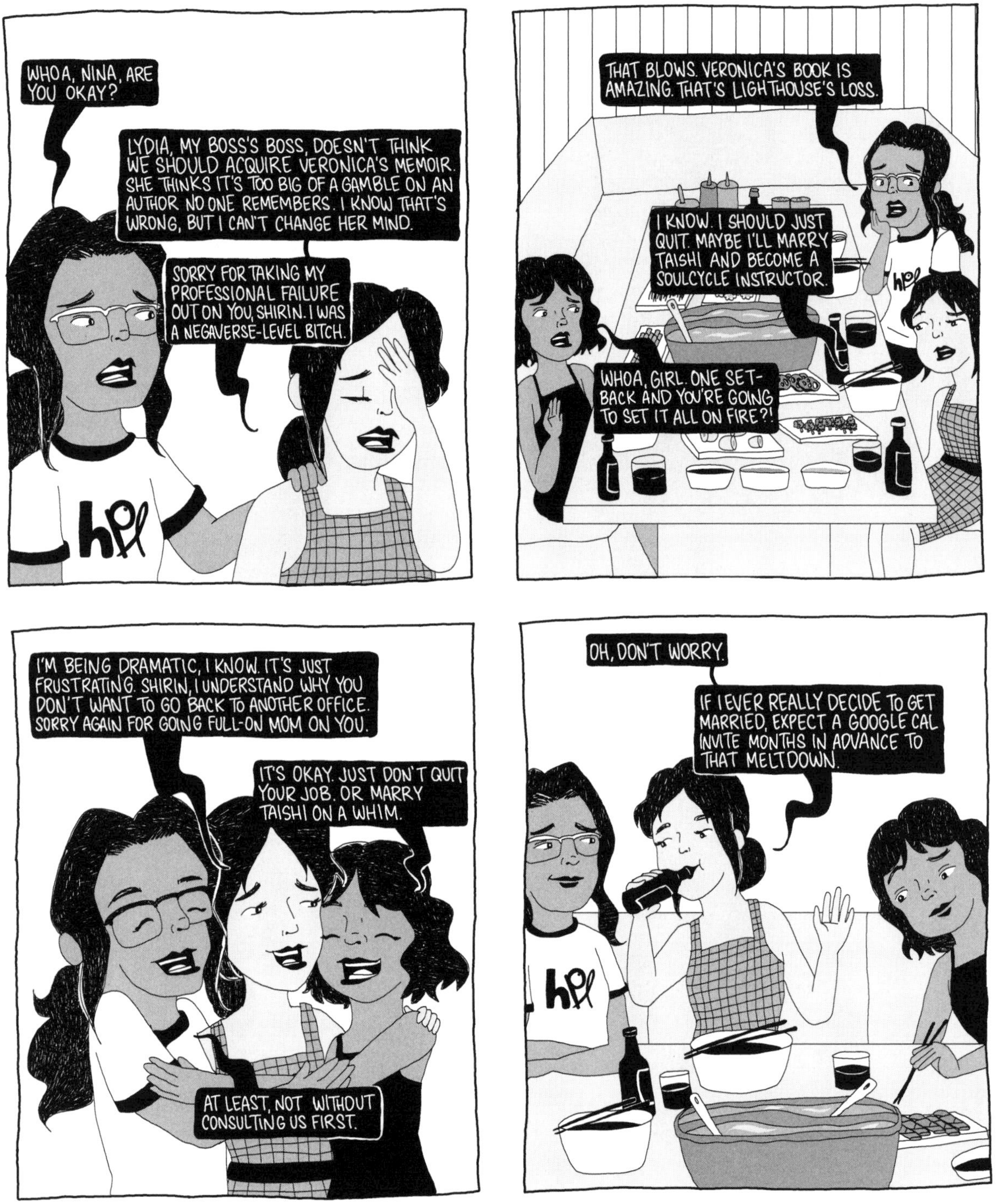
WHOA, NINA, ARE YOU OKAY?
LYDIA, MY BOSS'S BOSS, DOESN'T THINK WE SHOULD ACQUIRE VERONICA'S MEMOIR. SHE THINKS IT'S TOO BIG OF A GAMBLE ON AN AUTHOR NO ONE REMEMBERS. I KNOW THAT'S WRONG, BUT I CAN'T CHANGE HER MIND.
SORRY FOR TAKING MY PROFESSIONAL FAILURE OUT ON YOU, SHIRIN. I WAS A NEGAVERSE-LEVEL BITCH.
THAT BLOWS. VERONICA'S BOOK IS AMAZING. THAT'S LIGHTHOUSE'S LOSS.
I KNOW. I SHOULD JUST QUIT. MAYBE I'LL MARRY TAISHI AND BECOME A SOULCYCLE INSTRUCTOR.
WHOA, GIRL. ONE SET-BACK AND YOU'RE GOING TO SET IT ALL ON FIRE?!
I'M BEING DRAMATIC, I KNOW. IT'S JUST FRUSTRATING. SHIRIN, I UNDERSTAND WHY YOU DON'T WANT TO GO BACK TO ANOTHER OFFICE. SORRY AGAIN FOR GOING FULL-ON MOM ON YOU.
IT'S OKAY. JUST DON'T QUIT YOUR JOB. OR MARRY TAISHI ON A WHIM.
AT LEAST, NOT WITHOUT CONSULTING US FIRST.
OH, DON'T WORRY.
IF I EVER REALLY DECIDE TO GET MARRIED, EXPECT A GOOGLE CAL INVITE MONTHS IN ADVANCE TO THAT MELTDOWN.

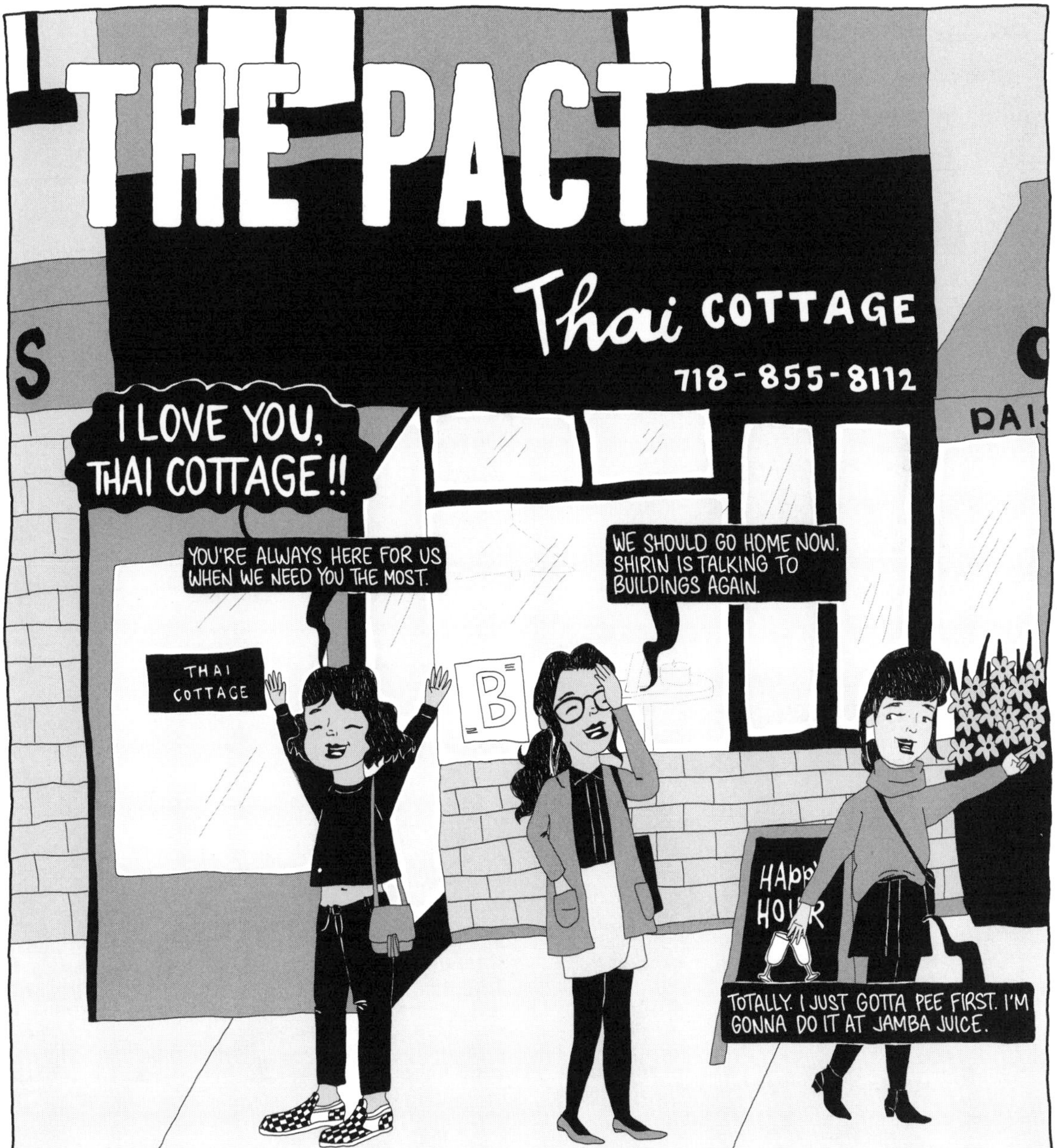
THE PACT
Thai COTTAGE
718-855-8112
I LOVE YOU, THAI COTTAGE!!
YOU'RE ALWAYS HERE FOR US WHEN WE NEED YOU THE MOST.
THAI COTTAGE
WE SHOULD GO HOME NOW. SHIRIN IS TALKING TO BUILDINGS AGAIN.
TOTALLY. I JUST GOTTA PEE FIRST. I'M GONNA DO IT AT JAMBA JUICE.

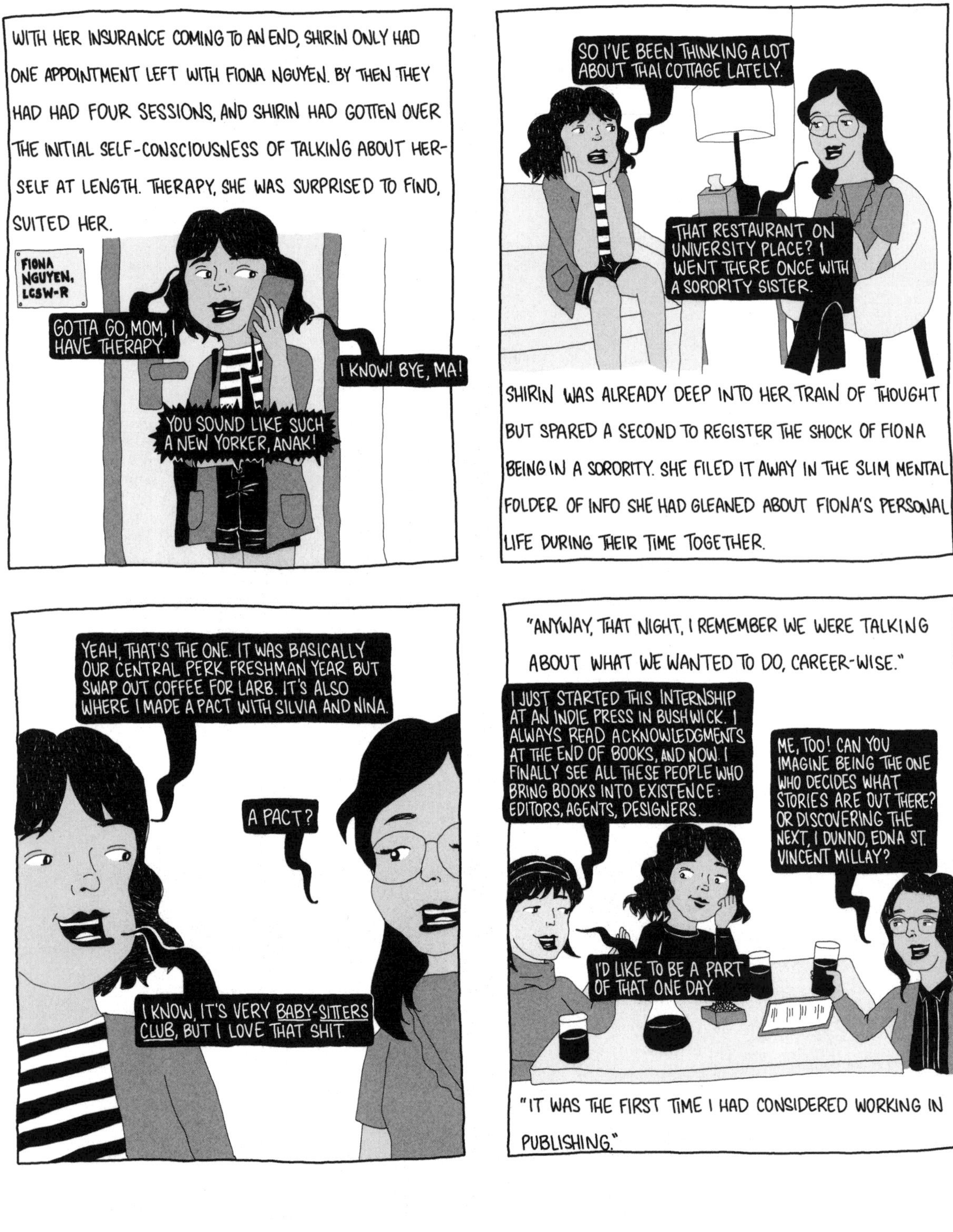
WITH HER INSURANCE COMING TO AN END, SHIRIN ONLY HAD ONE APPOINTMENT LEFT WITH FIONA NGUYEN. BY THEN THEY HAD HAD FOUR SESSIONS, AND SHIRIN HAD GOTTEN OVER THE INITIAL SELF-CONSCIOUSNESS OF TALKING ABOUT HERSELF AT LENGTH. THERAPY, SHE WAS SURPRISED TO FIND, SUITED HER.
FIONA NGUYEN, LCSW-R
GOTTA GO, MOM, I HAVE THERAPY.
YOU SOUND LIKE SUCH A NEW YORKER, ANAK!
I KNOW! BYE, MA!
SO I'VE BEEN THINKING A LOT ABOUT THAI COTTAGE LATELY.
THAT RESTAURANT ON UNIVERSITY PLACE? I WENT THERE ONCE WITH A SORORITY SISTER.
SHIRIN WAS ALREADY DEEP INTO HER TRAIN OF THOUGHT BUT SPARED A SECOND TO REGISTER THE SHOCK OF FIONA BEING IN A SORORITY. SHE FILED IT AWAY IN THE SLIM MENTAL FOLDER OF INFO SHE HAD GLEANED ABOUT FIONA'S PERSONAL LIFE DURING THEIR TIME TOGETHER.
YEAH, THAT'S THE ONE. IT WAS BASICALLY OUR CENTRAL PERK FRESHMAN YEAR BUT SWAP OUT COFFEE FOR LARB. IT'S ALSO WHERE I MADE A PACT WITH SILVIA AND NINA.
A PACT?
I KNOW, IT'S VERY BABY-SITTERS CLUB, BUT I LOVE THAT SHIT.
"ANYWAY, THAT NIGHT, I REMEMBER WE WERE TALKING ABOUT WHAT WE WANTED TO DO, CAREER-WISE."
I JUST STARTED THIS INTERNSHIP AT AN INDIE PRESS IN BUSHWICK. I ALWAYS READ ACKNOWLEDGMENTS AT THE END OF BOOKS, AND NOW I FINALLY SEE ALL THESE PEOPLE WHO BRING BOOKS INTO EXISTENCE: EDITORS, AGENTS, DESIGNERS.
ME, TOO! CAN YOU IMAGINE BEING THE ONE WHO DECIDES WHAT STORIES ARE OUT THERE? OR DISCOVERING THE NEXT, I DUNNO, EDNA ST. VINCENT MILLAY?
I'D LIKE TO BE A PART OF THAT ONE DAY.
"IT WAS THE FIRST TIME I HAD CONSIDERED WORKING IN PUBLISHING."

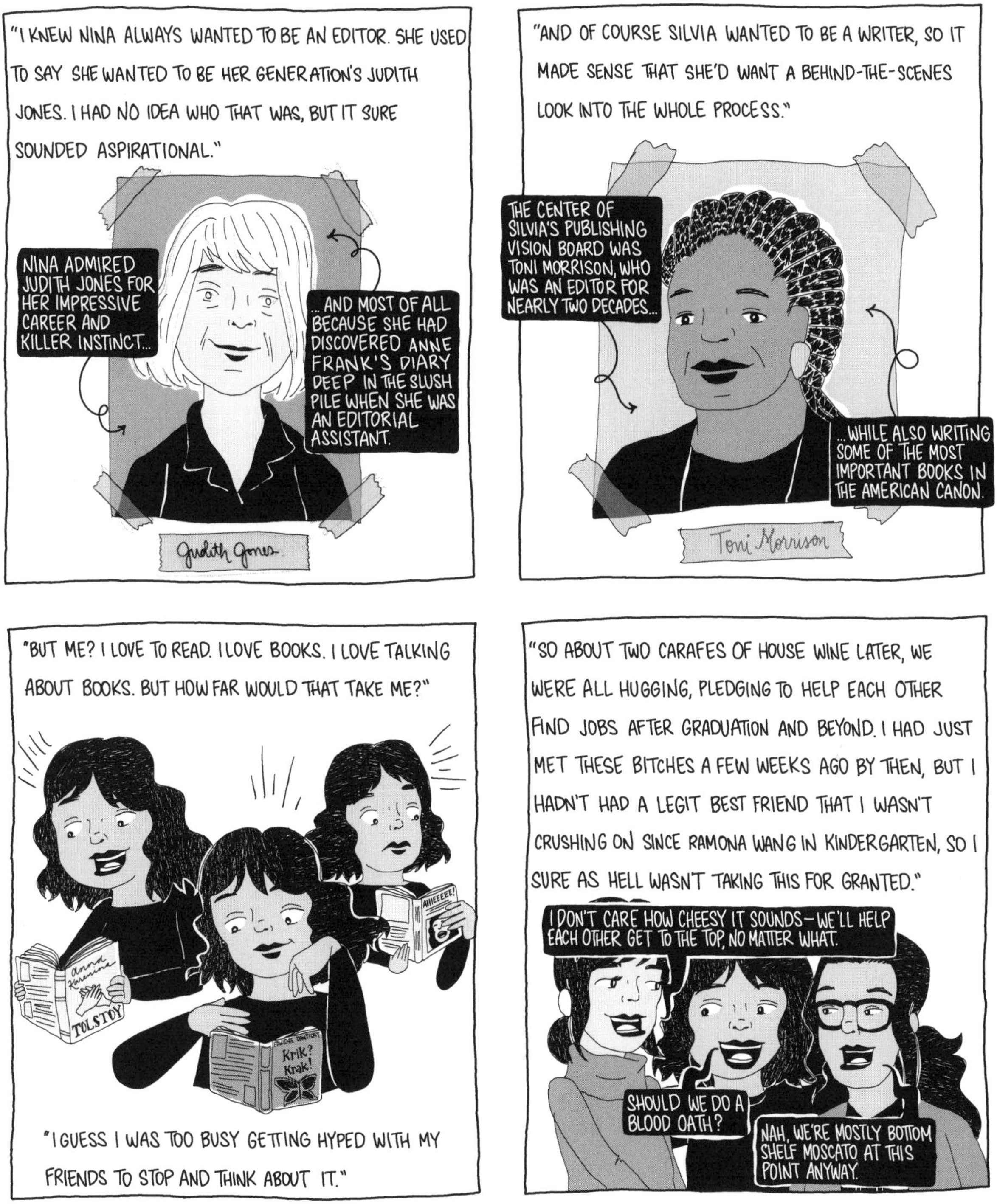
"I KNEW NINA ALWAYS WANTED TO BE AN EDITOR. SHE USED TO SAY SHE WANTED TO BE HER GENERATION'S JUDITH JONES. I HAD NO IDEA WHO THAT WAS, BUT IT SURE SOUNDED ASPIRATIONAL."
NINA ADMIRED JUDITH JONES FOR HER IMPRESSIVE CAREER AND KILLER INSTINCT...
... AND MOST OF ALL BECAUSE SHE HAD DISCOVERED ANNE FRANK'S DIARY DEEP IN THE SLUSH PILE WHEN SHE WAS AN EDITORIAL ASSISTANT.
Judith Jones
"AND OF COURSE SILVIA WANTED TO BE A WRITER, SO IT MADE SENSE THAT SHE'D WANT A BEHIND-THE-SCENES LOOK INTO THE WHOLE PROCESS."
THE CENTER OF SILVIA'S PUBLISHING VISION BOARD WAS TONI MORRISON, WHO WAS AN EDITOR FOR NEARLY TWO DECADES...
...WHILE ALSO WRITING SOME OF THE MOST IMPORTANT BOOKS IN THE AMERICAN CANON.
Toni Morrison
"BUT ME? I LOVE TO READ. I LOVE BOOKS. I LOVE TALKING ABOUT BOOKS. BUT HOW FAR WOULD THAT TAKE ME?"
Anna Karenina
TOLSTOY
Krik? Krak!
AIIIEEEEE!
"I GUESS I WAS TOO BUSY GETTING HYPED WITH MY FRIENDS TO STOP AND THINK ABOUT IT."
"SO ABOUT TWO CARAFES OF HOUSE WINE LATER, WE WERE ALL HUGGING, PLEDGING TO HELP EACH OTHER FIND JOBS AFTER GRADUATION AND BEYOND. I HAD JUST MET THESE BITCHES A FEW WEEKS AGO BY THEN, BUT I HADN'T HAD A LEGIT BEST FRIEND THAT I WASN'T CRUSHING ON SINCE RAMONA WANG IN KINDERGARTEN, SO I SURE AS HELL WASN'T TAKING THIS FOR GRANTED."
I DON'T CARE HOW CHEESY IT SOUNDS—WE'LL HELP EACH OTHER GET TO THE TOP, NO MATTER WHAT.
SHOULD WE DO A BLOOD OATH?
NAH, WE'RE MOSTLY BOTTOM SHELF MOSCATO AT THIS POINT ANYWAY.

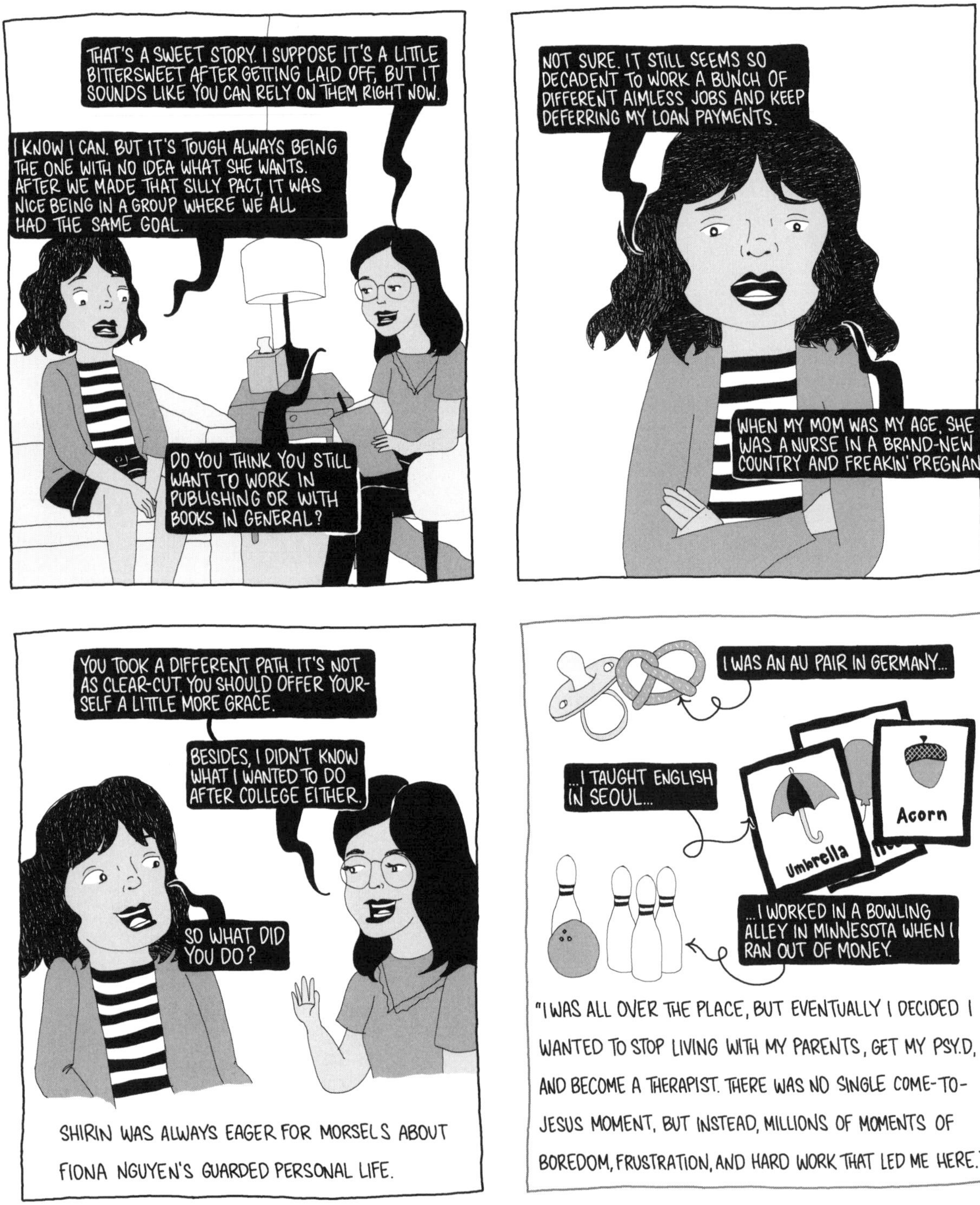
THAT'S A SWEET STORY. I SUPPOSE IT'S A LITTLE BITTERSWEET AFTER GETTING LAID OFF, BUT IT SOUNDS LIKE YOU CAN RELY ON THEM RIGHT NOW.
I KNOW I CAN. BUT IT'S TOUGH ALWAYS BEING THE ONE WITH NO IDEA WHAT SHE WANTS. AFTER WE MADE THAT SILLY PACT, IT WAS NICE BEING IN A GROUP WHERE WE ALL HAD THE SAME GOAL.
DO YOU THINK YOU STILL WANT TO WORK IN PUBLISHING OR WITH BOOKS IN GENERAL?
NOT SURE. IT STILL SEEMS SO DECADENT TO WORK A BUNCH OF DIFFERENT AIMLESS JOBS AND KEEP DEFERRING MY LOAN PAYMENTS.
WHEN MY MOM WAS MY AGE, SHE WAS A NURSE IN A BRAND-NEW COUNTRY AND FREAKIN' PREGNANT.
YOU TOOK A DIFFERENT PATH. IT'S NOT AS CLEAR-CUT. YOU SHOULD OFFER YOURSELF A LITTLE MORE GRACE.
BESIDES, I DIDN'T KNOW WHAT I WANTED TO DO AFTER COLLEGE EITHER.
SO WHAT DID YOU DO?
SHIRIN WAS ALWAYS EAGER FOR MORSELS ABOUT FIONA NGUYEN'S GUARDED PERSONAL LIFE.
I WAS AN AU PAIR IN GERMANY...
...I TAUGHT ENGLISH IN SEOUL...
Acorn
Umbrella
...I WORKED IN A BOWLING ALLEY IN MINNESOTA WHEN I RAN OUT OF MONEY.
"I WAS ALL OVER THE PLACE, BUT EVENTUALLY I DECIDED I WANTED TO STOP LIVING WITH MY PARENTS, GET MY PSY.D, AND BECOME A THERAPIST. THERE WAS NO SINGLE COME-TO-JESUS MOMENT, BUT INSTEAD, MILLIONS OF MOMENTS OF BOREDOM, FRUSTRATION, AND HARD WORK THAT LED ME HERE."

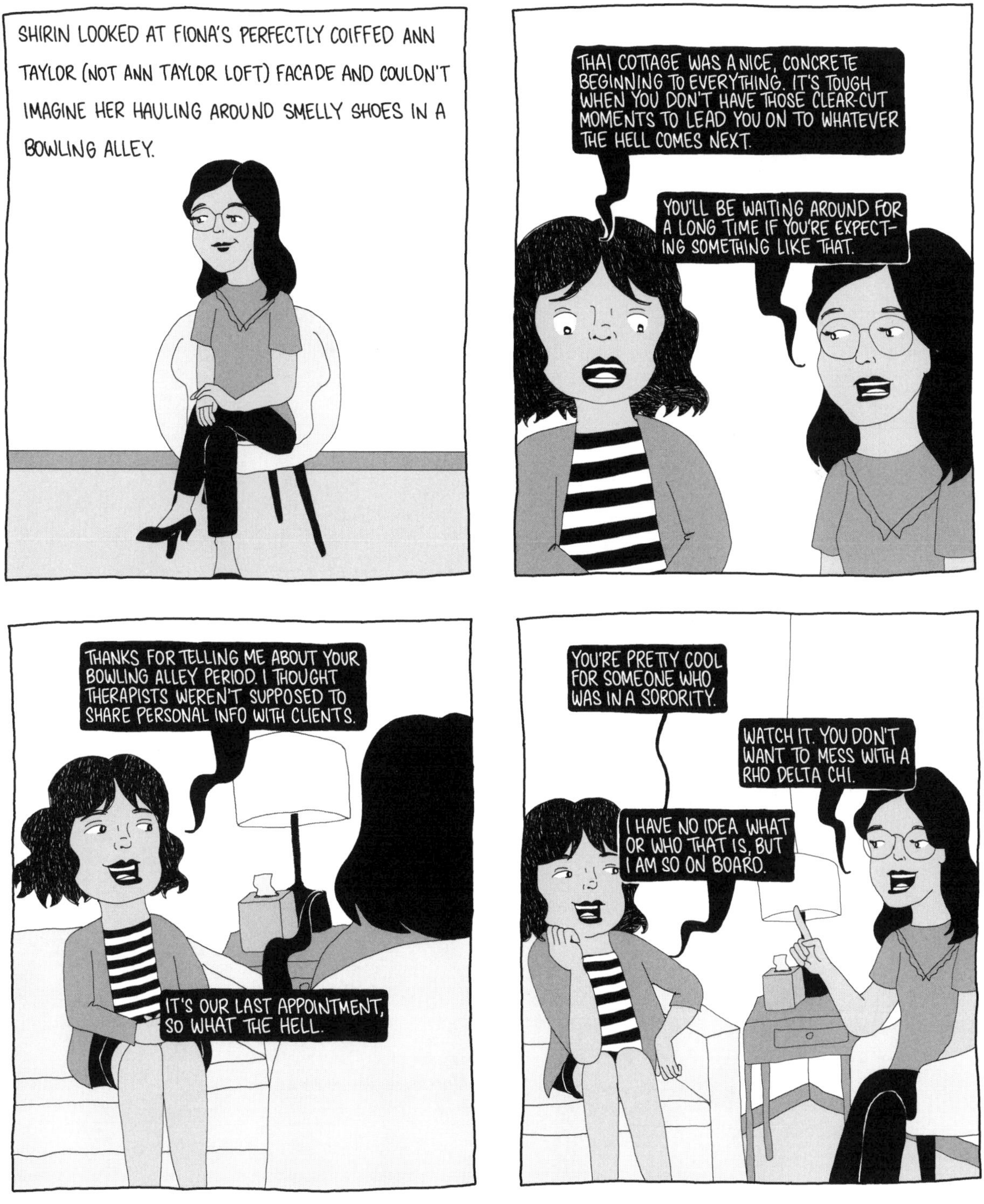
SHIRIN LOOKED AT FIONA'S PERFECTLY COIFFED ANN TAYLOR (NOT ANN TAYLOR LOFT) FACADE AND COULDN'T IMAGINE HER HAULING AROUND SMELLY SHOES IN A BOWLING ALLEY.
THAI COTTAGE WAS A NICE, CONCRETE BEGINNING TO EVERYTHING. IT'S TOUGH WHEN YOU DON'T HAVE THOSE CLEAR-CUT MOMENTS TO LEAD YOU ON TO WHATEVER THE HELL COMES NEXT.
YOU'LL BE WAITING AROUND FOR A LONG TIME IF YOU'RE EXPECTING SOMETHING LIKE THAT.
THANKS FOR TELLING ME ABOUT YOUR BOWLING ALLEY PERIOD. I THOUGHT THERAPISTS WEREN'T SUPPOSED TO SHARE PERSONAL INFO WITH CLIENTS.
IT'S OUR LAST APPOINTMENT, SO WHAT THE HELL.
YOU'RE PRETTY COOL FOR SOMEONE WHO WAS IN A SORORITY.
WATCH IT. YOU DON'T WANT TO MESS WITH A RHO DELTA CHI.
I HAVE NO IDEA WHAT OR WHO THAT IS, BUT I AM SO ON BOARD.

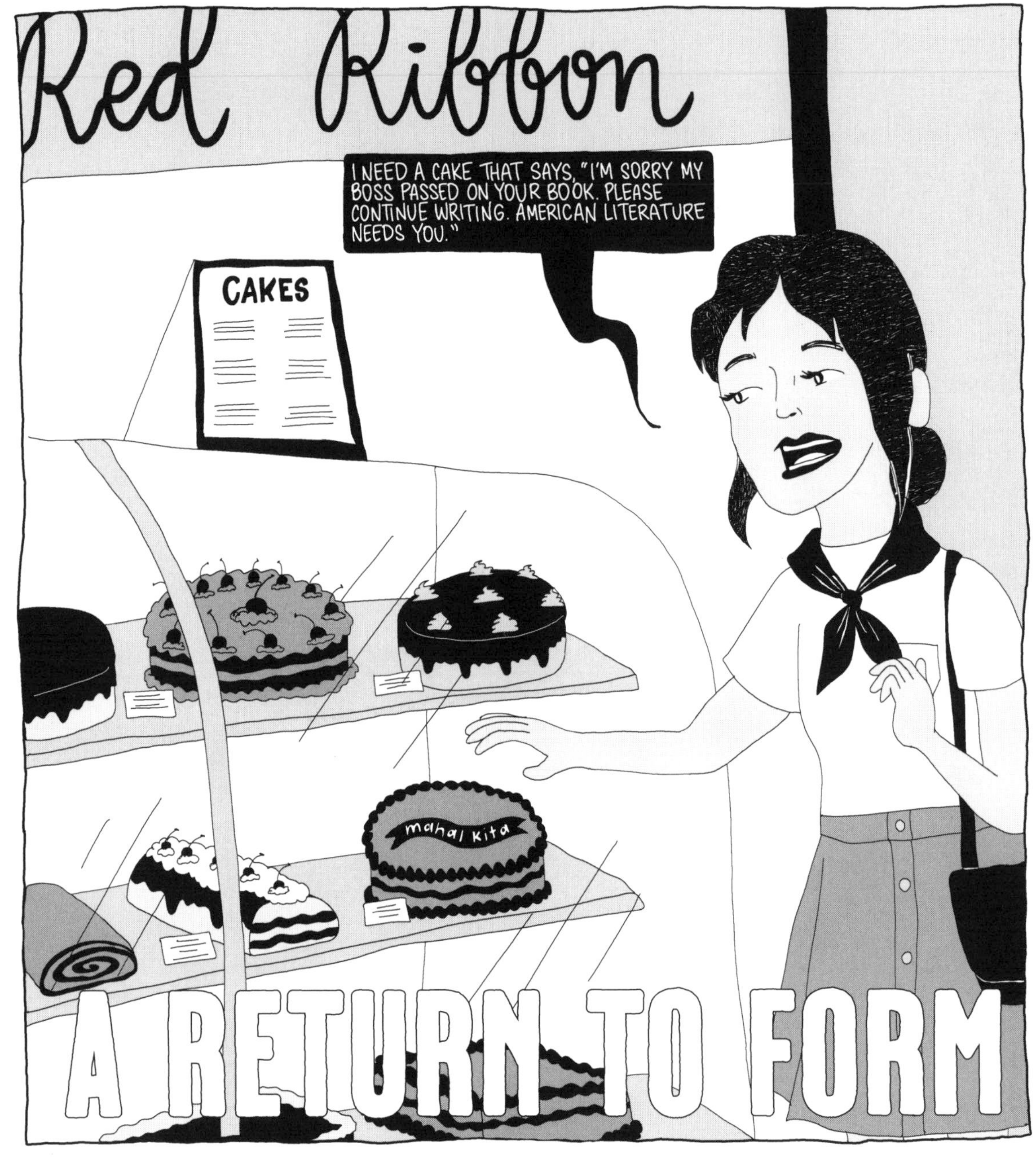
Red Ribbon
I NEED A CAKE THAT SAYS, "I'M SORRY MY BOSS PASSED ON YOUR BOOK. PLEASE CONTINUE WRITING. AMERICAN LITERATURE NEEDS YOU."
CAKES
mahal kita
A RETURN TO FORM

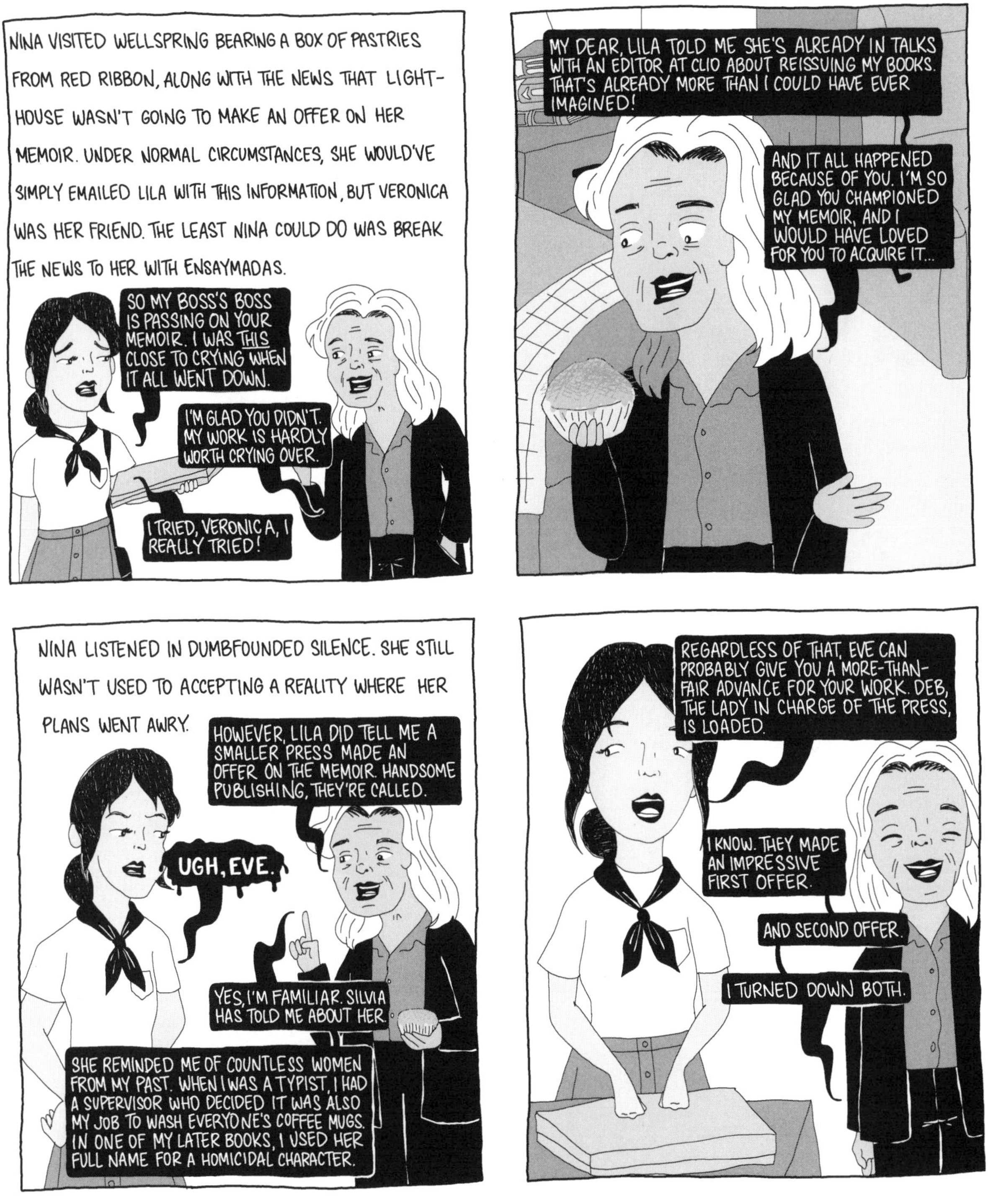
NINA VISITED WELLSPRING BEARING A BOX OF PASTRIES FROM RED RIBBON, ALONG WITH THE NEWS THAT LIGHTHOUSE WASN'T GOING TO MAKE AN OFFER ON HER MEMOIR. UNDER NORMAL CIRCUMSTANCES, SHE WOULD'VE SIMPLY EMAILED LILA WITH THIS INFORMATION, BUT VERONICA WAS HER FRIEND. THE LEAST NINA COULD DO WAS BREAK THE NEWS TO HER WITH ENSAYMADAS.
SO MY BOSS'S BOSS IS PASSING ON YOUR MEMOIR. I WAS THIS CLOSE TO CRYING WHEN IT ALL WENT DOWN.
I'M GLAD YOU DIDN'T. MY WORK IS HARDLY WORTH CRYING OVER.
I TRIED, VERONICA, I REALLY TRIED!
MY DEAR, LILA TOLD ME SHE'S ALREADY IN TALKS WITH AN EDITOR AT CLIO ABOUT REISSUING MY BOOKS. THAT'S ALREADY MORE THAN I COULD HAVE EVER IMAGINED!
AND IT ALL HAPPENED BECAUSE OF YOU. I'M SO GLAD YOU CHAMPIONED MY MEMOIR, AND I WOULD HAVE LOVED FOR YOU TO ACQUIRE IT...
NINA LISTENED IN DUMBFOUNDED SILENCE. SHE STILL WASN'T USED TO ACCEPTING A REALITY WHERE HER PLANS WENT AWRY.
HOWEVER, LILA DID TELL ME A SMALLER PRESS MADE AN OFFER ON THE MEMOIR. HANDSOME PUBLISHING, THEY'RE CALLED.
UGH, EVE.
YES, I'M FAMILIAR. SILVIA HAS TOLD ME ABOUT HER.
SHE REMINDED ME OF COUNTLESS WOMEN FROM MY PAST. WHEN I WAS A TYPIST, I HAD A SUPERVISOR WHO DECIDED IT WAS ALSO MY JOB TO WASH EVERYONE'S COFFEE MUGS. IN ONE OF MY LATER BOOKS, I USED HER FULL NAME FOR A HOMICIDAL CHARACTER.
REGARDLESS OF THAT, EVE CAN PROBABLY GIVE YOU A MORE-THAN-FAIR ADVANCE FOR YOUR WORK. DEB, THE LADY IN CHARGE OF THE PRESS, IS LOADED.
I KNOW. THEY MADE AN IMPRESSIVE FIRST OFFER.
AND SECOND OFFER.
I TURNED DOWN BOTH.

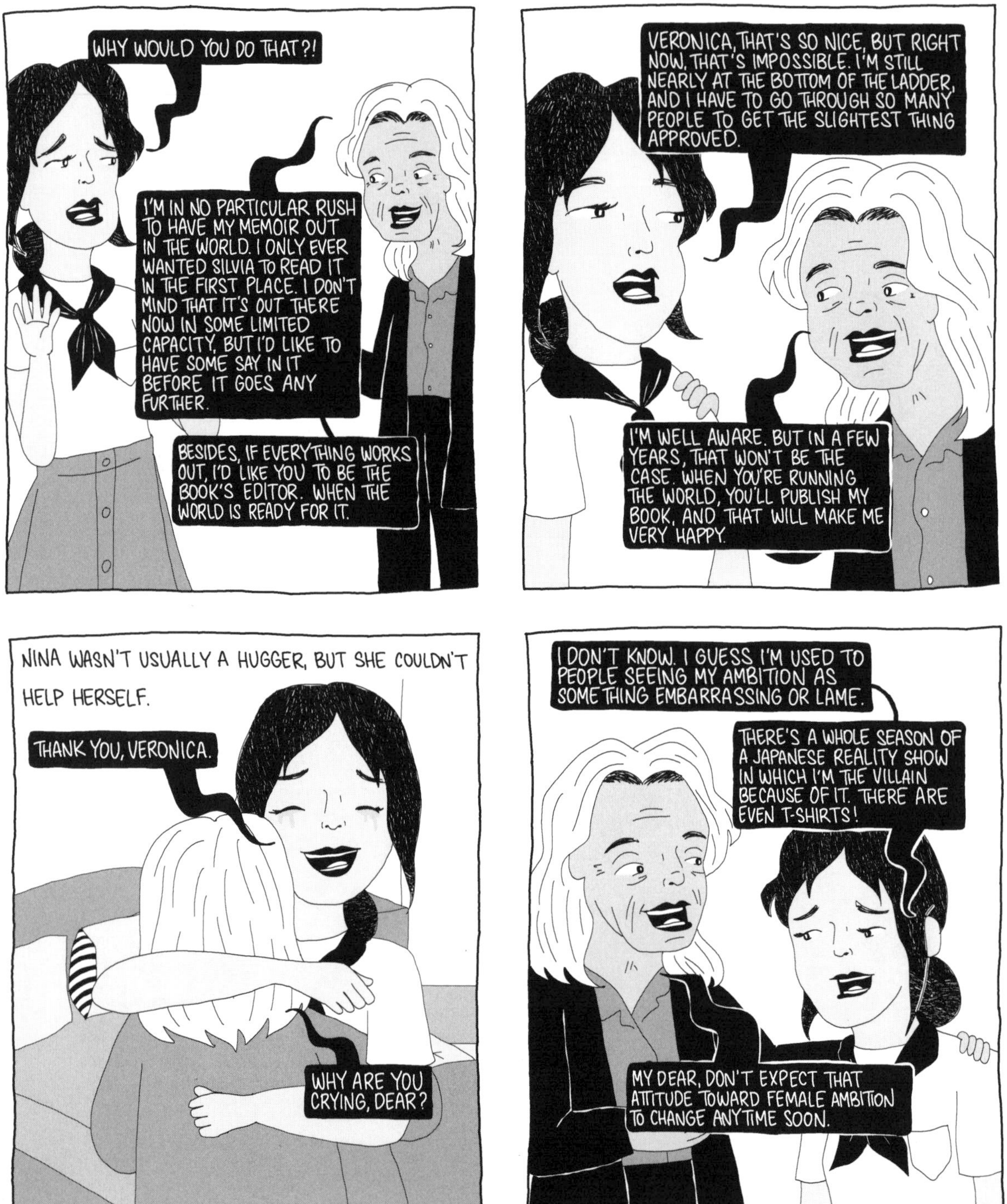
WHY WOULD YOU DO THAT?!
I'M IN NO PARTICULAR RUSH TO HAVE MY MEMOIR OUT IN THE WORLD. I ONLY EVER WANTED SILVIA TO READ IT IN THE FIRST PLACE. I DON'T MIND THAT IT'S OUT THERE NOW IN SOME LIMITED CAPACITY, BUT I'D LIKE TO HAVE SOME SAY IN IT BEFORE IT GOES ANY FURTHER.
BESIDES, IF EVERYTHING WORKS OUT, I'D LIKE YOU TO BE THE BOOK'S EDITOR. WHEN THE WORLD IS READY FOR IT.
VERONICA, THAT'S SO NICE, BUT RIGHT NOW, THAT'S IMPOSSIBLE. I'M STILL NEARLY AT THE BOTTOM OF THE LADDER, AND I HAVE TO GO THROUGH SO MANY PEOPLE TO GET THE SLIGHTEST THING APPROVED.
I'M WELL AWARE. BUT IN A FEW YEARS, THAT WON'T BE THE CASE. WHEN YOU'RE RUNNING THE WORLD, YOU'LL PUBLISH MY BOOK, AND THAT WILL MAKE ME VERY HAPPY.
NINA WASN'T USUALLY A HUGGER, BUT SHE COULDN'T HELP HERSELF.
THANK YOU, VERONICA.
WHY ARE YOU CRYING, DEAR?
I DON'T KNOW. I GUESS I'M USED TO PEOPLE SEEING MY AMBITION AS SOMETHING EMBARRASSING OR LAME.
THERE'S A WHOLE SEASON OF A JAPANESE REALITY SHOW IN WHICH I'M THE VILLAIN BECAUSE OF IT. THERE ARE EVEN T-SHIRTS!
MY DEAR, DON'T EXPECT THAT ATTITUDE TOWARD FEMALE AMBITION TO CHANGE ANYTIME SOON.

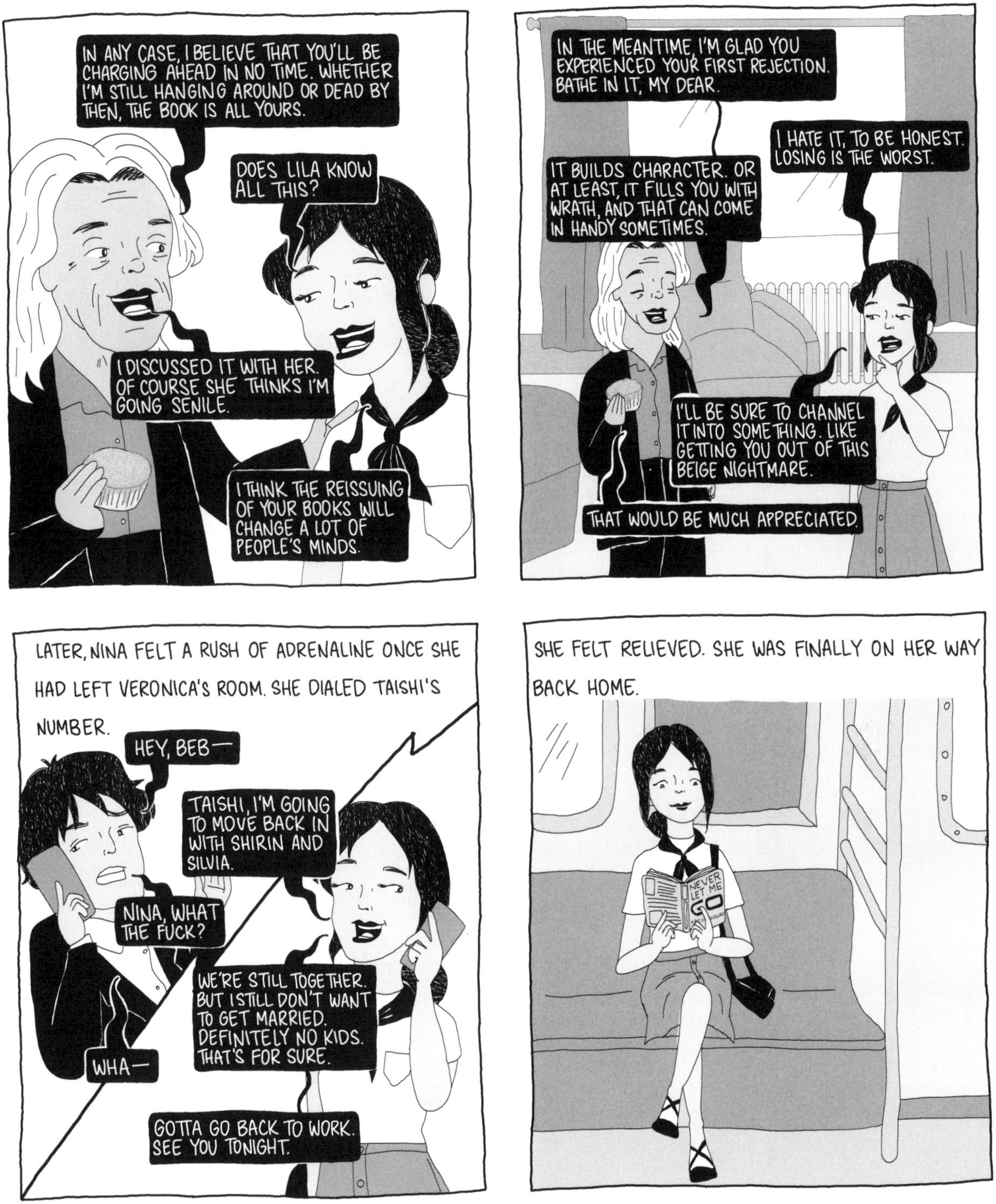
IN ANY CASE, I BELIEVE THAT YOU'LL BE CHARGING AHEAD IN NO TIME. WHETHER I'M STILL HANGING AROUND OR DEAD BY THEN, THE BOOK IS ALL YOURS.
DOES LILA KNOW ALL THIS?
I DISCUSSED IT WITH HER. OF COURSE SHE THINKS I'M GOING SENILE.
I THINK THE REISSUING OF YOUR BOOKS WILL CHANGE A LOT OF PEOPLE'S MINDS.
IN THE MEANTIME, I'M GLAD YOU EXPERIENCED YOUR FIRST REJECTION. BATHE IN IT, MY DEAR.
I HATE IT, TO BE HONEST. LOSING IS THE WORST.
IT BUILDS CHARACTER. OR AT LEAST, IT FILLS YOU WITH WRATH, AND THAT CAN COME IN HANDY SOMETIMES.
I'LL BE SURE TO CHANNEL IT INTO SOMETHING. LIKE GETTING YOU OUT OF THIS BEIGE NIGHTMARE.
THAT WOULD BE MUCH APPRECIATED.
LATER, NINA FELT A RUSH OF ADRENALINE ONCE SHE HAD LEFT VERONICA'S ROOM. SHE DIALED TAISHI'S NUMBER.
HEY, BEB—
TAISHI, I'M GOING TO MOVE BACK IN WITH SHIRIN AND SILVIA.
NINA, WHAT THE FUCK?
WE'RE STILL TOGETHER. BUT I STILL DON'T WANT TO GET MARRIED. DEFINITELY NO KIDS. THAT'S FOR SURE.
WHA—
GOTTA GO BACK TO WORK. SEE YOU TONIGHT.
SHE FELT RELIEVED. SHE WAS FINALLY ON HER WAY BACK HOME.
NEVER LET ME GO

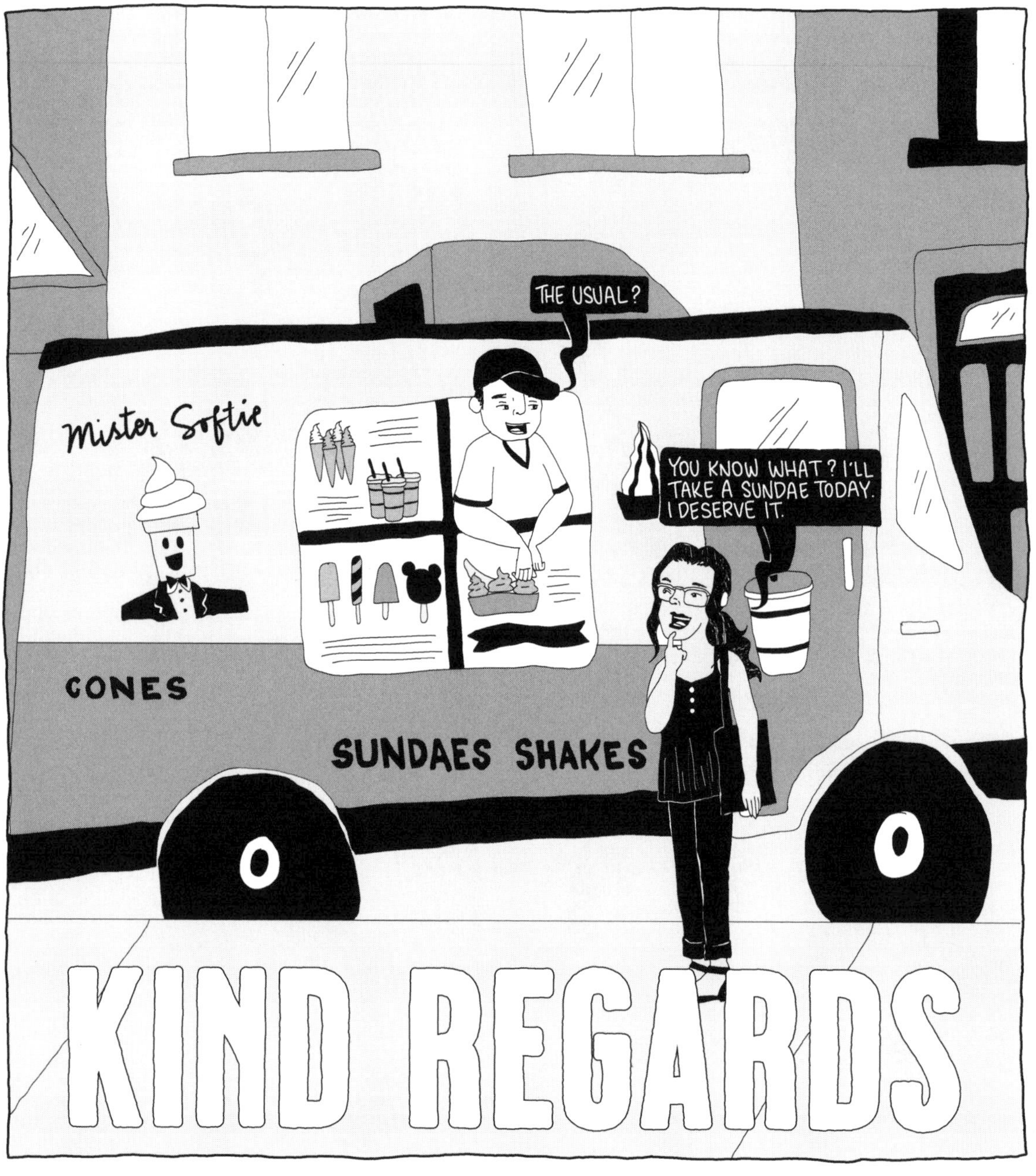
Mister Softie
CONES
SUNDAES SHAKES
THE USUAL?
YOU KNOW WHAT? I'LL TAKE A SUNDAE TODAY. I DESERVE IT.
KIND REGARDS

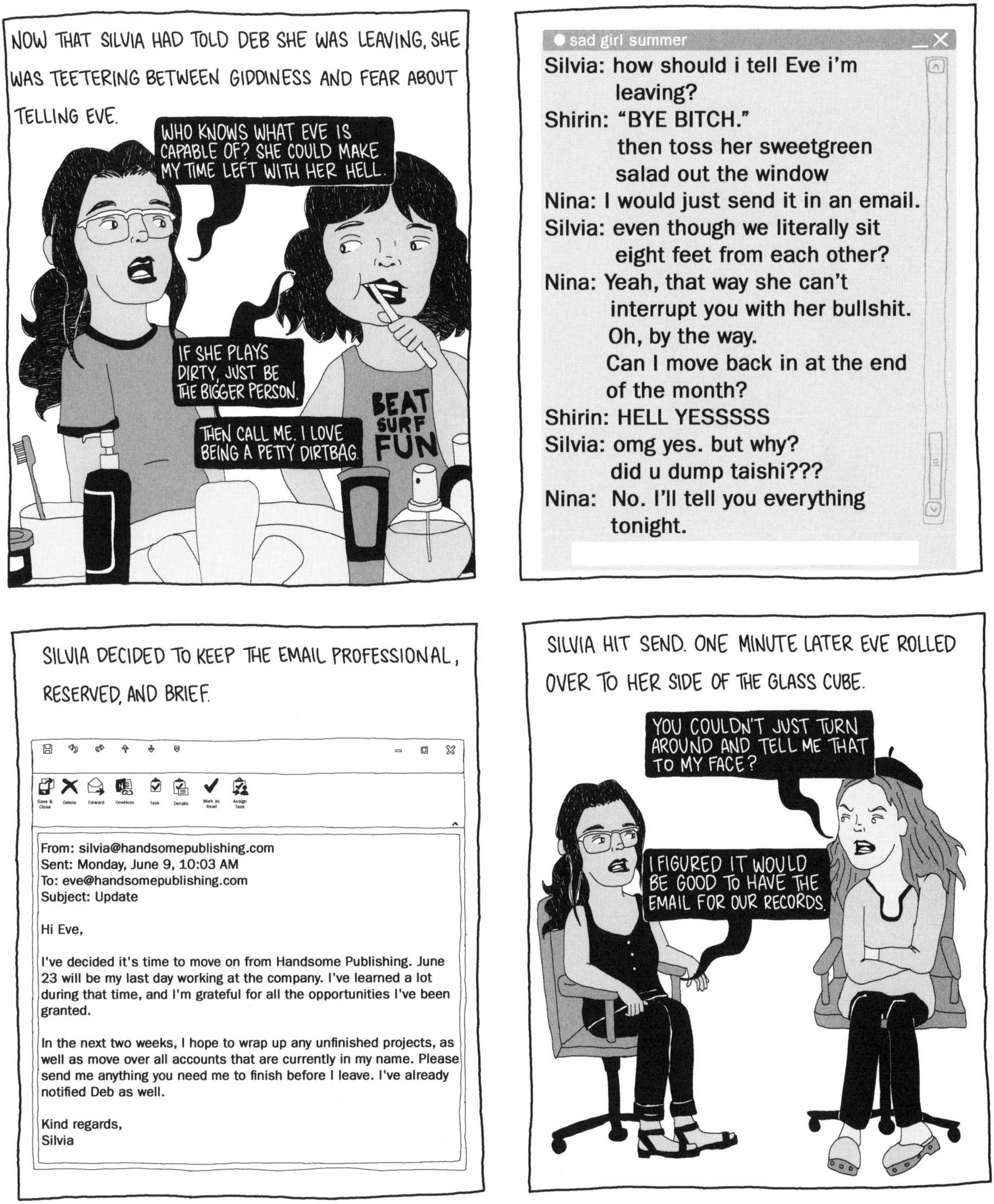
NOW THAT SILVIA HAD TOLD DEB SHE WAS LEAVING, SHE WAS TEETERING BETWEEN GIDDINESS AND FEAR ABOUT TELLING EVE.
WHO KNOWS WHAT EVE IS CAPABLE OF? SHE COULD MAKE MY TIME LEFT WITH HER HELL.
IF SHE PLAYS DIRTY, JUST BE THE BIGGER PERSON.
THEN CALL ME. I LOVE BEING A PETTY DIRTBAG.
BEAT SURF FUN
sad girl summer
Silvia: how should i tell Eve i'm leaving?
Shirin: "BYE BITCH." then toss her sweetgreen salad out the window
Nina: I would just send it in an email.
Silvia: even though we literally sit eight feet from each other?
Nina: Yeah, that way she can't interrupt you with her bullshit. Oh, by the way. Can I move back in at the end of the month?
Shirin: HELL YESSSSS
Silvia: omg yes. but why? did u dump taishi???
Nina: No. I'll tell you everything tonight.
SILVIA DECIDED TO KEEP THE EMAIL PROFESSIONAL, RESERVED, AND BRIEF.
Save & Close
Delete
Forward
OneNote
Task
Details
Mark as Read
Assign Task
From: silvia@handsomepublishing.com
Sent: Monday, June 9, 10:03 AM
To: eve@handsomepublishing.com
Subject: Update
Hi Eve,
I've decided it's time to move on from Handsome Publishing. June 23 will be my last day working at the company. I've learned a lot during that time, and I'm grateful for all the opportunities I've been granted.
In the next two weeks, I hope to wrap up any unfinished projects, as well as move over all accounts that are currently in my name. Please send me anything you need me to finish before I leave. I've already notified Deb as well.
Kind regards,
Silvia
SILVIA HIT SEND. ONE MINUTE LATER EVE ROLLED OVER TO HER SIDE OF THE GLASS CUBE.
YOU COULDN'T JUST TURN AROUND AND TELL ME THAT TO MY FACE?
I FIGURED IT WOULD BE GOOD TO HAVE THE EMAIL FOR OUR RECORDS.

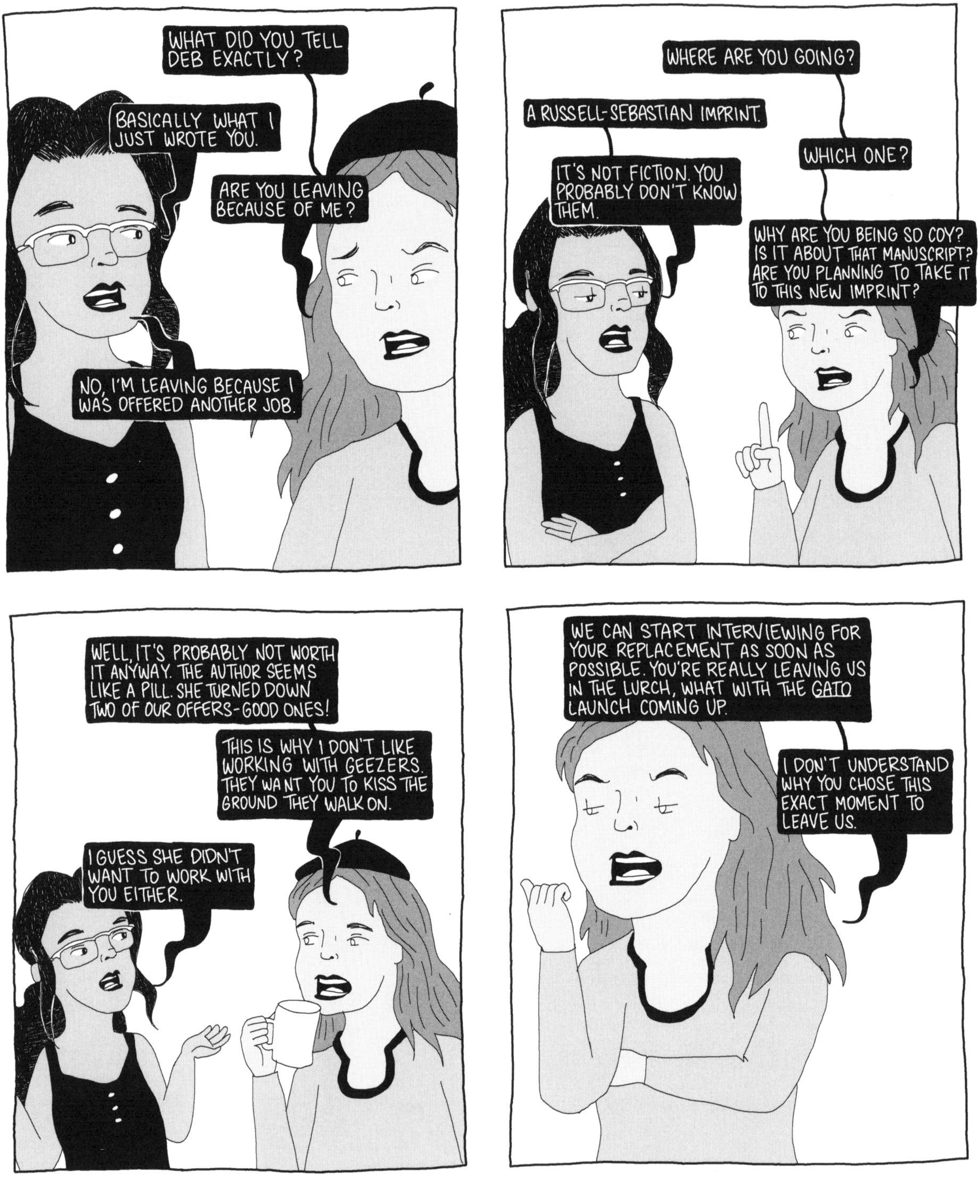
WHAT DID YOU TELL DEB EXACTLY?
BASICALLY WHAT I JUST WROTE YOU.
ARE YOU LEAVING BECAUSE OF ME?
NO, I'M LEAVING BECAUSE I WAS OFFERED ANOTHER JOB.
WHERE ARE YOU GOING?
A RUSSELL-SEBASTIAN IMPRINT.
WHICH ONE?
IT'S NOT FICTION. YOU PROBABLY DON'T KNOW THEM.
WHY ARE YOU BEING SO COY? IS IT ABOUT THAT MANUSCRIPT? ARE YOU PLANNING TO TAKE IT TO THIS NEW IMPRINT?
WELL, IT'S PROBABLY NOT WORTH IT ANYWAY. THE AUTHOR SEEMS LIKE A PILL. SHE TURNED DOWN TWO OF OUR OFFERS-GOOD ONES!
THIS IS WHY I DON'T LIKE WORKING WITH GEEZERS. THEY WANT YOU TO KISS THE GROUND THEY WALK ON.
I GUESS SHE DIDN'T WANT TO WORK WITH YOU EITHER.
WE CAN START INTERVIEWING FOR YOUR REPLACEMENT AS SOON AS POSSIBLE. YOU'RE REALLY LEAVING US IN THE LURCH, WHAT WITH THE GATO LAUNCH COMING UP.
I DON'T UNDERSTAND WHY YOU CHOSE THIS EXACT MOMENT TO LEAVE US.

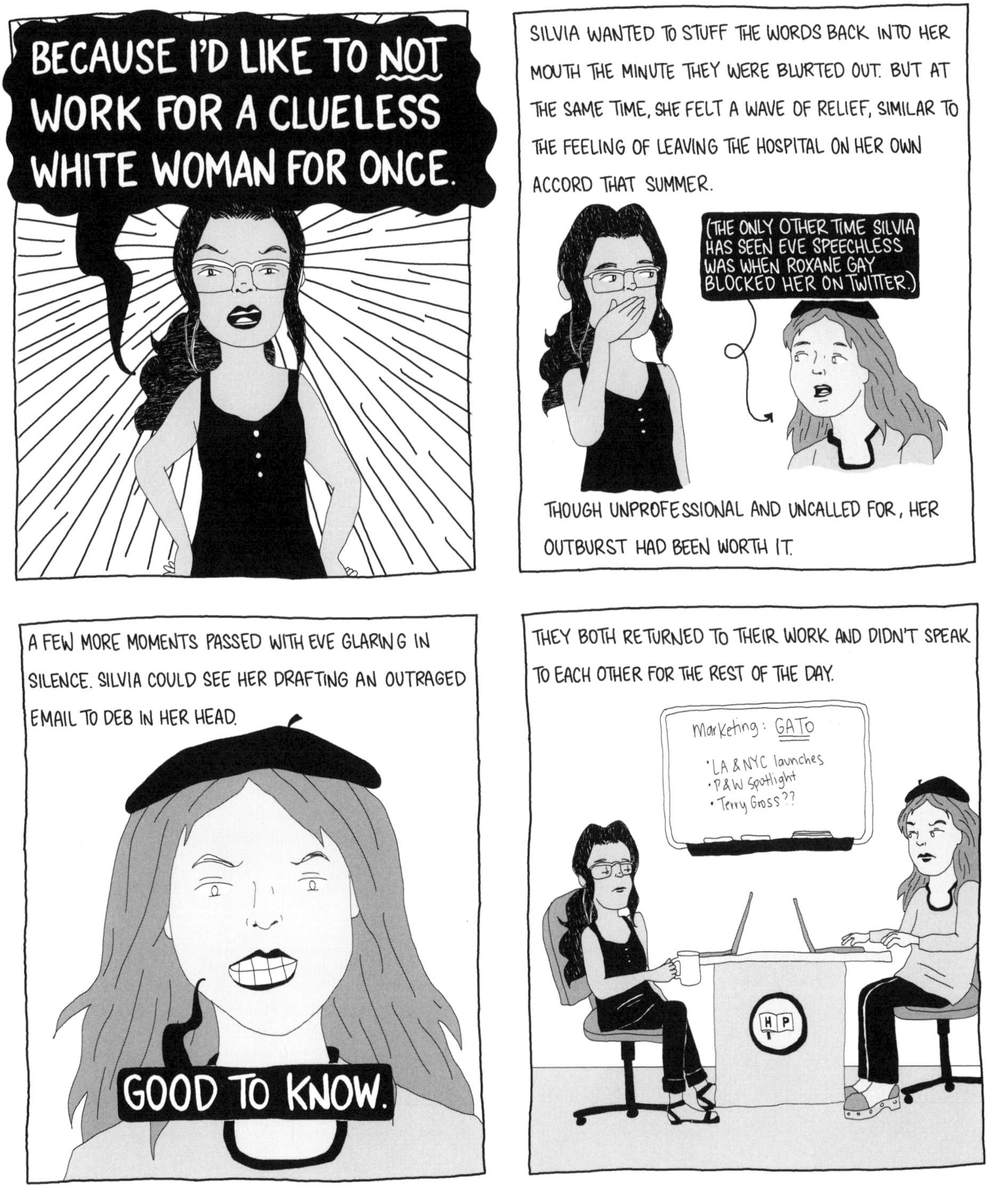
BECAUSE I'D LIKE TO NOT WORK FOR A CLUELESS WHITE WOMAN FOR ONCE.
SILVIA WANTED TO STUFF THE WORDS BACK INTO HER MOUTH THE MINUTE THEY WERE BLURTED OUT. BUT AT THE SAME TIME, SHE FELT A WAVE OF RELIEF, SIMILAR TO THE FEELING OF LEAVING THE HOSPITAL ON HER OWN ACCORD THAT SUMMER.
(THE ONLY OTHER TIME SILVIA HAS SEEN EVE SPEECHLESS WAS WHEN ROXANE GAY BLOCKED HER ON TWITTER.)
THOUGH UNPROFESSIONAL AND UNCALLED FOR, HER OUTBURST HAD BEEN WORTH IT.
A FEW MORE MOMENTS PASSED WITH EVE GLARING IN SILENCE. SILVIA COULD SEE HER DRAFTING AN OUTRAGED EMAIL TO DEB IN HER HEAD.
GOOD TO KNOW.
THEY BOTH RETURNED TO THEIR WORK AND DIDN'T SPEAK TO EACH OTHER FOR THE REST OF THE DAY.
Marketing: GATO
•LA & NYC launches
•P&W Spotlight
•Terry Gross??

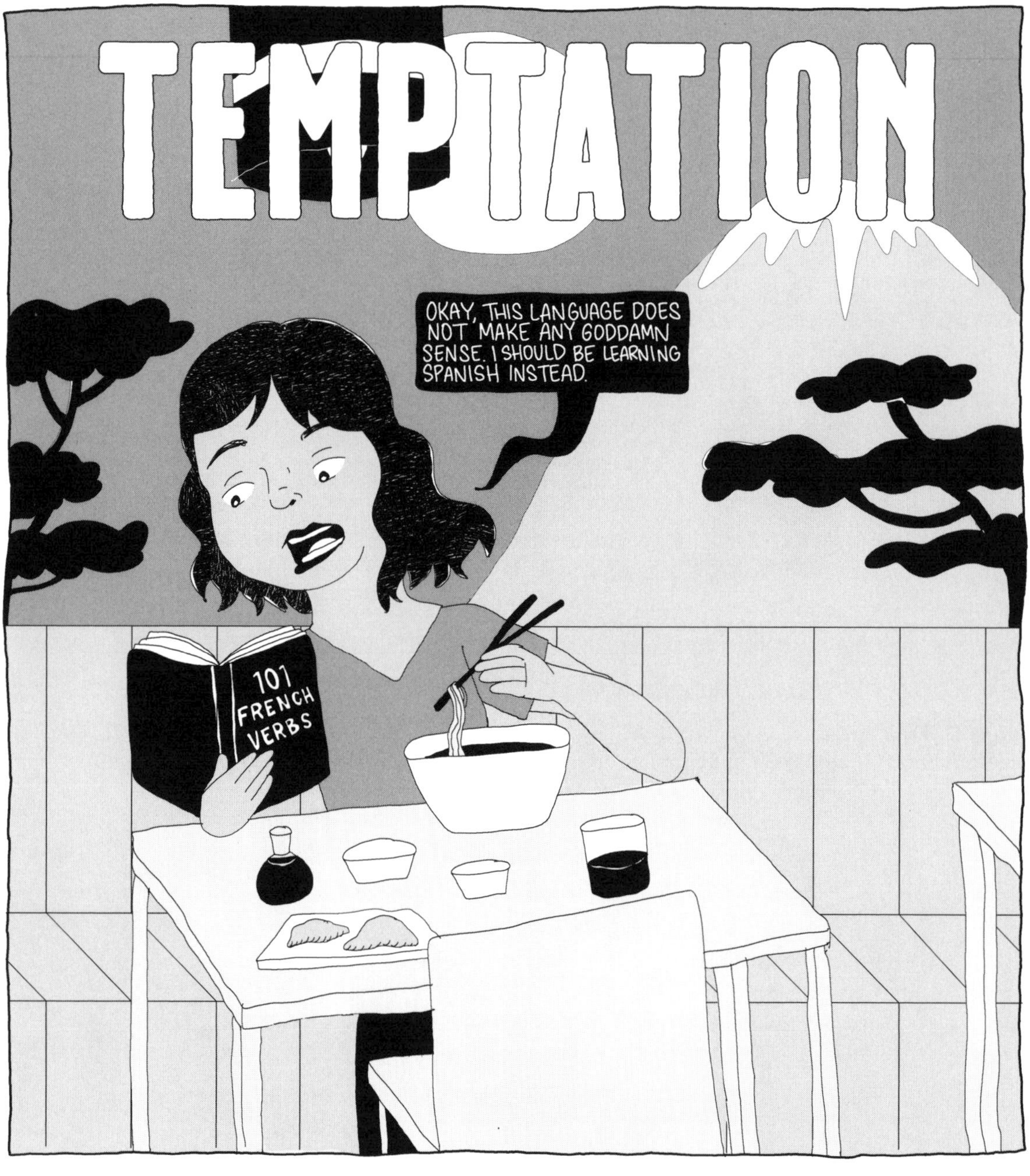
TEMPTATION
OKAY, THIS LANGUAGE DOES NOT MAKE ANY GODDAMN SENSE. I SHOULD BE LEARNING SPANISH INSTEAD.
101 FRENCH VERBS

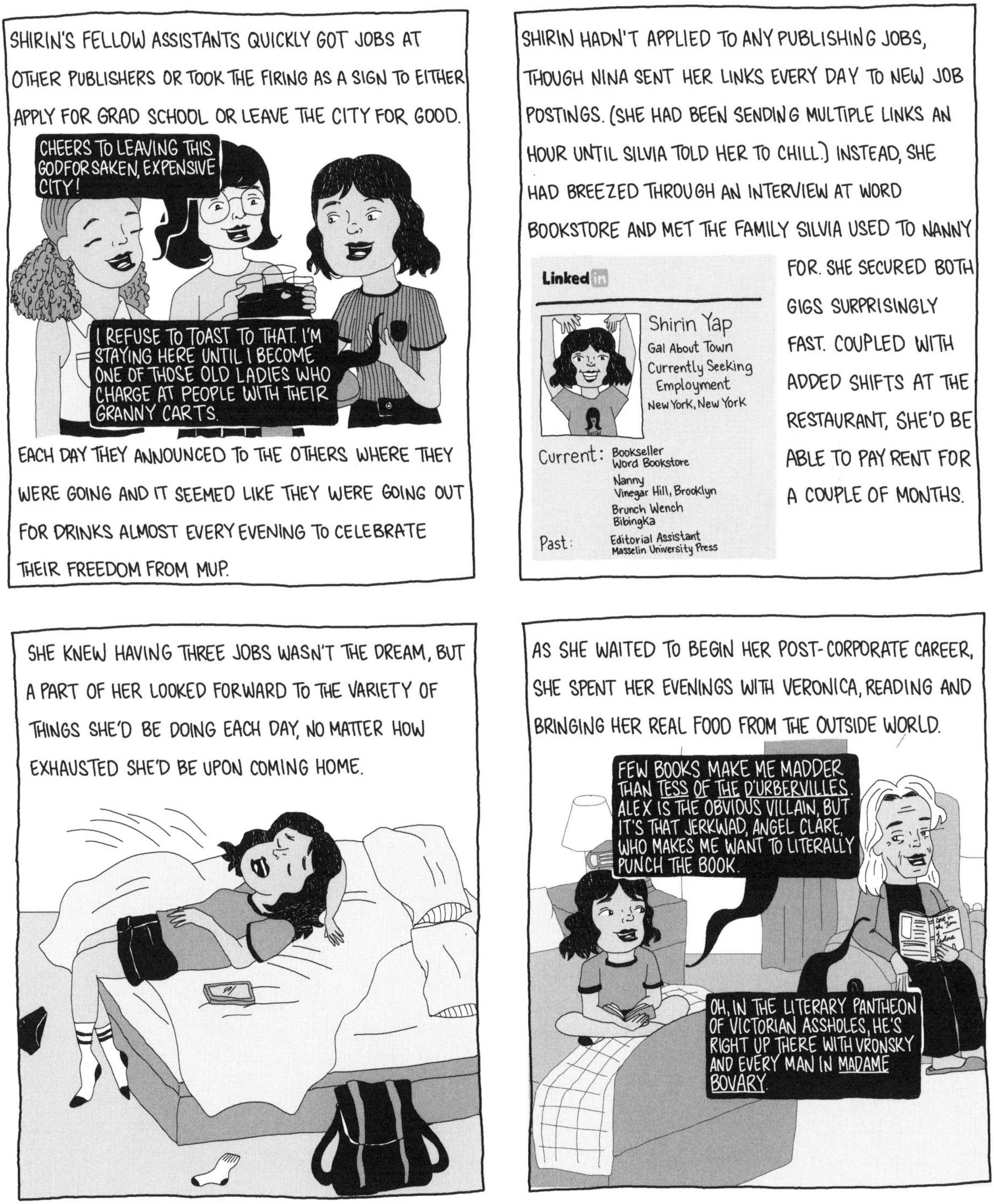
SHIRIN'S FELLOW ASSISTANTS QUICKLY GOT JOBS AT OTHER PUBLISHERS OR TOOK THE FIRING AS A SIGN TO EITHER APPLY FOR GRAD SCHOOL OR LEAVE THE CITY FOR GOOD.
CHEERS TO LEAVING THIS GODFORSAKEN, EXPENSIVE CITY!
I REFUSE TO TOAST TO THAT. I'M STAYING HERE UNTIL I BECOME ONE OF THOSE OLD LADIES WHO CHARGE AT PEOPLE WITH THEIR GRANNY CARTS.
EACH DAY THEY ANNOUNCED TO THE OTHERS WHERE THEY WERE GOING AND IT SEEMED LIKE THEY WERE GOING OUT FOR DRINKS ALMOST EVERY EVENING TO CELEBRATE THEIR FREEDOM FROM MUP.
SHIRIN HADN'T APPLIED TO ANY PUBLISHING JOBS, THOUGH NINA SENT HER LINKS EVERY DAY TO NEW JOB POSTINGS. (SHE HAD BEEN SENDING MULTIPLE LINKS AN HOUR UNTIL SILVIA TOLD HER TO CHILL.) INSTEAD, SHE HAD BREEZED THROUGH AN INTERVIEW AT WORD BOOKSTORE AND MET THE FAMILY SILVIA USED TO NANNY FOR. SHE SECURED BOTH GIGS SURPRISINGLY FAST. COUPLED WITH ADDED SHIFTS AT THE RESTAURANT, SHE'D BE ABLE TO PAY RENT FOR A COUPLE OF MONTHS.
Linked in
Shirin Yap
Gal About Town
Currently Seeking Employment
New York, New York
Current: Bookseller
Word Bookstore
Nanny
Vinegar Hill, Brooklyn
Brunch Wench
Bibingka
Past: Editorial Assistant
Masselin University Press
SHE KNEW HAVING THREE JOBS WASN'T THE DREAM, BUT A PART OF HER LOOKED FORWARD TO THE VARIETY OF THINGS SHE'D BE DOING EACH DAY, NO MATTER HOW EXHAUSTED SHE'D BE UPON COMING HOME.
AS SHE WAITED TO BEGIN HER POST-CORPORATE CAREER, SHE SPENT HER EVENINGS WITH VERONICA, READING AND BRINGING HER REAL FOOD FROM THE OUTSIDE WORLD.
FEW BOOKS MAKE ME MADDER THAN TESS OF THE D'URBERVILLES. ALEX IS THE OBVIOUS VILLAIN, BUT IT'S THAT JERKWAD, ANGEL CLARE, WHO MAKES ME WANT TO LITERALLY PUNCH THE BOOK.
OH, IN THE LITERARY PANTHEON OF VICTORIAN ASSHOLES, HE'S RIGHT UP THERE WITH VRONSKY AND EVERY MAN IN MADAME BOVARY.

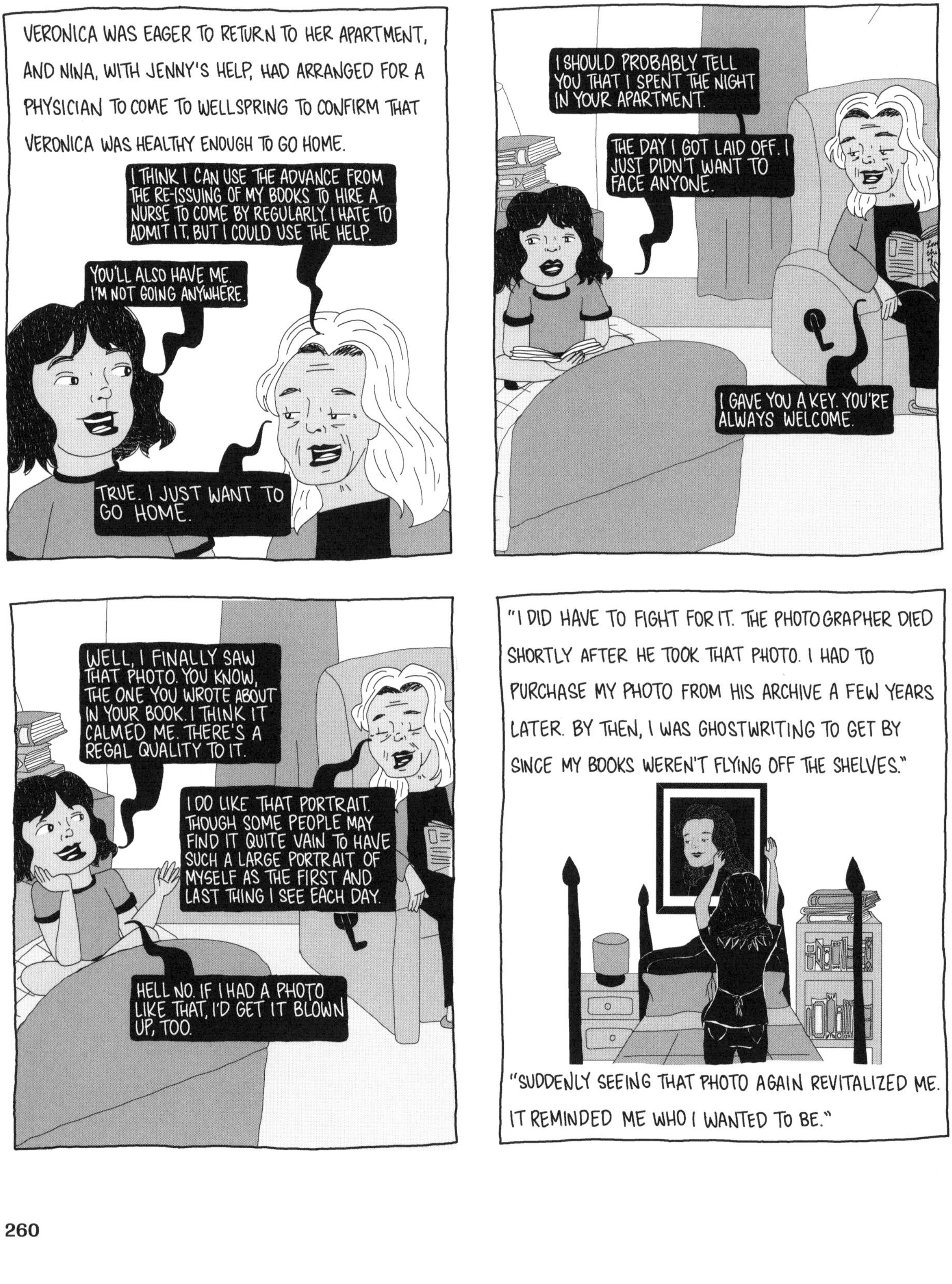
VERONICA WAS EAGER TO RETURN TO HER APARTMENT, AND NINA, WITH JENNY'S HELP, HAD ARRANGED FOR A PHYSICIAN TO COME TO WELLSPRING TO CONFIRM THAT VERONICA WAS HEALTHY ENOUGH TO GO HOME.
I THINK I CAN USE THE ADVANCE FROM THE RE-ISSUING OF MY BOOKS TO HIRE A NURSE TO COME BY REGULARLY. I HATE TO ADMIT IT, BUT I COULD USE THE HELP.
YOU'LL ALSO HAVE ME. I'M NOT GOING ANYWHERE.
TRUE. I JUST WANT TO GO HOME.
I SHOULD PROBABLY TELL YOU THAT I SPENT THE NIGHT IN YOUR APARTMENT.
THE DAY I GOT LAID OFF. I JUST DIDN'T WANT TO FACE ANYONE.
I GAVE YOU A KEY. YOU'RE ALWAYS WELCOME.
WELL, I FINALLY SAW THAT PHOTO. YOU KNOW, THE ONE YOU WROTE ABOUT IN YOUR BOOK. I THINK IT CALMED ME. THERE'S A REGAL QUALITY TO IT.
I DO LIKE THAT PORTRAIT. THOUGH SOME PEOPLE MAY FIND IT QUITE VAIN TO HAVE SUCH A LARGE PORTRAIT OF MYSELF AS THE FIRST AND LAST THING I SEE EACH DAY.
HELL NO. IF I HAD A PHOTO LIKE THAT, I'D GET IT BLOWN UP, TOO.
"I DID HAVE TO FIGHT FOR IT. THE PHOTOGRAPHER DIED SHORTLY AFTER HE TOOK THAT PHOTO. I HAD TO PURCHASE MY PHOTO FROM HIS ARCHIVE A FEW YEARS LATER. BY THEN, I WAS GHOSTWRITING TO GET BY SINCE MY BOOKS WEREN'T FLYING OFF THE SHELVES."
"SUDDENLY SEEING THAT PHOTO AGAIN REVITALIZED ME. IT REMINDED ME WHO I WANTED TO BE."

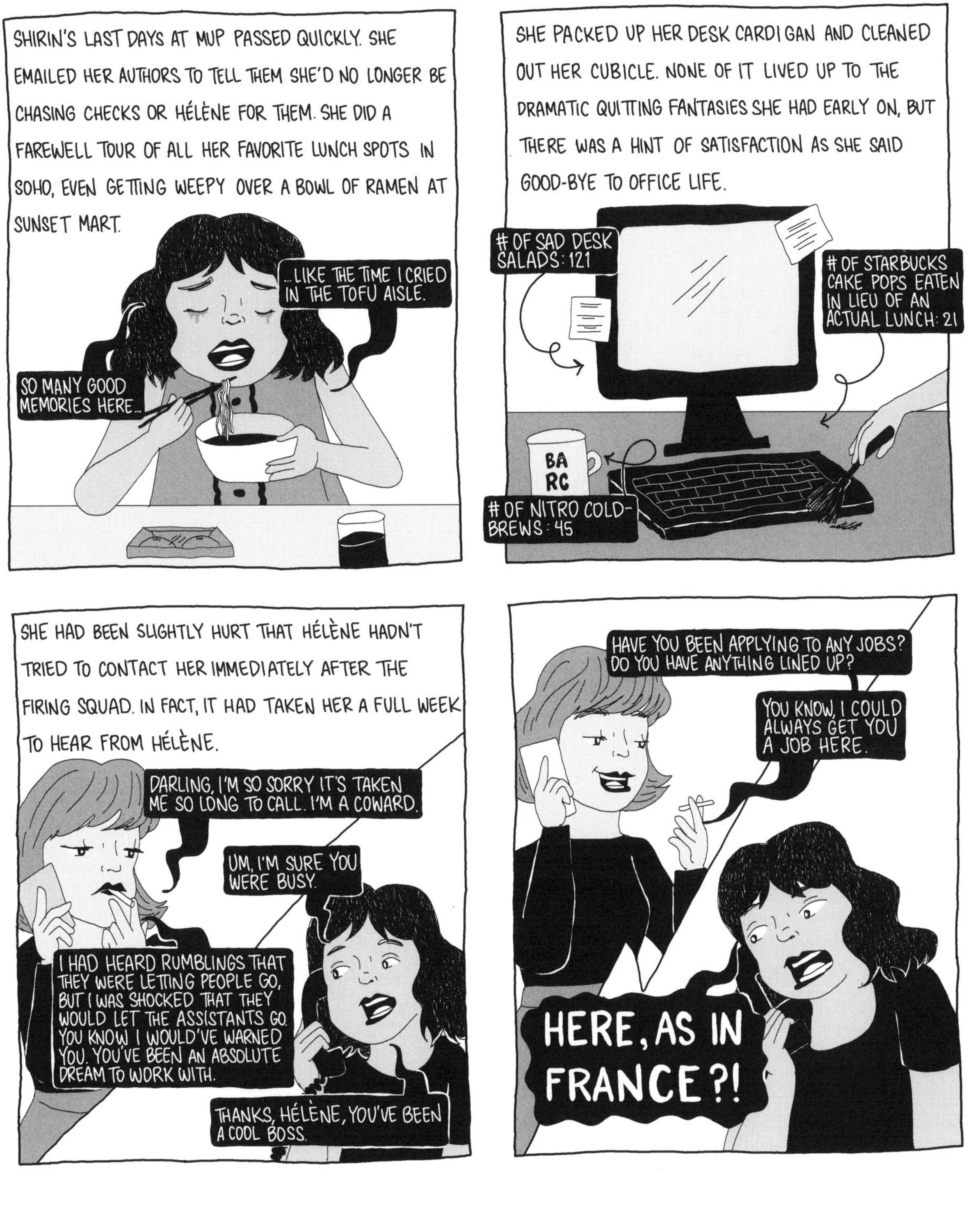
SHIRIN'S LAST DAYS AT MUP PASSED QUICKLY. SHE EMAILED HER AUTHORS TO TELL THEM SHE'D NO LONGER BE CHASING CHECKS OR HÉLÈNE FOR THEM. SHE DID A FAREWELL TOUR OF ALL HER FAVORITE LUNCH SPOTS IN SOHO, EVEN GETTING WEEPY OVER A BOWL OF RAMEN AT SUNSET MART.
SO MANY GOOD MEMORIES HERE...
...LIKE THE TIME I CRIED IN THE TOFU AISLE.
SHE PACKED UP HER DESK CARDIGAN AND CLEANED OUT HER CUBICLE. NONE OF IT LIVED UP TO THE DRAMATIC QUITTING FANTASIES SHE HAD EARLY ON, BUT THERE WAS A HINT OF SATISFACTION AS SHE SAID GOOD-BYE TO OFFICE LIFE.
OF SAD DESK SALADS: 121
OF STARBUCKS CAKE POPS EATEN IN LIEU OF AN ACTUAL LUNCH: 21
BA RC
OF NITRO COLD-BREWS: 45
SHE HAD BEEN SLIGHTLY HURT THAT HÉLÈNE HADN'T TRIED TO CONTACT HER IMMEDIATELY AFTER THE FIRING SQUAD. IN FACT, IT HAD TAKEN HER A FULL WEEK TO HEAR FROM HÉLÈNE.
DARLING, I'M SO SORRY IT'S TAKEN ME SO LONG TO CALL. I'M A COWARD.
UM, I'M SURE YOU WERE BUSY.
I HAD HEARD RUMBLINGS THAT THEY WERE LETTING PEOPLE GO, BUT I WAS SHOCKED THAT THEY WOULD LET THE ASSISTANTS GO. YOU KNOW I WOULD'VE WARNED YOU. YOU'VE BEEN AN ABSOLUTE DREAM TO WORK WITH.
THANKS, HÉLÈNE, YOU'VE BEEN A COOL BOSS.
HAVE YOU BEEN APPLYING TO ANY JOBS? DO YOU HAVE ANYTHING LINED UP?
YOU KNOW, I COULD ALWAYS GET YOU A JOB HERE.
HERE, AS IN FRANCE?!

"BIEN SÛR. THE PARIS OFFICE IS MUCH BUSIER AND BETTER ORGANIZED. WE GET A LOT MORE SUPPORT FROM THIERRY SINCE WE'RE RIGHT HERE WHERE HE CAN SEE US. I THINK YOU'D DO VERY WELL IN OUR RIGHTS DEPARTMENT, WHICH MOSTLY WORKS WITH THE UK AND US. I SHARE A COUNTRY HOME WITH THE HEAD OF THE DEPARTMENT, CELINE."

SHIRIN HAD NO IDEA WHAT CELINE LOOKED LIKE, BUT BASED ON WORDS LIKE "HEAD OF DEPARTMENT" AND "COUNTRY HOME," THIS IS WHAT SHIRIN IMAGINED.

JUST THINK ABOUT IT, DARLING.

BUT LET ME KNOW SOON. IF WE WORK QUICKLY, I CAN GET YOU A NICE POSITION HERE.

SHIRIN SAID NOTHING. SHE REMEMBERED HER SAD TRIP ABROAD, AND YET: THIS WAS STILL AN INTRIGUING OPPORTUNITY.

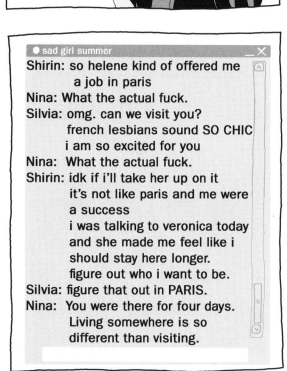

● sad girl summer

Shirin: so helene kind of offered me a job in paris
Nina: What the actual fuck.
Silvia: omg. can we visit you? french lesbians sound SO CHIC i am so excited for you
Nina: What the actual fuck.
Shirin: idk if i'll take her up on it it's not like paris and me were a success i was talking to veronica today and she made me feel like i should stay here longer. figure out who i want to be.
Silvia: figure that out in PARIS.
Nina: You were there for four days. Living somewhere is so different than visiting.

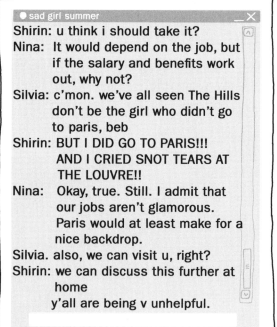

● sad girl summer

Shirin: u think i should take it?
Nina: It would depend on the job, but if the salary and benefits work out, why not?
Silvia: c'mon. we've all seen The Hills don't be the girl who didn't go to paris, beb
Shirin: BUT I DID GO TO PARIS!!! AND I CRIED SNOT TEARS AT THE LOUVRE!!
Nina: Okay, true. Still. I admit that our jobs aren't glamorous. Paris would at least make for a nice backdrop.
Silvia. also, we can visit u, right?
Shirin: we can discuss this further at home y'all are being v unhelpful.

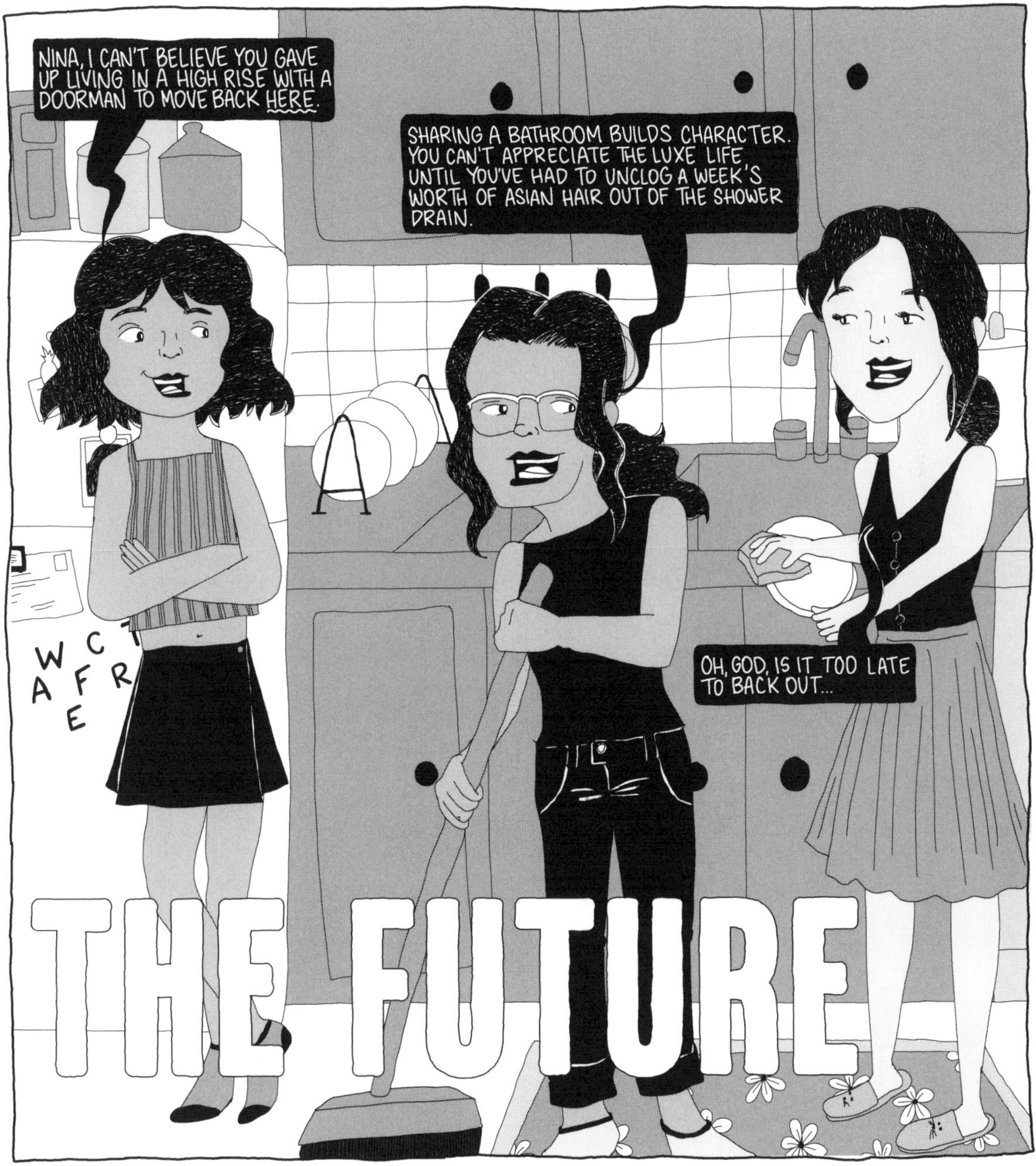
NINA, I CAN'T BELIEVE YOU GAVE UP LIVING IN A HIGH RISE WITH A DOORMAN TO MOVE BACK HERE.
SHARING A BATHROOM BUILDS CHARACTER. YOU CAN'T APPRECIATE THE LUXE LIFE UNTIL YOU'VE HAD TO UNCLOG A WEEK'S WORTH OF ASIAN HAIR OUT OF THE SHOWER DRAIN.
OH, GOD, IS IT TOO LATE TO BACK OUT...
W C T
A F R
E
THE FUTURE

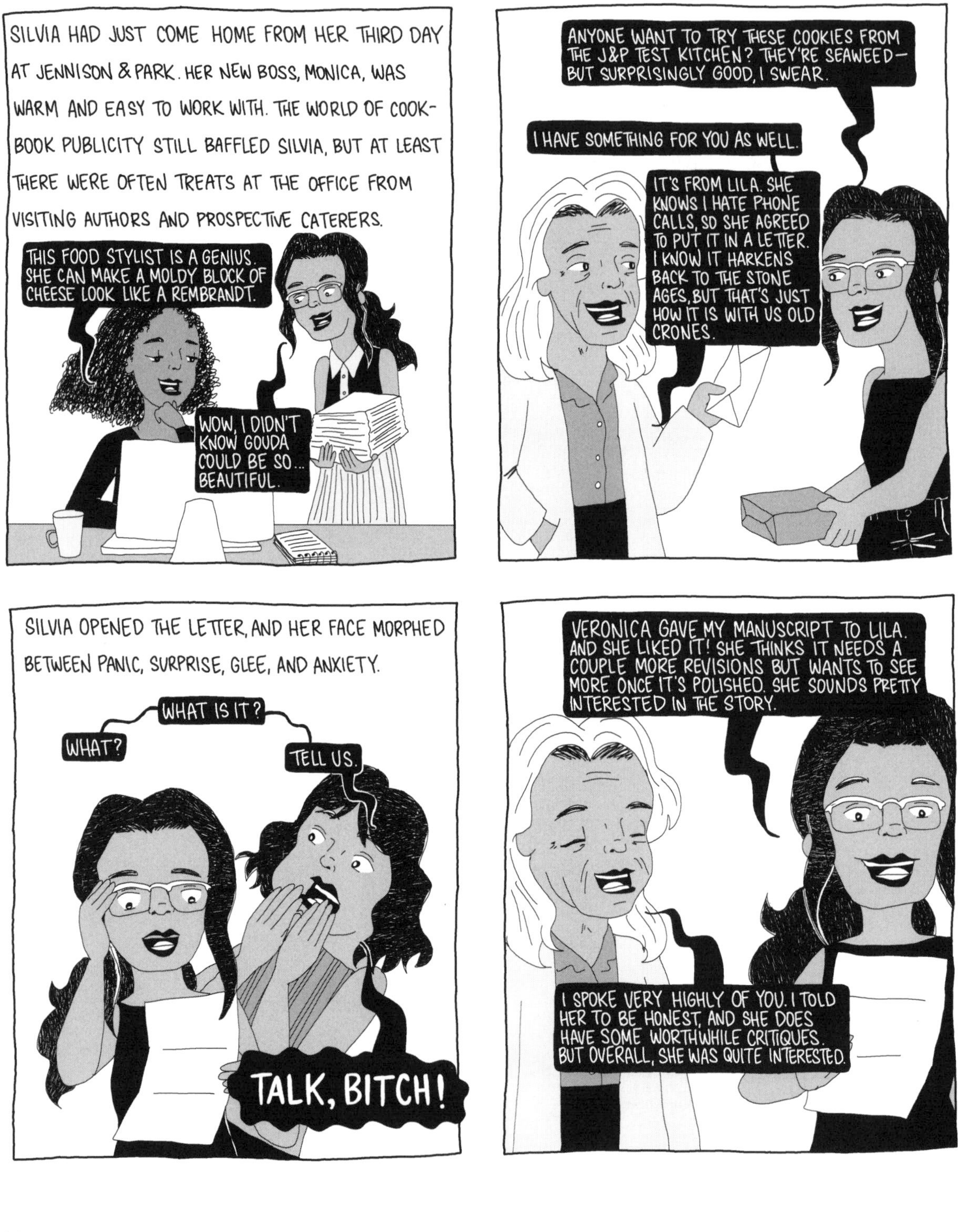
SILVIA HAD JUST COME HOME FROM HER THIRD DAY AT JENNISON & PARK. HER NEW BOSS, MONICA, WAS WARM AND EASY TO WORK WITH. THE WORLD OF COOKBOOK PUBLICITY STILL BAFFLED SILVIA, BUT AT LEAST THERE WERE OFTEN TREATS AT THE OFFICE FROM VISITING AUTHORS AND PROSPECTIVE CATERERS.
THIS FOOD STYLIST IS A GENIUS. SHE CAN MAKE A MOLDY BLOCK OF CHEESE LOOK LIKE A REMBRANDT.
WOW, I DIDN'T KNOW GOUDA COULD BE SO... BEAUTIFUL.
ANYONE WANT TO TRY THESE COOKIES FROM THE J&P TEST KITCHEN? THEY'RE SEAWEED—BUT SURPRISINGLY GOOD, I SWEAR.
I HAVE SOMETHING FOR YOU AS WELL.
IT'S FROM LILA. SHE KNOWS I HATE PHONE CALLS, SO SHE AGREED TO PUT IT IN A LETTER. I KNOW IT HARKENS BACK TO THE STONE AGES, BUT THAT'S JUST HOW IT IS WITH US OLD CRONES.
SILVIA OPENED THE LETTER, AND HER FACE MORPHED BETWEEN PANIC, SURPRISE, GLEE, AND ANXIETY.
WHAT?
WHAT IS IT?
TELL US.
TALK, BITCH!
VERONICA GAVE MY MANUSCRIPT TO LILA. AND SHE LIKED IT! SHE THINKS IT NEEDS A COUPLE MORE REVISIONS BUT WANTS TO SEE MORE ONCE IT'S POLISHED. SHE SOUNDS PRETTY INTERESTED IN THE STORY.
I SPOKE VERY HIGHLY OF YOU. I TOLD HER TO BE HONEST, AND SHE DOES HAVE SOME WORTHWHILE CRITIQUES. BUT OVERALL, SHE WAS QUITE INTERESTED.

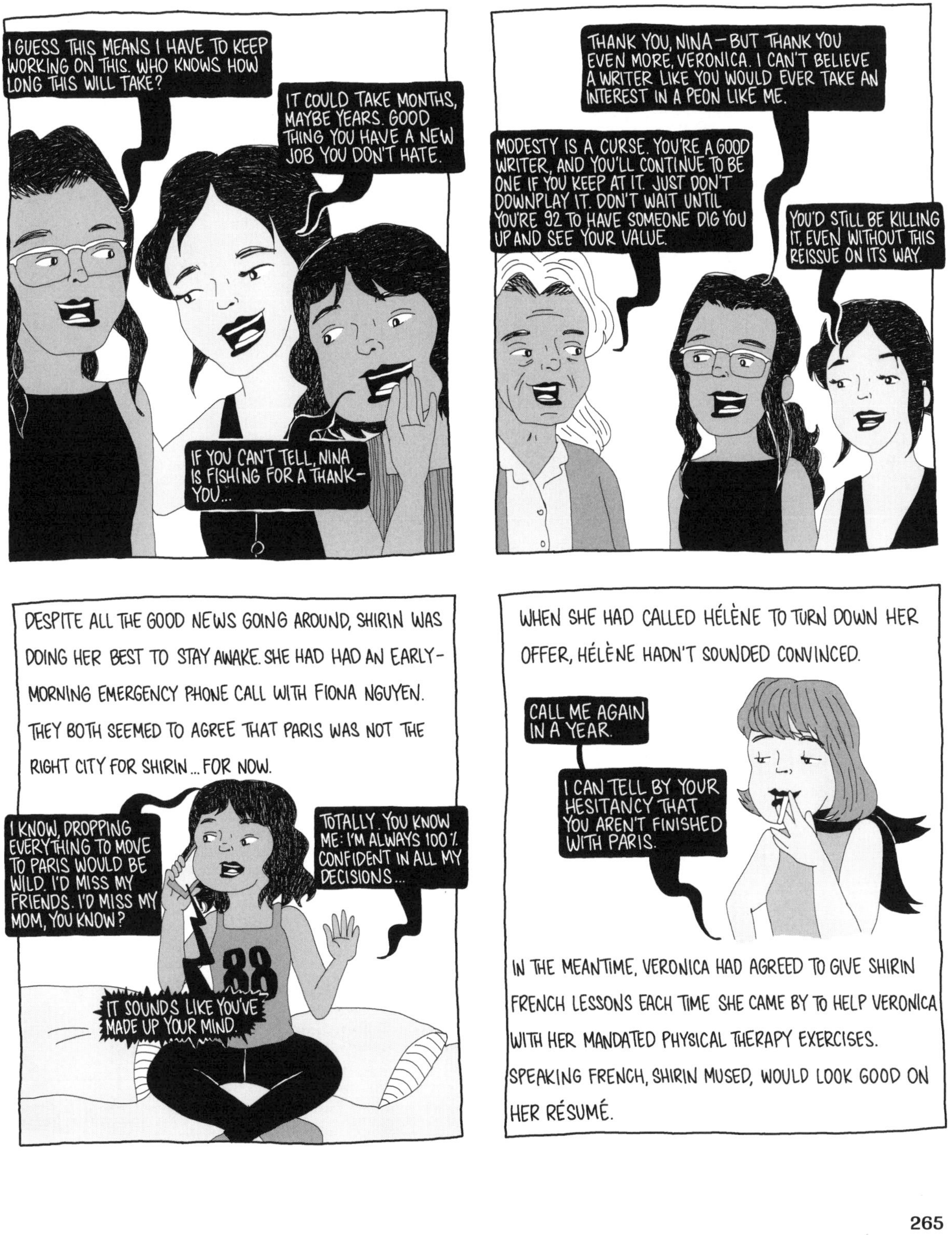
I GUESS THIS MEANS I HAVE TO KEEP WORKING ON THIS. WHO KNOWS HOW LONG THIS WILL TAKE?
IT COULD TAKE MONTHS, MAYBE YEARS. GOOD THING YOU HAVE A NEW JOB YOU DON'T HATE.
IF YOU CAN'T TELL, NINA IS FISHING FOR A THANK-YOU...
THANK YOU, NINA—BUT THANK YOU EVEN MORE, VERONICA. I CAN'T BELIEVE A WRITER LIKE YOU WOULD EVER TAKE AN INTEREST IN A PEON LIKE ME.
MODESTY IS A CURSE. YOU'RE A GOOD WRITER, AND YOU'LL CONTINUE TO BE ONE IF YOU KEEP AT IT. JUST DON'T DOWNPLAY IT. DON'T WAIT UNTIL YOU'RE 92 TO HAVE SOMEONE DIG YOU UP AND SEE YOUR VALUE.
YOU'D STILL BE KILLING IT, EVEN WITHOUT THIS REISSUE ON ITS WAY.
DESPITE ALL THE GOOD NEWS GOING AROUND, SHIRIN WAS DOING HER BEST TO STAY AWAKE. SHE HAD HAD AN EARLY-MORNING EMERGENCY PHONE CALL WITH FIONA NGUYEN. THEY BOTH SEEMED TO AGREE THAT PARIS WAS NOT THE RIGHT CITY FOR SHIRIN... FOR NOW.
I KNOW, DROPPING EVERYTHING TO MOVE TO PARIS WOULD BE WILD. I'D MISS MY FRIENDS. I'D MISS MY MOM, YOU KNOW?
TOTALLY. YOU KNOW ME: I'M ALWAYS 100% CONFIDENT IN ALL MY DECISIONS...
IT SOUNDS LIKE YOU'VE MADE UP YOUR MIND.
WHEN SHE HAD CALLED HÉLÈNE TO TURN DOWN HER OFFER, HÉLÈNE HADN'T SOUNDED CONVINCED.
CALL ME AGAIN IN A YEAR.
I CAN TELL BY YOUR HESITANCY THAT YOU AREN'T FINISHED WITH PARIS.
IN THE MEANTIME, VERONICA HAD AGREED TO GIVE SHIRIN FRENCH LESSONS EACH TIME SHE CAME BY TO HELP VERONICA WITH HER MANDATED PHYSICAL THERAPY EXERCISES. SPEAKING FRENCH, SHIRIN MUSED, WOULD LOOK GOOD ON HER RÉSUMÉ.

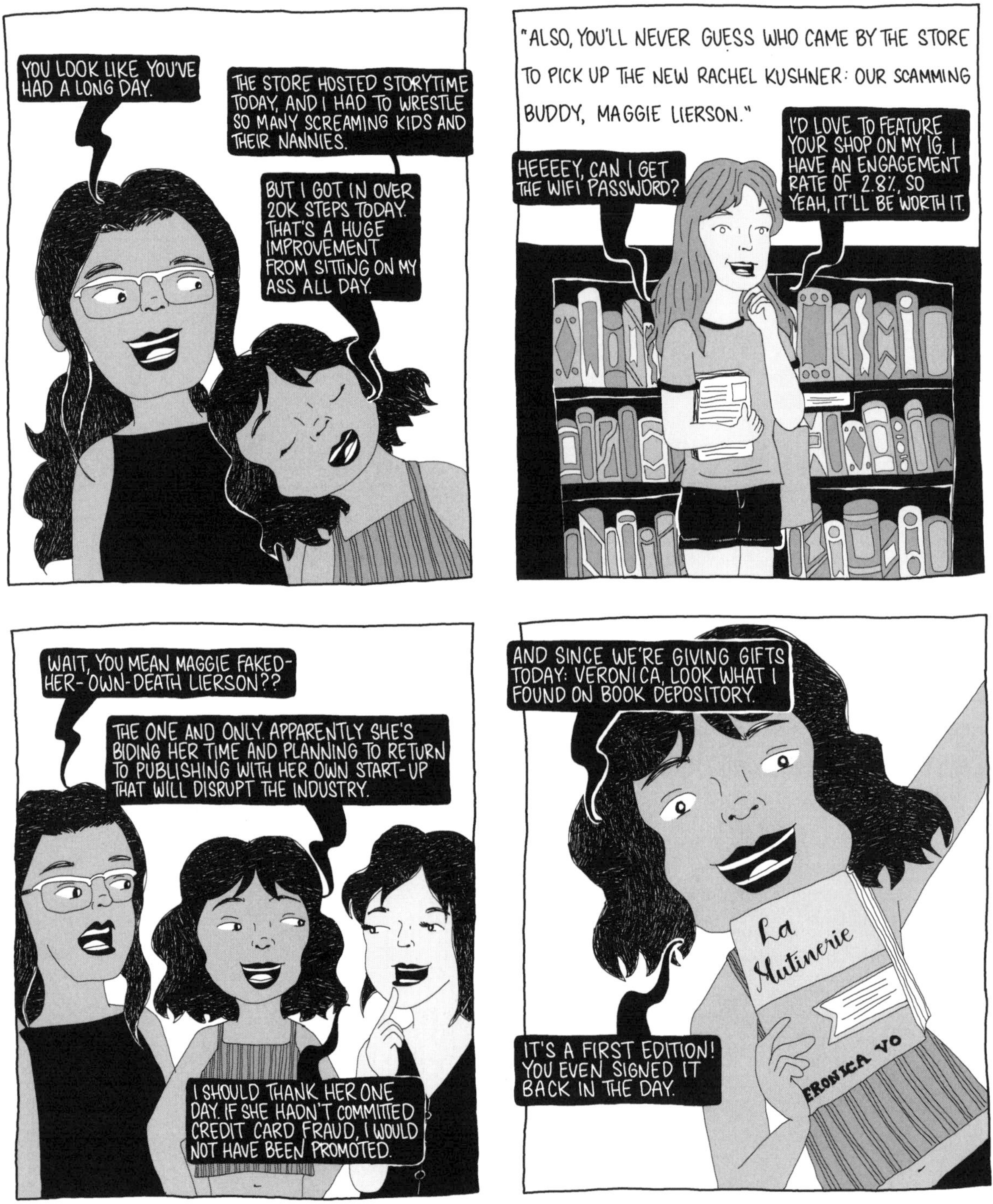
YOU LOOK LIKE YOU'VE HAD A LONG DAY.
THE STORE HOSTED STORYTIME TODAY, AND I HAD TO WRESTLE SO MANY SCREAMING KIDS AND THEIR NANNIES.
BUT I GOT IN OVER 20K STEPS TODAY. THAT'S A HUGE IMPROVEMENT FROM SITTING ON MY ASS ALL DAY.
"ALSO, YOU'LL NEVER GUESS WHO CAME BY THE STORE TO PICK UP THE NEW RACHEL KUSHNER: OUR SCAMMING BUDDY, MAGGIE LIERSON."
HEEEEY, CAN I GET THE WIFI PASSWORD?
I'D LOVE TO FEATURE YOUR SHOP ON MY IG. I HAVE AN ENGAGEMENT RATE OF 2.8%, SO YEAH, IT'LL BE WORTH IT.
WAIT, YOU MEAN MAGGIE FAKED-HER-OWN-DEATH LIERSON??
THE ONE AND ONLY. APPARENTLY SHE'S BIDING HER TIME AND PLANNING TO RETURN TO PUBLISHING WITH HER OWN START-UP THAT WILL DISRUPT THE INDUSTRY.
I SHOULD THANK HER ONE DAY. IF SHE HADN'T COMMITTED CREDIT CARD FRAUD, I WOULD NOT HAVE BEEN PROMOTED.
AND SINCE WE'RE GIVING GIFTS TODAY: VERONICA, LOOK WHAT I FOUND ON BOOK DEPOSITORY.
La Mutinerie
ERONICA VO
IT'S A FIRST EDITION! YOU EVEN SIGNED IT BACK IN THE DAY.

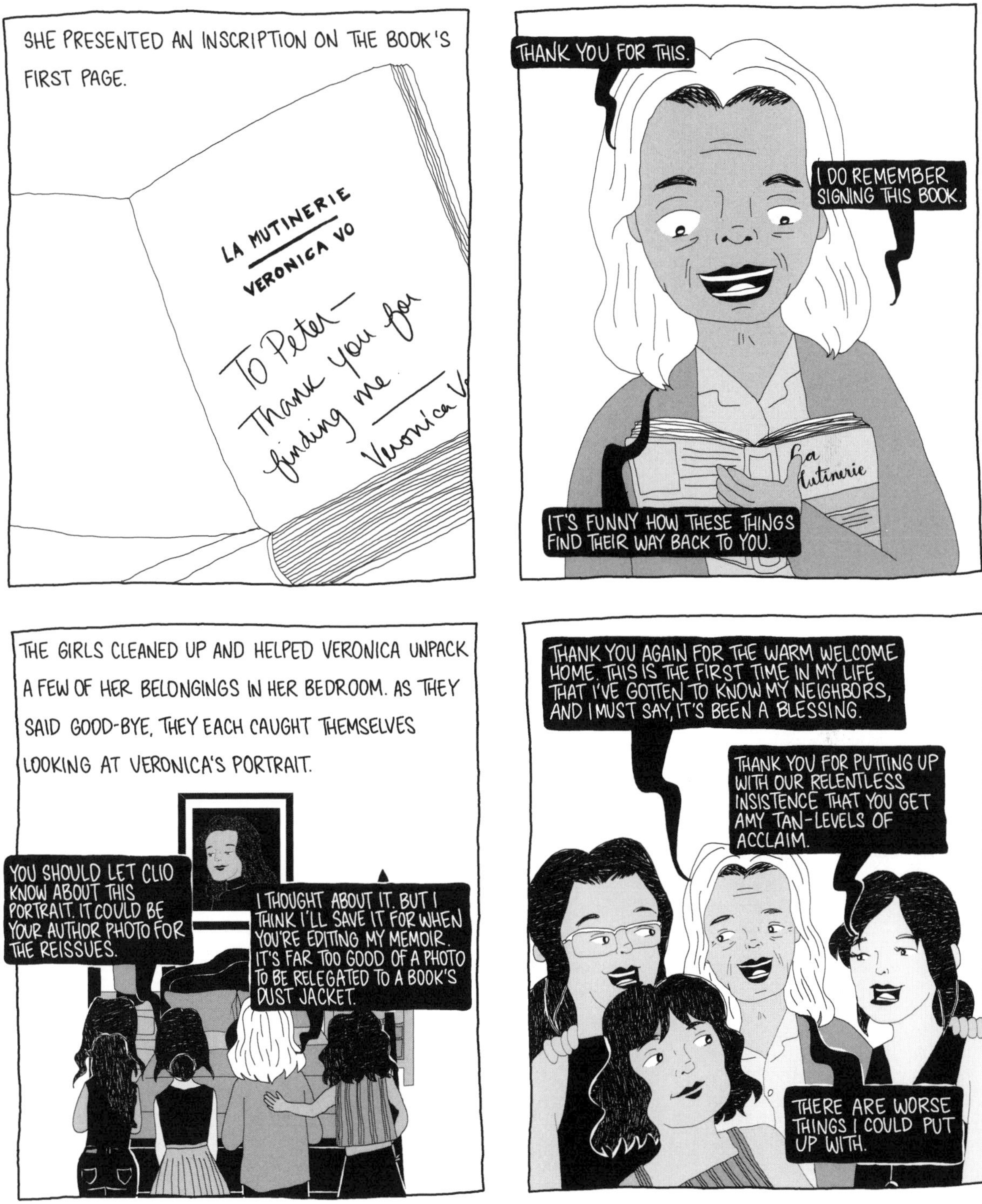
SHE PRESENTED AN INSCRIPTION ON THE BOOK'S FIRST PAGE.
LA MUTINERIE
VERONICA VO
To Peter— Thank you for finding me. —Veronica Vo
THANK YOU FOR THIS.
I DO REMEMBER SIGNING THIS BOOK.
La Mutinerie
IT'S FUNNY HOW THESE THINGS FIND THEIR WAY BACK TO YOU.
THE GIRLS CLEANED UP AND HELPED VERONICA UNPACK A FEW OF HER BELONGINGS IN HER BEDROOM. AS THEY SAID GOOD-BYE, THEY EACH CAUGHT THEMSELVES LOOKING AT VERONICA'S PORTRAIT.
YOU SHOULD LET CLIO KNOW ABOUT THIS PORTRAIT. IT COULD BE YOUR AUTHOR PHOTO FOR THE REISSUES.
I THOUGHT ABOUT IT. BUT I THINK I'LL SAVE IT FOR WHEN YOU'RE EDITING MY MEMOIR. IT'S FAR TOO GOOD OF A PHOTO TO BE RELEGATED TO A BOOK'S DUST JACKET.
THANK YOU AGAIN FOR THE WARM WELCOME HOME. THIS IS THE FIRST TIME IN MY LIFE THAT I'VE GOTTEN TO KNOW MY NEIGHBORS, AND I MUST SAY, IT'S BEEN A BLESSING.
THANK YOU FOR PUTTING UP WITH OUR RELENTLESS INSISTENCE THAT YOU GET AMY TAN-LEVELS OF ACCLAIM.
THERE ARE WORSE THINGS I COULD PUT UP WITH.

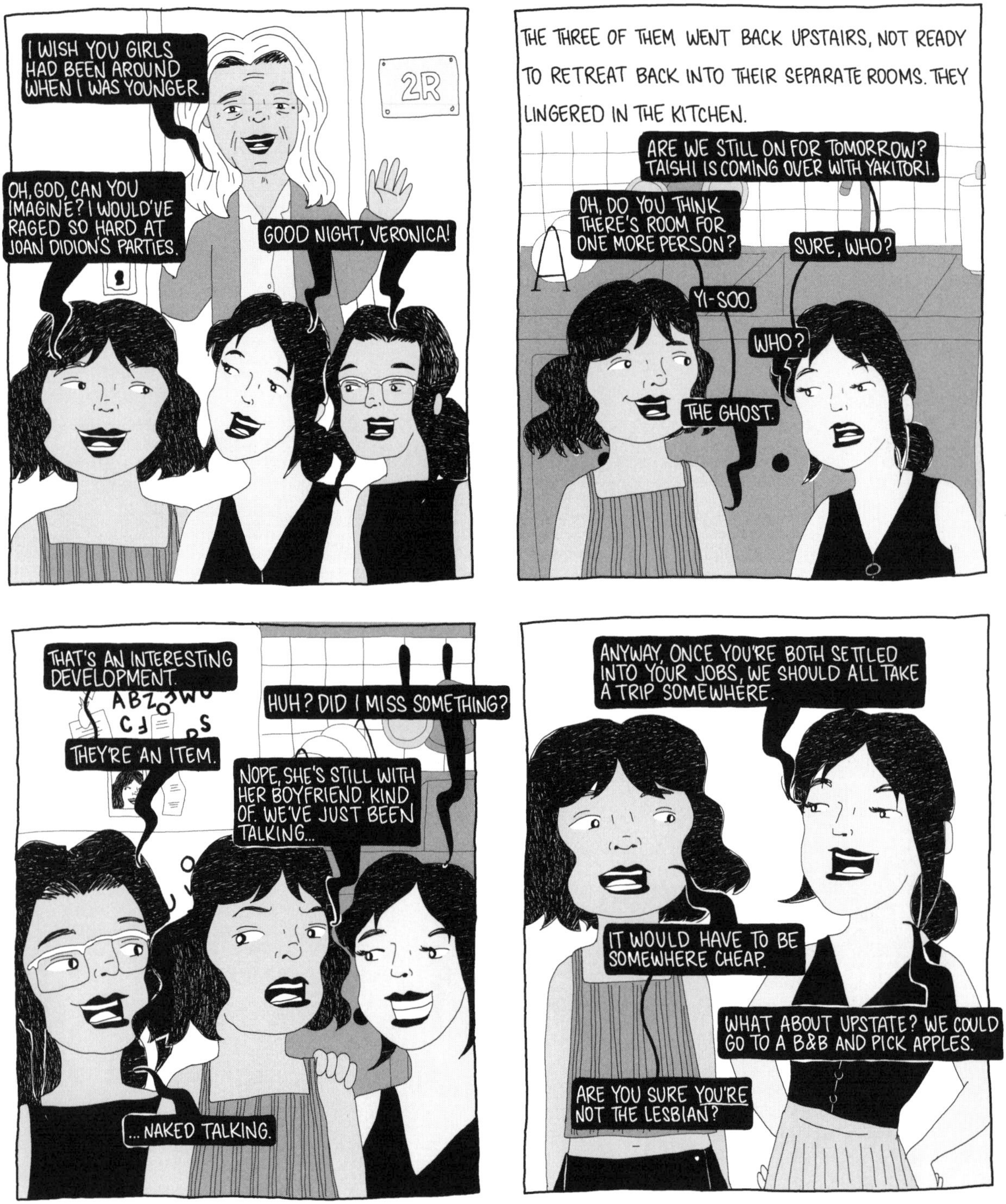
I WISH YOU GIRLS HAD BEEN AROUND WHEN I WAS YOUNGER.
2R
OH, GOD, CAN YOU IMAGINE? I WOULD'VE RAGED SO HARD AT JOAN DIDION'S PARTIES.
GOOD NIGHT, VERONICA!
THE THREE OF THEM WENT BACK UPSTAIRS, NOT READY TO RETREAT BACK INTO THEIR SEPARATE ROOMS. THEY LINGERED IN THE KITCHEN.
ARE WE STILL ON FOR TOMORROW? TAISHI IS COMING OVER WITH YAKITORI.
OH, DO YOU THINK THERE'S ROOM FOR ONE MORE PERSON?
SURE, WHO?
YI-SOO.
WHO?
THE GHOST.
THAT'S AN INTERESTING DEVELOPMENT.
HUH? DID I MISS SOMETHING?
THEY'RE AN ITEM.
NOPE, SHE'S STILL WITH HER BOYFRIEND. KIND OF. WE'VE JUST BEEN TALKING...
...NAKED TALKING.
ANYWAY, ONCE YOU'RE BOTH SETTLED INTO YOUR JOBS, WE SHOULD ALL TAKE A TRIP SOMEWHERE.
IT WOULD HAVE TO BE SOMEWHERE CHEAP.
WHAT ABOUT UPSTATE? WE COULD GO TO A B&B AND PICK APPLES.
ARE YOU SURE YOU'RE NOT THE LESBIAN?

WE'LL DO A GROWN-UP TRIP THIS TIME. SOMETHING CLASSY.

SPEAKING OF CLASSY, I FOUND THIS BOTTLE OF MALIBU FROM OUR LAST DAYS OF DISCO VIEWING PARTY.

I FEEL SO OLD. DOES ANYONE WANT TO GET A CHINATOWN MASSAGE WITH ME TOMORROW? I'M GOING TO REQUEST A MAN TO ELBOW THE SHIT OUT OF MY BACK.

NO, NO, NO. ASK FOR AN OLD LADY. THEY'RE THE ONES WHO REALLY TAKE OUT THEIR AGGRESSION ON YOUR BACK. THEY COULDN'T CARE LESS WHAT YOU THINK.

THAT COULD BE US ONE DAY...

...THREE OLD LADIES, SHUFFLING AROUND AND WREAKING HAVOC ON THE YOUTH.

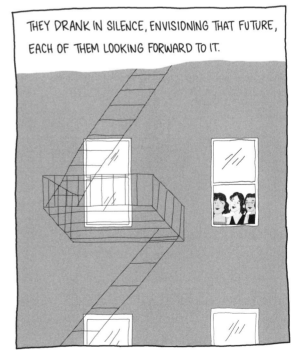

THEY DRANK IN SILENCE, ENVISIONING THAT FUTURE, EACH OF THEM LOOKING FORWARD TO IT.

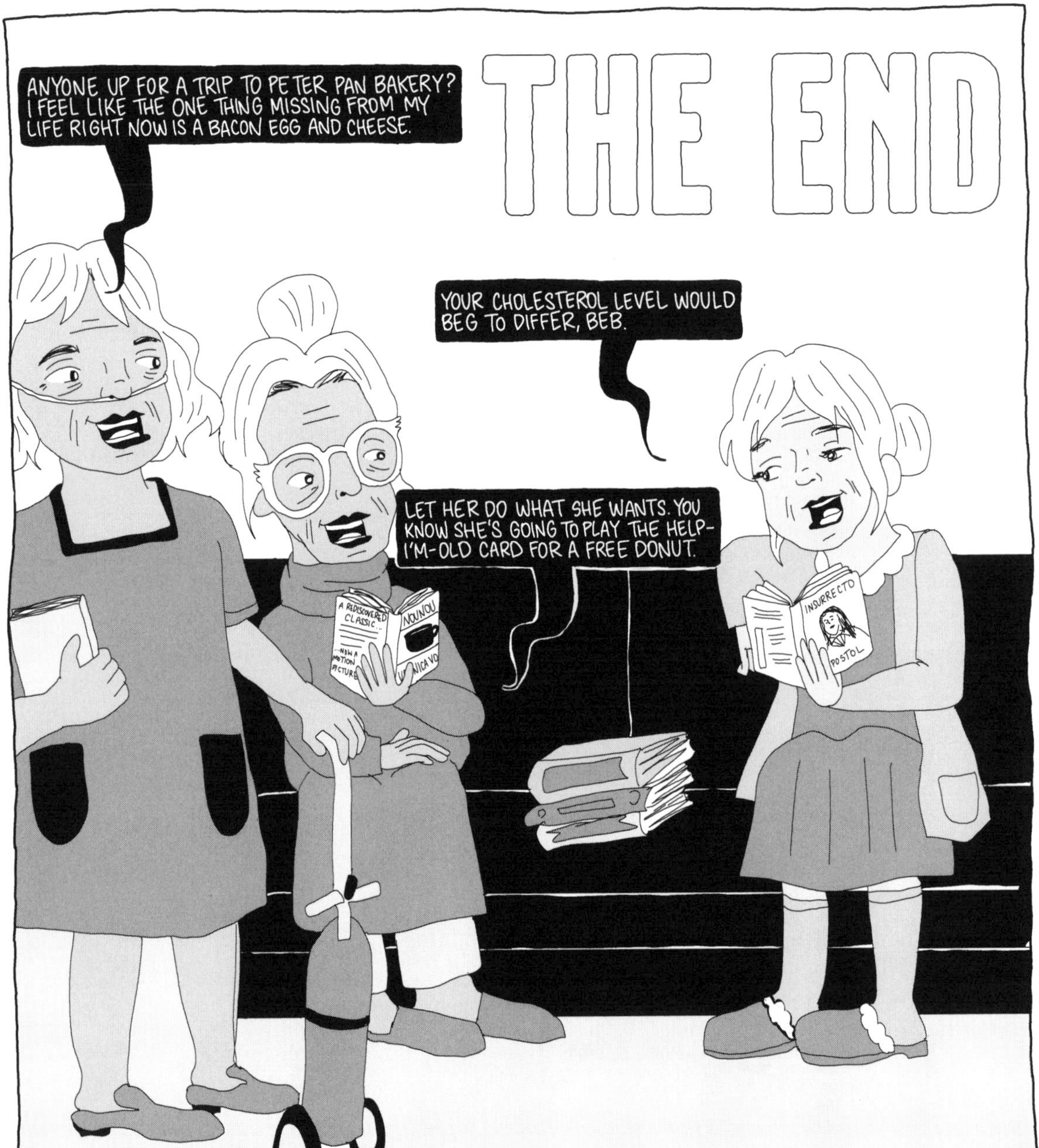
ANYONE UP FOR A TRIP TO PETER PAN BAKERY? I FEEL LIKE THE ONE THING MISSING FROM MY LIFE RIGHT NOW IS A BACON EGG AND CHEESE.
THE END
YOUR CHOLESTEROL LEVEL WOULD BEG TO DIFFER, BEB.
LET HER DO WHAT SHE WANTS. YOU KNOW SHE'S GOING TO PLAY THE HELP-I'M-OLD CARD FOR A FREE DONUT.
INSURRECTO
POSTOL

ACKNOWLEDGMENTS

This book wouldn't exist without friends and early readers like Kelly Lin, Nancy Nguyen, Thu Doan, and Lauren Rochford. Particularly Kelly for being a girl's girl. Most of the places in this book, from Chopt and Pocha to Peter Pan and God Bless Deli, would mean nothing without you.

Thank you to my agent, Kate McKean, for quelling all book-related anxieties. Thank you to the wonderful team at Plume for being a pleasure to work with: Jill Schwartzman, Marya Pasciuto, Lexy Cassola, Becky Odell, Tiffani Ren, Claire Winecoff, Tiffany Estreicher, Kristin del Rosario, and Vi-An Nguyen.

Thank you to Yukiko Miyakawa and Vivian Lee for providing important information for the book.

Thank you to all the assistants I've worked among over the years, especially for all the happy hours, bitchy chats, not-so-subtle code names, and good-bye lunches. Thank you to all the good bosses, too—especially you, KM!

Thank you to my family: Mom, Dad, Christine, JP, Silas, Lolo, and Lola.

Most of all, thank you to Dustin for giving me the time, energy, and support to create this book. You put up with a caffeine-fueled, sleep-deprived, moody monster for months. I love you. Lastly, for Lilou: for showing me what I'm capable of and occasionally resting your head on my shoulder.

ABOUT THE AUTHOR

KATE GAVINO is the author and illustrator of *Last Night's Reading* and the graphic novel *Sanpaku*. Her work has appeared in *The New Yorker, The Believer, Longreads,* Oprah.com, and more. She was both the greatest and the worst editorial assistant.